COLD FUSION

LADD GRAHAM

Crown City Company

ISBN: 978-1-54390-618-9 (print)
ISBN: 978-1-54390-619-6 (ebook)

CHAPTER 1

Preston Cook's life was on the cusp of world-changing promise. Cold fusion was not a wild fantasy. In October of 2005, Preston would make it work. He would make it work in spite of all the other failed attempts back in the late eighties when the disappointing premature announcements by other physicists were followed by paltry, empty findings in replications around the globe. The enthusiasm for cold fusion had been sucked dry after the nineties and the foci for energy research had moved on, gone in other directions, turned to bio-fuels, solar panels, and wind turbines. And, predictably, a boat-load of energy researchers got in bed with the hard money and were trying to squeeze more and more efficiency out of every drop of fossil fuel, desperately shoving back the inevitable day when there would be none remaining. Cold fusion had gone completely by the wayside. Everyone had concluded it was a pipedream. The concept could still generate a few sparks of interest here and there, but not enough to power a flashlight, much less save the planet.

As far as Preston Cook knew, he was about the last scientist who still thoroughly believed in cold fusion, as he tweaked his contraptions, and continued the pursuit. He knew in his heart that he could pull it off. He could taste success. He could hear the future breathing inside the equipment he built in his Pasadena garage, which was converted into a laboratory years ago for that very project. It was sound-proofed and air-conditioned, with precision lathes, a high-speed gas centrifuge, refrigerated lockers, and a fully-plumbed chemistry

1

bench. There was even a clean room that looked like something unearthly occupying the rear third of the garage, made from inch thick floor to ceiling glass, with a twin-door airlock. The garage lab smelled like warm electrical wiring and sulfates. It was half space station and half metal shop, with chemistry paraphernalia tossed in. Computer monitors were everywhere, tapping into a series of a dozen PCs Preston had linked together to make a powerful single brain that ran simulations day and night.

Much to his wife's everlasting dismay, a good deal of their retirement savings had gone into the lab. There was no money to be had at Tech-U, as California Technological University was frequently dubbed, because Preston was on hiatus. Nor was there money from anywhere else for Preston Cook and his God forsaken obsession.

Cold fusion was collateral damage on the international scientific front. The early experimenters in the enterprise – creating "nuclear reactions in thermos bottles", as detractors said – had gone straight to the press with their findings, rather than introducing them gradually by asking colleagues to vet the experiments, as is expected in the research community. Consequently, volumes of misbegotten information about cold fusion were already in the public domain. It was a common view among potential investors that nobody could successfully patent such a reactor. Not only was Preston Cook pariah to conventional research grants because of the concept's checkered history, but his research was equally off-putting to funding from venture capitalists. There was zero support in both directions. Nonetheless, Dr. Cook had pushed unwaveringly and heroically onward with his research over the years, all by himself and on his own nickel.

Preston's friend and research partner in the early going, Dr. Maxwell Umberto, had given up and moved on finally, two years earlier, returning to his dissertation love, gravity and the elusive "unified theory". Since then, Max's voice had mutated into yet another one in the chorus reminding Dr. Cook that his commitment to cold fusion was folly, advising him to return to his students, to his classes, and to more traditional bench research at California Technological University, CTU or Tech-U, a mile away in Pasadena. Preston's former partner had always had a weakness for popular science, anything that might prick up a few ears, and the unified theory was an edgy topic, always getting attention, like the ever-so mysterious beauty on the perimeter of a mixer who speaks to no one. One might expect as much from a fashion plate like Dr. Umberto, but Maxwell Umberto was also a smart scientist, no doubt there. Like Preston, his PhD was from MIT. In fact, they had known one another in graduate school and became strong friends amidst MIT's somber, granite, mausoleum-like buildings along the Charles River in Cambridge, Mass.

Dr. Umberto's curriculum vitae weighed a couple of pounds and it listed presentations at pretty much every major professional conference around the globe. It included publications in all the correct refereed journals, but it also included quite a few contributions to the likes of *Science Digest* and *The Los Angeles Times*. And that was because Max was a bit of a celebrity in the world of physics, which like nearby Hollywood had its own luminaries. He relished fame, notoriety, and the spotlight. Early in his career Maxwell Umberto had finagled himself into a very public spat with Carl Sagan, back when Sagan was on television holding forth on the vastness of the cosmos and its billions and billions of suns. Such a fight was not everyone's badge of accomplishment, but Max wore it that way. It got him onto the national stage at a fairly young age. Yet, in spite of the limelight and in spite of what some considered his superficial manners and pandering to the press, Maxwell Umberto had also recently earned a nomination to become the new Chair of the Physics Department at Tech-U . This was a highly a coveted spot soon to be vacated by a world-renowned scholar who was retiring, a stuffy white guy who had lost touch with the cutting edge years ago. But tenured professors tend to hang on too long and too late in their careers, embarrassingly similar to the vociferous drunk one is unable to shed at a cocktail party. For Max, however, this departmental Chair's impending vacancy was a propitious opportunity.

One is not considered for distinguished positions like the Chair of the Physics Department at Tech-U by being popular and by trading snipes with Carl Sagan. There had to be some meat on his bones. Still, because of Maxwell Umberto's irrepressible showmanship there was more opposition to his appointment than was really justified. Many saw his publicity shenanigans as sufficiently off-putting that they readily and vocally discounted him for the Chair's office. They had concerns about CTU's image in the professional community, but with that opposition having been noted, Max Umberto countered with substantial professional clout. Almost no one thought he was a lightweight in his field. Even his most vehement detractors reluctantly conceded Max was a worthy scholar and scientist when he put his talents to it.

The Parthaneum at the southeast corner of the CTU campus is a spacious dining and drinking accommodation for the faculty and important friends of the institution. Stucco walls and dark wood echoed the Spanish architecture on the rest of the campus, but it also had a luxurious and stately quality, standing as it did near the perimeter of the lovely grounds where tall California oaks shaded the greens. Across each of the surrounding streets were quiet upscale neighborhoods ensconcing the campus and the Parthaneum in legacy and lending an imposing affect usually reserved for an exclusive club rather than college facilities. Faculty members and their guests were welcomed to the Parthaneum's sanctuary through an open-air foyer that surrounded a gurgling baroque fountain. Heavy, white linen covered the dining tables spaced generously beneath a vaulted ceiling. Conversations were hushed with a dignity usually reserved for a library or cathedral. It was all contrived to provide a contemplative mealtime retreat that might honor the men and women who were guiding a goodly portion the next generation of the world's premier scientists and engineers through their arduous studies. They all took these traditions and presumptions quite seriously. This was a trait that Tech-U cultivated, lending a distinct snobbishness to everyone associated with the institution. Even administrative assistants and clerks were known to be rather snooty when dealing with the general public as though they were personally responsible for the institution's lofty credentials.

In September of 2005, Preston Cook still counted Maxwell Umberto as one of his closest friends and confidants, in spite of Maxwell's abandonment of the cold fusion project two years earlier. At least once a week they would have lunch in the faculty dining room in the Parthaneum. Their lunches would typically conclude after an hour or so, with Preston describing some recent near miss in his research, after which a puzzled and despondent Preston would hang his head at the linen covered table, where rested the crystal goblets and the CTU bone china, and he would mumble something about lithium, or diodes, or heavy water and high frequency sound. It had become miserably predictable.

That was the queue for Max to reach across and touch his friend on the forearm and affectionately assure him the Physics Department would still take him back. Preston Cook was a wonderful teacher after all. And somewhere in the conversation, Max would remind Preston that cold fusion is a grand and beautiful notion, but it just wasn't going to happen. Ever since Maxwell abandoned Preston to be as alone as Sisyphus shoving his boulder up the hill, Max repeatedly had compared the cold fusion idea to a search for a perpetual motion machine. The math on the energy involved just doesn't add up and it never will add up, he would say.

At those words, Preston would simply get more depressed and ironically more determined, too. He was a dog with a bone, guarding his stake. Preston was intellectually and emotionally overwrought with his project, wretchedly consumed by it. He had not quite plunged over the edge into madness, but sometimes he felt like he was teetering on the brink. Dr. Cook was definitely in dangerous psychological territory and the abyss was yawning right in front of him. To his credit, Preston's old friend, Maxwell, could see that and the only way he could imagine to help Preston was to suggest alternative realistic plans, like a return to the classroom.

It may have been Dr. Cooks' son who kept him sane, or at least sane enough to stay the course. Not long after his son, Dalton Cook, turned twelve years old was about the time Preston's cold fusion vision started to gel and his goal became a palpable possibility. That was when the reality of what he was trying to accomplish began picking up speed as if Sisyphus's bolder topped the mountain and quickly adopted a frightening momentum of its own heading down the farther side, rather suddenly introducing as it rolled forward a completely different kind of very serious dilemma for Sisyphus and a village below.

But in the months leading up to that fateful period, Dalton was often Preston's only fan, his only companion on lonely weekends in the garage lab, and his inspiration, too. It certainly wasn't Dalton's mother, Samantha Day-Steiner, mathematics genius and, like her husband, a Tech-U professor. She was no longer a supporter of Preston's weird obsession and she had not been a supporter since the day Maxwell Umberto backed away from the project in late 2003, saying he was sorry but he had to go. Max had also said he was afraid the Fields-Parker fiasco back in 1989 was all there was in cold fusion, the "lattice assisted nuclear reaction fantasy", he had snorted, quoting detractors from the earlier failed experiments. "Replications since then are interesting but no better. It's a blind alley", Max had concluded as he left.

In the very practical mind of Preston's wife, Dr. Umberto's arguments about her husband's research played so convincingly for her that she had drifted away from Preston over the next two years arguing about it. Samantha Day-Steiner could not fathom how any intelligent, balanced, and responsible grown-up would relinquish all that Preston seemed to be willing to relinquish on his quixotic adventure. It was unconscionable. It was beyond reason for her. But that was a worn minefield by 2005, cratered from many past altercations and there remained many more mines in that field, just below the surface, ferocious upheavals at the ready. The two of them, husband and wife, mother and father to Dalton, tried to steer clear of discussing the "project", as the minefield had come to be called. They managed to avoid it for the most part, but not always. Occasionally there would again be the deafening concussion and dirt hurled through the air. Emotional blood remained on the day's agenda from time to time, not planned for, but seemingly inevitable. Preston absolutely hated those days, but their son, twelve-year old Dalton, hated them even more.

CHAPTER 2

"Dad, why can't you and Mom get along?" Dalton asked, not looking up, sitting at a computer keyboard in the bright garage laboratory and generating a report they had programmed the dozen linked Dell, Gateway, and HP desktops to run. He would have rather been working the metal lathe, but it wasn't the time for that. There was something about a machine's tactile quality that drew Dalton in. Computers had too many degrees of separation from the actual item, although he was facile with computers.

"It's complicated, Dalt," Preston said from a wooden stool next to Dalton where he was reading printouts.

"No it isn't," returned the boy, typing commands briskly with two index fingers, conjuring up from the warm microchips arrayed before him a summary of the outcomes of a hundred virtual experiments calculated during the last twenty-four hours, even while the Cook family had slept. "Mom just does not think we should be doing this," Dalton added.

Preston studied his son and said simply, "You're right about that."

"Mom just doesn't love you," came back Dalton. He never did look at his father during this exchange. Nor did he load the conversation up with a lot of emotional baggage. It was a matter of observations to him, just like the experiments.

"No. That's not true!" returned Preston, taken aback. He lowered his printouts and stared at Dalton, who just continued calmly working, leaning toward the monitor that was recording his queries. The boy wasn't malicious or capable of being malicious. He merely told his father what he saw.

"She never says she loves you," said Dalton. "She has said she loves me sometimes when she's had some wine."

Preston did not know what to say. It wasn't the first time his son had stopped him in his tracks. Preston could feel his spirit sinking away from his body into the floor. He could not respond effectively. His romantic heart was in Samantha's pocket and always had been. He could not accept the idea that her love for him had gone away because of his research. He did not want it to be the case and he always rejected the idea.

"She loves me in other ways", he said.

"I don't think so," said Dalton continuing at the keyboard.

"Well, *I* don't say 'I love you' so often," returned Preston, trying to make a point. "Does that mean I don't love you?"

"You show it to me, Dad. Every time we say 'The center of stars!' to each other, you're saying you love me. Mom does none of that with you."

Preston just stared at his son. The boy's words were right on the money. He had not felt love from Samantha in a long time. Preston didn't know how to counter his son, so he simply returned to the print-outs.

Dalton seemed to understand his father's predicament and continued with his computer work while saying softly, "You love mom. I know that."

Young Dalton had asked about his mom's displeasure before, but never so directly. Conversations with Dalton had a way of repeating themselves in various forms. It's not that he didn't remember the last conversation. He remembered well, but he liked the repetition.

It was comforting to him. In fact, Dalton and his dad had numerous routines they had created. One of them might say, "Like the center of stars!" in reference to the subatomic reactions that were supposed to be occurring within their experiments, both live and virtual. And the other would nod in agreement and reply, "Like the center of stars!"

"But not nearly as hot," Dalton would say.

"Not as hot," his dad confirmed. "We hope!" Preston might add, and they would both laugh. In fact, "the center of stars" had become the primary key in their cold fusion composition inside that garage laboratory, a chord of mutual joy.

Sometimes they would repeat lines to movies they both enjoyed together. *Back to the Future* was one of Dalton's favorites and he sometimes teased his dad about making a "flux capacitor" in their garage and Preston would do his best Christopher Lloyd imitation with a breathy, "Ronald Reagan is President? Who's Vice President then? Jerry Lewis?"

Dalton was most often in the lab with his dad when he wasn't in school. He didn't really have too many child friends in the quaint but modest craftsman houses on their street in Pasadena. There were other kids his age but Dalton often steered clear of them because Dalton was a Down syndrome boy and making friends was not the easiest thing for him to do. He preferred being with his father. He was safe there from an outside world that was not always accommodating to someone like him, an odd youngster who was smart enough, but "not quite right" as folks would say. He was fortunate in that he had only the slightest facial characteristics of someone with Down syndrome. His brow was not so much flat as it was just off from rounded. He had the single crease on his palms, but no one would typically notice that trait. His ears were smallish, but not by much. There was one eye that would occasionally wander, yet he looked in no way mentally compromised. Dalton had the frame and musculature of a normal a boy and he never got a second glance amongst strangers. He could easily pass as a typical twelve year-old and he might have been considered an attractive boy, too, with thick wavy hair and broad shoulders for his age. Furthermore, Dalton made pretty good grades in the public school where he was mainstreamed. But after a few minutes around him, people could sense that something was amiss. He was sweet, but he was different. He was obviously very smart, but he was strange.

When it comes to Down syndrome, Dalton was blessed to be very much on the more normal end of the spectrum. Yet, he well comprehended his unusual condition. His parents had told him that he had 47 chromosomes and most people have 46 chromosomes and that was the reason he was different.

Dalton's mom, Dr. Day-Steiner, could never have fun with his condition in any way. For her, this turn of events a dozen years back was a heavy cross to bear and not pleasant by any stretch of the imagination in any situation. Dalton's dad, Preston Cook, took another angle on the matter altogether, as he often would in otherwise serious circumstances. He and Dalton had made 47 into their lucky number. Jack Morris, Detroit Tigers pitching ace, wore number 47. Andrei Kirilinko, star of the NBA, wore number 47. John Lynch of the Patriots and Buccaneers was another number 47. Preston would remind Dalton that 47 was one of Einstein's prime numbers in his Special Theory of Relativity.

What was truly magical and was definitely one of the most striking traits of Dalton's as both of his parents saw him, was that he had a certain kind of raw cut-to-the-truth intelligence that was sometimes quite amazing. There wasn't any literature they could find on this characteristic of Down syndrome children, but they were sure it was a product of his difference, of that extra chromosome. Now and then Dalton would bring the conversation to a dead stop with a lightning strike of insight. It was always rather unassuming coming out of Dalton's mouth, no big deal. He never was interested in impressing anyone. He had no capacity for that kind of behavior. Often he did not even look up from whatever he was doing. And after being around Dalton for a while, one could see the boy was perceptive in so many subtle ways that most normal people are not. Maybe it was just because he paid attention to every little thing - Preston and Samantha weren't sure - but that twelve year-old boy sensed the world keenly and there was no dismissing it.

Dalton was a planned-for child. He was born of Samantha and Preston late in their lives because they both wanted to get their careers off the ground before starting a family and each year it seemed there was one more goal to pass before they made the commitment. When they had been married fifteen years and they were both in their forties they finally did recognize it was time, if it was going to happen at all. Statistically speaking, at their ages they were rolling the dice on problems with having a child. The sonogram screening didn't show anything, not the lumpy neck the doctor was looking to find. Still, they wanted to be careful; so they went ahead with an amniocentesis and downplayed the risks. But the test results were messy, showing neither negative nor positive, only a one in ten occurrence. Sam and Preston chose to do the test again, and again there was no clear indication of a problem. Results remained vague. Their doctor shrugged and said this happens occasionally; it's not an exact science. There were other tests, he said, and more risks, too, if they wanted to continue. He simply could not provide assurances one way or another at that point in those days.

Upon hearing the murky and unsatisfying reports Preston and Sam had some rather emotional conversations about what to do – heated actually – with Dr. Day-Steiner always being the more reluctant. After all, as she would point out, it was *she* that was carrying the fetus; it was *she* that would endure labor, not Preston. In the end, however, with consideration for their ages and the dwindling chances that remained for them to have a child that was biologically theirs, they elected to go full term with the pregnancy and they cast their fates to the wind.

They were fifteen weeks into it by then anyway and even though Sam was somewhat ambivalent about having children, thinking of herself as, at best, a mediocre candidate for motherhood, her husband proved to be about as passionate on the subject as Sam had seen during the twenty-plus years they had known one another. She understood Preston carried a life-long desire to be a father. Samantha figured it was because Preston could then become his own father in a way, filling in for the missing dad that had been pretty much of a no-show during Preston's childhood, a workaholic Princeton University professor and classical scholar. When Preston was a youngster growing up in New Jersey, there had been no tossing the ol' apple around with his dad or going for hikes in the quiet and dappled woods so common in the countryside surrounding the university. All he remembered of his childhood was work and books.

But as it happened, when the decision was made, when Preston eventually talked Sam into having this baby boy, they went forward and denied to themselves that the winds of fate might blow an extra undetected chromosome little Dalton's way. Everything would be okay, they said to themselves. Denial, however, doesn't alter reality and with their decision the family's die was cast. As sometimes happens, that errant, eschewed extra chromosome did float their way and managed to finagle its way into the baby's genome.

Strangely however, Dalton's 47th chromosome was seriously and mysteriously corrupted in the process of its delivery. In fact, it was compromised so dramatically that it was unable to render the biological havoc inside the fetus that a 47th chromosome typically renders. Quite to the contrary, that peculiar stray and distorted chromosome may have bequeathed extraordinary skills of perception to baby Dalton. Was it good luck or bad luck at play in that curious late pregnancy, when genetic material was tossed around like dice at a craps table? Dalton was indeed unique, so perhaps in the broader scheme of things it was a positive outcome, but it did not feel that way to professors Day-Steiner and Cook in the early going when they realized what had happened, when they understood that Dalton was not normal, and it took one of them much longer - years longer - to come to terms with it all.

CHAPTER 3

When lunching with his friend Dr. Umberto at the Parthaneum, Dr. Cook was routinely reminded that he was an odd duck in the midst of aristocratic academic pomp. As one might anticipate, there were the fashionable members of the faculty at CTU and there were the nerdy ones, too, but Preston had his own style that wasn't welcomed in either camp. He was always an eclectic jumble of clothes, seemingly hauled randomly from a laundry hamper. It was yet another bane to Samantha Day-Steiner, who was a trim and handsome fifty-something woman, as presentation conscious as most aspiring and accomplished professionals.

Upon meeting with Maxwell Umberto one particular Wednesday, Preston was as usual wearing a tie. In fact, he wore ties when no else did in casual California, displaying some vestige of professorial appearance that had been hard-wired into him by his father. But his plaid button-down shirt was miserably wrinkled and Preston's tweed sports coat wasn't much better. Otherwise, it was rumpled cargo pants, argyle socks and oxblood wing tips. Preston's short beard was anything but manicured and he had combed his longish graying hair by running his hands through it a couple of times as he entered the dining hall. Furthermore, Preston Cook was over six feet tall and rangy, so you would never refer to that physical specimen as innocuous. He always garnered a double take or two wherever he went.

And there was Max, waiting for him, trendy, stylish, Max. You might think he was a theater professor, if CTU had such a program, wearing his camel cashmere Ralph Loren blazer draped across both shoulders as he would stride across campus, his fedora at a jaunty angle. Every item of attire was precise and correct. He and Preston made quite a pair as they clasped hands in greeting. They set the fashion curve at each of its extremes.

"Preston," said Max.

"Max," said Preston. And they sat down.

Deftly flipping his fifteen by fifteen linen napkin onto his lap, Max said, "So is there news? How went the sonofusion trial?"

Preston shook his head and stared at the table for a minute, fidgeting with his silverware, straightening, aligning, and straightening again. "It's the deuterium," he said quietly. "We're getting flashes with the sound waves. Nothing new. It's the deuterium, but…," and his voice trailed off.

"Did you think you can put a boom box next to a beaker of heavy water and light up a city, Preston?" asked Maxwell sarcastically. Then, not missing an opportunity to besmirch the higher education competition, he added with a twinkle in his eye, "But, once again, *that* idea was hatched at Rensselaer," and he earned a small smile from Dr. Cook. On a more serious note Max said, "Dr. Cook, I think we were getting some solid - if unexplainable - energy output with an electric charge in water two years ago. Go back there."

Preston lifted his gaze and locked onto Max's pale blue eyes. His friend was being frank about the project and without malice to Preston. He was even trying to make a suggestion. After all, Max had worked on the project for over four years. He had a strange residual stake in it that Preston had detected on and off, and the electrical charge model had always interested Max the most. "Maybe," Preston acknowledged. "Maybe what we got is all sound waves can do. Bubbles and sparks. But it still might be the deuterium…" and he looked so very sad. In truth, Preston looked sad, woeful and depressed, most of the time this last year as his dream continued to run ahead of his grasp, out of reach. He was not a lot of fun to be around.

"Chrysalis, Inc. has already built that tamperproof nuclear battery, Preston. Maybe that's as good as it gets. Not bad, actually," said Maxwell.

"Hmp!' grunted Preston. "That thing is filthy dirty, Max. It's smallish, yes – for a reactor – but it's water cooled and as big as a house. It has to be buried, for chrissakes! And 'tamperproof?' That's code for the reactor never going to where it's really needed. If you're selling bomb parts, Professor Umberto, some maniac will make a bomb. I can do better than Chrysalis. Smaller, cleaner, and no bomb parts."

"I admire your determination, my friend. I always have admired that."

Preston smiled faintly and retuned to aligning his utensils.

"I saw Samantha this morning," said Max, trying to turn to something more upbeat for minute.

"Oh?" said Preston and he looked up.

"She came by the office. She wanted to say 'Good luck' on this Dean thing."

"Any other internal candidates?" asked Preston about Maxwell's bid to become Dean of Physics Department at CTU.

"Brundi," said Max.

"Santosh Brundi?" responded Preston a bit more enthusiastically than expected. He knew Dr. Brundi well. They had shared an office for a while as newcomers to CTU. Santosh Brundi was a slight Pakistani man, freakishly tidy, a nitpicker to end all nitpickers, and loud. He couldn't speak in a civil voice. He confirmed in Preston's mind that it's the compulsively tidy people who are the most confused of all. They think they can arrange their internal lives by tidying up their external ones and loud people think they can make their opinions compelling by shouting. Brundi rankled Preston because he was always plying his way with diversity arguments on his own behalf, first it was in the faculty senate and later in committees, anywhere he thought he could make it stick. And all of that would have been okay, but in Preston's mind Brundi was a mediocre scientist at best. He had managed to gather up a PhD from UC Berkeley yet Preston could not fathom how that happened. It boggled the imagination. Furthermore, Dr. Brundi was born and raised in Santa Monica, California, by well-to-do immigrant parents who had made a fortune in the plastic packaging business. The guy was about as third-world and underprivileged as a Kennedy. Yet he unabashedly gave birth to a Pakistani accent while he was at CTU and cultivated it as the years went on.

"You'd be a much better choice, Max," said Preston.

"Well, I'm trying to be realistic. It's a national search, of course, and the department has always chosen stodgy leadership. I don't know what chance there is they will alter that pattern."

"Change is the only constant," said Preston.

"If I should be so fortunate as to become Dean – and even if not – I'll always be a voice in the department trying to keep the door open for your return to the classroom, Preston."

"Thank you, Max. But you know I've got to see this through."

Max understood there was no point in pursuing the futility question that day with Preston. After all, if his wife Samantha hadn't made any headway, then how in God's name, would a friend? "I know," he said softly to Preston. "I know."

That was the moment a known-to-them and spirited Jamaican waiter in a blindingly white and stiffly pressed, brass-buttoned porter jacket arrived at the table, providing Max with an opportunity to brighten things up a bit and change the subject. "Ah! So, what's good today, Henry?"

The gallon flask of distilled water, at the center of Preston's most current experiment in his personal clean room in his garage, was made from thick, tempered, leaded glass. Half full, all the air had been evacuated from the flask and it was sealed. Preston leaned down to examine the tiny heating element immersed in the water, an element whose simple mission was to warm the water sufficiently that nearly microscopic boiling bubbles would begin to form, at which point he would project a pre-calibrated sound wave through the flask. He'd gone through this exercise numerous times. It's an old laboratory demonstration from the early twentieth century that was not entirely understood, but was often thought to lend some credence to the plausibility of creating nearly room temperature nuclear reactions.

When the moment was right, Preston lightly touched a button that fired high-frequency sound waves through the flask. And in moments, as predicted, tiny flashes began to occur in clouds throughout the warmed water. Then they stopped and Preston turned off his equipment. He stood there staring at this contraption with his fists on his hips and with all his soul he summoned the gods of science to shed some light on the truth of what he was witnessing. He asked for a clue to spring from the now-quiet water before him, spring into his imagination, a clue that would become the key to solving the riddle of cold fusion. But no such key was to be uncovered on that day, nor had one been presented to him on any other day he ran variations on that experiment, using sound waves, or electrical charges, with distilled water, with heavy water, with platinum coils, with lithium coils. You name it. He used high charges, low charges, high frequencies, and low frequencies. Sometimes there were sparks and sometimes not.

On any given day, when he didn't have the specific materials on hand to try the concept in the flesh, he ran computer-generated mock-ups. But it didn't matter, the cruel and selfish cosmos remained silent and it tightly gripped its secret. He grunted or he laughed, but it wasn't fun. Somewhere, Dr. Cook imagined, some teenager at a high school science fair has an exhibit with a nine-volt battery and seltzer bottle that was not much different than the appalling *nothing* he had been contorting fruitlessly for months.

Lately Preston had felt the pressure of his advancing years and limited resources. How long could he continue to fund his own work? It was a timely worry as the afternoon would play out. His was certainly no hobby on the cheap. Fortunately, CTU still considered him a core faculty member on an informal extended un-paid sabbatical, which meant the institution could also provide access to some of the materials he needed that are very difficult to obtain, occasional tiny portions of isotopes and rare metals required for his experiments. Some of those materials were federally controlled. He knew he was respected but he also knew this informal arrangement with the university would not last forever. The blind eye that had been turned his way would eventually see.

And on that particular day, as Preston was struggling with these gnawing concerns, as he stood in his clean room behind the thick glass walls in the garage, the outside door to the garage opened slowly and Samantha peeked inside. When she saw Preston was alone, she came forward. He couldn't hear anything from within the clean room as she moved past his metal lathes, drills, kilns, the chemistry scaffolding standing on one of the research benches like a jungle-gym, and of course there were the stacked interconnected

PCs with as many screens as a broadcast newsroom. She walked unnoticed up to the glass wall of the clean room and knocked on it.

Her knuckles made only the slightest of sounds on the thick glass, but it caught Preston in the midst of his desperation and it startled him. He turned abruptly.

Sam waved in a little gesture of, "Hello," and she beckoned him to come out.

Preston collected himself from his surprise and he went through the air lock, sitting momentarily on a stool between the two doors, so he could remove his shoe covers. He hung his lab coat with a couple of others on an incongruous wooden hat tree inside the air lock, and then he came out into the front half of his funky garage lab.

"Hi," he said. "What's up? I had lunch with Max today."

"I know," she said. "I saw him before."

"He told me."

"Dalton's not home?" she asked.

"Not yet. You know... the bus... it sometimes runs a little late." He gestured to the door. "I expect he'll pop in before long."

"How's it going? Any developments?" she said in her perfunctory way.

"You would be the first to know," he returned, "after Dalton and me."

"Yes. Your little assistant," she said.

Preston nodded. What was she after? That's where their relationship had gone in those strained days. If she came into the lab she had an agenda, he figured. So he waited.

"I went by the bank yesterday, Preston," she said.

He raised his eyebrows and gestured as if to say, "So?" But he was thinking, Not this.

"There's not much money left in our joint savings. But, of course, you know that because you've been withdrawing from it for a long time."

"I told you I was going to do that," he said.

"Yes, you did. And we agreed on the lab here," she gestured around, "for your work. But now we are at an end. No more of our money for this project. Get a grant, Preston. Get an endowment. Get a foundation to back you. You know how it works! But not another penny of *our* money is going into this adventure. Enough is enough!"

He just stared at her.

She added, "Thank god, I've kept my own retirement account to myself or you'd probably go through it, too."

"We're doing okay," he said weakly, trying to keep it calm. He didn't want to get into anything hot and nasty as so often happened when they went down this path. It led right into that ol' minefield and they both knew it.

"Did you inquire about a second mortgage at the bank?" she asked like a prosecuting attorney

"Yes," he said. "But I would not borrow against the house without consulting with you, Sam."

"Well… actually, you *can't* do anything about the mortgage without consulting with me, Preston. So let's put that question to rest right now. *Forget it*! Sell that goddamn airplane, if you need the cash. It's got to be worth – what? – thirty thousand? *Sell it*!"

His Cessna Skyhawk was a rickety old aircraft by 2005, but it was one of Preston's few joys remaining in life, that bird and Dalton. The project was an obsession, to be sure. He had to do it, but joy wouldn't be the right word to describe his experience of it, at least not lately.

"Probably not that much," he said defensively about the Skyhawk's value.

"Well, it's worth something. Get rid of the damn thing!"

Preston was wishing there was as much heat generated in that flask in the clean room as between him and his wife. It's not the kind of heat one looks for in a marriage. They were clearly angling toward that loathsome cratered and dangerous minefield but he didn't say anything. When it got tense between them he usually clamed up. She, on the other hand, tended to go on a tear at that point, fueled by his silence in some inscrutable way.

"We are so different, you and I!" she said for the thousandth time. "Maybe we should never have gotten married in the first place. That's all blood under the bridge. I've known that for a long time. But after realizing how ill-suited we are for one another, why we went ahead twelve years ago and had Dalton, God only knows. We should've terminated that pregnancy, Preston!"

And suddenly the air in that garage laboratory took on a sweeping chill. The temperature seemingly dropped perceptible degrees the moment Sam uttered those words and they both felt it.

With the hair on his neck standing straight up, Preston was compelled to turn his eyes toward the lab's front door and Sam's gaze followed.

There, silhouetted against the bright afternoon, stood Dalton, his school backpack hanging in one hand by his leg and his other hand still clutching the lab doorknob. Neither Preston nor Samantha had heard the door open nor had they been the least bit aware of their son's arrival. They were already dug in by then. They didn't know at that moment what he had heard of their conversation, but because he was not advancing, they both instantly assumed the worst.

CHAPTER 4

It was yet another spectacular fall day in Pasadena, the home of the Rose Parade and shaded neighborhoods of earth-toned, Green and Green, redwood craftsman houses, with their luxuriously long eves and elephantine pillars protecting airy porches with wicker furniture. The city was sublimely reminiscent of a quieter America, an earlier America.

Maxwell Umberto had just entered his office at CTU, overlooking California Street and the athletic fields across the way. The men's and women's track teams were in off-season training. He stood at the window watching the athletes. Behind him his tailored cashmere blazer was hung on the Scandinavian hat rack adjacent to his office door and his Scala fedora was there, as well.

California Technological University had no athletic scholarships but it did boast a solid array of varsity sports for students who wanted to participate. The Beavers competed with a community of small well-respected private Division III colleges in the Los Angeles area, Whittier, Occidental, Chapman, and Claremont among others. Max had been an athlete himself in high school and college. He was captain of the swimming team at Yale and he was also *ATO* fraternity president in those days. Maxwell played intramural football and softball at MIT when he and Preston were in graduate school. Even in 2005 he still considered himself athletic, a power-biker who put in twenty mile rides twice a week. And he would enter long distance events several times a year, eager to plunk down the two hundred bucks entrance fee so he could peddle from San Francisco to Los Angeles in a three-day AIDS marathon. He would joke it was the only long distance race that had free leg massages at the rest stops, a bargain at twice the price! And for all this effort, sixtyish Max was a tan, taut and fit, a specimen of maturity suited to an AARP magazine cover.

His Yale experience had been the perfect prescription for the youthful Max. All the pieces were in place. The grooming was perfect. But the downside of it all, after his success in the classroom, with women, and in campus politics, was an insidious inability to accept failure, an inability that ran through him like his veins. He had neither a history with failing nor the acceptance of failing as any reality in life. It simply wasn't in his DNA. Naturally, he could speak modestly about himself. He knew that much about etiquette. But in his heart he was a prince-in-waiting and he truly coveted the crown. Maxwell Umberto could never completely comprehend why others did not see he was the most obvious heir apparent for any high position he sought.

Max watched the CTU runners on the other side of California Street rounding the final bend on the quarter-mile clay track. They were just beginning their kick to the finish line. He knew those young athlete's lungs were already on fire as they turned on the afterburners at that very moment and gave it everything their legs had had left for that final hundred yards. Max's own heart was pounding, too, just watching them from afar. Coming in second simply would not do!

The scene on the track flooded Dr. Umberto with his own college memories when his life was so full of promise. He smiled at the recollection of his Cambridge, Massachusetts days, almost four decades in the rearview mirror. His long-time friend Preston Cook, on the other hand, was no athlete and never had been one. Maxwell and Preston had played tennis together every Friday at MIT and Preston was about as graceful on the court as a platypus. But he did have heart. Dr. Cook was game and he hung in there in those days just like he was hanging in there in his garage lab in 2005. He was not a quitter.

Preston's and Maxwell's backgrounds were as disparate as their wardrobes. Preston had gone to public high school in Lawrenceville, New Jersey, not far from Princeton University where his father burnt the midnight oil. His public school education came to pass because Preston's mother, a high-minded, free-thinking poet wanted a diverse public school experience for Preston, not the rarified hoity-toity society found in the private schools surrounding Princeton, populated by strutting incarnations of various Princeton faculty dons. Actually, there had been a bit of a skirmish in the Cook household over the matter, but Preston's father retreated fairly quickly, always having other pressing scholarly matters on his agenda that concerned him well beyond parenting.

After public high school in Lawrenceville, Preston went on to Rutgers in keeping with his mother's philosophies, because it was the public state university of New Jersey. Then he headed off to MIT for his doctorate. Rutgers was an excellent institution but not private. It took only a couple of years at Rutgers for Preston to realize his mother had been right all along advocating for public education. Later in life he frequently defended his educational background by saying that he never felt one inch less prepared than any of his classmates at MIT or his colleagues afterward who had their imaginations and minds swaddled in the entitlement and curricula served up at premium prep schools. Preston Cook was not only content with his academic history and choices, but he was also militant about them whenever the subject was broached.

In spite of these differences, Maxwell and Preston were solidly good friends in the physics department at MIT. They would study together and they would hit the local college watering holes together, too, and share in an unending stream of jokes and jibes at the expense of MIT's neighbor along the Charles River, Harvard. Maxwell's friendship with Preston was genuine. Part of the problem, ironically, was that things always seemed to drift Maxwell's way so very easily. The same phenomenon was absolutely *not* true for Preston, who was as much a slave to his studies in those MIT days as he was a slave to his garage laboratory decades later in Pasadena. His all-consuming obsession with work was one of his father's undying legacies, one that his mother was unable to circumvent with her more carefree public school spirit.

Both of those young men, Max and Preston, had been valedictorians at their respective high schools, although at that time they had yet to meet one another. Max had gone to an expensive private high school. He had been the golden boy at Stonewall Academy outside Alexandria, Virginia. Athletic, handsome, smart, and funny, he was the kind of young man that makes his contemporaries say, "It's just not fair!" Maxwell's father was a well-known judge in stately Savannah, Georgia, where Max grew up among the aristocratic remnants of the Old South. But it was Maxwell's mother, Leah Umberto, who ran the show. She was on the board of numerous socially conscious organizations that served the under-served of the state, most of whom were black, although that would change over time with an influx of Mexican and Vietnamese immigrants. She was a volunteer who worked longer hours than her husband, but she ran all of her affairs with such precision that there was never a family dinner or a Sunday church service sacrificed to her other commitments. Matriarch was a word invented for Leah Umberto.

When Max went off to Yale University, he could not have found more fertile soil for his political ambitions, his scholarship, his social climbing, his fashion consciousness and his self-indulgent ego. He flourished!

There weren't that many girls at Yale in the sixties, but he managed well enough on long weekends in surrounding New Haven to find female companionship whenever he wanted it, a skill that stayed with him through to MIT, and stayed with him into his later years at CTU where he amazingly found a way to cross the great divide between the world of scientific research and the world of Hollywood movie glamour. In brief order after arriving in Pasadena, Dr. Maxwell Umberto began dating budding starlets from the other side of town, soap opera lookers who lived in Beverly Hills or Brentwood. They weren't A-listers, but they turned heads.

Several fateful arcs in Max's life commenced while he was at Yale. His *Alpha Tau Omega* adventures and friendships bore the keys to his future. Even as a freshman, after rush and hazing had gone by the boards, Max moved smoothly and quickly into a circle of the most insidious shakers and movers the university had to offer, all conniving within the *ATO* fraternity house. *ATO* was a cut above in that way, in spite of the fact that Yale was crawling with slick, smart characters possessing the most vulgar ambitions supported on the bluest of pedigrees.

Not the least among Maxwell's young colleagues in the fraternity was a deft political tactician by the name of Robert "Bobby" Skyler. He was from the Oklahoma Skylers, the deeply rich oil Skylars out of Tulsa. Max was cleaver and he was brilliant, but Bobby was a genuine silver-tongued devil. Together they cut a swath of broken hearts and debauchery wherever they went. Surprisingly, it was Max who often put the brakes on that run-away train, because almost nothing would stop Bobby when he got going. Had he been a flimflam man, he would have made his own fortune. Everybody loved Bobby. His laugh, his flirtatious eyes, and his boyish harmless manner, were irresistible to men and women alike.

While Maxwell Umberto was getting elected president of his *Alpha Tau Omega* chapter, Bobby Skylar was rigging the student government elections to make sure a Greek-system loyalist became president of the entire Yale University student body. This was occurring during the birth of the Vietnam War era, when America was in the process of shedding its role as military advisors in Saigon to a more aggressive involvement on the ground. It was when the hippy movement was incubating. Public opinion was barely formed on the immense questions the conflict in Vietnam raised. Suffice it to say, at that time, in those days, Bobby Skylar was not going to let any of those grassroots liberals steal away the student body presidency and ruin everything the good times had going. Bobby was a force and it was a force that carried him from Yale to Georgetown Law School where he surged forward in his C-student sort of way, but he was a C-student who was remembered years later by every one of his professors because of his brash assuredness and his seductive style. No mean feat.

Bobby and Maxwell gradually lost touch with one another during the ensuing decades after graduation from Yale, as their careers and graduate schools consumed their respective lives and pulled them in different directions.

Be that as it may, Bobby Skylar reappeared in Maxwell's story more than thirty years after their relationship at Yale University had faded away. By then Bobby was ensconced at the highest level of surreptitious federal government work, silently involved in focused activities about which few beyond the President of United States had knowledge. Mr. Skylar's dusty left-behind decades-old friendship with Dr. Maxwell Umberto, cum CTU tenured professor of physics, was prominent in the equation when Bobby was asked to fly to Pasadena to influence Dr. Umberto away from that silly business with cold fusion and return to his more promising work on a unified theory and the essence of gravity. Power brokers in Washington and elsewhere were not happy with even a remote possibility that cheap, unlimited energy was a possibility.

Those who sent Bobby to see his old friend in 2003 were sure that high-profile Maxwell Umberto had to be the prime mover in the cold fusion adventure reputed to be taking place in California, and removing him from the project would kill it. Some passable explanations had been trumped up for approaching Max about abandoning cold fusion, but what Bobby discovered at that time was that Dr. Umberto was already tired of it all and he was quite amenable to bailing on his friend Preston Cook. Bobby Skylar and his agency happened to catch Dr. Umberto at the exactly right time. It was amazing how the sudden appearance of grant money for Max could tip the scales with a thud and prompt Maxwell to bid a swift adieu to the cold fusion project.

Yet, as things evolved in Washington two years later, in 2005, long after this whole cold fusion exercise was thought to have been put to bed, attention ignited again around that strange and radical form of alternative, cheap, and nearly limitless energy. Attention came via recurrent sparks of gossip. The existence of ongoing cold fusion research was more of a mystery than a known reality, but Bobby's old relationship with Maxwell Umberto became an asset one more time. If the rumors about cold fusion had any substance at all, it was assumed Dr. Umberto had to be instrumental in the new developments. It was all happening in Pasadena, California again, just as before, so Dr. Umberto must be back at it, or so surmised the puppet masters.

Consequently, Mr. Skylar was summoned by his superiors in Washington, D.C. and again he was asked to surface in Max's life on the West Coast to find out what the hell was going on with cold fusion after two years of silence. Only Bobby Skylar could pull off such a hat trick. It would work because Bobby really liked Maxwell Umberto and he always had. There was Yale!

CHAPTER 5

Preston and Dalton Cook were at the Van Nuys airport where he kept the old Cessna Skyhawk. They would often go flying together, on weekends, just to get off the ground and away from the world and its crowds and aggravations. They rejoiced in soaring amongst the clouds both physically and mentally. They were alike in that way; they needed flight. Preston's entire life had been flight in a sense, his emersion in his work and his research. Dalton was not too different, given what the outside world so often offered to him, and it was not always acceptance. Rising high into the blue California sky was a liberating experience. They would grin at one another like two children because they would bounce gently along like a kite above the earth, riding on nothing but thin air. And along with all of that, young Dalton loved machines. He had an affinity for them, knew instinctively what they wanted, what made them purr. In Preston's lab, it was the machinery Dalton gravitated toward, the lathes, drills, kilns, and the sand molds that were needed to manufacture the precision equipment for the cold fusion experiments.

However, that particular flight on that particular Saturday had an ulterior motive. Preston had arranged it so Dalton might put into perspective the events of two days earlier, when the boy had arrived unexpectedly at the lab while Samantha and Preston were arguing. Dalton's presence on earth had been mentioned. This was not a subject that was easy to broach because most youngsters could well understand the meaning of the conversation Dalton had heard and he would never bring such a topic up for questions. It wasn't his way. He had retreated from the garage laboratory doorway that terrible day, going to his bedroom in the house to bury himself in the World Wide Web. Dalton had allowed the door to the garage to close slowly behind him when he left, shutting the lab once again into a place with no sunlight. Preston and Samantha had turned to each other that day and not spoken a word. They each knew damage control had to happen, but how? Dalton was not a kid to be placated with inane apologies. He was far too smart for that.

By abdication, nothing was said to Dalton about the incident immediately. Samantha had to go back over to the college because she was teaching multivariate statistics that night in a classroom loaded with freshman wizzes. It wouldn't be your run-of-the-mill stat class; it never was at CTU. But variables in the equations of her home life were not so comfortably handled by Dr. Day-Steiner. They tended to remain out of reach for her because she would quickly abandon their pursuit. She had always left the touchy-feely part of parenting to Preston and on the day she said out loud that Dalton should never have born, she seemed more eager than ever to drop the situation into her husband's lap.

Preston's own father, the workaholic at Princeton, relinquished the rearing of his son to his artist wife who imagined the colorful latitudes available to Preston. Quite to the contrary, Samantha's father was a captain of industry, the genuine article. He was a self-made man, who turned hundreds of square miles of California desert into thousands of three bedroom ranch houses for the masses that were flowing into the state in the fifties like an invading army after World War II. He had over five million dollars in his personal bank account by the time he was thirty years old and that was with no college education whatsoever, as he would repeatedly boast after two or three martinis at the Bel Air Country Club where he had been a member for the last four decades dining and golfing with Los Angeles's old blood. It was probably his belittling of college that ultimately drove Samantha to the academic heights she did achieve, just to carve herself out from her father, but in the end it was all for naught. He was an unforgiving role model in her soul and he had soldered her wires into place exactly like his own. Old Mr. Steiner turned nothing over to chance or to anyone else, including the indoctrination of his offspring. As the years would demonstrate, Samantha could be as controlling and as materialistic as her father had ever been. Never mind her PhD and never mind the sixties.

Samantha had scampered back to the CTU campus before she and Preston could even discuss any kind of strategy regarding young Dalton's interrupting them during such an untoward scene in the garage laboratory. So, once again, Preston was left to invent a plan of his own. His plan was indirect and it was delayed, which was common for Preston on such matters, but his plan was also genuine. Still, neither parent in young Dalton's life would be getting a medal for tending to his pain quickly when the boy was hurting as he was on that day. His parents were both inept in many ways.

Preston had traipsed to his son's bedroom after Samantha left for her class and he found Dalton mouse-clicking his way through scenes of far-away places. Preston walked up behind the boy and, not being a man of too many words in tough personal moments, he simply rested his hand on Dalton's shoulder.

Without looking up, Dalton said, "Hi, Dad."

"Hi," said Preston quietly. And after a beat, watching Pacific islands become Himalayan Mountains, and those becoming South

American rainforests on Dalton's wide flat-screen monitor, Preston added, "How would you like to go flying on Saturday?"

Dalton still didn't look away from the images but he said as happily as he could under the circumstances, "That sounds great, Dad."

"Okay, then," said Preston conclusively and patted his son's shoulder before removing his hand. On the way out of the bedroom, Preston stopped at the open bedroom door where he turned to look back at the boy whose head appeared to have a halo glowing around it from the bright screen he was facing. "We love you, Dalt."

"I know, Dad. I love you, too," said Dalton, as he kept clicking and moving the mouse. Beaches, prairies and cities sped past until he came to an ice blue arctic landscape where he paused and stared.

At the small community Van Nuys Airport the next Saturday, Preston and Dalton were going through their usual pre-flight drill with the Skyhawk. Preston would walk around the aircraft and Dalton would call out the items on the checklist.

Dalton yelled out, "Baggage door?"

"Closed and locked!" shouted Preston.

"Missing rivets? Dents?"

Preston walked by the cowling where "Lucky 47" was dramatically painted near the nose as though the little Cessna was a World War II fighter aircraft. All that was missing was a leggy vamp in a swimsuit. "Negative!" said Preston.

"Left elevator – leading edge?"

"Check!"

"Trailing edge?"

"Check!"

"Bolts in hinge?"

"Check!"

They went through the exterior inspection and then they climbed inside, continuing their countdown to take-off.

"Fuel selector value?"

"Both!"

"Mixture?"

"Full rich!"

Preston didn't allow them to skip any step. He wanted to emphasize safety at all times, even as they hit the ignition and the Cessna's engine sputtered into life and the single prop blurred before them.

"Throttle?"

"Open one-half inch!"

"Brake?"

"Apply and hold!"

"Radios, avionics power switch?

"On!"

In moments Preston was checking off with air traffic control, too, "Van Nuys tower, N5224K, at 29R, request take-off, departure to the North."

"Wing flaps?" continued Dalton.

"Up!" said his dad.

With the ground rushing by them at eighty miles per hour and the little airplane shaking and vibrating as it sped over the tarmac toward the mountains beyond the broad San Fernando Valley, the rush of air over the white wings suddenly and gently lifted Lucky 47 off the ground like a great hand had slipped beneath her. Even though Preston well knew the physics of aerodynamics, it was magic to him every time lift-off actually occurred. God damn it, they were flying! They were free as birds! Dalton let out a huge "Woo-Ha!" when they left the earth behind and they rose above the sprawling suburbs and rose above the sounds of the city and rose above the smog and rose like a song into a bright, bright sky. They grinned at each other. It was wonderful.

Whatever needed to be said about what happened in the lab a couple of days ago when Dalton appeared unexpectedly in the midst of an altercation between his parents was also left behind like the brown mundane San Fernando Valley. The blue sky was a canopy of limitless forgiveness. That part of Preston's fathering worked. He long ago realized the quality of flying time together with his son and its remarkable healing powers. He was musing, as he often did, as they slid between two clouds as thin as dreams on either side of their airplane, if only therapists could recommend flying for all of their troubled clients.

Up there, high over the San Gabriel Mountains, where hikers sweated and drank Arrowhead water as they crawled over boulders and pressed along narrow passages to achieve a summit that would give them a glimpse of vast Los Angeles County below, and where coyotes competed for a vanishing array of prey, slinking, boney and dangerous in the shadows of California pines, Preston did at one point say to Dalton, when they were quiet and the features of the land moved gently beneath them, as remote as a memory, his Mom loved him very, very much. She always had. And because of pressure at work she sometimes says things she doesn't really believe.

Dalton nodded, looking out the window at the earth below. "I understand, Dad," he said. And then the topic was behind them.

Preston always figured Dalton did understand in a relatively complex way. He always understood far more than anybody gave him credit for. Perhaps all children are like that. Elements can be thrown together with such ferocity in the lives of family there may be no true solving of them on one single day. The challenge of solving the cold fusion riddle was a snap compared to the challenge of rearing such a unique child in their obsessed household.

CHAPTER 6

Washington, D. C. is a magnificent city with a European feel. It mirrors the designs of Beaux-Arts Paris with grand rotaries and radiating avenues dramatically emphasizing the alabaster monuments and the beating heart of the nation's government. Statues and rotunda of marble and granite, paying tribute to America's iconic and heroic history, are lit by flood lights at night and present to even the most cynically tourist a moment of awe and respect. The city spreads around and absorbs a visitor as it should, the capital of a powerful and visionary nation.

But for Twenty-First Century automobile traffic, the rotaries and radial avenues make it a city of horrors, wrong turns, and slingshot, errant trips across the Potomac. Visitors to Washington looking to merely appreciate the corridors of power could suddenly find themselves carried on boomerang highways into the corridors of an impoverished America living only a stone's throw from the capitol rotunda and light years from its promise. Washington, D.C. is a city of brilliant contrasts. Ghettos decay just around the corner from the tony townhouses of Georgetown. In some communities you may find a street thug, in others a heavy-handed congressman, but a thug, nonetheless. Extortion and exploitation are two of the currencies on splendid display in the United States' capital.

Bobby Skylar and his family lived in a three-story townhouse in the new *haute* district of D.C.'s historic Foggy Bottom. He'd been working the Washington beat when Watergate undid his first Presidential boss back in the seventies, but unlike many of the denizens of the nation's capital, his fortunes didn't rise and fall with the results of elections. Many offices around Washington would change hands, family photos and furnishings endlessly coming and going, as candidates won and candidates lost. It was a revolving door. Very distinguished, intelligent and accomplish men and women would set up in the capital offices like they owned their space only to be packing boxes a few years later when a new President, senator, or congressperson took office. So many of the actual worker bees came and went, election after election, based on party affiliation, it's a wonder the federal government could really function at all. When leadership changed, gratuities and favors determined the occupancy of every building and every choice office space along the lettered avenues of Washington.

Yet, there was also a reliable army of career civil servants who weathered the changes. Among them, in a few carefully guarded buildings, were cohorts of protected men and women engaged in meticulously veiled activities. They were the kinds of activities that sailed on unabated, administration after administration, the shadow government that is not accountable to the electorate, handling business behind closed doors and with the lights dim. And these were the offices of government in which Bobby Skylar had found his home. He was an esteemed senior practitioner at his trade, too. And even though he was edging beyond sixty years of age, the twinkle had not gone from his clear blue eyes, nor had he lost the bright smile and dimples that had carried him into so many townie bedrooms back at Yale. His features and his charm could still earn a blush from a pretty administrative assistant thirty years his junior.

The Skylars had a pair of grown children, out of the house by 2005, and both Ivy League educated. The more rebellious son had gone to Brown just to be different and to pursue altruistic goals, but their daughter knew what was right to please her dad and graduated from Yale the prior spring. Still, Bobby had negotiated for each of them sweet jobs inside the beltway soon after their respective college commencement ceremonies. And, as it turned out, Bobby's Brown University son wasn't so altruistic that he would snub a brand new Porsche Carrera and a six figure income at twenty-three, thereby confirming his father's long held suspicion that everybody has their price. Bobby never deviated from his plan to groom his children for an aristocratic future. When he set his sights, he followed through and no intellectualized resistance from his boy was going to stand in Mr. Skylar's way. He had sown the seeds too well.

Bobby hadn't lost much of a step after the four decades since his own adventures as a college kid in New Haven, rigging the race for student body president. He was still a force in his own right, having been a storied agent with the CIA. But by 2005 he had moved on to a position with the lesser understood but very much coveted Special Group. It was an honor, actually, to be accepted as a part of that clandestine branch of the United States government's intelligence community.

Yet in spite of its unique and valuable niche, the Group had been very quiet in the years after nine-eleven. That was a time during which the nation's security focus turned fully toward two horrendously dysfunctional, uncooperative, and very visible agencies, the CIA and FBI. Those were the years in which Homeland Security emerged. But even during that eviscerating period for the United States, the Special Group still had value here and there because it could do things none of the other agencies could touch. The Special Group had always flown well below the radar of public scrutiny, including the press, and that's exactly why in the fall of 2005 Special Group agent Bobby Skylar was summoned to see his boss about a "unique threat to America's national interests". Those were the exact words used in the communiqué. Bobby noted his directive was even more oblique than was usually found in the obscure language so popular among Special Group operatives, language resplendent with euphemisms. At least Bobby was getting some manner of assignment during a prolonged lull in activities for the Group. With just over one year to go before his retirement almost any assignment was welcome to Agent Skylar. On the other hand, as it turned out, this particular assignment was rather complicated on a personal level.

CHAPTER 7

It was a bright autumn morning in 2005 when Bobby Skylar went to meet his boss, Digger Mac Brown, at a Special Group office hidden above a non-descript storefront Chinese restaurant, "Walk the Wok", frequented by many congressmen and congresswomen because of its proximity to the capitol. No customer at the restaurant would have remotely suspected clandestine and sometimes lethal operations were being orchestrated overhead as they rolled their mushu pork and drank their egg drop soup, but that was exactly the point. No Special Group meeting ever occurred in an actual federal building or even on government-owned property. The dimly lit space above the restaurant was rented in the name of a fictitious real estate company, "Potomac Title and Trust". There was a door adjacent to the Chinese restaurant which bore the phony company's name and that door opened to a narrow wooden staircase in serious need of fresh paint. The staircase climbed to an office on the second floor that would pass for a bona fide rag-tag title company on the verge of bankruptcy should someone happen to wander up the stairs looking to find an actual business, which occurred from time to time in spite of the off-putting entrance.

Special Group didn't leave anything to chance, however, so they had cross-trained one of their agents to occupy a front desk and do a pretty good job of fielding real estate questions should an unsuspecting stranger climb those stairs. Her task was to deflect inquiries as plausibly as possible and drive any customer back down the stairs and out into the street to find a real title business that would help them. With some of the stubborn visitors, it proved to be a much more challenging assignment for the front desk agent than anyone would ever have imagined.

Digger Mac Brown, the Director for Special Group, was a left over from the cold war if ever there was one. He had been part of the secretive 5412 Committee, named after the room number in which it originally met, a committee that was imagined to conduct covert operations in the years subsequent to JFK's assassination. In the beginning, Special Group was a subset of the 5412 Committee and it was designed to handle, as implied by its title, only the most special of assignments and the blackest of black operations that resided in an otherwise very black arena. Special Group had planned an assassination of Fidel Castro, who in those days was often thought to be behind the assassination of John Kennedy, but the Castro scheme was never initiated. Special Group continued on the fringe of government after the 5412 Committee was dissolved. Up to that very day in October of 2005, when Bobby Skylar was going to meet his supervisor, Digger Mac Brown still burned with the belief that Castro killed Kennedy. Nobody dared mention that old and abandoned Special Group objective around Digger because he would immediately fly into a tirade, ranting that we should go in and knock off that communist Cuban bastard while he's still kickin'. Even if Castro was on his deathbed, Digger Mac Brown wanted desperately for the United States to put a slug in the son of a bitch's forehead and be sure to let him know who was doing it before we pulled the trigger!

Yet Digger's hatred of the commies wasn't born with the 5412 Committee in the nineteen-sixties. He was nurtured on loathing the reds by his Marine Corps father, a bird colonel, who was a flawless guiding light in the admiring eyes of young Digger during the early Eisenhower years. But his dad, Colonel Mac Brown, was captured by the North Koreans during the police action there in 1953 and he was tortured to death. It was nasty, too. His disfigured remains were sent home after hostilities ended and the staggering power of that loss to Digger, with the lessons the boy had absorbed about the godless, inhuman communists, never faded in him over the years. The reds were the antithesis of everything Digger had been raised to value. Hatred was in his gut like a cancer. It wasn't abstract, either; the commies had hurt him personally.

The post-Kennedy 5412 Committee was long since gone by 2005, but Special Group lingered like spectral remains with little in the way of a body to inhabit. Yet the funding continued as an earmark, a footnote, an unexplored line item lost in billions of dollars spent on homeland security.

Digger's record in Special Group was astoundingly free of failures, which is pretty remarkable when one considers they did not trade in slam-dunk affairs. When he was a young agent he had personally put a bullet in the back of the head of a truculent Soviet general while he was sitting at his desk in the Kremlin. Digger had come and gone from Moscow undercover in twenty-four hours, parachuting into the Soviet Union at night and after his mission was accomplished he was gunning a motorcycle by dawn's early light through the Urals and out of harm's way. It was more in keeping with an Ian Fleming novel than something that could actually happen, but it did happen, and it happened to Digger.

By 2005 the United States was only fighting communists as a sidebar, more of a distraction after the collapse of the Soviet Union, but Digger used those old feelings of hatred to fuel any Special Group action that involved thwarting un-American activity and he had a lot of fuel and a lot of hatred to spare. He didn't go on missions any longer at seventy, but he would do it in a heartbeat, if asked. Plus he admired Vice President Dick Chaney, an admiration born from numerous clandestine alliances hatched during the fading decades of the twentieth century, alliances and plots aimed at outsmarting the commies. Digger missed those old days. He continued to see the world in black and white and could spot enemies to the American way of life around every corner. The anti-war train that roared through America with so many of their contemporaries during the Vietnam era had gone right by him.

Bobby Skylar was more than a decade younger than his boss and he didn't necessarily embrace the same mentality, linking communism to evil, but the belief that communism is evil was a throughline with Digger and Bobby knew how the conversation had to be framed whenever they talked. Bobby's views damn well better be painted in red, white, and blue or there would be trouble to pay. He knew Digger's history and Bobby always reminded himself that he might be just like his boss if his own father had been mutilated and murdered by communists.

There must have been an undiagnosed bi-polar disorder residing in Digger, or so Bobby Skylar strongly believed, because conversations with the man in what may have been a manic stage would often begin in the middle of things and it was up to the listener to scramble around and catch up, put the pieces in place, and respond appropriately. If one would fall behind in those conversations and choose to challenge, then Digger's withering glare would follow. No one wanted to be on the receiving end of those eyes in that kind of moment.

So, there was Bobby on that October day, climbing the run-down wooden staircase to the faux offices above "Walk the Wok", getting ready for what very well may be a dance requiring some really fast footwork. Even as Bobby opened the door to the would-be title office and saw his boss behind the worn oak desk toward the back, flanked by rows of well-used but empty filing cabinets that were nothing but props for the office, he sensed the game was going to be brisk that day. He nodded to Veronica, the curvy female agent who had been tutored on the rudiments of real estate and who was positioned like a receptionist near the front door. Before Bobby's eyes fully met Digger's, Agent Skylar noticed a phony Potomac Title and Trust wall calendar over Digger's shoulder with appointments scratched all over it. Attention to detail. His desk had an old-fashion CRT computer monitor glowing with a trumped up Excel spreadsheet.

"So, he's still at it, huh?" shouted Digger toward Bobby, going right to business and rolling back and forth in his squeaking wooden chair while he fiddled with a pencil between his fingers. He was not happy.

Bobby Skylar's mind was racing. *Who*, precisely, is still at it, was the question ricocheting around in his skull like a squash ball. He'd better know this one, because it was apparently the focus of the meeting. Digger always went straight to the chase when he was like this, on the manic side.

"How are you, Digger?" Bobby said coming forward. This was a normal question even in the strange world of Special Group and it might buy him a couple of beats to figure things out. Besides, Bobby knew Digger's wife, Dottie, had passed away last November, a week before Thanksgiving. Bobby had gone to the funeral. Digger and Dottie had been married forever, but there were no children. Even a man like Digger had to be suffering and lonely. But Digger was better at burying feelings than any human being Bobby had ever met, so one never knew for sure where his mood might be.

"Is he?" demanded Digger, skipping the pleasantries altogether.

As was the protocol with Special Group, this was a private meeting. All meetings were. Veronica had risen and disappeared out the office door as soon as Bobby had passed by her. Need-to-know was not a casually tossed about concept with these operatives. There was only one chair in front of Digger's desk, so Bobby slid into the chair and Digger snapped forward on his elbows, leaning across the worn oak surface of the desk, and he wiped a bit of perspiration off his high forehead, firing that fierce gaze of his directly into Bobby's eyes, waiting for an answer. He was way ahead of Agent Skylar at this point.

Tossing his hands apologetically, not knowing what else to do and not willing to confess ignorance, Bobby said, "That's what I've heard." Obviously, he was supposed to know what was going on and he was buying time. It was a gambit.

"I thought we provided some kind of incentive to let it go? Didn't we? Oh, shit, I don't understand this crap. Help me out here, Bobby! We made sure the guy got grants, other money, something, right?"

Bobby repeated the words to himself silently. Grants? And out of the fog, Bobby began to locate some images in his imagination. Incentive? Grant money means research, most likely. Okay. We're getting somewhere now. Of course! It was Max! He remembered they had made sure he got a substantial grant on.... what was it? Yes! Gravity and the unified theory! A geek favorite. It was all coming back. His old college buddy, professor extraordinaire, Maxwell Umberto, had been *bought* away from his cold fusion work to study gravity! But the bribe was a couple of years ago, wasn't it? And there was somebody else, another faculty member, an odd guy but really smart, according to Max.

"That's right," said Bobby after a beat and tossing the dice. "We paid off an old friend of mine from Yale with a grant we dug up from the Wicks Foundation. He was supposed to abandon his cold fusion research and go back to his work on *gravity*, of all things." Bobby chuckled. "I figure Newton covered gravity well enough when that apple hit him on the head."

"What about the energy apple, Bobby? Is your old college buddy still trying to work this portable nuclear reactor crap?"

"All I know as a matter of actual fact is that Max quit it two years ago."

"Well, we're hearing things."

It didn't surprise Bobby that words uttered somewhere in obscurity had gotten back to Digger Mac Brown, because whispered words or words written in invisible ink will find their way into Digger's fevered consciousness if they run cross-ways with his agenda and personal mission to protect America. He had his means.

"Max did have a research partner," said Bobby trying to make sense of the rumors.

"Why didn't we buy him out, too?" queried his boss.

"The guy's a nutcase. He can't piss in a swimming pool without Maxwell's help. Max assured me there is no chance in hell cold fusion can work."

"Whatever," sighed Digger. "I'm no scientist, but this research has to stay completely out of the public domain, Bobby. That was the original idea. The administration doesn't want it. America doesn't want it. This bullshit is a threat to industries that drive our country and our economy. We're thinking there may be hostile interests pushing it along. So, you're gonna have to go out to California again, Mr. Skylar, and conclusively take care of this with your friend. Either that or... tell us what needs to happen to end it all. Catch my drift? Sooner is better than later."

Digger Mac Brown leaned back in the creaky old chair that was used only a dozen times a year on varying Special Group assignments and he fiddled with his yellow No. 2 pencil, looking across it at Agent Skylar. These were never meetings where lengthy analytical discussions would take place, where the reasonableness of an action was going to be reviewed and debated. These were meetings where Digger would tell Bobby what to do and then Bobby would do it. Maybe a couple of exchanges would go down, as had happened on that day, but in the end, an order would be given and that would be that.

CHAPTER 8

On a gloomy day in late September there was only a lingering marine layer that left one feeling like rain was in the offing, but no rain would follow. A three month siege of Santa Ana winds in the summer had desiccated everything in their path, a relentless attack seemingly driven by the planet's determination to return the Los Angeles basin to a landscape of dirt and rocks and lizards, as was there before humans. But that day Preston and Dalton and the rest of Pasadena were experiencing an afternoon with nothing but dull gray sky more cool than hot.

Father and son were setting up to give their experiment another go in the clean room. Every time they went through this drill they told themselves that their old-fashioned analog ammeter would go wild when the water heated up, its needle would be buried to the right as thousands of volts would suddenly surge through output cables and, even if it was for the smallest fraction of a split-second, they would have succeeded! To that end, Preston chose not to repeat a failed experiment over and over again. He would always change something. Similarly, his virtual experiments ran twenty-four-seven on computers in the lab, introducing the slightest random adjustments each time. Research is a game of inches. Small movements can result in big differences. But lately it had all begun to feel routine. Preston made uninspired corrections, often mechanical, like raising the palladium rod a centimeter. And he would dutifully write it all down, every minor alteration that might finally be the secret of the matter, that might at long last lead to a break-through in his work and give birth to a realistic source of light and heat for every man, woman, and child on earth! Water, food, and shelter could very reasonably become quick byproducts of this kind of unlimited, clean and cheap power generation. Drilling and pumping, agriculture, mining, milling and foundries… they all require power and lots of it. If Preston Cook found what he was seeking, human kind might see the end of misery in short order. Or so Preston believed. That's what kept him going.

On that strange day, things would take an innocuous but remarkable turn. Preston and his young assistant, his son, were about to give their experiment another tweaked effort at getting sonic impulses to take them were the wanted to go. And Dalton, who had been charged with cleaning some laboratory glassware, said straightforward as usual, "Stars do not make any sound, Dad. Why not try more light. Stars are really, really bright! The center of stars!" he said enthusiastically, reciting their mantra.

Preston glanced at him and smiled. "The center of stars!" he returned.

"How is there sound without air?" said Dalton.

"Well, it's really the vibrations…" and he stopped and examined his boy. "We can go back to light," said Preston softly. He was ready to try anything.

In spite of the popular sonic driven cold fusion research that had gone before, the notion of using intense light instead of sound ate its way into Preston's brain like a worm after he heard it from Dalton, and he began connecting the concept of pulses of sound with pulses of light. He had tried laser beams before but he had been doing sound waves lately because the body of research shows sparks can actually be generated. He'd seen them. But instinctively it had always felt like a blind alley to Preston. So, after that day in the lab, even while Preston was running his last failed experiment trying to create cold fusion from sound waves, he was already calculating how laser beams might lead him to the undying brilliance that resides at the center of stars.

The Raymond is a restaurant that would not be seen by most passers-by in Pasadena. It is below street-level south of Old Town, tucked away in the shadows of Fair Oaks Blvd., fashioned from a hundred-year-old house that had once been the residence for the manager of the upscale Raymond Hotel in 1900. All that remained of the hotel in 2005 after an eviscerating fire nearly a century earlier were the little manager's house, some photographs, and a lingering memory of quality. The restaurant embodied that memory, where once upon a time those grounds were something special.

Maxwell Umberto and Samantha Day-Steiner were having a late lunch at the Raymond, graciously prepared by the chef an hour after the restaurant had formally stopped serving lunch and had turned its focus to dinner guests. But Max, as was his style, had personally cajoled Eduardo to provide them a simple meal. Eduardo was a Salvadorian immigrant who dazzled world-renown French chefs during his Parisian internship ten years earlier after he graduated from the American School of the Culinary Arts. He ran the kitchen at The Raymond like he owned it. For such special service, however, a generous gratuity was an unspoken expectation and Max would more than meet those expectations, because he could clearly see that by late afternoon he and Sam would be the only guests in The Raymond. All around them waiters switched out table settings for evening fare, but it didn't bother Drs. Umberto and Day-Steiner who were quite content to be enjoying succulent lemon and caper sand dabs with a bitter-sweet nutty endive salad that Eduardo had agreed to prepare for them.

In the old days Preston, Samantha, and Max used to go out to lunch together regularly, if their class schedules at CTU allowed. Actually the cuisine available on campus was rather special at the Parthaneum, not at all what one would typically find in a faculty dining hall. But getting off campus to some secluded restaurant was a treat in those days. Of course, Preston had been absent for a couple of years now, sequestered as he was in his private clean room and laboratory laboring over his journals and his work, like a monk determined to save the world. So, Samantha and Maxwell decided that they wouldn't let Preston's dreary obsession get in the way of enjoying some really good food from time to time off campus. Besides, when they left the CTU premises, there were no students waiting to bushwhack them and no ornery colleagues fit to be tied over a faculty senate vote. These lunches remained a delightful escape even though an observer might say they were happening more often now that Preston was not with them.

In fairness to Samantha, Maxwell Umberto was erudite and entertaining company. At home she had "The Man from Gloom" to contend with. In the best of times, friends may have thought Dr. Day-Steiner was a good family person, but her current unhappiness with Preston was palpable to everyone they knew. Nonetheless, she did love her son, little Dalton. What happened recently in the garage lab, she told herself, and during other stressed marital confrontations dating back to the boy's birth were simply beyond her control because she had always been reluctant to be a parent. Still and all, she was the boy's mom and her affection for him was not dismissible. She could feel the power of love for her child as part of evolution's imprint, even if it was extremely conflicted.

Nonetheless, without all of that complicated evolutionary analysis, Sam had observed that Dalton plainly preferred his father. After a number of years of being frustrated about her life with Preston's obsession, plus being second in line to Dalton's affections, she had backed off, choosing to allow herself some room to enjoy life, to laugh and not worry about competing with Preston over their son, or her husband's center of the stars mania, or even his damn Cessna. Maxwell Umberto provided for Sam an opportunity to escape, to smile, to be lighthearted.

Dr. Umberto also delivered serious circumspections for Samantha, political and practical, on so many of the issues enveloping both of their lives. After all, they were equally enmeshed in the competitive and highly charged world of CTU. And beyond the university, Maxwell had cultivated insights into LA's broader popular culture, insights that anyone would find fascinating. It wasn't for nothing this nationally recognized physicist and scholar was dating aspiring movie stars and slipping smoothly through the fast-paced partying on the west side of town, the *paparazzi* side of Los Angeles. He was also a fashion plate even at his age, tall, blonde, blue-eyed and handsome. At the very least, when he got together with Samantha Day-Steiner, he always had terrific Hollywood stories to tell.

CHAPTER 9

A wide-tire Heritage Softail Harley-Davidson makes a distinctive sound. It may be irritating noise to some people, but that deep-throated machine had presence; it had gusto. To lovers of motorcycles, it has a thunderous and wondrous voice. This was a bike that defined what motorcycles ought to be, or so believed Preston Cook's next door neighbor, Big Buster Bernard, a man as imposing as his Harley. He rode a classic vehicle. None of that pansy-ass molded fiberglass crap, no sleek rigid saddlebags that even Harley-Davidson went to, in later years. No, siree. Big Buster blamed all of that nonsense on Harley trying to compete with the Japanese bikes. Buster's Heritage Softail had black leather, studded and buckled saddlebags and his sumptuous tandem leather seat was soft and curvy as a full-figured woman. His ride had no tricked-out handlebars, either, requiring him to cruise down the freeway like he was hanging from a chin-up bar. He wasn't a freak. He wanted control of his machine when he was out on the road. So, in keeping with that thought, the front shocks didn't reach forward like the tines on a Bar-B-Q fork, the way a chopper's might. He wasn't *Easy Rider*, for chrissakes. His was a restored straight-from-the-factory bike, a purist's motorcycle, and it was all Harley-Davidson, through and through.

Buster himself was a straight-from-the-factory classic, too. He stood six feet, six inches, and his weight was headed toward three hundred, and neither of those measurements included his hob-nail, scuffed, black biker's boots or his thick and worn black leather, snapped and epilated, biker's jacket. He had "Mongrels" sewn in a faded arc across his back as a parody of a bad-ass biker gang, the Mongols. He clearly didn't give a shit. He belonged to no biker club, gang, or posse. He wasn't a joiner. The name Mongrels was also a private reference to his own blood line, because Big Buster Bernard was half Jewish, one quarter Jamaican, and one quarter Chinese. God knows what else was thrown in there. His voluptuous lady, Cloud Willow, was half Cherokee and half Irish. It was a nightmare for demographers, finding these two mosaics under one roof. They were like a couple of insect mutants that managed to hook up, sole survivors of DDT and everything else humans had poured on them, the very beginnings of an indomitable future. They were American that way, the power of a rainbow coalition distilled down to a single couple. Buster and Cloud loved each other as madly as teenage rebels in a fifties movie, with a Romeo and Juliet until-death-due-us-part passion. And they went everywhere on that damn motorcycle, leaving Cloud Willow's aging Ford F-100 pick-up in the driveway most of the time.

You could say there was a visceral connection between Preston and his neighbors, Big Buster Bernard and his girlfriend, Cloud Willow. They were all outsiders really, and they all chose it. Cloud was a college instructor, too, like Preston, but she worked at nearby Pasadena City College, a bulging community college with a very good reputation for sending kids on to four-year schools. PCC had an articulated relationship with CTU that would fast track science-heads to those prestigious corridors. It also had its share of community college ne'er-do-wells, youngsters who basically planned to hang out with no direction until external forces forced them to make a decision.

Cloud Willow taught in the art department at PCC, which meant none of her protégées were headed toward degrees in math or science of any stripe. Her job was to open up minds to the relevance of art in this world and to help students find their own voice in a creatively challenged and very commercial environment that pressured newcomers to copy what has already been done. Interestingly, it wasn't so far removed from the world of scientific research in that way, as Preston saw it. In fact both Preston *and* Samantha had once talked about collaborating on that very topic, writing an article or a book together, but they had never gotten around to it. They each observed that established paradigms want to sustain themselves in any discipline. Paradigms are guarded fiercely by stakeholders who refuse to lose position and who will fight to the death to prevent a new paradigm from dislodging them. Best practices and reason take a back seat to ego and control.

Art instructor Cloud Willow and Big Buster Bernard were an odd pair of throwbacks to the revolutionary sixties, but they were also about as sweet a pair of human beings as one is likely to encounter. Cloud wore more silver and turquoise jewelry than Preston had seen on any other human in four decades. Each finger carried a heavy ring and a single necklace was never enough. She often had so much silver and turquoise draped around her that she looked like an Aztec courtesan. Fortunately, Cloud was a substantial woman, as a man the size of Big Buster might require. She was a curvy, large breasted, long-haired broad, clearly a leftover from hippiedom. She didn't wear much make-up, but she was sexy and she didn't mind being sexy. She was the proverbial earth mother. Both Cloud and Big Buster had profusions of gray streaks in their hair, yet they didn't act gray at all. They were feisty and active, always on the move. Sometimes, on his way to the lab, Preston could hear them yelling at each other and, if he was not mistaken, the yelling would often be punctuated by the sound of breaking glass. Nonetheless, the next morning they would be a pair of turtle-doves, cooing and kissing and climbing onto that Harley Heritage Softail Classic and peeling off for parts unknown, as tightly wound as if they were a single body on the bike and loving every minute of it. They were one hell of a couple. They knew who they were and they knew how to settle their grievances. It was a quality that was completely missing in Preston's life with his own wife and partner, a woman he loved completely. Sometimes it felt to Preston as if the opinions of other people had become more important between him and Samantha than what they thought of themselves. Buster and Cloud didn't give a damn.

The fact that young Dalton Cook was fascinated with machinery only sealed the deal with the next door neighbors, because Big Buster's monster hit of a motorcycle was a true machine if ever there has been a machine. Dalton loved to ride on the back. Big Buster would never do anything foolish with the little guy in tow and Preston knew that, so almost every time there was a chance to let Dalton experience the freedom of the motorcycle world, Preston would nod and say, "Okay, but be back in twenty minutes." It was the closest thing to drifting among the clouds in the Cessna as could be found on solid earth.

Samantha felt differently.

"God damn it, Preston!" she screamed coming out of the back of their house, down the stoop, the door slamming behind her. It was the same day she had been lunching on sand dabs with

Maxwell Umberto at The Raymond. "What the hell do you think you're doing?"

The Heritage Softail was rumbling up the street by then with Dalton wearing Cloud's too-big, white, daisy-themed helmet and clinging to the huge leather-clad back of Buster Bernard. On the motorcycle neither of them saw or heard Samantha's outburst. They were too giddy to catch that bad energy, laughing and grinning in the wind as they leaned around the corner and took off in a roar.

"I've told you not to let him ride on that motorcycle!" yelled Samantha. She was livid. Preston could see this was not really about the motorcycle; it was about something else. He was standing in the driveway leading to his lab at the back of the property. He was speechless. He didn't even know that Samantha was home yet.

"Buster will be safe," he said and it was weaker than he would have preferred.

"I don't want Dalton riding on motorcycles!" she repeated.

"The boy loves it. It's an adventure for him, Sam."

"He doesn't need an adventure. He needs to be safe. You have such crippled judgment when it comes to Dalton. How could you possibly believe a twelve-year old boy should be out speeding around the city with... well... on the back of a motorcycle, for cryin' out loud?"

Preston looked to where the Harley had gone with Big Buster, and little Dalt hanging on, having the time of his life.

"We disagree. To me, it's okay. That's all."

Sam was furious now. Preston was simply closing the door to discussion. She knew him well and had seen this resolve before. It was part of their daily life lately. He had his mind made up. And she, too, had made up her mind. They were very alike in that way, smart, confident, and resolute, not the best combination for negotiation.

After a beat, with the two of them just staring at each other in the driveway leading to Preston's rather sophisticated homemade garage laboratory, situated behind their three bedroom, two story, ninety year-old clapboard craftsman house in Pasadena, Samantha sighed. She shook her head. Maybe there was no getting past this kind of difference, this gulf that had grown between her and Preston regarding their son. She knew her husband could be one stubborn son of a bitch and could dig in his heels like nobody's business. But stubbornness is the poorer relative of obsession, and Samantha realized in spite of her anger that it was obsession that was keeping Preston's research chugging down the tracks all these years. Consequently, stubbornness was a formidable obstacle with this man and it always would be. When Preston made up his mind, Samantha could see dialogue and discussion flying right out the window. It simply wasn't part of the equation any longer. Argument became a pointless exercise.

Life likes to deliver good news and bad news at the same time. One might be advised to cringe when something rewarding happens, when a grandchild is born, when one wins an award, when one gets a bonus check, because the next phone call will say somebody died. It is the equilibrium on which the human cosmos is built, or so Cloud Willow believed. That is why she benefitted from acknowledging a set of spirit guides to help her through life's maze of ups and downs. Her Native American ancestry figured this one out a century before white people brought their guns and viruses to the New World. Life is balance. No happiness can come without sadness. Preston didn't have spirit guides that he knew about, but he once conceded to Cloud and Buster that he did not trust feeling happy because he knew it only meant he'd be depressed soon. At least when you're bummed out, he had said, you know that feeling better is just around the corner. Cloud Willow had smiled. Preston must be part Indian, she thought.

So when the glorious miracle finally happened, Preston might have suspected and probably should have expected, an upcoming plunge into a baffling darkness that would provide the inevitable balance, the scales of irony tipping one way and then the other. But after all the years and after all the frustrations the actual event was just too overwhelming for him to feel anything other than wonder and joy. It was a tidal wave of happiness! All he wanted to do was let it sweep him away. Preston had tears in his eyes when the experiments finally came together. Suddenly there in front of him was the palatable, tantalizingly real possibility that human civilization, which had been struggling with the haves and the have-nots since time began, could lift the hopeless half of itself away from the muck and the pain and the irrepressible poverty that lack of energy inevitably bestows in the modern world. Humankind could leave the horror of the Third World behind… and the time was neigh!

Preston could envision a glorious future for cold fusion as it emerged from his thousands of trials and failed efforts, rise like an archangel in a blinding light contained within a glass canister that sat unassumingly on a table in the clean room of his small garage laboratory.

When the low heat and clean subatomic explosion in the upright martini-shaker-sized vessel in his laboratory actually occurred, it so startled Preston that he staggered backward away from it, raising a palm across his eyes to block the intensity of the light while he knocked over a stand of tools that went crashing to the floor, as he collapsed against one of the glass walls in the clean room. His eyes were wide in the shade of his hand, and his mouth hung open in disbelief. "My god," he had said.

Preston quickly pulled up the dark goggles that were always hanging around his neck during these experiments, but he could not look away. There it was! The laser configuration and pulse worked! The ammeter was nailed to the right peg as electricity surged at who-knows-what capacity since the power was well beyond the available scale. Acrid smoke rose from the cables and the dark, leaded glass canister of heavy water was as aglow as a welding arc. It was as brilliant as the heart of a star! It was like observing the birth of the universe right in front of him. It went on and it went on. Preston couldn't move. He couldn't speak. It was magnificent!

And then, as quickly as that, it all went dark and vanished when his built-in timer killed the reaction. Like a switch had been thrown, the light show disappeared. Preston almost wished he hadn't had the foresight to include a failsafe cut-off. The glass cylinder went silent and black. Preston remained there, against the wall of his clean room, unable to move. He dragged the dark goggles from his eyes. The ammeter continued to smoke and spark off to the right and Preston could smell the pungent aroma of burnt insulation. How long had it been, he wondered and quickly checked the clock? The reaction had gone on an amazingly brilliant seven seconds, the maximum he had planned. It was not a few flashes in the mist like he'd seen so many times before, not bubbles and sparks. What had happened appeared to be true, cold, nuclear fusion!

Pushing leg muscles that seemed to be filled with cement, Preston Cook managed to drag himself slowly toward his apparatus, where he reached tentatively out to touch the heavy-water cylinder. A less overwhelmed and emotionally spent scientist probably would not have done anything so foolish. What if that cylinder had been a thousand degrees and had carbonized his fingertips? But it was not a thousand degrees. In fact the thick, dark, leaded glass canister built to withstand traditional fusion-level temperatures was barely warm, no hotter than Dalton's baby bottle years ago. Jesus! He had done it! It works! The god damn thing works! He had created cold fusion right here in his lab! Light was the trick! A hundred focused laser beams! "Yes!" he finally screamed. "Yes! Yes! Yes!" He danced around in a little circle like a child, alone in his laboratory clean room. He was swarmed over by glee.

CHAPTER 10

Preston looked like he'd spent a long day at the beach wearing sunglasses. All his facial skin was red except around his eyes where the goggles had been. But there wasn't any life-threatening radiation emanating from the cold fusion reaction Preston had just created in his lab, no gamma particles that will turn human tissue into steaming jelly faster than a Flash Gordon ray gun. Safety was one of the primary objectives to inventing a source of clean plentiful portable energy. He had not created a dirty nuclear reaction, one could accurately say, but nonetheless, it was also very intense even through a nearly opaque glass canister.

In spite of the burn, cerise-hued Preston didn't know what to do as the reality of what happened began to sink in. Basically, he wanted to tell somebody, right away. He wanted to run out into the street and shout it to the neighborhood. He didn't feel the burn on his face at all as he stumbled around his clean room, straightening up, muttering to himself. Dalton wasn't home from school yet and Sam was over at CTU. But suddenly he realized his wife didn't teach that afternoon and Preston concluded he should drive over to the college, on the spur, and surprise her! He'd be there in a jiffy. Preston was like a school kid. He was so excited and so eager to share his success. Maybe it would do some good in their relationship, he reckoned, with the troubles they had been having. Maybe now Samantha would see that she had been too harsh and premature in her assessment of his efforts and the money he'd spent. He wasn't crazy after all! She surely could not say *that* any more. It will be the good old days for them again, he fantasized. He'll get back into a classroom and he and Samantha will finally write that book together on the tyranny of paradigms they'd always talked about.

Preston was grinning and he couldn't remember being so tickled in his entire life, as he climbed into his Corolla and backed out of the driveway of the Pasadena home, where something world-changing had just happened inside a converted garage behind the house. But in the florid rush of developments on that day, Preston had forgotten one of the guiding imperatives in life: balance. Good news absolutely has to be delivered on the same plate with bad news.

When he arrived at CTU, Preston passed his faculty card through the scanner at the faculty parking lot and when the gate lifted he wheeled inside a little faster than he might have on another day. He was definitely feeling frisky. Life was good. How long had it been since he and Sam had made love? Not recently.

Preston parked, climbed out of the little sedan and made his way across the campus to the math building, where his wife's office overlooked a small courtyard from a second story window. The Spanish architecture at CTU provided contrasts of pale plaster and dark wood. Roughly hewn heavy beams and doors were hinged by black ironwork befitting a Junipero Serra monastery. It was a scrumptious bit of real estate Preston found himself realizing as he strode across the dappled grounds shaded by two-hundred-year old California oaks that rose handsomely between buildings. He hadn't had a beautiful thought like that in years, it seemed, but that day the sky was clear and blue, and he could see detail again in the world around him, all of which apparently had slipped away in the more recent stress-filled and fruitless months. Preston could even hear birds in the trees chirping and he grinned like a fool. In some sense, his wife was right to be upset with him. He had been a zombie to his work and he promised himself, right then as he marched across campus, he would make it up to her. He loved her. That had not changed. He didn't mind that students passing by looked oddly at him, with his red face and white circles around his eyes. He just smiled back, nodded, and said, "Hello!" as he walked briskly forward and pushed his way through the monastery-like stained glass doors at the math building's main entrance.

Preston was up a flight of stairs in only a few bounds, finding energy he didn't know he had. Then it was a quick right turn and down the sparse hallway to her office door where he stopped, collected himself, took a deep breath, and knocked firmly, like a freshman calling on a sorority girl.

Rap, rap, rap!

No sound from within, but he gave it a second's pause.

Then, *rap, rap, rap*, again!

He could feel his elation slipping away when there was no answer. Why he had assumed Dr. Day-Steiner would be sitting there in her office waiting on his news didn't really make sense, but the fact that she wasn't there was a deflating moment to Preston nonetheless. He was all primed and ready to go.

"Sam?" he shouted leaning to the door, in one last hopeful attempt.

But there was still nothing.

Again Preston took a deep breath, but this one felt more like a sigh. She wasn't there. That was clear; so, now what? What was Plan B? Samantha could be anywhere. Then Preston thought, what about Max? And he instantly perked up. Of course, Maxwell Umberto, the smarty pants who had walked out on the cold fusion adventure two years ago, should be high on the list to find out what happened! This would be fun, Preston said to himself, telling Max that the ship had come in! "Oh, yeah!" he said out loud. Let's go see Max. And Preston immediately found that bounce in his step again as he pivoted away from the Day-Steiner office and pointed his shoes toward the physics building.

While Preston Cook was trying to find his wife on the CTU campus, while he was turning his attention to his good friend Maxwell Umberto as a colleague who would appreciate the wonderful news Preston was bursting to deliver, a jam-packed Boeing 757 from Washington, D.C. was dropping its landing gear and descending to the tarmac at LAX. Smoke billowed around the aircraft's great tires as they labored to bring the weight of the 757 and its cargo to rest in Los Angeles after a five hour flight across the continent. Federal agent Bobby Skylar was arriving in Southern California as he had been instructed, to speak with his old college conspirator, Maxwell Umberto, and to investigate some renegade scientist who may be working on this cold fusion nonsense when Special Group thought it had been put to bed a couple of years ago.

So, Bobby's arrival in LA took place while that very renegade, Dr. Preston Cook, was burning to scream his success from the rooftops at CTU. Agent Skylar's luggage was being carted to Delta's baggage claim while Preston was on the verge of grabbing strangers on the CTU campus walkways to exclaim he had, just that very afternoon, saved the entire world!

Preston did not actually act on that impulse, of course, because he was rational enough to see it was a sure-fire recipe for getting campus security to escort him off the premises. And, of course, premature announcements were not part of appropriate scientific process. But for heaven's sake, Preston was thinking as he headed toward the physics building hoping Max would be in his office, when the energy equation for humanity has just made a dramatic right-angle turn toward the good, somebody should hear about it!

Most regular citizens of the modern age would have called ahead on their cell phones at that point, but Preston rarely turned his cell phone on. Preston had a cell phone, like most people in 2005, because it made sense for emergencies. Smart phones were not yet on the scene and in a prescient maneuver Preston's inventor-self had jury-rigged all the family phones to do extra things that smart phones would routinely do later on. Still, Preston didn't think about his pocket phone very often in those days and he didn't use it much. He didn't even have his phone with him on that day at CTU. Basically, Preston thought any kind of telephone call was rude and intrusive. He was not a categorical opponent of communications technology; in fact he loved email, precisely because it is passive. You can take those messages when you're ready. And while he admired cell phones and had enhanced his own, he curmudgeonly saw the expansion of cell phone activity as one more step toward loss of privacy and autonomy in life. He did not like that aspect.

"Who the hell needs to have constant and immediate connection?" he opined out loud, in the moment, while he thought about his cell phone at home on his dresser, as he arrived in the shadow of the physics building where his own dank basement faculty office had gone unvisited for months. However, Preston's good friend, Maxwell Umberto, the Physics Department's Chair heir apparent and CTU's star on the rise, had a spacious second floor corner office overlooking California Street and the athletic fields beyond.

It happened that Samantha was not so hard to find as Preston originally feared because she was right there in Maxwell's office when Preston arrived. Serendipitously Preston was going to have an opportunity to share his wondrous news with two of the most prominent people in his life and two people who were very high up on his personal need-to-know list.

However, before Preston arrived at Dr. Umberto's office door, while Preston was marching determinedly across the campus with his strange red and white face looking like a kabuki mask to passers-by, Max and Sam were already having a weighty conversation of their own about Preston. They were also in a rather tight embrace, having just enjoyed a long, slow kiss, and it was not the first one they had shared recently. Their intimate lunches off campus had over time evolved into other intimate activities and now they were in a place where Preston's role as husband and good friend had given way to a new role as a serious obstacle and problem. They had already had the "What are we gonna do?" conversation a few weeks back, but no solutions had been found. Those kinds of solutions do not come easily. But on that very day, as oblivious Dr. Preston Cook excitedly climbed the stairs in the physics building and as he headed toward Maxwell's office, the two friends cum lovers were again reviewing their options about their relationship, groping for answers, but nothing they were able to invent looked promising.

Rap, rap, rap, suddenly came the sound of Preston's knuckles on the office door. He was somewhat more enthusiastic in his knocking this time, as though emphasis alone would conjure up the person he wanted to see. "Hey, Max, are you in there?" he shouted.

Max and Samantha froze where they were standing in each other's arms by the California Street window, where Max had watched the track teams sweat through their paces. Then they quickly stepped back from one another. Sam straightened her clothes and Max straightened his, but they didn't speak, collecting their thoughts simultaneously and after only a moment they had both raced to the same conclusion. There wasn't anything amiss about her being here. Max tossed his hands as he looked at her and she nodded. They were good friends. Preston knew they continued to lunch together after he'd stopped coming to the campus, after he had disappeared into his private project. Everything was cool.

So, Max went to the office door and opened it.

"Preston!" he said when he saw his friend and Max smiled as genuinely as possible. Then, after a beat, "What's wrong with your face?"

"Hi, Pres," offered Sam still standing near the window, unable to summon quite the cavalier tone as could Max, the showman.

Preston provided a small double-take, not expecting to find both of them there, but he knew his antennae in matters of human interaction were terrible, so he just pushed past any reservations a more attuned man or woman might have had, given the atmosphere of guilt that filled that relatively confined space. Preston did pick up an odd sensation in the thickness of the air but he chose to pass it by and he sprang into the office, eyes dancing above his Cheshire-Cat grin. After all, these were exactly the two people he was looking for! What good fortune they were together!

"I've done it!" he exclaimed just like that. "Thank heaven, you're both here!"

"You've done it?" said Max uncharacteristically dumbfounded, assuming Preston must be talking about the project because for several years it was pretty much all Preston did talk about. But the weight of these words – if they meant what Max thought they meant – were stupefying.

"Yes! Yes! It works! The damn thing works!"

It was right about then that both Sam and Max connected the odd coloration on Preston's face with what they were hearing from him and they both knew it was true. It was monumentally true. The reality of it actually took the breath right out of Max and he felt faint.

"Oh, my god!" he said and he folded downward into one of his own Scandinavian glove leather office chairs. "Oh, my god!" he said again, his eyes rolling around inside his skull.

Sam was totally speechless. She put her hands over her mouth and stared at Preston like he was an apparition.

"Ha!" exclaimed Preston. "Ha!" He went straight to Maxwell and knelt down in front of him. "You have to replicate it, Max! You have to do it soon, too. Okay? Will you? I'll give you my notes. As hard as it is, I'm not going to say a word officially about what happened until others have repeated it. Will you be the first, Max? Can you make it a priority? It *should* be you. You were part of it!"

"I... I... Of course, Preston. Of course, I will." He shook his head. He was in a Neverland of belief and disbelief. He knew this wasn't some mistake, not by a researcher like Preston Cook, and not with that damn burnt face right in front of him. Max could already see the awards, the prizes, and the accolades falling from the sky as plentiful as raindrops, and he also felt a twinge of jealousy. What a cruelly ironic knife-twist it was, too, in light of his current relationship with this man's wife, a man who thought of Maxwell as his best friend.

Samantha finally came forward. "Are you okay, Preston?" she said about the burn, touching his face.

"Am I okay? I'm great... fantastic!" said her husband and he stood up straight. He turned toward her and took her by the shoulders and looked into her eyes. He was happy in a way that Samantha could not remember seeing before. "I've never been better, my little cabbage! Never!" he said loudly. And, right there in Maxwell Umberto's office, in front of his former research partner, who was also his wife's lover, Preston grabbed Samantha's face and planted on her the longest kiss he had given her in years and he hugged her tightly. For Preston, it was passion, but it was awkward for Sam, who wasn't exactly prepared for his display, especially after what had been going on between her and Max just minutes earlier. Her husband was soaring with excitement and she well knew that even after all the acrimony, he really did love her. It was a feature of their unexpected and uninvited triangle that truly gnawed at her insides. Preston always had loved her, and Samantha Day-Steiner knew it.

She could clearly see that her husband wanted to share his moment of victory with two people who meant a great deal to him. So, she did her damnedest to respond appropriately, yet even then she could not help but get in her own way. "Preston," Samantha said quietly, "after everything that has happened... we *all* feel how deserving you are. It is wonderful for us." And Sam smiled at her husband, while she began to sense how she might redefine history of the project. She and Max had every right, she was reasoning, to be swimming in the rewards that would very likely flow plentifully from what Preston had accomplished. After all, they had each con-tributed a great deal to the effort over time, in various ways.

CHAPTER 11

Fuming for nearly an hour over the scarcity of cabs at LAX because of a taxi strike, Bobby Skylar finally got a cab to stop when he stepped out directly in front of a Red Top that was just pulling away from the curb. He basically hijacked it. That's the way he found a ride with a Haitian scab driver in dreadlocks who let him share his crowded car with three cornpone tourists from Minden, Nebraska, who were headed for Beverly Hills. They didn't seem to mind an extra body because they were already giddy with the prospect of seeing movie stars. Everybody got the full ticket in that vehicle, because they were charged by the head and didn't seem to understand the difference. That Caribbean cabbie knew what he was doing during the strike and all the rules were out the window. None of his licensing information was in sight and his meter was never turned on.

After the aggravation of that cab-nabbing adventure, after two hours in Los Angeles traffic with a team of babbling yokels, Bobby was immensely thankful he finally arrived in Pasadena, where a reservation had been made for him at the Double Tree. He even gave an extra twenty to the outlaw, picket-line-crossing, Rastafarian driver, if that's what he was. Breaking rules and crossing the lines were not foreign concepts to anyone in Special Group, so maybe there was a little bit of respect in Bobby Skylar for the ballsy entrepreneurial spirit of the cabbie.

The bellhop got a ten-spot for bringing up a couple of Polo suitcases on a brass rolling cart. After all Bobby was on a government expense account, so the money was not so much of an issue. It happened ten dollars was a jackpot compared to what many of the Double Tree guests tip bellhops, who have truck with convention-eers riding on their own nickel and not inclined to generosity, and neither are the Rose Bowl partiers during the holidays. They are not big spenders. It was Pasadena, not New York City, and definitely not Las Vegas. Service people, like the city college bellhop who had helped Bobby with his bags, had learned to expect tips based on a formula concocted during the Great Depression. It was yet another failed paradigm like so many collapsing scientific paradigms that Preston and Samantha had at one time wanted to bury, as revolu-tionary young investigators. Of course, Bobby Skylar knew nothing of their axe to grind on that count. When he arrived in Pasadena, agent Skylar knew next to zero about the lackey, Preston Cook, or the lackey's wife, Samantha Day-Steiner. He didn't even recall their names from his prior visit. He was there to see the man he thought was the prime mover in the cold fusion rumors, his old college com-padre, Maxwell Umberto.

But right then, after finally getting to his room, Agent Skylar was happy to just close the door to his suite like any other working stiff and have some quiet time to pull off his shoes, loosen his tie, crawl onto the king-sized bed, click on the television, and put in a call to his wife to say he'd arrived safely in California.

When he hung up, Bobby wished he knew about some quaint little hotel that regular tourists would never find, that only the gen-try in Pasadena knew about. Those are the best hotels. Not many rooms, small but elegant, "boutique hotels" they had come to be called, and with luck, a great little French restaurant might be tucked away on the ground floor. Well, that was his fantasy in any case, and the Double Tree was not it. Yet his accommodations filled the bill on that particular evening. He was exhausted and he wiggled his toes inside his socks.

Bobby Skylar had to remind himself he wasn't on vacation, even though he was really looking forward to seeing his old friend Max again. They had some great times together at Yale. But Bobby always kept in touch with his mission and he understood he wasn't in town for fun. He was in Pasadena to chat up an old drinking and carousing buddy specifically to uncover information for Special Group. This trip had a personal aspect that was genuine; but at the end of the day it was not truly a personal trip. If Bobby Skylar had been instructed to find his friend Maxwell and put the muzzle of his 9 mm Walther PPK against Maxwell's cranium and pull the trigger that is exactly what Bobby believed he would have done. He'd done it before, although never with a friend. He was a professional in a dangerous and often lethal game. Agent Skylar knew that the identity of the wayward, worker-bee physicist would surface in due time after he saw Max again. However, what Bobby did not know and could not have anticipated as he reclined on the Double Tree king-sized bed, was what extraordinary and dramatic events had transpired earlier that very day, and not far away from where he lay.

Bobby would soon discover that there was now something for those who feared cold fusion to worry about. It had all been hypothetical hand-wringing. Yet, on that California afternoon, those concerns turned into a cold fusion bullet flying straight at the palpitating hearts of the most worried. Although agent Skylar didn't know it as the sun began to set on the Pacific Ocean and the San Gabriel mountains to the north of the Double Tree were magnificent in magenta and rose, but he was soon going to have some very unwelcome news to deliver to his boss, Digger Mac Brown, in Washington, and the ante on his California assignment would be upped for sure.

Dalton was sitting at his computer in his bedroom when Preston got back from his revelatory meeting with Samantha and Max at the CTU campus. Still eager to share the news, Preston crept up to his son's door with a sly smile on his face. Maybe Dalt saw his father's reflection somehow in his flat LCD monitor and maybe not, because he always seemed to know when his parents were nearby. But before Preston could speak, and while Dalton was still furiously clicking away on his keyboard without looking, while he was responding to someone in a cyberspace chat room, Dalton said calmly, "Hi, dad."

"Hi, Dalt," said Preston, accustomed to this unexplained ability of his son to know when he was there, and he came forward and sat down on the one twin bed in the room where "Star Trek" and "2001 Space Odyssey" movie posters hung on the wall, along with a poster advertising "Monster Jam!" from a goliath truck competition they'd gone to at the LA Coliseum a couple of years back. It had seemed like demolition derby to Preston, but Dalton loved it.

"I've got some good news," Preston said, in as contained a way as possible.

Dalton stopped typing and faced his father. Something had definitely happened because his dad was acting really peculiar and he rarely sat down on the bed to talk.

"Boy, are you sunburned," said Dalton, eyes wide with excited anticipation. He never feigned anything like that. He didn't even know how.

"We did it!" said Preston. "The laser pulse? Remember? Like you said, light was what we needed." Preston was beaming with pleasure.

Dalton jumped to his feet and shot his hands in the air. "Yes! Yes!" He screamed and he danced around in circles very much like his father had done and then he gave his dad a huge hug. "Like the center of stars!" he shouted, as he had when he had originally suggested they go back to light. "I knew it! I knew it!" he yelled to the ceiling.

Preston nodded. "Yes… like the center of stars," he confirmed and regaled in the joy of his son, whose original advice was not born out of sophisticated understanding of the physical sciences, but wild out-of-the-blue imagination. Dalton had not suggested the multiple rings of lasers that Preston had used, but he had suggested light.

"Can we do it again right now?" said Dalton, breathing heavily and staring straight into his father's eyes. He could hardly stand still.

"Well… tomorrow maybe," said his father. "We'll be able to do it again tomorrow."

"Oh, boy!" said Dalton. "I can't wait to tell my teachers. Wow! They think we're crazy!"

Preston raised his palms and shook his head. "No telling your teachers just yet, Dalt!" he said emphatically. "In science we have to have other people do the experiment, too, before we talk about it. Remember?"

"Oh, yes. I know. 'Scientific Method,'" Dalton recited.

"That's right," confirmed Preston.

And at that moment there was the popping growl of a slowing Harley at their neighbors' house and Dalton ran to the window. He could see Big Buster Bernard and Cloud Willow pulling up in their driveway behind Cloud's pick-up. "Can I tell Buster and Cloud about it, Dad? Okay?"

"Alright," said Preston smiling. His son was so excited. "But be sure and tell them it's a secret for now, until we run some more tests. Got it?"

"Got it," said Dalton. "I will tell them about the Scientific Method. Wow!" Dalt said again, and he hugged his dad one more time before bolting out his of bedroom and down the stairs to scamper next door.

This alone is worth all of it, Preston thought as he heard the front door slam. He found he was smiling to himself with a profound inward satisfaction that he had not experienced since...*ever*, actually. He'd never felt like that in his life. Everything had always been a hope, a struggle, a possibility, but so little closure. Such a feeling of abject accomplishment was so very rare in his life and that day his work was worth all the pain and heartache.

Unfortunately, the scales of joy and sorrow needed balancing in Dr. Preston Cook's life and that cosmic mandate was, as always, just around the corner like the next bus. The following few days would hold their own special life-changing surprises.

CHAPTER 12

"Well, that's pretty darn cool, Dalt!" said Big Buster Bernard sitting on the velvet couch he and Cloud Willow had proudly added to their oddly decorated home, a mish-mash of fifties modern and Victorian. Dalton didn't notice. This was his neighbors' house; that's all. But his mom always had wondered if Cloud and Buster were going for some kind of kitsch, retro blend. She'd even mentioned this theory to Preston, but he wasn't any more interested than his son. It was one more of those curiosities that flew over the heads of the two males in the Cook household and left Sam alone to speculate. Maxwell Umberto would easily have seen the neighbors' decor as notably strange which prompted Samantha to ask, why can't Preston see it, too?

"Oh, it is way cool," said Dalton sitting across from Buster, confirming what he had just told them about the cold fusion outcome. "But don't tell anyone right now," related Dalton dutifully and seriously. "In the Scientific Method other scientists have to repeat the experiment before anyone can talk about it. We have to prove it wasn't just us."

"Ah! I see," said Big Buster. "That sounds like a good system."

Cloud meandered in the background, watering some half-dozen hanging plants in macramé, and as many other potted plants on the floor, and she was sort-of listening all along to Buster and Dalton. She was an artist, after all, and physics was about as far off her radar screen as anything could be, but she adored little Dalt and she even liked rumpled professor Cook. The math-teacher wife, however, was a bit of a cold fish, but there were no hard feelings.

The huge turquoise stones in the silver rings on Cloud's fingers moved like shiny blue-green beetles as she tilted the watering can, and gently lifted the sumptuous leaves on every plant. She even spoke to them like they were conscious individuals while she moved from one to another. Outside the house there were always flowers and there was color everywhere. All the vegetation thrived with Cloud Willow's touch. She had a gift for this kind of care. Some people do. Nothing of that sort was happening in the Cooks' garden and never could. There wasn't much beyond large low-maintenance bushes all around the property.

"Oh, look at you. What's going on here? Are you thirsty?" she said softly as she tilted the thin spout of her watering can toward the potting soil of a philodendron that appeared about as robust as a philodendron can appear. But she saw something else.

"We're going to bring light and heat to villages all over the world," Dalton said in earnest to Buster. "We are going to give people water where they are thirsty and give people food where they are hungry," recited Dalton proudly. "All it takes is energy!"

"Hard to argue with that," said Buster, smiling. "By golly, nobody can argue with that!" he repeated and he slapped his knee. "You guys are special," he said, and that was something he could say with no reservations whatsoever, because that's what he thought. He liked them. Still, he didn't really know what to make of the things Dalton was saying about this cold fusion accomplishment. After all, Dalton was twelve years old. But Buster had talked with Dalton's father enough to know what was up over there in that back-yard laboratory. Whether or not the old dude had really pulled it off... well, that was another matter. It was rather unbelievable, for sure. Buster didn't know what to make of the news he was hearing from his young neighbor.

Buster was an ox, a massive imposing physical specimen of a man, who once on a bet at a biker bar had bent a length of rebar around his back! But he was also innately intelligent. An avid reader, even though self-educated after the tenth grade, he knew as much about atoms and nuclear reactions as most smart and informed non-physicists, meaning he wasn't totally lost on the topic.

"What if the rich people don't want any cheap energy that'll give water to the thirsty and food to the hungry," said Cloud Willow from the side without looking toward Dalton, as she moved to another plant. She had a husky sensuous voice bequeathed to her by years of smoking cigarettes, which she had quit a decade ago. Cloud continued to singe her vocal cords from time to time by burning marijuana, although she never did so when the boy was around, only late at night, working on her art. "Some people don't care about hunger and suffering. It's not their problem," she added calmly.

Dalton had turned in her direction when she first spoke, but he didn't understand what she was saying. It didn't compute to him. "Nobody wants people to be hungry," he countered resolutely.

Cloud put down her watering pot and she went about getting some indoor fertilizer from a box. She used her hand to sprinkle some of it in a couple of the pots while Dalton watched. "Well, okay... maybe you're right about that, darlin'. It's not that they want people to be hungry, exactly. But I would bet there's a lot of money involved in gettin' food to people. They don't want that money to go away," she said. "Not everybody cares about who is hungry and who is not hungry like you and your daddy do... or like Buster and me. We're on your side, hon."

Dalton just looked at her. This was not a consideration with which he was familiar and it just didn't make sense to him.

"No," he said assuredly, "people want to help each other most of the time, especially when they know better." He'd received his own share of cruelty at school, but that was just from mean spirited boys who didn't know better. The world could be a better place, which is what he'd been taught. "If people have a choice, they will do what's right," Dalton said and that's what he believed. That's what Preston believed, too.

Cloud Willow had the most wonderfully warm smile. It was genuine, too. Dalton was not fooled by insincerity; his antennae were good at sorting out the phonies. Life had taught him that much in his twelve years dealing with people. Cloud smiled at Dalton and she said, "Darlin', I hope you are right about that. Those are thoughts that can change the world. People will do what's right, if they have a choice." She kissed her finger tips and touched Dalton's forehead as she drifted by him on her way toward the kitchen, her long light cotton skirt was flowing around her like the air and she left behind a wake of sweet fragrances that smelled of citrus and bath powder.

Buster watched Cloud move away from the living room. He was in rapture with this woman and had been since the moment they met thirty years ago. "She's somethin', ain't she?" he said to Dalton, who could only return a perplexed gaze. Dalton knew nothing of what makes a woman "somethin'". Kids in 2005 may have been maturing more quickly than earlier generations, but not Dalton. He really liked Cloud and Buster and he loved their motorcycle and that's all he knew. Buster saw the confusion in the boy's eyes and he grinned, "You'll understand someday, my young friend."

Dr. Maxwell Umberto followed Dr. Preston Cook's cold fusion notes to the tee, in a laboratory at CTU. He held some sway at the University, given he was a candidate for Chair of the Psychics Department and he knew pretty much everybody up to the college president, by first name. Not too many of the faculty members at

CTU could call their shots, and there were some heavyweights there, to be sure; but Max was different. He always got what he wanted just like he did at Yale and as he did in graduate school at MIT. Max was an artist at both the business *and* the politics of science, when most researchers are so far behind the curve in these matters they offer virtually no competition to denizens like Dr. Umberto. He was the fox in the henhouse and always had been. No wonder he and Bobby Skylar had hit it off as undergraduates. Their hearts beat in unison when it came to strategic instincts.

Max, of course, had no clue that Mr. Skylar would be reappearing in his life in the not too distant future and the replicated cold fusion experiment he was about to run for his friend and former colleague would be the match in their powder keg of a reunion. That day in the university lab ^2H_2O (heavy water) waited at the center of the spherical configuration of laser guns that would provide the flash from a hundred converging beams, a convergence that had been proven to be the trigger to the whole phenomenal success in Dr. Cook's garage laboratory. All it took was a micro-second of stellar-like heat in the heart of the canister and the result would be a cold fusion controlled reality, not a ten thousand degree furnace burning on and on dangerously getting out of hand, as detractors popularly theorized. Before the first A-bomb was detonated, similar fears led to a popular warning that the entire atmosphere of the earth would ignite in a chain reaction. But it didn't happen.

At CTU, Preston's friend and colleague, Max, figured he would see for himself if the contraption really worked. He knew there would be no explosions. He wasn't afraid. Yet in spite of Preston's burnt face, Max could not help but be skeptical. Maybe something else had happened, he thought, that wasn't cold fusion. He was a complicated man and the scientist in him was intrigued but questioning. After all, he'd worked on this project. Max was keenly aware of the very real possibility that unprecedented international fame was waiting just beyond that day's events at Tech-U, if cold fusion was real. Newton, Darwin, and Currie came to mind. Maxwell reckoned he had been part of the enterprise for years and he had only abandoned it due to promises and encouragement from the very Mr. Skylar who was, unknown to Max, again orbiting his world. An explanation of gravitational pull, had been Dr. Umberto's personal focus since MIT, but in 2005 it remained as much a mystery for him as it did when he jumped at the Wicks Foundation grant money that appeared two years earlier with Bobby Skylar. The possibility of a cold fusion break-through had Max as atwitter as a white rat in a small cage. That was when Preston Cook showed up nervously at the CTU lab, prior to the actual throwing of the switch, before the world and the course of humanity might very well shift directions forever and for all time.

"Want me to check it out?" said Preston coming forward and looking protectively at the apparatus situated to one side of the room. The physics department's pristine laboratory space was so different from Preston's garage lab with his piles of pieced-together equipment, looped computers, and metal-shop hardware, that he almost thought cold fusion couldn't work at CTU. But that didn't make sense, so he swallowed his anxiety. The experiment was a contained set of steps and if the steps are followed cold fusion should occur anywhere. That was the whole idea of having other scientists reproduce the event, standard Scientific Method. It was what makes for acceptable science and was exactly what went all askew during the infamous Fields-Parker debacle back in the nineties at the University of Nevada. Other researchers could not reproduce what Drs. Fields and Parker claimed they had accomplished. The whole thing went down the toilet after that, with only a few die-hards like Preston Cook refusing to let go.

"No. I've followed your notes scrupulously. You were pretty damn detailed, Preston, as I knew you would be," said Max.

"I see you've gone to an opaque canister," said Preston.

"I didn't care for your skin tones, frankly, after the light show in your lab. Instruments will tell us whether to duck, run, or laugh."

"We won't need to do any of those things," said Preston, not able to call up his sense of humor at the moment. He was wound tighter than Gordian's knot. What if it fails? He'll feel like a fool, no better than Fields-Parker.

"Relax," said Max, who wasn't doing the best job of relaxing, himself, as he spoke. "Let's say, what the hell, and throw the switch." In the Scientific Method, a confirmation is every bit as critical as a debut.

CHAPTER 13

When the lasers focused trillions of photons at heavy water molecules in the center of the canister that day at CTU, when the light beams pulsed for less than one-thousandth of a second, the lasers inspired a short exchange of neutron bullets at the heart of the canister. Neutrons fired around in subatomic chaos, slamming together at such force that new elemental molecules were created instantly inside that canister. Hydrogen and oxygen were released as waste, soon to recombine as trace amounts of standard H_2O and pure oxygen. Even though the experiment only ran for ten seconds until the timer shut it down, and even though it was miraculously absent significant heat or radiation beyond the canister, atomic fusion had definitely occurred. The voltage, the amperage, the total wattage produced in those moments astounded both of the investigators. There was no doubt. A small, contained, and controlled nuclear fusion reaction nearly as fierce as any within the heart of our own sun had just taken place in that laboratory, in the stainless steel cylinder that stood modestly upright with gyroscopic-like circles of small laser guns within. The entire installation was too simple and too clean to be real, yet it *was* real.

The two long-time friends and scientists were dumbfounded, to say the least, when the reaction flared, burned, and then vanished inside the vessel Max had manufactured for the experiment. Neither of them knew how to explain it exactly, but there was enough energy generated in that brief display to have illuminated all of Pasadena for an entire week. Even Preston was flabbergasted. He had no idea of the magnitude of the reaction based on his own limited home-spun measurements in the garage clean room, where wires melted and the ammeter smoked. The gages at CTU recorded all of it, and it was stupendous.

Neither Max nor Preston could speak. They robotically went about carefully examining the results captured by the instruments. They checked the cables, which were warm but certainly not hot, and neither was the canister where the solar furnace had done its work. Had dangerous radiation been emitted, they wondered?

This was a major concern from the beginning, but the resounding answer was, No. There had been no more dangerous radiation around that metal canister even at the height of the reaction than one would get in equal time at Santa Monica beach.

The quick follow-up experiment at CTU was also a staggering success. On that laboratory bench right in front of Drs. Maxwell Umberto and Preston Cook in 2005, a technological and far-reaching social revolution was seemingly being born. They smiled, but they were also cautious. After an hour of reading various computer reports and double-checking the equipment, they crumpled exhausted into a pair of stacking chairs not far from where the two experiments had been conducted. They had hardly shared a word since the first sub-atomic controlled explosion took place in the canister and now they sat there like two asylum inmates in a Thorazine stupor, with glazed-eyes and their limp arms hanging between their knees. There were no high-fives or knuckle-bumps or little dances on that day, it was just too overpowering for anything but awe.

"Everything in this world will be different from here on, Preston," said Max softly, his eyes fixed on the device which, disassembled, could fit inside a smallish sized suitcase.

"I know," said Preston, also mesmerized.

"Unlimited cheap energy with zero dangerous radiation, and with potable water and pure oxygen for waste?" said Max rhetorically.

"I know," said Preston.

"My god," said Max. "You must be Jesus Christ."

"No, I'm not," said Preston.

"Well, Satan will think so, and he'll be after you for sure," said Maxwell. "This is just too damn good."

CHAPTER 14

The war in Iraq wasn't going well and Osama Bin Laden seemed to be as good as lost to American justice, somewhere in the mountains between Afghanistan and Pakistan. Americans were not pleased. President Bush's approval rating had plummeted in counterpoint to rising military efforts righting the wrongs in Baghdad and all the while gasoline prices were climbing and climbing at the pumps in the U.S. None of this was making your every-day Joe in the United States happy and the popular suspicion among citizens was that in a handful of oil-producing third world countries the pockets of none-too-friendly Muslims were being stuffed with American dollars and they were laughing while they were getting rich. There doesn't have to be truth to these suspicions to have made them significant forces in the political landscape. American oil companies were scrambling to redefine themselves as environmentally friendly and to prove they were just as much victims to the strange economy as was the average consumer.

Riding a wave of perceived foreign culpability, some American oil companies actively distanced themselves from the Arab nations and pointed to OPEC as being guilty of artificially driving up the price per barrel of crude oil, increases that American companies vociferously opposed. It was a war of finger-wagging in those days. There was also a tightrope to tread, because many of those same U.S. companies were buying Middle-Eastern oil by the supertanker-full every day. Politics may make for strange bedfellows, but mountains of cash will do it just the same.

Digger Mac Brown, chief of Special Group and Bobby Skylar's boss, was meeting informally with the CEO from United States Petroleum, a conglomerate with a big tent under which half a dozen gasoline brands were collected, as well as twenty other substantial companies connected to the family business by virtue of their reliance on petroleum products. United States Petroleum was a serious player and Buckley Wicks, the CEO and major stock-holder, was a self-described party-crashing maverick. He loved that picture of himself, although he didn't look like a party-crasher. Before reaching the national stage with United States Petroleum, he had long been a supremely influential man in Texas and he figured with pretty good reason that George W. Bush may have never been governor of the state, and ergo, President of the United States, if it had not been for Mr. Wick's dark money spigot. Debts between Buckley and a few players in the Bush administration ran deeper than a Texas oil well. He figured he was damn near a silent partner at the White House. Although he wasn't a personal friend of the President – they didn't talk – what Buckley wanted in Washington, D.C after George W. Bush had taken office, he pretty much got through connections. And that's why he was meeting with Digger Mac Brown on that sunny afternoon in the nation's capital at the toney French restaurant *La Rive Gauche* in Georgetown on the Potomac.

Buckley Wicks was an odd man by appearances. You wouldn't necessarily know that the short, thick, rather rumpled guy, in a suit that didn't fit right, was the dominating fearsome individual he actually was, having muscled his way around Capitol Hill, an environment that had more than its share of demanding men and women. Buckley wasn't showy and he never had an entourage. That wasn't his way. Usually he traveled only with his wife, Arvella, a stout dowdy woman with curly gray hair that matched Buckley's. Digger wondered about couples that grow to resemble one another, like these two. He had noticed that he and his own wife were creeping in that direction before she passed away. Digger figured it was some interpersonal gravity that over time relentlessly drags the countenances of some aging couples toward a surreal and genderless center. Buckley and Arvella could have been twins, brother and sister they so much resembled one another before 2005. And they behaved like siblings, a man and women raised with a common sensibility. Neither of them had the slightest tolerance for inept employees, waiters, or service people of any stripe, nor did they have tolerance for the elected officials in Washington whom they saw as an extension of the servant concept. Digger Mac Brown, admired this quality in the Wicks because it was a trait he shared, but he also knew any meeting with Mr. Wicks was going to involve a lecture of some kind about the sorry state of U.S. business and the intrusion of foreign influences into the American way of life, punctuated with a few "Harrumphs" along the way.

"Isn't that right, dear?" Buckley would say, glancing to his spouse. Arvella would soberly shake her head with her eyes downcast because she was just too disgusted at the awfulness of it all.

Digger had mused once, evidencing a characteristic, dark, Special Group humor, that maybe Arvella Wicks was the real puppet-master in that twosome. Buckley did all the talking but you could not help but notice Arvella was always present and you never saw her lips move. Special Group dwelt in such a shadowy realm that most of the agents rather enjoyed predicting the strangest developments. They were even trained to watch out for them. "Expect the unexpected," they liked to recite. "Nothing is as it seems."

Buckley Wicks' predictable and quite emotion-laden patriotic lecture would usually be trailed by a request to Digger, which would inevitably include implied consequences should his request go unsatisfied. Digger had worked with Buckley long enough to know the pattern and to know the consequences were not simply smoke and mirrors. Consequences would arrive as surely as a FedEx package.

Digger understood clearly that Buckley had always been concerned about the cold fusion hocus-pocus out in California, which included rumors touting a run-away researcher trying to conjure up a genie in a bottle to save the world. United States Navy work in San Diego on cold fusion had sputtered along for a while, but Buckley managed to pull the plug on that strange science some time ago. So, Digger already knew what was on the table for discussion. It had been two years since the primary suspect, Dr. Umberto, had been lubricated down another path into research on gravity, so what is it with this other peculiar fellow? Umberto still had to be the driver, reckoned Digger. He must have remained quietly inside the cold fusion work. There wasn't anyone else.

Buckley and Arvella Wicks were frumps, but they were not stupid frumps, and even though cold fusion was a ridiculous long-shot, they knew the implications that came with any viable nuclear reactor that could be carted around in the trunk of a car. Simply put, the implications were disastrous for almost everything United States Petroleum was doing and disastrous for everything it could see itself doing in the future. The stakes were too high to ignore even the most remote possibility of a threat.

When destiny finally arrives, one can never know what irony will arrive with it. Both Buckley and Arvella Wicks were going to live into their late eighties, well into the twenty-first century, and both of them were diagnosed with Alzheimer's disease in 2017. Buckley never really walked correctly from damage done to his right foot in 2005, but otherwise, the two of them would be remarkably vital for a man and woman approaching ninety. They would still be able to get around in later years, albeit slowly and with aid. However, by 2019 they would barely recognize each other and had even elected to take separate apartments in the same posh assisted living facility, not far from Crawford, Texas, where George W. Bush had retired, painting and mumbling to himself about yellow cake.

In a bizarre twist, both Buckley and Arvella recalled the former President quite well, even though Buckley and Arvella could not remember each other. Living a fantasy that came from god-knows-where, Arvella would like to tell folks at the assisted living facility that George W. and she had been lovers back when he was an up and comer in Texas.

In fitting unison, Buckley and Arvella Wicks were going to die in the same month, January of 2020, only two weeks apart. Arvella went first, but Buckley didn't grieve for the loss of his wife because he didn't remember they had been married. When he heard of Arvella's demise, after a long pause while he struggled with the recollection of her, he finally said, "Arvella? Yes. I remember her. She always cheated at bingo."

CHAPTER 15

Maxwell Umberto lived in a spacious three bedroom town home on Orange Grove Boulevard in Pasadena, shaded by rows of mature California oaks and street lamps that bordered the boulevard like soft spheres of light marking a runway for a lovely mile. It was considered a most desirable location for those not interested in owning single-unit family dwellings, as the realtors liked to call regular houses. Max's town home had one hundred feet of trimmed lawn and shrubbery spreading out toward the boulevard, separating him from the traffic noise. His expansive floor to ceiling paned windows overlooked that lawn. The colonial building bore brightly polished blonde hardwood floors on which its well-heeled tenants tread and high moldings framed every room. A white-brick hearth sheltered crackling fires in the winter months. His choice in furnishings was modern. Soft leather was plentiful. He had one magnificent pale and curvy teak rocker that cost two thousand dollars. The entire space was clean and neat with paintings and statuary aglow from track lighting. His quarters perfectly matched his trendy wardrobe and self-conscious lifestyle.

Only a few Pasadena miles away, the rag-tag, two story bungalow, in which Preston Cook and Samantha lived with its homespun laboratory in a garage and a sweet but somewhat peculiar twelve year-old boy hanging around, did not compare on any artistic level to what Max had created for himself on Orange Grove Boulevard. Yet the two residences seemed to precisely fit each of the men occupying them. They were both sufficiently circumspect to appreciate and understand what was going on with the other and neither of them wanted to trade places in almost any way whatsoever, with only a couple of notably raw exceptions. Max did feel a twinge of jealousy buried somewhere in his brain over the events of that very day, when cold fusion actually happened. The other exception had to do with his best friend's wife, Samantha Day-Steiner.

"It was a jaw-dropping experience. Truly." said Max into the handset of one of his cordless phones, as he stood silhouetted before his wide living room window watching the silent commuter traffic gliding by on Orange Grove Boulevard as dusk slowly enveloped the scene. He was speaking into the phone while a scotch on the rocks in a thick cocktail glass was caught in his fingertips like a weight at the end of his left arm. "We blew out every expectation we had!" he said and then he listened for a few beats, his eyes dancing and his heart still racing from what had happened over at CTU with the success of the cold fusion reenactment.

"Yeah," he said agreeably, "I guess that's true, Sam, Preston and I haven't talked about an announcement. That would be presumptuous. But I know he thinks we should wait. It *is* protocol to have several replications... *you* know that. But the damn thing works. And it'll work every freakin' time! The science is good."

Then he listened again to Dr. Day-Steiner who had already heard about this validating replication from her husband and had given Maxwell a call as soon as she could do so discretely. She was as thrilled as they were, but waiting on more experiments was not on her agenda at all. Sam had sacrificed enough already to her husband's project and now they were sitting on a gold mine!

"When can I see you?" Max said suddenly and that question had come to have only one meaning between the two of them.

In that same moment at the Cook-Day-Steiner residence, Samantha was using her cell phone to speak with Max and she was doing it surreptitiously while she paced back and forth in the back-yard next to the very garage-laboratory that may have changed the entire world. She clutched the small phone in two hands and spoke softly into it while her eyes darted around. "Maybe tomorrow," she said. "I don't know exactly. I've got a department meeting in the morning. Oh, I don't know. I'll have to call you." Then she listened and paced. "Okay. That's good, I'll…"

She was interrupted by Preston calling her from inside the house.

"I've gotta go," she said quickly. "Bye." And she shut the phone as Preston came out the back door onto the stoop, looking for her.

"There you are," he said standing in the light of a small carriage lamp by the door. "What are you doing out here?"

She held up the phone, "I was just talking to Max about the experiment. He is *so* excited, Preston!"

Preston suspected nothing awry. People walk around outside for fresh air and privacy, talking on their cell phones all the time. He'd done it himself. Preston just nodded and smiled, but he was surging with excitement, too. It had been a momentous afternoon. "Well, he *should* be excited. He was part of it."

"Yes," agreed Samantha emphatically as she came toward the back stoop where Preston was standing. The carriage lamp cast a skirt of light into the back yard and Samantha entered that circle acting as innocent as a child while night settled across the city. "He is a good friend and colleague," she said and she came up the steps, walking into the house past Preston.

He held the door for her and said, "Hey, why don't we go out and get a bite to eat… you know… to celebrate. Club 39 in Old Town. I could really go for a nice cabernet and Oysters Rockefeller! What'd you say? Buster and Cloud are home, so Dalt'll be okay for a couple of hours," he added. His shirt buttons were still about to pop from pride. He really wanted his wife to be exuberant for him, but exuberance from Sam just wasn't in the cards and Preston could see it and, more so, he could feel it.

"Gosh, Pres, I'm really exhausted tonight," said Sam. "This weekend, we'll do something special. As we should! Okay?" Without making eye contact, Samantha headed further into the house and left Preston standing at the back door.

CHAPTER 16

Max put down his phone after speaking with Samantha pacing around in her back yard, and he lifted the glass of scotch in his left hand. He shook the ice and he sipped. It was twenty-year-old single malt Glenfiddich, his personal choice, and he did enjoy it. Unfortunately, it was the end of the bottle, he realized, as he savored the velvety sensation as the warmth of it ran down his throat and the memory of the day's events warmed the cockles of his imagination and, even more so, his ambitions. Damn it, he thought, there are such possibilities! He could feel the power of what was happening and it was a struggle to wrap even *his* facile brain around all of it; there was so very much potential.

But Max didn't have any more time that evening to revel privately in the adventure that had just begun, because his reflection was interrupted by a solid knock at his door, not loud, but firm. Then it came again.

As Dr. Umberto walked to his front door he was actually a bit perturbed at an intrusion on this special evening, but he was wholly flabbergasted when he opened the door and saw his old friend, Bobby Skylar, standing there with his usual irrepressible grin, the signature twinkle in his eye, and a liter of twenty-year old single malt Glenfiddich held forth in his fist!

"Good god, Bobby!" said Max quickly regaining his composure and regarding the bottle of Glenfiddich his friend had thrust toward him. "It's a *miracle*!" Max continued as he hoisted the almost empty glass of scotch in his own left hand for Bobby to see, and without missing a beat Max added, "You're barely on time! This was the last of it!"

They embraced in the doorway and Max ushered his old Yale buddy inside. Bobby never called ahead. That wasn't his style. Of course, he already knew Max was there and alone. He'd been watching Max since earlier in the day, although Bobby knew nothing about the fantastic experiment that had been conducted at CTU. On the other hand, Max would not ever have imagined Bobby would be observing him all afternoon, nor would Max have suspected that he had been staked out this way the last time he got together with Bobby Skylar over two years ago, even though Bobby had shown up unannounced with a bottle of Glenfiddich on that occasion, too. Suspicions of that stripe were simply not part of Maxwell's world with humans. With subatomic particles, he would ask hard questions, but not with humans. He was innocent like Preston in that way.

"You know, my friend," said Maxwell, "you're either gonna have to bring several of these at a time or show up more often. I've actually had to *buy* scotch since you were here."

"I'll try to do better, professor," said Bobby.

In truth, Bobby's unannounced visits didn't really bother Max. He was basically glad to see his old friend. And what is also true is that incredibly charming Bobby Skylar could show up without announcing himself at almost anybody's front door and in no more than ten minutes he would manipulate his surprised host into laughing with him, totally delighted Bobby had dropped by. Forget normal boundaries. Bobby simply had the touch. He could get away with the most outlandish behavior and it had always been so. That was one of the reasons he was of such value to Special Group... *that* and the fact that he was also absolutely cold blooded when he needed to be, a totally unexpected trait in such a warm, sociable guy, a family man, a loving father and friend. Both of these sides of him worked because neither of them was phony. He had learned to compartmentalize his behavior with astoundingly rigid walls. It was the only way he could keep his sanity. When he was with friends and loved ones, the some-times-killer and government agent Bobby Skylar was nowhere to be found. That was his job, but the assignment in Pasadena was unique in that it blurred the compartmental walls he had built so fastidiously.

In minutes they were seated on Maxwell's wide leather couch, having opened the liter of Glenfiddich and having poured each other an inch of the amber nectar into two glasses. They raised the glasses and recited on the same beat, "Good men are scarce!" clicked glasses and downed their drinks. It was a ritual they had followed since their Yale days.

Max never really understood what Bobby Skylar did for a living, beyond the fact that he worked in Washington and that his work was mostly confidential. He knew Bobby was connected to power-ful interest groups in some way, because Bobby had been the one to suggest that Max abandon the cold fusion project two years ago. And mysteriously Bobby had been the one to indicate there was sig-nificant money to be found in Maxwell's old love, research on grav-ity. The argument had successfully turned Dr. Umberto's head at the time, and in fact the money quickly appeared in the way of a Wicks Foundation grant, a coveted award. It was a grant of such propor-tions that Max was able to secure lab time, plus a graduate assis-tant at CTU to further his research, not a common occurrence in such short order. By then Max had become impatient with the cold fusion concept anyway. He and Preston just seemed to be repeating the mistakes of prior failed work, with no end in sight. To ambi-tious Maxwell Umberto, it was beginning to feel like a pipe dream.

Preston, on the other hand, was dogged and was not going to quit, no matter what. Inevitably, the two friends chose to severe their ties and part company with no ill will. These things happen all the time in academia; plus they had known one another for decades

Preston had said to Max, as Max packed up his few personal items in the strange little private laboratory behind Preston's house, that Max had contributed immensely to the project and Preston thanked him. He wished Max good luck in snaring the ever elusive unified theory and the dark secrets of gravity. What Preston said to his friend and partner that day was not convivial baloney, because Max had truly contributed to the cold fusion work. Furthermore, Preston understood that no physicist worth his salt would fail to be intrigued by money available to pursue the unified theory.

Before Max finally did beg off from the cold fusion work, his grant money had fallen right out of the sky onto his lap just like Bobby Skylar said it would. The arrival of Wicks Foundation funding was especially strange because he actually submitted his application to the Wicks Foundation through the Contracts and Grants Office at CTU *after* he had been mysteriously assured in a phone call that his research was already on track for financial support from that foundation. It was a shadowy development and definitely not customary. In truth, Max suspected from the wink Bobby had given him when Bobby said he might be able to "do something," that Bobby, or Bobby's people, had an invisible hand in making the Wicks Foundation grant appear. But Maxwell was generally pragmatic in life and he didn't really care how it came to be. He got the money. That was the main thing. A less self-interested and less ambitious scientist might have moved more cautiously in those circumstances or even backed off, but that was not Max. On the contrary, he was ecstatic about the grant and he did everything he could to get his friend Preston to abandon cold fusion and join him in his adventure at CTU. But Dr. Umberto's repeated overtures were respectfully declined by Dr. Cook.

By 2005, after damn near a quarter of a million dollars and thirty months of work in the gravity research business had gone by the boards, while coming up with some curious and intellectually provoking observations, Maxwell's efforts had not really brought the world significantly closer to uncovering the holy grail of physics, a unified theory and the nature of gravitational forces, than was true on the day he bid adieu to cold fusion. The entire enterprise had been extraordinarily frustrating to Maxwell Umberto, the golden boy, the constant winner.

And after that October day's revolutionary cold fusion developments in the CTU laboratory, Dr. Umberto's pursuit of a unified theory and the nature of gravity were clearly headed for the filing cabinet. Max was again infused with the religion of cold fusion. He could not ignore the pull of what was occurring right under his nose and *that* was the kind of gravity that began to control his orbit.

Two years ago Maxwell Umberto did not really understand Bobby Skylar's suggestion that chasing cold fusion had powerful and dangerous opposition. There were vague references to "following the money in this world, if you know what's good for you." Max knew the Wicks Foundation was funded by an oil conglomerate, but on the other hand he also knew the Wicks Foundation had varied interests supporting high-profile altruistic environmentally friendly projects, wind and solar energy stations as alternative energy sources at both of the earth's icy poles. The foundation seemed egalitarian to Maxwell. He had no clear reason to think his sponsor, the Wicks conglomerate, United States Petroleum, was an adversary to cold fusion. Maxwell did not know in those days that the Arctic Circle projects for United States Petroleum were little more than explorations for drilling opportunities hidden behind pictures of a seal pup, happy with its mom, photo-shopped next to a wind turbine on the ice.

Max was a scientist, not a politician, and as brilliant as he could be, his sensitivities to the moves in an industrial chess game were not developed to the degree needed in those circumstances. Scientists, like artists, often wear their thoughts and their goals on their shirt sleeves because hidden agendas are usually counterproductive in their worlds. Secrets don't help; they hinder. The minds of Washington politicians, corporate chieftains, and the minds of everyone in an organization like Special Group were cut from an entirely different cloth than the minds of Dr. Umberto and Dr. Cook.

When Bobby Skylar appeared smiling on Maxwell Umberto's threshold that evening with a liter of Glenfiddich, Max did not suspect that he had anything to worry about. His delight at seeing his old college compatriot was bald-faced and true. Plus, he was presented with an unexpected opportunity to share that day's momentous life-changing events with someone he had known since their intellectual childhoods.

So, on that propitious evening, Bobby Skylar became the first person to hear it was California Technological University's Dr. Maxwell Umberto, with some minor help from his rogue colleague Dr. Preston Cook, who had actually solved the problem of cold fusion. And in that simple exchange, Max planted the lie that would be his ultimate undoing. Max said to Bobby that he had produced a small nuclear reaction on a table top at CTU just that afternoon, with very little heat generated and no dangerous radiation whatsoever! Agent Skylar could not believe his ears, hearing his long-time friend wax magnificently during the telling of the tale.

What a serendipitous occurrence it was, thought Max, Bobby showing up that very night to share the victory. Maxwell was totally oblivious to the consequences of what he had just claimed, when he took credit for a discovery that wasn't his. Perhaps he had re-written history to the degree he believed it. When he mentioned the cold fusion success, he thought he saw a flicker deep in the center of Bobby Skylar's green eyes that was disturbing for reasons Max did not fully comprehend. Nonetheless, Dr. Umberto smiled as humbly as he was able, before the many subsequent ounces of Glenfiddich took hold.

After the power of the cold fusion revelation had passed, Dr. Umberto and his old friend from undergraduate school began laughing together in Maxwell's trendy, modern Orange Grove town house in Pasadena, recounting their adventures at Yale. Max convinced himself his future was as bright as the sun. On the other hand, Bobby filed Umberto's astounding accomplishment out of sight so he could genuinely enjoy the evening with his friend, because in the back of Bobby's mind he saw a dimming of the future for his good friend Maxwell Umberto.

CHAPTER 17

Preston ran the experiment one more time in his own patchwork lab, mostly for Dalton's benefit, who was beside himself with enthusiasm to see the center of stars in their garage, but Preston had learned enough from his earlier bout with radiation to purloin the concept of an opaque canister Dr. Umberto had used for their confirmation run at CTU. The sunburn Preston earned the first time was just beginning to heal and there were patches of skin on his face that were peeling rather dramatically. He thought he looked like a two-tone, cream and brown, '54 Chevy.

Their experiment went swimmingly with the heavier canister and some newer instrumentation that was up to what it was going to get from the reaction. Big Buster Bernard and Cloud Willow were also invited to be on hand as witnesses to the spectacle. Preston felt a bit like a showman this time, a trait more suited to his friend Maxwell, as he tried to explain in lay terms what his audience was going to see. Then he flipped a switch and a subatomic reaction instantly lit the tiny slit windows in the silver canister Preston had manufactured, with brilliance sufficient to make the witnesses cover their eyes in spite of the dark goggles Preston had purchased for that very encore. It all lasted no more than ten seconds this time with the controls Preston had added. As before, the energy created seemed galactic in magnitude!

When it was over, only nominal smoke rose from the newer heavy cables. Young Dalton began running around the small clean room screaming. It was better than Christmas morning for him. He was as energized as any particle in that canister. Cloud and Big Buster slowly lowered their goggles and looked at the readings on the instruments, which Preston proudly pointed at with his index finger. The gauges clearly indicated the massive quantity of amperage and voltage that had been manufactured there in only a few ticks of the clock.

"That's more than a hundred million amps," said Preston quietly. "We could have powered the San Gabriel Valley."

Big Buster and Cloud said simply and simultaneously, "My god!"

The energy from that fusion reaction went through the roof. Transformers had kept the equipment from melting this time, but the numbers were immense, like the distance to far away regions of the universe, mind numbing figures for something so brief… and to all appearances so small!

"You saw the center of a star!" exclaimed Dalton wild-eyed to his neighbors.

"I guess so," said Big Buster resting his huge hand on the boy's shoulder. Cloud Willow, beside her husband, just nodded in amazement. There were not many words for that kind of experience.

Considering the reaction they had just witnessed, thrown in with popular knowledge about nuclear energy, Cloud did eventually say, carefully trying not to be offensive, "Are we okay standing here so close?" It's entirely possible she did not actually believe they would really see what they saw that day, and that's why she hadn't asked the question prior to the demonstration, when it would have made more sense.

Preston smiled toward his neighbor and said, "If it were dangerous, my friend, I would have told you to come in here and watch, while I waited outside."

They all laughed.

"Bless you, Preston Cook", Cloud finally added softly to her neighbor, when everyone had gone quiet. "You have always wanted to change the world for the better. Well, now it seems, you are actually going to do it."

CHAPTER 18

"I don't know exactly," Max said to Samantha as they lay on his thick and expansive feather bed that half swallowed them both in white Egyptian cotton sheets beneath a northern window with flat October light that filled his contemporary bedroom and its black lacquered Japanese furnishings. A pair of large and bold abstract paintings splashed two walls with primary colors. "Bobby and I are ancient friends, back to Yale," he continued. "But, by Jesus, I damn near felt a chill when I told him I'd… that Preston and I… had cracked the formula for real cold fusion. Something was not right." Max was visibly shaken by the memory and he didn't know why.

"Is he a physicist, too?" Sam asked, putting one leg half across Max.

"No, not even close," replied Max, "he's a government man of some kind. I don't even know what. But he was the one who suggested I get out of cold fusion a couple years ago and he was the one who directed me toward the Wicks Foundation."

"Didn't he understand what's been accomplished?" she asked.

"Oh, yes. He acknowledged that and said all the right things. 'That's great,' and 'It's a fantastic breakthrough.' But then he asked me if I'd told anybody else about it. Isn't that an odd question? I think it is."

"Eh… I wouldn't make too much out of it," said Samantha relaxing again as she reframed it for Maxwell. "Never mind what you thought, Max. Your friend was just shocked by the news. That's all.

Who wouldn't be? And remember he may have had some skin in the game when he got you to quit the project in the first place. That would mean your return to it upsets his apple cart in some way."

"I guess," said Max, studying Sam. She certainly had a suspicious streak. He could not recall Bobby Skylar specifically asking Max to abandon cold fusion and get back to the unified theory research. Maybe it just wasn't noticed at the time because Max was so weary of the work in Preston's peculiar little lab and he was primed for a change. Maybe time had eroded Maxwell's memory.

"It doesn't matter, Maxwell!" insisted Samantha. "You've accomplished something really, really terrific, astoundingly terrific... you and Preston. Even your old Yale buddy can't argue with that!" Then she added half in jest, "You don't have to give the Wick's Foundation money *back,* do you?"

"No, of course not, I've done my work," returned Max who found decidedly less humor in the question.

"Well then," she said with a dramatic waive of her hand dismissing all concerns and adding with the exuberance of someone who had actually solved cold fusion herself, "I'd say it's time to *tell the world*! You know, Maxwell, there is a fucking boatload of spanking fresh money waiting for us."

"A fucking fleet-load, I would say" amended Max wryly.

"A goddamn king's fortune!" shouted Samantha.

It didn't take long for word of the cold fusion success story to pass through an assortment of academic grapevines to distant ears with very keen interest in such developments. It was particularly strange because Dr. Preston Cook and his back-in-the-fold colleague, Maxwell Umberto, had not made any formal announcements about the work, nor had they published their findings in any professional journals. Nonetheless, the news was amazingly available and it was available so very quickly, not just available to key stakeholders within the U.S., but energy hounds around the globe were almost instantly alert to what had happened in Pasadena only a few days earlier! The speed of communication about cold fusion was a fantastic curiosity. It was as though the findings had been published in the *Los Angeles Times*. It was as though there had been a story on CNN. But the hot paradigm-shifting item of cold fusion was not traveling by public channels in any way whatsoever. The news flashed like lightning around the world simply by word of mouth.

Showing off to his non-scientist neighbors Buster and Cloud was one thing, but Dr. Cook had been steadfast that information about cold fusion be kept on a need-to-know basis, even at CTU, until it was properly vetted by colleagues elsewhere. He generally acted like the discovery was the darkest of military secrets. Nonetheless, and in spite of Preston Cooks' wishes, the awesome potential of the achievement had heads from Peru to Peking nodding as they listened to the tidal wave of gossip that flowed outwardly from Dr. Cook's findings. Overnight, with the muscle of the Internet, six degrees of separation had suddenly become two degrees. Secrets of that magnitude had faint hope of remaining aloof from common conversation.

The senior advisors to the President of the United States in 2005 knew about the cold fusion developments in Pasadena because they had been advised of the developments by Special Group's Digger Mac Brown. The information had been passed on to the President swiftly, the very morning after Agent Skylar had surprised Maxwell Umberto with a bottle of Glenfiddich, when they reminisced over their conquests of yesteryear and inebriated Max had unwrapped the extraordinary events of the day. It didn't make very many figures in the administration happy when hearing of these cold fusion discoveries and that meant it didn't make Digger Mac Brown all that happy, either, because in the federal government distress runs downhill hot and heavy.

From the White House, word flew straight into corporate America and by mid-day on the same morning the President had gotten wind of what happened in Pasadena, the cold fusion news had United States Petroleum's Buckley Wicks leaning all the way back in his great leather home office chair with one of his plump hands sweeping across his sweaty brow. He rolled his eyes toward the ornate ceiling of his study in the 10,000 square foot, three story, sprawling edifice that his sometimes silent wife, Arvella, had insisted they acquire in Alexandria, Va. She had successfully argued, when they were calculating where to settle, that it is Washington, D.C., not New York and not Los Angeles, where all the real deals are consummated.

On the other end of the line Wick's favorite ally in the west wing was relating what had been reported to President Bush about cold fusion's birth. To Buckley Wicks, the news of cold fusion's success was like the coming of the anti-Christ.

My god, this has gotten way out of hand, Buckley was thinking as he listened to an explanation of how it all went down. His White House contact was saying, "There was one screwball that wouldn't let go. But we also know Umberto is the one who made it all happen. He pulled together the missing pieces, even after we paid him to stop."

"Shit!" said Buckley Wicks.

United States Petroleum was not just your regular friend to the President's staff. Buckley Wicks knew them from the inside out and the current administration's rapport within the oil industry both domestically and abroad was reliant on a solid relationship with Buckley Wicks and with United States Petroleum. George W. Bush, himself, did not even have to get involved directly. Mr. Wicks was the most significant, hard-wired conduit to the global oil producing community in all of the administration's connections.

"What are we going to do about it?" said Buckley on the phone.

"Digger's workin' it," came the reply in reference to Special Group and to Bobby Skylar's deployment, but Buckley's contact could offer no more and Buckley was not happy with that inadequate response. "We'll get it cleared up," the contact said confidently.

"Not good enough."

What he wanted to hear was that cold fusion research and development would be unequivocally crushed! Furthermore, Buckley Wicks was sufficiently sure of his clout even when talking to the White House that he hung up the phone on that very beat. Without saying another word, he left a powerful advisor to the President of the United States holding a handset to his ear and listening to the dial tone.

CHAPTER 19

Bobby Skylar's rented Ford Taurus moved slowly along the street in Pasadena where Preston Cook and his family lived their unpretentious, but now fuse-lit lives. The strange little laboratory configured from odds and ends was barely visible to passers-by, wedged into what had been in 1923 a two-car garage at the end of a long narrow driveway. When the house was built the neighborhood had been surrounded by stunningly fragrant commercial orange groves, but there were no orange groves in Pasadena by 2005. Those days were gone.

Agent Skylar was not yet interested in speaking with this apparently self-reliant albeit odd partner of Maxwell's. Bobby just wanted to know where the guy lived. He even had a peculiar admiration for the man's stick-to-it-iveness which he guessed was just as critical to the final solution of cold fusion research as Maxwell's *coup de grace* toward the end. Skylar knew he had a wide stubborn streak in himself, like this curious zealot. In fact, two years ago Bobby was a little disappointed on some visceral level when his old friend from Yale, Maxwell Umberto, so quickly abandon the cold fusion research and leapt at the grant money, even though it was Bobby's mission to make that happen. The whole episode was a complicated message in Skylar's life. But Umberto was clearly back in the thick of it, so what did all the subterfuge from two years ago finally deliver? Not much.

Agent Skylar didn't personally give two winks about the cold fusion business, one way or another, but he was not a simple man. He could appreciate the whole adventure from afar, with a fairly intellectual and rather moral assessment all around. But one shouldn't conflate that ability with a lack of resolve in what needed to be done to get an off-the-tracks enterprise back where it belonged, out of sight and under wraps. The good of the nation always trumps. The future of his country prevailed beyond all other reckoning. That's the way it had to be in Special Group. A fundamental faith in the United States had to be alive and fervent for Skylar if he was going to follow through on the many messy things he had been asked to do in recent decades. Americans weren't perfect, he believed, but everybody else was less so. He was a patriot first and last, and as superficial and charming as Agent Skylar could be, he was also a reflective and thoughtful patriot.

As his Enterprise rental Taurus slid quietly by, outside of the Cooks' residence, Bobby examined the simple façade of the building. He could see all the way down the driveway, flanked on one side by tall hedges, to the remodeled garage. Across the front of the garage laboratory a wall to match the house had been built, but the frame of the original garage door remained like a memory of automobiles long gone. Bobby's imagination was flooded with images of what was inside that old, remodeled garage. Was it a lab with Erlenmeyer flasks and beakers boiling over with smoke and electrical devices sparking and sputtering? Was it a scene right out of a Frankenstein movie? That's what he imagined, anyway, and the monster that may have come from that little lab was evidently just as threatening to townsfolk as Mary Shelly's, even though both may have been well intentioned by the men who brought them to life.

It was right about then a rumbling Harley-Davidson motorcycle came slowly by in the opposite direction, with about the biggest human specimen agent Skylar had seen recently astride the machine and giving him a long hard stare. Maybe Bobby had been too obvious in his surveillance, so he just nodded and smiled toward the stranger and then Bobby stepped on the gas a bit and moved on. Yet, in his rearview mirror Bobby could see the big man lean his bike into the driveway adjacent to the house with the peculiar backyard laboratory where very serious lightening must have flashed. Apparently, they were neighbors.

"It's alive!" Skylar heard himself mutter, thinking of Boris Karloff, as he pulled away from the Cook house. Bobby and the mad scientist in Pasadena would meet soon enough, he said to himself, but not that day. The federal agent believed it was Max who had been the catalyst to cold fusion success. So, thinking right-brained once again, Bobby figured getting Max back on board and shutting down the whole damn misadventure, would be the A move. Silencing the fanatic in his funky Frankenstein lab was of secondary importance. After all, if this Dr. Cook character could not accomplish much while Max was out of the picture, then he was not a significant threat to the energy equilibrium in the world. Preston Cook, the wayward one, could be handled later. On that October day in 2005, Bobby Skylar just wanted to know where the guy lived.

During those minutes, while Agent Skylar's car paused outside the Cook house before little Dalton had come home from school, Preston was attempting to discuss with his wife what the next steps should be following the cold fusion success. He so very much wanted her to be joyful with him, to appreciate his victory after so many seasons of defeat, and to share the next planning phase with him. Preston wanted them to make a new start as a couple now that the heavy lifting on his project was done. He knew that if ever there could be a fresh dawning in their lives they were in that moment. He hoped and imagined good things would blossom for them.

Unfortunately, the two of them were not at all close to the same thoughts on the question of a fresh dawning in their relationship after the miracle in the CTU lab earlier in the week, nor were they in agreement on what the next steps should be. The degree of difference was out of the blue to naive Preston Cook. He was stupefied by what he was hearing from his wife when the topic was broached.

"Preston," Samantha began, "Maxwell had a lot to do with this thing, don't you think? He got you working with sound and then the deuterium… jeez, I don't know this stuff. I'm not a physicist. You could not have pulled it off without him."

Preston was confused. For long seconds he actually could not form words. After he was able to summon up the wherewithal to move, he took Samantha gently by both of her shoulders and stared as deeply and directly into the dark pupils of her eyes as he could, as if he was drilling down inside her to find the woman who loved him, the woman he married. "What are you saying, Sam? Max was a terrific help… but those things… the sound waves and deuterium… that was all from work that'd been done in the past… at Nevada and down in San Diego. Max was *not* a part of what we finally did. He's been gone for *two years*. A lot changed. No deuterium rods. No sound waves."

Sam pulled away and moved back from him. She rolled her shoulders, not really wanting to make direct eye contact again. Samantha was angry about her failed dreams and the future she had once imagined with her husband. When Preston tried to come toward her, she held up a palm to keep him at bay. She had resolve. "Look… the ethical thing is for you to wait until you can *both* make the announcement… you *both* deserve the billing here, Preston."

"Why are you saying this?" he said, truly flummoxed by what he was hearing. Why she would champion Max so fervently? "Of course, Max can stand with me, Sam, when it's time to make an announcement," continued Preston. He was a bizarrely unassuming man in matters of personal ambition. He was childlike in that regard. He had not the foggiest suspicion that Maxwell had been playing up his role in the recent developments to Samantha and likewise playing them up to his old Washington buddy, Bobby Skylar when Skylar happened by Maxwell's stylish townhouse on Orange Grove. Preston did not know that Max had been saying the breakthrough on cold fusion was his own doing. But how such a claim by Maxwell made the slightest sense to Samantha would be a total mystery to Preston.

Max had successfully muddled Dr. Day-Steiner's judgment because he was all the things to her that Preston could never be. Umberto was an irresistible concoction of intellect and glamour. Dr. Samantha Day-Steiner was a handsome and brilliant female mathematician who was starving for a bit of what Maxwell offered. Maybe his lifestyle was the ticket she was looking for, a way to legitimize her infidelity and escape to some kind of fantasy life that Maxwell embodied. Maybe she'd thought this through and knew what she was doing in a calculated Lady Macbeth kind of way. Or, maybe she was just being swept along by what remained of her estrogen.

In any scenario to Preston – even though he and Sam had not been getting along well in recent time – her championing Maxwell Umberto was a mind-boggling change of direction in her and he was at a loss. His thoughts of reigniting something between them seemed misbegotten to him on that day. He didn't know what to do and he was in pain. He loved his wife with all his heart, a feature of Preston Cook that would never go away.

"I… I don't want to make an announcement at this point," continued Preston softly, trying to reason with Samantha. "I'm thinking maybe we get another physicist, or maybe two, to replicate the experiment and if it continues to work, then we should publish our results and let the world have them."

"*Are you a mad man*?" recoiled Samantha. The distress on her face was something Preston had not seen since they discussed continuing with her pregnancy thirteen year ago. He physically stepped back from her. Samantha's eyes were wide and her face was flushed. "There is too much at stake to be doing more experiments or publishing a paper, Preston. I don't care if that is a common practice among you guys… you and your science colleagues. But Max and you… you've brought a revolution to the world! There's no turning back. This is not something you give away in a journal article… or in a presentation at one of your conferences. *No, no, no, no*!"

Preston went white and stared at his wife of two decades. Who was she? What was going on here? Why was she acting this way?

"Sam", Preston pleaded, "this research was always for the betterment of *everybody*. Remember? Remember, I said, when I started this, when I got inspired before Max was with me and I could see cold fusion could work, I said it's *not* about money. Do you remember that? Do you? It's about fulfilling our responsibility to the world. Those of us blessed with the capacity to do these kinds of things have a moral obligation to everyone, not just ourselves. And you agreed with me!"

She responded, "If you and Max don't take the money, Preston, you can bet that somebody else will… and the people… the 'everybody' you want to help… they'll all get screwed anyway. That's what will happen. Let's not be idiots!"

"We are many things bad, but idiot is not among them," said Preston.

"My father said you've got your head in the clouds, Preston."

"Your father had a limited imagination, Sam. I've got my head in the *stars*!"

"By the time he was *your* age he had *six* successful companies and had retired a very rich man. I don't think limited imagination was his problem."

"Spare me," returned Preston. He had heard all of the accolades about her father so many tedious times before.

CHAPTER 20

"Loose lips sink ships," Americans used to recite during World War II. Ahmad Mulham was already on a jumbo jet headed for Los Angeles from Saudi Arabia and his father had only heard of this supposed cold fusion experiment one day before from a European businessman. But his father had remarkable connections everywhere in the oil world, even in the United States, and critical information like that wasn't going to wait. If only ten people on the entire planet knew of anything that might have a deleterious impact on petroleum based energy, Ahmad's father, Mahudin Mulham, would be one of those ten.

Ahmad had not been back to the United States in years and that feature of his assignment was particularly pleasing to him. It was precisely because he had gone to college in the U.S. that made him perfect for his father's mission. He fit in so nicely among the yanks. In fact, when he was attending the University of Miami a decade prior, he had been dubbed "Skip" Mulham, the preppy handle having been bestowed upon him when he was a freshman by several of his rowdy American friends, who were so tickled by such an unexpected nickname for a handsome but very dark Arab, that it just had to be, and it stuck. So, he was Skip Mulham throughout his five years in Miami and he loved every minute of it. He loved his classes. He loved the balmy ocean breezes and soft evenings in Coral Gables, Florida. He loved the parties and the pretty girls who were not wrapped head to toe in yards of cloth. He even learned to love American football.

The Hurricanes were a powerhouse at the University of Miami in those days, and he would play touch football with his friends on the university green in Coral Gables during the fall semester. And none of this fondness for the United States was hypocrisy to Ahmad, not blasphemy. He would have happily stayed on, perhaps gone to graduate school, if his father hadn't pulled the plug and said to Ahmad in a visit that his son needed to finish his studies and come home. Enough was enough, his father had said and he had said it in a voice that was only used when he was deadly serious. Time was up.

Ahmad Mulham sat in his first-class seat on the British Airways airplane that was returning him to the U.S., looking like a clotheshorse corporate attorney in his thousand dollar Italian suit, the heir apparent to his father's oil conglomerate, and he still thought of himself as a "Hoorocane." He grinned. All those years and miles later, he was still "Skip".

These were concepts that were lost on most of his family and friends in strictly ruled Islamic Saudi Arabia, but strangely not so much on his father, Mahudin Mulham, who was always somewhat of a liberal and Americana aficionado, even though there were no western clothes in his wardrobe. That's why going to the University of Miami had been a slam-dunk in Ahmad's father's game plan. They lived in the ancient port city of Jeddah on the Red Sea, which was the business center of Saudi Arabia and a cosmopolitan city, too, which was relatively unique in that country in 2005. Jeddah was thought by many Saudis to be a place of western decadence. But it was an absolutely appropriate site for the somewhat iconoclastic Mulham household to thrive.

Circumspect Mahudin Mulham thought he might have behaved just like his son if he had been born when Ahmad was born. The Mulham family was Muslim, to be sure, and they believed themselves to be devout; but they were not fundamentalists, they were secular Muslims. They were like secular Jews who may say "Merry Christmas," and secular Baptists who drink alcohol, and secular Catholics who have forgone confession. Mahudin Mulham believed in the prophet Mohammad, and he believed in daily prayers, and he believed in the teachings of the Koran, but like other secular deviants from various stripes of fundamentalism around the world, he simply had decided for himself and for the rearing of his children what was important and what was not. It's better to get along in the world, he figured. So, he chose to shed the weight of what he saw as antiquated and unenlightened demands and taboos that belonged in an earlier era. He had no time for the Sunni-Shiite ancient disagreements about the profit Mohammad's son and who was or was not the rightful leader of the faith. He had even less time for the totalitarian, reason-crushing Taliban. He was like an educated Christian who does not feel defrocked by the reasonable consideration that the historical Jesus may have simply passed out from agony and dehydration on the cross and woke up later. It doesn't really matter. An abiding philosophy of love and forgiveness still holds up.

So, it's not surprising Mahudin Mulham's only boy, Ahmad "Skip" Mulham, was so very available to western ways when he went off to school in the United States and that a real affection for those western ways had taken deep root in the boy's heart, so much so that his years at the University of Miami were now a part of his life he cherished. Like many American men and women who traipse off to college to be born into adulthood intellectually and emotionally, those days were remembered by Ahmad as some of the richest days of his young life.

As Ahmad leaned back in his wide first class seat, as the pilot announced that they would be landing in Los Angeles in about forty-five minutes, he wished he were headed to a class reunion or a get-together with old American school mates, men and women he did not see often enough. But that's not the kind of trip it was on that day. He was there on business related directly to his father's oil interests, which were significant. His liberal father, Mahudin Mulham, was a very a powerful figure in the Mid-East, a man who had been present during the founding of the Organization of Petroleum Exporting Countries, OPEC, in 1960. Ahmad's father had by the sheer force of his will and vigorous emotional persuasion, helped cobble together the charter for OPEC. Saudi Arabia had been included among the original six member states. Mahudin Mulham was a forward-thinker in a land where he figured the future is too often something left to the will of Allah. A passive strategy had never been for Mahudin Mulham. In another time, in a democratic Saudi Arabia with no absolute monarchy, he might have been the president. But he was a relatively old man by 2005 and so he fantasized that might be the destiny for his son; perhaps it would be Ahmad.

Sadly, there was not going to be any kidding around with many old college chums for Ahmad Mulham on his trip to the United States. He was on a heavily weighted "diplomatic" mission, one might call it, to discover with greater certainty what the devil was going on in California with this cold fusion rumor that had the underground wires in OPEC alive with activity and had his father, a usually calm and contemplative man, pacing around in his Jeddah high-rise wringing his hands.

Ahmad had been briefed prior to his departure. He had names and he had addresses. He knew what he was supposed to do and who he was supposed to see and what he was supposed to find out and he had far too much respect for his father and his family to not give it his best.

At one point Ahmad's father took his son aside after two of his father's business associates had been stuffing Ahmad with information like he was a Cornish game hen. It was information that may or may be of use on the trip he was about to take, but they had to pour it into Ahmad's head anyway. And Mahudin Mulham looked into Ahmad's eyes afterward and said rather ominously that it's possible other OPEC parties were investigating the situation, too, and maybe the Russians. Maybe the Argentinians. "Many parties have a stake. Expect anything", he said. "You know America and you'll get along fine, but be very careful", he added.

It was such loaded advice from his father that it actually made Ahmad pretty nervous, as he packed for the trip and as he reviewed the possibilities, imagining scenes out of some Hollywood espionage thriller. Was he in real danger? And right before he was to be driven to the airport in the family's huge black Mercedes Benz sedan, Ahmad tried his Americanized sense of humor, to defuse his concerns, and he asked his father if perhaps he should have packed a gun.

In truth, Ahmad was a bit taken aback by his father's slow and thoughtful answer when he responded quietly, "No. No, I don't think so." Ahmad would have preferred a hearty laugh and slap on the back.

Something was up, for sure, and pleasure was not on the agenda.

CHAPTER 21

Dr. Maxwell Umberto had already spoken with the President of the California Technological University about a truly astounding, mind-boggling, outcome from an experiment in one of the physics laboratories, which he had personally conducted. There would be unlimited energy for the entire world! Max had allowed that some preliminary work had been conducted by Dr. Preston Cook in a laboratory at his home, a man who was known to the President as a full-time faculty member on leave. But the *coup de grace* on this research happened at CTU, emphasized Dr. Umberto in relating developments.

Max told the head of the prestigious institution that he and Dr. Cook had been close to success all along until he had eventually suggested to Dr. Cook that they introduce multiple focused laser beams and it did the trick. But Maxwell did not want to extend his lie to dismissing the work of Dr. Cook altogether, and he said that nothing could have happened if Preston hadn't stayed the course on his own money. Except for me and him, he'd added, everybody else around the globe seemed to be tossing in the towel on cold fusion. Still, Max did not hedge too much on lauding his own contributions and he lied about those contributions as convincingly as he had lied about them to Samantha, effectively stealing the thunder on the remarkable accomplishment. Maxwell had nothing to do with the laser beams, but intellectuals are strangely self-centered creatures and it was entirely possible he had re-written the history of the research so thoroughly in his mind that in some perverse way he now saw his role as pivotal.

There was no doubt that President Charles Trenton Holcomb believed Max had been the prime mover, believed Dr. Umberto had cracked the nagging, frustrating puzzle of cold fusion and the world would be forever different because of it. Max sheepishly acknowledged this was a momentous development, and it didn't take Max to fill in the blanks for the president on what cold fusion could mean to CTU and the president's personal cachet.

Maxwell had ambitious Dr. Holcomb's full attention standing in his elegant suite at the University and even as Umberto was speaking with the President, Max could clearly see himself as the Chair of the Physics Department, a position he had come to truly covet. While he struggled to be as humble as his rather inflated sense of self-importance would allow, as he figuratively nodded in the direction of his long-time friend and colleague Preston Cook, as he asked the President of CTU if there could be some kind of formal announcement and press release as soon as possible, Maxwell was also envisioning himself in that spacious endowed Chair's office in the physics building. He was salivating with anticipation.

CTU's President Holcomb, was much more of a politician and fund-raiser than he was an academic. That's why he was the president and not a dean or a teaching member of the faculty. Oh, sure, he was an engineer; he had to be something like that to get the job. He earned his PhD in electrical engineering at Virginia Tech decades ago, and he had written his dissertation on power generation, but of the hydroelectric kind, not nuclear. He had published a slew of forgettable papers, too, which were good for his curriculum vitae but not much else. Mostly Dr. Holcomb had continually positioned himself for administrative advancement during the thirty years of his academic life, which meant he moved around and then moved around some more. Keep your ear to the ground and do not be afraid to "do the ask," as people in development like to say, which was something at which Holcomb excelled. He had no compunction whatsoever about pointedly saying to a wealthy science enthusiast, "How about helping us put a rover on Venus, like the one we're going to put on Mars?" And it worked for him. He had money pouring in from deep-pockets, would-be scientists on every continent, which is the primary reason Charles T. Holcomb had eventually managed to earn that plum President's job at CTU.

For an engineer, the President of CTU was as close to the top rung in academic administration as one is likely to reach. If he could nail down another Nobel Prize winner in another CTU department, it would be one more colorful feather in the grandly festooned cap he already wore, and that's what he sensed might happen via the story Dr. Umberto told to him.

Therefore, Max had Dr. Holcomb's attention right off the bat and, yes, a press conference and announcement was absolutely possible. Rushing ahead, as the CTU President was envisioning it, with the implications related to that particular breakthrough, such an affair would have to be a bit more extravagant than academic announcements usually would be at CTU. Umberto's research had such an intoxicating over-the-top outcome that President Holcomb was nearly glassy-eyed while he mentally laced the next step in his career together with Maxwell Umberto's.

When Max left his meeting with the President he was floating. He could hardly keep his feet on the ground. The announcement would be in a week or two, tops. President Holcomb had said it should be done quickly, "Let's not waste time on this *shattering* news!" He didn't know how the miracle had been accomplished, but he trusted Maxwell Umberto completely.

As Max drifted several inches above the pavement, levitating his way back to his office at CTU, he was imagining how he would inform Preston of developments. He was never planning to leave his friend out. He wasn't trying to steal the discovery, he said to himself. But Max was so overcome with the entire evolution of the experiment that he didn't even consider that Preston might not agree an announcement should occur at this early stage. Max, either ignorantly or hopefully, pictured Preston as being delighted with it all. A press conference at prestigious CTU!

It wasn't unlike Maxwell to be wrapped up in his own world and his own ambitions to the degree that he was out of touch with others and this was definitely one of those times. He was a child in that way. He simply could not fathom there would be a problem with Preston. By then, Dr. Umberto had said to so many people that he had been the trigger to the success of the research that Maxwell realized bringing his full-speed locomotive to a halt would be a very difficult maneuver. He had convinced his old friend Bobby Skylar, and he had convinced Preston's wife, Samantha Day-Steiner, and god knows how many others at CTU he'd run into in the last few days. One could argue Maxwell had purloined the whole project before Preston Cook even knew Max had been speaking of it to anyone!

Dr. Umberto really had no idea how far and wide news of the discovery had traveled and he had no inkling as to just how riled some factions in the outside world had become on rumors alone, without a formal announcement. On that count both he and Preston were equally unaware. Maxwell could hardly keep his trap shut about what had happened and with each telling his role in the research seemed to grow like Pinocchio's nose. Repeat the same lie often enough and it becomes the truth. There wasn't going to be an official press conference for days at the soonest, but as Max returned to his office after speaking with CTU's President there were already strangers on the other side of the continent and strangers on the other side of the globe who had been informed that Dr. Maxwell Umberto had created a portable and clean cold fusion nuclear reactor in California. Many of those strangers had grave concerns about Umberto's research and its outcome, an outcome that would seriously upset the status quo in the highly lucrative energy world. Many of those strangers wished the discovery would go away and they were willing to take action to facilitate that wish. Some of them were willing to take rather aggressive action. Trillions of dollars were on the table.

CHAPTER 22

Responding to the doorbell, Preston strode from the kitchen with a dishrag in his hands to the front where he found Cloud Willow and Big Buster Bernard standing on the porch, crowding the Cook's quaint threshold.

"Buster's got something to tell you," said Cloud Willow while her large partner swayed at her side waiting on permission to enter. His size notwithstanding, Buster had learned some time ago that Cloud saw him as a bit too assertive with his opinions, so he had chosen to let her lead in certain situations.

They were a pair clearly with something to say that day and it might have struck someone else as strange that they would begin with a proclamation. But Preston well understood Cloud and Buster were not your run-of-the-mill twosome. Any interaction with these neighbors was going to be odd by any conventional standard. Cloud Willow was in her customary flowing ex-hippie dress, with arms, fingers, and neck bedecked by silver and turquoise jewelry. And there was gigantic Buster Bernard next to her, with a red bandana tight over his head and knotted at the back. He wore a black tee shirt under a worn and sleeveless denim jacket, as bikerly as he could be. The two of them were an offline but perfect match, as Preston saw it, and he liked them for their lack of pretense. Buster and Cloud were also so very sweet with Dalton, which was always a big plus in Preston's book.

"Okay. Why don't you guys come on in?" said Preston and he stepped back so they could enter.

Cloud was still in charge. She obviously had hauled Buster over for something that he wanted to share and she was trying to make it happen in some way resembling normal behavior, which was not always a characteristic you could rely on with Buster.

"Buster saw something," she announced as they came inside and selected seats in the mission-style living room created by Samantha two years ago when she finally tired of all the collected hand-me-downs they had lived with for the previous two decades of their marriage. "He saw someone outside and you should probably hear about it. He's got a good sense of these things."

It was unusual for Samantha to be around at that hour, in the afternoon on a weekday, but she'd forgotten something at the house she needed for her late class, so she'd come back that day to dig it up. She was home in an office that had been fashioned for her out of a first floor spare bedroom. Samantha and Preston had agreed some time ago that because Preston had staked out the garage for his laboratory, any in-house work space went to Sam.

So, upon hearing voices in the living room and wondering what was going on, Samantha drifted out from her office where she had been collating handouts for her students.

"Hi, Sam," said both Buster and Cloud nodding toward her.

Preston turned around to see his wife emerging from the rear of the house.

"What's up?" she asked.

"We're just about to find out," returned Preston as they all took seats. "So… '*What's up?*'" he recited jocularly.

"Buster?" said Cloud turning to the large man, who at that moment looked like a school kid about to give a book report. He was aware of his limitations, but his limitations were not intelligence; they were sensitivity to boundaries. It was often touch and go with Buster.

"Late yesterday there was this guy out front in a Taurus, checkin' out yer place," said Buster. "I was comin' home 'round five or so, and there he was, stopped across the street in his car, really lookin' things over. I mean checkin' it all out!"

Preston and Sam glanced at one another quickly.

"Did he say anything?" asked Sam. "We get realtors around here all the time."

"He was no realtor," said Buster confidently. "The way he acted when he saw me lookin' at him… it just wasn't right. He was up to somethin'. I know for damn sure, he was up to no good."

Cloud added, "I've been trying to get Buster to consider other possibilities, but he's convinced about this and I believe him. Primal skills get shoved so far away in most of us that we don't trust our instincts anymore. Buster still has it."

"It's good of you to let us know about him, Buster," said Sam, quickly trying to get a control of a suspect conversation, without offending well-intentioned neighbors. "What do you think we should do?" she asked earnestly.

This time it was Buster and Cloud who exchanged glances.

"The guy wasn't a gang-banger or anything like that, ya know. But he was casin' the joint. Count on it."

"What did he look like?" asked Preston.

"Looked normal," he said. "A white guy in a four-door Taurus. He looked like a cop, to tell ya the truth. Civvies, though. He looked like a detective. Regular build. Some gray hair. Late fifties, maybe sixty, I'd say."

At that point, nobody knew what else to say and they just fired glances around at each other for a couple of beats.

"I think there's trouble," added Buster deadly serious.

"Buster," admonished Cloud, "Easy…" She held up one finger.

"No. I'm serious. I don't know what it's about, but somethin's goin' on," continued Buster.

"Well, thanks," said Preston. "We'll keep an eye out."

Buster suddenly reached into his denim jacket and he hauled out an Army issue Colt .45 caliber handgun. The mere sight of it jolted both Preston and Samantha!

"Put that away!" said Could Willow reaching over to her husband's arm.

"You might need this," said Buster offering it to Preston. "Sombitch's not too accurate over a hundred feet, but ya can stop a truck anywhere close."

"Oh, no!" said Preston holding up his palms. "No. No guns."

Samantha sat there with her eyes about to pop out of her face. "We… we won't be needing any weapons or anything… but thanks. Thank you," she said.

"I'm so sorry," said Cloud. "Really I am. I didn't know he brought that damn thing over here. Put it away, Buster."

"You may wish you had this handy, my friends," insisted Buster to the Cooks.

"They don't want it, Buster!" said Cloud firmly.

Buster finally tucked the firearm away inside his jacket and he said, "Well, if you need anything… you know I've got it. That individual was *not* a friendly," he concluded.

"Yes, thank you, Buster, and you, too, Cloud," said Sam. "We will definitely keep our eyes open."

"Okay," said Cloud, "We won't bother you anymore this afternoon," and the two neighbors stood up and headed for the doorway.

Cloud stopped just before leaving and said apologetically that she has been trying to get Buster to trust his intuition and she repeated that she didn't know about the gun.

At that point Buster blurted to Dr. Cook, "I thought this might have somethin' to do with yer experiments and all, Preston. You could really tip over a big apple cart with this reactor you've invented!"

Preston smiled. "I certainly hope so," he said. "But nobody knows about it yet, Buster."

Samantha felt blood rise in her face upon hearing those words. She knew a host of people at CTU and elsewhere around the country had already heard about the experiments with Maxwell advertising his success all over the place. As the guilt crawled through her, she realized she'd actually encouraged it.

"Well… this creep was up to somethin'," repeated Buster Bernard underlining his eye-witness account. "That much I know! Be careful."

"We will," confirmed Preston.

And with that, the neighbors went out the door into the late afternoon daylight.

As Preston closed their craftsman house's wide solid front door behind their neighbors, he looked at Samantha. "What do you think that was about?" he asked having been more than mildly disturbed by the report he'd just heard from Buster but not for any identifiable reason.

Sam shook her head. "All I know is we don't need any guns in this house."

She had never cottoned much to Buster's survivalist mentality and conspiracy theories, and while she was sociable with their neighbors she was generally not so accepting of their peculiar ways and lifestyle. What bothered her most that afternoon was her private knowledge of Maxwell's meeting with CTU's President Holcomb and Maxwell's unilateral movement to publicize the cold fusion accomplishment. So, Samantha figured a mysterious Ford Taurus drifting slowly by with someone scoping out the house may very well be related to Preston's work. That last suggestion springing from their big, awkward neighbor's suspicious mind made sense to her.

"Oh, who the hell knows?" she finally chose to say dismissively, covering-up as best she could as she went back toward her office, speaking across her shoulder. "Those two were probably smoking dope and got a wild hair. I'm sure it's nothing." And as Samantha disappeared around the corner toward her office at the back of the house, Preston could hear her fading words. "The world really *should* know about what you guys have done, Preston, and *soon*!"

CHAPTER 23

Max was an exuberant man when he arrived at his townhouse the evening he had spoken with President Holcomb and was still walking on air. It was the same evening Big Buster was offering the Cook household a U.S. Army .45 caliber semi-automatic pistol for protection. Maxwell hadn't yet said anything to Preston about a press conference, but Umberto had that very conversation on his agenda for the next day. Max was fantasizing about the upcoming announcement as he fiddled with his keys to find the right one for his front door. He envisioned Preston and himself sitting at a table with a CTU banner behind them and a tangle of microphones in front of them, television cameras aimed like spotlights, a crowd of reporters, and flashes popping in box cameras. His fantasy was all in black and white. But academic press conferences of the day didn't look like Joe DiMaggio announcing his retirement. The scene that Max had in his mind could never happen, but he swam in it nonetheless.

Dr. Umberto's dreams were put to a sudden and wholly unexpected halt the moment Max opened his front door. "What the fuck?" is about all he could say as he entered his Orange Grove townhouse.

The entire living room had been upended by an exceptionally thorough intruder. At first glance, it seemed like everything in the place was thrown over in some way. All of his paintings were down, on the floor and leaning against the walls. Most were worth significant money, too, so Max was quite unnerved by what he was seeing. They had been man-handled like so many worthless posters, but at first glance it didn't seem any had been stolen. Max immediately figured the imbeciles didn't know valuable art when they had their mitts on it!

He came forward into his trendy residence rather slowly and totally in shock. He picked up a heavy replica of the Reclining Buddha that had been dropped onto the sofa. It was solid jade, for crying out loud! These guys were total idiots, he was thinking, as he collected his senses and went to telephone the Pasadena Police Department. He put his hand on his forehead. "Why *now*? Why *today*?" he yelled. This couldn't have happened at a worse time... not that there's a good time, but this was *the worst*. It had been such a stupendous day until then.

When the cops arrived, not twenty minutes after Maxwell's call, it was two detectives with several uniformed officers in tow, and the team went straight to work checking out all the rooms and looking for anything that might have been inadvertently left behind by the intruders. Max actually thought he recognized one of the men in uniform, a skinny police officer named Sigopian who had a strangely crooked nose. Max remembered the officer because he had pulled Max over and ticketed him for going 40 in a 35 zone along Orange Grove, not a hundred yards from his own townhouse a couple of years ago, but this was not a connection he wanted to bring up right then. The cop didn't seem to remember, or he didn't say anything. But Maxwell's memory of it pissed him off all over again.

Lieutenant Stanley Lau was a stranger to Max, rather short and on the plump side, a fortyish Chinese-American detective with only wisps of black hair remaining on his head, evenly dispersed across his scalp and reminding Max of someone undergoing chemo therapy. He had an assistant who was as strange a creature as one is likely to find: tall, gangly, and silent, moving about the scene like a large insect, sniffing and ogling items. Lau asked if Max knew what was missing and Maxwell looked around his ransacked home, rather befuddled by it all.

"I... I haven't really had a chance to take a good inventory," he said.

"Well," said the detective, "do you have any valuables?"

"*Yes*!" said Max perturbed. "Pretty much every damn thing! The artwork! All of the pieces are originals... or most of them, anyway. My furniture!"

"Is it famous art?" asked Lau, who knew almost nothing about it.

"No... no, not famous like the *Mona Lisa*, for chrissake, but I do have sketches by Picasso and Chagall, among others," said Max almost defiantly. "And some superb but less well known artists in oil," he went on. "But I must say," he added, somewhat at a loss, "I cannot see anything missing right off. I'll have to check. Ah!" he proclaimed suddenly, spying a piece and crossing the room to where he picked up an acrylic sculpture in sharp geometric shapes which was cock-eyed on its base because it had been tossed aside to the floor. "This is probably worth five thousand dollars! It's an original Bergson!" Max said, assertively. "And look at it!" He was incensed.

Stanley Lau was not really interested and not especially impressed by the acrylic sculpture or the paintings but he digested what he had heard as a kind of evidence. "Mr. Umberto," he said forgetting that Dr. was the appropriate title, "hope you have insurance. Seems to me like this person or these people were looking for something specific and it obviously was not the artwork."

"What do you mean?" replied Max weakly. He could see there was disarray throughout the town house and yet it appeared that nothing was missing. Max suddenly could understand how strange that might appear to the police officers.

"Do you have a safe?" said Lau.

"No. I have nothing to put in a safe."

The detective nodded and made some notes on his small pad.

"Do you have any enemies?" he said, surprising Max.

"Enemies?" came back Max with his version of a deer-in-the-headlights face. "No. I don't have any enemies," he added. He did not consider recent events. He did not connect the research on cold fusion to the invasion of his home. How could it be connected? He was as naive in his own unfortunate way as were the police investigators. Scientific research was so far off the radar screen for the Pasadena Police Department that they would have never thought to ask about controversial scholarly work or anything related to it. Their world was not so esoteric. It was far more earth-bound and concrete.

"Do you do recreational drugs?" the detective asked suddenly and as a matter-of-fact, without judgment.

"No!" said Max, stunned at the thought. "No, there are no drugs here! I don't do drugs!" It was a true statement.

"Well," said Lau, "these guys went through your kitchen cabinets, your refrigerator, and your dressers. Follow what I'm saying? When this kind of domestic search occurs, whoever does it has a target. They didn't do this for fun. This wasn't mischief. It's a mess, sure, but there's not much reckless damage. They didn't slice open sofa cushions. For me, Mr. Umberto, *you* are in the best position to guess what it is they wanted."

Detective Lau watched Max blink and contemplate what was said, and then Lau calmly said to Max, "So, look around, okay, while we finish up. Let me know if any kind of motive comes to mind."

Maxwell Umberto nodded and tried to organize his thinking, tried to redefine his possessions in light of what among them might be worth taking. He still wasn't connecting the dots between the cold fusion research and the bizarre development in his home. He wasn't considering hidden floppy disks or zip drives. It was baffling because the usual robbery booty was still there, the flat screen television, the digital state-of-the-art sound system, the artwork. Isn't that what burglars usually take? Items had been tossed around but not carted off. Actually, Maxwell's noting of this peculiarity was beginning to give him the willies more than if his Bose stereo was gone. He could see what the detective was saying. What in god's name were these people after?

Less than an hour later the Pasadena Police had done what they could do at that time. Before leaving, Detective Lau asked Maxwell Umberto to lend serious thought to what had happened. Try to guess who might have a reason to ransack his home. Was it just to scare him? That's a possibility, if there is somebody out there with a bone to pick. Is there an angry woman in the picture, the detective asked, and that made Max shiver a little bit, because of his relationship with Samantha. He didn't want to be confessing to the detective that he's been screwing his old friend's wife.

"Well… I can't think of anything right now," Max said.

"Okay," said Detective Lau. "Here's my card. Call me if anything comes up. If you think of something, or if you find out that something is missing that you hadn't noticed before, give me a call."

"What happens next?" said Max as Detective Lau was leaving. Max didn't really know what to ask. He'd never been burglarized before.

The detective stopped in the doorway and looked back at Max, who was a healthy guy but appeared strangely frail in that light and at that moment. Skinny crooked-nosed officer Sigopian and the other uniformed officers were already gone, as was Lau's partner, the tall, peculiarly mute man who had been sniffing around and looking for evidence.

"In this situation, my guess is, *nothing* happens next," responded the detective to Max's question. "I hate to be so blunt. We'll review what we've seen here and get back to you if we need to. We'll poke around. But, I'll be truthful with you. I'm thinking we won't come up with much. If there's another break-in around the neighborhood and it looks kind of like this one, maybe we'll start to piece things together. But what you've got here tonight is pretty unusual, Mr. Umberto. Unless you tell me different… so far, nothing has been stolen. All we have is trespassing and vandalism. And I don't think this was vandalism."

Max nodded. He had nothing else to say. He was dumb-founded.

"I'm sorry," said Detective Stanley Lau and he left, leaving Max standing in his doorway with one hand on the door knob, watching the cops retreat into the night.

What a hellish way to end a day that in many ways had been one of the best in his life.

CHAPTER 24

Detective Lau didn't walk away from that crime scene and simply shelve everything he had seen hoping that Maxwell would call him after having discovered his diamond tiara was missing. Something was fishy there. Lau had been around the block on break-ins and the one at the town house on Orange Grove only fit one pattern. It had all the earmarks of an illicit drug deal gone sour. The detective would've bet the deed to his mother's house that a bundle of cash or drugs had been hidden there and now the stash was gone.

Clearly the professor wasn't a street thug, nor did he likely have affiliations with organized crime because Dr. Umberto didn't think twice about calling the cops when he got home to find the place ransacked. That's what middle-class white folks do when they get robbed, even when it might not be such a good idea, even when they may have been up to something illegal. Following Maxwell's footprints was very much the order of the day for Detective Lau and his quiet partner, the silent awkward sleuth, who never spoke much even around the Pasadena police station. But that gangly and strange detective reared amongst Louisiana bayous could find a suspect's pubic hair in a New Orleans' cat house if he was told to, and everyone at the Pasadena Police Department knew it.

Maxwell Umberto and his academic life may need some surreptitious looking into, reckoned Stanley Lau, to tidy up any loose and curious sets of possibilities about what happened in the professor's town house. The Pasadena police lieutenant had been over to CTU on business before. Three or four years earlier he busted another professor who liked to run around Victory Park on moonless nights, butt naked, darting from tree to tree and scampering in front of women jogging along the lighted paths. Lau had taken the streaker into custody as he stepped down from his lectern after delivering a presentation on quantum mechanics to a hundred and fifty freshmen physics majors. There are peculiar goings-on everywhere in the world, it seemed, and CTU was no exception. This Maxwell Umberto fellow might be dealing smack right out of the prestigious Parthaneum, thought the Pasadena Detective. Weirder things have happened and he didn't want to leave stones unturned.

The morning after Maxwell's residence had been burglarized, or at the very least broken-into, Preston Cook and his son, Dalton, were "getting away from it all" as they liked to say to each other when the urge to take to the skies overcame them. The cold fusion success story was already creating stress in Preston's life, but to his knowledge only a handful of people knew about it. He didn't have the foggiest idea that word of his achievement had gears in motion near and far. Preston had not yet heard about the ransacking of Maxwell's town home. Only the bizarre report from Big Buster, in which someone was giving the Cook household the once-over, presented even the flimsiest indication anything was amiss in their peaceful world. Preston had chosen to eschew any connection between that drive-by event and his research. Such a notion was ludicrous, he figured. At the end of the day, Preston was as ignorant about these things as his colleague, Maxwell Umberto, who had more than a suspicious drive-by on his hands. Max had real intruders and an upended town house to get his attention and even then Dr. Umberto had not considered the cold fusion research was relevant.

Although Max could scheme in his own devious ways, he was always a scientist, and scientists, like artists, can be woefully disconnected to what motivates your garden variety ambitious man or woman. As a result, the treachery most healthy adults might recognize pretty quickly can parade by in full regalia before many a scientist or artist and go totally unnoticed.

In that vein, the pressure Preston was getting from Samantha came from an unknown source, right out of the blue, but not the wild-yonder kind of blue he was enjoying that morning with his son, as the white Skyhawk leaned to the starboard and banked across the San Gabriel Mountains.

Dalton's nose was pressed against the starboard window as he scrutinized the various activities on the earth below them, where thousands of garden variety men and women shoved forward in their daily routines.

"Do you think you'll like being famous, Dalt?" said his father, smiling.

"I dunno," said Dalton, glancing over his shoulder at his father, half listening, and then looking out the window again.

"Well, you will be when the world knows you're the one who solved cold fusion."

Dalton looked back at his dad and grinned, "The center of stars!" he said enthusiastically.

"The center of stars!" said Preston.

"Are we going to be rich?" his son asked.

"Rich? Why would you ask that?" said his father.

"Mom says we can make a lot of money from what we did."

"Oh," said Preston. "Well, that all remains to be seen. We'll reimburse ourselves, but that's not why we did it, remember?"

"I know. We want to leave something good behind in our lives."

"That's right. Everyone should leave something good behind… and everyone *can*. We just happen to be in a special place where our contribution can help a whole lot of people."

"Yes," said Dalton, looking out at the traffic on the 210 Freeway, thick in both directions and slicing Pasadena across its middle, east to west. "But I guess being rich would be a nice thing."

Preston looked at his son as the youngster reviewed the city below and to the south. Preston studied the back of the perfectly round head and soft brown hair at the window. Preston was thinking what a difficult time that sweet and very smart boy with an extra chromosome had known in his few years of life. Looking at Dalton, Preston also realized Samantha had been talking to the boy about developments in the lab. 'Are we going to be rich?' was not Dalton's question. But Dalton was not so removed from the regular world by his specialness that he did not understand how money can have an impact on the way people live and what they can do.

"Hey," said Preston changing the subject, "why don't *you* drive!"

"Okay," said Dalton excitedly and he sat up straight in his seat, rested his hands on the copilot's yoke in front of him, and stretched his toes down to the peddles.

"Are you ready?" said Preston.

"Aye, Captain," returned Dalton in another of their rehearsed maneuvers as Preston turned the plane over to his son. The aircraft went wobbly for just a beat as Dalton found his bearings at the controls, but Preston said nothing and the Cessna leveled out quickly to where it was once again throbbing gently through the cool early October air, smoothly floating above the landscape.

"Well done, Master Cook!" said Preston. "Well done! Steady as she goes."

CHAPTER 25

Things weren't going to get a lot easier for Maxwell Umberto after his surprise the prior evening at his town house. He'd gone into his office at CTU the next morning, still rather shaken by the whole episode and disheartened at Detective Lau's discouraging forecast about solving the case. It didn't dawn on Max that he himself was a suspect in the callously cultivated imaginations of the police investigators, just as it didn't occur to Max that his involvement in the research might have something to do with what happened. He could be brilliant, but he was in the dark on these matters. And when he arrived at his office on the second floor, the office that overlooked California Street and the athletic fields where future scientists and researchers kicked soccer balls and sweated away their afternoons, Max had another unexpected visitation, but at least it wasn't on the sly and this visitor didn't leave his office in disarray.

As Max turned the corner at the top of the stairs and as he was hauling his office keys out of his pocket, he couldn't help but notice a young man sitting on one of the benches in the hallway, just beyond but near to his office door. Max was particularly sensitized that morning after what had happened in his apartment, so he slowed slightly as he came forward, and he eyed the stranger suspiciously. He didn't look familiar. At twenty paces, the young man turned and stared directly at Max. He had a dark complexion. Max guessed him to be Mid-Eastern. The stranger appeared to be around thirty, a lanky attractive man, wearing a CTU sweatshirt and blue jeans. Max suddenly wondered if this guy was one of his own students. Had Max become so befuddled by everything that he didn't recognize his students? The young man certainly seemed to recognize Max, smiled and continued to stare right at him as Max stopped to unlock his office door. It made Dr. Umberto rather uncomfortable to say the least on that particular morning and he was eager to get inside his office.

"Dr. Umberto?" said the dark young man suddenly, standing up and slightly advancing, but he was appropriately tentative and quite respectful in his affect.

Max remained nervous with his key in the lock, trying to figure out who this young man was. "Yes?" he said.

"My name is Ahmad Mulham and I'm wondering if I could have a few minutes of your time this morning. I apologize for not making arrangements." Ahmad's English was perfect in spite of a modest Mid-Eastern accent.

"I'm rather busy, truthfully," came back Max, preferring no off-track encounters to start his day. "What is it about? Are you a student?"

"No, I'm not a student… just yet!" he volunteered with a self-conscious laugh, gesturing to his own chest where "Tech U" appeared on the sweatshirt. "I just want to ask you a couple of questions about the physics program. It won't take a minute." He flushed darker brown and looked sheepish.

Maxwell studied the young man. The stranger's embarrassment over his sweatshirt ploy was actually quite disarming, sufficiently so that Max said, "Sure. But I really do not have more than a short minute right now."

With that, Dr. Umberto opened his office and the two of them went inside.

"Have a seat," said Max, gesturing to one of the four chairs surrounding a table where he would have conferences with his graduate students over their various research interests and he rested his briefcase on that very table.

"What can I do for you?" Maxwell said.

Ahmad was earnest and he gazed directly into Maxwell's eyes. "I'm trying to decide between graduate programs in physics."

"Have you been admitted?" said Max.

"Yes," Ahmad lied, "here, MIT, and Rensselaer. I don't know which is best for me. I'm visiting all of them. I just flew in from Saudi Arabia the day before yesterday. I'm making a 'whirlwind tour', I think you call it."

"Ahhh," said Max still uncertain as to where this was going. "Your English is pretty good."

"I went to the University of Miami," said Ahmad. "I'm a Hoorocane," he added and he grinned.

"Good football team," returned Maxwell cordially, thinking Miami is not your usual undergraduate feeder school for CTU.

"I understand you have done a lot of work in the area of cold fusion," said Ahmad just like that, and the words thumped Max in the middle of his forehead like he had been hit with a rubber mallet. No paper had been published on the research and no announcement had been made. The press release would be next week. How would *anybody* outside of his academic community come up with that notion, especially an international student fresh from Saudi Arabia?

"Cold fusion?" repeated Dr. Umberto, numbly. "That's your area of interest?"

"Yes," said Ahmad and he didn't need to lie for that part of the conversation. "My father is a very powerful man in the oil business and he is forward-thinking. Unlike so many of his colleagues in the Middle East, he accepts that oil is going to run out some day, so he would like to lead change, rather than chase it. Change is a wild stallion that many would not ride. It is too risky. But if the stallion is a winner, one *must* ride, says my father."

"I see," said Maxwell, and that is where he should have asked the young man *why* he had come to him about cold fusion. How did he know about it? But Maxwell's critical mind went off-line after he heard the young Saudi man's words about his father. At that point Maxwell began to see lights flashing and he began to hear cash-registers ringing as dollar signs spun around in his head like the cherries on a slot machine. A Saudi oil baron was interested in the cold fusion work? Sound judgment was often replaced in Maxwell's head by glee when there were early winnings. He was a fool for good fortune and a terrible gambler. He attempted restraint, but it was a hopeless effort.

"Well…" Dr. Umberto boasted carefully to the young Arab, "all I can say is, I've been involved in cold fusion research for some time and I have been the principle investigator in a project that has undoubtedly gone much further than any other project in that area has ever gone."

Ahmad's eyes were beginning to light up. It's true! He was rejoicing within himself. I can tell my father, they have done it!

"That havening been said," offered Max attempting to bring the conversation back to earth, "I am not free right now to say any more about the work. So, let me just answer your primary question. If you want to do research on cold fusion, there isn't anywhere in the world that is going to be more deeply and critically involved in its development than at CTU in the upcoming years. That much I can guarantee," he said and he smiled.

Ahmad Mulham took a very deep breath and leaned back. He rightly sensed it was about as far as he could go in the discussion at that moment, but he'd gotten his foot in the door, as his American friends in Miami used to say. "Okay," he replied to Dr. Umberto. "I thank you for your time."

"You're welcome" said Max, sending the signal that he had other things to do and Ahmad understood.

"Uh… if I have a question, can I call?" said Ahmad impulsively, with his large, dark and imploring eyes studying Maxwell's face.

"Here," said Max grabbing a business card from his desk, "shoot me an email. I'll do what I can."

"Thank you! Thank you, very much!" said Ahmad taking Maxwell's hand and vigorously pumping it. They both went to the door and Max let Ahmad out into the hallway from whence he had come. After shutting the door Maxwell reckoned he had just met a peculiar but pleasant young man whom he believed to be a Mid-Eastern graduate student in physics, a young man whose family may hold interesting opportunities for Preston and himself. And some of what Max was thinking was true.

Max smiled to himself and figured the young man would be shocked when the announcement about cold fusion occurred the following week. But naive Max had no clue the Saudi boy had been sent to him by parties who already believed cold fusion may have been accomplished and the young man was there on a mission to find out if it was a fact. And the mission had been a slam dunk because what Maxwell said to Ahmad pretty much confirmed everything. All the while, Max thought he was being oh so cautious.

But Americanized Ahmad Mulham insightfully calculated as he left the physics building, any cutting-off-at-the-pass of the galloping cowboy, Maxwell Umberto, was going to have to occur without delay. In that same moment of clarity, Ahmad realized the cold fusion success story would be public soon and likely very soon. Once it goes public, he figured, getting a rein on cold fusion and a partnership would be near to impossible. Ahmad was on his cell phone to his father before he got back to his rented convertible.

Of course, Max didn't know interested parties were zeroing in on him over the cold fusion research even before an announcement hit the airwaves. And Ahmad didn't know he, too, was being studied and watched, zeroed in on, as he enthusiastically updated his father with a cell phone mashed against his ear while he walked across the CTU campus. In the shadows of a forest-like collection of California oaks at the university, Maxwell's government friend, Bobby Skylar, followed the young Saudi man all the way to his Toyota Solara rag-top in the CTU visitors' parking area.

It had all occurred serendipitously, because like Ahmad Mulham, Bobby had also come by to drop in on his old friend Max that morning, but he found Ahmad was already waiting in the hall outside Maxwell's office. So, Agent Skylar backed away from his original plan. His curiosity about this Middle-Eastern interloper was piqued by that chance encounter. Bobby knew right away the young man was not one of Max's students even if Max wasn't sure himself. With the aid of Special Group's tentacles, Bobby knew more about Maxwell's life at that juncture than Max knew about his own life. No time had been wasted. Information is power, they say, and it was absolutely currency of the realm in Special Group.

In a matter of hours Bobby would know everything important there was to know about Ahmad Mulham, details that Ahmad himself would not have imagined anyone knew, such as the terminated pregnancy of a Tri-Delt named Lorraine, whom Ahmad dated while at the University of Miami. It was an unfortunate side story of Ahmad's life in America that would have devastated his mother and father.

Ahmad's unexpected appearance and intervention with Dr. Umberto was not a development Bobby exactly cherished. He already knew about the ransacking of Maxwell's town house and he knew that a Pasadena detective was on the case. He knew Max had been boinking Dr. Day-Steiner, the wife of his research partner, and it probably wouldn't be long before the Pasadena Police knew about it, as well. Bobby Skylar understood several hostile oil interests on the other side of the planet, besides the Saudis, had their ears up and were sniffing the wind, such as Russian and South American oil interests. And Bobby knew America's own oil conglomerates were on the trail, too. There was already an international assortment of snoops, agents, and tough *hombres* in the game. All the players clearly saw the future of the world's energy market was at stake. Far too much money was on the table and Agent Skylar understood quite clearly only one thing can happen in his business when there is that kind of traffic in a hot situation. A rogue was going to appear and break up the logjam.

CHAPTER 26

Lieutenant Stanley Lau knocked on the door to Preston Cook's garage laboratory. It was a Saturday so Dalton was with his father in the lab running some computer simulations, changing one little thing and then another little thing each time to see what margin there was for error in their wildly successful results on cold fusion. The two of them were in fine fettle because the computer tests were telling them this was not a frail or temperamental outcome, easily derailed, or likely to fail if some miniscule variation found its way into the formula. They had tried many variations in the most likely places for errors to occur. And as was typical for them, Preston and Dalton made a game of their work. Every time they ran the virtual experiment with positive results, they would high-five and dance around in what they had come to call their "center of the stars dance." They generally acted silly and laughed a lot even though it was genuine research. Preston would show Dalton what they were looking for in the simulations and the boy was quite capable of deducing whether or not the simulations worked.

They were in the midst of one of their center of the stars dances when Detective Stanley Lau's knock came at the lab door. Samantha would simply have entered. A loud, demanding rap on the lab door was actually a rare event. Preston and Dalton stopped their dance and looked at each other quizzically.

Then Preston said, "See who it is," so Dalton went to the door and opened it.

Two strangers were standing on the original old and cracked cement driveway which led to the garage laboratory. It was a bright day, so Dalton had to hold a hand over his eyes like a visor to get a good look at them. The closest man was a short and slightly overweight Asian in a dark suit, a man with not much hair on his head and a squint on his face. The second man was a tall, white guy in a gray suit and bone-skinny. He was wringing his hands compulsively like someone from an asylum as he dodged around in a disturbing sort of way behind the Asian man. They were an unexpected and odd pair standing there in the sunlight, but it didn't deter Dalton.

"Yes?" Dalton said, like he owned the place.

"Is Preston Cook here?" said Detective Lau.

"Who's asking?" said Dalton. Preston heard his son challenging these guys and was actually quite proud of the boy for his assertive stance. Confidence wasn't usually Dalton's strongest asset when he dealt with strangers.

Lau was trying to look beyond the youngster into the dark laboratory, but he decided to cooperate and hauled out his badge from his coat pocket and said, "I'm Lieutenant Lau with the Pasadena Police Department and this," he gestured to the furtive man behind him, "is my partner. Now, young man, is Dr. Cook around today?"

Dalton still held his ground standing like a tiny blockade in front of the two police officers, with his arm holding the door open. He yelled over his shoulder, "Dad, there is a guy who says he is a detective here to see you!"

Preston came forward from the interior of the lab, which was to Detective Lau a dark and ill-defined space beyond the little sentry standing in front of him.

"I'm Dr. Cook," said Preston approaching from directly behind Dalton and resting his hands reassuringly on both of his son's shoulders. "What may I do for you?"

"Well… we just have a few questions we'd like to ask you about your research partner, Dr. Maxwell Umberto," said Stanley Lau, just as plainly and as drama-free as he could muster. "He *is* your research partner?"

"We've done work together," returned Preston.

"May we come inside?"

"Sure," said Preston as he and Dalton backed up.

The two cops adjusted to the change of light as they came in from the brilliant afternoon. They both looked around at work benches and computers and contraptions of mysterious design to them.

Gesturing toward the rather prominent white and orderly space so distinctly set apart from the rest of lab by its floor-to-ceiling glass walls, Lt. Lau said, "What's that?"

Preston didn't look and didn't want to get into explaining every piece of equipment in the laboratory, "It's a clean room."

"It sure is," said the detective. "What's it for?"

"Experiments. That's what one does in a laboratory," said Preston. "But, I'm sorry; the tour is at noon. You can catch a tram from parking lot B," he said more sarcastically than was his custom, but he'd always had issues with police authority since his college days in the sixties.

"I see," said Lau. He was accustomed to being unwelcome. That was the birthright of being a cop and his agenda was, as Preston surmised, under wraps. How could he conduct an investigation otherwise?

"When was the last time you saw Dr. Umberto?" said the detective.

Preston noticed that the gaunt and awkward second officer was roaming around the lab examining various devices, but Dalton was right there at the man's hip scrutinizing his every move, not saying a word but he was clearly making the detective nervous, a sleuth accustomed to operating on the perimeter and out of focus.

"I don't know," said Preston. "A few days ago, I guess. Why?"

"Well, he's had some trouble," said the lieutenant.

"Is he okay?" asked Preston, concerned that something bad had happened to his friend. Maybe he had been hurt.

"He's alright. But somebody decided to turn his apartment upside down. Do you have any idea what that might have been about?"

Preston was taken aback by this news. He'd been over to Maxwell's town home on Orange Grove on numerous occasions, social and otherwise; both he and Samantha had been there not that long ago for a dinner party. "Oh, my god!" he said. "Max has a ton of valuable art!"

"The artwork is still there," said Lau, matter of fact.

"What did they take?" came back Preston.

"That's what I'd like you to tell me," replied the detective. "What would your colleague have there that somebody would want very badly? Try to imagine something less obvious than the art. What would you say?"

"I… I… don't know," said Preston. He backed up and sat against the edge of a chemistry work bench. He was racing through his memory, trying to recollect the kinds of oddities and interests that Maxwell acquired. Preston was truly trying to be helpful, but he just couldn't come up with anything. The research he and Max had conducted together wasn't in his mind at all.

"Did Dr. Umberto participate in recreational drugs that you know of?"

Crash! That was the moment the lanky second detective inadvertently knocked over a liter beaker, which was empty, but it shattered the thick air in the room when it hit the floor.

The skinny nervous cop looked up, clearly embarrassed, and tossed his hands. He shifted foot to foot not knowing what to do.

"Be careful!" Dalton admonished him, the little guard right there, scowling at the detective, making the boney investigator even more jittery.

Preston waived off the broken beaker, "Forget that. I'll get it later."

"Why don't you wait outside?" said Lau to his colleague who was delighted to get away as he scampered out of the lab to escape the scrutiny of Dalton. Then Lau turned back to his investigation. He didn't repeat the question but stared at the scientist and waited for an answer.

"Drugs, you say?" returned Preston, rolling around in his head what he believed was a preposterous question. "No, detective. Dr. Umberto has a coveted faculty position at CTU and he is in line to become Chair of the Physics Department. No, absolutely not. I've known him a long time. No."

"Do *you* do recreational drugs, Dr. Cook?" said Lau suddenly.

Preston's answer came back firmly and angrily. "No! No, I don't do drugs, either, Lieutenant! Now, if you have any other questions, I'd appreciate it if you'd get them over with. We have work to do here!"

"I'm sorry. I have to ask. It's my job. There's something odd about a break-in where nothing is stolen, wouldn't you say?" said Lt. Lau.

Now it was Preston's turn to toss his hands. "That is more in your line of work than mine."

"I suppose," said the cop. "I suppose it is." And the exchange, such as it was, came to stop.

"Is that all?" said Preston. "Like I said, we've got work to do," he repeated as he gestured over his shoulder to the substantial array of patched-together equipment that surrounded them.

"What kind of work would that be?" queried Lau.

"Cold fusion," said Dr. Cook.

Stanley Lau had no earthly inkling what cold fusion might be, but he elected not to get into it right then. He just nodded and said,

"One other thing… you say you've know Dr. Umberto a long time. How long?"

"Oh, we were friends in graduate school back in Boston. 'A long time', is an understatement."

"Has your wife known him that long, too?"

"My wife?" This question caught Preston off guard and it showed. "She met him after we were all working together at CTU."

"I see. Are they friends? I mean do they see each other separately, from when you are there? She's still teaching over at the school right now, isn't she?"

There was something about this line of questioning that made Preston uneasy. He didn't suspect his wife was doing anything wrong but Preston's instincts picked up on a sleazy undercurrent to the questioning and having his son standing right there probably upped the amperage in his answer. "Yes, she is a tenured faculty member at CTU, as am I, and as is Max. They do see each other sometimes. They are friends, as I have said, and they are also academic colleagues. What is it *exactly* that you are asking me?"

"Oh, nothing really. I just wanted to know, if *you* know, they see each other sometimes, over at the college."

"Yes, I know that!" said Preston.

"I see," said the detective and stuck his hands into his trouser pockets and stared at the floor as though he could shovel up further questions with the toe of his shoe on the cement, but nothing came to him.

"So, if that's it…" said Preston.

"Yes. I think that'll do for now, Dr. Cook. I appreciate you taking the time to answer my questions today. I know it's an inconvenience. If you think of something, in the middle of the night or whenever, that might inform us about the ransacking of Dr. Umberto's residence, give me a call. Okay?" And he handed his card to Preston.

Preston nodded soberly when he took it.

"I'll find my way out," said the detective. The door was only a dozen feet behind him, yet he paused to glance at Dalton and say, "Good day, young man," before being absorbed by the bright sunlight outside.

CHAPTER 27

A Desert Eagle is a fifty caliber, gas operated, semi-automatic pistol made in Israel. In 2005, it was the largest caliber handgun available on the general market and was advertised by its manufacturer as a sporting handgun. But with a ten inch barrel, making it a six-plus pound monster to hoist, a Desert Eagle was far too inaccurate for target competitions. So, as for sports, that leaves only hunting and, in truth, nobody would want to go out sneaking around for deer or lying in wait for quail with a pistol like the Desert Eagle. That cannon was more suited for Rhino. Hunting is a business for rifles and shotguns. Stealthy hunters, who like to creep right up on their prey at a range suitable to the Desert Eagle, favor bows and arrows.

Very much like the Army issue semi-automatic .45 that Big Buster Bernard had tried to hand over to Preston Cook, a Desert Eagle is a weapon that is designed for one single practical purpose and that is to blow the shredded internal organs completely out the opposite side of another human being, and preferably at close range. The ten inch barrel does give a Desert Eagle more accuracy at modest distances than some smaller semi-automatic pistols, and the mammoth magnum cartridges work well because the weapon is re-chambered like an assault rifle, with expelled gasses.

This was a formidable firearm, to be sure, and not for the faint of heart. The mere report can drop a Nelly-kneed, gun-control freak right in his tracks, unless the weapon is silenced. But a silencer adds another four inches to the overall length and several more ounces to the weight; meaning one would be carrying an fourteen inch very heavy pistol, rather like a shortish, large-bore rifle, actually, and it would not be something your typical marksman would want to discharge while holding it straight out at arm's length. A Desert Eagle certainly has its set of drawbacks.

Martin Speck, however, was not your typical marksman and the Desert Eagle was his hands down tool of choice. Maybe his name was Martin Speck and maybe it wasn't, not that it mattered much. Martin Speck was the handle he was carrying with him on that particular trip to Los Angeles. He never used the same name twice. One name, one job; that was his rule. Even his employers didn't have a real name for him, or a reliable fake name that would be available tomorrow. All they had was a cell phone number and an email address, both of which changed randomly and regularly, so nobody knew where he resided or how to contact him on the spur. No name, no residence, no agency, no nationality, nothing.

Over the years Martin had worked for various political groups and he had worked for various nations and he had worked for various private individuals, too, because he was a free-lance contractor and had no lasting loyalties whatsoever. He would surface whenever it was made known he was needed. The whole of it was about the job. Martin Speck didn't believe in anything beyond commerce and his angle in the free market world was his service. He removed obstacles, as he liked to put it. On that day the obstacle involved something he'd never heard of, "cold fusion." It was the obstacle he was contracted to remove and the seven-digit proceeds from the arrangement were to be sitting in his Swiss bank account after he set out to fulfill his obligations. He did enjoy visiting his money in Switzerland, because he had gone to a private school there as a young man and he knew it to be a beautiful country. He tried to spend as much time in Switzerland as he could manage.

Martin Speck didn't know much about nuclear physics, but it didn't really matter. He recalled from early science classes that weight multiplied by velocity equals mass, and a .50 caliber slug traveling at twice the speed of sound has the mass of a cannon ball. That was all the physics he needed for his work.

He was medium build, not light-skinned and not dark-skinned, not tall and not short, not handsome and not plain. Martin Speck spoke six languages fluently, including Chinese, Russian, and Farsi. He had a lyrical but complex accent when he spoke English, an accent that nobody recognized. From his school days a touch of Swiss was laced into his captivating voice like an herb you can't quite name, but it was only one of many other flavors. Women in particular found his words mesmerizing and he would smile when asked by hotel personnel where he was from, and he would often challenge them to figure it out. On occasion he would hand over a twenty dollar bill on the spot to a bartender, a waiter, or a stranger he'd been chatting with, when they would venture a guess after his challenge, but only if it had some remote connection to reality. Martin would lie and tell them they got it. But no one ever guessed correctly. And it was not exclusively by his voice that people were confused, but by his appearance, too. Martin Speck seemed to be a human compendium of races and backgrounds from around the globe and almost any suggestion as to his true make-up might be convincing upon hearing it, but wrong.

Over the years he remained an enigma to numerous professionals who were pretty good at solving mysteries of that sort. And suddenly he was there in Southern California, staying at the Beverly Hills Hotel at fifteen-hundred bucks a night, enjoying room service with a bottle of merlot and *escargot 'en cruet*. Of course, he wasn't paying for any of it. Mr. Martin Speck never paid for his hotels or his expenses and he always stayed at the very best establishments.

He was never listed on the hotel registry, either, that was for sure. Someone out of sight with a very big wallet and an equally big need to have an obstacle removed subsidized Martin Speck wherever he went. Records like a hotel registry can be misleading or erased.

He checked in at the Beverly Hills Hotel on the same Saturday that Detective Lau was questioning Preston Cook and while Detective Lau's assistant was bumfuzzled by little Dalton. On that day, Mr. Speck had taken a suite overlooking the fabled hotel swimming pool and its adjoining Polo Lounge. Between sips of merlot he was carefully unpacking his Louis Vuitton suitcase and religiously removing the teak box that contained his precious Desert Eagle.

Martin Speck knew how to handle plastique and other explosives, such as the ever so exquisite powdered napalm. They all have their place he believed. And he had used some exotic modern poisons in his past and some ancient ones, too, right out of a gothic novel. Knives are crude and dirty, he would say, but they are quiet and he could throw one with precision. He understood his job. Martin could cite every line in the most current edition of the *Lethal Methods Handbook*, but almost all of those strategies involve some kind of paraphernalia and usually a tenuous window of opportunity. Handguns, however, add that oh so sweet spontaneity and power to the recipe, like no other ingredient provides.

Most of the few men and women in his shadowy trade selected lighter, more easily concealed weapons, but Martin Speck didn't operate that way. He was a neat man and he was a scrupulous man in his work and in his preparation, yet he was not delicate when it came to the end game. He didn't hesitate or dance around when he had his chance and he never went on a business trip without his Desert Eagle.

CHAPTER 28

Ahmad Mulham was not staying at a fancy hotel, although it was well within his expansive budget. His father was lenient with his children when they traveled and he didn't want them to suffer poor appearances, which was very important in the Saudi culture but appearances were far less critical to Americanized Ahmad "Skip" Mulham, the "Hoorocane." So, unknown to his father, Ahmad changed plans when he arrived at LAX and cancelled his hotel reservations after the first night. Instead, he made arrangements to crash with a friend from his Miami days, a hefty Jewish guy in med school at UCLA. He lived in a non-descript stucco two story apartment building in Culver City, with car ports around back. George shared his modest apartment with a gigantic nameless goldfish that could eat just about anything and had, in fact, consumed a series of tank mates; so the ferocious goldfish just meandered the tank alone devouring whatever was available, frighteningly like his owner, George the Gorge.

It happens that George was the only person in LA that Ahmad really knew, aside from a couple of pretentious sons of distant family relatives, whom Ahmad never really liked. His Americanized sensibilities saw those boys as giving his country a bad name in the United States, with their gaudy jewelry and pushy behavior. Therefore, Ahmad was loath to look them up. But strangely enough, George the Gorge, so named at Miami for his prodigious ability to consume large volumes of food, was quite okay for Ahmad. George was a true U.S. southern boy from Alabama and he was smart and he was funny and Ahmad was delighted to see him again, especially in the midst of the peculiar mission in which he was involved at that time. Ahmad knew he would be revisiting the physicist at CTU soon enough. But that second night in Los Angeles Ahmad wanted to simply kick back, and kick back he did with George the Gorge and six tall-boy Coors accompanied by an extra-large deep-dish pizza supreme delivered from the local Round Table.

. Ahmad wasn't a true espionage agent of any kind. Consequently, and perhaps unwisely, that evening he entertained George with an overview on his visit to the States, including mention of world-wide interest in a new kind of portable nuclear reactor that had sneaky people crawling around everywhere, behind bushes and in disguise, like he himself had been that afternoon over at Tech-U. Many of these sneaky types were bent on halting the whole process any way they could, according to his father, said Ahmad.

After a half-hour rendering, Ahmad's tale of adventure was reviewed with a combination of intellectual incredulity and school-days' raunch. It inspired a critique from the surgeon-to-be in the way of a seriously extended fart that had Ahmad accusing his host of recklessly defoliating the neighborhood. He called it a "real leaf blower" in University of Miami vernacular.

"I know a few physics guys," summarized George, "and cold fusion is a total crock. Whatever this CTU lunatic thinks he's done, it's *not* cold fusion." George tossed a chunk of pizza crust across the room into the fish tank and the unnamed freakishly large goldfish that had been staring hungrily at Ahmad and George all evening through his glass prison wall did not hesitate, tearing into the pizza crust like a piranha.

George the Gorge was a bright guy, articulate and well educated for all his adolescent affectations. What he had to say about table-top nuclear reactors would be a pretty common opinion in the minds of many educated folks at that time. The failed Fields-Parker experiment at the University of Nevada had been newsworthy and it was heavily publicized. George's debunking commentary actually succeeded in bringing Ahmad down to earth for the remainder of the evening, which felt good to the Saudi man as he moved away from the espionage adventure he had been sharing. He was happy to let go of high intrigue, danger, and spies. That whole nefarious business was really not what a mild mannered affable guy like Ahmad was cut out for, in spite of his performance earlier that very afternoon with Dr. Umberto. He really only wanted to help his father and be a good son.

After the brief exchange about cold fusion and because they were three-quarters looped anyway, the two friends slid toward a more musical mood. They were both early alternative rock fans from the eighties, their college years, so they threw a couple of CDs into the changer and cranked up *Nine Inch Nails* all the way to the ceiling. However, their revelry lasted less than fifteen minutes before a sixty-year old perturbed neighbor lady showed up in a pink velour sweat suit and she managed to wither their entire evening with a threat of calling the cops.

That was enough for Ahmad, who pictured himself hand-cuffed and phoning his father from a west side police station with the entire cold fusion plan in ruins. That was a scene he needed less than strangling to death on a wad of pepperoni soaked in beer, about the most hellish death a decent Muslim boy could imagine. And there was George the Gorge, a Jew, who had grown up in a modest Jewish community in Birmingham. During their school days in Miami, George had Ahmad as a guest to his Alabama home during Thanksgiving weekend and it had been clearly noted for Ahmad that there would be no pork under that roof on the holiday. But by 2005 when they were together again, pork clearly did not worry George the Gorge or Ahmad. When they were out on their own, they were both more keenly interested in enjoying epicurean delights than observing religious traditions.

Ahmad's and George's muted reverie continued until after two in the morning before they both gave up, Ahmad settling onto George's beyond-repair, three-cushioned vinyl couch. It delivered a night's slumber which Ahmad reported in the morning as being spare. Sleeping on that implement of torture was less satisfying than sleeping on a sack of doorknobs, he had said. After George had said, "Nightie-night," the prior evening and turned off the lights, a clean and spacious bed at the Sheraton was looking rather desirable to Ahmad. Maybe his college days were finally over.

CHAPTER 29

At home, Professor Samantha Day-Steiner was at her desk in the office that had been created for her out of a former bedroom, where French windows stretched across two walls. The October Bougainville was brilliantly purple, spreading densely outside on a fence that separated their home from neighbors' property. She was reviewing student papers and finding them to be distressingly poor when Preston came quietly to the door behind her. Samantha was thoroughly consumed by her dissatisfaction as Preston walked up and touched her on the shoulder.

She jumped!

"Oh, Jesus!" she said. "My god, Pres, don't sneak up on me like that!"

"I'm sorry," he said meekly. "Can we talk?"

"I… I've really got a lot of work to do here. These theorems are so *sloppy*! What do you want?" she said impatiently, which was not a rare affect for Samantha in recent time.

Preston loved his wife. He knew he had given her short shrift during these last crucial years as he struggled to finish his research. He also understood she had sacrificed a great deal to an obsession that was not her own. Whether she was actually in the lab with him or not, she had paid a very high price. Preston had passed on promotions and other opportunities at the university. He had wasted multiple other research offerings at one of the premier engineering and science academies in the entire world, so he could continue with his ego-driven cold fusion vision. Nobody knew if it would play out favorably. It was always a long shot. Preston didn't even know himself if it would really work for sure. What he did know for sure was that Samantha had been frustrated and angry about all of it for quite a while. He knew that success in his work did not provide a magical antidote to his selfishness. To sacrifice one's self for a personal vision is understandable, but to expect others to sacrifice themselves for your vision is absurd. He understood that.

Practicality is a massive force in marriages. During the years of cold fusion research Preston hadn't let practicality into the picture at all. The strange and unexpected inference Detective Lau had made about Samantha's faithfulness clung to the inside of Preston's skull. Was it a mean-spirited bit of grist thrown by the detective into the mill of Preston's ruminations about the state of his marriage? Preston wanted Sam to see he cared and that he truly, deeply appreciated everything she had gone through. That's why he'd come up behind her on that day while she worked on students' papers.

"Well, Preston?" she said staring at him as she waited on some explanation for his sudden appearance.

He smiled sheepishly, almost like a schoolboy, and he slowly produced a couple of airline ticket envelopes from his hip pocket.

"Let's get out of here," he said to his wife. "How does Hawaii sound? Five days!" And he grinned.

Samantha didn't know what to say, but she could clearly see this was a genuine gesture on her husband's part. She thought it was ill-timed, but it was genuine, so she moved cautiously. She was far more political, far more careful than Preston had ever been at CTU, and she knew how to avoid ruffled feathers in a sensitive environment, how to slip between the mines in a field, when it wasn't the Cook household minefield.

Dr. Day-Steiner had always been a bit more shoot-from-the-hip and abrupt with her husband at home which is one of those things that comes with matrimony. Yet, in that moment, when he approached her, Sam tried to be as careful and deferential as she might have been at work. She could see immediately it wasn't a time for recklessness.

"Oh… my god, Preston! That sounds wonderful! Why… what made you do this? Right now?"

"You know… I've been kind of distant lately. For a long time, really. Not like a husband should be. I've let my work take over… and I'm sorry, Sam. I mean, I'm glad it all turned out the way it did, of course!" He chuckled. "But you have had to put up with a lot from me. Not just recently… but for a long, long time. I guess I want to say I know that, and I'm sorry. But mostly, what I want to say to you is," he looked at the blue and white airplane ticket envelopes in his hand, "I love you, Sam. I haven't stopped loving you since the day we met."

Dr. Day-Steiner was speechless at hearing this. And for that moment, the love she had for him way back in graduate school came flooding into the room and her eyes welled.

Samantha came to her feet and went to her husband. She was winging it now and she didn't want to slap that man across his face. He did not deserve it; so she hugged him tightly. "Preston, Preston, Preston," she said softly in his ear. "You are such a dear man. So sweet. I know where Dalton gets it from. It's you, not me."

She pulled back and looked at her husband directly into his eyes. "Thank you, Preston," she said. "We absolutely should do this… but I think, with the earth-shattering announcement that you and Max are going to be making soon, maybe now isn't the best time. My god, you and Max have changed the world! Hawaii will be there next month. We'll go then! Okay?"

Preston looked down at the tickets in his hands. He was hurt that she hadn't said she loves him back, the customary response in a couple. But maybe that was too much to expect, given how they had been with each other lately, all business and confrontations, plus that unfortunate exchange in front of their son not that long ago.

She embraced him again and hugged him as tightly as she could, and the reassuring hug was true and heartfelt. They had been together a lifetime, it seemed, and they had sailed through many dark nights and rough seas together. Finding Down syndrome in Dalton was only part of it over twenty-plus years. "Yes, yes, my darling. We *will* go to Hawaii as soon as possible, okay? Right away! When it's right!" she said.

Preston saw what Samantha meant about the timing, vis-à-vis the cold fusion results, even though making an announcement wasn't in the cards as he saw it. But he didn't want to get into that conversation right then, not again, not at that moment.

"Okay," he said quietly to Samantha before retreating. "We'll wait."

Preston was a brilliant physicist. He was obsessed with analyzing minutia. Sub-atomic particles were part of his everyday intellectual life. But he was also a child in so many other ways, and choosing to whisk Samantha away to Hawaii on impulse with everything that was swirling around them at that time, as sweet and disarming as his gesture might have been, was an example of how totally naive he could be.

After hearing from his wife that an announcement about cold fusion would soon be coming via CTU, Preston was suddenly eager to visit his old comrade, Maxwell Umberto. What the heck

was Max doing making plans about announcing the research findings? Preston actually bristled at the thought. Maybe his reaction was juiced by what the Pasadena plainclothes cop, Lau, had
implied about Max and Sam and maybe it wasn't, but the thought
had lingered.

CHAPTER 30

Life events had escalated in Maxwell Umberto's new topsy-turvy world. The day that Preston was attempting to lure his wife off on a romantic excursion to the Hawaiian Islands, Max was standing at the door to his CTU office, positively dumb-founded. He had just opened the door and in a bone-chilling *déjà vu* he found that his office had been given the once-over by someone who manhandled it in exactly the same manner as his apartment. Things were not broken, so much as gone-through. Files were open, artifacts were off the walls, and his desk had been plundered. Books were off the shelves. To some degree, this was more startling to Max than his home break-in, because Tech-U has a security force. There are campus foot-patrols throughout the night. Maxwell had seen them with their flashlights and batons, as well as in their cars cruising by on California Street, at all odd hours as he finished up professional and sometimes recreational interludes in his office. This ransacking happened right under their noses!

Max went right for the phone and called the campus police. He didn't have to dial up his new Pasadena City Police acquaintance, Detective Stanley Lau, because the campus security officers were required to contact the PPD on a break-in, even though the campus cops did not know Max and the local constabulary were already familiar. In fact, Lieutenant Lau appeared at Preston's office door only a handful of minutes after the campus security team arrived. None of the campus cops had touched anything before Lau slid into view. They had been trained to wait on the "real" authorities in such matters. The campus cops only attempted to calm Dr. Umberto and reassure him that the culprits would be swiftly apprehended, which was a fanciful notion at best, but it was part of their script.

Umberto was not so easily placated, as it turned out. He was pretty much at his wits' end after what had happened to his town house. And when Lau arrived the scientist was livid and grilling the two campus cops on the scene, who stood there with their hands by their sides, nodding.

"Where were you guys last night when this was going on? I thought we had a security force here on campus, not the Keystone Cops! This had to be noisy! Look around!"

The two uniformed campus security men just listened. They'd had training. They didn't like taking abuse and it probably didn't make for the best strategy if one wanted prompt service out of these two guards in the future, but the security officers acted like professionals and they let Max ramble on, tossing his hands in the air and gesturing toward the mess that surrounded them.

"We're sorry, sir, but the campus is large and we can't be everywhere at once," said the more seasoned of the two. He had corporal's chevrons on his sleeve to account for the gray in his hair. He'd actually been on the security force at Tech-U for twenty-eight years, was coming up on retirement and certainly wasn't going to offend any distinguished faculty members at that point. By chance, he'd also been with Detective Lau when they handcuffed the quantum mechanics professor in his classroom, who'd been running around a local park in the buff a few years ago.

"Hmp-hmp," came a throat-clearing sound from the office doorway and Max pivoted to find Lau standing there. The boney assistant detective was in tow like a kite behind Lau, taller than Lau, and drifting back and forth in the hallway looking over his boss's shoulder into the scene of the crime, but he would not move forward until given a nod.

"Patrolling isn't as easy as it might seem," said the Detective to Max, in defense of the campus cops. "Do you mind if we come in?"

Maxwell Umberto was shocked that the Pasadena Police were here and were here so quickly. "Uh… sure," he said, meaning they could enter.

"Hi, Corporal," said Lau to the campus officer, recognizing him from that episode with the streaking professor. "How are you?"

They shook hands. "Oh, not too bad," said the Corporal. "Seems we had a bit of break-in."

"What are you doing here?" demanded Max.

"Whenever we have a possible felony, Dr. Umberto," said the soon-to-be-retired Corporal, "we always call the city police."

"Hello, again," said the Detective shaking hands with stunned Maxwell Umberto and then Detective Lau vigorously scratched his scalp and patted down the sparse black hair scattered across his cranium. "So… what happened?" he asked of no one in particular. He also gestured to the skinny assistant who immediately flew to work like a giant insect passing up the men gathered inside the office.

"Door's okay," said the Corporal, pointing to the open office door. The physics building was old and the door was solid oak. "Professional," he added.

Lau nodded. No crowbar entry here.

"Let's try this again," said the Detective to Umberto. "We've got to stop meeting like this," he said and he chuckled. It was about the only regular joke he used, but he found ample opportunity for it over the years in his profession. "Do you know what's missing this time?"

Maxwell was frustrated. He didn't have a clue about these break-ins and he was starting to get angry, too. "I don't know that anything is missing yet, Detective. I haven't really had a chance to look around… but… but at a glance…" he turned and surveyed the disheveled scene. "Look at those files!" he exclaimed. "If something was missing from there… I wouldn't know it for weeks!"

"So, what would be in there?" asked Lau.

"Classroom materials. Articles. Presentations. Grant contracts. A lot of pretty boring paperwork."

This investigation was really beginning to get Lau's attention. He was a regular cop and events in his business were fairly routine, at least they were in Pasadena. You can change the faces and the neighborhoods, but people in Pasadena managed to screw up in remarkably similar fashions, give or take. A hardened cop's sense of highbrow vs. lowbrow got a make-over in garden-happy Pasadena. Everybody came out looking like they belonged to one large predictable family. Originally, the break-in at Maxwell's Orange Grove town house was casually chalked up by Lau to be some kind of academic drug deal gone south, or a more conventional white-collar crime like embezzlement. Maybe it was a Ponzi scheme. Who knows? But on that day, in the professor's turned-over office, the situation started to look unique. The detective's antennae were twitching and telling him that something larger was underway, something really outside the norm.

"Is there *anything* at all… anything that is new and different that you've been working on, Dr. Umberto, that somebody might have an interest in getting? Is somebody jealous of anything you've accomplished? People are people." said Lau just taking a wild stab.

A light went on inside Maxwell's head and it showed on his face. There was clear recognition and there was incredulity, too; but for the first time he began to think that the cold fusion research – which was monumental – might play into what had happened. Why hadn't he thought of it before? Probably it was because he didn't believe anybody of with an axe to grind knew about it. But this realization did not make him feel any better. He began to connect dots in his head rather quickly and if the magnitude of the research findings had anything to do with the magnitude of the interloper's motive, then there was good reason to be really afraid. Life threatening fear was palpable and appropriate and his face went paper white.

"What are you thinking?" inquired Lau.

Even the two security officers could see that some switch had been tripped in the professor's brain and they leaned toward the conversation to hear his answer.

In the background, the gangly, goggle-eyed, insect-like detective continued to buzz around in the office debris, making notes, while his antennae ears followed every detail of the conversation near the door.

"Nothing," said Max weakly to Detective Lau, while he looked at the floor. "There's nothing." Umberto's mind and imagination were racing through scenarios. Max reminded himself that he and his long-time friend and research partner Preston Cook were going to make an announcement about the discovery in a couple of days, so leaking everything to this detective right now wouldn't be good. If he did say something, the whole story would be headlined in newspapers tomorrow. It's best to just keep everything quiet, he concluded, racing through possibilities like his life depended on it. He did not have much of a recollection about his own indiscretions regarding the research and his loose-tongued revelations about it. These burglars, he was thinking, who are they? What do they want? Where do they come from? How do they know?

"Dr. Umberto," said Lt. Lau in his most official voice, actually startling Max out of where he had gone in his mind. "If you have anything to share with us about what might have happened here, or at your home, I think it would be in your own best interest to share it with us right now." He waited a beat before his punch line, "We can take you to the police station, if that's what you would prefer."

Maxwell was a deer in the headlights, if ever there was one. "Do what you need to do, but let me call my lawyer," he said, straight out of television.

But Lau was just playing cards with Max. He was beginning to see that the professor was actually a victim, just as he had claimed from the start, and now Max was a visibly shaken and frightened victim. It was also becoming clearer to Lau there were some *bona fide* bad guys out there that were after this scientist. But for what?

"Okay, professor. You let me know if you think of anything," said the detective, signaling his strange assistant with a hand gesture, as though the assistant was a blood hound. And with that, both Pasadena police officers turned and slipped away into the hallway, leaving Maxwell devastated and afraid, with the security guards staring at him,

"Please leave!" Dr. Umberto demanded uncharacteristically after a beat. And the campus cops left.

CHAPTER 31

While George the Gorge was out scavenging for their breakfast, Ahmad Mulham was reclining on George's lumpy couch, where he had ended up spending yet a second night because he could not bring himself to insult the hospitality of his friend, who wanted Ahmad to save the expense of a hotel. It was all very endearing in each direction. George didn't really have a grasp of the financial resources available to his Muslim friend from the University of Miami, and Ahmad had his own cultural baggage that prevented him from rejecting the offer of a roof for the night.

A Blackberry was shoved up against Ahmad's cheek while he waited for the international radio-wave satellite phone system to patch him through to his father on the other side of the globe. It was early morning in Los Angeles, so it would have been early evening in Saudi Arabia at the time, but his dad always worked late and Ahmad figured his father was very likely still at his desk wrestling with complex OPEC concerns. And as it turned out, Ahmad's father was only wrestling with a more mundane demand from Ahmad's mother, who needed several items picked up at the market, a woman who was as liberated as her husband and, in spite of her head scarf, was as vocal, fashion conscious, and flamboyant as any western counterpart. Not many Saudi wives would call their husbands at work and ask them to pick up something on the way home, like they were in an episode of *Leave it to Beaver*. So, when Ahmad connected with his father, he could hear the frustration in his dad's voice, perhaps only a nuance, but his son could detect the subtlest inflection in the voice of either parent, as children everywhere can.

"Hi, father, what is wrong?" Ahmad yelled into his phone like he'd just cranked up long distance in 1936. There was something about overseas calls that made people shout, even in Farsi.

"Oh?" he said listening to his father explain, but that was not new. Ahmad had watched the back-and-forth between his parents since he was a pup. "Just pick it up, father. It is an easy thing to do. Everybody already knows she is the boss," he said switching to English, which his father spoke well. But such jokes were absolute anathema to Saudi men. Ahmad had to immediately pull the phone away from his ear as his father launched into an emotional rant disclaiming any truth to what his son had just implied about his mother being in charge!

"Sorry, father, I was just kidding," said Ahmad, back to Farsi, which was the language he would use for the balance of the phone conversation while he listened to his father lament, after calming down, how it might have been a terrible mistake to send his son to American schools. In America Ahmad had learned to disrespect his elders and that was not the lesson his father had intended or financed for him.

For generations, money was never far from any conversation in the Mulham household and it probably explains why they possessed so much of it. They were savvy and practical in matters of business and they always had been. This teasing exchange between father and son was actually an oft rehearsed affair; it was ground the two of them had covered on well-worn tracks. Both of them understood the hidden and important themes in these kinds of interactions, too, themes that involved a blend of honor for traditions along with "the times they are a'changin.'" The two of them understood deeply that their family, the Mulham family, and all of their western-minded comrades in that part of the world, comprised the only viable future for their people and their way of life. It wasn't the U.S. invasion of neighboring Iraq and their military presence in the Middle-East in those days that had the Mulhams of the Mid-East thinking that way. Their views were embraced in spite of American missteps.

Most often what they believed was because Western reason had won the day and the magnetic compelling lure of freedom of thought had infected them, as a small presage to uprisings and revolutions that lay ahead for several Arab nations less than a decade hence during the "Arab Spring". The insipient revolution was not a bellwether they took lightly and the family's influence in the oil producing world made their position all the more critical, particularly because they and a few others in that region understood profoundly that the their reliance on fossil fuels had to come to an end eventually.

"My medical school friend at UCLA tells me cold fusion cannot have happened, but I am not so sure," said Ahmad moving to a more business-like demeanor when the preliminaries and family dys-functions were past. "I have not seen anything, myself, one way or another, but I have met with Dr. Umberto and he said he would help me," related Ahmad. "So, I am going to set up an appointment with him as soon as I am able. Like I told you, father, I think he is going to make an announcement very soon, so time is not our friend. If that happens, who knows what villains will appear."

He listened to his father ask if he had seen curious people hanging around and the question carried a foreboding quality that reminded Ahmad of the handgun question he'd posed when he was packing for his trip. It was the same quality that had him referencing "villains" a moment earlier. "Do you have someone in mind?" asked Ahmad and he waited while his father tried to defuse concern while re-enforcing caution.

"Oh," hedged his father, "anyone who might have provocation in mind."

"No, I haven't encountered suspicious or... *dangerous* people, if that is your meaning."

His father quickly replied, "Good. Dangerous people are like heart attacks... by the time you sense them, it is often too late. So, be careful, my Ahmad. I fear that maybe I should not have asked you to do this."

Ahmad could hear his father's worry. "I'll be fine, father," said Ahmad and just as he was saying those words the door to the apartment opened suddenly and in came George the Gorge with a sack of Egg McMuffins and a box of Krispy Kream doughnuts.

"Salt, sugar, and lard! The basic food groups!" George yelled heading for the kitchen and not giving a rat's ass that Ahmad was on the phone.

"What is that?" said Ahmad's father.

"Oh, just room service with breakfast," said Ahmad.

"They are loud at that hotel," said his father.

Ahmad smiled, "Yes. Yes, they are. Tell mother I miss her," he said.

"No pork!" yelled his father to his Americanized son.

"Okay, father. I'll call you tomorrow with an update, alright?"

"No pork!" said his father again.

"Good-bye, father," said Ahmad and he hung up.

CHAPTER 32

As he came down the hallway on the second floor of the CTU physics building, toward Maxwell's office, Preston noticed the door was standing open, sunlight falling on the hall carpet from those windows in Maxwell's office that overlooked the athletic fields. With bright light illuminating the hall carpet Preston could not help but notice how worn it was. And that's what he was thinking as he turned into Maxwell's office doorway and halted dead in his tracks.

"Christ, Max!" he exclaimed looking around at the mess.

Maxwell was sitting on the floor, back to the door, sorting through files that had been strewn about and he looked over his shoulder at Preston. Maxwell Umberto appeared as disheveled as the room. He hadn't even combed his hair and he was a man who prided himself on how he looked, but there Max sat, pathetic as an orphan, distress carved into his usually bright countenance. "I'm redecorating," he said with a weak stab at glib.

"Interior design meets chaos theory," said Preston stepping carefully forward.

"If only you'd dropped by about an hour ago, you'd have heard a sparkling review from the Pasadena Police," said Umberto.

"Funny you should mention that," said Preston as he pulled around a wooden chair from the small conference table. "Mind if I sit up here?" he added, gesturing to the chair as an alternative to the floor. "I had a visit from the constable, myself," continued Preston, sitting down.

This news had Maxwell's attention immediately and he let the papers in his hands fall to his knees as he turned his red puffy eyes directly toward Preston.

"A detective came by the lab," continued Preston glancing around at the upheaval.

"Let me guess: Detective Stanley Lau," said Max.

"Umm," said Preston agreeing, "and he had a rather odd bird with him," added Preston about the boney assistant. "Detective Lau told me this ransacking happened at your home. I guess he meant your office."

Maxwell shook his head and looked even more miserable, if that was possible. "It's all true. My home, too," said Max. Then he struggled to his feet and took a chair, while Preston recorded how very exhausted the poor bastard looked. "What in heaven's name did that cop want with *you*?" Max asked after they were sitting eye to eye.

"Seemed to think I might know something about what happened," said Preston. "Now there's *this*!" Preston tossed a hand toward the upending of the office, which had been scrupulously tidy one day earlier. Preston knew Max liked to maintain order in his surroundings. In fact, the prevailing disorder in Preston's homemade garage laboratory surely had hastened Maxwell's exit from the project.

"What the hell is going on?" asked Preston, totally flummoxed.

Dr. Umberto suddenly became very serious with his friend. He visibly darkened and leaned forward with his elbows on his knees and he spoke very softly toward Preston. Up close, his tousled blonde hair above his intense blue eyes, made him look a bit on the mad side.

"I think it has something to do with our research, Preston," he whispered.

"What?" replied Preston.

"Yeah. Me, too. I didn't go there at first. The detective was asking me about drugs and crap."

"Why?" said Preston, quite taken aback by this change in direction.

"I didn't really know... until *this* happened!" said Maxwell throwing out his hands at his upside-down surroundings. "First, it was my house... and now *here*. And nothing seems to be missing. My art may not be Norton-Simon worthy, but it ain't Kincade," said Max about his pricey collection. "What they wanted wasn't *there*... and it isn't *here*. Clearly, it's not cash. And... and..." Max actually got quieter and leaned toward Preston, "remember, I gave you all the notes, charts, photos, drawings, even my hard drives from our experiments? All of it." His pale blue eyes glinted. "I think *that's* what they are after, Preston. They want the invention!"

Preston collapsed where he was sitting and slouched there, more confused than comprehending. "No," he said quietly. "That doesn't make sense. Who could know about the research?" he added reflecting his honest bewilderment.

"I don't have a fucking clue," said Max. "I've been trying to recall who I mentioned it to and it's not that many people. I thanked President Holcomb for letting us use the facilities, but I didn't get into details. I was thinking our announcement would make a bigger splash here at the University, don't you?" asked Max in an incongruous moment of enthusiasm looking into Preston's eyes. He had not, until *that* moment, shared his announcement plans. "Other than Holcomb... I don't know, really."

Preston just stared at his friend and colleague. He did not like what he was hearing about these disclosures or plans to make an announcement, but confrontation was not Preston's long suit, and that day in Maxwell's ransacked office did not seem to be the optimum moment. All he could say was, "You *told* people?"

"No, no, not really. Only a couple," said Max.

In truth, Dr. Umberto had practically advertised the accomplishment. It wasn't like him to keep his trap shut if he could shine a spotlight on himself and impress someone, but in his mind he could not imagine he had told anybody who would constitute a true "leak", anybody who might be competition. "*But…*," he said suddenly remembering the Saudi student who had stopped by. Maxwell couldn't recall the Saudi's name at that moment but he went on, "… there was this one very odd thing that happened," he said and he leaned forward on his knees and again, he began to speak softly, a gesture that made Preston really nervous because it made him feel like there was actual danger in these goings-on. "A young man came by to see me, here in my office. No appointment. He just showed up. He's a graduate student and he is thinking about coming to Tech-U. Already been accepted. He wanted to know about my cold fusion research!"

Preston's eyes got wide. "Whose research?"

Max shrugged and bypassed the question. "His daddy is a big wig in Middle-Eastern oil and somehow got wind of it. Right now… it's really creeping me out." Not being the most self-aware man and fairly blind to just how much he'd tipped his hand that day with Ahmad Mulham, Maxwell added for Preston's reassurance, "But I didn't tell him we'd done it. So, don't worry about that."

Preston was almost afraid to ask, so he timidly inquired, "Do you think I might be next in line for a ransacking?"

His former research partner just stared at him for a beat, contemplating that likelihood. Preston would have far preferred a quick dismissal of his concern.

"I haven't mentioned you to anyone," said Max finally as naively as a child. "So, unless they know us from before, then I'd say, no. They think it's me that's done this. You're safe."

Preston did not comment right then. He couldn't bring himself to say anything, because his friend Max had clearly undergone a psychological beating already with what had happened to him *twice*! Just looking at him would tell you that. This was not the usual Maxwell Umberto, *bon vivant*. Yet, here he was taking credit for work he didn't really do and as much as admitting to it. But in that moment there were other irons in the fire for two scientists who seemed to be the targets of god-knows-whom because of research they had conducted. Consequently, at that moment Preston didn't want to call Max out on his usurpation of the work; but it was conversation that was going to have to happen, sooner or later.

"Let's back off on any plans to announce anything," said Preston, using the situation to get where he wanted to go on that matter at the least. "We've clearly drawn too much attention to ourselves."

Max dropped his face into his hands. He was so looking forward to the news release and press conference. He could already feel the heat of the flash bulbs popping away; but he could also see Preston was right. Low profile had to be the order of the day and he looked up. "Okay," he said. "I'll get in touch with Dr. Holcomb and request a stay on the announcement. It'll be fine."

"Don't say 'stay', for chrissakes. Sounds like an execution," said Preston.

CHAPTER 33

Martin Speck was sporting a Tommy Bahama silk Hawaiian shirt and cream linen trousers. The blousy shirt sufficiently concealed his baby, the Desert Eagle, on a horizontal holster along the back of his belt, easily hauled out for business if need be, but it was not too obvious to the casual observer as he walked along the open corridor Westside apartments where George the Gorge had been harboring Ahmad Mulham for the last three days. Speck had international information about who was doing what around this cold fusion matter, as did Special Group agent Bobby Skylar. In fact, rumors were flowing pretty freely by then, all around the globe for interested parties, some with a more aggressive agenda than others, and all of the attention was focused on Los Angeles as though there was an upcoming Cold Fusion Convention. The success of cold fusion research was, after all, monstrous news for many international players and monstrous money was in the balance, too. Greed is an equal opportunity employer.

Speck knew where he was going and he went straight to George's door. There was no hesitation and he authoritatively knocked on that door like he was the landlord. There was no answer, so he knocked again, only louder. You can't be furtive in those situations. It only brings suspicion, so you have to act like you belong there. The next time Martin Speck actually pounded on the door, but still there was no sound from within. And as swiftly as if he had a key to the apartment, he pulled out a little tool from his pocket, stuck it in the keyhole and opened the door. He didn't look left or right to see if anybody was watching him. Why give a witness a full face view?

The apartment was empty. Martin did shout a couple of "Hellos," just to make sure. Then he went around and checked out the space, finding Ahmad's luggage neatly arranged in the living room near the lumpy couch that had managed to provide for Ahmad a very tender lower back. As a result, Ahmad had already decided he had to get out of his friend's apartment, grateful for the hospitality, but he realized another night on that couch might render him immobile.

So, while Martin Speck was digging around in Ahmad's belongings in George's living room, Ahmad Mulham was checking into the Hilton Hotel in Pasadena, on the other side of LA County, where he would be much closer to his target, Dr. Umberto at Tech-U, and it would also provide significantly more comfort. He could collect his luggage later from George.

Martin flipped through Ahmad's suitcase quickly and then sat down on the lumpy couch, grimacing when he did so, and touching with his fingertips the bumps on the cushions. His face registered disapproval, but he did not have to endure the couch for long, because George came home right then. Martin didn't know who was rattling keys at the door and he didn't really care; he just sat there waiting.

George burst into the apartment from the afternoon daylight with one arm full of groceries, because he always stopped at the store on his way home. He frequently forgot something and Ralph's supermarket was always *en route*. What was not typical that day was to find a stranger sitting on the couch in his living room. George let out a scream when he saw Martin Speck relaxing there with his legs crossed.

"Ahhhhh!" yelled George as he fumbled awkwardly with the paper grocery bag, which got the best of him and fell to the floor tumbling bananas, Oreos, Doritos, and a large plastic jar of Prego spaghetti sauce across the floor near the entrance to his apartment. He dropped back against his own door, wild-eyed. "Who are you?" he said.

Martin Speck stood up from the couch and smoothed his clothing. He stepped coolly forward with his hands crossed non-threateningly in front. "It's okay," he said. "Come on inside," he gestured calmly, like it was his apartment and not George's.

George the Gorge was terrified. He moved very cautiously into the living room. "What to do you want?" His voice was cracking as he spoke.

Cutting straight to the chase, Speck said, "Has your friend here, Mr. Mulham, said anything to you about cold fusion"?

George's eyes were as big as hard boiled eggs. He stammered. How did this guy know anything about Ahmad *or* cold fusion? "I don't really have any money, but you can take everything I've got," said George, and he pulled his wallet out from his hip pocket and held it out for the intruder.

Martin Speck waived off the wallet and asked, "What about Ahmad Mulham and cold fusion?" he repeated. He wasn't one to waste time.

George was at a loss. He wanted to provide whatever this son-of-a-bitch wanted, but he didn't know what that was. "Cold fusion? Uh... uh... Ahmad said that some scientist he knows had done that... but I told him it's not possible," said George.

"Did he have any documents, or anything?"

"Documents?" said George. "Uh... no... no documents that I know about. I've got nothing for you, sir," he said.

"Who was the scientist?" asked Martin Speck.

"I... I dunno," said George truthfully. "He's at CTU."

Martin nodded. Seeing there was nowhere for this interview to go, he reached to his back and pulled out the Desert Eagle and he aimed it directly at George's forehead.

For a split second George thought the nickel-plated weapon was some kind of electrical device, a Taser or something. Then he saw the gun's muzzle.

"I…." was about all George was able to say before Martin killed him. George never heard the silenced report or even noted the smoke that rose up as the fifty caliber slug hit him squarely in the forehead right above the bridge of his nose. It made a neat puncture about the size of a dime, but the exit wound on the back of George's head was larger than a softball, assorted bits of his cranium and flesh hit the wall behind George in a spectacularly uniform pattern. George crumpled to his floor with a thud louder than the muted gunshot.

Martin stood there for a moment looking at the splattering of blood and other solid matter across the wall. It was quite remarkable, evenly spread from left to right as if an artist had purposely cast various hues of crimson paint and bits of unidentifiable material in an abstract statement on a wide canvas. There was not much dripping. The pattern made a dense and glistening, very bright red, three-foot diameter circle on the wall, surrounding an inch sized hole where the bullet had gone through. The entire installation was almost as balanced as if it had been measured.

"Well, well," Martin Speck said out loud as he returned his Desert Eagle to its clip holster behind his back. "I've never seen that before," he added. And then he causally left the apartment while George's remarkably large goldfish rose to the surface of the water in its tank directly below the red circle on the wall and it began to tear at pieces of George's gray matter floating there.

CHAPTER 34

Fitzgerald Jack, with the Los Angeles Police Department, was about as different from Detective Lau as two police investigators could be. Detective Jack was tall, handsome, and looked more like a matinee idol than the real-life detective he actually was. And he was successful, too, having solved a number of high-profile homicides in Los Angeles, building quite a reputation for an officer in his forties. He certainly came by his chops honestly enough, through his now-retired mom, Sally Jack, who was herself a force to be reckoned with as a detective back in the day, when female detectives on police forces were few and far between. Furthermore, his father was a working English professor at UCLA, so "Fitzy", as his parents and best friends called him, had the right gene pool delivering to his constitution the determination and sharp intelligence that made him the right man in the right job. He was no fluke. And in the fall of 2005 as events were to unfold on the murder of George the Gorge he would wind up working closely with the Pasadena Police Department, and in so doing he would also work closely with Lieutenant Stanley Lau. But on the day George was murdered on LA's west side, neither of the two detectives saw their relationship on the horizon. Their investigations were miles and jurisdictions apart.

The killing of this UCLA medical student was as odd and inexplicable as any homicide Detective Jack had seen in his career. It had all the earmarks of a professional execution and none of the reasons. Why whack an overweight Jewish kid from Birmingham, Alabama?

Mistaken identify? Sadly enough, cops kill the wrong people more often than professional assassins. Nothing around the place appeared to have been touched, so it wasn't robbery. It bore an uncanny resemblance to the ransacking of Maxwell Umberto's residence and office, but on that day Detective Jack knew absolutely zero about what happened in Pasadena.

LAPD's first responders got there only minutes after the killing when a rubbernecking middle-aged neighbor lady in a pink velour sweat suit dialed 911. She'd heard the silenced gunshot and she'd heard George's body fall. She said there was an A-rab staying in that apartment. She'd seen him with her own eyes when they were all juiced up and playing loud rock and roll music in the middle of night. She said she knew something bad was going to happen. Those two were up to no good, she'd concluded. The pink sweat suit lady said she had not seen anyone else leave or arrive.

It happened that the pink sweat suit lady was on the phone to the cops when Martin Speck breezily walked out of the complex and strolled around the Culver City street corner to his rented white, BMW 745i. As Fitzgerald Jack and his colleagues poked around the apartment for clues, the pink sweat suit lady loitered outside the door wringing her hands and trying to get a peek at the crime scene which was mostly hidden behind a stern uniformed officer in the doorway.

"They were up to no good!" shouted the lady into the apartment just to emphasize the point she'd made earlier, prompting the police officer in the doorway to politely ask her to go back to her own apartment. Detective Jack had already interviewed the lady and he had thanked her for making the call and he also had already concluded that she wasn't going to be of much help outside the very limited possibility she would be able to pick Ahmad Mulham out of a line-up of A-rabs. Of more interest to Fitzgerald at the moment was the neat suitcase on the floor to the side of the living room. There was a rumpled blanket and pillow, so apparently someone had been sleeping on the sofa, which Detective Jack tested with his fingers and winced. The suitcase still had its airport baggage tags showing that it had come to LA from Saudi Arabia, so figuring out this guy's identity was not going to be a problem. All of his clothes were designer Italian, and they were meticulously folded, none of which was consistent with the meager lifestyle of the corpulent corpse sprawled in front of a living room fish tank, where a really big goldfish hovered, its fins moving rhythmically, watching the police activities. Fitzy looked at the fish for a beat. My god, that's one huge goldfish, he said to himself. Was it eyeing him back?

Then Fitzgerald Jack's gaze climbed the wall behind the fish tank, a wall splattered liberally in a symmetrical circle of blood and tissue. It was a feature of the detective's life that was never pleasant, yet that particular blood splattered wall was unusual. In noting the prominent near-perfect circle of red surrounding the bullet hole and the bizarre uniformity of the display, Fitzy shared a cosmic moment with the killer. Whoa, he thought. That's different.

CHAPTER 35

In Maxwell Umberto's scrambled and increasingly confused mind, it was not a day for unexpected visitors. There had been enough surprises and upheaval. Why did his CTU office suddenly become Grand Central Station? He had no clue. But it was not fifteen minutes after Preston had departed that Preston's lovely and brilliant wife, Samantha Day-Steiner appeared at Maxwell's office door, breathy with concern. Max was gradually beginning to realize that along with intelligence and sophistication, this woman could also be demanding, probably not a trait unknown to her husband, Preston. The last thing Dr. Umberto wanted to get from her in the midst of what had transpired was pressure about the progress he was making on announcing the discovery.

Samantha had received the news on this latest break-in from her husband who cell-phoned her about the awfulness of it all as he was heading back to his car in the CTU faculty parking lot. Preston still didn't accept the untoward relationship his wife may have had with Maxwell Umberto, or he refused to see it, and he continued to behave as if they were all simply long-time friends and colleagues. That was what he wanted it to be. When Preston called, Sam was only two minutes away, working in her own office in the Mathematics Department; so, she scampered over to the physics building immediately upon hearing the news.

"Holy shit, Max!" she said heaving deeply as she got a glimpse of Maxwell's office when he opened the door, a door that had previously been standing wide open all morning for fresh air in the troubled space, even while Lieutenant Lau grilled him about the second edition ransacking. But Max had finally closed that door after Preston's suggestion, not fifteen minutes earlier.

"You'll have noses in here all day as soon as word gets out," Preston had joked when he was leaving. And reminded of the cold fusion announcement he knew Dr. Umberto was keen to deliver, Preston added, "But, I guess that's something we'll both have to get used to down the road."

Max was in no mood to find any of these developments humorous. People who don't have a rectal hernia might joke about it, he thought, but if you've *got* a rectal hernia, there's nothing to laugh at. It was a classic Maxwell Umberto self-absorbed interpretation of the work. *His* drama was the primary drama; it had always been so.

"Hi," said Max to Sam, a rather understated choice of greetings given the circumstances.

"Are you okay?" she asked coming into his office and touching Maxwell's face with the tips of her fingers and looking into his blue, puffy eyes. "You look like death warmed over," she added.

"Not so warmed," he said as he returned to the job of cleaning up.

"What do you think is going on?" she asked, earnestly. Of course, Dr. Umberto had been racking himself over the weird scenario since his previous encounter with a hooligan's wreckage.

"I don't know for sure," he said and collapsed in a chair, the same wooden chair he'd heaped himself into across from Preston half an hour ago. And Sam took the chair Preston had occupied, so now there they were looking at each other in the disheveled office just like he'd been with his research partner earlier, face to face. But this time it was his research partner's *wife* sitting there, a woman who had become his lover. The musical chairs aspect of it all made Maxwell feel a little creepy, so he stood up and paced over to the California

Street window, the window that had given him reflective moments so often before, when he would watch the athletes go through their drills. But on that day the field was empty, not a runner, or a ball of any shape, or even a lone, melancholic wanderer to be seen in the expanse of patient grass while a cool October breeze silently disturbed the thin spruce trees on the far boundary of the field.

"What do the police think?" said Samantha from behind, hauling him back from his reflection.

"They want me to tell them who did it," Max said flatly turning toward her.

"*You*?" she said.

"Yes," he said. "But I couldn't."

"You couldn't tell them because you don't know! What a bunch of yokels," said Samantha rising from her chair and coming to Max. "Isn't that *their* job, to find out who did it?"

"Usually," he said with a frightening touch of fatalism, a dark edge that was not like the usually effervescent Maxwell Umberto.

She put her hands on his shoulders and rested her cheek against Maxwell's chest. "What are you saying Max?"

"The police don't know about the research, about the cold fusion and all that," said Max flatly.

"You didn't tell them, did you?" said Sam, pulling upright. She well understood that leaks of that kind to public officials could very well undermine the impact of the official announcement they were planning.

"No. No, I didn't say anything, Sam. But I do think what has happened here has something to do with the research. I don't know how or why, but they are connected. It's got me a little frightened, to tell you the truth."

"Look here," she said, grabbing Maxwell's face with both of her hands and firing her line of sight straight into his pupils. "Nobody important other than Holcomb knows about your research, Max. *Do they*? You realize you're being silly. What makes you think these break-ins have anything to do with it?"

"What else? Even the Pasadena Detective wondered if it was something related to my work."

Samantha laughed. "Is he a physicist?"

"He deals with crimes, Sam. That's his life. We have a crime here. I should listen to what he says."

"No, you shouldn't. You shouldn't listen to somebody with a BA in Criminal Justice from an online diploma mill. Just move forward with our plans for the announcement. Which, by the way, is set for when?"

Maxwell grew noticeably gray at the question. There it was, just as he feared. "I've had too much on my plate lately, Sam, to be worrying about announcements," he said with a firm and final edge that did not escape Samantha.

"Okay. Alright," she returned calmly, trying to accept the momentary derailment. "You clean up here," she said and gestured at the office. "We'll get back on track… but we shouldn't waste time. Time is both money *and* power," she added, ramping up the old saw.

Max didn't want to get into it. She'd retreated a little bit and he already knew enough about Samantha to know that's as much as he was going to get from her.

"I'll speak with Preston about it, too," she said.

"He doesn't think we should announce yet. And it has nothing to do with the break-ins, Sam. He wants other researchers to prove our findings first. That's the model."

"I understand *all* of that. I'll talk to him," said Dr. Day-Steiner.

"What is it, these bastards are after, if it's not the research?" asked Max directly to Samantha, hoping this self-confident and very analytical woman would have an answer.

Sam just stared back at him. She did not know what to say. She actually had no counter to his question in spite of being exceptionally quick on her intellectual feet. The simple unavoidable fact that nothing sprang to mind, gave her pause. And that was the first time Samantha Day-Steiner started considering that maybe the research was in fact what these thugs were after. At least the possibility could not be dismissed out of hand. Then, for no rational reason, Sam saw a fleeting mental picture of Big Buster Bernard sitting in her living room not that long ago, having reported a suspicious car on the street and hauling out his old Army Colt .45 side arm for Preston's protection.

CHAPTER 36

Ahmad Mulham was trying to find a place to park on the streets surrounding the Tech-U campus because the visitors' lot was full. This was not easy. In the ritzy neighborhood that bordered three sides of the Pasadena campus, cars that didn't belong were towed away in minutes, leaving the vehicles' owners with a bureaucratic gauntlet to fight, fines to pay, and hours to be lost, just to get their cars back. It wasn't worth it. So, there was Ahmad in his Tech-U sweatshirt going up and down streets looking for that precious legal and empty slot to store his rented convertible before he traipsed, once again, up to the office of Dr. Maxwell Umberto.

Ahmad did not know that Max's world was upside down at that time, both figuratively and physically. Nor did Ahmad know that the Los Angeles Police were sifting through his belongings at George the Gorge's apartment while George lay cold dead with the back of his head scattered across a wall. Right then all Ahmad wanted was a parking place at CTU, and in only a few minutes he found one when a pretty Japanese female student jangled her keys for him to see and courteously hurried to her car because she'd been in his situation many times. She jumped into her Volkswagen and pulled away with a quick waive in the mirror, arousing the flirtatious Ahmad in a most pleasant way. The girl was pretty and she offered her metered parking space. On that day it felt to Ahmad like she was a saint.

At eight minutes a pop, it took as many quarters to give him just over an hour, but he ran out of quarters, so it had to do. Ahmad left his car and headed toward the physics building. Who knows why Ahmad thought just dropping in would be the best idea, since he'd already tried it and found the strategy wasn't received so well. He was westernized, to be sure, but he also sprang from a family of privilege in Saudi Arabia and perhaps somewhere in the shuffling of those two worlds he lost track of the idea that an uninvited appearance was a *gauche* maneuver. On the other hand, Ahmad was an exceptionally sweet and likeable man, a characteristic that was discernable to any human with active antennae. Consequently, Ahmad had gotten away with a lot of missteps in his days at the University of Miami. Therefore, on that day in October Ahmad walked single-mindedly toward Dr. Umberto's disheveled office, even though the state of the office was unforeseen.

When Ahmad's knock came at Maxwell's door, it was just about the last straw for the professor. He threw the files he was holding into the air and they scattered to the floor all around him. Could he *ever* get his office straight! He rolled his eyes, tossed his hands again and yelled, "Jesus Fucking Christ!" When he yanked the door open, he must have looked like a wild man to Ahmad, who quickly backed away across the hall until he bumped into the farther wall!

Dr. Umberto jumped back, too! They retreated immediately away from each other. This was *that guy*, thought Max, that Arab guy who had been here asking questions about cold fusion! What did he want now? The sight of Ahmad practically scared the pee out of Max and he stammered, shifting from furious to frightened right before Ahmad's startled gaze. "What are you doing here?" asked Max. He saw threats everywhere.

Ahmad was trembling, too. "I… I… I just wanted to ask you about… you know…," he almost couldn't speak and his voice broke. Plus he could now clearly see the disarray in Dr. Umberto's office because Max had backed away from his door in terror. There were files and papers everywhere. This was not the way the office looked when Ahmad came by two days ago. Something was amiss.

"You're going to have to go," said Max as firmly as he could, pointing the way with a stiff arm and index finger.

"What happened?" said Ahmad in total sincerity.

"You *know* what happened!" yelled Max.

"*Me*?" said Ahmad, shocked.

"Did you or your friends find what they wanted?" said Max sarcastically, sensing a little less threat than he'd originally imagined, and straightening his spine as he spoke.

"Me?" repeated Ahmad. He had no earthly idea what this professor was talking about.

"Yes… *you*! When you broke in here and did this!" said Max, now more confident and grandly offering up the panorama of his upended property.

"I had nothing to do with that!" said Ahmad and he was becoming more and more afraid. He was, he would admit, deceitful in his approach to Dr. Umberto two days ago, but he pictured his deceit as relatively benign and he certainly intended no harm. He had things to find out. That's all. The possibility of his father's company striking an alliance with Max was very real; it was all about energy for the future. He did not believe his motives were bad. He had no ill will.

"You had better be on you way, young man," said Maxwell acting tough now, sensing the young Arab's trepidation. "The police will be by here any minute," he said, but it was a total lie. The cops were long gone and CTU security officers only make routine rounds at night, not in the daytime. Campus cops were not prison guards and CTU was not the Pentagon.

Similarly, Ahmad was not an undercover agent or even close to being one. He had accepted the job to please his dad. Even so, he very clearly understood that some of the players in his adventure might be quite serious individuals and might be quite dangerous, as well. That was the basis of the whole gun joke he'd made with his father before leaving Saudi Arabia for the U.S. But at that moment, on that day in Pasadena, Ahmad wanted only to alert this stranger, this angry misguided American researcher, Dr. Maxwell Umberto, to the facts. If Dr. Umberto's office was being burglarized, and if he thought a Saudi kid, a Hoorocane, who partied his way through his years at the University of Miami, was the culprit, then the professor would be overlooking all the serious threats entirely.

"Dr. Umberto," said Ahmad stepping up, showing real gumption, "I can understand why you are upset. I can see that something happened here, but I did not have anything to do with it. Yet I might have some information for you that you would find of real value." He surprised himself as the words spilled across his lips. He was still very afraid, but he also wanted to help. Ahmad had no idea how his offer would be received by the disheveled and distraught Dr. Umberto, but he gave it his best amateurish shot. These were two off balance but bright and for the most part good men trying to find a way to come to an understanding.

CHAPTER 37

Ahmad Mulham had rushed away from the office of Dr. Umberto after finding it topsy-turvy and finding Umberto maniacally suspicious. Nothing was settled between them about cold fusion, which was Ahmad's mission in the U.S. In spite of best intentions, no meaningful connection between them could possibly have been settled on such a bizarre day. During his brief visit with Maxwell, Ahmad had done his best to assure a disoriented professor that he, Ahmad, was in no way connected to the ransacking of the professor's office or his home. But it was clear when they parted that Dr. Umberto was not so convinced. Still, Maxwell did not telephone the police and have Ahmad arrested on the spot. Ahmad consoled himself with that one small victory as he drove his rented, brilliantly red Toyota convertible with its top down across the city and back to his host's apartment near UCLA. He had no idea his old friend, George the Gorge, had been shot dead.

The chilling weirdness of it all didn't really introduce itself until Ahmad actually arrived at the bland apartment complex where he had been hanging out with George. There Ahmad was confronted with a phalanx of LAPD black and white sedans, pretty much blocking off the entire neighborhood. Ahmad got out of his car and stood there with other spectators watching the drama unfold. There was a KQLA news van already setting up for the evening broadcast and men were pulling cables and lighting equipment out of the wide open side doors of their van like they were disemboweling a large animal. At first, Ahmad didn't know that this activity had anything to do with him or his friend, but he could see from his distance that the front door of George's apartment was wide open and cops were coming and going through it. As he watched, he saw two paramedics bring a gurney out from George's apartment and on the gurney was the covered body of a large person. Ahmad's heart dropped down into his shoes. It had to be George! Ahmad's instincts screamed for him to get the hell out of there fast, while a very powerful notion was surfacing in him that his whole adventure in America was headed seriously in the wrong direction. The LA Coroner's vehicle parked on the street did not make Ahmad feel any easier as that body in a zippered bag was loaded into it.

After driving away, Ahmad phoned home from a Starbucks three blocks from the crime scene and he relayed to his father what he had witnessed. On hearing these developments Ahmad's father advised his son to get on an airplane right away and head back to Saudi Arabia. Forget the original plan, his father had said forcefully, and his father added that they could always try to join forces with Dr. Umberto later. All was not lost. He emphasized, as he had before Ahmad left, he did not want his son to take any chances.

However, Ahmad wisely forecast if the activity at the apartment complex had implicated him in anything illegal, the police would already be looking for him. It was clearly a crime scene! He remembered all his clothes were in George's apartment, plenty of identification, and the police might already have alerted authorities at LAX and probably travel alternatives, as well. Ahmad did not know for certain foul play was in the equation, but it sure as hell looked that way.

Ahmad dropped his face into his hands thinking Dr. Umberto was probably also spilling his story about a Saudi man to the police, which would double the heat. When paranoia really attacks, that damn beast can tear away at a mind from every direction. Consequently, Ahmad concluded after speaking with his father that trying to go home at this time was not a reliable option. Those were not good days after 9/11 for Muslim men in America, but Ahmad had no other option in mind. What the hell was he going to do? He had placated his father temporarily by reassuring him he was okay and would be in touch soon. Ironically enough, his imagination and his fears in this situation were right on the money. Real things had taken place in George's apartment that put Ahmad in very serious jeopardy even if Ahmad did not yet know the magnitude.

All the cloak and dagger espionage business was not for Ahmad and never really could be for a man like him. He was a happy-go-lucky kind of guy, not an undercover agent! Ahmad was more frantic and at a loss than he had ever experienced in his rather privileged, money-swathed life. Ahmad was frightened and on the run but he didn't really know how to do "on the run." After coming out of the Starbucks, after he had called his father, Ahmad stopped and looked at the car he had rented, a red convertible! When he got in, he put the top up immediately and pulled away, still trying to figure things out. Ahmad knew to stay away from his room at the Pasadena Hilton. Authorities would be on to that move in no time.

Mindlessly driving into Hollywood, he eventually checked into a sleazebag motel on Sunset Boulevard to hide, guessing a hooker-haven would be off the cops' radar screen in looking for him. He was in no way prepared for the situation in which he found himself and he desperately tried to regroup and calculate next steps.

Ahmad barely slept that night at the Del-Mar Motel. There were loud voices in the hallway, shouting, and random heavy thumps against the walls on all sides. He was startled by every noise, and he woke in a sweat at 3:15 a.m. fretting about the shiny, red Toyota convertible he'd rented. Ahmad immediately concluded that driving that vehicle around the city was no longer safe. A bright convertible was the worst of choices. He so very much wanted to get out of Los Angeles, out of the United States, and get back home. Why in Allah's name did he come here in the first place? Ahmad didn't sleep a wink from then on. Maybe, he was thinking, he should sneak back to George's apartment to see if George was okay. Maybe the cops would be gone in the morning. He was jumpy until dawn after realizing that hiding, even in a gigantic American city, was a tenuous exercise at best. His soaring anxiety and his terror-fraught speculations on what might have been going on back there at the apartment complex near UCLA were already wreaking havoc on him. It was a torture that was well underway long before he opened up the next morning's *Los Angeles Times* at 7:00 a.m. in a booth at the International House of Pancakes next door to the Del Mar Motel and he discovered his good friend George the Gorge had been shot through the forehead in his apartment and that a Saudi man, named Ahmad Mulham, was a "person of interest" in the crime!

He practically passed out in the restaurant booth when he read it. This was worse than his wildest nightmare! It's true! George was murdered! Ahmad was light-headed after reading it and he actually had to hang on as the lights all around him in the IHOP grew dim and the sounds from other tables faded far away. He was literally two heartbeats from toppling totally unconscious in a crumple of newspaper pages onto the worn House of Pancakes' carpet while a steaming cup of coffee waited for him next to the carafe that a cheerful black waitress with one solid gold incisor had just delivered. What was he going to do, he said to himself, as he started to come around and regain full consciousness? He inhaled deeply. He drew in several great lungsful of air and struggled to recover. "Breathe, breathe,"

Ahmad repeated to himself. What was he going to do? Then he looked around. Were people in the restaurant staring at him? He concluded he'd better get out of there and right away.

CHAPTER 38

Undeterred by recent strange developments, Preston Cook was moving forward day by day with his research, exercising the best practices of standard scientific protocol, as he understood them from a lifetime at his craft. There had been the startlingly successful work in his odd little back-yard laboratory, followed by a more sophisticated and delightful rendering of the results over at CTU, with Maxwell's assistance, and then Preston and young Dalton, his most-trusted assistant, had replicated it all yet again at home. But at that point in time as Preston saw it, a more remote, a more detached and less directed reproduction of the experiment would be the appropriate next step prior to going public. Perhaps there should be two more replications elsewhere. That was an accepted procedure. Preston dismissed out of hand Dr. Umberto's suggestion that an announcement about the project was imminent. Preston had no such plans. He had no clue where that cockamamie idea came from and he continued to see himself as the principle investigator in spite of Maxwell's insinuated joint ownership of the cold fusion project.

Dr. Cook fancifully reckoned the next trial might take place at the University of Nevada as a deferential nod to where cold fusion first caught the nation's attention in the Fields-Parker debacle, where a ton of good work had taken place and where some measure of redemption was perhaps the ethical thing to offer where a pair of decent researchers had suffered terribly under onerous and sensationalized reportage. Preston knew, as he fantasized about this process, that Maxwell would disagree vehemently and that Samantha, for whatever unknown reason, would be absolutely apoplectic about any delay in announcing their success at achieving cold fusion.

Of course, Preston acknowledged nothing to himself about the possibility of his wife's more intimate involvement with his long-time pal and colleague, Dr. Umberto, and Preston also acknowledged nothing to himself about a swelling international interest in his cold fusion work. This remained true in spite of his recent visit with Max who was beginning to imagine foreign agents and Middle-Eastern terrorists and god knows who else snooping around, hiding behind trees, and crawling through his windows. He was not the cool sophisticated Maxwell everyone had come to recognize but was instead beside himself with worry over the mysterious activities swarming around him in those days. Max was a man whose life and possessions had been turned upside down and who had been visited by suspicious exotic characters right out of *film noir*. To Preston's observation, Max was a physical and emotional wreck, half-crazed and exhausted. Still, Preston did not grasp the magnitude of the problem.

In Maxwell's defense, Preston had already interacted with the primary police investigator in Maxwell's worry-riddled story. Pasadena's Lieutenant Stanley Lau and his gangly praying mantis assistant had engaged Preston Cook inside his own miniature laboratory. So, at least *those* characters were not imaginary, a product of Maxwell's increasingly fragile mind.

Although Preston was concerned about Umberto's deteriorating mental state, he could not help but note there was truly something very real, very strange, and new in the air. Although undefined, it was palpable even to a naive Dr. Cook, and it was not at all a typical feature of the map a research project follows as it is being delivered to the world. Maxwell was clearly afraid and he had said openly to Preston, in an unexpected change of direction, that he suspected this whole ransacking business was only an indication of what might lay ahead if they continued with the cold fusion research. But after consideration and a day's passage, Preston could not bring himself to agree. It was too much of a stretch for him. He continued to be rather dismissive of it all in spite of the strange goings-on, as one who had *not* had his home ransacked might be. Nonetheless, something nagged Preston subconsciously and led him to question whether or not he should take greater interest in what was happening with his friend and former research partner.

Bobby Skylar really enjoyed his Starbucks latte every morning back in Washington, D.C. But in Pasadena, not knowing where a Starbucks might be near his hotel, he dropped into a local independent coffee house, the retro fitted Has Bean, at around 8:00 a.m. He purchased a latte, grabbed a copy of the *Los Angeles Times*, and caught up on the news after flopping into an over-stuffed chair and cranking up his lap top to connect with his triple-encrypted Special Group email. Bobby also had the opportunity to flirt with the flouncy and cute twenty-something barista who worked Has Bean's early shift and he would wend his ever so charming ways, even for an aging fart. Sometimes he scored a free scone that way, not that Bobby was in need of any gratuities with his generous government per diem, but it was the challenge that counted. He hadn't lost his touch.

On that day, on the second page of the *Times*, a particular headline burst into Bobby's eye balls: "Saudi Suspect in UCLA Murder." As he quickly scanned the article describing the west-side shooting of a med student, Bobby zeroed in on the name "Mulham," found on baggage tags at the scene. Bobby Skylar knew that was the kid he followed while hidden in the shadows of the California Oaks on the CTU campus after the young man left Maxwell Umberto's office.

Bobby also knew the young man was from a powerful OPEC family. Agent Skylar damn near spilled his precious latte as he went to open his Special Group email to see if anything related to this late-breaking news had popped up at headquarters. And the very first message in Bobby's mailbox was from his boss. "You'd better get your ass back here right away," it said simply and there was no need to reply. That kind of email from Digger Mac Brown meant Bobby Skylar should be buckled into a seat on a flight to Washington before noon.

CHAPTER 39

There sat Bobby Skylar and Digger Mac Brown in the rarely used Washington, D.C. office, the old run-down "Potomac Title and Trust," the second story phony real estate company that waited inconspicuously over the non-descript but busy Chinese restaurant, Walk the Wok. It was the same site at which, a few weeks earlier, Bobby and Digger had discussed agent Skylar's trip to see his old chum in California, Dr. Maxwell Umberto. In that prior meeting, Digger and Bobby had skimmed across the rumors about cold fusion research that apparently continued to stumble forward, even though it was supposed to have been abandon two years earlier when they bought out Dr. Umberto with some drummed up grant money. The cold fusion research had never been popular with many in the Bush administration and it was not popular with other powerful people very close to the President in 2005. And cold fusion research also happened to be exceedingly unpopular with many other influential individuals all around the globe. So, during the second meeting, on that fall day in the offices over Walk the Wok, it was the newly realized very intense world-wide interest in Umberto's research that was highlighted on Digger's agenda. It seemed the ante had been significantly upped since their first meeting.

Digger was slumped back in his chair on the opposite side of his desk from charming Bobby, and to say Mr. Mac Brown was rather gloomy would be an understatement. If a shadow can cross one's face, then a shadow was settling down on Digger's.

As he always did, before meeting with his mercurial boss, agent Skylar had speculated if his boss would be in the manic phase of his bi-polar world and a frenzied fire-storm would be one second away from his lips, *or* would Digger be drooping into a dark state of mind, unable to really cope with what was transpiring out in California and looking for leadership from Bobby as someone to show the way out of his problem. Both of these scenarios had played out in the past; so either of them was an ever-present possibility.

Upon arriving and taking one of the chairs across from Digger Mac Brown in his customary way in that fabricated title and trust office, Bobby inquired how Digger was doing. It was a genuine question and it was received as such. On Digger's morbid days, Bobby would then become audience to a worn but honest love story. Digger would quietly mention dead Dottie Mac Brown, the woman who had been his sole corporal passion for fifty years. Things were not the same in Digger's life after Dottie died and he had resigned himself to the cold hard fact that they would never be the same. This reality would weigh on Digger for the remainder of his life and especially so on his darker days. Beyond congenial Bobby Skylar, very few at Special Group who knew the seemingly unflappable Digger Mac Brown would have ever pictured him to be a man who, years after his wife's death, would clutch a photograph of her to his chest and sob away the evenings alone in the house they had shared, knocking back shots of Wild Turkey until he passed out.

When George W. Bush and Dick Chaney relinquished the White House in 2008 to the Democrat who followed them, it would be the last straw for Digger. He didn't give a flying fuck if the President was black or polka-dot, he just knew that with that change in leadership his way of life in the agency would never be the same, and of course he continued to miss his Dottie. So, after getting all of his affairs in order one year later Digger climbed the stairs into his attic and he found a foot locker that held, among his collected memorabilia, a single cyanide capsule that was issued to him when he was a wet behind the ears agent a lifetime earlier at the height of the cold war. He'd always imagined he would be chomping on the capsule after having been beaten half to death and thrown into a dark dank cell in Eastern Europe, having had to dig around in his own rectum to retrieve the pill. Digger even managed a chuckle at the thought. At least the damn capsule was clean on that particular day, so he popped it into his mouth and burst the capsule between his molars.

When Bobby Skylar was summoned back to Washington in October of 2005 over developments in the cold fusion adventure, George W. Bush was still the President and Agent Skylar found that Digger Mac Brown was not in an upswing. He was struggling to surface from his gloom and it was very clear in his affect. Digger made little eye contact, but he was able to muscle through the meeting and in spite of his compromised condition, there was no doubt he knew what needed to be said because he was one very dogged patriot and soldier.

The most import item on the agenda was a clearly understood message that multiple national and private entities around the world were involved in attempts to squelch this threat to the status quo, this apple-cart-upsetting cold fusion research. There was far, far too much money on the table at that point for any of the players to toss in their cards. They were doubling down, if anything. This was a game of brinksmanship that took Digger back to the cold war years. To the degree it could, in his mental state at that time, the situation excited him and perhaps transported him back to classes on global strategies during his time in the U.S. Army's War College. Digger imagined his long time cold war colleague, Vice President Dick Chaney, was surely salivating over the whole confrontation. Hot damn! This was the Cuban missile crises all over again! Who's gonna blink first?

Once cordialities had been passed, such as they were, Digger Mac Brown attempted a cut to the chase, but there was a passive quality to his efforts this time that bespoke of his depression. He was clearly not on speed dial.

"We've got company, Bobby," Digger said, swiveling slightly left, then slightly to the right, as he spoke. "Out there in Los Angeles, have you seen anyone you recognize from other assignments? Anyone suspicious?"

The secret agent business was an odd cross-cultural social club, one might say. Many of the agents from various nations gradually came to know one another, by sight, if nothing else, from their respective intelligence files. Yet, when an agent became too well known, he or she might be finished in the field, but not always. Bobby Skylar was fairly well known among professionals around the globe and he was still sent out on missions. It was a very unique line of work.

"Not beyond that Arab kid I mentioned, who'd been to see Dr. Umberto. Ahmad Mulham."

"He's the one might've killed that med student, right?"

"He's a person of interest."

"Well, you're not alone out there in California," said Digger as a matter of fact. "This whole adventure seems to have grabbed the attention of quite a few agencies, east and west."

Bobby sat there and waited for the report he knew was coming.

"We have learned," continued his boss, "that there are operatives from Russia... from China... one from Venezuela... and we know one is from Kuwait, too."

"Kuwait?" said Bobby, and he smiled at the irony of it, because the U.S. and other coalition countries saved Kuwait's bacon not that long ago, saved their asses from Saddam Hussein and his Iraqi

Imperial Guard in a United Nations sanctioned military intervention called "Desert Storm". Now those Kuwaiti bastards have some agent snooping around in the United States because of rumored research that might be a threat to their precious oil fields? Ridiculous and insulting! Bobby didn't care for it and Digger nodded appreciation for the expression he saw on Agent Skylar's face.

"Ain't that a kicker?" said Digger.

"Yes. I would say so, sir," said Bobby.

"And... Cain is out there, too," said Digger soberly and finally.

This gave Bobby pause. Cain was the name Special Group had given to a free-lance operative who didn't have a real name in any country's data banks. He was a global mystery. The biblical Cain was the world's first killer and in some religious lore he was fathered by Satan, a child of evil. And like every other clandestine intelligence operation among the industrialized nations around the globe, Special Group had a file on Cain. He was smart and he was a professional and he had no known allegiances whatsoever, because that was the Achilles' heel to most agents in the espionage arena. Cain could never have existed in the years before current technology. His cell phone numbers would last only a couple of days, as would his email addresses, before they vanished into the ethers. But that's how potential clients usually contacted him, through his quickly opening and closing electronic windows. It was a lightening game of hide and seek. Days later, after a query had been posted to his one of his ephemeral phone numbers or email addresses, Cain would get back to potential clients at his leisure and in his own very controlled and untraceable way. Yet as elusive as he was, Cain did leave tracks. For instance, he had fingerprints which were on file. And a Desert Eagle was his weapon of choice. Cain also frequently killed everyone in his immediate path, without compunction, just to get to his primary target. Then again, occasionally he made inscrutable exceptions to his killing. He was like God in that way. He had no concern for the dimensions of the swath he cut, but he would always cut it fast and cut it precisely. Cain invariably won his prize, too, and it seems his benefactors were satisfied with his efforts because there were always more contracts to be had. Given Cain's predilection for expeditious resolutions, it was reasonable to assume the clock was already ticking in California on cold fusion, and it was a fast clock.

For an odd inside-out moment, upon hearing that Cain was involved, Bobby wondered if Digger Mac Brown and Special Group had contracted Cain themselves. It sounds so bizarre, even paranoid, to outsiders, but Special Group like most organizations in those years was a data-driven entity. It had crunched the numbers and found that two agents working separately on the same mission, not being aware of one another, would accomplish their objective 32.80% more efficiently than one agent working alone. So, it had become all a matter of expediency after that surprising statistic was exposed. The "two-separate-agents" plan had been put into play numerous times. Typically the two agents didn't get in each other's way, but in a couple of instances one Special Group agent killed the other Special Group agent, not knowing the other guy was friendly. But to Special Group that was defined as a cost of doing business in a very lethal theater. The surviving agent almost never comprehended what he had done, because agents did not get to know one another in Special Group. They were segregated. They knew less of each other than they might know of agents from other countries. Special Group was iron clad in its individualized work and training. In Special Group, the agent involved in the misbegotten death of another agent was congratulated and lauded for his work, all orchestrated so he would never even suspect what had actually transpired.

So, Bobby Skylar understood clearly he could not ask his boss, Digger Mac Brown, if Cain was on the U.S. payroll. Inquiring was clearly not an option. Perhaps Cain was contracted by the U.S. and perhaps he wasn't. Bobby didn't know of a time that Cain had been hired by the United States, but one never knows for sure. Maybe some Special Group internal agent was on the assignment along with Bobby and not Cain. Cain could be foreign paid and maybe Bobby was the sole American agent involved. Anything was possible.

Agent Skylark's job was in front of him and it was clear; that's all he needed. He had to stop the cold fusion research and keep it under wraps while watching out for operatives from other countries, even from his own country. In Bobby's ever active survivalist imagination he was thinking he needed to be on the watch for Cain, in particular. That independent operative would blast him to smithereens in a blink if their paths crossed.

Bobby Skylar knew how to be a professional in his trade. He could do some pretty nasty things when he had to, and he had done quite a few of them over the years, but at the end of the day he did possess that old weakness, loyalty. Cain had nothing but a contract. Cain was no more than a cipher. With available prosthetics and cosmetics, nobody really knew what he looked like. In fact, nobody knew whether he was male or female. Nobody knew where he came from. Cain was ephemeral. Bobby Skylar had to consider the real possibility of being blown to eternity in his own hotel suite by a Jamaican housekeeper wielding a fifty caliber Desert Eagle, or the possibility of a Pakistani cab driver turning around suddenly and putting a bullet in his face right after pulling away into the night. That was the complexity that Cain brought to the equation for Agent Skylar. Anything was possible.

CHAPTER 40

On the west side of Los Angeles there were police matters that would eventually be tied to the curious and growing lightning storm swirling around Preston Cook's cold fusion research. The Los Angeles Police Department's Detective Fitzgerald Jack and his investigation were specifically focused on the strange and inexplicable killing of a medical student, known as George the Gorge, and his missing houseguest, one Ahmad Mulham, a foreign tourist.

As far as anyone knew in the early investigation, the west side murder had not the slightest relationship to any peculiar developments way over in Pasadena at that elitist science college. The events in Pasadena were as far off the radar screen for LAPD Lieutenant Jack as one of Tech-U's missions to Mars, but it wasn't because he couldn't make the intellectual leap. Detective Jack could make any kind of intellectual leap that was needed. In fact, that is what made him a cop phenom. It's what set him apart. This west-side LAPD detective was cut from an entirely different cloth than was Detective Lau, as well as almost every other gumshoe on the beat in the LA area. He was modest, deferential to his fellow cops, yet everyone saw he was an unusual man and a rare detective. Fitzgerald Jack was more courageous when it came to the chase than most cops, and more willing to follow his instincts. And in this particular murder investigation, Fitzgerald Jack's instincts were telling him right away that this Saudi Arabian youngster was not in California to catch up on old University of Miami shenanigans with George the Gorge only to blow the back of his head away with a heavy duty handgun. This was a conclusion reached by Detective Jack very soon after he had left the murder scene. So what *did* happen in that apartment?

"Fitzy" had gotten his *chutzpa* and his outsized instincts from his mom, former Detective Sally Jack, who'd cracked her own share of thorny cases over the years and who had taught her son that you had better move with stealth, you had better maintain respect for your colleagues and their turf, you had better move quickly, and you also had better move decisively.

In that sense, Detective Jack shared an ironic similarity to Cain, aka Martin Speck, even though neither of them knew of one another and came from different worlds entirely. Martin Speck, had created for himself a cold and calculated life of international intrigue and espionage, while Fitzgerald Jack put down roots in the grit of street gangs, dime bags of crack, hookers, and the occasional movie-mogul gone berserk who shoves the muzzle of a snub-nosed .38 in the mouth of a starlet and pulls the trigger. Yet, beyond the dirt and the glitz that leavens what cops cook up every day in Los Angeles, there was something in these two stranger's compositions that matched, that made them mirrors of one another. Perhaps it was the complexity, the unexpected juxtaposition of interests and talents that both of them possessed. Perhaps it was something else that only destiny would tell.

Fitzgerald's mom was a former police officer and his dad a professor of English at UCLA. On the other hand, Martin Speck's father was a Belgian diplomat and his mother an Indian opera singer. So many languages were spoken fluently and frequently during Speck's childhood that he almost didn't know which one was his native tongue. On the other hand, Fitzgerald Jack had gone to a small

California private school, Chapman College in the City of Orange. He was exceptionally smart, on a full academic scholarship with a double major in Psychology and Art. As for foreign languages, Fitzy managed Spanish pretty well and that was all, but he was a natural with a paint brush and demonstrated a stunning sensitivity to both classical and contemporary compositions in oil and water color, a passion he continued to nourish into his later years. At the same time, Martin Speck had gone to the Sorbonne in Paris where he was a stellar student, majoring in world history. His professors saw him as a future faculty colleague. He had a wise-beyond-his-years grasp of the confluence in historical events, of cultures, and the *zeitgeist*. But that being said, it was actually gardening that captured his heart. He loved to see beautiful things grow out of the earth from seeds and to know he had made it happen.

There was raw intelligence, fearlessness, and unbridled gall that drove both of those men, all of it set intractably within a commitment to what they each set out to accomplish every day. That was what made them tick.

Martin Speck, of course, did not give a tinker's damn who he might be like, but Fitzy Jack felt differently. He hated to see himself alongside Cain when the picture finally came into focus in front of him some time later, like a photographic print in a tray of developer, a ghostly image emerging slowly on glossy white paper. When Fitzgerald finally got to know this mysterious lethal man with a .50 caliber Desert Eagle on a clip holster at the small of his back, when the blood was finally let, Fitzgerald Jack realized he wanted to be superior to his enemies, but in this particular case, on many levels, he wasn't. At the end of the day, that would be the take-away for Detective Fitzgerald Jack, a lesson to be carried in his hip pocket for decades to come.

CHAPTER 41

Dr. Charles Trenton Holcomb, CTU's President, appeared at Maxwell's office on campus not long after Max had been visited by the police, by Samantha Day-Steiner, and by that Arab kid who knew too much about the cold fusion research. Furthermore, Max had also been recently visited by his research partner, Preston Cook. This was all because of an altogether different kind of visitation by the midnight marauder who made Dr. Umberto's life a disaster at home and at the college and had generally scared him shitless.

President Holcomb was wearing a most suspicious face when Maxwell greeted him, surprised to find the president standing there in what seemed to be, as always, a freshly pressed dark suit. In spite of things, Max was sufficiently collected to know how he should act in the presence of his boss. Holcomb was moving cautiously, which was not at all behavior that was typical of the man on whose whims the fates of so many turned, but the president had gotten word about the break-in and he figured bulldozing his way onto the scene might not be productive. The president had heard nothing whatsoever from Dr. Umberto since their meeting when they roughed out a plan to announce something important to the world, something that had transpired in a CTU laboratory in the physics department. The heft of what had happened in the lab was not lost on Dr. Holcomb.

His original meeting with Max had not at all been a throw-away footnote on the president's busy agenda, which was often the case in the fluffy ego-driven world at CTU. Instead, after the meeting, Holcomb had highlighted it on his calendar for follow-up. This was true even though Dr. Umberto had not supplied any details of the research to the president, but that isn't to say the ebullient Dr. Umberto had not left behind a strong impression with President Holcomb, one that promised a sea-change in the world's energy equation. Otherwise Umberto had managed to be tantalizingly mysterious.

Such a scenario could have only played out with so little concrete information for Holcomb because even before their meeting, Max was not a dismissible member of the faculty, lined up as he was to become the chair of the physics department and connected as he also was to news-worthy folks over on the other side of town in Hollywood. All presidents of colleges and universities are in love with the press, when it suits them, and high-flying, sophisticated Maxwell Umberto carried impressive media cache for a scientist, just like his old foe, Carl Sagan. Maxwell had been a public-relations jewel.

However, on that strange day, the high-flying, sophisticated Maxwell Umberto seemed to have given way to a rather frazzled, but working-to-get-it-under-control, Maxwell Umberto. Clearly, this was not business as usual, which President Holcomb could see right off the bat. Even though Umberto's office had by then been mostly reassembled following the ransacking, it was still disheveled. Holcomb was taken aback when he came inside and found he couldn't even take a seat at first. He had to wait on his host to clear a chair, after which Max grinned gamely and ran a hand through his wild blonde locks, a grooming concern heretofore unknown to the former boulevardier.

"Are you okay, Maxwell?" said Holcomb after sitting and crossing his legs as he tried to act normal in the wake of the chaos that had recently flooded Umberto's world.

"Oh, sure," said Max, attempting to be as cavalier as possible. "We've had a bit of a stir here, as you can see; but it's alright. I'm alright." And he smiled again as best he could before he too took a chair.

"What happened?" Holcomb asked, trying to be friendly, yet sounding too much like one of the investigators.

"Oh… I don't know. Maybe I shouldn't have kept that bag of South African diamonds in my filing cabinet!"

"Diamonds, you rascal!" said the president, trying to be light, which was not his strong suit. "Sounds like a Hollywood movie."

Max indulged his boss and chuckled. Holcomb wasn't a funny man, but he was trying. "No, Dr. Holcomb, unfortunately there're no diamonds, rubies, sapphires, or even quartz crystals for karma," said Maxwell. "I'm afraid we are rock poor around here."

They both smiled. Dr. Umberto tossed a hand and prayed they were beyond the awkward niceties.

"Well, what *did* happen?" queried the president, turning sober, a more comfortable affect for him.

"I don't know," said Max as honestly as he could.

"No idea at all?" said Holcomb.

"Not much," said Max, "but I'm thinking it might have something to do with the research we've been talking about."

"How's that?"

"I don't' know," said Max. "I'm working with the police. They don't seem to have an ability to go further than drugs and organized crime. Smuggling jewels has a certain *joie de vie*, don't you think? But, I'm afraid the research might be it. That's the only thing that connects the dots."

President Holcomb uncrossed his legs, placed his hands on his knees, and looked at his own long fingers curling over his dark worsted trousers. "So," he said, "what do you suggest, Dr. Umberto?"

"I hate to say this, but I think we should hold off on our announcement, wait until the air has cleared and the police have had a chance to figure out what's going on."

Holcomb nodded and thought about what was being said to him. He wasn't happy, but there wasn't anything in Maxwell's words that departed from what he'd already heard from CTU security or from the Pasadena Police Department which had always been very respectful of the place Tech-U occupied in the community. They had been in touch with the president from the beginning. Detective Lau had been quite forthcoming with President Holcomb in his report earlier that day. To the president, the detective didn't seem in any way to be the melodramatic drugs-and-mafia nitwit Max depicted.

"Okay," said the president to Max. "Let's back off for now. Please let me know when we can move forward." And he tried to smile, but it wasn't genuine.

Max knew his words were code for let's make the announcement as soon as possible.

"I will, of course," said Max. "It won't be long."

As he stood, the president said, "This is about as strange a thing as has ever happened at CTU. I don't know what I'm going to tell the Board, but I'll figure it out. Unfortunately, I've already spilled the beans to several members that something big is coming."

Max nodded . He knew that the President's concerns were likely very real in his highly charged political world, but Maxwell did not know how on earth to respond, so he simply turned up his palms and shrugged to show he was empty of suggestions.

"Stay in touch," said the president as he left.

CHAPTER 42

You don't have to be a master hacker to get inside CTU's database to find out the home address of a faculty member, particularly if the faculty member in question had never thought about protecting his privacy. Preston Cook had always believed his students should be able to seek him out on a weekend if need be. He had never chosen to hide from anyone.

Likewise, Maxwell Umberto was a cinch to locate. He had managed to commandeer all of the attention around the cold fusion research, in spite of his two year absence during a stretch of heavy lifting and sweat-work that had moved the experiments to where they successfully landed. So, because Max was drawing the spotlight during those days, Preston didn't really know he was of particular interest to anyone. The strange things that had happened recently to his research partner, the break-ins and the investigations, had nothing to do with Preston Cook. He was, and had always been, a naive man who saw the best in everybody. He did not believe nefarious characters might be lurking about and he was definitely not expecting Ahmad Mulham when the bedraggled Arab appeared on Preston's doorstep. This was after Ahmad had abandoned his leased, bright red Toyota convertible in the Del Mar Motel parking lot and taken four different MTA busses from Hollywood, so he could find his way to the house of a nuclear physicist that he did not know and on whose lap he would place his trust and very possibly his life.

Ahmad did not think he had many choices. Despite his oh-so-cleaver contrivances to find out from Dr. Umberto what was up with cold fusion by donning a Tech-U sweatshirt and claiming to be a graduate student, deceits of any other kind were long gone. There was no secret agenda in Ahmad's mind. He wanted to go home. That's all. He had simply run out of options.

By way of information on the cold fusion research that had been spoon fed to him before he left, Ahmad had Dr. Preston Cook's name as an ancillary figure. But it was the only other California name he *did* have after George the Gorge and Maxwell Umberto. Ahmad did not count those two Saudi boys who lived flashy lives somewhere in Beverly Hills. The Hoorocane had come to believe gaudy was repugnant, meaning the pair of Saudis he knew in LA were less reliable to Ahmad than an American stranger who lived in Pasadena.

"Will of Allah," Ahmad said to himself when he pressed the doorbell button while standing on the front porch of the Cooks' Pasadena craftsman home, waiting at the wide, solid redwood door.

This was happening in the very same minutes LAPD officers were opening the trunk of his rented convertible, left behind in Hollywood. It was in the same minutes Detective Fitzgerald Jack was poking around for evidence in Ahmad's shabby Del Mar Motel room. And his sweat-soaked sheets were as good as a urine sample to forensics, so the LAPD took a pillowcase when they left.

Ahmad was expecting a professorial man, a scientist, to open the door at the Pasadena residence where he was standing, damn near shivering from fear, not knowing if he was doing the right thing, but not knowing what else to do. However, to his surprise, when the door opened he found himself looking down at the unusual face of a twelve year old boy. It was not an unpleasant face, at all, but it was not quite the typical boyish Caucasian face. The face was bright but different.

"Yes?" said Dalton. Assertiveness was a lesson that had been delivered regularly to the boy by both Preston and Samantha. His mom and dad did not think reticence would serve him well in the world he would be facing on his own, after they were gone.

"Uh…. I… was looking for Dr. Cook," said Ahmad.

"So, who is asking?" said Dalton just as he had with the Pasadena detective who had appeared at the garage lab not that long ago. His affect was like a man in his forties, a guy from a gangster movie, which was the true source of the question and his inflection, too.

Ahmad's eyes were wide. He was clearly taken aback. "He… he… uh… wouldn't know me," said Ahmad.

"Are you a salesman?" demanded Dalton.

"No! No! I have nothing to sell. I… I… know Dr. Umberto," said Ahmad quickly trying to find something reasonable to explain why he had arrived at the front door.

Dalton just stood there staring at Ahmad and not giving away anything. He was becoming pretty good at this. "And?" he demanded finally.

"Well," stammered Ahmad, "I have something to tell Dr. Cook… about the cold fusion experiments." He was just grabbing ideas by then, out of thin air.

Dalton stared at Ahmad a moment longer, but the last comment did the trick sufficiently. "Okay," he said. "Wait here." And Dalton closed the door, leaving Ahmad standing, as he had been before, on the front porch of a house belonging to a family he did not know, in a foreign country, and he was wondering if going there was a good idea after all. Ahmad knew full well George's murder was already in the news and his own name would show up there, too, sooner or later.

However, serendipity is occasionally a better ally than judgment and this was one of those cases for Ahmad, because nobody in the Cook household watched that much regular television unless it was sports, movie classics, or *Masterpiece Theater*. They rented the occasional DVD from the local Blockbuster, but there would be no six o'clock or eleven o'clock news in the Cook household. Current events came with the morning newspaper and National Public Radio. That meant Ahmad would have at least twelve hours to explain himself.

When Preston Cook came rather slowly and suspiciously to the door to meet the "guy who knows Dr. Umberto", as Dalton had put it, there was no thought of a west-side murder or international flight in the equation, just the usual defensive posture that any homeowner would adopt when a stranger shows up asking questions. In the back of Preston's head, however, were the warnings of his friend and neighbor, Big Buster Bernard, who had said somebody up to no good was sneaking around. Preston briefly pictured Buster's .45 Army handgun just as Samantha had pictured it not that long ago. Something out of the ordinary was clearly going on in their world.

"May I help you?" said Preston cautiously when he saw the lanky, young and nervous Middle-Eastern man on his front porch. All the while, Dalton hung by his father's side, eyeing the stranger.

CHAPTER 43

Before Ahmad Mulham appeared at Dr. Cook's doorway that day in October, Special Group agent Bobby Skylar was already ahead of the game in some respects after visiting his boss, the lonely, bipolar widower, Digger Mac Brown, in Washington. Skylar understood there were other serious players at the table, a development that had to come about eventually, but a development he'd hoped would not surface so soon. Skylar also had the very sobering news that Cain was sniffing around in the pack, too, and he sincerely hoped Cain wasn't on Special Group's payroll, although there was no way to confirm or refute that possibility. The formula for Cain as a Special Group team member didn't seem to work well from an agent's point of view, if the fuzzy numbers gleaned from other sovereign countries' spooks were valid at all. It seemed Cain's teammates around the world would inevitably end up in a zipper bag alongside the zipper bag holding the mission's target. Cain was not what one would call the ideal partner.

When Bobby Skylar got back to Los Angeles, he reckoned he shouldn't waste any time. He had to give his old college *compadre* another visit right away to get the ball rolling, but this time Bobby would precede his visit with a phone call rather than showing up suddenly at the man's doorstep like a prodigal son returned, which is how their rendezvous usually occurred. Frankly, in the past that's the way Bobby wanted them to occur. He had carefully orchestrated each one of those meetings. But to be fair, the encounters with Max did provide genuine hours of reminiscence for Bobby even though he invariably had a Special Group agenda in his pocket. His adventure in Pasadena was a complicated and quite conflicted assignment for Agent Skylar. He really did value the good times that he and Max shared at Yale University, back in the day, and good old Maxwell had always played his part in their get-togethers perfectly, never suspecting any untoward motives from his college pal. He never imagined he was being used by his long-time friend, Bobby, even when the grant money suddenly appeared and took him away from the cold fusion research. To Dr. Umberto it was a reward for networking and hard work. He'd earned that grant money all the way. There were no bad actors in his view of developments.

But when Bobby phoned Max in October 2005, Bobby was not greeted with the usually upbeat Dr. Umberto who had dated Hollywood starlets and had wooed the CTU community leaders into making him the front runner in their search for a new chair of the physics department. In fact, Max was damn near disoriented, or that was the way Skylar perceived it after hanging up. The truth was Bobby knew far more about what had transpired in his old friend's life than Maxwell knew himself. Bobby understood there was good reason for confusion and anxiety in his friend, very good reason. So, when Max indicated he wasn't up to much at the moment because of all that had happened to him lately, and when Max suggested they meet for lunch in the faculty dining room at the Parthaneum on campus, Bobby immediately said, "Sure. That sounds great."

So, the next day, there they were, sitting across from one another in that stately Spanish setting with the vaulted ceilings and thick white table cloths, with Bobby doing his best to resurrect the good-old-days, their carousing years at Yale. But Max would have none of it and he sat there variously distracted and otherwise morose. He barely made eye contact with Bobby, which was not like him at all.

"What do you recommend?" said Skylar as upbeat as possible after failing at all other angles of connection, and scanning the leather bound menu.

"Pear salad," Max said with almost no inflection whatsoever.

Bobby raised his eyes to the professor who was looking over to his left, then over to his right, like he was in the Secret Service scanning the crowd for an assassin, and strangely enough, he wasn't that far off the mark.

"Pear salad?" said Bobby. "*Salad*?" he repeated with emphasis for fun and he finally got Max to look his way. "No pastrami on rye… or some other pile of salted grease, like real men eat?"

"It's good," said Max flatly.

"Do I have to click my heels twice to get back to Kansas?" said Bobby.

"You're in California. We eat pear salad here. It's got walnuts," said Max and even though he was trying to be funny, Bobby could barely tell. His friend's face remained rigid and stressed.

"Hey," said Agent Skylar, putting down his menu and leaning forward on top of it. "What is the matter, Max? What's going on? Is it the burglaries?"

Maxwell rubbed his eyes and took a deep breath trying to calm down. He looked exhausted. "It's also everything else. I… don't know what the hell is happening, Bobby."

"Look," said Skylar softly and seriously, "I have extensive experience with this kind of thing. I really do. *Extensive*."

Maxwell's eyes got wide. It was the first time Bobby had ever made reference, so directly, to what his professional activities might involve. He'd always been vague in talking about what he did to bring home a paycheck. And from brief conversations with Bobby's wife over the years, Max understood his old buddy was just as vague at home. Based on these observations Max had concluded Bobby must be up to his eyebrows in confidential stuff with the government and it was always on the hush-hush. But Maxwell had never gone into any imaginary James Bond scenarios about his friend, guessing instead Bobby was a bureaucrat who worked on state secrets of some kind. However, in a wild, surreal sense, the James Bond scenario would have been much closer to the truth, but only if the famous Mr. Bond had a very dark, nearly sociopathic side, because only in that case would James Bond have qualified to be an agent in Special Group.

What Agent Skylar actually did for a living wasn't noble and it wasn't heroic and it wasn't the romantic stuff of Ian Fleming novels. Special Group was an elite, efficient, and pragmatic agency created to eliminate international problems for the United States' government. The job of Special Group was unique compared to the rank and file security and enforcement crowd from Washington. For instance, typical Special Group agents had learned from experience that the FBI was not much more than a collection of federal Keystone Cops, especially evident after the Twin Towers fiasco. Those guys were jotting down information on pocket notepads. Where was their database? Where were their laptops? And, since Special Group was actually kin to the CIA, Special Group agents had learned their CIA counterparts were bogged down in an immobile bureaucracy that was no more than a cumbersome heavily politicized anachronism from the old cold war.

Special Group was uniquely lean, and it was uniquely mean, and its agents were the genuine articles, technically savvy American commandos in a fifth column war. Shoot first and *never* ask questions.

The Parthaneum waiter, Henry, arrived jovially and Bobby looked up at him, smiled and said, "Pear salad, please."

Maxwell did not look up. "Me, too," he said gruffly.

Henry studied Dr. Umberto for a beat, realizing something was amiss, and then he confirmed, "Two pear salads," and he departed.

At that point the two men got down to business and looked at each other across the table. Bobby confided in Max that he thought what had happened at his home and office clearly had something to do with the cold fusion research. He also informed Maxwell that he knew about the Saudi man, who had come to Max's office in a CTU sweatshirt. Bobby said the young man was from a powerful OPEC family. The young Saudi man's name was plastered all over the *Los Angeles Times* as a suspect in a murder on the other side of town.

Maxwell wasn't aware of this; he hadn't read the morning paper. He almost could not breathe upon hearing it. His eyes were round and wiggling in his head as he watched Skylar relate the horrible news.

Of course, Bobby had his information about Ahmad before the murder story hit the newsstands. Info had come pumping through his Motorola cell phone as quickly as it was available. Agent Skylar had trailed Ahmad following the young man's impromptu meeting with Max only a couple of days ago, which by then felt like a week. That was the very day Bobby popped by to see Max in his office only to find his plan derailed by this Ahmad Mulham fellow, who had beaten him to the punch.

Aside from highlighting the Saudi connection, Bobby continued to play his cards close to his chest for the most part at the Parthaneum with his friend. He did not explain he'd been snooping around outside the day Ahmad had surprised Max at his office. He did not explain he knew specifics about the ransacking of Maxwell's home and his office. Bobby was a creature of a clandestine world and he would be that creature to the day he died. Nonetheless, Bobby did say to Max that government sources suggested the cold fusion research was, in fact, at the root of all that had happened, just as Maxwell suspected.

Dr. Umberto received the news silently. He just sat there with eyes like saucers, waiting on more.

But Bobby could not get into exactly how familiar he was with all of the shenanigans, the ransacking episodes and the array of men and women zeroing in on Pasadena from governments around the globe. As he spoke, agent Skylar imagined Cain out there somewhere in LA, probably not too far away at that very moment, looking for his opportunity to terminate the cold fusion threat and satisfy his employer, whomever that might be. Bobby could see clearly that Maxwell did, indeed, have serious things to worry about and Bobby knew his very best advice would not be received well, because it involved asking Dr. Umberto to distance himself from these world-changing findings, findings that would undoubtedly put his name in the history books alongside Edison's. What scientist would follow such advice?

To protect Maxwell Umberto, Agent Skylar was going to have to advise Max to disavow the research, explain that it doesn't really work, that it was a flash in the Petri dish. Bobby would have to suggest that Max discard any connection to it. That was going to be the advice Bobby had to give to Maxwell Umberto, the ambitious, renowned, and dedicated CTU physicist. In Agent Skylar's mind, to guess advice like this would not be welcomed by Max would be a catastrophic underestimate.

"The research is it, Max. That's what they want," said Bobby frankly. "These guys who broke into your apartment and your office… they want this whole thing to go away."

For a few seconds the two old friends just stared at one another across their pear salads.

"What? That doesn't make sense," said Max in disbelief.

"I'm saying that what you… and your research partner, I guess… what's his name?"

"Preston Cook."

"Right. What you and that guy have accomplished is… well, it's wonderful… it's stupendous! Really, it is! But it upsets a lot of business interests, if you catch my drift."

Max began to withdraw a little bit and he sat up straight. He sensed in that conversation more about his friend's government life than he had gleaned over a hundred shots of Glenfiddich. "You're talking about big oil," Maxwell said finally.

"Among other things. But the oil industry would certainly be concerned by such a development, don't you think?" said Skylar. "Put one of your contraptions in a car and you could drive for a hundred years without filling up!"

Agent Skylar folded his napkin, rested it beside his plate and continued, "Many oil people are very worried about a sudden change like this. And it isn't just foreigners, Max. Domestic players are worried, too, and some of them are very influential people, I might add. Some of them are connected in Washington. Some of them see this development as deadly serious. They don't take kindly to threats."

Max just sat there, still ramrod straight in his chair with his fingers clutching the table to either side of his salad like he was hanging from a ledge.

"Providing cheap clean power to the entire world is not a threat," said Max.

"They aren't ready for it," said Bobby Skylar. Bobby knew about threats and he knew about the lividity of this one. He did not have to go to the crime scene where the UCLA med student had his cranium blown in half to recognize the handiwork in that grisly piece of business. Bobby already knew it was Cain and not the Saudi boy who killed the med student. He knew it from recent information provided by his support people in Special Group. The poor bastard, Ahmad Mulham, was as trapped in this spiraling situation as was

Bobby's friend Maxwell. Ahmad's well-respected family aside, this was a lethal game that the Saudi young man's father had put his son into, and the fact that Ahmad was not really a danger to anyone didn't matter at all. He was in the line of fire and collateral damage was predictable on that kind of stage.

Right then Bobby Skylar could only give his best advice to Maxwell when he said the cold fusion research was definitely at the vortex of all that had happened lately. The unspoken reality was, in Special Group's universe, if things started jumping, Max could quickly become a liability. At that point, all bets would be off for ensuring his safety from any direction.

Although he didn't say it to Maxwell on that day, silencing the cold fusion results and deep-sixing the records was precisely Agent Skylar's current job. It was also the self-same mission for a handful of international counterparts who were gathering in Los Angeles while Bobby and Max sat in the Parthaneum having a pear salad lunch.

Even as Bobby and Max tried to commune in the Parthaneum's serene dining room on the campus at Tech-U, while a wistful Bach chorus swam faintly around them as light as the air, those foreign operatives were planning their moves. And there was Cain, out there somewhere, already plotting his course of action in his customary way. That UCLA med student was just the beginning.

One huge difference between Bobby and the other secret agents assembling in Southern California was that privately Bobby Skylar really wanted Maxwell to survive. None of the others in the hunt gave a good god damn about Maxwell's future. The sad truth – as Bobby well understood it – was that his personal feelings about his friend in that kind of situation was a handicap and it might very well compromise his spontaneity, which for a Special Group agent is most often a fatal compromise. To disavow emotional involvement in any operation was an iron law.

After neither Bobby nor Max uttered a word to each other for what seemed like a full minute, while both of them stared into their waiting pear salads, Maxwell ventured for the first time a quiet inquiry of his old friend, "What in god's name do you do for a living?"

Bobby responded equally quietly and he said, "Just take it from me, Max, you are in the gravest of situations and I want to help you."

CHAPTER 44

Detective Fitzgerald Jack had already been on the phone with Detective Stanley Lau and they both quickly figured they had something worth talking about. When a crime is committed in one jurisdiction, such as the one that occurred in West LA with the slain UCLA student, and then the suspected perpetrator moves into another jurisdiction, such as Pasadena, then some negotiation and cooperation between separate law enforcement agencies usually takes place. So, Fitzy was simply following due diligence when he contacted the Pasadena Police Department. A flurry of handoffs about "who should take this call" at the Pasadena police station eventually gave way to Detective Lau as soon as a mention of a CTU physicist came up in the conversation. Fitzgerald Jack did not know about the cold fusion research and the tsunami that was rising slowly and irrepressibly in far-away regions, but the bits and pieces Fitzy could put together from Ahmad Mulham's suitcase did lead the LAPD detective to the name of Maxwell Umberto. Why that professor's name was implicated in Ahmad's life, Fitzgerald Jack didn't have a clue, but this Dr. Umberto guy lived and worked in Pasadena, and a few tips here and there gleaned from standard cop grunt-work after they found the Saudi kid's rented convertible in Hollywood's Del-Mar Motel parking lot, put young Ahmad Mulham in Pasadena. And that was enough to have Detective Jack on the phone chatting with Detective Lau.

"Okay," said Detective Jack after he and Stanley Lau had sorted through enough of the fuzziness to see there was a connection worth pursuing. It hadn't taken them long to link up as city law enforcement officers and in fairly quick order they actually rather liked one another, even though they'd never met. "I'll come up there in the morning and we'll hash this out. I'd like to do some homework, though," said Fitzy. "What kind of research does this Dr. Umberto do?"

"He's a nuclear physicist and that's pretty much all I know. Respected. No problems in the past. At first I thought it was drugs – you know, when his residence was ransacked – but that doesn't add up. He won't talk much about his work," said Lau. "Trade secrets, I guess."

"Hmmm." said Detective Jack. "See you tomorrow."

Martin Speck wasn't too far behind the Los Angeles Police Department in following the Saudi desperado's footprints to Pasadena. Speck had riffled through Ahmad Mulham's belongings before leaving George the Gorge's apartment, quickly taking notes without removing anything. Ahead of the LAPD detective who had just reconnoitered the murder of George over on the west side and was figuring a trail to the young Arab man, Martin Speck was going after the physicist who was Ahmad's objective in the U.S., the savior of an oil dependent world, Dr. Maxwell Umberto.

Ensuring the Saudi Arabian youngster had not gotten his mitts on the secrets of the research could come later. Martin Speck was not the least bit hindered by jurisdictions, like Detective Jack. Speck was free to go straight to the Tech-U professor who had started the whole fuss with his research. The entire planet was within Martin Speck's jurisdiction.

If fairness is defined as equal treatment for all, then fairness was absolutely the grim largess of Cain. He would eliminate anyone between himself and his objective without the slightest compunction, regret, or pleasure. It definitely wasn't that he wanted to kill or that he enjoyed killing. He simply pulled the trigger the same way a bolt is tightened by a garage mechanic. You don't want your hard work to fall apart. Another job was always waiting and Cain had a reputation to maintain. He was a not a prejudicial man – dispassionate, maybe – but he was fair and he rendered equal treatment to all. That is to say, he usually eliminated everybody in the path to his objective, man or woman, friend or foe. Ironically, Cain and Bobby Skylar were similar in that respect, but Cain had taken the game to the next level of disassociation and clarity. Bobby and his fellows in Special Group had lingering tendrils to the normal world, even when they shouldn't have. Cain, or Martin Speck, had very little of that.

After their pear salad lunch at CTU, during which they had delved into the assortment of dangers growing quickly out of the ground around them, Bobby and Max repaired to Dr. Umberto's town home on Oak Grove, only a few miles west of the campus. Bobby had been there not that long ago, when he surprised his old friend and had shown up at Maxwell's doorway bearing a bottle of Glenfiddich. That was before the two ransackings, before the tumultuous bizarre goings-on with police interviews and strangers asking all kinds of questions about Maxwell's research, his unpublicized research. Nobody should have given a tinker's damn at that point.

Bobby and Max rolled into Maxwell's Oak Grove town house like college dorm roomies, shedding jackets, and mumbling. The two of them were already up to their ear lobes in a heavy discussion of options for Max. Without missing a beat and still running the tape in his head, still expressing his total dismay at developments, Max went to his kitchen and resurrected from his liquor cabinet what remained of the Glenfiddich liter Bobby had provided the last time he was there. Fortunately there was a goodly portion remaining, sufficient to get them through the evening and through the topic that descended around them like the night, an unshakable gloom in Dr. Umberto's world.

"And what if I do... give it all up... as you say, and destroy any records of what I've discovered? Not that I am inclined to do it, you understand. Would that stop these assholes? Wouldn't they become concerned I might wait until the dust clears and then do it all over again?" He plopped down on the wide modular leather sofa and put an inch of Glenfiddich in each of two wide heavy whisky glasses.

"Good men are scarce!" they said in unison, clicked glasses, and knocked back the booze.

"Well?" pressed Max as he poured two more drinks and urged them to plunge back to his question.

"You're right. The bad guys may figure they aren't safe from you until you're no longer in the picture. You may have to disappear for a while."

Max looked at Bobby like he'd just been told to sequester himself in a cave for the next ten years. He pictured a few odd friends surreptitiously bringing him the occasional basket of bread and fruit and leaving it for him to find when he would sneak out at night like a leper.

"Disappear? What do you mean?'" said Maxwell.

"You know, Max... become less visible. What do you eggheads call it? Sabbatical! Take a lengthy sabbatical and get back to your... your *gravity* research again. That's not solved is it? Forget this cold fusion crap. Keep a low profile. The main thing is to stop looking like a threat to these lunatics."

Bobby saw Maxwell drop his face into his hands and groan.

"Max, old pal, we absolutely *can* do this. It'll be okay," said Bobby reassuringly as he put a hand on Maxwell's shoulder.

"I didn't discover cold fusion," said Max lifting his face. "That's the problem."

The confession caught Agent Skylar off guard and he pulled back. "What?"

"The real work was by Preston Cook. I helped… but when I left him a couple of years ago for my own research on the unified theory… we had not done it yet, not accomplished cold fusion. We were just repeating the mistakes of others. It was Preston who broke through. *He* discovered how it works. Not me."

Bobby just stared at Maxwell. He didn't know what to make of this. "I… I thought he was your assistant. You're saying *he* did it? It was *him*?"

"Yes, that's what I'm saying. I'm not only up to my god damn ass in life-threatening shit I also appropriated credit for research that wasn't mine. *Hah*! Look where that's gotten me!"

Bobby knew about Preston Cook. He'd already checked out the man's dowdy house in northern Pasadena. Skylar figured he'd have to deal with Cook at some point down the path, but much later, after Max had been protected or "taken care of," in Special Group lingo. This new information presented a change in direction for everything.

"How many people know it was Cook and not you who cracked this?" inquired Bobby coldly serious as he rested his glass of scotch, that only a moment earlier he was going to toss back.

"I don't know," said Max. "Really… nobody should know right now. We haven't announced it yet."

"Well *I* know about it," said Bobby, a little testy, not being one who took well to surprises. "*You* just told me."

"Well, Preston hasn't said anything. He's very conservative. He wants to have further replications of the experiment, before we go public. He wants to publish an article about the work in a scientific journal. Preston can be a total nerd. He doesn't understand the money and acclaim that can come from this. He doesn't seem to care. He wants to give the god damn results away! He wants to help the world! And, hey, I'm alright with helping the world, but I want my slice, too!"

"Oh, shit!" said Bobby, and it wasn't facetious. His words actually frightened Maxwell. "Oh, fucking shit Christ almighty!" said Skylar. He knew right away that dealing with an idealist changes the game, changes it dramatically, and not in an advantageous way for his interests. He probably cannot negotiate successfully with a man like that.

With tears welling, Maxwell looked up at his old college chum, Bobby Skylar, and said, "I love the guy. I really do. He's my best friend. This has been like a razor that I've swallowed and it has been cutting away at my insides."

Skylar was feeling a bit betrayed, too. Never mind his own daily duplicity, Bobby had always trusted Umberto's claim to be the lead in the discovery, so a quick and bitter retort was easy to locate. "Oh? Do you love him so much you decided to bang his wife?"

Maxwell's eyes were wet and as wide as silver dollars. He didn't know what to say, but he didn't try to hide it. Max was childlike and added faintly, "It's not what it seems."

"Yes it is… and everybody knows about it… except your partner, of course, her husband."

"I feel terrible," said Max and he was on the verge of bawling. His lower lip trembled. "Jesus," he said.

Agent Skylar had gone totally sober and ashen. "You should've thought about that before, buddy. This is going to get really nasty and really fast!" He picked up his glass of Glenfiddich and slugged it down.

Even as Bobby was enunciating those prophetic words, outside in the fresh darkness covering Orange Grove Boulevard, a white BMW moved slowly along the street. Inside that car was Martin Speck who scrutinized the glowing windows of Dr. Umberto's town house, windows through which Speck could see only the shadows of human activity thrown against the curtains by table lamps, where Bobby Skylar and Maxwell Umberto were coming to terms. That night was clearly not the night for Martin to make his move, so he turned back toward his hotel, the pink Beverly Hills Hotel on the other side of LA, a prestigious accommodation as was his preference when on assignment in cities around the world.

On the same evening Martin Speck was gliding by Maxwell's town house in the privacy of his rented BMW and Dr. Umberto was in the midst of confessing to Bobby Skylar that he had insinuated himself into a research success that was not rightfully his own, there were international agents afoot in Los Angeles sent from various invested parties bent on silencing the work forever, even if it meant killing the researchers. Such a development was wildly beyond the imaginations of either Maxwell Umberto or Preston Cook when they set out years ago to save the world. And death was certainly not what Max was looking for when he got back into the cold fusion business a few weeks earlier, but according to his old carousing buddy, Bobby Skylar, the terrifying possibility of death was suddenly right in front of him.

CHAPTER 45

Fitzgerald Jack had always liked Pasadena, "the Crown City," and the very first incorporated city in all of California. The city hall was magnificent, a towering columned Spanish dome worthy of Madrid, a signature sight, particularly after dark, gloriously lit against a black sky. Pasadena had old residential neighborhoods nestled along the San Gabriel Mountains north of Los Angeles and it was filled with old-growth oaks and fragrant, flowering vegetation. There was shade on the streets and in the parks, not the most common feature in Los Angeles County where asphalt and concrete had taken the place of grass and had erased trees in so many neighborhoods. The needs of business and the demands for rental space took precedence in LA, but in 2005 that had not yet happened in the Crown City.

To meet with Pasadena's Detective Lau, LAPD's Detective Jack drove up the Pasadena Freeway from downtown LA. He had always enjoyed that particular route. It wasn't far between the two municipalities, but the 110, the Pasadena Freeway, was a quaint and naively designed freeway, the original U.S. freeway actually, and it was acutely serpentine. There were green hills rising up on both sides of the route, with the roofs of many houses jutting out from a lush tree canopy. It was arrestingly pretty, but the Pasadena Freeway was so much fun to drive precisely because of its many curves and it was the only fun freeway that remained in Southern California.

With the inexplicably brutal and seemingly senseless murder of a med student on the west-side, Fitzgerald's gear-shifting sprint up the 110 freeway in his black jeep was a very welcome diversion and strangely relaxing. He wished the trip would have been longer than fifteen minutes.

When the two detectives, Lau and Jack, met they were as different as their histories, yet they hit it off rather well, just as they had on the telephone. Maybe it's cop stuff, and that's certainly some of it, but Fitzgerald Jack had known numerous police officers and detectives that he did not like over the years and those men and women were sometimes within LAPD and occasionally within his own unit. The fairly new Police Chief at LAPD, who came from New York to set things straight in Los Angeles' law enforcement, seemed to be on the right track and Detective Jack was hopeful a different police department would emerge from his leadership, but one never really knows. At the Chief's level, it's all political.

Perhaps it was that mixed bag Fitzgerald had found himself digging through during his time with LAPD – a much publicized scandal at the Rampart precinct and more – that gave him particularly sensitive antennae to good cops and bad cops. He could see soon after meeting Stanley Lau that he was in the company of an earnest lawman, a professional.

They came from entirely different places in life, Jack with his cop mom and professor dad, and Lau with parents who ran a take-out Chinese restaurant not far from Pasadena. Lau was short, over-weight, with his balding head showing lonely black hairs glued across his pate, while Jack looked like he had stepped out of a movie, tall, athletic, articulate, and witty. But it was *focus* which pulled these two together. They quickly saw in each other another police officer who was committed to making justice happen, who was committed to finding the cooks, and who was committed to honesty in the process.

"So what kind of guy is this Umberto?" said Fitzgerald Jack just after he and Stanley Lau had slipped into their chairs at the California

Pizza Kitchen on Los Robles, not a stone's throw from Lau's office at the Pasadena Police Department. It was very bright outside that day, and cars were zooming by with sunlight glinting off their windshields onto the ceiling of the restaurant, making for shards of light flashing left and right above the detectives.

"Prima donna," said Detective Lau. "He's kind of a celebrity over there at CTU, dates movies stars and things like that." Lau was reviewing the menu while he spoke. His words were not really judgmental; it was just his point of view.

Fitzgerald let his eyes wander across his menu, too, and said, "Do you know of any connection to this Ahmad Mulham, the Saudi youngster in the papers?"

They had cut right to the chase, not wandering around, but saying right out what each wanted and what each had to offer.

"Dr. Umberto told me a student had come to see him and had been asking about his research. He said the kid was Saudi and knew more about Umberto's research than Umberto expected. This student – maybe he was just applying to school – said he and his father wanted to be partners with Umberto. But Umberto didn't give me a name. Umberto may not even have a name. I'm guessing it's the same guy you're looking for." The waiter arrived and they each ordered an individual pizza.

"So what *do* you know about the research?" asked Fitzgerald.

Lau looked up and shrugged. "Like I said on the phone, not much. We didn't think the break-ins were related, until recently. Last time I spoke with Umberto, he was still very protective of all that."

"Ahmad Mulham is from a very wealthy oil producing family in Saudi Arabia," said Fitzy to Stanley. "Do you know if the research had anything to do with oil?"

"I'm sorry, Detective."

"What the heck would a Middle-Eastern oil baron's son care about research in the physics department at CTU?"

"I haven't the foggiest," said Lau.

"Here's some more grist for the mill," said Fitzgerald. "That murder of the student over in my neck of the woods was not some random frivolity-turns-to-frenzy affair. The med student was killed with a fifty caliber slug, not everyday hardware. It wasn't pretty. This is serious business."

The pizzas arrived while Detective Lau was looking across the table at the Los Angeles detective. When the waiter was gone, Lau said, "What kind of serious business?"

Fitzgerald Jack shook his head. "I don't know yet. Serious is all I can say."

"You think we should call the feds? See what they've got," said Lau.

Detective Jack looked at Detective Lau for a long beat before he answered with bald-faced candor. "Not yet. They tend to take over and then muck things up."

It happened their experiences with the FBI were strikingly similar. Stanley Lau smiled and offered a knuckle bump. "Let's wait," he said.

"When those guys imagine something is in their bailiwick, they're not going to be shy about it," said Jack.

At that point, they both examined the thin-crusted pizzas that sat in front of them on the table. They didn't know exactly where to go with the conversation just then, having shared what they had to share at the moment. Lt. Lau spontaneously grabbed the check that had been left by the waiter and he announced, "This one's on Pasadena."

"What is going on with you, Max?" said Sam, pacing in Maxwell's office and running a hand back through her thick auburn mane. "You're as frightened as a puppy! What do you mean we're not making the announcement? Where did *that* come from?"

Max was trying to be reasonable, but he was also aware that recent events did have him on his heels, so perhaps he didn't appear too assertive. He was, after all, truly frightened by what he had heard from his college buddy, Bobby Skylar. And he'd been cautioned by Skylar to keep things on the QT for the time being. Max, quite frankly, didn't know what to say or do at that point.

"Things have gotten out of hand a touch," he said vaguely.

"What things? What's out of hand?" asked Samantha Day-Steiner, and she was capable of being intense when she wanted to be.

"Word about the research has gotten out of hand. Preston doesn't want to announce at this time. You know that, don't you?"

"Look," said Samantha, and she walked right up to Maxwell Umberto and stood there, staring into his eyes. She was an imposing woman at 5' 9", not mousey in any dimension. "What Preston wants is not all there is. *You* own this discovery as much as he does. Unless we take some control he will be tickled pink to share everything with everybody, and he will largess us all right out of the picture. Do you know what I'm talking about here? If *we* announce it first, then *we* own it! Otherwise, heaven only knows who's going to come up as majority stock holder!"

Max remained cautious. "Sam... there are people involved here that we don't want to mess with. Trust me on this."

She just looked at him like he'd said there were kangaroos on the moon. "I do *not* trust *anyone* with a billion dollars of my retirement account, Max. Who are these 'people' that are involved?"

"I... I have informants. I can't tell you who, but this has become very dangerous business, all of a sudden."

Samantha knew there were dangers. She had sensed it, too. But at that moment she had enough of Maxwell's smoke and mirrors routine. She needed concrete answers. And, as it happened, there was just enough of Maxwell's good sense remaining in his addled brain that he did not blab to her everything Bobby Skylar had explained the night before. That meant Samantha was not going to get the hard answers she wanted... not on that day, in any case, although an avalanche of unexpected, horrific evidence would present itself soon enough.

"I can't tell you my sources," said Max.

Samantha was incredulous. "Oh, so it's Deep Throat, is it?" she said. "Well, I can tell you *my* sources," she continued, "if I tell Preston about *us* – you and me – there will be a price to pay for sure, but I'm the mother of his son. And I can guarantee you, Maxwell, *I* will still be around on pay day. On the other hand, you are a cheat, a johnnie-come-lately, and you will be out professionally and in every other way! There will be nothing for you, Maxwell, not the tiniest footnote of appreciation."

Max had backed away from Samantha. His eyes were wide and he was utterly defenseless. He did not know what to do. The whole drama had gone so far south and was so very different from his expectations when he'd gone to the CTU President's office only a few days ago looking to make an announcement about the research. His prospects all seemed so innocent and bright on that day with the President.

Maxwell raised the palm of one hand in surrender, a pathetic gesture to get Samantha to stop. "Okay... okay," he said weakly. "We'll make an announcement. We'll go ahead," he said and he could feel his knees trembling, so he slipped down into a nearby chair so he didn't collapse onto the floor.

Samantha stood up straight and looked down at Max, who sat there utterly defeated, in his roomy comfortable faculty office on the second floor of the physics building at CTU. How could she have gotten so involved with this man? Letting Preston know about her infidelity was absolutely *not* what she wanted to happen, but relationship-mending was in order at home just in case the unhinged screwball, Umberto, did something radical and crazy.

"So… are you going to speak with President Holcomb about resurrecting the announcement?" she said.

"Yes… yes, I'll speak with him."

"When?" said Samantha like a salesman closing a deal.

Maxwell looked up from where he sat. It was the first time Samantha had ever seen hatred in this affable man's eyes, but it was there at that moment. "This afternoon… or as soon as he is available," said Max.

"Good," said Dr. Day-Steiner.

Beyond Maxwell's office window, across California Street, Sam caught a glimpse of female students playing a pick-up game of soccer on the athletic field. One young woman deftly kicked the ball in a long, low graceful arc across the smoothly mowed grass, past defenders, to a young goalie who took immediate control of the ball with one touch. As Samantha walked out of Maxwell's office, she was wondering what her own next shot should be.

CHAPTER 46

When Preston asked the young man who had come to the front door if he could help him, the man unexpectedly answered by saying, "Maybe, we can help each other."

"Each other?" said Preston to Ahmad.

Ahmad shifted nervously. He looked down at his hands and did not meet Preston's hard eyes directly. "Well," he said, "My name is Ahmad Mulham and I have spoken with Dr. Umberto about his research on cold fusion, about the success he has had with it."

Ahmad looked up and found Preston to be waiting, but Preston's gut was tightening at the notion of this stranger's knowledge of cold fusion.

"My father is one of the founders of OPEC," continued Ahmad, a statement that hit Preston with a jolt! They know about the research *in Saudi Arabia*?

Ahmad continued, "My dad understands the problem with reliance on fossil fuels. Many in OPEC ignore this."

Preston didn't speak.

"We have influence," said Ahmad. "We want to assist with a transition away from oil. If cold fusion is real."

"Oh, it's real," said Preston softly, and he waited.

Ahmad nodded. "That's what everybody is saying. But… there are a lot of people who don't want it to happen."

"A lot of people?" said Preston, still reeling from hearing about the astounding reach of the gossip.

254

"There are people here from all over the world. They want cold fusion to go away. To disappear. You could be in trouble," he said and glanced quickly at young Dalton to see if he had said anything to alarm him, but Dalton was standing stoically by his father. "I think Dr. Umberto is in serious danger right now for having invented this."

Preston looked at his guest, allowing the words "for having invented this" float around in his head. First, Samantha seemed to give Maxwell's contributions more weight than they deserved and Maxwell, too, seemed to continually suggest he had a driver's seat on that same bandwagon. And, now, here is this young man from the other side of the planet, thinking similar thoughts about the primary investigator. Preston was reevaluating. Had he missed something? Why does everybody believe Maxwell Umberto cracked the cold fusion mystery, when he left the research two years ago? The fact that distinguished, respected, sophisticated, popular, and renowned Dr. Maxwell Umberto may have coveted what Preston had accomplished and stolen the credit for it did not enter Preston's equation and, instead, befuddlement entered.

"But there's more I have to say," said Ahmad, since he was on a roll right then and might as well give the full monty about what happened to George the Gorge. It was already in the news.

Preston held up a palm to get him to stop. "Wait! Let's not stand here in the doorway like this. Come in. This is my son, Dalton." The boy quickly stuck out his hand to shake and said immediately, "We are about to have supper, can you join us?"

The invitation caught Preston by surprise and he looked at his son who defended himself quickly by saying, "I'm hungry, dad. We should not eat in front of him."

Ahmad shifted foot to foot just inside the house and said, "Please. It's okay. I'm fine."

"No. No," corrected Preston. "Dalt's right. We were about to sit down and we have plenty."

The Cooks had a vintage O'Keefe & Merritt gas stove in their kitchen of which they were quite proud, and that's where the steaming ingredients for dinner where simmering. The three of them slid onto stools around a butcher block table in the kitchen.

When they had a moment to get situated, Preston said quietly, "What else?"

With that queue, the Arab man took a deep breath and plunged forward. "I am wanted for a murder that I did not commit."

This was another bomb of a statement, delivered by a stranger sitting in the kitchen of their house. It stopped Preston in mid-thought. He was not expecting such a turn in the conversation and he stared at Ahmad for a very long beat. Preston pushed away from the table slightly. Even Dalton blanched, his eyes gone wide as he stared at the dark man sitting in front of him. Dalton certainly knew what "murder" meant. Strategies for calling the police were quickly forming in Preston's imagination. How can this be happening?

"What?" is about all Preston could muster and rather weakly at that.

Ahmad was more nervous than ever, shifting on his stool, and he began to sweat across his brow. "It will all be on television," he said, "and I didn't want you to find out like that," he added, his eyes searching the expressions of the man and boy who looked back at him with shocked, stony faces.

He continued, "That's how I know there is danger. I came to Los Angeles to meet Dr. Umberto and then someone shot my friend. I was staying with a college buddy who wanted to be a doctor. UCLA. I had no idea this was coming." Tears were formed on Ahmad's lower lids. "I would never have hurt that guy," he said about George the Gorge.

Dalton methodically handed Ahmad a paper towel. Children understand tears.

"It's the job of the police to clear you if you did not do this thing," said Preston slowly. It was a recitation, but he actually believed what he was saying, having no real comprehension of the epic, oceanic swell that was growing right beneath his little boat. "If you turn yourself in… it will all be figured out," he said naively.

Ahmad suddenly stood up from the table and a flash of panic crossed his face. "I am an *Arab!*" he said firmly. "After what happened in New York there will be no fair dealing with me in America. Through my father I am directly connected to OPEC, Dr. Cook. And I have already spoken with Dr. Umberto about it. The police will know this. It will be opened and shut for the cops. The one who killed my friend - of this I am sure - he will also kill anyone between him and the silencing of your work. That means Dr. Umberto and… that could mean *you*, as well, because you might know something important."

"Who do you *think* killed your friend?" asked Preston.

"I don't have any idea," said Ahmad. "My father was afraid there may be this kind of reaction to Dr. Umberto's discovery. He told me to be careful when he asked me to come here. He wants to embrace the new energy, not bury it. But others with fortunes to lose think differently."

At that moment with this frightening information spilling forth, Preston did not think it was a good idea to correct the young Arab's misconception about who actually solved the cold fusion puzzle. If somebody had truly pinned a bull's-eye on the back of the inventor of workable cold fusion, then with his behavior Max had certainly earned the right to wear it. Overall, Preston did not know what to make of the stranger's story. Preston's adult advice to himself was to find a way to surreptitiously call the cops. Yet, at the same time, Preston's instinctive more innocent self was not at all sure that dropping the dime on his visitor was the right thing to do.

God damn it, Preston admonished himself, why am I such a freaking dupe? But in spite of all the good reasons to throw an unknown Arab interloper out on his keester or have him arrested, Preston decided to let things remain as they were, temporarily. It would probably be best *not* to let Samantha in on everything when she got home from her class later, he figured, because she would surely be far less hesitant about contacting the authorities.

"Ahmad," said Preston softly, "please do *not* repeat what you have told us to my wife when she comes home, okay? Let *me* explain it to her."

Ahmad had seen his own father interact with his mother enough to understand what he was hearing and he nodded. There was not *that* much of a gulf between the cultures.

Preston was willing to deal with her inevitable wrath later when she found out. He was fairly confused at that point, actually. There were the break-ins at Maxwell's home and office; there was Maxwell's very unexpected assumption of centrality to the whole cold fusion investigation; there was Samantha's peculiar insistence on making the research results public; and now there were international thugs shooting people and there were agents of foreign powers showing up all over Los Angeles in pursuit of the cold fusion chalice. And one of those foreign operatives was sitting in his kitchen! Preston was damn near short of breath.

CHAPTER 47

The morning after Ahmad had chosen to appear on Preston Cook's front porch was the morning after Samantha had pressed Maxwell about not being aggressive enough in securing a press release on the cold fusion. On that morning, Dr. Umberto trudged to his office on the second floor of the physics building to follow Sam's bidding. He was a beaten man. He'd lain awake practically all night. Dark circles swept beneath his bloodshot pale blue eyes, the azure irises that had captivated so many women and students, too, over the years. His life was out of control, totally beyond his reach. As magnetic as the cold fusion development was, and as earth-shattering as were the implications around it, Max was beginning to wish he had no part of the freaking invention, now or ever. Things would have been wonderful he fanaticized, if he had just remained inside his world of unified theory, a life spiced now and again with the occasional movie-starlet romp. He was lined up to be Chair of the Physics Department! Who needed this? And that's what he was thinking as he sullenly and fatefully stuck his key into the lock of his CTU office at around 8:30 a.m.

When Maxwell shoved open his office door, the room was already filled with morning light. But completely unexpected was a trim man he did not know sitting quite calmly in one of his chairs. It really scared the bejesus out of Max, who was already emotionally threadbare, and he dropped the Gucci leather briefcase he was carrying and he audibly gasped! Adrenalin zoomed through his veins and he was suddenly wide awake and alert. His lips remained immobile, however, and he couldn't form words for a couple of very strained seconds.

The mysterious man just sat there without moving, rather serenely with his arms crossed on his lap while Maxwell fell back against the door jam, his heart racing and his eyes wild. "What do you want?" Max finally uttered, more loudly than he intended as the words jumped out.

"Shhhhh," said the seated man and he calmly put a finger to his lips. "Close the door," he added softly. The stranger was one very spooky individual.

Terrified, Maxwell did just what he was told as he began to examine the unexpected visitor. The intruder was of indiscernible nationality, trim but not thin, dark but not that dark. His shortish hair was streaked blonde and Max also saw the man was wearing creamy Tommy Bahama shirt and slacks, with woven-top loafers beneath the trouser cuffs on his causally crossed legs. Clothing was a feature of the high life with which Max had some familiarity and strangely enough even in a surreal and scary situation such as that one, he could not help but notice the man's attire.

"How did you get in here?" said Dr. Umberto standing absolutely still just inside his office door with his briefcase lying on top of one foot. So much had happened recently that his head was swimming. He wanted to be organized, to be logical, to ask the right questions, to not offend, and to take mental notes. He knew that much. But the overriding sensation at the moment was gut wrenching terror, and he was fearful he was about to lose his bowels as he stood there.

But the man in the chair had nothing whatsoever to sacrifice in answering Maxwell's question. He already knew how this interview would turn out and he said slowly in his unidentifiable accent, "I came in through the door, Dr. Umberto. It wasn't difficult. And you may call me Martin Speck, if you would like a name."

As fate would have it, on the very same morning Maxwell Umberto had routinely inserted his key into the lock of his office door and had been stunned by the sight of Martin Speck waiting for him, Bobby Skylar had coincidentally elected to make one of his patented surprise visits to his old friend at his Tech-U office. Bobby wanted to find out how their recently exchanged views on his situation had fermented in Maxwell's compromised brain. He was genuinely worried about his scientist friend but he was also conflicted about it because in Special Group business he was not supposed to personally care about anyone. But Bobby had managed to convince himself the Pasadena assignment was different. He'd known Max forever. He was still rationalizing the whole thing even as he slid his rental car into a slot in the visitor's parking lot at Tech-U. Then he headed on over toward the physics building to see Max. Perhaps 8:30 a.m. was early for an unscheduled visit, but Umberto had clearly stated he was in his office at the crack lately because he could not sleep.

As Bobby Skylar was walking across the CTU campus toward his impromptu rendezvous with his old friend, Cain, aka Martin Speck, was already getting down to business with the rigidly horrified Dr. Umberto, who had yet to move a muscle after he closed his office door. He was frozen where he stood at the threshold, with his briefcase where he'd dropped it.

"Tell me, Professor, where are your notes and research results on this portable nuclear reactor you have created?" said Speck to Dr. Umberto, speaking about things that were foreign to Speck's life but using phrases and words that had been suggested to him through his research for this very conversation.

Max realized then that it *was* without any doubt the cold fusion research people were after, whoever the people were. And that intruder was likewise in pursuit of records about the development of cold fusion, just like Bobby Skylar and that Arab boy had foreseen.

"I… I don't know what you mean, Mr. Speck," tried Maxwell feebly and unconvincingly.

That was when Martin Speck hauled out his Desert Eagle from behind his back and he methodically began so screw on the four inch silencer.

Maxwell's mouth went totally dry. His eyes were huge and staring at that weapon in the hands of this very frightening individual, who was terrifying at a level that Max had not known in his entire life in spite of what had happened to him in recent weeks. His knees went weak as they had with Samantha's anger, and he was afraid he might fall down, but there was no chair nearby to support him. He realized in a late-blooming flash of insight that he was such a pussy. He thought he might throw up.

"What do you want?" he managed with a weak voice.

"I want all of it," said Speck as he finished tightening the silencer. The weapon was like a small artillery piece in the man's hands. "I want everything you have, related to the experiment. I don't want anyone, anywhere to be able to do this again." And that was when he turned the muzzle of his weapon toward Max.

"Oh, please," said Dr. Umberto. "I'll give you what I've got, but… but it's not much. I haven't got much," and suddenly his legs worked again and he went over to a blue file folder on his desk. It wasn't very thick but Maxwell was telling the truth. It was all the documentation he had. Preston Cook kept all the findings in his odd little lab in his garage. "Here," said Max trembling and handing the file to Martin Speck, who stood up when it was handed to him. He did not look happy.

Maxwell backed away, leaving his briefcase on the floor by the door. He could barely stay on his feet. "Please... please, Mr. Speck," he said. "My partner has the rest." The words just popped out.

"Your partner?" said Speck, who was by then directly across the room from Maxwell, who had moved nearer to his desk to collect the blue file and stood directly in front of the wide window that looked across California Street, and Speck was near the office door. They had rotated positions within the room. "Your *assistant* has more of the data on this reactor than *you* have?" Speck asked rather incredulously. It all sounded to Martin Speck like a ruse.

"Yes! Yes! *He* actually did it... *he* solved the cold fusion problem! Not *me*," said Maxwell shrinking into abject cowardice, admitting for the second time in two days that he'd stolen the glory. "That's why *he* has the notes on how it's done and I don't!" Max added emphatically. Dr. Umberto was flamboyant and he was brilliant, too, but he was not a brave man and this was the worst case scenario for someone with his constitution. Even as it was happening, Maxwell saw that he was pleading.

"That would be Preston Cook?" asked Speck.

"Yes, that's right" confirmed Max. "But... but I can get in touch with him and... and we can destroy the evidence... just get rid of *everything*! You don't have to worry about that, Mr. Speck. You won't see any more of this from us," said Max in his best effort at protecting his colleague and himself.

Martin was efficient at his job and he was not one to waste time. Torture was not his game or his intention. He just took care of business when it was time, and this was the time. He raised his fifty caliber handgun quickly and immediately fired a muffled round that went straight through Maxwell's chest, straight through his beating heart. The bullet ripped out a wet and messy crater the size of a softball in Maxwell's back. Dr. Umberto staggered rearward a couple of steps, a wide-eyed dead man standing upright, before crumpling in a pile under his favorite window.

But as Maxwell was falling to the floor that morning, Martin Speck's antennae-like ears were picking up sounds behind him as the office door opened, and as smoothly as a cat, he pivoted on a foot, swiveled to his side and knelt down on one knee while he brought up the Desert Eagle toward a startled individual standing just outside in the hall. But in a sliver of an instant the startled man in the doorway was producing a Walther PPK 9 mm handgun from inside his jacket. Time virtually stopped between these two men and not a half second truly passed, feeling like a full minute, as they eyed one another before Speck got off a round! But Bobby Skylar was a professional, too, and he saw what was coming as he dropped to his left out of the doorway at the very instant the .50 caliber bullet tore half the door jamb away in splinters and blew a sizeable hole in the plaster wall across the hallway. Bobby elected not to get into a weapons war with this assassin, already concluding the stranger was probably the notorious and mysterious Cain.

Bobby Skylar backed away down the hall with his Walther PPK raised on stiff arms, firing a couple of measured shots across the doorway just to keep Cain at bay in the office and then Bobby sprinted down the staircase and out of the physics building. His heart was pounding and the image of his old friend falling backward with blood spurting from his chest was vivid in his mind. Unfortunately, Bobby continued to make errors in Special Group judgment as he heard himself audibly vowing to "get that bastard, no matter what," while his professional voice was reminding him he should have no emotional involvement in those events. Emotional involvement was usually fatal. At the same time he was realizing he may be one of the very few living Special Group agents who had actually seen Cain in the flesh and lived to consider it.

Martin Speck waited a beat after the initial shots were fired, and then he moved toward the hallway and carefully looked toward the head of the stairs, the stairs down which Bobby Skylar had escaped. But Speck wasn't worried. Those things didn't bother him. He'd been intruded upon before in the middle of his business around the globe and he knew he would not be lingering. None of those earlier sightings had coalesced into a cogent picture of him. Generally, his adversaries didn't even know his gender. Martin walked back to where he had been standing when he killed Maxwell Umberto and he looked at the dead man's face for a moment.

Maxwell's bright blue eyes were still wide open. Then Speck noticed that a chunk of Maxwell's heart tissue had hit the glass on the window behind him after he was shot and it was sliding slowly down the window pane leaving a greasy trail like a big crimson slug. The bullet itself had deflected, as bullets do, and exited into the wall below the window. Martin Speck examined the piece of muscle on the glass. Each time the killing is different and each time it's unique how the bits and pieces fly. Then he saw students playing American football out on the athletic field across California Street, some eight or ten young men running plays and tackling each other in a pick-up game. He shook his head in dismay as he watched them and he thought to himself how crude American football is compared to European football, or soccer. American football is just not civilized, he thought. It has no finesse and it is so violent.

Before leaving, Martin Speck opened the window for oxygen and then he distributed some pale gritty powdered napalm that looked like beach-sand around Maxwell's CTU office. He also uncoiled a small length of fuse, inserting one end into a small mound of the powder and he lit the free end of the fuse.

Speck walked out the door without looking back. Powdered napalm wasn't really napalm in any way chemically and it was really too coarse to be a powder, but it was called powdered napalm because of the violent and billowing conflagration that could be rendered with very small quantities. It was extraordinarily intense. Martin Speck had carried his small supply to CTU in a zip lock bag. By the time he was in the courtyard heading for his car, the entire office space was engulfed in furious brilliant flames. Expansive black and orange clouds poured from the open window. The young men across California Street stopped their uncivilized game of American football to watch the fire in the physics building while at the same time Bobby Skylar stealthily tracked Martin Speck across the campus toward his car.

Speck was fast-forwarding on this agenda in his mind and he calculated the intruder with the Walther PPK was another agent who was most likely following him even while he walked to his car. CTU faculty members and staff don't sport semi-automatic handguns and campus security guards wear uniforms. But Martin Speck didn't care. The guy wasn't going to get in his way. Agent, or cop, or nosey civilian, it did not matter.

Martin Speck had little difficulty ditching his shadow, Bobby Skylar, and it would have been the same if roles were reversed. Both of these agents knew what they were doing and cutting off a tail in traffic is elementary training in their line of work. High speed, rubber-burning car chases, and acrobatic foot pursuits across rooftops are usually only a phenomenon of the cinema. None of that happened when Cain lost Skylar in minutes after leaving Tech-U.

By nightfall, Maxwell Umberto's stylish townhouse would also be gloriously in flame just as had been his Tech-U office. His DeKoonings and Dalis were going up in sparks and smoke of volcanic coloration. Even with the Pasadena Fire Department deployed in force, the powdered napalm would do its job beautifully and nothing tangible would survive. If any records of the research had been there, they were history by then, which was altogether the point.

Agent Skylar did not choose to put Maxwell's town house at the top of his list of locations where Cain might turn up. Following that brief exchange of bullets in the physics building, after Martin Speck had dumped Bobby using quick and unexpected turns on yellow lights and gunning his rented white BMW 745i along routes concocted for the sole purpose of cutting off a tail, Bobby Skylar repaired to his Doubletree hotel room to connect with his boss in Washington. When news of Dr. Umberto's murder was sent to Digger Mac Brown, there was a longer than expected delay in response, several hours of delay as reconsiderations at Special Group were undertaken. And when instructions did come back over the agency's secure network, Bobby's mission had been altered significantly. He was still supposed to quiet the buzz about cold fusion, take it off the market, but he was supposed to *protect* the remaining individual who may know how it worked, Preston Cook. Now it seemed that Dr. Umberto's assistant in the discovery was seen has perhaps having some value going forward.

So it was late in the day of Maxwell's murder that Bobby Skylar went to see the reclusive, rather unknown physicist, Dr. Preston Cook, who was tucked away innocently in his modest craftsman house with his homemade laboratory in northern Pasadena. Digger had agreed that is where Cain would be going soon enough, so that's where Skylar went later that morning, rolling his leased Taurus slowly to a stop by the curb not far away from where Preston, his family, and the suspicious Saudi man were struggling with recent tragic developments and wondering what they should do next.

CHAPTER 48

It was unimaginable to think things could go well when Samantha came home the night of Ahmad's arrival, the night before Maxwell was killed. Preston was going to have to explain to his wife the presence of the heretofore unknown Arabian young man in the house, a young man who, by the way, was also on the lam for murdering a UCLA med student! There was *no* possibility Samantha would just say, "Oh, okay." A fight erupted almost instantly right in front of Ahmad and Dalton. Sam was not having any of it. She didn't accept the wild stories of danger brought into the house by this interloping Arab any more than she accepted them from Maxwell earlier in the day. After half an hour of incriminations, Samantha said she had enough. She said she was going to spend the night at the college and she left, remarking over her shoulder that when she came home in the morning she didn't want to see strangers in house. And she didn't want to hear any more about spies and intrigue, either! Samantha had retreated to university before, upset after a scrap, but this felt different to Preston. He wondered if it was the last straw.

It was quiet in the Cook house after Samantha was gone. There was no chit-chat and no more discussion of events. After calming Ahmad, who was thoroughly embarrassed and tried to leave, Preston persuaded Ahmad into remain until the next day. Preston knew the young man had nowhere to go, so he said Ahmad could sleep in Dalton's room on a sleeping bag. Perhaps Preston Cook's reasons were not sound, but he believed Ahmad. There was strangeness everywhere. Preston did make an effort to assure both Dalton and their guest that Samantha would be better in the morning. "She's emotional," he had said, but for the most part, it was wishful thinking. Things remained tense in the house, but Preston did succeed in getting the threesome through to dawn.

Samantha surprised Preston when she staggered through the front door early the next day after having slept in her CTU office, gushing tears and sobbing! She was thoroughly distraught, beside herself with worry and fear, and she was burbling something about a fire at CTU and Maxwell having been killed in it! Christ almighty, thought Preston, catching her in his arms as she stumbled toward him in the kitchen where he had been making coffee.

Preston was disoriented by the unbelievable words he was hearing from his wife as he wrapped his arms around her. It couldn't be real, he thought. Fear and confusion were not familiar states for either Preston or Samantha, and whatever actually happened over at the campus, it was obviously overwhelming to Sam. But what the hell was it? Max could not have been killed in a fire? That seemed absurd. Had the world run amok? A Saudi man on the run from the police appeared out of nowhere with conspiracy stories, and then Maxwell dies in a fire at the university? Samantha Day-Steiner was collapsing in sobs while Preston was trying to hold her up. "Sam… Sam", he was saying.

Fortunately in those first minutes, young Dalton was still upstairs in his room with Ahmad. They weren't immediately confronted with the scene in the kitchen.

Whimpering, sobbing, crying, Samantha was carrying on in a way that Preston had never seen from her. He could hear her insisting it was the *research*! It's all about the *research*! Maxwell's murder and the ransacking and the arson were all about the *research*! She was clearly scared. "You were right!" she said. "Max was right! Something horrible is happening!" she cried. She was trembling. Samantha Day-Steiner was in such of an out-of-control state that Preston realized he had to take charge of her and calm her down… which was not the easiest of tasks and not his customary role, but that's what had to be done. It took him time to decipher what she was saying through her sobbing. She was a mess.

Preston took his wife by the shoulders when they were finally sitting on the living room sofa. He was trying to be as in-charge as he was able and he lifted her face so he could look into her puffy reddened eyes. "Samantha!" he said. "Samantha, I know something terrible has happened, but I'm having trouble understanding you. We are all going to be okay. Do you hear me? You are saying there has been a fire at the school and Max was involved. Tell me exactly what has happened." He spoke firmly, which was not like him when talking to Samantha.

Strangely, this seemed to help and Preston's wife began to slow down, choking up here and there, but able to speak a bit more clearly. And eventually the situation, the story that bubbled up from Samantha, very clearly aligned with the story that Ahmad Mulham had been feeding to Preston and Dalton the night before. Ahmad had said that Maxwell was in danger. Secret agents representing various invested parties around the world were after the research results. Samantha's and Ahmad's two stories fit together in a horrific way and were consistent. Ahmad had said it was a lethal game, because the stakes were so very high, globally high. The process of destroying cold fusion along with any memory of it may already be underway. It didn't look good.

As he let Samantha unload what she had heard that afternoon and earlier from Dr. Umberto, and as he continued to stare into her eyes and present himself as stable a partner as his wiggly, gelatinous insides would allow, Preston was already beginning to consider avenues of escape and how to protect his family. If this *was* about the research – and it certainly seemed to be – then how long would it be before some maniac showed up at their door with a flame thrower to incinerate everybody!

By different means it had become evident to Samantha and to Preston, too, that many powerful people were not going to embrace the staggering world-changing potential of what had been discovered in their converted garage laboratory. Why a discovery of such monumental humanitarian proportions would be quashed by various antagonistic commercial interests was beyond comprehension to Preston. Not so for Samantha Day-Steiner, who was up to her neck in a personal understanding of the whys and wherefores: an unimaginable sum of money.

Dead Maxwell Umberto's press release to the world had never taken place. And professional papers had yet to be published by Preston Cook. Nobody at CTU, including President Holcomb and Umberto's and Cook's closest colleagues in the Physics Department, knew anything significant about the cold fusion research and how it worked. Maxwell Umberto's uncontrollable braggadocio had apparently and unfortunately spawned curiosity all over the globe. But if all the rumors and implications were added together, they amounted to zilch about how the miracle had come to be.

CHAPTER 49

Pasadena Detective Stanley Lau and Los Angeles Detective Fitzgerald Jack were sifting through the remarkable, thoroughly charred remains of Maxwell Umberto's town house on Orange Grove Boulevard in Pasadena. Unbelievably, no one in the affluent complex was injured as the intensity of the fire seemed to be quite focused, absolutely consuming nearly every item that Maxwell Umberto had owned, leaving each a black, brittle variation of itself, while adjacent residences had been mostly spared. There was smoke damage and some charring next door, but amazingly very little nearby property had been seriously damaged given the conflagration in the Umberto unit. Neither Fitzgerald nor Lau had seen anything like it before, but they had no experience with the effects of powdered napalm.

The awkward, gangly associate that Lau brought along on his investigations like an exotic pet was roaming in the background, twitching and mumbling, nervously touching debris here and there with his toe, as confused as everyone else. Fitzgerald Jack could not help but glance at the peculiar specimen every now and then out of curiosity, as any normal person would, but he didn't ask Stanley Lau about him. There was clearly a bond of some kind between them.

Arson experts, borrowed from the county, were on hand, too, shaking their heads, perplexed at the way this volatile event had contained itself. They were selecting samples and examining the ruins in ways that neither Lau nor Jack could do. But as two police professionals with an odd bent and stranger still *the same* odd bent, Lau and Jack wanted to commune with the scene as though inspiration would float up to them from the ruins. It was a bit of hocus pocus, maybe, that they couldn't defend rationally if pressed, but both of the investigators wanted to do it, and the technique, imagined or not, had worked for each of them in the past. So, they were brothers of a unique sort, reviewing, discussing, contemplating, and fantasizing what might be going on in these strange developments and what they might portend.

The two detectives had already hashed over the fact – unknown to the public – that a fifty caliber bullet had knocked a hole through now-incinerated Maxwell Umberto's chest before he burned and the bullet had lodged in a fractured, solid oak stud inside the stucco wall behind Umberto. It appeared that a matching slug had penetrated the hallway wall across from Umberto's office door, passing through another professor's office, where it destroyed an autographed photo of the 1942 Manhattan Project team. The photograph had been hanging on the farther outside wall for thirty years. Afterwards the heavy bullet had exited the physics building, leaving a four inch hole in the masonry behind the Manhattan Project photo. The spent projectile finally struck something it could not penetrate somewhere downrange. Desert Eagle bullets have scary momentum.

Lau and Jack had already discussed the connection between the dead UCLA student and his guest, Ahmad Mulham, and now this dead physicist at CTU. But they couldn't yet pull together the whys and wherefores that made them a whole.

A call from the State Department indicated a federal agent would be coming because of what had happened, but as it turned out the two detectives would not in any way be relieved of the investigation when the agent arrived. After a couple of telephone conversations with Washington, the two police chiefs in LA and in Pasadena, informed lieutenants Lau and Jack that they would both be up to their ears in this highly confidential investigation. They were not going to be reassigned. The messages to the two detectives from their respective departments were remarkably similar.

It was all a matter of government resources. Unlike some federal agencies, Special Group did not have nor did it want a phalanx of G-men descending on a situation, with Washington experts kicking up a cloud of dust wherever it went. That's not the way Special Group operated even though the developments in Pasadena were especially sensitive with highly charged international implications. Strangely, the California adventure was wholly within American borders and in recent decades Special Group missions had exclusively migrated overseas. But, overseas or not, the fewer investigators on the scene the better was the way Special Group figured. They were not the Army, the Navy Seals, the FBI, the CIA, Blackwater, or any other platoon-driven arm of the United States' government. They usually relied on quiet, well-informed professionals doing their jobs with surgical precision. Cain's preferred solitary style actually fit very snuggly into the strategies of Special Group.

Consequently, the only person Lau and Jack had to anticipate flashing his federal badge was a single agent named Bobby Skylar. At the time, they didn't know he was already in town. Nor did they know he was a personal friend of dead Dr. Umberto. They knew nothing at all really except they had some very strange and inexplicably related crimes on their hands, one on the west side of Los Angeles and the other in Pasadena. In any case, both Lau and Jack were told by their bosses that Agent Skylar would require the absolute cooperation of the local police departments to fulfill his mission. Patriotism had been evoked somewhere along the line in those Washington phone calls, but patriotism lost its mojo in the police chiefs' retelling because both chiefs hated it when the feds intervened.

Catching the bad guys, however, was a resonating note for Lau and Jack and any other clean cop on a beat; so that part of the objective came through loud and clear. They were eager to see how and why those very big bullet holes in West LA and in Pasadena could be connected.

As Bobby Skylar prepared himself to walk up to the front door of the Cook house, as he sat contemplatively in his rental, he knew an LAPD Detective named Fitzgerald Jack and a PPD Detective named Stanley Lau were waiting on him to get in touch. He figured he'd get to them soon enough.

"Poor, poor Max", Bobby said to himself out loud while he reviewed images in his mind of them back at Yale, whooping it up. Then Bobby Skylar heaved a deep sigh, another rarity for him when on the job.

Maybe he'd been in this kind of work for too many years. He missed his wife and his family tremendously and these were sentiments that had not plagued him so much on past assignments. He was a professional and he had always maintained strict boundaries in his work-life balance, as the touchy-feely folks liked to say.

Bobby's original mission was to stifle the cold fusion research. He was to help maintain the energy-world's status quo. But now, Agent Skylar's job had pivoted one-hundred and eighty degrees, as he understood it from the last words he heard from Digger in Washington, D.C. The twist on his assignment was welcomed by Bobby because it was easier to pursue in a new and more nostalgic mood. In truth, he was beginning to realize that perhaps it was time to retire from the chaos of his job. But on that morning in October 2005 there was still work to be done before retirement could enter the picture. As the agent glanced at the Cook house not far away, he

shook his head. It was the first time in his Special Group career of
more than thirty years, Bobby Skylar came to the conclusion he just
wanted to go home. He'd had enough.

When Agent Skylar heard a thump on the passenger window of
his Taurus and he looked to his right, he found a very large bearded
man pointing an Army issue Colt .45 semi-automatic sidearm
straight at him, Bobby knew right away his assignment had taken yet
one more bizarre and unexpected turn. Who was this guy? The man
was gesturing with the .45 for him to get out of the car and Bobby's
imagination ran quickly through a rather extensive collection of
strategies he'd learned for exactly this kind of situation, and most
of them led to killing the other guy. But for whatever reason, maybe
related to his melancholia and longing for his family, Bobby chose
not to terminate this large fellow outside his passenger window. So,
Skylar climbed deliberately out of his rented Taurus and raised his
hands just as he had been told.

In case it was a robbery, Bobby said as simply as he could, "I
don't have much money".

With both hands Big Buster Bernard held his Colt straight at
Skylar and said, "What are you doing out here?"

"Nothing," said Bobby, "just about to visit some folks here."

"I've seen ya here before. You ain't no visitor, pal!" said Buster.

That was when Bobby Skylar dragged up a memory of the biker
going past him in the opposite direction the day he'd drifted by the
Cook residence just to see where it was. Ah, yes, he thought, this is
that burly guy! He remembered they had actually made eye contact
at the time.

"I know who you are," said Bobby, deciding to go straight at it
and not mess around. He spoke with assurance.

His strategy worked because Buster pulled back ever so slightly
and asked, "What the fuck are you talkin' about?"

Bobby continued to stand there with his hands in the air like he was being robbed while the .45 was leveled at him across the roof of the rented Taurus. "Well… I recall a couple of days ago I was driving by here and *you* came along on your Harley-Davidson motorcycle and you pulled into that driveway… right over there." He gestured with an elbow toward the house next to the Cook's. "You really gave me the once-over!" said Bobby trying to be light. "Do you remember that?"

"Are you a cop?" said Buster.

"No," said Bobby.

"What do you want?" said Buster, the interrogation having been momentarily turned around.

"It's a long story," said Agent Skylar. "But… I'm trying to protect your neighbor."

"*Protect*?" said Buster, sarcastically.

"Yes, I'm trying to protect him. Like I said, it's a long story and I'd be happy to explain, but this isn't the best way to do it, standing here like this in the middle of the road. Do you know if Dr. Cook is home?" Bobby said, figuring that cutting to the chase might be best.

CHAPTER 50

Opening his front door to find yet another stranger, an older preppy guy standing there, was yet another surreal experience for an already shaken Preston Cook. Behind Preston in the living room of his house was his ashen, grieving wife, Samantha, still distraught from Maxwell's fiery death. There seemed to be no relief for thread-bare souls on that October day as over-the-top events and sudden turns in the road just kept coming. The newcomer had both hands in the air like he was under arrest. The world was going mad.

"Here's the asshole been snoopin' around!" said Big Buster, from his wide-legged stance to the side. His Colt .45 was raised directly toward the preppy stranger's head. "Found him out there eye-ballin' yer house again."

Ahmad Mulham had crept onto the scene with Dalton when they heard activity at the front door. Preston and Sam had already carefully shared with them the story of Maxwell's death in flames at the University. Samantha had sped right past her concerns about the Arab's presence in the house and had moved on to broader worry for the safety of the whole family. A more convoluted set of circumstances and characters coming together in one setting would be difficult to imagine outside a French farce. No one at that address in Pasadena, including Buster with his Army .45 at the ready and the preppy stranger with his hands in the air, was normal.

Ironically, twelve-year old Dalton was probably the most stable person in the Cook household, because for the Down syndrome boy complication was a normal day. Life was never predictable for Dalton. He had learned to cope.

"I can explain," said Bobby as calmly as he could, while he was standing on the porch with his hands raised. "You are in grave danger," he said directly to Preston Cook.

"Oh, Jesus," thought Preston but he didn't say it. His knees did go weak for a second upon hearing the words, but he regained himself before his eyes rolled up into his skull. None of this adventure was what Preston imagined being a nuclear physicist might involve when he and his dead friend, Maxwell Umberto, earned their PhDs those many years ago at MIT, after they had crossed the commencement stage, wearing the same new doctoral hoods, laughing like idiots, and threw their mortar boards high into the air. In those days they wanted to change the world for the better. Improve life for everyone.

It took Preston Cook a beat to respond to the stranger while all those thoughts were rushing through his memory in a torrent. No one else had moved a muscle.

"Alright. Come inside," Dr. Cook finally was able to grunt as he gestured toward Buster to lower his weapon, which the big man did, reluctantly.

As Bobby came into the house, he instantly recognized the Arab young man standing to the rear of the living room with Dalton. After all, the agent had followed Ahmad across the Tech-U campus from Umberto's office, but Bobby Skylar kept that fact to himself. Yet it did give him pause when their eyes met even though Ahmad could never have recognized Skylar. Bobby already knew the young Arab was a suspect in a murder on the Westside and he guessed rightly that the Arab would soon become a suspect in Umberto's death, too. The police would likely connect the two homicides. It was logical. But Agent Skylar happened to be on the scene when Dr. Umberto was killed, having confronted Cain in a brief exchange of gunfire, so

Bobby Skylar knew to a certainty that the Arab young man was not the killer of Umberto, no matter what implications surfaced in the news. And in quick non-scientific reckoning, the fact that Ahmad hadn't committed the *second* murder led Bobby to think he probably didn't commit the *first* murder. More likely it was just more debris left behind by Cain, of which there is customarily quite a bit when that particular operative was moving around aggressively. Bobby had been witness to the carnage just a year earlier in Johannesburg where two Chinese businessmen were found executed in their jail cells only days prior to their opening testimony in a trial that involved serious money and unlicensed gold mines. A pair of fifty caliber projectiles had truncated the men's interest in gold and had saved Cain's employer from some embarrassing explanations to the South African government. Cain had only been in Johannesburg forty-eight hours to accomplish his objective. His targets were under heavy guard and collateral damage left four guards dead, who happened to be in the way. That was how Cain operated.

Bobby knew there had to be some connection between Cain and the murdered UCLA student. This young Arabian's interest in Umberto's involvement with cold fusion research might be the link. Skylar's thirty years of sneaking through convoluted conspiracies had given him a pretty good nose in this kind of situation and his knowledge of Cain cemented his theory. It also put a little juice into what he was going to have to say to Preston Cook and his family as soon as possible on that strange day.

Agent Skylar had not actually seen Dr. Samantha Day-Steiner in his reconnaissance, but he certainly knew who she was - sitting there with her puffy eyes - and what role she played in Maxwell Umberto's life at the end. In spite of the genuine affection Agent Skylar had for his old friend, Max, Bobby Skylar did not think this last chapter in Umberto's time on earth had been handled in good form. Stealing the credit for the research of his partner was not like the old Maxwell, who was ambitious, but always ethical. And having an affair with his colleague's wife… well, that was totally off the scale for the Max that Bobby Skylar had known in college, even though they had certainly done their share of skirt chasing back at Yale. In those days there were always rules, and buddies' girlfriends were definitely off limits.

Bobby wondered if it was the Hollywood connection that had jaded Umberto in recent years, or was it simply envy for Dr. Cook's over-the-top accomplishment. Was the highly regarded mathematician, Samantha Day-Steiner, as vulnerable and needy as Maxwell? A quick scan of faces and body language, plus a very fast feed from his internal antennae, led Bobby to the conclusion that Preston Cook knew zero about the love affair between his wife and his best friend, Umberto. And, of course, *none of them* in that living room that evening had the slightest inkling about murderous Cain on the prowl. These poor souls were babes in the woods, every one of them, commiserating there in that little house in Pasadena. They may realize there is danger, but they had no idea of how imminent it was. Not a clue.

Skylar looked at all the people staring straight at him. How much time did he have? If Cain took out those incarcerated Chinese in forty-eight hours, anything could happen, at any moment, even here in residential Pasadena. Bobby was getting sweaty-nervous as the clock ticked away with this particular adversary on the move out there. Agent Skylar scoped this neighborhood in the first place because he knew Cain would show up sooner or later looking for the research assistant. Cain may or may not know that Cook was actually the principal investigator. Bobby Skylar wouldn't have known about it, either, if Maxwell hadn't spilled his guts in a fit of terror as worldwide resistance to cold fusion writhed around him and slithered up his legs like snakes.

Amazingly, Dr. Cook had remained fairly oblivious to the excitement about his invention around the world. Maxwell had stolen Preston's research and by so doing he had turned the spotlight completely on himself. But all of that was history when Bobby Skylar was forced at gunpoint into the Cook living room, where everyone looked at one another, mystified.

While looking at those naïve faces, Bobby shivered because he knew without a doubt that the killer Cain was on his way. There was absolutely no other scenario to consider. It was a matter of time. Still, he'd been in more tight spots than a reckless gigolo and he had his job to do. There he was with a lot of fantastical things to tell these unknowing innocent people, to win them over, and to get their butts in gear. It was a very tall order, even for charming Bobby, but he had to find a way.

Skylar glanced at the burly biker whose military pistol now hung downward in his right hand as if it might be needed at any second and provided only a steely glower as his version of hospitality. Maybe the young Arab man would understand, calculated Skylar. Maybe *he* could be converted into a quick ally thought Bobby as he sat down on a dining room chair that had been hauled into the living room for him by the strange boy, Dalton.

The federal agent knew quite a bit about the Saudi fellow, information collected through Special Group intelligence, which included Ahmad's respected OPAC family's roots and his rather distinguished father. Therefore, Skylar strategized that he should zero in on the Arab.

CHAPTER 51

Soon after he was back at the Beverly Hills Hotel, following the world's least spectacular car chase in which he'd easily eluded the man who had interrupted his clean-up at CTU, Martin Speck had collected the intruder's identity. It didn't take him long, because he had noted the license plate number of the rented Ford Taurus that made its feeble attempt at keeping up with Cain's BMW after he departed the killing scene. Speck wasn't the least concerned about anyone jotting down his own license plate number. He knew it would only lead to a planned dead end, a planned dead end Special Group had failed to put in place for their Agent Skylar.

Cain had his own kind of intelligence on his payroll. It was fascinating to Cain how much information was available in the world when the purchase price reaches a critical mass. Everyone has his or her price, they say, an old saw that had been repeatedly validated throughout Martin Speck's career. Even the United States' Special Group, as small and innocuous as it had labored to remain over the years, cutting corners, limiting personnel and exposure, was nonetheless partially visible on the international espionage radar screen. Yet by the time Speck was lying on his back in a softly lit spa at the Beverly Hills Hotel having his high back muscles stretched gently by a Filipino masseuse, by the time the aroma therapy fragrances where filling his nostrils with their herbal scents and strong oiled hands ran up beneath his cervical vertebrae, rhythmically pulling out the stress of the day, he was beginning to realize that Special

Group, unlike so many government agencies around the world, did manage to maintain a modicum of secrecy in their operations. For instance, there wasn't *as much* information about Bobby Skylar as perhaps there might have been for one of the more storied FBI men and women, or one of the ubiquitous CIA agents scuttling around in every troubled corner of the world. That said, there *was* a low level quantity of information on Cain's new opponent.

Martin Speck discovered where the Special Group agent lived and he discovered information about the man's family in the upscale townhouse neighborhood of Foggy Bottom in Washington, D.C. Cain even uncovered some operations they had in common, including the one involving the pair of jailed Chinese businessmen in South Africa who simply had to go. At that point, in Martin Speck's mind, it seemed Bobby Skylar might have to go, too, if the American agent continued to stand near to Speck's targets. There would be nothing personal in the killing that might happen, only cleanliness. But Cain understood sophisticated government agents like Skylar can take a little extra attention in getting the job done and that was what Martin Speck was visualizing as he closed his eyes and relaxed into the steady pull of the masseuse.

Detective Fitzgerald Jack lived alone in Hollywood, on Gower, in a quaintly indigenous two-bedroom apartment nestled within his LAPD precinct. He didn't really have much business on the Westside. The UCLA med student's murder was the exception, not the rule on his beat. Most of his investigations fell within a five mile drive of where he lived modestly in an older building that had "character" as the realtor said to him when he went to look at it years earlier. The complex was all Spanish stucco with graceful archways, surrounding a small, quiet and well-tended courtyard with a gurgling fountain where numerous fan-leafed ferns and ten-foot dense fichus trees protected the courtyard from the world beyond the wrought-iron gate that led inside. The fountain space was sequestered, if one could ignore the occasional helicopter, or the occasional siren echoing along the deteriorating brick buildings on Hollywood Boulevard, or the odd midnight shouting match in the street. If one could look past all of that, it was really quite serene.

At forty-plus years of age, Fitzgerald's reputation in the department had lifted off and he'd been promoted recently, too, after a couple of high profile busts, so he could actually afford a sweeter upscale environment to which he might retreat at night, but in October of 2005 he still favored a low profile. Maybe it was a conservative sensibility bequeathed to him by his college professor dad, who taught English lit at UCLA. Or maybe it was because Fitzgerald Jack was a frustrated painter, an artistic side of him that relished the edgy, restless environment of Hollywood. Or maybe it came from his gritty, retired, police detective mom who had little patience for the high life. In any case, the tony upscale world of Los Angeles held no appeal in those days to Fitzy, as his friends called him. He was more in tune with reality right where he was.

So, while Martin Speck, a man whom Fitzgerald Jack had yet to meet, was relaxing in the spa at the Beverly Hills Hotel, LAPD Detective Jack was pulling off his tired herring bone sports coat and tossing it across the back of a chair in his hardwood-floor living room in Hollywood. His taste in décor was a work in progress, one might generously say, not that he didn't care about his living space but his police life had simply gotten in the way of that concern. So, he continued to live in an apartment that was furnished with a minimalistic hodge-podge of accoutrements. There was no longer a special woman in his life at that juncture having had his heart seriously broken twice, so sprucing up the place sank to lower priority. He absently considered he would attend to that feature of his lifestyle further down the road, when it mattered. Right then, it didn't. His only concessions to personal comfort were his easel and his oils, which were not so prominently displayed because he used the second bedroom as his studio where many an off-duty hour was spent with brushes and canvas. In truth, he was tormented by the pull between his career and his art. Humans are complicated animals. He shared far more with the assassin Cain than he could possibly have known at that time but, while it would take years, those commonalties would eventually unfurl.

Fitzgerald went to his refrigerator and pulled out a Samuel Adams lager while he puzzled over the fact he had heard nothing from this federal agent Bobby Skylar character on whose signal the entire investigation turned. Everybody involved was in a holding pattern. Lt. Jack had been working on his own impatience issues, after the captain to whom he reported at the precinct had highlighted that flaw for him on his annual performance review. The captain had suggested to Fitzgerald that impatience was not considered a virtue in police work. It was a criticism that came in the wake of Fitzgerald Jack having laid open a movie industry drug ring that resulted in multiple press-worthy arrests and generated some political heat. A relaxed lets-see-what-happens quality was always elusive for Detective Jack. Getting to the bottom of things was simply one of his natural inclinations. It was in his genes. He was a brilliant law enforcement officer and privately he no longer believed he was going to embrace patience.

On that October evening in 2005 Fitzgerald was stewing over the UCLA and the CTU killings, the whereabouts of the Ahmad Mulham character, and the whereabouts of a Special Group agent named Skylar. The lieutenant wanted to get things done and his tendency toward action never would dissipate over the ensuing years.

As a result Fitzgerald would often be the first one in the face of the bad guy, for better or for worse.

Lt. Jack plopped down onto his well-worn couch in front of his 27 inch analog television and he began clicking through the cable channels, while he reviewed in his mind the facts of these two homicides and the involvement of federal agents.

Suddenly, a huge blonde tabby cat, as fat as a summa wrestler, jumped up on the coffee table where Fitzgerald had crossed his stocking feet after kicking off his shoes, and the cat meowed loudly and demandingly and it turned this way and that right in front of Fitzgerald to make sure he was noticed.

"Well! There you are, Watson! Where have you been?" said Fitzy expansively to the hefty feline named after Sherlock Holmes's curmudgeonly assistant. The big cat balanced his way up the LAPD detective's legs and settled on his stomach as though he should have been there all along. The cat spread completely across the detective's midsection. He was as big as a bed pillow. Watson weighed twenty pounds. This was the largest domestic cat that anyone, who had ever met Watson, had ever seen. Guests would be slack-jawed at the sight of the portly creature moving silently around Detective Jack's apartment like a plush toy that had come alive.

Fitzy began stroking the cat's back immediately when it settled down, their ritual together. Then Detective Jack said, "I've got a puzzle for you, my fat, fuzzy colleague. I guess you could say this puzzle would be from the 'science' category. Okay? Are you ready, Watson?" Fitzy looked at the large cat dead in the eyes and got another loud meow in response. "What do the words 'cold fusion' mean to you? Huh?" he said to the cat.

He continued to run his hand gently along the cat's spine and he waited, as if an answer might be forthcoming. Fitzy's touch was greeted with a slightly arched back and a loud purr, but there was no cogent answer from Watson just yet.

"Ah. I see. Yes, it *is* mysterious, Watson. I understand. Still... I *know* I've heard that phrase somewhere," continued Fitzgerald, "but I'm not sure where. Maybe I just read it. Is that it? Did you read it, too?" he said and scratched Watson's ears. Watson purred even louder. He sounded like an outboard motor. Fitzy sometimes wished he had named him Evinrude. "Cold fusion," Fitzgerald repeated to his associate, Watkins the cat. "What the hell *is* that?"

It didn't take too much poking around online for Fitzgerald Jack to find out enough information on the dead professor's research efforts to start to see a picture of the problem. Sitting at his laptop in his Hollywood apartment, while his 27 inch analog television mumbled in the background, Detective Jack discovered what "cold fusion" means. Google didn't keep secrets. Fitzgerald ended up refreshing himself on the Fields-Parker flash-in-the-pan phenomenon that was in the news a decade earlier. Fitzgerald recalled that he read about table-top nuclear reactors. It was sensational news at the time and had a lot of folks hopeful for a nano-second before the entire adventure turned out to be unsupportable by further investigation. Although Fitzgerald only had a mild understanding of the physics involved, he could easily see how such a development would catch the attention of the world. Cheap, portable, clean, and endless energy for everyone would be a revolution! Is that what Maxwell Umberto had done? Why wouldn't everybody in the scientific community be applauding such a stupendous achievement and regale in it? Umberto was at venerable CTU, for heaven's sake! The whole thing was all very peculiar. If cold fusion had happened, how could it be so quiet? Of course, at that time, Detective Jack did not know the real work had been carried out in a back yard garage by a loose cannon researcher who wouldn't give up. That's why nobody knew about the findings. That's why it had not been in the newspapers. Yet, at the same time, Fitzgerald Jack instantly saw the development as a formula for heavily funded and powerful resistance and it had a strong potential for murder, as well. There would be many a fortune in the swing of things, if Umberto had solved the cold fusion puzzle. Detective Jack's instincts were not far off the mark. A very possible international dynamic was beginning to take shape in Fitzgerald Jack's verdant imagination and this was without LAPD intelligence and without one word from the wayward Agent Skylar. It grew out of Fitzy's speculation alone. He was sure something nasty was forming out there in the fog of strange events and it was most likely well underway.

Detective Jack creaked backward in his chair and stared at the bright laptop screen where his cold fusion findings remained before him and he took a long swig on his second Samuel Adams. Once again, huge Watson jumped from the floor onto the detective's lap and Fitzgerald grunted from the sudden weight before he ran his hand across Watson' silky blonde back again and the tomcat settled down like Fitzy's lap was going to be his evening's nest.

While Fitzgerald stroked Watson, he was beginning to see more clearly why the feds would be involved. He was beginning to wonder why they were not there sooner and why there were not more of them. Heavyweight forces had to be in the works. Fitzy was beginning to see the magnitude of the research outcome… if it had actually occurred. These killings would seem to be random and peculiar to any regular city cop, who was assigned to them, but Lt. Jack could see the deaths may have been linked. He was thinking they may be anything but disconnected and random. The killings may have been the coldest of fusions.

CHAPTER 52

Sitting on the wooden dining room chair that had been dragged into the living room to face the team of inquisitors in Dr. Preston Cook's home that evening, Bobby Skylar at first kept his cards close to his chest explaining why he had come to the house. He was there to" help", was what he offered in the beginning. Bobby did not choose to report right away that Maxwell Umberto had been murdered and that the fire at the college was no accident. Nor did Bobby choose to mention that murdered Max had been *schtuping* Preston's wife. However, agent Skylar *did* reinforce to the gathering in that modest house that oil interests with Herculean power in Washington and other global capitals might be aroused if Preston's revolutionary energy invention came to the market without proper delivery, using words suggested to him by Digger Mac Brown.

So, in that vein of conversation, Bobby did lead to revealing he was, in fact, a government agent. He said this without getting bogged down in what Special Group was, but Bobby did not miss a chance to emphasize there were agents from foreign governments in town and they all had the same mission, which was to put an end to the cold fusion threat. These words were received by Dr. Cook and Dr. Steiner-Day with debilitating dismay. Both of their faces went white. It was their worst fears confirmed.

"Can you show us credentials?" asked Sam softly.

"In my profession, credentials are a death sentence. You'll simply have to believe what I say," said Skylar.

"Why would anyone be our enemy?" said Preston honestly in his naive best.

"It's the *money*, Preston, dear." said Samantha quietly.

"Damn it!" shouted Big Buster, jumping to his feet and waiving around his .45 Army-issue sidearm. "I knew there was somethin' goin' on that weren't right. Somethin' fishy… and it's the damn government, *ain't it*?"

"Whoa, whoa, whoa! Hold on there, pardner!" said Preston, standing up, too, coming back into focus and trying to calm down his survivalist friend, his neighbor and frighteningly large human specimen. "Put down the gun, okay? Let's hear what Mr. Skylar has to say."

"They're out to get us all!" said Buster a bit wild-eyed and a bit scary, but he did sit down again and lower his weapon.

"Okay," said Preston to his biker friend. "Take it easy. Let's listen. And please put your gun on the floor."

Buster studied the Army .45 in his hand, which he hesitantly rested near his foot.

Then they all turned their attention back to their captive, the graying, unshaven preppy guy, who was tired and who sat there with his tie loose in his oxford cloth button-down shirt, watching the action around him and sizing up his situation.

And at that point, Bobby Skylar decided it was the correct moment to look the young Saudi man square in the eyes, the one person that Bobby hoped to recruit as an ally out of this bizarre suburban squad of confused and nervous people. Bobby decided to say directly to Ahmad that he knew who Ahmad was, where he came from, who his family was, why he was there in Pasadena, and why he had been seeking audience with the murdered Dr. Umberto at CTU. Some of it was guesswork and some of it was Special Group intelligence but Skylar's commentary quickly plunged the entire room into a numbed silence. Bobby elaborated on each of his points, including the key role that the elder Mr. Mulham, Ahmad's father, had played in the formation of OPEC decades ago. Bobby Skylar's words came forward in a steady very credible stream that took at least fifteen clock minutes to unfold. His in-depth knowledge of Ahmad Mulham lent credibility to his claim he was a government agent.

Ahmad was like stone during the rendering of his life and purposes, but he was also thankful, because when Agent Skylar was done, Bobby's story fit hand in glove, snugly and convincingly, with the explanations that Ahmad had been offering to his hosts since his arrival. Ahmad was an honest young man. What Bobby Skylar related that afternoon in the Pasadena living room led everyone to believe that the young Saudi was innocent of the charges supposedly floating around out there in the world, charges they had yet to officially hear. It led to them believe in Skylar, too, because all the key points matched the young Arab man's story explicitly. Their stories lined up like stars in the heavens, tales from two complete strangers dropped into their midst. Trust may not have been the most reasonable outcome, but because consistency and predictability were such rare qualities on that extraordinary and exhausting day, a powerful coincidence of information was good enough.

There was a long silence after Bobby's revelations were placed on the table for consumption and although everyone in the room believed what they heard, they also remained stone quiet, contemplating what it meant for each of them. Unease mounted in the room while eyes darted and no one spoke. It felt like there must be one more shoe to drop and there was. Skylar seized the silence to return to his opening proclamation. He only wanted to help. He did not think he should admit he had been sent to Los Angeles to destroy or sidetrack this cold fusion invention like the foreign agents. His original orders where a thing of the past. What Bobby said to those people in

Pasadena about helping them had become his new truth and his new mission and it was one he was personally pleased to embrace.

Agent Skylar found himself disclosing information which he would never have done previously. It was behavior that went entirely against the grain of his training in Special Group. Maybe the training all started to come unglued when he was sent once again to work with his old school chum, Maxwell Umberto, to cajole him and perhaps manipulate him… maybe even terminate his operation with lethal force, if needed. Perhaps that was the final straw, so to speak, in Bobby's professional life. After arriving in Pasadena he had been refreshed by how much he enjoyed his time with his old friend during those long-lost days at Yale, when the sky was the limit and their futures lay at the rainbow's end. What fun they had together! A couple of weeks ago Bobby could feel a shift in his energy toward protecting Dr. Umberto and, by extension, now that focus had moved to the Cook household. Maybe it was the ravages of the years in his grueling dangerous line of work; but for whatever reason Bobby slumped in his hardwood dining room chair in the warm light cast around the living room of that modest three-bedroom home in Pasadena and he studied his hands before speaking, possibly reviewing what those hands had done over the years. Then he said softly, with as much candor as he could muster, "I have a beautiful wife back in Washington D.C. I love this woman with all my heart and soul. And…I haven't been all that present for her during our marriage. I wish I had. If it's at all possible, I want to make it up to her, to spend more time with her, and do things *she* wants to do. She's a wonderful, intelligent, caring woman, an absolute joy. I also have two children, grown up now and on to lives of their own. I want to kiss the soft checks of my grandkids and not end up dead in a ditch somewhere in the Third World. I have *nothing* to gain by coming here tonight and lying to you. My career is at an end. I want to help you and then go home and retire from all of this."

There was something so totally unexpected and sincere in the man's words and manner that even Big Buster Bernard sat back with his Colt .45 lying on the floor. He was surprised and sympathetic, exposing the down-deep creampuff that anyone who really knew him understood. For Preston Cook the sentiments struck so closely to home and to regrets about his presence in his own marriage that he shivered slightly upon hearing them from a stranger.

Samantha was the most cautious. She had far more to lose through investigations into Maxwell Umberto's personal life than anyone in the room. She did not know the agent already had the goods on her, regarding the affair and the wealth she had been pursuing through her lover, her husband's now-dead research partner. So, it was understandable that Samantha spoke first when Bobby's testimonial had come to its conclusion.

"I hope you find what you're looking for, Mr. Skylar," she said sincerely. "How can you help us? Tell us what to do."

"There's at least one significant piece of the scenario that I haven't shared," responded Bobby. "I've said there are agents here, agents who want to quash your cold fusion research, Dr. Cook," and he looked directly at Preston for the first time during his sharing of information. "That part I've told you."

Preston waited, where he sat on the couch, next to his son who was as rapt as everyone else.

Bobby continued, becoming distinctly more assertive with his agenda and with his urgency. "I don't have a real name... we call him 'Cain' at the agency. He is on this assignment." Agent Skylar looked around and found that he had everybody's full attention. "Cain is no one to mess with. He is absolutely deadly. He takes no prisoners. He accomplishes his mission. He kills everyone in his path. And then he disappears."

"Who does he work for?" said Preston rather weakly.

"Any person or government who will pay him. I don't know who has hired him this time. It doesn't matter. This assassin is here in Los Angeles. I saw him at CTU. Your friend Maxwell Umberto did not die in an accidental fire at the college. He was murdered by Cain prior to the fire."

Everyone was stunned. Their eyes were as big as boiled eggs, even Dalton's.

"Cain also murdered your college friend, Ahmad," said Bobby, nodding toward the young overwhelmed Saudi man. "This I believe."

The group held their breath in unison. They glanced back and forth at each other's frozen expressions. "Why don't you go to the police?" injected Samantha, quickly and incredulously.

Bobby Skylar smiled. "We trump the police," he said. "But... I am supposed to be working with a couple of detectives, one from LAPD and one from Pasadena. I have not met them yet... because I'm being held prisoner," he said gesturing toward Buster, while trying to add a lighter moment.

"You're free to go," said Preston, not finding jocularity within his reach at that moment.

Then Agent Skylar's face went sober, which did not look like a good sign. "You have to get out of here," he said frankly. "Sooner is better than later. Cain will not waste time; it's not his style. He will come *here* just as I knew to come here."

"Where should we go?" asked Preston.

"Somewhere completely off his radar screen. Out of town. Not to a relative's, because he will figure that out in a New York minute," said Skylar.

"New York minute?" said Dalton, the first words from his child's mouth since Agent Skylar arrived.

"It means 'quickly,'" said Preston.

Dalton fell silent again. His antennae were probably the most sensitive in the room that day and they were collecting intense signals all around that the grown-ups were scared. He did not like what he was sensing at all and he understood from what was said that his dad was in danger.

"I know where!" said Big Buster Bernard, suddenly from his wing chair near the front door. His baritone caught everyone by surprise emanating from where he sat, off to the side. He leaned forward on his knees with his .45 Army issue handgun once again firmly gripped in his right hand and he certainly had everyone's attention. Buster was ready for action. "I know where we can go before this freak shows up!" he added. "Cloud and I have a place."

CHAPTER 53

LA Police Detective, Fitzgerald Jack, was back in Pasadena the morning after the Cook household had been filled with tales of espionage and assassins swirling around the cold fusion research like demons. Everything else on Fitzy's plate, except the single assignment related to Agent Skylar's arrival, had been shoved aside by order of his supervisor at LAPD, a squeamish and proselytizing Christian man, named Peavey, who never really made any decisions on his own. Detective Jack had noticed Peavey would lift his chin, puff out his chest, and tell anyone who asked him about anything that they should "stand down" and he'd get back to them. "Get back to them" meant he would scurry off to contact the Chief's office and find out what he should say. Eventually Captain Peavey relayed to Detective Jack as authoritatively as he was able, that Fitzgerald's association with the Pasadena case was "from the top." Word had come "through high channels." Government agents needed assistance from local police departments on the matter. "Homeland Security was involved and re-prioritizing was not an option," Peavey had said to Lt. Jack.

The previous evening Detective Jack had been mulling over various possibilities in the case with his insouciant partner, Watson, and digging around on the Internet to see if he could come up with any leads about the research the dead CTU professor was pursuing. Jack still figured the whole thing was ultimately out of his hands. And it happened Pasadena's Detective Lau was of similar mind. Neither of them cared to be ladies-in-waiting for the feds, but that had clearly been defined as their jobs for the time being by both of their precinct bosses.

A more frustrating dilemma was that there were no federal agents to support! The Skylar fellow was a no-show at that point and there was not one syllable of explanation about his absence from the Washington puppet masters.

While Fitzgerald Jack and Stanley Lau were sitting around the Pasadena police headquarters drinking Kirkland coffee out of Styrofoam cups in a cubical arena where all the detectives worked on the second floor of the Police Department's east wing, with the magnificent dome of the Pasadena city hall a spectacular sight three hundred yards away, Fitzgerald shared with Stanley his speculations that it *was* the research, after-all, for which Maxwell Umberto had been murdered. It was not a jealous Preston Cook, inflamed over his wife's infidelity that killed Umberto. Fitzy speculated the homicide was a deliberate attempt to silence the scientist and control whatever it was he had invented. Umberto's intellectual property was sufficiently threatening to someone out there in the world that murder seemed the best way to control it. Lau and Jack were both playing catch-up to the drama unfolding in the Cook household not that far away.

The strange gangly assistant who always seemed to be at Detective Lau's side was never far away, lurking near the water cooler or a filing cabinet, throwing them furtive glances like a homely schoolgirl afraid she would be left out of the fun. Fitzgerald Jack couldn't help but notice the odd detective, but he remained on task.

Jack went on to say he didn't believe that the young Saudi man the LAPD was chasing had murdered his friend over at UCLA. It didn't compute the way killings usually do. The dots didn't connect. Why would he come half way around the world to shoot a college buddy?

So, in Jack's mind the Saudi guy didn't kill either his friend at UCLA or Umberto. Why would he?

The man they understood to be Umberto's research assistant, Preston Cook, didn't murder Umberto, argued Detective Jack. It appeared Cook did not know his wife was unfaithful. Without that motive, why would *he* do it? Again, things just didn't add up.

It all stuck in Fitzgerald's craw. And when you do investigative work long enough, you begin to trust your craw. In that way, the two men were like Preston Cook, although they didn't know it. They trusted their instincts. If it didn't feel right in your guts, it probably wasn't right.

Detective Lau connected to Jack's thoughts, nodding agreement with almost every sentence. They understood there was a ton of missing information and they knew they were fabricating possibilities left and right as they sat there drinking coffee in Pasadena, but those two city cops were experienced in their business and neither of them were fools. They allowed that blank spots were going to be there, because blank spots are always there. Sometimes you put together one corner of the jigsaw puzzle and then the diagonally opposite corner. The empty space will eventually fill up.

Martin Speck scrolled with an index finger through his email on his thin Apple laptop after his full body massage at the Beverly Hills Hotel, where he ruminated about what his next intervention would be, as he liked to call the steps toward his target. But for some reason he could not focus. Maybe it was because he was swathed in the luxury of that legendary pink hotel while he reviewed the electronic correspondence appearing before him, or perhaps he was merely sedated by the sunlight in his suite which seemed almost liquid. It spilled through wide open French doors and washed the walls in southwestern pastels. Who would not be seduced by it?

Just below his balcony laughter rose from cabana conversations near the swimming pool, sounds that drifted up to him through palm leaves and gardenias.

He inhaled the varied scents deeply, smiled, and he kept scrolling, with the wide flat screen of his Mac glowing as brightly as a Cinemascope feature. He grinned as he read the whereabouts of this other wayward scientist, the reclusive assistant, Dr. Cook. Maybe he stashed his findings and he may even have the research results in hand. Wouldn't it be nice if there was nothing more important to uncover, Martin Speck fantasized, and the whole case would be closed by finding this Cook fellow?

Maxwell had so thoroughly stolen the spotlight, whether he really intended to or not, nobody thought that Preston Cook was the mastermind. Cognoscente around the world believed only Maxwell Umberto could have managed the miracle of cold fusion.

In truth the primary investigator on the cold fusion breakthrough was still quite alive and kicking. While he was no secret agent or martial arts expert like the men and women in hot pursuit of him, Dr. Preston Cook was nobody's lackey. He would prove to be a hard and stubborn nut to crack, a characteristic that would never have come as a surprise to anyone who really knew him. Preston wasn't your run of the mill opportunist who might spill his guts about a colleague's work for a nice sum of money, or spill his guts about his own work even if he found himself staring into the business end of a Desert Eagle. That wasn't him. It would take more than that.

There was nothing Martin Speck eschewed faster than targets with strong principles, targets that would rather die than cooperate. He tried to avoid going after ideologues. Martin knew from a few prior, unsatisfying, contract episodes, you almost cannot get real closure on those assignments. The results Martin's employer wanted in this situation were primarily to shut down the progression of these cold fusion research findings into the marketplace, but as a less likely but ironically *preferred* second outcome, Martin was to bring the whole concept home, bring the newly discovered treasure back to his employer as spoils of war!

The legacy of ideologues in Speck's experience was that they were the exception in life to the rule that everybody can be bought. Principles can be unyielding. Yet, on that lovely Beverly Hills morning, his hopes remained high that all could be negotiated and done-with in forty-eight hours or so. If he had to shoot another egghead, that was okay, and if he didn't have to shoot the egghead, that was okay, too. Martin Speck had no personal interest in killing. It meant nothing to him. He just wanted each intervention to be accomplished quickly and cleanly, but he also had observed over time that cleanliness usually meant dead bodies. It just works out that way.

Speck's contemplations were interrupted by female laughter from outside, which came through his open French doors leading to the balcony. The laughter was more pronounced than before, so it caught his attention. He smiled. There had been three rather beautiful women in the lobby the day before, one spectacular lady with waves of ebony hair down to her shoulders, so much luscious hair that a man could smother himself in it, and she had legs that didn't end. She and her lovely friends were clearly on the hunt with furtive glances and sly smiles. Through a fleeting and flirtatious exchange of pleasantries in the lobby, Martin Speck had discovered she was a long haul from the Chock-Full-A-Nuts where she'd worked in Manhattan before she and her spirited pals decided a year earlier that warmer weather and movie stars sounded like a preferable option. So, there she was at the hotel, gaming the system with a paid-for apartment off Wilshire and enough freedom to play on her own time.

Upon hearing that poolside laughter, Martin's eyes lit ever so slightly and he figured the svelte, long-legged delight he'd seen in the lobby may be available that afternoon. Perhaps there was time for him to glide downstairs and see what might develop. Maybe it would just be the tonic he needed to press forward on a nasty assignment. Martin Speck had found that such diversions gave him a boost during dicey interventions. Events had certainly gone sideways on this mission thus far, given Cain's penchant for swift action and closure. He grinned in recalling an American expression he'd picked up somewhere along the way in his upper-crust education: "All work and no play makes John a dull boy". Perhaps this was a time for play.

That morning turned out to be a detour in Martin Speck's plans for the day. It was a detour that was extraordinarily beneficial to Preston Cook and his new entourage, who, with Bobby Skylar's urgency, was at that time planning an escape route and hatching a strategy to protect the Cook family and the research. There was no telling exactly how it might have gone if Martin Speck had shown up early that very morning at the Cook residence in Pasadena, with steel in his eyes and a fourteen inch .50 caliber Desert Eagle in his hand. Cain was a professional in his strange business and if he had appeared in Pasadena on task, there surely would have been blood, death, and mayhem. Not a picture of serenity. Martin Speck's wandering eye that morning had given those at the Cook house in Pasadena a few blessed hours to get their logistics in order. The blood, death, and mayhem had to wait.

Preston and his new cadre of resistance fighters would never know that they had a comely, long-legged, young woman at the Beverly Hills Hotel to thank for their reprieve that day, as well as the tedium of her having worked endless shifts a year ago at Chock-Full-A-Nuts in New York City.

CHAPTER 54

Detective Stanley Lau had been out to visit Dr. Cook before. He had gone there with his peculiar assistant, who had twitched and sniffed around in the background before he smashed a beaker and was hounded out of the lab by the professor's intense young son. During that first visit, Lau fancied that Preston Cook might be a suspect in the Umberto events, but that angle had long since been put to bed.

Now Lau was headed back to the Cook house with his LAPD colleague Detective Fitzgerald Jack riding shotgun in an unmarked Pasadena Police Crown Victoria while the wired and wiggly associate detective sat in the back seat bobbing and gawking. But Dr. Cook was no longer a suspect. Stanley Lau's return to the Cook home was for an entirely new reason. It was because neither Stanley Lau nor Detective Jack had heard one peep from the wayward Special Group agent named Skylar who seemed to have sailed off the edge of the map. Maybe Preston Cook knew something.

Therefore, contrary to what their respective bosses would have wanted, they both figured they may as well minimize imminent calamity by heading it off at the pass. After all, calamity was precisely what Washington had promised was headed their way. That was why a government agent had been sent to aid them. But Lau and Jack reckoned you can either sit on your butt and wait for calamity to strike, or you can confront the situation head on. They were of an absolutely similar mind in this kind of thinking and, consequently, they were on the move. The lines connecting the dots they had drawn up in their conversations crisscrossed at Umberto's assistant's residence in Pasadena, so that's where they were going. After all, they were both police officers, and *not* ladies in waiting.

In their Crown Vic, the three cops rolled around the corner toward the Cooks' house in the clapboard-house neighborhood in north Pasadena and they parked their plain white police cruiser unknowingly right behind the missing Agent Skylar's rented four door Taurus. There wasn't anything strikingly unusual about a Taurus sedan sitting on a street anywhere in America in those days and Detectives Lau and Jack did not choose to waste time by running the license plates on every car they saw. Ironically, it would have led them directly to the name of the missing fed, Bobby Skylar. Instead, they sat in the cruiser for a few minutes studying the quiet, Cook house. These men knew absolutely zero about Martin Speck or any of the other foreign agents prowling southern California in search of information about the cold fusion experiment, but Lau and Jack did know there was some weirdo on the loose with a very big gun who was not reluctant to use it, a weirdo who was familiar with precision methods of quickly and utterly incinerating a defined physical space, a capability that was heretofore unseen by either of the detectives and rather impressive in its own frightening way. So, it seemed to them that caution was the better part of valor in these circumstances.

Once again the ever vigilant neighborhood watchdog, Big Buster Bernard, noticed strangers lingering nearby on the street and scrutinizing the Cook house. He was always alert, but after a fresh conversation with the federal agent his antennae were twice as sensitive.

He was a large mass of nerve endings. Buster could feel when an interloper was in the neighborhood without looking.

When the white unmarked Pasadena Crown Victoria police sedan pulled up and parked, Buster was at his own house next door to the Cooks. He went to explain to ethereal Cloud Willow what was up and to say that he had offered their personal little fort in the mountains for a retreat. Buster and Cloud had a cabin high up the San Gabriels, above the community of Crestline, up where there was no plumbing, power, or even roads to mention. Rustic is for tourists; their cabin was *frontier*. That's where Buster had offered safe haven from whatever monsters were out there trying to crush Cook's marvelous discovery.

Buster, the survivalist, imagined this was the beginning of the end for society. He shared his fears with Cloud and she was right with him on most points. If it wasn't the actual end, it wasn't good, she figured. They both believed horrendous change was inevitably going to roll down the pike and they were ready. Buster and Cloud had constructed their safe-house in the mountains as a survival stronghold. The squat roughly hewn dwelling was stocked with canned or dried food and it had a clean water well with a manual pump leading up to a water tower that when nearly full would provide enough pressure for the faucets and one shower to work adequately. There was sufficient fuel oil they had accumulated in tanks along the side of the house to get them through a significant period, perhaps two years, depending on rationing. That was the goal. Cord wood was stacked to the ceiling in an adjacent shed, enough to provide heat in two fireplaces they'd built in their emergency home for a pair of snowbound winters. They were ready.

As for armaments, Buster and Cloud only thought to purchase a Remington twelve gauge pump action shotgun, which they figured would be used for hunting in desperate times, but it was handsomely displayed like an artifact over the fireplace in the cabin's living room. Otherwise, Buster's U.S. Army issue .45 was the only remaining weapon that might be counted in their modest arsenal. There were boxes of ammo for each.

Buster and Cloud had been working on their bunker for the better part of the last decade, building most of it themselves. When the world's economic order collapsed and heaved its last breath – which Buster and Cloud knew for a certainty was bound to happen – it would then become everyone on their own. Open warfare, however, was not in their personal script, hidden as they would be high in the San Gabriel Mountains. That's why they had not stockpiled guns for the apocalypse.

Big Buster Bernard was not one to let a failing civilization on its way down the drain drag him and his wonderful Cloud along in its final anguished swirl. Skylar had discovered that aspect of Preston Cook's neighbor the instant he found himself looking at the black bore of an Army issue .45 the evening before. The big guy had principles. And detectives Jack and Lau and their peculiar back-seat partner were going to learn the same lesson from Buster as they sat in their big, city sedan and watched the Cook house. In this case, however, Buster had made note of the city tags on the Crown Vic and he thought to himself, "Who the hell drives full-sized American cars except cops?" And with that conclusion he circled around behind the big Ford. "Okay," he continued inside his head, "it looks like we've got three plain-clothes guys here, but I've got a license for this .45, so let's just see what's goin' on."

Buster knew he couldn't ferry Preston and the Special Group agent up to the mountain cabin with these gumshoes sitting out here ready to tail them. Something had to be done if they were going to get out'a Dodge before light in the morning, which was their freshly hatched plan.

God damn it, Big Buster was a veteran of the United States' armed forces! He had served his country honorably in a war he didn't believe in, and as an American citizen he had his rights! And that was the frame of mind that Detectives Lau and Jack and the odd bird-man saw on the face of Big Buster aiming a Colt .45 side-arm at them. They all knew over-the-top behavior when they saw it. Experience and training had taught them to be careful, to play along, and don't antagonize.

Therefore, the three detectives rousted from inside the Pasadena Police Department's Crown Victoria found themselves standing on Preston Cook's front porch, ringing his doorbell, and holding their hands in the air as night descended, just like Bobby Skylar had been standing there a few hours before.

Vigilante Buster Bernard was once again positioned squarely to the side of the three suspects with his gun aimed at their backs, knowing in his heart that he was saving a potential national hero, Dr. Preston Cook, from who knows what manner of harassment, disrespect, and perhaps even arrest. With the gaunt, peculiar detective wiggling and twitching and unable to stand still, the entire scene was even more dreamlike than Skylar's arrival at the same threshold.

CHAPTER 55

Preston did not exactly display the expansive approval that Buster was looking for when Dr. Cook opened his front door again to find three more embarrassed captives in coats and ties standing there like nabbed peeping toms. Ahmad Mulham was simply too overwrought by now to be much more than catatonic as he sat off to the side of the Cook living room, with arms on his lap and with eyes like two shiny white orbs in his brown face. Samantha Day-Steiner was not much better.

"Are you rounding up everybody in the neighborhood?" inquired Preston of Buster.

No!" said Big Buster Bernard. "These lugs were scopin' out the house, too. And after what Agent Skylar said, I figured we shouldn't take any chances."

At the mentioned of the name "Agent Skylar", Detectives Lau and Jack shot glances at one another. "Skylar" was the name of their federal contact! And in that same millisecond of recognition, Preston recalled the face of Lau from their brief conversation in the garage lab, not long ago. And who could forget the gangly, peculiar cop, swaying with his eyeballs about to pop out of their sockets?

"Detective Lau?" said Preston and Stanley Lau nodded.

"Will you tell your friend to put the gun down?" said Lau and Preston gestured toward Buster, who again reluctantly lowered his .45.

Buster wanted some kind of appreciation for apprehending these guys. He was a bit of kid in that way. He was huge but he really needed a pat on the back, probably the pat on the back that he never got from his alcoholic and abusive father fifty years ago, who preferred to slap Buster and his younger brother around. It was a hot imprint from one generation to the next. But consciously tossing aside the torch of abuse his father tried to pass on, Buster had learned to forgive the old man before his liver did him in some twenty years back. Big Buster Bernard had chosen for himself a kinder and gentler path. Nonetheless, he still hungered for approbation here and there. Fortunately, Preston had figured this out about his biker, gun-toting neighbor some time ago. So, in spite of how unwelcome and bizarre it was to find yet three more captives standing on his modest porch, Preston did his best in his frazzled state to reward Buster by saying, "Good work. Excellent. Thank you."

With that, Preston ushered the new hostages into his house to blend with the haphazard band of prisoners, family, and lone refugee gathered there to save the future of energy for what increasingly seemed to be a less than enthusiastic world. Precocious Dalton eyed the weird, skinny assistant suspiciously while the jittery birdman refused to make eye contact with the boy that had sent him scurrying.

Bobby Skylar was the only one among this rag-tag collection of people in the house who had any interrogation training at all, such as it was, from Special Group. So, with appropriate humility he gestured to their host, Preston, and asked if he might speak to these new arrivals standing awkwardly in the living room by then with Buster armed and at the ready directly behind them. Bobby winced at his recollection of having been in their shoes not that long ago. Bearded Big Buster Bernard with a gun in his hand is an unknown and scary quantity for the unsuspecting and that odd house full of random strangers did not lend any more comfort.

"Do you chaps happen to have any ID?" Bobby said calmly to the men.

All three of the cops quickly produced their badges. But iconoclastic Big Buster did not relax when he saw the police shields they all displayed. Preston had to gesture yet again to get the big guy to stow his .45. Buster suspected these new strangers to be law enforcement from the get-go with that Crown Vic in the street, so badges were no surprise to him. And then there was, Ahmad, who was on the run for a murder he didn't commit. He was not in the least comfortable with this development.

"Key-rist," mumbled Buster. "A federal agent and now three cops!"

Meanwhile, Bobby Skylar was recognizing the names of two of the officers: Stanley Lau and Fitzgerald Jack. He personally knew no one on the Los Angeles police force or the Pasadena police force, but he *did* recognize these two names. These were the two detectives he was supposed to contact so he could lean on the resources of local law enforcement, if needed. Bobby remembered quite clearly that he had been assured by his boss, Digger Mac Brown, that all the connections and arrangements had been made. But Bobby had not reached out to these men yet. His Special Group aversion to excessive boots on the ground was hard-wired. In his reckoning, it wasn't yet time to contact the officers.

Bobby Skylar looked up from the new arrivals' badges and studied the men standing in front of him. One was a tall unshaven white guy, with his tie loose, and another was a shorter Asian man with thinning hair. The third was a wiry, odd-looking fellow who could not stop wiggling inside his baggy suit. It all seemed magically unreal, thought Agent Skylar, to have this collection of men and women, coming from different directions, in that house all at once. It was a coincidence that could not happen. Yet, at the same time, it was eminently logical because in many ways they were all on the same case. That house in Pasadena was where the trail of evidence led them all!

Bobby stood up and stuck out his hand. "Hi, gentlemen, I'm Agent Skylar. Good to see you finally." And they cautiously shook hands.

Both Jack and Lau were as overcome with the strangeness of the gathering at the Cook house as was Bobby Skylar. The others in the room could sense that something very peculiar had just taken place and they each searched amongst their comrades' faces.

Skylar and the detectives eventually relaxed into their conversation, but it was after the recently apprehended men were allowed to sit down, after they were served potent French roast coffee brewed compulsively by increasingly nervous Samantha. The gangly assistant detective did not contribute much, but he did sit down and weave around where he perched at the perimeter, once again an observer on the margins. Dalton and the skinny wiggly detective managed to make eye contact for a millisecond but the strange man's eyes repaired instantly to his hand wringing.

In short order, the confluence of these cops' stories in the Cook living room became as compelling as the terrifying vision Skylar had provided. Soon, they were all picturing this "Cain" character crashing through the front door any second, followed by the deafening report of his legendary Desert Eagle.

The entire unlikely cast assembled in the Preston house was drawn together by a cold set of rather furious conditions. That group *had* to come together. There was really no other way. It was all quite predictable. The overarching curiosity was that it all happened in such short order, but even that swift sequence was driven by tangible reality which was the unexpected murder of Dr. Umberto, an event that swamped their situation with urgency. Now, there they all were on what became a dark and moonless night, trembling with anticipation that a veritable explosion was about to occur. And when the realization finally sank in, it truly cranked up the burner on getting the hell out of there as quickly as possible! Cain's next move was totally predictable. All paths in that unwanted adventure led directly to Preston Cook's doorstep and his laboratory. Cain had to be on his way very soon.

CHAPTER 56

It was breakfast with New Yorker long-legs for Martin Speck, all provided via room service at the Beverly Hills Hotel, which had delivered perfect soft boiled eggs in cups with buttered toast strips and rich coffee. Women were perhaps one of the assassin's few weak spots, women and gardens, although he'd managed to overcome his flaw regarding women on numerous occasions over the years when members of the gentler gender had to be eliminated. When that was the case, there certainly was no evidence of sympathy or consideration, just business as usual.

That morning, however, had not been business of any kind and had followed an evening of indulgence. Martin Speck was exhibiting the caring and affectionate side of his strange personality that would be wholly off the charts to those around the globe who knew him as Cain. At almost 10:00 a.m. that morning, after savoring the soft-boiled egg breakfast, Tiffany and Martin Speck sat quietly in their plush white terrycloth Beverly Hills Hotel bathrobes near the open window through which he had heard the laughter of this former Chock-Full-A-Nuts waitress from Manhattan and her friends the prior afternoon. Martin kissed the tip of his index finger and he reached gracefully across the small table between them and placed that finger-borne kiss gently on the full lips of the woman with whom he had just spent a playful night. Then he said, "I am truly sorry, my lovely, but I must go. I have a very important commitment."

She was not in the least surprised by this turn and she asked, "Will I see you again?"

"I don't know," he replied honestly in his unrecognizable but magnetic-to-women foreign accent. "But I certainly hope so. You'll be here for two more days?" he asked and it was no ruse. Generally, he did not find lying to be ethical behavior.

"Yes," she said, smiling coyly. "After that, I have... an important commitment, as well."

There was no one in the Cook household that morning who actually wanted to be there other than Preston and Dalton both whom wished the world would return to where it used to be, to normal, so they could go out to the lab and toy with wonders. The strange team had spent the night planning, packing and preparing to depart before light.

The most recent arrivals, the three cops, never really pictured themselves as the supporting cast to a federal agent of any stripe, so that was not their ideal gig by any stretch. And Bobby Skylar had his own set of frustrations. He knew that things had gotten out of hand on the assignment. He hadn't come to Pasadena to do anything beyond dissuading his old friend, Maxwell, from pursing a line of research that was unpopular with powerful Washington players. He'd done it once before. But his friend was dead and his whole assignment was off the tracks.

Big Buster Bernard was ready, bristling with his evangelical fervor, preaching that the end of the economic world we have come to trust was crumbling and they were standing at the epicenter! Cloud Willow, had come over, too, that morning to help any way she could and was perhaps the most relaxed of anyone. She was confident that their celestial spirit guides would protect them and get them through the awful situation in some unfathomable way. Cloud believed each of them simply had to stay the course and be true to their beliefs and values.

Samantha Day-Steiner was edgier than a burned cat. She didn't know what the heck to do with herself. Some of her antsy behavior was born of guilt related to the as-yet-undisclosed liaison she had with Maxwell Umberto. But much of it was self-pity, too, complicated by genuine fear for her family's safety, which under those circumstances was not unrealistic. Nonetheless, for an intelligent educated woman, Sam did possess a remarkable capacity to blame others for her set-backs in life, but this morning was different. She was not blaming everyone around. There was no question that Samantha was a brilliant mathematician, but underneath she was a fearful and anxious woman, which was on display that early morning. That's probably why she married Preston in the first place. It wasn't just the intellectual promise he held out to her as one who might accomplish magnificent things but he also supported her on an emotional level. He was in touch with the frailty in her that so many others were not. Self-absorbed Preston understood forgiveness as being *quid-pro-quo*. Sam was flawed and so was he. He loved her in spite of her personal struggles and fears.

Ahmad Mulham had begun to suspect, since his unannounced arrival two nights earlier, that he was embedded in a patch-work team of completely mad Americans. He had been sent on a mission concocted in his father's ever-hopeful mind, a conceit that was collapsing around Ahmad like it was beset by flood waters. How was he to get home? Can the murder charges be shed without a long trail of misery and incarceration to endure? There were more questions than answers in his mind and the confused and frightened group around him didn't engender confidence that he would be safe for long.

Of course, there was the boy, Dalton, center-of-the-stars Dalton, who did not know what to make of any of the frantic activity in his home the night before or that morning, with strangers showing up, policemen, a secret agent, and guns! Guns had never been allowed in the Cook household. Before finding his way to bed the prior evening, Dalton managed to corner his father as soon as he could do so and whisper earnestly, "Is everything going to be okay, Dad?" Dalton really did not know. His eyes were wide with concern and his heart was beating a mile a minute. He was a courageous boy, overcoming physical and mental obstacles every single day that normal men and women cannot understand, and now there was *this*! Even the adults were mixed-up.

"Yes, Dalt," Preston had said, while he stroked his son's head. "We're gonna be alright. We're just figuring it out right now. You're going to have to be strong, though," said Preston to his son. "We've got a few rough days coming up. But we'll be okay." And Preston smiled. Dalton tried to smile back, but it wasn't the usual beam of light his dad had come to know from that boy when he was truly happy. It was something different, something cautious. A shadow crossed his son's magical face that Preston hated to see.

CHAPTER 57

There hadn't been much sleeping the evening before in the Cook household, with everybody on edge. After Skylar's arrival they each anticipated some kind of horror erupting around them any moment. It felt like the last night at the Alamo. All that was missing was a campfire and the plaintive moan of a harmonica. Their numbers had been increased by three after the detectives had been hauled into the house by Big Buster, but since the recent newcomers were police officers, they mostly calculated extra cops couldn't hurt. It also didn't hurt that Agent Skylar had some kind of connection with those particular cops, even though it was not entirely clear to everyone what that connection might be. Generally, they viewed the three recent additions to their anxious band as more good than bad. After all, everything had gone so very strange.

By 6:00 a.m., Bobby Skylar was getting really nervous and he was insisting they were on very thin ice by staying in that house. It was time to confirm how they would divide up and where they each were headed. Preston already knew he was going with Buster to their survivalist hide-out in the mountains. That was settled. Federal agent Skylar insisted on going with them, because his official assignment from Washington was to protect the cold fusion research, which was how it had evolved after the murder of Maxwell Umberto.

Then, out of nowhere, LAPD Detective Fitzgerald Jack found himself partnering with the rag-tag team by saying he would take Samantha and the boy with him to his apartment in Hollywood. No one would look for them there, he said. When the smoke cleared, he added, a future move could be arranged.

Preston sparked to Lt. Jack's suggestion instantly. "Thank you!" he said, surprising himself with the emphasis in his own words. His family would be safe!

Dalton, however, wanted to be with his father. "I want to go with you, Dad!"

"No. No, Dalt," said Preston to his son, kneeling down in front of him so they could see eye to eye. "You've got to take care of your mom. Okay? Detective Jack is a policeman, so you and she will be alright with him. I'll meet up with both of you later."

"But, Dad…" complained Dalton.

"No whining, 47! You escort your mother! Understand?"

Dalton didn't say yes, but he didn't say no, either. He was not rebellious. That wasn't his nature. Perhaps it was a product of his condition and perhaps he would have been cooperative no matter what. But Preston knew Dalton would do what was requested of him. He always had. Preston turned to the LAPD Detective and said again, "Thank you, detective."

"And, I'll take Ahmad, too," Lt. Jack added, looking at the frightened young foreigner who was wanted for murder and was, ironically, the man Detective Jack was originally out to track down. Nobody's plan was going according to Hoyle on that morning in Pasadena.

"Don't worry," said Fitzgerald suddenly toward Ahmad. "I know you didn't do it. We have to get you home." Ahmad was stunned. Lt. Jack had no earthly idea why these commitments were popping out of his mouth. Had he gone loony? Was he caught up in this spirit of camaraderie and collusion? Was he really just a softy, like his English professor dad? Or was it his mom in his blood, a strong-minded police investigator ready to run on gut feelings?

"Well," exclaimed Stanley Lau grinning like he'd won the lottery, "that means *we* get the *collar*!" They all looked at him and at his weaving bobbing assistant to see what he was talking about. Lau couldn't have planned the whole outcome more to his liking. It was his moment to shine. With the LAPD dick taking care of the kid, the wife, and the Arab, he and his peculiar partner were left to take care of real police business. "I think we will just hang out right here and when this Cain character shows up… well there you have it."

"Uh… Detective Lau," said Bobby stepping forward. "I'm not sure that's such a good idea. This guy, well, he's different than your usual gang-banger or drug dealer. He can inflict serious damage and do it quickly."

"Why, Agent Skylar," Lau said in mock amazement. "It sounds like you don't have much confidence in the abilities of a city police officer."

"It's not that," said Skylar.

"Stanley," said Fitzgerald Jack, having taken quite a liking to his Pasadena colleague, "maybe we should listen to what the agent is telling us. He has experience with this individual."

"Oh, I'll get some back-up. Don't' worry. I'm not going to try and do this by my lonesome."

"Still…" said Bobby.

"You don't think a Pasadena SWAT team can take this guy? What is he, The Terminator?"

Bobby Skylar didn't know what to say. Actually, the way Special Group operated, there were never heavily armed paramilitary teams trapping their targets. They were almost always working solo in a foreign environment and often on the run, too, so he wasn't quite sure what would happen in this scenario. But, overall, Bobby was apprehensive. He'd seen the carnage.

"I suggest you just kill the bastard at your first opportunity," said Agent Skylar finally. "Don't mess around with reading him his rights."

"Is that what you guys do?" said Lau. "No due process?" he added with an edge of righteousness that he'd been waiting years to display to federal agents.

"Where I work, Detective Lau, we like to come home in those comfy first class seats, not in the cargo bay. That's all I'm saying," said Skylar.

"Well, if at all possible, we'll get cuffs on this boogieman. Don't worry your pretty little Washington D.C. head about that, my friend." And then he turned patronizingly toward Buster, "I'll let you know when the coast is clear and you can all come down from your tree house in the mountains."

Fitzgerald Jack said nothing more at that point. They were on Pasadena Police Department turf and Lau had already claimed he saw city police as second-class citizens in the world of federal investigations, so Fitzy wasn't going to get involved further. He understood very well why Lau bristled. Yet, there was something unexpectedly brazen about his Pasadena colleague's demeanor on this matter. Personally, Fitzgerald Jack didn't think that trying to apprehend an unknown and sophisticated international adversary by confrontational means was a good idea. There were too many unanswered questions. Fitzy rather accepted the federal agent's warnings. Plus, Lt. Jack's job had been clearly defined to help the federal agent and that's what he was doing as best he could. Fitzgerald Jack had already committed to taking care of Dr. Day-Steiner, little Dalton Cook, and the Saudi young man, so all Fitzy could muster at that juncture was, "Be careful, Stanley," and as he spoke those words he wished he could have sounded more carefree than he did.

"Okay!" shouted Agent Skylar all of a sudden and he clapped his hands together, *smack*! It actually startled Preston and Sam. But it flicked the switch in everyone and got them moving. The eastern sky was already beginning to glow with the rising sun. "Grab whatever you're gonna grab and let's get out'a here!" he shouted like a Wagon Master. "Forward ho!"

"Dr. Cook and Dr. Day-Steiner," Skylar said to his hosts, you'll have to leave your cars here. Cain knows what you are driving and leaving the cars will buy us time."

"What?" said Samantha weakly.

"Trust me," said Bobby. "Your husband and I will go up the mountain in my rental and we'll call a cab for Lt. Jack to take you to his place. The unmarked cruiser will stay right out front, too. This man notices everything."

"I don't think…" said Day-Steiner, before Preston butted in.

"Sam! Let's do what these people tell us to do! Okay?"

The logic resonated with her even if she didn't like it and she fell silent.

"I'll see there's nothing left in the lab," said Preston at that point. He'd already stowed the device into an aluminum, carry-on suitcase ready to go, but he wanted one more look around.

"That thing isn't likely to blow up is it?" asked Bobby Skylar apprehensively.

Preston looked at the federal agent for a long beat. He knew this was one of the fears and questions he would be facing on a daily basis for a long time, if he ever got a chance to actually tell the world about the wonderful things that had been accomplished in his laboratory. "*No*, Mr. Skylar. It cannot blow up. It's perfectly safe. In fact, safety is exactly the point in having this kind of portable nuclear reactor. Safe, clean, unlimited energy for everyone!"

Bobby was out of his element on cold fusion even though Max had told him a few things. Why in god's name would *anyone* want to destroy such a wondrous discovery, he thought? Bobby's jaded Special Group mentality was clearly on the wane. He shouldn't be getting intellectually or emotionally involved in the right or wrong of things. At that point in his career, such a trend was yet another reason to retire.

"Okay," Skylar said to Preston. Destroy whatever you can't bring with you," he added.

"It's all in my head," said Preston. "There's nothing more to destroy. Between Dr. Umberto and myself, there was maybe one file's worth of scattered notes… scribbling, really. So much of what we did earlier was worthless. We were too close to Fields-Parker, so we had to…"

"Preston," said Samantha, "you don't need to give us a history."

Preston looked hurt, but under the circumstances, he did get her point. They were in a hurry. So, he gestured to Dalton and said, "Common partner, let's take care of business," and the two of them marched out the back door toward the strange little laboratory where so many amazing things had occurred and where a utopian promise had been fulfilled.

At the same time, Cloud Willow turned toward Big Buster and said, "Hey, my lovely man, I'm gonna stay home. You don't need me up there hangin' around that cabin. I'd just get in the way. This maniac fella isn't lookin' for me." She smiled. "So, I'll have a nice dinner for ya when you guys come back down the mountain in a couple'a days and I'll have some ice-cold beer in the fridge."

"Cloud?" said Buster suddenly wary. He didn't want to leave her. He was as imploring as a child. Maybe that's why he and Dalton had always hit it off so well.

"Now, you *shush!*" she replied sternly to Buster with a finger to her lips. Then Cloud smiled again and kissed Buster quickly on the back of one of his large hands before she pivoted on a foot and went flowing out the front door, her full and colorful skirt billowing as she crossed the Cook porch and then the driveway that separated these two unremarkable but pleasant Pasadena homes on the shaded avenue where such extraordinary events had taken place and where such violence was soon to occur.

CHAPTER 58

Preston and Dalton entered their small back-yard private laboratory carefully, respectfully. They looked around at the jury-rigged collection of desktop computers they had linked together for their computations and reports. There was the chemistry table with its beakers and burners, the lathe, the fine grain grinders, the centrifugal equipment, the metallurgical molds, the welding stand, and the clean room they had built as perfectly as any at the Jet Propulsion Laboratory, which was not that far away up the freeway. The garage was half science lab and half metal shop. All of it was there waiting like a faithful servant for its next assignment. It had been their sanctuary for several years, the two of them, conspirators out to the change the course of history, to change the world! Somewhere in each of their hearts they knew that part of their lives was over, the comfortable place where they worked together and shared disappointment and shared inspiration was coming to a close for one shy but very accomplished CTU scientist and his compromised but enthusiastically brilliant young son. They hated to see it end, but they silently knew it had to end. Both of them knew it and both of them pretended it wasn't happening. They tried to act like they would be right there in their own special lab before long, pushing the envelope and embracing the majesty of the subatomic world and star-filled heavens. What could ever replace an emersion in the awesome power of the universe flowing from the hearts of faraway galaxies straight into that tiny lab? They had replicated God's handiwork and they knew it.

"Awright," said Preston, getting back to business. Let's see what we've got around here that explains what we did." And they went to the mismatched filing cabinets lined up against one wall and started going through drawers. Dalton would haul out a file occasionally and more often than not it was only nostalgic for him. He might have stumbled upon a record of something that didn't work but had been fun in its collapse, like the time two years ago when the cold fusion canister ruptured in the clean room because they simply had overlooked a residue in it and they had a private fireworks display worthy of New Year's Eve.

After less than half-an-hour, the door to the garage lab cracked open and Skylar appeared. "We really should be getting on our way," he said with urgency. "How is it going?"

"There's nothing here," returned Preston. "Max and I had pretty much cleaned it up already. You know… *before*. There are snoops in academia, too."

"That I do know," said Bobby although Preston hadn't meant anything as global as Agent Skylar envisioned.

"He took only a few notes with him," continued Preston softly in reference to Max while shaking his head. It was all happening so fast. He still hadn't really processed the murder of his good friend and colleague. "But I've got in my head what worked. *This*," he said gesturing to the filing cabinets, "is all failed attempts."

"And the computers?" said Skylar looking at the odd collection of desktops connected like a grotesque multi-bodied animal with arteries drooping one to another.

"Clean", said Preston, "even the shadows".

"You're sure?" said Skylar and he got a really tired and fed-up return gaze from Preston, a man who had spent his entire life working with computers and data retrieval. "Okay, then," conceded the Special Group agent. "Let's get going."

Preston and Dalton put down the files they were holding and they glanced at one another understanding a thousand memories were captured in that space. Then, with resolve, Preston put his hand on his son's back and they headed to the garage-lab door for perhaps the last time.

CHAPTER 59

It was late-morning at the Beverly Hills Hotel. Martin Speck tipped the parking valet ten dollars and climbed into his wide, white BMW 745i sedan and pulled slowly away toward the Sunset Boulevard exit. Speck was not, as one might say, diminutive. He was six feet tall and weighed in at a taut 190 pounds. Compact or even mid-sized automobiles were not for him. Furthermore, he truly did relish the rush of speed and acceleration that a powerful car can deliver. He also had money, which is the end of the argument for men and women of means who simply want to regale in the moment and the machine they are driving.

Martin smiled at the throaty ripple his Beemer uttered as he arrived at the boulevard. He quickly scanned the FM radio stations until he found KUSC where Vivaldi's "Four Seasons" was appropriately in mid-autumn. "Ah!" Martin pleasantly exclaimed, and then he floored it, squealing out into surprised traffic with the scent of burnt rubber rising on the southern California offshore breeze as he aimed his bright Bavarian missile toward Pasadena and his new target.

In getting out of town, Preston saddled up with Bobby Skylar in his Taurus. But Big Buster Bernard did not go anywhere without his hog, so when they left Pasadena, a huge bearded figure on a Harley-Davidson Fantail Classic rolled ahead of the rental Taurus at some distance. They were going east on the 210 Freeway toward San Bernardino and the mountain resorts when Agent Skylar finally internalized for himself that saving Dr. Cook had officially become his new assignment. That truth sank in while Skylar was taking note of Bernard's massive black leather jacket that mocked a real biker gang, with his arched "Mongrels" across his back. Buster was fearless in his world.

As they rode, the big biker was always monitoring where his charges were in his wing mirrors as they motored onward toward the mountains in the east toward a potential hiding spot well up into the forests above San Bernardino. Agent Bobby Skylar did experience some anxiety during their accordion-like progression along the freeway, because he had only an adversarial history with the gun-toting giant ahead of them on his Harley, a man who had rested a semi-automatic .45 sidearm on the windowsill of the rented Taurus, not that long ago. The memory was fresh.

While Skylar nervously twisted the steering wheel, Dr. Cook sensed the agent's anxiety and gently reached over touched the right driving arm of Special Group agent and said, "Buster is not going to leave us behind, Mr. Skylar. He's a good man."

Bobby was simply too programmed by a world of subterfuge and violence to settle down on command into a simpler trust. He wanted to believe what he was hearing from Dr. Cook, but he was skeptical. Even at home he kept an emotional distance from neighbors. Nonetheless, after an hour of trailing the big biker, Bobby began to relax slightly at the steering wheel of his rental and accept his fate. He found himself thinking that trust *should* be the glue in society, not suspicion. It was a line of reasoning that was anathema to his Special Group mentality. More and more, as this unexpected detour in his assignment evolved, Bobby more and more clearly could see his days with the agency were at an end. He wanted real friendships again in his life. It was time for change.

At the Cooks' Pasadena residence that morning, getting Dalton to agree to go with his mom, Ahmad, and Detective Jack did not go smoothly. Samantha was too emotionally ragged to persuade her son to stop moaning about not going with his father. She tried to reason with Dalton, but he was not receptive. And Fitzgerald Jack was a total stranger to the boy. He hadn't met this family until last night! Nor did he have experience with children in any environment. He had no nephews or nieces or even neighbors with kids at his Hollywood apartment. So, there he was with this stubborn youngster who obviously was very connected to his dad. Before Fitzgerald could conjure up an intervention, Ahmad spoke.

"Hey, my friend" Ahmad said to Dalton, totally surprising everyone while they waited on the front porch for a taxi cab to arrive. "I never did ask you if you know where my *own* home is, Saudi Arabia." They had an incipient relationship from having gone up to Dalton's room for two nights, where they played some computer games before going to sleep. So, they had talked privately before.

Dalton looked at Ahmad Mulham suspiciously. The boy typically took things at face value. He didn't understand deceit. "I think so," he said to Ahmad. "I've seen it on Google maps."

"Okay. Where is it?" said Ahmad while Fitzgerald and Samantha Day-Steiner watched.

"Top of Africa?" said Dalton.

"Close!" came back Ahmad impressed.

"No," corrected Dalton. "It's to the right. Other side of the Susie Canal," said Dalton picturing the map in his mind.

"Excellent!" said Ahmad. "The Suez Canal separates Egypt from my homeland, Saudi Arabia! And it's a long, long way from here. You see, I want very much to see *my* father, too. So, you and I have something in common. We have the same goals!"

"Time to go, Dalton" interrupted Dalton's mother when the Yellow Cab they had summoned pulled into the driveway. They all made their way down to the taxi from the front porch, lugging the belongings they had selected.

Detective Jack followed the young Arab's lead and said, "I wouldn't want to leave my dad *or* my mom, either. I would be exactly like you and like Ahmad," he said to Dalton as Fitzy climbed into the front seat of the cab. Samantha and Ahmad nudged Dalton along so that he ended up in the middle of the rear bench and they pulled the doors shut. Fitzy looked over his shoulder at Dalton, squarely into the boy's eyes. "It will all be okay, Dalton. You will be back with your dad very soon."

Samantha was imagining the international killer coming around the corner any second. She clutched her son's hand and said, "Okay, Detective, let's go."

"Thank you, Ahmad," said Lt Jack. "I'll see that you get back to your family, too, as soon as possible."

At that point the Yellow Cab backed out of the drive-way and drove away from the Pasadena craftsman where the Cook family had spent the last twenty years. Dr. Day-Steiner, Dalton Cook, and Ahmad Mulham were abreast in the back and Detective Jack was riding shotgun. It was quiet in the car, with only Fitzgerald giving simple instructions to the cabbie as they headed toward Hollywood.

On that very peculiar day an effective and proven detective, Fitzgerald Jack, was at a loss as to how he might size up the situation. He could not even begin to estimate probabilities, an integral part of planning in his world. International agents and assassins were wholly unfamiliar quantities for him and he was doing his damnedest to conceal a creeping and uneasy feeling when he had glanced back at the Cook house as they drove away from where Detective Lau and his very odd partner were electing to take a stand. Fitzgerald was worried for them and he had good reason.

CHAPTER 60

The cabin Buster Bernard and Cloud Willow had assembled for Armageddon was only slightly homier than an army barracks. The first of the mountain roads leading to this hide-away was a fairly heavily traveled serpentine four-lane highway on which the locals in their pick-up trucks would squeal through tight blind curves at freeway speeds to the abject horror of tourists slowly maneuvering their way up or down the mountain. That stretch of road was designated Rim of the World Highway because of the sweeping panorama off to the south where thousands of irrigated agricultural acres insulated the city of Los Angeles from an expanse of arid desert patiently waiting to the east, waiting to reclaim what rightfully belonged to it.

The four-lane blacktop rising away from the community of San Bernardino in the foothills soon narrowed into two lanes carved tightly against the mountain's southern rocky exposure. It was all boulders and scrub at lower altitude. At an elevation of about five thousand feet the road suddenly peeled around a bend and presented a spectacular panoramic view of the sprawling San Gabriel Valley far below. The image was similar to what a passenger on a jetliner from LAX would see, a tabletop of flat farmland in rectangles of varied green hues and protective snow-capped mountains in the hazy distance. It was an expansive topography that appeared as a breath-taking surprise.

Forty-five minutes farther uphill, the Taurus was continuing its pursuit of the Harley-Davidson when the bike leaned northward to its left onto a much narrower blacktop that departed from the Rim of the World Highway. In a mere hundred yards the road became the main drag to the very small community of Crestline. They rode past a Chevron gas station with a strangely large hand-made sign reading "Mechanic on Duty". There was also a wide rustic general store dubbed The Crestbear Store. Bobby Skylar's fleeting glance toward the log-cabin styled building noted a Starbucks decal in one of the establishment's paned windows. He would love a latte, he thought, but in seconds without slowing they had blown by the handful of enterprises serving Crestline. The Tree-Topper sports bar and the Quality Cleaners blurred by them as they flew onto Old Mill Road exiting the farther side of Crestline. And with that, the Pasadena escapees found themselves roaring up the mountain once again but by then they were surrounded by a thick evergreen forest. Clearly, there was no pause button on Big Buster's trajectory.

Weathered and washed-out billboards from long ago popped up here and there along the roadside, advertising ski resorts at Arrowhead and Big Bear. Old Mill Road had been the 1950's route to those resorts, but it was no longer used after Rim of the World Highway was completed. And when they finally arrived at a faded, falling-down sign featuring a largemouth bass leaping from blue water in pursuit of a lure, Big Buster throttled way down and leaned his Harley to the left, parting company with Old Mill Road onto a gravel easement in the heavy forest. The easement was not wide enough for two passing cars. It was at that very intersection opposite the bass fishing sign that the refugees left comfort behind.

Once on the easement Bobby Skylar's Taurus slowed and fell behind slightly because of the dust Buster's Harley was kicking up ahead of them. They jostled along, grinding through ruts and small washes that were barely passable for the mid-sized sedan, bottoming out more than one time; but they pressed onward. They were well above the tree line by then, somewhere in the neighborhood of seven thousand feet, so the rugged slopes rising on either side of their dirt and gravel route were dense with towering pines, interspersed with an occasional redwood. Only now and then, when the bend in their ascent was just right, could they get a glimpse again of the agricultural valley they had left behind, a chessboard of greens.

After half an hour of bouncing along, wondering if the Taurus was really up to that kind of abuse, Bobby and Preston saw Buster pull his bike off to the side and wait for them. They soon rolled up adjacent to the Harley and Skylar put down his window.

"Christ! Is it much further?" said Bobby.

The big guy wiped his lips with the back of a fingerless biker's glove and he said, "We're gonna be leavin' the road up here in about fifty yards and it's gonna get kind'a bumpy; so hang in there. Won't take long," he added as he put his bike in gear and went ahead.

Preston and Skylar looked at each other. They figured they had *already* left the road! What in god's name could "bumpy" mean?

The Taurus followed the now slow-moving motorcycle off the gravel route onto something that was hardly wide enough for the Harley. Remarkably, Buster and Cloud Willow, with some Mexican day-laborers, had cleared that very pathway themselves to get to the site where they wanted to build their safety zone. It was on no map. It was barely a trail, nothing but holes and ruts. There was not even gravel for traction. It was weeds, rocks, and dirt, with some muddy hollows in which the car's tires would spin wildly and the Taurus would fishtail slightly as they ground forward. Each time that happened, Preston and Bobby thought it was a damn miracle they didn't get stuck. Four-wheel drive would have been nice right about then. Tree limbs were scraping and scratching both sides of the car from the moment they began this stretch, and suddenly one sturdy branch knocked the driver's outside mirror clean off!

"Shit!" exclaimed Bobby.

"Did you get the extra insurance?" asked Preston about the rental.

Gripping the steering wheel for dear life, Skylar just glanced back at Preston finding no humor in their situation.

Then, after another twenty minutes of a kidney-busting ride, they found themselves facing a steep grade that the Harley had ferociously mounted moments earlier. But an automobile was no match for the obstacle which was taller than the Taurus. It looked like a damn cliff! And at that moment of defeat, Buster suddenly appeared at the top of the grade, on foot and standing there gesturing for them to go around. As it happened, there was a less steep, but quite overgrown and easily overlooked passage to the right of the rise. They had to pass a massive granite rock that rose out of the earth like a sentry and was some fifteen feet in diameter. So, Bobby Skylar gritted his teeth and he gunned it! The car moved forward, slipping and drifting, digging and hurling dirt and mulch and chunks of vegetation in all directions, but the car also pulled ahead as it was told, eventually passing the huge boulder which inscribed its slow and painful signature along the entire length of the sedan's side. Both passengers grimaced as it was happening, but they also knew they couldn't stop and Bobby kept his foot on the gas.

Suddenly they breached the top of the grade and *there* was the cabin directly ahead! It was tight among trees. There was no deforested property in the front or in the back to give occupants elbow room, nor was there a vista-view of any kind. In fact, there was no manner of landscaping whatsoever. The structure was simply planted there in the mountain forest, with a shed and small water tower nearby. It was clearly a sanctuary and that had always been the plan.

The Taurus came to a stop twenty paces from the cabin and Bobby shut off the engine. Buster's Harley-Davidson was already parked near them. Without saying anything to each other, both

Bobby and Preston were imagining how in hell they were going to get this busted car back down the mountain. What kind of damage had been done to the machine underneath? This worry was not because it was a rental, but because they wanted the car to operate if needed!

They could see Big Buster climbing the slope ten yards ahead toward the cabin. There were no steps or pathways. It was not a vacation spot for Buster and Cloud. Hidden on the mountain in a forest, their cabin was a squat log building with small windows and a heavy door. It looked more like a bunker than a house. However, Buster and Cloud, the two erstwhile survivalists, *had* indulged in a small, covered stoop at the entrance which was the sole concession to hominess that could be seen from the car.

Buster Bernard stopped near the cabin and looked back at his two charges who remained shell shocked inside their sedan and he wondered in his child-like way why they were not bounding eagerly out of the car to join him, like they were on a camping trip. So, he beckoned with a wave of one of his massive arms and yelled, "Common, ya wankers!" before turning again toward the cabin's door.

CHAPTER 61

Dalton had not spent much time in Hollywood even though it was relatively near to his home in Pasadena. It simply had not been in the get-away scheme of things for the Cook family. So, like many out-of-towners, the boy was mesmerized by the chaotic, daytime street scene in Hollywood with its peddlers, prostitutes, and pretty-boys among the tourists, all such a radical departure from the sedate flow-ered neighborhoods to which he was accustomed. He crawled from the middle of the back seat across Ahmad's lap to where his nose was practically glued to the taxi's window!

Unfortunately, Dalton's adventure in Hollywood was all trans-piring under the fearful countenance of his mother. She sat in wor-ried silence, with her arms crossed on her chest like armor as they cruised along Sunset Boulevard toward LAPD detective Fitzgerald's apartment in the very heart of tinsel town. She was timid on this day, a characteristic that was anathema to her carefully planned life and to the future she had imagined for herself with Maxwell Umberto only a few days earlier. Everything was out of control.

There was also an irony in the Hollywood sojourn for Samantha. To Dr. Day-Steiner, Maxwell Umberto's fascination with the film industry was one of the few things she never could reconcile within herself about him. There were all those starlets he used to date! It was so below him, she thought, as she looked out the cab's window at the tawdry storefronts. But her son, Dalton, was of an entirely different mind and he kept hoping he would see famous people strolling along the sidewalks. He was just like the thousands of visitors who come to Hollywood from around the world and magically believe celebrities will be everywhere.

"Where are the movie stars?" he asked.

Detective Jack heard the boy and said, "You don't see many, Dalton. I've lived here for years and I've only seen a few in all that time".

But that was just the spark Dalton needed! "Where did you see them?" Dalton said energized and wide-eyed, leaning forward toward Fitzgerald, thinking that if they drove to that spot right then, a movie star might be there. It must be a movie star hang-out! The idea was unrealistic, but it worked for Dalton's twelve-year-old imagination. He was smart beyond his years in science, but he remained a child in other ways.

"It was a long time ago," said the detective, "but, I'll tell you what… I know some people who work at the studios, and I'll bet I could get you to meet a movie star… if I asked them… if you'd like that."

Dalton was apoplectic with excitement!

"Yes! Yes! Yes!" he screamed.

Fitzgerald saw he'd connected with the little researcher, an odd but charming youngster who had evidently played a role in the discovery of what makes this cold fusion business actually work. Quite obviously all the right chromosomes were available to him in spite of that one gimpy interloper, number 47.

"When can we do it?" the boy exclaimed.

That was when Fitzgerald Jack glanced at Dalton's mother. The puffiness around her yes was diminished by then and in the morning light she looked much better than she had the night before. She offered her first small smile of the morning, and nodded to the detective.

"Well… when the coast is clear and you're back home, we'll do it then," said Fitzy to the boy.

"Super!" said Dalton and returned to scrutinizing the neighborhood.

But that was right about the time they rounded the corner at Gower, off Sunset, and pulled up in front of Detective Jack's detailed Spanish apartment building, which was actually about as quaint and desirable as they came in older Los Angeles and was quite a find for him in a fiercely competitive, urban marketplace. But none of that meant anything to his adult charges, who had other life-threatening concerns on their minds that day.

The cab came to a stop in front of an arched wrought-iron gate-way hiding what appeared to be a forest of long palm leaves, ferns, and thick ancient grape vines, all fortified by rough stucco walls. The four of them exited the taxi and collected their limited luggage. Dalton was in a near frenzy at being in Hollywood. Fitzgerald discovered the boy had barely traveled at all. He'd rarely been outside of Pasadena in spite of his parents' where-with-all and worldliness. Perhaps this limitation in the boy's history was because his parents had chosen to protect him, but the detective calculated it was more likely because dad and mom were so wrapped up in their careers that the notion of a vacation and new experiences for their son played a nominal role in family life. Dalton was distracted by his Hollywood surroundings, yet he remained keenly aware something bad was happening.

The boy watched as Fitzgerald went to unlock the wrought iron gate that separated the apartment complex from the outside world. Dalton was impressed with the courtyard he could see through the gate, overgrown as it was, with a large gurgling mosaic fountain at the center. Dalton had never been anywhere like it, except for a remotely similar faculty dining room at CTU, which had a fountain, too. But that facility didn't have a helicopter thundering low over-head in the pale blue afternoon sky, a helicopter which slowed to a hover nearby, drawing the boy's eyes toward it. Most kids could not resist a helicopter and certainly not Dalton.

None of them except Fitzgerald Jack knew the chopper belonged to the LAPD and had been providing protection to them since they had entered Los Angles jurisdiction, even as they wound their way down the Pasadena Freeway past Chavez Ravine, where Dodger Stadium waited for the boys of summer. The low altitude pause above them at that moment was an acknowledgement to Detective Jack that the air-team was heading back to their helipad, having seen that the escorted subjects were safe. Fitzy stopped before opening the gate and waved skyward toward his colleagues to thank them for answering his surreptitious phone request earlier that morning. Naturally, Dalton thought it was all in good fun, so he vigorously waved at the helicopter, too.

"That's a Bell 206B Jetranger!" Dalton exclaimed at the top of his small voice. He could see the pilot's smiling face, beaming within his LAPD helmet. His gloved hand was visible and waving, too, in the window of the cockpit.

Fitzgerald was ignorant about helicopters and he looked oddly at Dalton.

"He knows everything about stuff that flies," shouted the Samantha Day-Steiner while the aircraft continued pounding the air overhead.

The aircraft's pilot, Sergeant Agopian, was fairly well known to Fitzgerald Jack, and he actually lived in Pasadena, not that far from the modest Cook house where Detective Lau was settling in to trap the assassin Cain. Coincidentally, Sergeant Agopian's daughter attended the same public school as Dalton Cook and she happened to be in Dalton's sixth grade class. The two kids knew one another.

They weren't good friends, but she was one of the few girls in class who did not make fun of Dalton's peculiarities. Dalton knew her as the pretty, curly-haired girl on the front row, who had a beautiful voice and could sing like an angel during music lessons. But Sergeant Agopian was not aware of that particular association on that particular morning. He had simply volunteered for the helicopter assignment because he wanted to help any fellow Pasadenian who might need assistance and he'd always rather liked good-natured Detective Jack. Before climbing away, Sgt. Agopian smiled down at the four refugees below and he could see that next to Fitzgerald was a youthful Middle-Eastern man. Agopian also saw a white woman who was covering her head from the copter's down-draft. And there was that one enthusiastic shiny-faced boy who grinned and waived toward the helicopter and who happened to think the Sergeant's daughter could sing like an angel.

CHAPTER 62

Stanley Lau's superiors at the Pasadena Police Department did not think that an entire SWAT team was required to arrest one single man. The lieutenant had called his boss immediately after everyone at the Cook house had sped off to their sanctuaries, hidden from this Cain character like he was a gun-slinger in a B-western. Detective Lau wasn't going to run from the bastard. Stanley was going to take him down! Forget Miranda Rights, he'd finally concluded. The son-of-a-bitch was a cold-blooded killer. Lau had never come across a murder scene like the one at CTU the day prior. It was emotionless; it was inhuman. Stanley wanted to put the reptilian international menace out of operation.

Cain had Lt. Lau's blood pressure up. But in spite of the fact that his supervisor at the department had specifically directed Detective Lau to help the federal agent, Skylar, and had directed Lau to support the government operation, the old police department resentments toward Washington intervention surfaced. And it did not work in Stanley's favor.

So, when Lau called with a request for a back-up SWAT team based on the testimony of Skylar, a fed, Captain Charles Jorgen, Lau's direct boss, rolled his eyes with incredulity and said, "Isn't apprehending this thug the agent's job?" He didn't want any complications on his final watch at the PPD. Putting a respected veteran, Lieutenant Lau, into the action was done merely to avoid the inevitable heat that would come his way if he didn't cooperate with Washington.

Charlie Jorgen had been with the Pasadena Police Department for thirty years. He was "one of the guys". He'd come up through the ranks. He was there during the LA riots and the fires after Rodney King's beating. He'd been through the law enforcement mill during his years as a sworn officer and most who knew him believed Charlie to be a damn good cop and a stand-up guy.

But now he was looking forward to retirement, a goal that was not too dissimilar to that of federal agent, Bobby Skylar. However, clouding Jorgen's sunset was the fact that he happened to have been surprised two years ago in his city office with his jodhpurs down, grunting over a thirty-year old, curvy, front office admin assistant who was on her back across his desk with her legs wrapped around him, yelling, "Captain, Captain, Captain!" as Charlie hammered away while a strand of drool dangled from his lower lip.

It was a stupid, idiotic maneuver that almost destroyed Jorgen's career and left him with a situation at home that was anything but healed. Two years is nothing after that kind of transgression. His grown children still gave him the cold shoulder. Charlie Jorgen certainly did not want to hear about international assassins and a SWAT team in that final stage of his career. The Captain was impatient and he wanted a clean, smooth ending to this federal episode and the CTU murder, too. He was tired and he was done. Jorgen wanted nothing but calm from here on out – an oddly selfish wish for someone in his line of work – and Detective Lau was not helping him by upping the ante, bringing serious attention his way on that strange day in October, 2005.

"Well, Skylar hasn't done much at this point regarding this assassin," said Lau flatly to the Captain's question about what the federal agent's role might be in the emerging drama. And that answer was the opposite of what Charlie Jorgen wanted to hear. "It seems Agent Skylar's assignment is to protect Dr. Cook and his invention

– whatever that hell that is," said Lau. "And right now they are off with a crazy-ass survivalist headed for a cabin somewhere in the San Gabriel Mountains, up toward Big Bear," added Lau. "Skylar doesn't seem to give a shit about capturing this assassin. All he says is we should stay out of the guy's way. The feds are very different than we are, Captain," Stanley concluded.

"Who is this…alleged assassin?" said Jorgen, his fatigue and frustration not well hidden.

"All I know is the code name 'Cain,'" said Lau.

"*Code name*?" said Captain Jorgen in disbelief, collapsing into his chair at headquarters. Holy Jesus, this is really getting out of hand, he was thinking.

"The feds don't know who the fuck he is," added Stanley.

"What does he look like?" asked Jorgen.

"They… don't really know," said Detective Lau. "Skylar saw him once, briefly."

"Nobody knows what he looks like? And you don't know his name? And you want to *arrest* him?" said the Captain feeling the whole police action slipping away like sand between his fingers. He was getting far more exercised over it than he wanted.

"I… I know it sounds very odd, Captain Jorgen, but Agent Skylar said, without equivocation in the slightest, that this… I don't know… this foreign fucking agent, Cain, killed our professor over at CTU two days ago – that's when Skylar saw him – *plus* this Cain guy also probably killed that UCLA student two days ago. The connection to it all seems to be an invention. But I'm a little vague on that part."

"Agent Skylar *saw* this man kill Dr. Umberto?" asked Jorgen.

"The agent told us he arrived just after," said Lau.

"Christ!" said the Captain.

"Yes, sir," said Detective Lau.

"You know I don't cotton to helping these prima donna federal assholes do their job, don't you, Stanley?"

"Yes, sir. Neither do I."

"And I sure as hell don't like 'vague' connections!"

"No, sir."

"Was it an invention at CTU?"

"No, it seems to be Cook's personal research at home," said Lau. "Some kind of nuclear reactor."

"*Nuclear reactor*!" said the Captain reeling and going pale.

"I can't tell you, sir," said Stanley. "It's all physics and shit like that. It's a portable reactor. The important thing is this killer is going to show up here *today*… any fucking minute really. We need to hurry and I need help." Lau was actually beginning to sweat a little because time was ticking away.

The detective had not much more to offer his boss in his plea to get a SWAT team dispatched pronto and yet he had to wait while Charlie Jorgen mulled it over.

Eventually the Captain came back reluctantly but firmly. "Okay," he said. "We *did* get a strong request from Washington to provide support. So, I am going to send over *three* SWAT officers – not a whole team. Got it? *That's it*! And don't get all trigger happy, Stanley, and go blowing the bejesus out of the wrong son-of-a-bitch! You've got these men for *one* day only, twenty-four hours, and then we're done with all this espionage crap! I don't give a shit what they want in Washington. It makes me *very* nervous," said Jorgen and he hung up the phone, hard.

Nonetheless, Detective Lau had managed to acquire most of what he wanted: three crack shots from the SWAT detail, three men who would not hesitate to drop this asshole in a wink and Detective Lau felt pretty good about that part, pretty confident. He knew in his heart that he may well get the biggest collar in recent Pasadena police history and he grinned at the thought.

He glanced over to his odd partner, who had been watching the conversation from his perch across the room like an eager pet emotionally riding the ups and downs of his master.

"We're gettin' 'em!" said Lau, confirming the arrival of the SWAT members.

His silent partner's head wobbled on his thin neck and his upper torso oscillated slightly. He rocked where he sat while his boney hands drifted around like large leafs across his knee caps. The gaunt bird-like face smiled and his eyes wiggled in their sockets. God damn it, Lau thought, looking at the gangly man he'd known and worked with for years, as long as his partner had been by his side Detective Lau had never seen the man at rest.

In Hollywood, Fitzgerald Jack opened his front door with a sweep of his hand offering up his spacious, sparsely furnished apartment for his impromptu guests and trying to be as grand about this development as he could be.

"It's not the Ritz Carlton, but it's what I've got!" he said expansively.

His paintings were mostly stored in his studio, the second bedroom, so beyond a pair of wan female figures in oil in the living room there wasn't much evidence of Fitzgerald's passion for art and he didn't plan to hold forth about it to those particular guests on that day.

Samantha Cook was the first to enter the apartment and she didn't really look around much. She was preoccupied with worry about Preston.

Dalton was right after her, quite alert, with sparkling eyes. "Wow," he said. "Nice digs," a phrase he'd picked up from watching television.

"Thanks," said Fitzy, smiling, entering with Ahmad, who had no luggage, as it was in police custody over on the west side of LA, having been collected as evidence at a murder scene. But he did have a zip lock bag with toiletries he'd purchased while on the run.

"May I use the restroom?" said Dr. Day-Steiner politely. She wanted to throw some cold water on her face and have a minute alone to collect her thoughts.

"Of course," said Detective Jack, "just down the hall."

"Oh, my gosh!" said Dalton, eyes wide when he spied gigantic Watson, curled complacently on an ottoman near Fitzgerald's bulky old television. The animal did not move when they all traipsed inside. He may have passed for a large plush-toy at first glance.

"Watson," said Fitzy to the cat, "meet Dalton. Dalton, this is my partner, Watson."

"Like Sherlock Holmes?" asked Dalton.

It was unexpected insight. "Why, yes," Fitzgerald said, "exactly."

"Hi, Watson," said Dalton and he went immediately over to the large animal and knelt down beside the ottoman. The plump and docile feline rolled over expecting affection and that's precisely what he got, as Dalton stroked him.

"Watson's great!" said Dalton quickly and sincerely.

"That is one big cat!" said Ahmad in amazement.

"Yes, he is," returned Fitzgerald with equal honesty. "Plus, he helps me figure things out."

"Smart cat," said Dalton, absolutely going with it.

"I bet you don't want to argue with him," said Ahmad.

"Well, he does sit where he likes," said Fitzy.

Samantha had returned from the bathroom by then and she stood at the entrance to the living room watching the three of them and the cat. She did look a little refreshed, and she said, "How long do you think this will last, Detective? Do you think we're really safe here?"

"Please have a seat, Doctor," said Fitzgerald relaxing onto his sofa. "I don't know when it will be okay to go back to Pasadena, but I hope not long. We are safe here. Don't worry."

It's not likely the assurances satisfied Dr. Day-Steiner, but she did tentatively sit down near her son, who was transfixed by languid Watson. "I'd like to call Preston as soon as I can," she said, absently fiddling with her cell phone. "But they're probably still on the road."

"Reception can be spotty in the mountains," the lieutenant said. "Are any of you hungry?"

CHAPTER 63

At the Cook house in Pasadena, three members of the PPD special weapons team soon arrived. They drove their massive black and white GMC Suburban right into the driveway. Unfortunately, they had been led to believe they were basically slumming it on their assignment that day and they weren't the least bit concerned with concealment. Detective Lau had to rush outside and intercept them as they piled out of the vehicle laughing and carrying-on like they were on vacation, clearly the derivative of unhelpful instructions they had received from Captain Jorgen.

"Whoa, whoa, hold it, gentlemen!" Stanley Lau exclaimed standing in front of them in the driveway with two stiff-arms up like a traffic cop at a Rose Bowl game. "Don't you think this might be a bit conspicuous?" He gestured to the huge SUV with a bold Pasadena Police Department logo on each of the front doors.

Lau knew these guys, every one of them, but SWAT team officers had an air about them. Driving the SUV was a smart-aleck, Sergeant Roosevelt Dixon, named after Rosie Grier, a famed member of the Los Angeles Rams' Fearsome Foursome. Sergeant Dixon had once been a promising quarterback at Pasadena City College but he busted up his knees before he could go on to Division I-A. Dixon yelled back at Lau, "Well, *yeah,* it's conspicuous, Stan! The bad guy sees we're here and he leaves us alone!"

Lau isn't taking any of Dixon's baloney and he shoos them away with a flick of his wrists. "Park this thing out of sight, Rosie. Around the corner! *Now!*"

"Hey, detective, so what's up?" said Sergeant Dixon, who was clearly confused, just like his partners. All they could see was a quiet suburban neighborhood in north Pasadena. It surely didn't look like a place where all-out war was about to erupt.

"Just do it!" said Stanley. "I'll explain later."

The SUV rolled back out of the driveway and went to the nearest corner, rounded it and parked some hundred yards down the adjacent street, not really out of sight but at least not directly in front of the house. It wasn't five minutes before Roosevelt Dixon and his SWAT comrades, two joined-at-the-hip special weapons experts who had come to be known as "Mutt and Jeff", after comic strip characters from another generation. Mutt was the short, thick one of the two. He was Italian, or Armenian, or Greek, it was hard to tell and no one knew. But wherever he came from he had his misogyny down pat. From the front porch of the house Detective Lau could hear Mutt as they walked down the street from the corner toward the Cook house.

"Ju see them bitches, man?" said, Mutt, looking over his shoulder, glancing back at a pair of giggling high school girls they'd passed at the corner. "Hot 'n nasty!"

His counter-part, Jeff, was a tall, southern boy and his speech customarily ran about four beats behind the actual conversation. He wasn't dim-witted, just painfully deliberate. He and Mutt made the very oddest of partners. The police trio from the GMC Suburban had almost made it all the way up to the house before Jeff finally responded critically to his friend Mutt and said, "They're only teenagers. So, shut up." They had been assigned their monikers when they were in police training together. They were each twenty-two at the time and now they were in their early thirties, but those handles stuck. Most of the officers at the head-shed on Walnut didn't have a clue what Mutt's and Jeff's real first names were.

As they approached the house, Lau saw that none of the three men were really outfitted for serious work. They hadn't even brought their Kevlar vests! Detective Lau watched them coming toward him, each lugging a black canvas bag with a couple of weapons and ammo inside and Stanley shook his head in dismay. What in heaven's name did Jorgen say to these guys? They looked like they were coming to play pick-up basketball, not confront a professional assassin! It scared Lau, actually. Bobby Skylar was not really a known quantity to Detective Lau, but the federal agent was sufficiently convincing in his description of Cain and what he was capable of doing that Skylar successfully bestowed to Stanley Lau a sobering respect for their opponent. He was apparently a ruthless, skillful, and a mysterious murderer, who was going to arrive at that house in Pasadena as surely as a clock ticks.

Lau could not help but inquire, with a rather disturbed look on his face as the three SWAT team members trailed into the house, "Do you men have *any* idea about what we're doing here?"

"Relax," said Rosie Dixon. "It'll be okay, detective. Jorgen told us you got some really tough *hombre* headed this way, a foreigner, and our job is to cancel his act. That right?"

The men immediately made themselves at home. Mutt picked up the remote and turned on the television. Stanley was livid. "Turn off the god damn TV! This isn't a picnic!" he yelled, while his wide-eyed bird-like quiet partner stood in the background in the shadows, shifting foot to foot.

The three SWAT members stared at Lau, a bit shocked. They thought his was an over-the-top reaction, but the television did go dark. They all could see something wasn't right with the Lieutenant, so Rosie stepped up and took charge of his team. He wanted to give the detective time to vent, if he needed to, and get whatever was eating him off his chest. Cops deal with people on the edge every day.

"Awright, Stanley, awright," said Sergeant Dixon. "Tell us what we're missin' here. We don't mean to be out'a line."

Detective Lau looked at Mutt and Jeff and said sternly, "Sit down, men. Let's act like professionals for a minute."

Roosevelt could see Detective Lau was upset, so he was scrambling to regroup. It was an honest effort. The sergeant could be a smart-ass but he was also a very capable Pasadena police officer. Dixon did recognize his small team was being a bit lighthearted about what was now shaping up to be more serious than they had been led to believe. Perhaps Captain Jorgen hadn't presented the situation with sufficient gravitas, a failing he'd been known to display more than once in those final months at the helm of his precinct. Everyone understood he didn't want a crisis.

"Okay, okay. Tell us," said Rosie as the three men sat in the living room and waited attentively for the real story.

Although it was second-hand information from the federal agent, Detective Lau believed what Skylar had said when he described the sophistication and cunning of this internationally known professional killer tagged "Cain" by American intelligence. Lau described to his SWAT colleagues the strange unknown combustibles used to incinerate Dr. Umberto's town home and his office on the campus. He told the SWAT contingent about the heavy caliber handgun this man carries and they also heard from Lau about the variety of killing strategies Cain reportedly had used all around the globe for years. Cain was feared by people in the secret services on six continents, men who don't usually disclose fear. Nobody, until Skylar's very recent encounter with Cain, knew what the guy looked like and nobody knew his real name. Stanley explained they were up against a lethal, almost invisible, and nearly unstoppable assailant. Then he added in an effort to show some kind leadership, they should take the intelligence to heart and embrace their assignment on that day as a challenge.

Lau continued in his best Knut Rockne, "Are we up to it, gentlemen? Are we going to take down this son-of-a-bitch mercenary? He doesn't care who he kills. Our job is to make sure it doesn't continue. We have an opportunity to silence him and jocularity has *no* god damn place in what is going to happen. Even as we speak the maniacal bastard is on his way here."

Stanley's words were not what Rosie or Mutt or Jeff expected to hear, while the bird-man paced in the background. None of the SWAT team members knew how to weigh the news, but the stakes may have been far higher than they expected and, Sergeant Dixon, in particular, as the officer in charge of the SWAT detail, wished they had been given the straight skivvy by Captain Jorgen. The three arrivals didn't know if what they heard from Lau was true or hyperbole, but to play it safe Dixon calculated that more men would have been a good idea, particularly if what Lau said was known at the precinct. But no more men would be coming on that bright morning. Maybe tomorrow reinforcements could be arranged, if it wasn't too late. It clearly wasn't shaping up to be the leisurely afternoon the SWAT team had imagined.

CHAPTER 64

In his 700 series white BMW sedan, Martin Speck rolled slowly and quietly by the retrenched Cook household. He'd already driven past the Pasadena City Police Department's GMC Suburban situated like a billboard around the corner. Martin had to ask himself, "Who are they fooling?" City police world-wide are so clumsy, he thought. Perhaps around Los Angeles it's because they are usually dealing with baggy-pants, tattooed gangbangers, Mexicans and Negros, he wasn't really sure. But from country to country, region to region, Speck always found local police interventions to be lacking. As a matter of routine, he would survey the lay of any location, "case the joint" they might have said in old American crime movies, of which he was a great fan: Cagney, Edward G. Robinson, Bogart. As a standard practice, he would note anything amiss.

When his car cruised beyond the Cook house, Martin couldn't really see much activity because in those very moments the SWAT team was in the living room with Detective Lau at his wits' end trying to get those unfocused officers' attention and get them to understand they were up their ears in very serious business! Yet, to an outside observer, the house looked like a quiet, craftsman house with a wide front porch. Martin did see the garage, toward the rear of the property, down the driveway, where all the scientific magic had taken place. It was an unremarkable free standing structure, modified with a wall where the lift-up garage door had once been.

Cain drove on, believing other perspectives on the environment were definitely in order before he made any move. Every intervention requires at least two reconnaissance angles. In his line of work, no trait was more fatal than impatience. And he drove inconspicuously around to the far side of the residential block where Dr. Cook's house waited with its compliment of SWAT officers.

Turning his steering wheel gracefully, Martin Speck moved beneath the spreading limbs of trees that lined the streets, patches of sunlight and shade flashing across his windshield. Pasadena was a lovely American community, he was thinking as he slowed his car to a stop in front of the house that was back to back with his target, the Cook residence.

It was a quiet and restful neighborhood, he thought as he looked around at the vintage houses on either side of the well-maintained and shaded street. Many of the trees were beginning to show their October colors. It was a sweet scene, just like the leafy hometown in that *Halloween* movie. And he realized as he sat there enjoying the neighborhood that he'd found his angle of attack.

Cain zipped open a small leather satchel adjacent to him on the passenger seat. He withdrew a pair of opera glasses, a bag of powdered napalm, a roll of twine, a perfectly balanced throwing dagger that he attached to himself via sheath on his lower leg and, of course, his Desert Eagle which he clipped behind his back as he exited the car. That was all he needed.

He smiled and inhaled deeply when he was standing in the open on the sidewalk adjacent to his BMW. "Ah," he said. It was truly a beautiful autumn day, one that reminded him of his play-filled childhood, with blue skies, a cool breeze, and sunshine everywhere. He straightened his ample jungle-toned Tommy Bahama shirt so that it concealed the weapon at his back and he strode to the front door of the house in front of which he had parked his car. There were no other vehicles around at that time of day and he guessed that no one was home, but he certainly didn't want to go sneaking around in the back yard if someone *was* inside the house, an angry property owner who might come charging out the rear door with a pump shotgun. You never know.

So, Martin went up to the front entrance of the small stucco house, which was not nearly as quaint as the Cook craftsman on the other side of the block, but Martin did notice that somebody who lived there was a gardener, because the front rose bushes were heavy with fragrance and blossoms. He drew in the surrounding air deeply with his eyes closed. How lovely, he thought, and then he knocked as loudly as he could on the door. It was close to pounding, actually. He also shouted, "Hello? Hello?" a couple of times. And then he knocked again, but there was no answer. Perhaps luck was in his favor and the house was vacant.

But just as he started to leave, to go around toward the rear yard, he heard the front door open. "Yes?" came a feeble voice from within, an elderly woman's voice, it seemed.

Martin did not care for this turn in events. It ruined the smooth quality of his plan as it was going, and it upset his good spirits, too, on a sunshiny, fragrant day in such a delightful neighborhood. But there she was.

Returning to the front door, Martin tried to be as congenial as possible and he smiled at a housecoat-wearing elderly woman who could not have been much over five feet tall, bent from osteoporosis and smelling strongly of medicine detectable even from the stoop where Martin stood.

"I am sorry to bother you, madam," he said as pleasantly as a church deacon.

"What do you want?" she came back, really not wanting to be bothered.

"Perhaps I should talk to someone else and not disturb you?"

"No. I'm it! Tell me what you want," said the woman, getting a bit perturbed. It was clearly difficult for her to be answering the door.

And that was all the information Martin Speck needed. His dagger was out of his leg sheath in less than a second and it came across the woman's throat with such force that, as the coroner would find nearly ten hours later, the blade's tip actually scraped her vertebrae. Every vessel in her neck was severed and she fell straight backward, struggling slightly when she hit the floor, but not for long. There wasn't even that much blood for such a catastrophic laceration because she was dead so quickly her heart stopped pumping.

Martin Speck leaned inside and quickly cleaned his knife blade on the woman's housecoat. Then he pulled closed the door and left the crone for her daughter to find, who would come by that evening with groceries. Cain just wished the old woman had not answered the door or hadn't been home. It was an extremely unpleasant detour and it had thoroughly spoiled his heretofore sanguine mood. He loathed ancillary killings.

Inside the Cook house, a new orientation had taken root. An air of sobriety had supplanted the cavalier attitude that had arrived with the SWAT detachment only half an hour earlier. Detective Lau had taken charge and put one of the men, Mutt, out in the back, as rear guard. There was a patio adjacent to the rear stoop, not far from the laboratory garage, and on the patio was a glass-top table and a set of strap-frame Browne Jordan chairs used for the bar-b-ques Preston and his family enjoyed in a less tumultuous period, with young Dalton occasionally wielding tongs over smoking ribs or burgers. Those were good times, but they were history.

After walking around the small perimeter of the enclosed back yard, Mutt fairly quickly assumed a seat on one of the patio chairs and put his feet up on another. There were large shrubs covering the six-foot cement block walls squaring off the rear property line. He couldn't imagine any one individual charging the house via that awkward route. Still, Mutt had heard what the detective said about their adversary, so he kept his AR-15 handy, resting on the glass table where he relaxed. The idea of being attacked in that Pasadena neighborhood really did stretch the imagination.

Meanwhile, Stanley Lau, SWAT team officers Rosie Dixon and Jeff, plus the strange, wiggly assistant detective, were all situated in the living room in anticipation of a knock at the front door. What else could happen? The assassin was coming to the house to locate Dr. Cook. That was his mission. He wasn't going to crash through the front wall with a truck. He wasn't going to kick down the door and storm into the living room with an M60 machine gun across an arm, hot cartridges flying, blowing to bits everything in front of him. A lone operative like Cain had to be subtle to get what he wanted; at least that's what Detective Lau believed.

A six foot fence separated the Cook's backyard and the back-yard of the house directly behind, but on both sides of that concrete wall there stood many years of healthy vegetation, massive camellia bushes on the Cook's side of the fence and a tended confection of plants on the other side. The cinder block fence on the property line was not visible from either residence.

Martin Speck was impressed by the care that the residents of that stucco house had shown in their private rear garden. He paused to ever-so-gently finger the flowers he encountered, taking time to investigate the irrigation and found a nutrient-enriched drip system woven around the entire property. He smiled. They knew what they were doing, whoever they were. It certainly could not have been that frail, old woman. There was someone else.

Most men and women have an alternative occupational path they might have followed if events in life had gone a different way, and for Martin Speck the alternative path would have involved horticulture. Even on that serious and lethal mission, Martin wished he had time to visit the Huntington Botanical Gardens before leaving Pasadena. Orchids were a special passion of his, as they are with many who value beauty found in the delicacy and symmetry of flowers, and he knew that while he stood there in a stranger's backyard the Botanical Gardens had a traveling exhibition of rare orchids from around the world! Sadly, that stop was not on Speck's itinerary. There was other grim business in front of him that day and he pressed himself back to the agenda.

A dense, brilliantly blooming but nasty-with-thorns Bougainville covered a goodly center span of the block fence of Cook's rear neighbor's house. Tall Hibiscus bushes were there, too, colorful and with broad pink blossoms, flanking the Bougainville's thorns and adjacent to deeply-rooted old camellias, like the Cook's, but rising eight feet skyward and squared-away like sentries at the rear corners of the property, dark and as impenetrable as the wall. The whole array was balanced and thoughtfully groomed on Cain's side of the fence, where he was now moving stealthily to find a small aperture for reconnaissance, a vantage point from which he could assess the perimeter defenses the law enforcement team had chosen to establish. Someone had to be covering the back entrance to the Cook house and that's all Martin Speck wanted to see. He already knew the situation called for *blitzkrieg*.

CHAPTER 65

Mutt was bored in back of the house on the patio and he'd only been there twenty minutes. He stretched and yawned, trying to wake up as he leaned back in the Browne Jordan patio chair that he filled listlessly. What if this so-called international assassin is a no-show, he thought? Was he going to have to sit out here all day staring at the goddamn shrubbery? He was hungry, too. The breakfast burrito he'd grabbed that morning didn't do the trick and he could still taste it every now and then with a burp. He wouldn't go back to that joint, a shack he'd noticed on his way to work many times and never stopped, but Mutt had seen a crowd of customers there every day, so he tried it.

He gazed at the thick decades-old growth that covered the cement block wall at the back of the Cook property. Mutt didn't know one bush from another. Horticulture was about as far off his radar screen as writing an etiquette column for the *Pasadena Star News*. He certainly had no inkling that through those overlapping leaves covering the rear fence someone was looking back at him, someone with opera glasses and someone who was very experienced at sizing up situations where suddenly, and in seconds, multiple lives meet bloody ends. There was only a collage of foliage along the perimeter of the property, bushes and black shadows wholly concealing a pale gray wall and everything else beyond. It gave Mutt the creeps a little bit because the overgrowth was so very dense.

"Christ almighty, I'm goin' fuckin' nuts!" he said out loud at one point, chiding himself after he realized he'd spent five minutes with his eyes struggling to drill down into the darkness of those bushes where he had imagined movement.

"Anybody want coffee?" said Rosie Dixon in the living room having gotten up from where he'd been stationed with Detective Lau and his lurking assistant. SWAT officer Jeff was there, too, planted on the soft couch. "They've gotta have a coffee maker," added Dixon meandering toward the rear of the house and the kitchen.

"Double sugar and cream," said Jeff, but Lau passed on the offer.

Rosie found the rather spacious farm-house kitchen with a chopping block table and stools situated at the center of a no-nonsense space. The windows overlooked the back patio where Mutt glumly slouched.

Rosie cracked the window and shouted, "How's it goin' out there?"

"Oh, it's just freakin' terrific out here. I can almost see the weeds grow."

"Want some jo?"

"Yeah," exclaimed Mutt, "and a jelly roll, too!"

Sergeant Dixon closed the window and he went about the business of making coffee in a kitchen he didn't know. The stainless steel Braun coffee and espresso machine was obvious on the counter, but where were the grounds and the filters? So, he started rummaging through cabinets.

In the living room, Lau was silently contemplating what lay ahead that day while drifting now and then to more mundane conversation with the other officers. Then suddenly he would be jolted back to the reality of the violence that may appear any second. It was a mental rollercoaster. Waiting is the worst part. Staying focused can be a monumental chore as Mutt was discovering where he relaxed on the back patio.

But right about then, while Rosie Dixon was trying to figure out how to make coffee in an up-to-the-minute Braun coffee machine, and while Mutt was nearly asleep on the back patio, the next door neighbor, Cloud Willow, made it her business to wander over to the Cook house for a visit. She didn't know everybody was gone by then because both of the Cook automobiles were there.

Only Lieutenant Lau had met Cloud before. Taut, athletic Jeff did not have the slightest clue who she was, when she came to the front door. Her graceful figure drifting into their world was wholly unexpected and it could not have happened at a less propitious moment. In her angelic way she had crossed the front porch of the Cook household, startling both Detective Lau and SWAT team member Jeff, into high alert when she knocked on the door! When the officers heard the knock, neither of them rose to greet her but instead they looked at each other in disbelief and quickly took their positions.

"Hello?" said Cloud from the front porch.

"Samantha? Sam?" said the woman loudly assuming Dr. Day-Steiner was still at home. Cloud knocked again. Of course, she knew Buster had gone up to the mountains with Preston and that federal agent, but Samantha and Dalton may still be around, she was thinking.

In those same moments, on the far side of the back fence that for years had protected the Cook residence and provided such comfortable privacy while they entertained or relaxed on the patio, Martin Speck moved silently with precision and experience. He had been observing Officer Mutt from within the thick covering of a tall trimmed Camilla, guarding a property corner. Speck had slipped quietly to the opposite corner of the garden, to the matching Camilla on that side of the property, and he carefully fastened a length twine to one of the heavy branches that leaned across the concrete wall into the Cook's property. Speck had a simple plan of distraction in mind, not complicated. He always thought simple and direct strategies were the most efficient and effective, and over the years Cain had confirmed his theories with success. So, after tying the twine to the farther Camellia, Martin retreated silently to his original vantage point, unrolling the twine as he moved, until he was back where he had been, where he could see the short, thick policeman reclining in a patio chair and looking like someone who wished he were home watching TV, which was not that far from the truth.

But Martin Speck had also overheard the offer for coffee from someone inside, words that came through the kitchen window, so he had to sit it out for the moment, and wait for the coffee to arrive before initiating his plan and getting the show under way.

CHAPTER 66

Stanley Lau opened the front door protectively, his sidearm in hand, hanging by his thigh. Tall Jeff was ready and out of direct sight, with his AR-15 assault rifle raised. Lau was surprised to find a glowing smile from Cloud Willow outside. She had no idea the house would be fortified with police officers and had simply assumed the woman of the house, Samantha Cook, was still at home.

"Oh!" she exclaimed, upon recognizing Stanley Lau peeking round the door from within. At that point, she didn't know exactly what else to add and she stood there pleasantly enough, collecting her thoughts.

"Yes?" said Detective Lau.

"May I speak with Samantha?" returned Cloud Willow, tentatively at that point, trying to get back to her mission.

"No," said Lau. "What can I do for you?"

Cloud was not often one to mince words, showing little fear, so she blurted without hesitation, "Why not? It *is* Detective Lau, right?"

This caught Lau a little off guard, the assertiveness of the woman, and he returned, "Yes. But Dr. Day-Steiner is gone."

"I'm Cloud Willow, the neighbor? Remember?" she prompted and smiled again as warmly as one can smile in such circumstances. She was not a woman of devious means, honest and genuine whenever possible, a characteristic that caught many more cynical men and women off balance.

"I remember," said Lau guardedly.

She already knew the general plan for the day. Bernard had motorcycled off with Preston with the federal agent in tow; but the boy and his mother were going to be ushered somewhere else with police protection. "Are you sure Sam and Dalton have already left?" Cloud asked straight up.

"Why?" said the detective.

"Oh…. well, you know… since I live next door," she said, pointing to her house, "and my boyfriend is with Preston. I was just wondering if Sam had left yet. Maybe she and Dalton could just stay with *me*?"

"They're already gone, Ms. …uh, Ms. Willow. With the LAPD officer. So, perhaps you should go home. Things are not really safe around here right now," said Detective Lau hoping the woman would walk away, but she seemed planted right there at the front door.

As Stanley Lau wrangled with the very determined neighbor lady, Rosie Dixon was out back taking a mug of hot coffee to his SWAT team partner, Mutt, stationed on the patio.

"Here ya go," Rosie said.

"Where's my fuckin' jelly roll?" said Mutt.

"Where's my fuckin' tip?" said Sergeant Dixon as he turned to go back inside.

And just at that moment the shrubbery over to the left corner of the back yard moved and stopped!

Rosie halted dead in his tracks. He and Mutt both stared at the spot where the bushes had shifted, near the top of the wall in the corner, but it was still again. Everything was quiet.

"Must be a squirrel or cat," said Mutt.

"That was no god damn squirrel or cat," said Rosie, as he gently lifted his Glock 9mm out of his leg-strapped holster while his eyes searched the darkness around the bushes in that corner. Mutt stood and followed Sergeant Dixon's lead. Lifting his AR-15 easily from the glass patio table where he sat, he pulled back the bolt seating a cartridge in the chamber. He released the safety on his weapon and focused on the corner of the back garden where the bushes had rustled. Mutt fully absorbed the seriousness of the moment; he'd been in dangerous situations before. There would be no jokes about jelly rolls now. The tone had changed.

On the other side of the backyard fence, Martin Speck watched the developments he had initiated with a single tug on the twine that ran from him to the tall Camellia bush at the opposite corner of the property. He'd then gently put down his end of the twine because he figured another tug would be too much. The tease was in place. Let it ride. Let it draw them in, he was thinking as he watched the two men, some thirty-plus feet away consider the disturbance they had seen. Through his opera glasses, Martin watched the squat man, who had been slouched on a patio chair moments earlier, lift his AR-15. Martin had watched the African guy, draw this Glock from its holster. They were both zeroing in on the rustling from the far corner that Martin had created with nothing more than a length of twine. Simple is always best he confirmed again in his mind. His heart was racing at that point because real action was neigh. *That* was what brought him back to his assassin's world again and again or he would have abandon the killing business years ago and gone to tending his own beautiful garden in Europe not that far from the blue Mediterranean Sea. But gardens don't get your heart exercised like this. Neither his beloved Orchids nor Monet's floral testament to a fecund world could do it.

Before the shrub had been wiggled by Cain and had become a magnet, the two police officers were too far away for a good shot. A Desert Eagle is a fine instrument of death, but distance is its nemesis, plus Martin Speck already knew that with perimeter guards, the killing always has to be fast and it has be certain. From the outset, he calculated he had to lure them closer. And now his targets were moving slowly toward him and coming into reasonable range, with the black policeman in the lead and the stout fellow lagging a step or two behind.

Neither of the police officers was wearing a radio to call for backup, which was such a serendipitous benefit for Martin Speck, a gift bequeathed to him by the fact *this* SWAT detachment had not taken the call today seriously, so they did not even bother to pack their walkie-talkies. It was either good luck or bad luck depending upon which end of a fifty caliber projectile you might find yourself, but it should not have happened.

Martin, hidden behind the dense Camellia at the other corner of the property and leaning against the cement block wall, hauled his Desert Eagle from the clip at his back and he gently screwed on its silencer. As the two cops moved closer to investigate what had happened at the opposite corner, Martin leveled his fourteen inch weapon across the top of the wall. He brought the gun sights around pinpointing the right temple of the black officer who was moving in the lead about twenty feet away, stepping oh-so-carefully toward the farther corner of the Cook's backyard. The shorter police officer circled more toward Cain, but he was still focused on the farther corner.

Speck knew everything had to happen in less than two seconds. He squeezed the trigger and a muffled *thwump* sent a bullet into the right side of Rosie Dixon's skull, just above his ear killing him instantly and removing most of the left side of his cranium while hardly altering its flight path and penetrating the free-standing garage laboratory wall some fifteen feet beyond where Rosie dropped to the ground. Mutt heard the gun's silenced report off to his right as he saw Rosie falling and Mutt pivoted, lifting his AR-15 but not before a second *thwump* sent a fifty caliber bullet through Mutt's neck, right below his jaw, crushing his larynx, and severing his esophagus and his spinal cord, but leaving his carotid arteries and jugular veins unscathed. Mutt collapsed on the lawn not far from Rosie Dixon, sputtering blood, immobile and mute, but still alive.

Martin was over the fence in a flash, a strange looking commando in a Tommy Bahama Hawaiian shirt. And he went straight to gurgling Mutt, glancing for a second into those terrified eyes, reminiscent of the terrified eyes he had seen dozens of times. Martin covered the officer's dilated eyes with his left hand because he hated those eyes. Terror was not his game of choice. He quickly slipped his knife out from his ankle sheath and with one swipe he severed all the primary blood vessels in Mutt's throat as surely as he had severed them on the old woman in the house across the fence where they had such a wonderful back garden. Mutt was dead in seconds.

CHAPTER 67

While Mutt and Sergeant Dixon were collapsing to the backyard turf, while Martin Speck was expeditiously dragging their bodies off to the side of the yard where a glance from the kitchen window would not reveal them, Cloud Willow was pressing Detective Lau for information about Samantha Day-Steiner and Dalton. Stanley Lau rolled his eyes trying to rid himself of this woman who just did not comprehend the gravity of their situation and would not go away. How could he have planned for this, Lau lamented?

In less than a minute after firing two rounds from his silenced Desert Eagle across the back fence, Martin Speck had stowed the dead SWAT officers and he had slipped silently up to the rear stoop of the house where he was positioned for his final phase.

No one would accuse Detective Lau of being a silver-tongued devil, so allowing Cloud Willow to come inside the house that precarious afternoon was not a pretty exchange. "Come in! Go away! But please get off the damn porch!" a frustrated Detective Lau had exclaimed to the stubborn female and latter-day hippie from next door, who was poking her nose where it didn't belong and who refused to back down from Stanley's petulance and who remained steadfastly there on the front porch. It was not at all what Lau wanted in those minutes with a killer on the prowl.

"Okay! Okay! Then *please*, *please* come inside," Lau had finally conceded and by grabbing her wrist he basically dragged her through the wide front door into the living room to get her out of public view in case the assassin, Cain, would come cruising by.

Lau had no idea the beast was already at the back door, waiting and listening carefully to everything. It was a small home and enthusiastic conversations in the living room were quite audible from the rear stoop, if one were to pay attention. Of course, Martin Speck did pay attention. He was passively learning all kinds of information about where his target and his target's family had gone. It was embarrassingly easy. Martin Speck was smiling as he replaced the spent cartridges in the clip from his Desert Eagle. When there's a gunfight, you never want to come up one bullet short.

Samantha Day-Steiner began pacing in Detective Jack's Hollywood apartment. The worry was on the rise again, as she fretted and wrung her hands, which was very distressing behavior for Dalton who was trying to play chess with Ahmad, but who could hardly take his eyes off his mother. Her distress was gradually absorbed as his own worry and distress, a capillary action that was not lost on Fitzgerald Jack as he watched. Watson, the detective's gargantuan cat lay contentedly next to the chess board on the dining table and he examined with extreme focus as the chess pieces were moved, as though he knew what they were doing and what the superior move might have been. The cat would also look up with unblinking judgmental green eyes as Samantha paced by the game and Watson would issue a curious deep-throated purr each time. Her troubled energy did not sit well with him.

"Professor," said Fitzgerald, finally, from where he relaxed on his worn sofa, "why don't you sit down again? There is nothing to do right now, but wait."

"But I have no idea as to what's going on back there. Where Preston is and where that… that… *man* might be!"

"Preston has gone to your neighbor's mountain cabin. Detective Lau may have already arrested the bad guy – we don't know – but at the very least, that guy is not here. He doesn't know we are here, and he doesn't know how to find us. So, why don't you sit down and try to relax?"

"Why doesn't Preston call?" said Samantha, holding out her cell phone as a visual aid. She'd called at least half-a-dozen times since they arrived at the apartment.

"I don't know. He will when he can," said Detective Jack. "I'm sure of that."

"Mom?" said Dalton, looking over to her from the game. "Are we okay?"

She did her best to look like she was in control and she smiled back, "Yes, Dalton, we are okay. We're good."

"We're here, you know," said Dalton to his mom, being as grown up as he could. "Fitzy is a *police officer!*"

She glanced at Detective Jack and then returned to her son. "Yes. Yes. I know," she said trying a wry smile. "We'll be fine."

Dalton returned to the chess board and he stroked the large animal lying royally next to him. Watson arched his back ever so slightly to receive the gesture and he purred as loudly as an outboard motor.

"You are a very good chess player," said Ahmad to the boy, trying to offer a change in mood.

"That's what my dad says," returned Dalton. Still, he was not to be placated so easily and he added matter-of-factly pointing to the taken pieces, "But I think you're winning by half a point."

Cain could see his moment of action was taking shape. He could hear the frustration in one of the officer's voices as he spoke to someone who had shown up at the front door unexpectedly. Apparently it was a neighbor lady. There were no other voices from within, so Martin wasn't exactly certain as to how many policemen might be waiting inside, but he guessed two or three and his guesses in these matters were usually pretty accurate. He wasn't specifically aware of the praying mantis man, the bird-like man, because that officer so rarely uttered a word. But he'd distinctly heard a woman and two others speak.

"Jeff," Martin could hear an angry man yell in the front of the house, "check on your teammates and see what the hell is keeping them?"

My god, thought Speck! It was manna from heaven; and he dropped away from the back door and squatted near the wall. He could hear the footsteps of the officer called "Jeff" coming through the kitchen toward the door leading onto the stoop. Cain remained still, pressed against the outer wall, and he held his breath.

Jeff had glanced out back through the kitchen windows, but he could see no one outside, so he opened the back door and walked onto the stoop. He foolishly didn't even have his AR-15 raised for action. It had not even been locked and loaded. This was too much, thought Martin, when he saw Jeff come into the sunshine and glance around the yard. The police officer was not three feet away. Martin could see him breathing and could discern his serious curiosity as to why no one was there.

"Sergeant Dixon?" yelled Jeff out into the yard.

But those were the last two words he would ever utter because a muted, fifty caliber bullet went *thwump* through his skull, splattering gray matter, blood and bone fragments across the driveway to his left. Jeff actually did not have time to see anything in the back garden or hear anything, either, because the world and everything in it went suddenly dark and silent. His lifeless body tumbled forward down the five steps leading from the rear stoop to pavement, and his AR-15 clattered along those same steps, bouncing to rest next to him where he sprawled below Martin Speck, who was still squatting against the wall and gripping his Desert Eagle in both hands. At that point Cain rapidly reconsidered his options. The clattering of the weapon was not to his liking. Not good.

"Jeff?" Cain heard a shout from inside the house in a voice pitched by concern, leaving little doubt the shouter had heard the assault rifle clanking in a summersault down the steps. Cain should have grabbed the weapon at the moment of the kill. It could have gone that way, he admonished himself, but he didn't visualize it properly.

CHAPTER 68

Nearly eight thousand feet above San Bernardino, in his squat rudimentary cabin buried among towering firs and pines, Big Buster Bernard was building a fire beneath the broad stone hearth in the center of the cabin that opened on two sides, one warming the galley – as he called it – and the other serving the living room. The wide meticulously stacked tower of granite rocks that created the fireplace and chimney, plus the broad cement foundation on the earth below the fireplace, provided the primary weight-bearing support for a single, twelve-by-twelve inch hewn hardwood beam that ran the length of the cabin at the roof's peak. Every other structural element of the cabin relied on those two fundamental features including the exterior log walls.

"Took Cloud and me two solid months haulin' up rocks every day and settin' 'em just so, to build this fireplace," said Buster. "But it works great, draws the smoke and puts out considerable heat when ya need it," he said, arranging fire wood and not paying that much attention to his guests.

Skylar watched Buster, hands stuffed into his pockets and wondering what the hell he was doing there in the mountains. Two days ago he imagined this would be his last gig with the agency. Quickly over. Instead, he was buried in the woods with a crazy survivalist and a geeky scientist who seems to have managed to fit a nuclear reactor into a carry-on suitcase. To Bobby, it was a world gone mad.

He glanced at Dr. Cook's small, alloy luggage near the farther wall among the mismatched furnishing in the living room of the cabin. The suitcase was precisely where Preston had deposited it when they first came inside not much more than an hour ago. Cold fusion was absolutely a mind-boggling concept to the Special Group agent. Did the small reactor really work? Was it safe? Bobby's murdered, brilliant but foolish friend, Maxwell, said it was all true and it was as safe as baby formula. Max would have been alive that very day and still *shtupping* his partner's wife, if he had not tried to appropriate the discovery. Most likely in that scenario, the cuckolded Dr. Cook would be the dead one. Agent Skylar could see Preston Cook outside the cabin. He was trying desperately to get a connection on his cell phone, eager to speak with his wife to find out if she and Dalton were okay, if they had gotten to the LA cop's residence in one piece. Preston was looking at the lit display on his Sanyo flip phone, disgusted that it was scanning for a signal and there was nothing to be found. He moved around the property, walking past the busted Taurus, hoping to pick up even the faintest connection, but to no avail. Neither Buster nor Bobby knew Preston had juiced up his family's cell phones to communicate directly with satellites when necessary among other things, but it wasn't working from where they were ensconced in steep mountains.

"Told him, ya can't use those phones up here," said Buster standing up straight, dusting off his hands from stacking the firewood and glancing outside at his Pasadena neighbor. "And that's the way I like it," he added. "Cloud and me, we don't even have one of them infernal devices. Gov'ment listens in…" said Buster before he regarded Agent Skylar and remembered Skylar *was* the government. Their eyes connected for just a second but Big Buster deftly skipped ahead and added, "Have'ta be on the phone twenty-four-seven. I see the kids. I don't get it."

"Yeah," said Bobby absently and he let go of the government conspiracy thread. "I know what you mean," he added, but he desperately wanted to check in with Digger Mac Brown and he wanted to call his wife, too, just like Preston out there wandering around. But Skylar also knew his own family would not be in Cain's crosshairs as Preston's might have been on that afternoon.

Of course, if the phones didn't work, Bobby reckoned he had his laptop in the car. He typically communicated with his boss via satellite and the Internet, but he quickly discovered the laptop problem was just like the cell phone problem that Preston Cook was having. Skylar had no dish on the mountain and he had no clear line of sight to the south where the telecommunications satellites swung through the heavens and where the cell phone relay stations stood like sentries across the landscape. Accessing an internet pathway was not likely going to happen from their location. They were electronically marooned, which apparently pleased the bejesus out of the big guy, Buster Bernard. But Bobby's world was different. Isolation for him was a serious problem. He absolutely knew Cain was *not* isolated. Cain was undoubtedly on the move and dining on all the information he needed to complete his mission, served up by a very wealthy and sophisticated adversary somewhere on the planet. No matter how safe Buster thought his cabin was, there in the mountains, his crazy conspiracy theories were right on the money about the reach of government intelligence. Bobby Skylar knew it was just a matter of time before, one way or another, Cain would be coming up that miserable dirt trail to find Preston Cook and his carry-on suitcase. It was inevitable.

In Pasadena Martin Speck was guessing correctly that the clattering of the AR-15 on the steps had drawn the attention of the officers inside the Cook residence. He knew a another cop was going to come to the back of the house to investigate what had happened and that officer was not going to be casual about it, like the first one. He would be ready, locked and loaded. Cain did not know for certain that only two officers remained inside, although he had concluded it was not more than three given what he had heard. For Cain three was a very manageable number.

The house was small and it only took Speck a few seconds to scoot from where he had been crouched on the back stoop, around the side of the house along the driveway. He pushed past some unattractive and not-so-well-tended shrubs that were nearly wild and overgrown to make his way to the wide front porch, where he paused again just around the corner and he listened quietly. He could hear the muffled voice of the detective calling for his colleague. "Jeff?" Cain could tell from the sound that the officer had already gone to the rear of the house and was likely in the kitchen looking into the back yard at that moment.

Cain recognized he had successfully outflanked his opponent. He accurately anticipated that when the third cop he had killed was spotted in a pool of blood on the pavement at the base of the stoop, with his AR-15 next to him, the wind would shift very quickly and the remaining officers inside, however many there were, would regroup at the front of the house in the living room.

Detective Lau had told Cloud Willow to stay put when he dragged out his 9mm Glock, holding it stiff-armed in front of him as he went to the back of the house looking for the SWAT team members he had requested for support that morning, *all* of whom were now missing. It was not the way he envisioned the afternoon going and he knew something was dreadfully wrong. Perspiration was beginning to appear across Stanley Lau's bare scalp and forehead as he moved toward the kitchen and listened as carefully as was possible for any sounds.

"Jeff?" he said loudly one more time and there was no answer.

Lau went to the kitchen window. He didn't stick his face right up to the glass like a round pale target for someone to put a hole in it. Instead, he leaned to the side of the window and eased a glance from the edge. He could see nothing from that angle, the first two bodies having been heaved into a pile out of sight.

So, the detective stepped toward the back door that led onto the stoop, but he only had to barely crack open that door before he could see Jeff's body lying at the bottom of the steps with his AR-15 right next to him. The entire left side of the officer's head was missing. The wound had come from the same gun, realized Stanley Lau in an instant that had killed the professor over at CTU, a fifty caliber Desert Eagle.

"Oh, shit!" he said to himself as he retreated from the door.

He knew he had to get back to the front room immediately, to where Cloud Willow and his strange partner were waiting. He also understood in that moment that the other officers, Mutt and Sergeant Dixon, would not be helping him any more than bloody Jeff. Lau quickly calculated they had all better get the hell out of the house and call for more back-up. Why in god's name did the precinct send just three men that day, and three men who didn't really have their heads in the game?

Lau eased through the kitchen and the dining room toward the living room and he continued to hold his Glock at the ready. The bastard Cain was out there somewhere! Lau saw Cloud Willow standing directly ahead with her arms at her sides. The insect man was off to the right, wiggling and alert as he shifted foot to foot where he stood.

"We've gotta get the fuck out'a here," said Lau as he came into the living room. "Common," he gestured and he headed for the front door. But then he realized neither of the others budged. "Common, damn it!" said Lau, yelling at them.

Then he heard the click of a hammer being drawn back, as a weapon was cocked directly behind him. The blood in Detective Lau's veins went instantly cold as ice. He knew Cain was inside. In that first second he raced through his choices. Turn quickly and step sideways while unloading as many rounds as possible at this man, who he had yet to see? What about the civilian woman standing right there? And his partner, who seemed immobilized? Lau realized fairly quickly that if he didn't kill Cain immediately, in that first fusillade, the uninvited neighbor lady and his partner were both dead. Why in god's name did she come over here? Nothing was going right in his misbegotten plan to capture the assassin.

Lau saw he was trapped, so he raised his hands, pistol still clutched tightly with his finger on the trigger, and he turned slowly around to face his adversary. Maybe a negotiation would work. Maybe he could bluff his way out of this, and if not, he was a pretty damn good shot on impulse.

By then, Martin Speck knew for a certainty there were only these two cops remaining in the house. What good fortune that was, because they were both standing only a few feet beyond the muzzle of his Desert Eagle. Not so fortunately, there was an unknown civilian woman right between the two officers. Cain already had overheard Dr. Cook and his family had been spirited away.

CHAPTER 69

Preston Cook came back inside the cabin, rubbing his shoulders and hands. It was starting to get cold. They were at a high altitude and it was late in October. And Preston was not pleased with his inability to make phone contact.

"You can't get anything up here," he said, holding up his cell phone as a visual aid. "I've tried it all around the property... *and* half-way down the road. There is no signal to be found. Not a flicker."

"Should' a asked," said Buster stoking the fire that was just beginning to come alive beneath the rather substantial stone hearth, small flames in the kindling, reaching upward, wanting desperately to enjoy the bark-covered logs crisscrossed above them. He blew on the hints of the fire to come and the flames liked it. "No cell phone is gonna work up here," he said. "The hills knock out the radio waves. There's no connectin' to no cell phone antennae 'til yer half way back to Old Mill Road. Don't ya know how that works?" said Buster a little surprised he had to explain it to his physicist friend and neighbor. "It's line'a sight."

Of course, Preston knew about radio waves. He'd explored radio waves, microwaves, x-rays, and gamma rays in his cold fusion work over the years. But at the moment he wasn't calculating like a scientist. He was a husband and a father who wanted to know if his family was safe. Like any guy with a cell phone, he just wanted it to do its job. "Yes," he said glumly to Buster, "I understand how radio waves work. I hoped that I'd get a bounce somewhere."

"Well, ya can't," said Buster.

"What's the chance of us getting away from here to a place where we can make some calls?" said Preston looking at Skylar, since the federal agent seemed to have the better handle on dangers.

"Believe me, Dr. Cook, I want to touch base as badly as you do," said Bobby. "I'd like to get a sense of what's going on with Cain."

"How do you 'get a sense of what's going on with Cain?'" probed Preston. "Do you get a sense of him when he's at our door? That's when I would get a sense of him."

Preston and Bobby just stared at one another. The agent didn't try to answer. It was a sarcastic question, anyway. Skylar figured he was looking ahead to a very tedious seclusion with this scientist, even if it only lasted two days. Pasadena's Detective Lau had not appreciated how seriously dangerous Cain could be and apparently neither did Professor Cook.

"So... anybody up for Navy bean soup?" said Chef Buster Bernard suddenly, trying to get beyond the heated words. "Not exciting... but hot and filling," he laughed. Buster was limited in the kitchen but he could throw together passable chow and his Navy beans with chunks of canned ham made a stout meal.

"Sounds delightful, my friend, but what else you got?" said Bobby Skylar, eager to go with a shift in attitude and who, after all, was a bona fide Washington, D.C. yuppie and a foodie, too. He had learned to invent simple but savory dinners over the years. In fact he had a really good nose for combinations from scratch, using random ingredients, and when he was home he made most of the evening meals. His wife marveled at his instincts in the kitchen. Truth was, Bobby really enjoyed the challenge of creating a dinner out of nothing. As he stood there in the heavy, timber hide-away in the mountains above San Bernardino, he was pining to be back in Foggy Bottom with his family, sipping a mellow merlot, while his whisk rattled in a bowl, creating something tantalizing for the people he loved. He could not help but slide into the galley along with the big biker just to see what might be cooked up on the spur.

When Detective Lau had turned fully around with his hands raised but with his gun still clutched in his right hand just in case he chose to go for it on impulse, he found a tallish attractive man of indiscernible lineage, standing in the corner of the living room. The man looked like he was on vacation, wearing a Hawaiian shirt and beige linen trousers. He had short, tousled, bleached hair as trendy as any serious LA player. It was not what Lau expected at all. The detective didn't really know what kind of man he would find, but it wasn't that guy. Of course, it would have been impossible to expect anything, since there was no official report available as to what this creature looked like. Cain did, however, hold the large nickel-plated handgun Lau knew would be waiting for him, a fourteen inch .50 caliber Desert Eagle with a silencer. However, the weapon was pointed, not at Detective Lau, but at the neighbor woman, who was frozen in place and strangely expressionless.

What a son-of-a-bitch, thought Lau. She'll be the first to get blasted if I try anything. The bastard knows what he's doing.

Martin Speck said softly in his mysteriously accented but precise English, "Put the Glock on the floor and kick it over toward me, please."

Lau leaned down and did as he was told, shoving the gun across the hardwood floor with his toe. Cain gave it little heed as the weapon slid up next to his soft webbed, brown leather Italian loafers and he kept his attention riveted on his captives, with the muzzle of his Desert Eagle aimed at Cloud Willow. Cain had already collected significant information while listening from the back of the house; so he knew what questions he was going to ask.

"Are you both police officers?" said Martin Speck glancing back and forth between the lieutenant and the peculiar, thin assistant.

"Yeah," said Lau while the sweat that had been forming on his brow sent a droplet down the side of his face.

"Do you know who I am?" asked Cain, not boastfully but simply framing the conversation.

"You're some kind of assassin hired by a foreign government to kill a couple of American professors," said Lau.

"Interesting," said Martin Speck oddly amused. "I don't think of myself as an assassin… but it doesn't matter." Then he went right back to business, "I understand that Professor Cook has gone into hiding."

"He's not here," said Lau.

"Where is he?"

"He's gone up into the mountains. I don't know where."

"Surely the professor did not leave on foot and alone… into the mountains. He must have been in the company of someone."

"He has guards," came back the detective, "but I don't know where they went."

"His family, on the other hand, did not go with him, did they?" said Speck, using the conversation he had overheard while on the back stoop.

"His family is also guarded, and I do not know where they went, either," returned Detective Lau.

"So, everybody is guarded and you don't know where any-body went."

"That's the size of it," said Lau.

"Then what do you suggest? Since there is nothing here for me, should I dispose of you all right now and be on my way?"

"Listen…" said Lau, kicking it up a notch in his voice. "There're a couple of things. First off, you should understand that there are more police officers on the way right now. That won't be good for you. Second, this woman," he gestured with an elbow toward Cloud Willow, "has nothing to do with the professor or anything you might be after. She's just a neighbor. That's all. So… so, I'm offering you a deal. You let her go home… and I will make sure you get away even if our back-up arrives first. Okay? I'll do it, too. Just let her go. You have my word."

"As an officer and a gentleman?" smiled Martin Speck.

"She's of no use to you," repeated Lau.

"I have a different thought about that," said Martin. "You don't want anything to happen to this lady, do you?"

"What do you mean?" said Lau.

"Tell me the name of the police officer who is protecting the Cook family. Do that, and this will be over. Be assured, I can confirm what you tell me."

Lau thought about it. He considered lying to Cain. How could this guy from another country confirm anything? On the other hand, he wasn't a street thug and maybe, as a foreign government's agent, he did have access to some kind of intelligence or databases. This situation was out of Stanley Lau's league. Lt. Lau's face was drained of color and he began to feel faint as he raced through alternative scenarios before saying, "Look. I don't know the man. All I can say is he's with the Los Angeles Police Department. A detective. Last name is Jack. That's all I know." It was a partial lie.

"Where did they go?" said Cain calmly.

"I don't know that, either. A safe house somewhere in LA, I imagine. I don't have an address."

"Somewhere in Los Angeles?" repeated Cain.

"Yes," confirmed Lau.

"Like his home?"

"That would be stupid of him," said Lau.

"But that's what I heard you say. You said they'd gone to this cop's apartment."

Christ, thought Lau, a chill racing up and down his spine as he realized he actually did say that to this daffy broad, only a few minutes ago. Obviously the bastard was outside and listening. What else does he know? "Well, I'm not sure," Lau mumbled. He knew he was losing ground. "Maybe I thought that's where they would go… but I don't know if that's where they really went! And, if they did go there, I don't know where the hell it is!" He was trying to be as persuasive as possible.

"Detective Jack with the Los Angeles Police Department?" said Speck, confirming what he had heard.

"Yes," said Stanley Lau. And that was his very last word.

Cain quickly pivoted his Desert Eagle toward Detective Lau, catching a glimpse of Lau's widening eyes and dilating pupils, as Martin Speck fired one round directly into the officer's chest, instantaneously pulverizing his sternum and sending a cone of ripped internal organs flying out of Lau's back, the bullet hardly slowing as it burst through the house front door leaving a two inch hole in the center of a three foot smear of lumpy scarlet blood. The heavier bits of tissue were already beginning to slide slowly down the inside of the door. Lau was lifted off his feet by the impact of the bullet and he dropped heavily, like a butchered steer's hind-quarter, just as he had been standing with his hands raised. He came to rest with his balding head against the base of the door and his dead eyes wide open. Stanley's hoped-for front page arrest story had suddenly turned into an *LA Times* front page story of bloody mayhem in Pasadena and Stanley Lau's father's dreams of his son giving up this police work to return to the family's restaurant business were lost forever.

The gangly, awkward assistant had backed up flat against a wall and when he saw Lau blown backward, he tried to quickly haul out his own .38 snub nose from his belt holster, which he had rarely even used at the practice range, but he immediately lost control of his quick-draw and the short weapon tumbled forward through the air and out of his twitching hands. The .38 hit the hardwood floor and bounced a couple times before stopping nearer to Cain than to the quirky Pasadena officer. Speck watched the entire clumsy, pathetic maneuver. He studied the strange man who had attempted to avenge his partner's killing, who shifted where he stood against the wall with both hands stretching toward Cain, wiggling there like they could summon the snub nose pistol up from the floor and into his grasp. After a couple of beats looking at the odd creature, Martin Speck discharged his Desert Eagle once again, blowing a hole in the insect-man's chest, too, but he didn't tumble backward because he was already up against the wall, nor did the bullet rip through his heart. So, Lau's peculiar assistant just stood there for a moment with a large bloody hole in his right pectoral and with his hands still outstretched and wiggling like he was holding two live fish. He expired while still on his feet. The assistant's arms dropped to his sides, his eyes closed, and he toppled forward like a plank, hitting the floor flat and loud. There wasn't much splatter behind him because the odd man had been standing against the wall, but there was a four inch aperture in the plaster and the redwood siding through which daylight could be seen.

Then Martin Speck turned toward the woman who had not moved a muscle since Cain first entered the room. They were alone. Frankly he was surprised that she had not screamed or cowered when he killed the two police officers. He wrongly concluded she was in shock, stunned to speechlessness, because Cain did not know Cloud Willow. During that entire interaction, from the moment he had slipped quickly through the front door and caught her and the strange officer from behind while they craned their necks to see where Lau had gone toward the rear of the house, from when Cain had concealed himself in the hallway while they waited for Detective Lau to return from discovering his slain colleagues out back, Cloud had deliberately reframed herself emotionally. She had to do so. She transitioned from the worried, helpful neighbor she was when she first came over to see what she could do, to the centered, committed, and spiritually-minded being that was always at her core. So, at that moment, when Cain turned toward her, although she was pale from the sight of what had happened, she was not intimidated and she stood firmly there in the living room staring at Martin Speck. Cloud looked directly into the eyes of the monster with his fifty caliber handgun leveled in her direction as she said firmly, with condemnation laced by sorrow, "These are horrendous acts." She uttered the words like they mattered to the assassin. "They are inexcusable. And I feel pity for you."

Martin Speck nodded ever so slightly. He actually admired the unflappable courage he was seeing in this woman. He hadn't been reprimanded by anyone in a long time. "I know you live with the man who escorted the professor to where he is hiding," he said to her. "Do you know where that is?"

"Yes, I do," said Cloud and then she fell silent. Martin Speck could hardly believe what he was seeing. Was this a challenge?

"Well," said Martin, "where did they go?"

Cloud Willow stepped forward slowly, her light cotton dress swam around her curvy body as she moved and her eyes were absolutely clear and unwavering. She nearly floated across the room until she was standing directly in front of Cain. She continued to stare into his eyes, which appeared to shift from green, to hazel, to blue, as indeterminate as his nationality or race. Then she reached out gently with her right hand and took the silencer of the Desert Eagle between her thumb and silver-ringed index finger, and she guided the muzzle of the weapon to where it rested between her breasts, right on top of her heart. Standing ready and waiting patiently in front of the killer, Cloud Willow said clearly, "I am not going to tell you." Their gazes were fiercely locked when Martin Speck raised his left hand and gently covered her eyes.

CHAPTER 70

Buster Bernard and Agent Skylar surprised themselves with what they managed to concoct in the primitive cabin's galley, serving up a meal that was quite reminiscent of Beef Stroganoff, while not being the actual thing. It was certainly not beans and ham, as originally envisioned. This collaborative effort had become a small challenge to Bobby that lifted him out of his most immediate worries and bonded him, to a degree, with Big Buster Bernard. They were having a good time together in that mountain kitchen. They were laughing. It happened there were fettuccini noodles and a canned roast in the larder. Fortunately, Cloud and Buster had been up here in July with supplies, so Buster and Bobby managed to dig up not only onions, but mushrooms, butter, and passable sour cream from a non-electric cold locker that was right out of the *Survivalist Handbook*. Of course, there was salt and pepper. And the resulting meal wasn't bad at all, Bobby thought, as the two men served their repast to their sole, glum bunker-mate, while the fire under the central hearth began to pop and crackle, reaching out with warmth to the refugees on a night that promised a goodly chill. Skylar wished his wife could see what had been done with bare rudiments in the kitchen. He was proud of himself.

Big Buster Bernard was enthusiastic, too, with their surprise entre. "Damn, Mr. Agent Man, we done good!" he said. His beans had ended up as part of a salad. In spite of his peculiarities and paranoia, Buster was basically an appreciative and generous soul.

However, Dr. Preston Cook was much less enthused. "Thanks," he said simply as he began to eat. It's not that he wasn't grateful, but food was never that important to him. Some days, working in his garage lab while Sam was teaching, he would forget to eat altogether until his son found him after dark and asked if dinner would be ready soon. The question would yank Preston back into the real world and his responsibilities in it. On those evenings Preston quickly assembled macaroni or potatoes and a meat, not fancy, but it filled the bill for Dalton and they would eat together and tease one another. Cooking was no more than chemistry to Preston, not art. Read the formula and follow it.

Buried in a mountain fortress, as he was on that day with Skylar and Bernard, Preston Cook would have eaten something right out of a can and he would have been quite content, lost in his world of subatomic particles, gamma rays, cold fusion, a son he loved dearly and a wife who continually broke his heart. His mind was almost never in the here and now, only coming and going enough to drive a car, get dressed, and sometimes enjoy young Dalton. Maybe that's what was wrong with his marriage, he analyzed, upbraiding himself as he forked down a mouthful of the Skylar-Bernard impromptu faux Beef Stroganoff. When would he be able to contact his lovely, wonderful Samantha and set things right?

Fitzgerald Jack was on the phone, having gotten a call from downtown moments earlier. Dalton and Ahmad were well into a second game of chess and well into a second bag of Cheetos, too, with six empty Diet Coke cans making a neat line nearby. Samantha Day-Steiner had gone outside for fresh air. The phone call and the information had Detective Jack instantly up from his slouched position on the couch to leaning forward totally engaged. His eyes became focused and intense, moving right to left in their sockets, seeking answers to what he was hearing. The energy in his attitude even brought huge, waddling Watson all the way across the room from the table where the chess game continued. The large animal sat down in front of Fitzy on the coffee table, a favorite spot of his, and he purred softly while he watched Fitzy on the phone. Like many domesticated animals, Watson was miraculously attuned to the most complex moods of his keeper.

"When?" said detective Jack

And he listened.

"All of them?" he said.

He continued to listen.

The telephone message from his boss made his blood run cold. He actually felt light-headed. There had been a gunfight in Pasadena at the Preston Cook residence, he was told. Detective Stanley Lau, of the Pasadena Police Department had been killed as had several other police officers that had been dispatched to help Lau. There were bodies everywhere and there had been a fire, too, at the residence but not much more information was available at that time.

Lt. Jack's supervisor, the Homicide Division Captain at LAPD, said the news would be breaking on television any minute. The Captain added that the Arab man who killed the UCLA kid might be involved. It was all unclear at that point. Fitzy's Captain continued by saying Washington people were asking questions about the whereabouts of their federal agent. The Captain asked Lt. Jack if he'd heard anything recently from Agent Skylar or the scientist and Fitzgerald replied he had not, repeating they'd headed up to a cabin somewhere above Crestline. Were the scientist's wife and kid still with him, his boss inquired? And Fitzgerald said they were. At the end of the conversation with the homicide division captain, Jack was told that what went down in Pasadena appears to be related to some bizarre international intrigue that had the feds' panties in a bunch. The Captain concluded by saying someone would phone Fitzgerald with developments as soon as more information was available.

"Damn!" said Fitzgerald under his breath as he put down the phone, thinking that he should never have been so compliant with Detective Lau's plan to lag behind, to arrest Cain. The federal guy, Skylar, had been pretty convincing in explaining that it was a different game with this kind of enemy. The risks and stakes were far higher. Cain wasn't going to retreat to the barrio like a gang-banger, where he could be picked up the next day in a sweep.

Detective Jack was allowing personal responsibility for what happened to his Pasadena police colleague dig into his soul, as if he had any control whatsoever over what that stubborn Pasadena detective would choose to do. Unfortunately, this self-recrimination would become a mounting burden for Fitzgerald to carry, as the years rolled onward. This was one in a mounting number of guilt episodes for a conscientious, smart, and hard-working LA detective, the conflicted offspring of a cop and a professor. He was alone in life partly because every girlfriend in forty years of Lt. Jack's life had found his cross too heavy a burden.

Fitzy looked to where his two young guests were playing chess and having a relatively good time near the window, but Fitzgerald Jack's heart was sinking because he was harboring a fugitive. It seemed to be the right thing to do, but it ran against the rules. He had to remind himself that he had a plan for the Saudi man and he had promised he would get Ahmad Mulham home to his family. Fitzgerald knew in the depths of his investigator's heart the young man had not killed anybody. Nonetheless, with the latest developments in Pasadena it was getting very complicated. Turning in Ahmad to his colleagues at LAPD would likely lead to a lengthy legal process that could last for months and perhaps become an international spectacle given the prestige enjoyed by the young man's family. Lt. Jack also figured, with a powerful father like Ahmad's and with his connections, a lot of red tape may fall by the wayside if they simply cut to the chase and reached out to him for help. That was the plan.

Over the ensuing years, Detective Jack would become a master at cutting to the chase and avoiding red tape. He'd actually learned the strategy from his mother at an early age and it would serve him exceedingly well during his decades of spectacular success within the Los Angeles Police Department. But right then, in the twilight hours of that October day in 2005, Fitzgerald Jack was painfully wrestling with the question of whether or not he was doing the right thing. Even at forty-something, he hadn't learned to fully trust his instincts and he was agonizing about his future in law enforcement after what may become a fiasco. After all, he was giving safe haven to a wanted Muslim in the wake of 9/11. In those days, the western world was not that friendly to Muslims on the run, especially if they were implicated in murder. He could easily find himself behind bars along with Ahmad.

CHAPTER 71

One hour before Fitzgerald Jack received his report on the horror at the scientist's house in Pasadena, Martin Speck stood in the living room of the Cook residence with his Desert Eagle pressed against the slowly rising and sinking chest of a woman he had never seen until a few minutes prior. And even though he had his left hand covering her clear dark brown eyes, in his mind he could still see them looking at him. He was perplexed and fascinated by her determined demeanor. Neither of them spoke during that interval until he suddenly lifted the muzzle of his weapon from her chest, removed his hand from her brow, and gestured for her to get out.

Cloud Willow did not question that development and she gently backed away a step or two from the assassin-for-hire. For Cloud to actually leave that bloody scene, Cain had to grab the foot of Detective Lau and drag his body from where he had fallen with his head against the door, blocking the exit. Cloud and Cain regarded one another for a long moment and then she stepped calmly beyond Detective Lau's body, opened the bullet-punctured front door on which thickening blood and bits of flesh slipped slowly downward. She gracefully departed onto the wide front porch and into the late afternoon, walking past the sedate wicker furniture, not hurrying in the slightest until she disappeared from sight. Martin Speck and Cloud Willow had no further contact that day.

Cloud had never really been the ice queen she had seemed to the assassin after the killings and when she reached her own front porch next door she immediately threw up into the flowerbed. Of course, Martin understood the neighbor lady was going to telephone the police as soon as possible. That fact didn't escape him, but neither did it trouble him. His job there was mostly done as he removed the silencer from his weapon and secured the Desert Eagle to the clip on the back of his belt. Then, moving briskly, he went out the back door of the house, negotiating the sprawled corpse of the officer Jeff and his clattering AR-15. Martin went straight to the door of the garage laboratory which was merely a footnote when he first accepted this assignment. In those early intelligence reports the garage had not played much of a role in the cold fusion research. It was Dr. Umberto who had been conducting the research at CTU, so the story went. Clearly, the intelligence was faulty. Martin now understood this little garage was the primary research venue. He had to kick open the door, splinters flying, and he went inside.

This part of his mission wasn't going to take much time, but Martin Speck could not help but hesitate on entering what appeared, from the outside, to be an old-fashioned, free-standing two-car garage. But inside, with the lights on, the space was transformed into an uneven yet impressive small scientific facility, concocted by Professor Cook for his research. It was an arresting sight even to a layman like Speck, who was educated enough to understand the linked-together array of computers, the metal-shop equipment, a chemistry scaffold befitting a college classroom, and of course the glass enclosed clean room to the rear with instruments defying his recognition. The laboratory would give anyone a moment's pause. How could the professor possibly have created this laboratory by himself? It was almost incomprehensible. But that was all the reflection and appreciation Martin could afford at that time with the police certainly on the move, so he went quickly forward with his task, tossing around the same powdered napalm with which he'd

razed Dr. Umberto's office and home. The single, filled, plastic bag-
gie from Martin's trouser pocket was quite sufficient and a Bic lighter
did the rest.

By the time Martin Speck had leapt across the back wall of the
Cook property, basically retracing his steps, the garage and its contents were already significantly involved in a billowing fire. Martin
didn't look back, but in the garden of the Cooks' rear neighbor, he
did stop for a second to contemplate the archway of pink roses that
had so taken him when he passed by before and he was once again
pleasantly reminded of Monet's fragrant and gentle garden six thousand miles to the east. But Martin did not have the luxury of dwelling on that memory, so he jogged down the driveway to his white
BMW 745i waiting in front of the house where the old woman lay
with her throat slit.

As Speck turned his ignition key in the big sedan, he could
already hear sirens in the distance as police and emergency vehicles sped toward the Cook residence. He glanced over the roof of
the old woman's house, beyond her lovely rear garden, and he could
see thick, black smoke rising from the garage laboratory, which he
imagined was now fairly well consumed in very intense and crackling flames.

That powdered napalm is such a magnificent tool, he was thinking, as he pulled away from the curb. At the end of the block, where
Martin turned onto the next residential street, two Pasadena police
cars with lights whirling screamed past him. Like any normal man,
he watched the vehicles race by his window. In fact, with all the commotion and sirens in the air, mouths-agape citizens were wandering
out of their houses like they were dazed or hypnotized to investigate the heavy police activity and the tower of black smoke not far
away. The Pasadena police in their cruisers were keenly focused on
their objective as they tore by, paying Martin Speck and the other

neighborhood rubberneckers no heed whatsoever. There's nothing like a building ablaze to get everybody's full attention, he thought.

When news was breaking on the television about the conflagration at a house in Pasadena and the bloody mayhem that had taken place at that address, it had everybody's attention in Los Angeles and especially within Lieutenant Jack's apartment. After watching the horrible news on television for twenty minutes, Samantha Day-Steiner whispered in a terrified voice to Fitzgerald that she needed some more fresh air and stood up, but before she could leave, Fitzgerald nabbed her with his most earnest and reassuring voice, "Your husband was not there, Doctor. He is safe."

"For now," she said. And with that she went outside again while the LAPD Lieutenant, her son, and the Arab man hung fast to the TV news.

Sam did not take well to hearing there had been a slaughter that afternoon at her home in Pasadena. It was shocking. It made her shiver thinking they may have left just in time. She was already a nervous wreck of a woman, conjuring up in her imagination all manner of calamity and horror that may be pursing them and her husband. This was too much. She pictured Preston and that federal agent both murdered somewhere en route to Buster and Cloud's mysterious cabin in the mountains. She was unsure of the plan. She was beginning to feel cornered. How could they turn Preston's personal safety and the safety of the research over to Buster Bernard and his cabin? Shouldn't the federal agent have known better? It all felt like madness, total madness.

When Samantha returned from her panic-fueled pacing outside the apartment, above the fountain in the courtyard, Detective Jack could immediately see the terror in her eyes. "It's going to be okay,

Dr. Day-Steiner," asserted Fitzgerald preemptively. "If your husband had been involved in what happened, in *any* way, we would have heard about it by now. I assure you."

"You don't know that," she said. "We don't know what has happened. I can't get Preston on my cell. I think something is wrong." Samantha appeared to be unaware of the impact her words were having on her son, sitting ten feet away. But she had always been direct in her speech and she was rarely circumspect when she shared her thoughts, even with Dalton in the room. It wasn't her nature.

"Mom...?" said Dalton. "Is dad hurt?" He was really afraid. Fitzgerald could see it clearly on the boy's face.

"No. No, Dalton. Your dad's okay," said the detective standing up from where he'd been sitting on the couch, trying to restore some order. "Let's not get carried away with our imaginations," he added stepping over to the frazzled, unpredictable woman, who was clearly coming unglued. Fitzy didn't really know her well enough to sense exactly what kind of strategy would be appropriate if she was seriously losing her grip. Still, he did reach out and touch her very gently on the shoulder to reassure her, and he tried to make direct and stable eye-contact, like he was trained to do with people on the edge. "It's going to be alright, professor," he repeated.

But she was too skittish for contact and turned away from his hand, rubbing her face vigorously with her finger-tips and moaning softly, "Oh, no. Oh, no. We've gotta get *out* of here, detective. That maniac will be headed our way."

Her husband's touch would have resulted in an entirely different outcome in this kind of ramped-up situation; it would have worked. In spite of how much he aggravated her, Preston had learned how to calm this bedeviled woman over the years of their marriage, because he really loved her. But that night in Hollywood she was not to be consoled by a stranger.

"Mom?" muttered worried Dalton.

Fitzgerald didn't want to treat Samantha like a child, so he tried to be honest by saying, "Staying calm is important. It's always the first thing," he said to her. Then he glanced at the two chess players now sitting near the television and he tossed them an encouraging wink. They were saucer-eyed and hanging on his every word. "Remaining in my apartment," the detective went on, "is the safest alternative right now. I can get officers here in a snap if we need them."

"I'd say we need them." said Samantha turning toward him, practically trembling where she stood.

"Well… I could do that, but it's a little bit complicated because we have a fugitive here," said Lt. Jack. Ahmad blushed but the detective followed up quickly to reassure him. "It's all cool, Ahmad. I know this is hard right now, but we're going to get you back home." Juggling as best he could, Fitzgerald returned to Samantha Day-Steiner to hold the situation together and he said to her, "It'll be dark soon. Let's sit tight 'til dawn. Okay? I can get help in two minutes with one phone call, if we need it. Believe me."

She looked at Fitzgerald Jack. Her composure was gone. She glanced at Dalton and then returned her gaze to her host, "I don't agree," she said. "Didn't that Pasadena detective promise safety? My son and I cannot stay here. Ahmad, you can do what you want."

CHAPTER 72

By six o'clock the same afternoon that he had put a fifty caliber bullet through the chest of Stanley Lau and he had incinerated the Cook garage laboratory, Martin Speck was back in his Beverly Hills Hotel room, thinking fleetingly of the Chock-Full-a-Nuts woman with whom he had shared the same bed the night before. What a naive and sweet woman she was, he thought, but so out of touch with the reality of her situation in Los Angeles. She should go back to New York and marry a kid from the neighborhood.

Then he flipped open his Mac laptop and made a crypto connection, looking for information. Almost anything could be had through his favorite international hacker cum researcher, who for this assignment had adopted the online moniker Breadcrumbs. Still, a reply to queries was rarely instantaneous and Martin Speck hated the delays even though he tolerated them. This job was already taking far too long. His custom was to enter an objective's territory and slice right through to his target, using surprise and swiftness to his advantage. Local police were almost never an issue because the motives and behaviors in an international operation did not comply with their parochial experiences. This time, however, the game wasn't playing out that way and the cops already had a bigger role than Cain preferred. And at least one more damn policeman was still in the picture, if Martin Speck understood correctly from his eavesdropping and the Pasadena plain-clothes officer's confused last sentences. There was still an LAPD detective named Jack in Cain's path and it seemed the scientist's wife and son were holed up with that detective.

Cain was eager to move forward. He wanted to get it done and he sure as hell wasn't going to let the descent of the sun and the growing darkness swarming the city slow him down. He could move in the pitch-black of night just as well as daylight. He was getting perturbed and that was not usually a good sign for his adversaries. Martin Speck called for room service and ordered a brie omelet with orange juice and coffee. He wanted the protein, sugar, and caffeine. He didn't take pills and he had work to do, which in those minutes involved firing off a few encrypted messages to Breadcrumbs. Cain's messages would prompt digital inquiries that raced round the globe, satellite to satellite, dipping into the most obscure corners of human life looking for bits of information that would guide Cain on two fronts. One involved the location of Preston Cook and where he had gone into hiding. The other involved the policeman who had spirited away the professor's wife and son. Martin Speck reckoned that when the data came back from Breadcrumbs, he could realistically formulate a hypothesis on how this cold fusion drama was unfolding and he could fashion his strategy.

The reach of the Breadcrumb's work on the Internet was mind-boggling. And it didn't take as long as Martin Speck expected before the answers to his questions and other useful information began to fill his inbox. This pleased him endlessly, because he truly felt stuck in his knotty little odyssey in America, which was not a country he cared for in the first place. He believed the United States for all its purported liberties was an arrogant, selfish, vulgar and violent nation. No other supposedly peaceful group of citizens on the entire planet shot each other to death at the rate that American citizens did. The shorter his stay in that toxic society the better, he figured. There were sensitive and cultured people Martin Speck knew in many other places around the globe and he would rather be spending quality time with them.

While finishing his cup of a bold African dark roast coffee with a touch of cream and sugar, Cain found through Breadcrumb's research that the partner of Cook's strange neighbor lady, the one who had put Cain's Desert Eagle up to her heart, was a motorcycle enthusiast. As it turned out, the partner's big Harley had a No-Jack computer chip planted on its frame, ostensibly so he could locate the vehicle if someone sneaked up under the cloak of night and hauled it away. Martin had to smile, because Harley-Davidson motorcycles were one of the few American artifacts he really *did* like. They are unique. He owned two of them, a quick little Sportster and a heavy road-hugging Duo-Glide, an older model, that seemed made for Switzerland where he spent as many of the summer weeks as he could when he wasn't working. Unfortunately, for Big Buster Bernard and every other No-Jack customer, this anti-theft technology was not secure. The bike could be tracked at any time by an outsider with sufficient hacking skills to get inside the No-Jack software and Breadcrumbs had just such hacking capability readily available. So, an hour after Martin had asked how he might find this particular Harley-Davidson Softail Classic, it was as good as located. Satellites can be oh-so wonderful, he thought and he smiled, thinking of the silvery servants whirling through cold space a couple of hundred miles above our lives, base stations for billions of data bits per second. What would he do without them?

The motorcycle was apparently on a southern slope in the San Gabriel Mountains, high above the San Bernardino plains, not far from the resort towns of Arrowhead and Big Bear, but seemingly not accessible by any known road. That was as close to his objective as Martin could get without actually going there himself. Still, it was information that was sufficient to him, because he was a man who regaled in a challenge and he figured he could find the bastards now, even with that limited direction. Martin Speck knew he would be headed up that way, sooner or later. He was confident and had always been confident since he was a child, traveling with his parents and visiting foreign capitals, frequently left to his own devices in strange lands with strange languages, yet even as a young boy he invariably found what he wanted. Perhaps that is why he was still breathing in October of 2005 and so many of his adversaries were not. And that was why he wasn't worried about locating Dr. Cook on that mountain.

The other interest to Martin was an LAPD detective named Jack. He'd been identified by the late Pasadena Detective Lau, a bit of information offered up to save the neighbor lady, or so it seemed at the time with a Desert Eagle in the picture.

This Detective Jack, according to what Martin heard and observed at the Cook residence, may have taken the target's family under wing and had gone off to seclusion at his *own home*! How odd is that? But then Speck found official confirmation through Breadcrumbs that there *was*, in fact, a real Detective Jack – first name Fitzgerald – working in the Los Angeles Police Department, Hollywood Division. So, the dead Pasadena cop's story held water.

At that point Martin Speck didn't know the Saudi young man was in the equation, the man whose suitcase Martin had found in that college boy's apartment on the other side of town. In fact, during those same minutes in which Martin ruminated over the information he gathered from Breadcrumbs about Lieutenant Jack, the young Arab was playing chess with Professor Cook's son by a kitchen window in the LAPD police officer's Hollywood apartment. It was before news broke on television about the murderous developments in quiet Pasadena.

Breadcrumbs reported to Martin Speck that Detective Jack was a budding star with the Los Angeles Police Department. The cop-on-the-rise lived in the heart of the city near the intersection of Hollywood Boulevard and Gower Street. A specific street address was provided by Breadcrumbs, too. This was better than half-a-mountain as a location, which was as close as Martin could get to the biker's hideaway. The LA detective's residence was specific.

Cain could not help but be pleased with what he'd gathered from the ethers and his contact there. Life was good. Information is strength. The guests this Los Angeles police officer was protecting could provide powerful leverage in delivering the man Martin Speck was after, the shy professor, the inventor of viable paradigm-changing cold fusion. After all, everybody loves family, even brilliant scientists, and surfacing an actual street address and apartment number that held the wife and child of the elusive physics professor was an irresistible opportunity.

Half an hour after Bobby's remarkable beef stroganoff and the screw-cap jug of the jaw-tightening burgundy Buster had managed to produce from his larder had been consumed, Professor Cook and Agent Skylar were pacing like leopards in the mountain cabin. The full onset of darkness brought a renewal of their worries and perhaps the wine enhanced those worries. Once the earthenware dishes were washed and put away, both of these men wanted desperately to make contact with the outside world. The federal agent was positive that information on the whereabouts of Cain would be available through his Special Group connections and Preston was simply out of his mind over concern for Samantha and Dalton, the most critical elements on his life's periodic table. All the while Big Buster Bernard sat in one of the overstuffed chairs in his cabin with his feet on a worn coffee table, trying to get his guests to calm the fuck down!

"Nobody'll come up here." he laughed. "It damn near killed *us* and we knew where we were goin'!" But Buster's good humor was not that comforting to Preston and to Bobby.

At the time, Buster Bernard had no idea what his lady, Cloud Willow, had been through earlier in the day, the horror of that afternoon, but Buster and Cloud were not the kind of couple to fret over the well-being of one-another when they were apart. They had a long-standing sense of individualism between them, so Buster was able to sit there in the secluded cabin with his legs crossed on the coffee table and believe comfortably that it would all work out somehow. That's the way he and Cloud had always been with each other. There are forces at play in the universe, they would say, that they cannot control. Both Cloud and Buster would agree that their cabin, hidden away as it was high in the mountains was an attempt at being in charge, but they were not so naïve as to really think it was foolproof.

Buster tried to convince his guests there wasn't anything that could be done until tomorrow anyway. Then he said if they absolutely *had* to move down the road for a cell phone or laptop connection perhaps in the morning they could very carefully find a line-of-sight to their distant base stations that were out of reach from the mountain cabin. The whole idea of it was mind-boggling to survivalist Buster. He shook his head in dismay. The need to be in-touch may be their undoing, he thought. Those two men reminded Buster of all those teenagers he'd see walking around in Pasadena everywhere with cell phones clapped to their earholes. Can't anybody be alone for five minutes, he wondered? Buster didn't quite see technology as a strength multiplier in the world. On the other hand, the killer Cain was connected, wired, and savvy to the internet's power.

"Hey, fellas," said Buster. "Why don't ya just sit yer asses down? Okay? We can't do nothin' till dawn anyways, so yer just gettin' yerselves all worked up walkin' back and forth like that!"

Neither of the men had actually noticed their pacing and they looked at one another on Buster's command, and stopped in their tracks.

Then out of Preston's fervent and mysterious mind he blurted, "Did you know that electrons move from one orbit to another orbit without traveling in between? They just show up at a new place. That's what we call the 'quantum leap' you've heard about. Stuff happens around us all the time that is totally outside human comprehension. Today has been like that for me," he added. And in that spirit of wonder and amazement, he stared through the window into the darkness outside. "The last forty-eight hours have been beyond my ability to understand."

Preston did recognize the other men's quizzical facial expressions at that point. He'd seen that look before on Samantha or students when he'd offer similar thoughts about life, subatomic particles, and the collision of distant galaxies. He had learned to avoid speaking this way in public most of the time. But on that night in the mountains Preston was blurting because he was tired, worn out, and afraid. All things large and small were always connected in his mind. His perception of human behavior was inextricably tied into his perception of drama on the smallest of stages. He couldn't help himself. Electrons, atoms, molecules, quarks and an endless array of excited waves and particles defined the universe in which he lived. Without his family to keep him on keel, Preston was often pretty much lost in the human world. He saw the force of atoms in all things the way Mozart may have heard musical notes in everyday cacophony. Preston was mad in a sub-atomic sort of way and he probably always would be. Yet he clearly wanted a normal life, too, and his heart was capable of mountainous love. Were his wife and his son okay? Were they safe? He was in agony over them. Preston understood both Sam and Dalton were off-kilter in their own inexorable ways, just as he was, but he also believed they needed him the way any dad and husband is needed. It was all mysterious and it was inexplicable, just like the quantum leap.

CHAPTER 73

Tucked between Tiffany's and Gucci in the row of boutiques off the lobby of the Beverly Hills Hotel, Martin Speck had noticed an FTD florist available to guests for that last minute thank-you. So, he stopped by the tight but well-positioned florist's shop before slipping away from the hotel into the night and he purchased a simple pair of fresh gardenias wrapped in cellophane. Martin thought their lush aroma would add a welcomed sweetness to his troubles while he sought out the home of Detective Fitzgerald Jack in Hollywood, where he also expected to find game-changing leverage in the form of Dr. Cook's wife and son.

Cain reasoned that going after the researcher's family was perhaps the most direct and least fussy route to accomplishing his mission. It was certainly more appealing to him than pioneering up the side of some strange mountain in late October to hunt out a cabin well above the tree line. Although that trek was likely to occur, Speck also knew that a threat to family makes for powerful leverage. Other efforts would be like wearing a gorilla suit to nab Sasquatch. As he paid for the gardenias he contemplated how to finish his job. The assignment, he sighed, was most assuredly a far more convoluted undertaking than he had pictured when discussing the project with his employer, and this in light of the fact that Cain will work in any circumstances for the right money.

Not so long ago, Cain had sent a fifty-caliber Desert Eagle bullet through the forehead of a would-be Indonesian despot while he was theoretically protected by a cohort of highly paid mercenaries. To build his empire, the despot had foolishly introduced fees and tariffs that disrupted an established narcotics trade route. It was the drug dealers who hired Cain. That bizarre and treacherous adventure was more easily negotiated than catching up with one lone American physicist on the lam. The whole California scenario was becoming ridiculous.

Of course, when Martin had accepted this assignment his employer and everyone else he'd spoken to believed it was only Dr. Maxwell Umberto who had the goods on this cold fusion business. At the time, nobody knew Max was a pretender. Only later had it become really complicated and somewhat out of hand. U.S. agents, possibly several other foreign operatives, and local cops were already in the action. It was messy and Martin Speck didn't handle his own frustration well. He could feel little tendrils of frustration starting to snake around in his chest. He knew he had to keep those feelings in check; they could only interfere. So, he held the gardenias to his nose as he pulled away in his white BMW into the night and away from the hotel valet. Those heavenly flowers' wondrous fragrance, as rich and thick as the darkness, was soothing to him, practically intoxicating, and he inhaled deeply, relaxing almost immediately as he drove. The scent temporarily took him home.

The seasoned Sony television in Detective Jack's apartment glowed with an update on the killings in Pasadena. Fitzgerald and his three refugees from that bloody site were collected around the sofa and they watched in silent, cold horror while, at the city courthouse, Pasadena Police Chief Charles Jorgen extolled the contributions of Detective Stanley Lau and the SWAT team members who had acted so heroically in giving their lives to assure the CTU professor, Dr.

Preston Cook and his family were safe from a killer on the loose. The
Chief was obviously a very fatigued man. Stress creased his face and
dark circles swept beneath his eyes, circles that had not been there
twenty-four hours before. He was selfishly tortured by these events
rising like spirits from the graves of his transgressions, events that
would surely consume the closing days of his watch at the Pasadena
Police Department. Charlie Jorgen was somber in his delivery, perhaps even depressed, as he explained to the news crew gathered
around him that details regarding the killer were not available at that
time and no motive had been ascertained. Still, he assured his television audience that whoever committed the horrible crime would be
apprehended. "Justice will prevail," he added unconvincingly.

Following the Chief's statements, KQLA News cut to an attractive thirty-something tan reporter, Rose Rios, who looked straight
into the camera with the Cook's craftsman house visible directly
behind her as night descended on the modest neighborhood. Smoke
drifted skyward from the smoldering remains of the garage laboratory toward the rear of the property, but the primary residence
appeared to be remarkably untouched. Rios observed for her listen-
ers that the scene had been chaotic only a few minutes earlier and,
gesturing over her shoulder, she noted that for reasons unknown
the free standing two car garage behind the house had been burned
completely to the ground. The reporter moved gradually around as
the camera's lens followed her, allowing fire trucks, police cars, and
ambulances to come into view. Emergency vehicles were crisscrossed
in the narrow street. Rose Rios said that she had managed to speak
briefly with a neighbor, an art instructor at Pasadena City College,
Ms. Cloud Willow, who had actually seen and spoken with the suspected killer. Ms. Willow was the very witness who had originally
called the police. In fact, this witness had evidently been a captive
in the home for a short time and was released by the killer before

he escaped. Ms. Willow related that the murders had something to do with Dr. Cook's research, but it wasn't clear what that connection might be. KQLA News reporter Rose Rios also related that Ms. Willow had said there was a federal agent at the house earlier in the day, but why he was there remained a mystery.

"It is all very strange, indeed," said Rios to her television audience. She went on to add that Ms. Willow was currently in the custody of the Pasadena City Police and, although Ms. Willow had declined to be interviewed on the air, she did say the professor who had lived in this house was safe and so was his family. However, Ms. Willow refused to divulge where the CTU researcher was hiding because, she had said, with the U.S. government involved, she didn't feel comfortable speaking further about it.

"'Government involved' – those were her very words," said pretty Rose Rios to the camera. "Whether Ms. Willow was connected in some way, and whether she can explain why she alone survived with four dead police officers at the site, and whether she will divulge the whereabouts of Dr. Cook is – tonight – in the hands of the Pasadena city police. This is Rose Rios, for KQLA, in Pasadena."

When the broadcast rolled to a weather report, Dr. Samantha Day-Steiner stood up abruptly from where she had been sitting on the arm of the couch in Detective Jack's apartment while they had been listening to Rose Rios. "It's time to leave," she said immediately, beginning to gather up the few things they had brought with them. "This isn't safe for us."

"Mom?" said Dalton, confused and scared. Dalton and Ahmad were sitting side-by-side adjacent to Fitzy.

"Come on, honey," Sam said to her son. "We're getting out of this place."

Detective Jack clicked off the television. "Look," he said. "I'll take you to wherever you want to go *in the morning*, but don't go out into the night. Please! Do you even know where you'll go? You don't have a car!" he said as earnestly as he could, attempting to convince her to remain with him and calm down.

She halted where she was and stared at him. She had plenty of practice at confrontation. "Are you saying you won't take us?"

Fitzy collapsed. He didn't know how to respond. Preston had been maneuvered by Samantha for years, but Preston had learned to counter.

"Please stay. At least for the night," Fitzgerald said.

"I'll call a cab," she said and got out her phone. She was frightened but determined, too, after having watched the report on the horrible events at their home in Pasadena.

Fitzy sighed. "Okay," he said quietly. "I'll drive you. Where in heaven's name do you want to go?" He was at a loss. He was doing his best to help these people.

"I think we should stay here, mom," said Dalton. "Fitzy is a policeman!" he said, convinced that a cop was good thing to have around given what had happened. The boy had seen his mother upset many times, but unlike his dad, Dalton could not perform the magic he'd witnessed from him to calm her down. He was just a boy, a smart boy, but no match for this emotional woman.

Samantha went over to her son and squatted in front of him and looked into his eyes. "I know he's a policeman, Dalton. But so was Detective Lau and Detective Lau was not able to stop the madman out there. I'm not going to let anything happen to you. You are the most important thing in the world to your father and me," Samantha said. And hearing such a direct, unqualified expression of caring from his mother was, strangely enough, very unusual for Dalton, and it was powerful.

"I'm scared, mom," said Dalton beginning to cry. "Is dad okay?"

Samantha didn't know what to say, but she did her best. "I believe your dad's fine. He's up in the mountains in a safe place."

Tears ran down the boy's cheeks and Fitzy came over to him quickly and knelt down next to him, beside Sam. He looked into Dalton's watery eyes. "I *know* he's okay," Dalton. "You, and your mom, *and your dad* are going to come out of this good as new! You'll be home playing in the neighborhood before you know it!" He said and he smiled.

"I don't play in the neighborhood much," said Dalton softly, but he understood what the detective meant as he rubbed the tears away with the back of a wrist.

"Oh?" said the detective. "Well, neither did I! That's something else we have in common!" he said and he stroked Dalton's head, managing to get a little smile to cross the boy's face.

"What else do we have in common?" said Dalton, not one to miss a slight of hand.

"Well…" came back Fitzgerald, remembering the boy's saucer eyes at the taxi cab window, as the foursome rolled down the boulevard earlier today, "you obviously like Hollywood. I noticed how you were looking every which way when we came here today." He grinned again at the boy. "And obviously… I like Hollywood, too!"

Dalton Cook smiled again, but rather sheepishly. He liked this detective. "When are we going to meet movie stars?" he asked.

"It won't be long. I promise," said Fitzgerald.

"We don't need movie stars at the moment," said Samantha. "We need to be on our way," she said and she zipped up the two soft bags they had brought.

Fitzgerald stood and looked at Ahmad Mulham who appeared rather abandon having not budged from where he sat the couch. He was clearly wondering where he fit into these developments. Dalton dutifully followed his mother's marching orders and positioned him-self near the door next to her, just like their canvas bags.

"I guess we're accelerating our plans, my friend" Fitzy said qui-etly to the young Saudi man. "I can't leave you here alone; so, you'll have to come with us and I'll get you to your consulate as soon as I can. Okay?"

Ahmad nodded. "I appreciate that," he said. "I want to go back and play in *my* neighborhood, too," he said and smiled. At least Ahmad still had his sense of humor.

"Why don't you call your father now?" said Fitzgerald to Ahmad, knowing his family was influential. "Let him know what's going on. I'll bet he can help."

To that Ahmad said soberly, "Lieutenant, I am thinking it would be better for you to drive the professor and her son to wherever they want to go. I'll catch a taxi after I call my father."

"Thank you, but no. It won't be safe for you that way. I'll take you. You saved an important man's life today. We came here together and we'll go on together," said Detective Jack in the most firm voice he had used since he first met the odd-ball collection of strangers at the Cook house. It had only been a few hours since then, but it felt like days.

CHAPTER 74

Night had fully settled on the Los Angeles basin and Hollywood was coursing with traffic like motorized corpuscles. Neon storefronts along Hollywood Boulevard didn't rival Las Vegas, but Reno was fair game. This pulse of an entertainment capital was only a short walk from Fitzgerald Jack's shaded and quiet apartment complex, where rustic walls and wrought iron gate protected a verdant courtyard and softly spilling fountain. Even though the famed Hollywood and Vine intersection was just around the corner, Fitzgerald's apartment setting was swathed in the Los Angeles of the thirties when life in that city was as full of promise and hope as were the hearts of the starlets streaming to California. The slower pace of those long-gone days survived in special corners of the city and that is precisely why Fitzy lived at that particular location, in that particular apartment building, because it was one of those few sanctuaries protecting a serene world where dreams could come true.

The romance of it all was not the least bit lost on Martin Speck, who left his 745i BMW a block away. He walked slowly up to the front gate of Fitzgerald's complex and looked around at it as a wonderful testament to a bygone era. Martin nodded appreciatively at the detail in the Spanish architecture of the building, dark oak beams protruding from each floor along the pale stucco walls three stories up, and the louvered shutters latched open at each window. He peeked through the vine encumbered wrought iron fence to glimpse the lovely, fountain atrium, which he could by then actually hear. Its flowing water gurgled seductively above the city's din. He noted a tall spreading and flowering Oleander, as beautiful as it was poisonous, and he smiled. Very, very nice, he said quietly to himself, before getting back to business. He had actually seen residences not too dissimilar to this one in Madrid and he relished them even then. The setting also led him to reflect on moody *film noir* from his younger days at university, particularly the Americans films. He loved the genre: Bogart, Peter Laurie, Claude Rains, Ingrid Bergman. It was a fascination he shared with Detective Jack.

When Mahudin Mulham answered his son's phone call, he had been sipping rich, black tea and looking out the window of his eleventh story, spacious office above the sprawling and very mixed skyline of the city of Jeddah where glistening steel and glass towers are interconnected by wide modern boulevards flanked intermittently by centuries-old red coral and earthen shops in open-air markets that were gradually crumbling to dust. It was a city of contrasts. People said the tomb of the world's first woman, Eve, resided somewhere in Jeddah, leading to the city being known as "The Ancestor of Women." Yet, because of a vulgar and thriving commerciality, Jeddah was also thought by many traditional Saudi Muslims to be as decadent as it was sacred. In 2005, Jeddah was the most cosmopolitan city in that conservative, staid Islamic monarchy. Jeddah's expansive port provided the principle access from the sea into the Saudi Arabian Kingdom and to its capital at Riyadh. Calls to prayer from minarets around the city ricocheted off the mirrored glass walls of towering office buildings such as the one in which Mahudin

Mulham conducted his business. That was the world of contrasts in which young Ahmad, the "Hoorocane," had been raised.

"Thank Allah," Mahudin exclaimed, and he sat bolt upright in his chair, spilling some of his black tea on the desk top. "Are you alright, my son? Where have you been?" he said as he mopped up with Kleenex tissues from a box.

Ahmad quickly explained he was okay and he said it was a long story, but that it seemed the cold fusion research was out of reach. "There were killings," Ahmad told his father soberly.

"Ahmad, come home immediately. I should never have asked you to do this. It was foolish of me…"

Ahmad tried to calm his father, telling him he was safe. It was okay. They could not have known how it would go.

"I knew… I knew… it might not go well. I should have sent someone else," said Mahudin. "Forgive me, son," he added, which is not a sentiment that many traditional Saudi fathers would ever say to a son. It would have been thought to show weakness, but to Ahmad and his father it demonstrated modernity and strength.

"Father, that's alright," said Ahmad trying to rein in the conversation and get back to the point of the call, "I need other help right now. I am with a Los Angeles police officer…"

"Have you been *arrested*?" shouted his father panicked!

"*No, no*! It is not that," Ahmad said. "I will explain later. He is my friend and he wants to take me to the consulate here and… I have lost all of my identification…"

"Ahmad! What have I done? How are you in custody?"

"I am okay, father. I am *not* in custody! Not to worry. It is a long story. Maybe you could assist me with a ticket home. I will need help when I get to the airport without a passport. This is because some – *not* my friend – of the Los Angeles police are looking for me… and it might be a problem with the airport security here in America."

"The American authorities are looking for you?" said Mahudin in shock, his mind reeling, trying to piece this together. He felt faint. What had gone wrong?

"It is *very* complicated, father. I can explain later," said Ahmad. "You know how Americans are these days, when dealing with Arabs. I've done nothing." Ahmad was practically in tears, but he held them back. "My policeman *friend* tells me it is okay. He *knows* it is all a mistake. But at the airport they may find it… *difficult*… if I show up. Can you call someone to help?" asked Ahmad cutting to the chase, and he waited.

"Of course… *of course!*" said Mahudin Mulham after running possibilities through his mind. "I know you did no wrong. You are a good boy." He was swaying in his chair, rubbing his forehead with his free hand. "Your mother has not turned her eyes toward me since I asked you to do this," said Ahmad's father. "Praise Allah, you are safe. I will call. The ambassador can arrange things. He owes me a favor. We'll bypass the consulate and get you on an airplane."

"Thank you, father," said Ahmad.

"Praise Allah," said Mahudin.

"Praise Allah," said Ahmad and he rang off.

Mahudin Mulham fell back into his chair. He was relieved but he was also filled with new worries. Why was his son wanted by the police? Mahudin could see the King Fahd Fountain from his office window. It was a glorious exhibition of hydraulic engineering and it could thrust a column of water more than two hundred meters into the sky and the mist drifting inland from the man-made geyser was like a gossamer veil carried on an early morning offshore breeze. At night, lit by twin thousand-watt spotlights, the glistening column of water and its silvery flag were visible for many miles along the flat coastline. Mahudin prayed that the fountain would become a beacon, a tower of light that would guide his son back home safely to his family.

CHAPTER 75

When Martin Speck chose a plan of action, he didn't hesitate. He moved forward and that's what happened on the evening Samantha was planning to escape from the detective's apartment while Fitzgerald Jack was doing his damnedest to help her in the safest possible way. But he still wanted to keep their troop, such as it was, intact. His instincts told him that was best.

Cain was deft. He quickly negotiated his way inside the court-yard at the Hollywood apartment complex, aided by the comings and goings of residents on that cool October evening. He merely had to smile and say, "Good evening," to a would-be Errol Flynn who was headed out into the night to see if he could hook up with an aspiring Jane Russell somewhere in one of the many dens of pulchritude the city had to offer. That simple "Good evening" was his key and he easily slid beyond the iron gates as the departing tenants left. No one suspected anything.

Martin Speck moved nearer to the central fountain. He could not help but be partially seduced by the lush flora surrounding it. The courtyard was so dense with blossoms and so fragrant that he almost lost track of his mission, but Cain was yanked back to reality when he heard the door open to an apartment on the second level toward the rear of the courtyard and he heard excited voices on the move. They emanated from where he calculated the detective's residence would be, given his apartment number.

"Come on, come on!" Cain heard Samantha's urging.

"Shush, please," came back Fitzgerald, hauling bags and trying to corral his party into a cohesive unit as they went forward. He knew this was not a good idea. They should stay put.

"I... we should hurry," she said.

Fitzgerald nodded, "Okay. But let's be quiet."

Martin Speck could not help but smile as he hid in the shadows of the lower level. Indeed, he thought, other people *can* hear. It was all too easy right now, after the frustrating collapse of his plans in Pasadena. He held back in the darkness and slowly withdrew his Desert Eagle from the clip at his back, and he carefully fastened the silencer to his weapon.

It's that scientist's wife, Martin Speck reckoned, upon hearing the voices.

Fitzgerald and the boys were on the second floor walkway that surrounded the atrium and the central fountain. They were moving toward the staircase some thirty feet ahead of them. Samantha was already at the stairs and she waited nervously. The lieutenant was trying to help Dalton with the pair of canvas bags to be thrown into the back of Detective Jack's Jeep, which was parked in the adjoining lot skirting the southern perimeter of the old building. When the Vista Grande apartments were built eighty years earlier, automobiles were an afterthought and vacant lots were plentiful. Fortunately the original building owners bought a lot next door for cars, a decision that was worth millions by 2005.

Dr. Day-Steiner was trying to hurry everyone along, away from the detective's apartment to the stairs where she waited, when the first .50 caliber bullet from Cain's Desert Eagle hummed through the night air directly between her and Fitzgerald. He was ten feet away with Dalton and Ahmad as the heavy slug hit the stucco wall with a shuddering *thud* and fragments of plaster flew around like shrapnel. Both Fitzgerald and Samantha dropped away in opposite directions, crouching for a moment trying to figure out where the shot had come from. The bullet was flattened by its impact with the wall but it had barely slowed when it exploded the screen of a 50" rear-projection television dominating the living room of the apartment on the other side of the wall, a television that was the pride and joy of the Errol Flynn wannabe who had unknowingly let Martin Speck into the courtyard only a few minutes earlier.

"Stay down!" yelled the detective from where he squatted. Dalton and Ahmad crawled up close to the detective, not knowing what had happened. Samantha had gone to her knees, too, and she looked back at Fitzgerald and her son, with terrified, wild eyes! She was still near the top of the staircase.

"We have to get back inside!" said Fitzy toward her, gesturing for her to come back but she didn't listen and she began scrambling slightly down the stairs.

"Common!" she said over her shoulder to them. "We have to get out'a here!"

One more .50 caliber round burnt the night, buzzing like a wasp, shattering plaster and wood over Samantha's head as she moved a few steps further down the stairs. The huge slugs were practically explosive on impact with those old walls.

"Ahhhhh!" she yelled as masonry scattered across her in fragments and dust. Fitzgerald heard her scream in the stairwell. Terrified, she continued down the stairs and disappeared from sight.

"Come back!" yelled Fitzgerald after her, but Samantha was gone and Fitzgerald fell back against the wall along the open-air walkway next to Ahmad and Dalton. He examined Dalton in particular, whose eyes were huge and horrified when his mother had gone on without them.

"Is someone shooting at us?" the boy asked.

"Yes. We have to go back," said Fitzgerald. "Everything will be okay, but we need to get inside!"

"What about mom?" said Dalton and he was beginning to cry.

"She'll be okay," said Fitzgerald. "She'll be okay," he repeated no more convincingly than the first time. Although he tried not to show it, Lt. Jack was seriously concerned about Samantha as they crawled back toward his apartment. He wished he could be more positive when Dalton glanced toward the stairway where his mom had disappeared. But Fitzgerald could not take the time right then to attend to Dalton's feelings. The assassin was there for sure and they needed cover immediately. A phone call for help had to be made, pronto.

Inexplicably, there were no more shots fired right away. From his crouched position Fitzgerald unlocked his apartment door and the three of them scuttled inside. Once across the threshold, as he turned to close and lock his door, he caught glimpse of another tenant, the elderly bald Mr. K., as he liked to be called, a retired haberdasher in his satin, monogramed bathrobe, emerge from his apartment on the other side of the atrium to find out what the infernal ruckus was about. Fitzgerald did manage to catch Mr. K.'s eye and wave him back inside. The neighbors all knew Fitzy was a policeman and they actually liked having him nearby, so with that signal from Detective Jack the monogramed haberdasher retreated quickly from view into his apartment.

After the front door was bolted, Fitzgerald and boys all collapsed on the floor in the lieutenant's apartment and breathed heavily. Lt. Jack wondered what Samantha Day-Steiner was doing. She was frightened and maybe she thought she was heading for safety. Both of his young guests were searching his face for clues as to their next move. He knew he would have to go after her as soon as he called for back-up. He hoped to god she'd found a crawl space and was staying out of sight. Fitzgerald stood up and went for his telephone.

Samantha was strong headed and scared, so she did not seek a place to hide or a crawl space as the detective had imagined. Instead her flight instincts were in high gear and very soon she was sliding along an exterior wall on the first floor of the building trying to find a path away from the maniac with a gun. She knew that Dalton was with Fitzgerald Jack back there at his apartment, so she tried to focus on taking care of herself in those terrifying minutes. She realized she should be as concealed as possible while she felt her way along the rough stucco wall on outer perimeter of the complex. She did not know the building's layout but she wanted to escape. Perhaps the parking lot would work, she thought. Samantha had no clue what she might find around any corner or in any direction. She was guessing. She'd only briefly noticed the courtyard when they arrived, as they walked through it, and that's where the gunman appeared to be waiting, so she was trying to avoid the area altogether. That was pretty much the entirety of her on-the-spur plan. Horrible things were happening too fast.

Dr. Day-Steiner was not only totally unfamiliar with the layout of the Vista Grande apartment building she did not know anything about the methods of the man called Cain. He had fired gunshots right out in the open, brazenly drawing attention to his presence. She didn't think he would be hanging around with police back-up surely on its way, but all was calculated, every move was planned by Martin Speck.

After seeing the foursome creeping along on the second floor, Martin chose to carve the woman away from the others with a couple of shots, and it worked perfectly. He always moved boldly and swiftly, finding it far more effective than stretching out a violent situation which inevitably invited complications. His internal algorithm told him he had to be out of there in three more minutes, no more. So, when he saw that the scientist's wife had separated herself from the others, he smiled and said, "Perfect". The LAPD detective was no doubt already in touch with his law enforcement colleagues, so speed was critical for Speck. The woman wouldn't be coming through the courtyard, because he had fired his shots from the courtyard. So, Cain sprinted past the fountain and darted through a quaintly arched corridor that cut beneath the second story apartments on the south side of the building. He'd already noted the private parking lot on the farther side of the complex and he guessed the woman may try to find a route in that direction, a guess that was right on the money.

As he moved into the darkness of what was equivalent to a short tunnel, away from the fairly lit courtyard, Martin Speck could soon hear Samantha's rapid breathing just around the corner where there appeared to be a perimeter walkway that was protected from the world by a seven-foot hedge. The parking lot was on the other side. Samantha was scraping against the sharp stucco walls as she inched forward trying to find a gate to the parking lot just as Cain had anticipated she might. Her every movement was audible to him. The panicky woman wasn't paying sufficient attention to the details of what she was doing but, after all, she was not a professional in stealth operations. Silly girl, Cain thought. It was far too easy, which for him was a common finding. In life-threatening situations, people simply don't think.

He waited near the farther opening of the dim, arched corridor and he leaned back calmly in the darkness as the terrified mathematics professor sneaked her slow way into view. For a moment, Martin Speck could see distant streetlights reflected on her round moist eyes in profile. She had no idea he was there until he raised the silenced Desert Eagle from the shadows and placed it against her temple.

"Stop," he said softly.

She spun toward him. "*Ah!*" she exclaimed. Her mind was racing and she backed off a step. Her eyes were big and pale in the night. She felt faint. She nearly evacuated her bladder down her leg right there. Blood drained from Samantha's head. Her knees went weak and she almost collapsed onto the terra cotta tiles beneath her feet.

Cain casually raised a finger to his lips and he quietly said, "Shhhh," while he held the large handgun straight toward her. And when Cain saw she had regained her balance, he added in his velvet accent, "All I want is your cooperation, madam".

CHAPTER 76

Before dawn Preston was up and he was into his third cup of Maxwell House by the time Buster and Bobby stirred an hour later. By then daylight in thin shards was barely finding its way to them, which is what happens when a cabin is nestled between the outstretched arms of a mountain, where night lingers. Ridges on either side protected the hand-hewn structure from wind and also from sunlight until much later in the morning. Those same ridges and the orbits of telecommunications satellites were at odds, too, and kept both Preston and Bobby out of modern contact with the world. Preston had found the coffee percolator in the galley and he was old enough to remember how a percolator works in the wake of drip machines and Starbucks' baristas, and he managed to bubble up a pretty stout pot. But when Buster and Bobby finally arose, Preston was so eager to get in touch with his family that he hardly gave the other men a chance to rub their eyes and savor his brew before he was on them about moving to a location where they could make contact via cell phone.

"Hold yer horses, professor!" said Buster emphatically, standing in the living room vigorously scratching his backside, sporting the sagging white long johns he had worn to bed. "Give us a god damn minute to wake up, if you don't mind. Jeez!"

Bobby was shivering. "Hey, man," he said, "If we're here tonight, I'm going to need an extra blanket. I'm freezing may ass off!"

"Aw, you'll get used to it," said Buster. "This is October. You should be here in February!"

"We will *not* be here in February," said Bobby soberly, like it was a possibility in someone's mind, as he made his way to the coffee pot and poured himself a solid black cup. "Umm." he uttered inhaling steam from the dark liquid. "Hello, joe!"

"Where can we get cell phone connections?" said Preston impatiently.

Big Buster Bernard had climbed into his patched Can't Bust 'Em bib overalls by that point, the daytime clothes he preferred whenever when he was in the mountains. In fact, he'd worn these very overalls through pretty much the whole construction of the cabin, a period during which he'd clomped around with nails in his pockets and a hammer swinging on his thigh. That was a fond memory for Buster. He was doing something for the future and for Cloud. Yet, the overalls looked odd on him that day to these men, because Buster never wore bib overalls in the city. The huge, urban biker had transformed himself into a Nebraska farmer right before their eyes.

"Oh... not that far down the trail," said Buster while he went to fetch his own mug of coffee. "When the sun's up full, we'll head on out. You guys can connect to yer hearts' delight."

Bobby was regarding Big Buster in his *American Gothic* attire. "If it ain't 'Grandpa Amos, the head'a the clan,'" he said.

When Buster came back with his steaming mug he did so with the hitch in his step that Walter Brenan used in *The Real McCoys*. "Luke, dad gum it," Buster added in a pretty fair rendition of Brenan's raspy voice, "I reckon Kate and Hassie ain't gonna take kindly to yer city slicker ways."

Bobby smiled and lifted his mug in a salute. The big guy had a sense of humor.

Preston had never watched television regularly. He didn't know Grandpa Amos from Ralph Kramden. Instead, he just slumped into one of the worn overstuffed chairs in the living area of the rough cabin Buster and Cloud had fashioned by hand as protection against a mad world and Preston waited sullenly until his cabin mates were ready to head down the mountain. He could not get Samantha and Dalton off his mind, not even for a minute. Preston was consumed with worry.

Characteristically, Big Buster seemed much less concerned about Cloud Willow. Perhaps it was their *laissez-faire* lifestyle. He loved her, absolutely, no question there; but he seemingly was not worried. And as he rested his boots on the resin covered cross-cut pine coffee table in front of the threadbare plaid couch that had creaked when he lowered his large frame onto it, Buster had not the slightest clue as to what kind of danger his lady had found herself in on the previous afternoon. Yet, in true metaphysical accordance with the easy-going view of reality he embraced in those higher altitudes and thin air, it happened that Cloud Willow was quite okay, miraculously okay. And in true metaphysical accordance with Preston's gloomy and feverish obsession about his own loved ones on that day's dawning, it happened that Samantha Day-Steiner was not okay; she was not okay at all.

In Hollywood the night before, after a magnum .50 caliber bullet had shattered the widescreen television of Fitzgerald's neighbor, but prior to the arrival of police back-up, Lieutenant Jack had asked Ahmad to stow himself in the bathroom tub for a little while. Ahmad was a wanted man and Fitzy's urgent call to his uniformed colleagues was not intended to throw his Saudi charge into a tunnel of diplomatic horror. His call was simply to get protection from the assassin lurking outside in the courtyard. However, it was very dangerous for Lieutenant Jack to conceal a high profile fugitive from the law, a courageous – or foolish – move to say the least and definitely a career gamble.

In spite of a lightening quick response from the LAPD, Cain was already gone by the time they arrived. Not only was Cain gone, but there was also no trace of Samantha Day-Steiner. She'd been sucked into the ethers along with the killer and Fitzgerald knew without a doubt that Cain had her. Fitzy could feel it in his guts and he also felt it was his fault. He should have prevented it. That was his job. That's why he was the one to escort the Cook family away from Pasadena. But on that night, with the investigation swarming around him, he could tell no-one what happened. Lt. Jack had to keep to himself the pain of losing Dr. Day-Steiner while lying to his cop friends, saying that luckily Samantha had gone out for some female things, so she wasn't there when the shooter turned up. And why did Fitzgerald make that up? Because he happened to have Ahmad Mulham hidden away in his bathroom! It was a fact that changed every interaction with LAPD that night. And right there in the Lieutenant's living room was wise-beyond-his-years Dalton Preston, sitting primly like the perfect child playing along magnificently with Fitzgerald's story. The boy understood what was happening and why it was happening and he intuitively knew that Lt. Jack was the best opportunity to get his mother and father back to him safely.

When the investigating officers finally left the apartment complex they were mumbling, which was not usually a good sign with the LAPD. These officers knew there was something funny about what they saw that evening but they weren't going to grill a fellow officer. They took notes enough for a report. The two officers in charge knew Fitzgerald Jack very well. They also knew Fitzgerald from the LAPD softball team where he could deliver an over-the-fence hit when it was needed. They knew him at Langer's Deli after hours, chewing the fat. And they knew him as a regular cop, which was the most important point of view, because he was an authentic, reliable, impeccable law enforcement officer. So, they were not about to bust his chops on that night in Hollywood, in spite of suspicious loose ends. They let it go for the time being and trusted him. If Fitzgerald Jack said the assassin that killed those cops in Pasadena had been in Hollywood that night, outside his apartment and shooting up the place, then that's what happened. There were, in fact, the large twin bullet holes in an outside corridor wall to prove it. If officer Jack said it was okay for them to go away, then it was okay for them to go away. No further questions. They privately realized something might be happening out of sight, but that was alright, too, if everything turned out okay in the end. That was the rule between officers who lived in a real world with some pretty nasty characters in it. All's well that ends well.

In the early morning, a white BMW sedan was speeding along the 210 Freeway toward San Bernardino, passing signs directing interested traffic to "Arrowhead, Big Bear, and Mountain Resorts." With the completion of the 210 Freeway, the mountains were an hour's drive from LA, an hour to the ski slopes and the lodges, not a difficult trip for most mountain cabin owners and southern California snow freaks. There was a steady stream of vehicles going in both directions every weekend, but rarely did one of them have a 14-inch silenced Desert Eagle lying ominously between the driver and the passenger.

Samantha was grey and silent as stone in the right front seat. She was terrified. She could feel the blood pounding through her carotid arteries. She wasn't even blinking, just staring straight ahead. For the emotional, mercurial Dr. Day-Steiner traumatic sudden events could send her into a downward spiral pretty quickly and

after her confrontation with this man on the dark perimeter walkway at Lieutenant Jack's Hollywood apartment building, she was still
in shock. She could not comprehend what was happening to her.

Martin Speck, on the other hand, looked in his Hawaiian shirt
like an everyday motorist out for a drive to the mountains, leaning
back casually with one palm resting on top of the leather bound
steering wheel. There had not been much conversation between
Martin and Samantha since he intercepted her in the midst of her
escape from the detective's apartment. He hadn't needed to interro-
gate the scientist's wife on where her husband and his holy grail of
an invention were to be found. From the No-Jack data he'd received
via Breadcrumbs, Cain already knew, roughly, the whereabouts of
the Harley-Davidson motorcycle that had taken the scientist to his
safe-house. But a little fine tuning in those unfamiliar surroundings
would do nicely if Cain could coax it out of Dr. Day-Steiner. Cain
was not the least bit interested in developing a relationship with what
he saw as a pernicious hostage. He was a provincial man privately
and he didn't care for her disloyalty to her husband. To Martin Speck
this woman was merely collateral and nothing more. She could be
jetsam just as easily. His world was black and white in these circumstances. He basically did not like using human leverage because it
introduced too many unknowns. Cain could barely recall the last
time he had manipulated live bait to get what he wanted, but he was a
professional and he knew to apply the resources that were presented
to him and not question them. His only rule was to move quickly.
That had been effective in every kind of circumstance. Even a sec-
ond-rate plan can work if it is implemented with alacrity. Delay usually equals death.

The BMW turned onto Route 18, which was an off-ramp from
the 210 Freeway and it led them onto a trafficked suburban surface street. But after one mile Route 18 began to climb into the San

Gabriel mountains and leave the suburbs of San Bernardino behind. At that point it became a genuine highway.

"Crestline, you say?" said Cain to Samantha while he smoothly guided the big German sedan along the winding, rising road.

She could barely speak. Her mouth was dry from fear and confusion. "Yes… I think so. I've never been there."

"But that's what he said?" came back Martin Speck to his captive, without pressuring her. He knew better. For all her lamenting her husband's lack of ambition and her philandering opportunism, he could now see she had a very fragile side. He wanted all the information he could get from her, so he moved with stealth, a trait that came as naturally to him as to a cat burglar.

"He told us it's above Crestline," mumbled Samantha recollecting conversations she and Preston had with Big Buster in recent years, "on some undeveloped roads. I really don't know." Her voice was very weak.

Martin Speck calmly said, "We'll figure it out. Relax and try to remember everything you can."

"You're not going to hurt my boy or my husband?" she asked feebly.

Cain glanced at the woman who was on the far side of her seat and leaning stiffly against the door. "I have no interest in your son, professor," he said to the woman. "Isn't he with the detective? I want the device."

"Does this small reactor really work?" Cain asked after another fifteen minutes of steadily climbing the winding highway, in his first show of actual interest in the science involved in his assignment. He was an educated man and he could see it was an amazing accomplishment, if true.

She looked at her captor oddly. "Of course, it works," she said quietly. "Preston is a true genius," and then she added, "but he can also be a true idiot. The thing is worth a fortune and he wants to give it to the world for free. You don't need to steal it, mister." And those words were probably the first indication there was any kind of gumption remaining in the woman since he had abducted her.

Martin nodded. His employer didn't want this apparatus available in any form unless he had it himself, especially not *free* to everyone!

Dr. Day-Steiner was not worthy of such a brilliant selfless husband, thought Cain. Nonetheless, Dr. Cook apparently did not see it that way. It seemed that Samantha and Dalton meant a great deal to the physicist, which also meant Martin Speck's frightened captive was the precise leverage he needed to pry Dr. Cook out of hiding.

What an odd world it is that would put Dr. Day-Steiner and Dr. Cook together, Cain thought. And what an odd world it is that would have his own employer wanting such an extraordinary, remarkable, revolutionary invention either purloined or erased. Those were the curiosities that made Martin Speck glad he was outside the fray. He was never a stakeholder in his assignments. His life and his objectives were simple and he felt better off for it.

CHAPTER 77

By the time Cain was driving the Rim of the World Highway the police had come and gone from Fitzgerald Jack's apartment in Hollywood. Lt. Jack's colleagues interviewed him as they had to do, and then they interviewed neighbors about what had happened, including the monogramed-robe, retired haberdasher across the courtyard. The detectives took pictures of the bullet holes in the Errol Flynn wanna-be's wall. And then, with a nod and a wink, the investigating officers went back to headquarters with their report. Fitzgerald knew the moment to reciprocate would someday arrive. It always did. On that evening, the tightening of the thin blue line saved Lieutenant Jack's skin.

Ahmad had remained in his dark hiding place in Fitzgerald Jack's bathroom, in the tub, sitting on the drain, a drip from the shower tapping him on his scalp for half an hour while his knees were pulled up to his chest. In the near black of his little space, he was terrified, expecting the shower curtains to be yanked back any second by an LAPD SWAT team with flashlights and assault weapons. He'd seen it in the movies.

Fortunately, none of that happened.

Lt. Jack went quickly to the bathroom when his LAPD friends had departed, when the various interviews were over. Fitzy cracked the bathroom door very slowly and said softly into the darkness, "Ahmad? Are you okay? They're gone now." And he clicked on the lights.

435

A yet unseen morning sun was rising beyond an eastern ridge in the San Gabriel mountains and was already casting brilliant October light onto dense forest farther up the mountain's slope to the west. Buster and Cloud's retreat remained in shadows, purposefully hidden in a crook between two of the mountain's great arms. It would be difficult to locate them even from the air and that was wholly by design. The three men emerged from their hideout, rumpled and unshaven, and they looked upward into a cobalt sky spanning the heavens above the lofty spruce, pine, and redwood needles that moved so gently in the slight breeze. It was quite cold already there at the higher elevations. Clearly winter could not be that far away and the air was invigoratingly fresh for those men, perhaps because they had just come up the day before out of the tainted atmosphere blanketing LA and the valleys. Whatever the reason, they all inhaled deeply and stood motionless and silent for a beat or two, each privately regarding the birth of that new day and the adventures it may hold for them.

"Okay, guys," said Buster, jump-starting their momentum. "There's a clearin' 'bout half an hour trek down the road," he said and pointed toward the crater-riven path they had maneuvered the day before. Both Preston and Bobby Skylar thought the use of the word "road" to describe that narrow horror was generous, to say the least. Looking at the Taurus that morning, they wondered how the hell they got the car up there at all. It was a ruined automobile and wasn't going anywhere again on that day or any other.

"Ya should be able to find line-a-sight for yer cell phone connections at the fork," Buster added about their destination and then he stepped on ahead. "Asses in gear!" he yelled over his shoulder as he left them behind.

"Oh," replied Bobby Skylar, recalling their carnival ride from the day before. "The fork must be where the rutted, pothole, dirt-shit trail, turns into an axel busting, rock strewn, steep mother-fucking footpath. *That* fork?"

Retired detective Sally Jack was as intuitive and no-nonsense at over seventy years of age as she was when she was a working LAPD dick two decades earlier, talking smack with fellow cops and delivering the goods, as she always did. Fitzgerald's mom was a one-of-a-kind mentor for a young man who was destined to become a detective and a heralded investigator, as accomplishments would play out in his career.

Fitzgerald showed up at his parent's Brentwood Tudor house with Ahmad and Dalton in tow, both of them wary, standing behind Detective Jack as he rang the doorbell at his parents' heavy oak arched front doorway.

Each time he came to that address, Fitzgerald thought of the first house they'd had, when he was a boy. It wasn't in a posh suburb like Brentwood. They lived on a simple ranch out on undeveloped land where Thousand Oaks and other prefabricated communities had sprawled by 2005. Even though they loved the rural feel of the ranch in those years, eventually his mom and dad were drawn closer into the city by the ease of their respective commutes. House prices in Brentwood were nothing in 1983 compared to what they had become a couple of decades later, so it had been quite manageable even on modest professionals' salaries.

When Ms. Sally Jack opened the door and found this trio standing there on her threshold, she whooped and gave her son a hearty hug and a kiss, exclaiming how good it was to see him. Then they repaired to the dining room where family conversations always occurred, rather than the living room. She had known instantly something was up because Fitzy always called ahead. Beverages and food were quickly recruited, as was also the custom, a trait hauled to California from the deep south where Fitzgerald was born and where his mom and stepdad grew up. Eating was always on the agenda.

Fitzy's English professor stepfather, Thomas Murdock, PhD, meandered into the dining room upon hearing his son's voice. After a hug from Fitzgerald and a sweet greeting, Dr. Murdock positioned himself at the end of the table to listen. He was the only dad Fitzy had ever known after his biological father had up and split when Fitzy was a toddler. It was merely coincidence his stepdad was home on that October day in 2005 researching the arcane notions of William Wordsworth. As usual, Fitzgerald's adopted father remained quiet during the conversation because it was police business, but he remained at the table because he was always concerned about Fitzy's well-being. Furthermore, the adventures of cops were always much more interesting to him than his own work-a-day literature research. It was an accepted fact in the Jack household that the old man would eavesdrop on all the police stories. Fitzy's parents, while aging, were in pretty good physical shape for an elderly couple and they were very obviously the wellspring of Fitzgerald's own stick-to-itiveness, creativity and lively intelligence.

That day, however, it was a different kind of story Fitzgerald was bringing home. He had not crossed his parents' front doorstep for many reasons beyond good cheer and affection after he went off to college. But that day he came to ask a serious favor, an element of parenting that had faded entirely from the family formula over the years. Fitzgerald Jack was well established within the Los Angeles Police Department, homicide mostly, but thorny larcenies, too, especially if high-profile names were involved. He had a knack for subtlety and good sense in delicate matters, which both the Chief of Police and the new Los Angeles Mayor greatly appreciated. When wealthy people commit crimes the tendrils of culpability often stretch into the most unexpected quarters. Lt. Jack's finely tuned skills in those affairs were inherited directly from his mother, who in her time could always play the most treacherous political poker game and still enforce the law when the cards were finally turned up.

So there Fitzgerald, Ahmad, Dalton, Sally Jack and her English professor husband, Tom Murdock, were sitting around the dining room table in Brentwood with cold fried chicken, potato salad and glasses of iced tea, while Fitzgerald cranked out their tale. He tried to omit elements which might put his parents in serious legal jeopardy if they knew about them, but even that was a difficult tap dance since a fugitive was sitting at the table, a fugitive who played a central role in the favor about to be requested.

"Take Ahmad to the airport?" repeated Sally to her son, after he'd lobbed the question toward her. "That's all?"

"Basically," said Fitzgerald. "But it is more complicated than it sounds," said Fitzy not wanting to betray his own mother.

Sally Jack smiled. "My darling boy, this is not my first rodeo."

Fitzy's mother may not have been directly told that the LAPD and many other local and federal agencies were on the look-out for the young Arab man, but she picked up on unspoken queues in the dining room conversation. She already knew about the UCLA murder, even though she had missed Ahmad's name as a person of interest. Sally Jack took it on faith she was informed by her son there were reliable assurances that Ahmad would be accepted at the Bradley terminal without difficulty or questions. She was told it was all part of an international web of connections and favors that were owed to his very influential father. Fitzgerald was running with that assumption because it was his only option. He knew Cain was on the move and that clock was ticking. Fitzgerald Jack was strangely like Cain in emerging ways: certain, efficient, and fast. It was expedition that brought Fitzy to his mother for assistance.

"And this assassin you mentioned, isn't he a problem?" asked Tom Murdock, listening in on his stepson's story and contributing his customary cautionary note.

"Don't worry, dad. *Everybody's* on that guy by now," said Fitzgerald lightly covering the situation with a fabrication. "He was flying under the radar for a while, but after what went down in Pasadena, that's all changed."

It was true in the sense that everybody wished they were onto Cain, but it was a lie in the sense that no one knew who Cain was or where Cain might be, riding in his big white BMW 745i in the San Bernardino mountains with Dr. Samantha Day-Steiner as a captive. Fitzgerald was about the only person alive who had reason to suspect something like that had happened based on his understanding of the man's objectives. But in his mother's house Fitzgerald's suspicions hadn't gone further than his own head. Telling his boss at the precinct about his theories would have generated an action plan as nimble and fast-moving as an oil tanker, which was not what was needed if lives were to be saved. Sometimes you have to go with your instincts. Above all else, the gut-check lesson was the most important lesson he'd learned from his mom about police work. Sometimes you have to risk ruining your career and be bold, or you might as well stay on the sidelines.

Sally Jack looked at the young Saudi Arabian man and patted him on the back of his hand and it made him blush. "Sure," she said. "I'll get you back to your family," she added and she smiled.

"Thanks, mom," said Fitzgerald. "Tomorrow would be great, if we can spend the night here. Things are jumping right now on the street. And I've got to go find Dalton's mother and father a.s.a.p.," he said without explaining. Fitzgerald glanced over to the strangely intelligent, doe-eyed Down syndrome boy whose dad was gone somewhere and now his mom had disappeared, too, vanished into the night. Just looking his way brought tears to Dalton's eyes, tears that he had been struggling to contain with all of his young heart.

"Oh, honey," said Ms. Jack, moving as quickly and smoothly as a cat from her chair to kneeling by the boy at the table upon seeing his tears. She hugged him. "It's going to be alright, sweetheart," she said. "You couldn't be in better hands than my son's," she said. She had always been half hard-case and half nurturer and she could turn on a dime from one to the other when needed, both genuine.

But young Dalton did not really know what hands were safe for him anymore, what promises were true, and what the future held. He was trying to be brave, but he was twelve years old. His lip trembled after Sally Jack wrapped her arms around him and he started to cry.

"I want my dad," he said into her shoulder. "I want my mom."

Ms. Sally Jack held him and kissed his hair and rocked with him slowly.

"It's going to be alright, sweetheart" she whispered. "It's going to be alright."

CHAPTER 78

Right after the turnoff from Rim of the World Highway at Crestline, there was a general store that appeared quickly on the right hand side of the road. "Crestbear Store" it called itself in a name that married two communities high above San Bernardino, Crestline and Big Bear. The larger and more popular Big Bear City was further up Rim of the World Highway, beyond the towns of Arrowhead and Blue Jay. Tiny Crestline didn't have the spreading clear lakes and the ski lifts boasted by those other tourist destinations, so it ranked well below them in desirability. But it was absolutely perfect for survivalists like Buster Bernard and Cloud Willow. It was off the beaten track.

Crestbear Store was the kind of mercantile enterprise that was popular in the west a hundred years earlier, not really committed to a specific line of products, but attempting to be a one-size-fits-all retailer with groceries, clothes, sports gear, hardware, and gift items, all distributed in various corners and aisles within a beamed and rustic building. The Crestbear Store even had a couple of coffee tables off to the side near the front with soft chairs and magazines strewn about, because they recently had added the ubiquitous Starbucks logo to one window, acquired to serve newer residents in the community. And as it happened when Martin Speck wheeled his sedan into a free space fronting the store, through the large, paned windows he could see a couple of locals relaxing with cappuccinos or lattes, reading and chatting in their own Starbucks coffee corner. The scene was cute in an innocent way. The fiftyish home-grown owners of the Crestbear Store managed to create an environment that was perfect for Crestline.

When Cain pulled in, half a dozen other vehicles were already aligned in the gravel parking lot like horses tied to hitching rails that were actually in place. He looked up at the sign reading "Crestbear Store" and he said, "Do you think the proprietor would remember a giant of a man riding a Harley Fantail?"

"I don't know," said Samantha quietly.

"Well, if your neighbors built a cabin near here, madam, I would guess they spent some time at this establishment," surmised Cain as he glanced around at the threadbare commercial options around them in Crestline. There was a Chevron station down the way, next to a café. He could make out a tavern, too, advertising billiards which he took to mean pocket pool, more popular in the U.S.

"They're very independent," Samantha offered, in answer to Martin Speck's assumption that Bernard and Cloud had shopped at the Crestbear Store.

"Why don't we find out?" said Cain taking his gaze from the far off billiard hall. He looked over to his hostage while he fastened the Desert Eagle onto the back of his belt. "I don't know how many people are in there," he added coldly, "but a lot of them could be dead in ten seconds if you do anything I don't like."

Samantha knew that this man meant exactly what he said.

In the same minutes that Cain and white-as-a-sheet Samantha Day-Steiner were standing in the rustic Crestbear Store that smelled of cedar, and were asking questions of a skinny, punk cashier who displayed one full colorful sleeve of tattoos, Preston Cook, Bobby Skylar, and their host, Big Buster Bernard were trudging down the narrow, steep, rocky trail that led away from the squat cabin hidden among the trees above them.

On foot the going was treacherous. The men had to watch every step to keep from twisting an ankle. Preston was shaking his head marveling at how the Taurus had managed to negotiate that god-awful route the afternoon before. Surely the rental car would never be the same, he mused picturing the undercarriage of the vehicle with a cracked oil pan and bent drive train and god knows what else. In fact, there were droppings of thick crankcase oil on the ground even where they were walking.

Preston's musings, as he trudged down the mountain to find a spot where they might connect with the outside world, were happening while charming and mysteriously handsome Martin Speck was sweetly manipulating the tattooed employee of the Crestbear Store to find out if she knew anything of a large guy riding a Harley-Davidson, who may have been building a cabin nearby, somewhere up on the mountain.

With plastic shopping baskets slung on their arms, customers were roaming around in the cedar and redwood general store. Crowded shelves created maze-like aisles, and the whole of it was silently surveyed by the great head of a snarling grizzly bear mounted high on the wall at the rear of the building. It was a fixture that had been purchased and shipped from Canada years earlier, as grizzlies were not native to southern California.

The skinny punk cashier looked at the two tourists in front of her, who were inquiring about the big biker. They were an odd pair she thought and very City. The man was friendly and good-looking but the lady was a cold fish, standing back, rigid as a statue. "Yeah," said the cashier. "Man, if you're talkin' 'bout that awesome old hog, then, yeah, I seen 'em. Hippie lady?" she asked.

Martin Speck nodded and smiled. "That would be them," he said smoothly recalling the fearless free-spirited women he had faced in the house in Pasadena.

"Great bike." she said. "My boyfriend's into Harley's."

"Me, too," said Cain truthfully.

"They've been in here a bunch'a times. Sure. Over the last couple'a years, I'd say. Kind'a private folks, but real nice."

"Do you know where their cabin would be?" said Cain and he glanced quickly over his shoulder at Samantha who had not budged. "We're their next door neighbors in Pasadena," he said and smiled again. He was very capable of becoming as pleasant and enjoyable as a spring afternoon.

The girl regarded him quizzically for a moment and rubbed her unadorned right arm with the hand at the end of her colorful left arm. She was wearing a tank-top, even though it was October and getting quite cool outside. "You got an unusual accent, mister," she said. "Where're you from?" She did not sound the least bit suspicious, merely curious.

"Oh, I was raised all over Europe," Martin Speck answered agreeably which was good enough for the clerk. "Nice art," he said gesturing to her sleeve. "All floral. I don't see that often. Beautiful," he added sincerely, thinking for a moment of his own garden at home.

The young woman glanced at her arm, "Thanks. Yeah. Designed it myself. No snakes, knives, or skulls for me. None'a that tribal shit, either," she said and laughed lightly, and so did Martin.

"Good for you," he said and meant it. "You're an artist."

"Not sure where they live," the clerk said getting back to the question. "Nice folks but, man, they really want'a get away from everybody. Ya gotta go up Old Mill Road quite a ways. There's a split-off somewheres up there. Sorry, can't tell ya more."

"It's okay. You've been very helpful," responded Cain. Then, after a beat, he said, "We'll take two cups of black tea to go, please, ma'am," he said, "and a splash of cream in one, if you don't mind."

"English style," noted the cashier as she headed over to the coffee and tea bar toward the Starbucks corner.

"That's right," said Martin and he smiled again.

At that, one of the Starbucks customers spoke up, interjecting himself from where he was relaxing near to where the tattooed clerk was fetching tea. He was sunk into one of the comfortable chairs and his legs were crossed. An *LA Times* was crumpled in his lap. The man was short and heavy-set, in baggy jeans and a faded UC Berkeley sweatshirt. He seemed to be seventyish with a closely cropped beard and thinning wild white hair.

"Howdy, friends," he announced, rather loudly in a gravel voice, "I couldn't help but hear you askin' about the big guy with the motorcycle and his girlfriend."

Cain stopped and waited and tried to appear cordial while he contained his brain's natural reptilian suspicions.

"Like our little missy told you" continued the old timer, "they're really swell people. Chatted with 'em a couple of times myself."

Martin Speck's eyes lit up. Perhaps serendipity was shining on him yet again. "Oh?" he said passively.

"Yup," said old wild-hair, "When you head up Old Mill Road some six or seven miles you'll get to a falling-down billboard with a faded picture of a bass on it. Only one like that on the whole stretch," he emphasized. "Turn-off's less than a hundred yards further. Easy to miss."

"Thanks," said Martin Speck. "Thank you very much, sir."

The old guy craned his neck to look outside through the wide paned window toward the cars lined up in front of the store. "What you drivin'?" he asked. "That turn-off is not well kept. I know this mountain."

Cain didn't answer the question about his car, but he accepted the old guy's words in the most appreciative way and his chameleon-like self slipped into its colloquial form. "Whoa," he said, as he pretended to review this new important information and how it affected their plans. "Well, thank you, my friend. We have to rethink things." Martin glanced over his shoulder at Samantha, who remained as motionless as when they'd arrived. "Let's just find the road today, hon, and rent an off-road vehicle tomorrow. What'd you think?" Then returning to the old guy and throwing in a red herring he said, "We're staying in Arrowhead, so we have to get back anyway."

The punk cashier brought two black teas in go-cups. "Cream's in this one," she said.

"Thank you," said Martin Speck and he handed her a twenty. "Keep the change," he said and winked.

"I thank you," she returned enthusiastically at the oversized gratuity, "and my little boy thanks you, too!"

Jesus, thought Martin Speck, this young girl already has a child! His European Catholic upbringing was always a millisecond from his judgment about society and people, but he fought that opinion down. Turning to the wild-haired newspaper reader, he said in parting, "I appreciate the head's up, about that road."

The old guy nodded and plunged back into an article in the business section while Cain and Samantha headed for the door.

CHAPTER 79

Just as Bobby Skylar had recounted, precisely where the steep narrow miserable path leading to the cabin met the slightly wider miserable path leading down the mountain to Old Mill Road, Preston, Bobby, and Buster halted their descent. The October morning was brisk and clear and they were breathing heavily even though they had been heading downhill. Their trek had consumed more than half an hour and it was anything but casual on the irregular downward grade. It was all small careful steps for the men.

"I'm thinkin' ya can pick up a signal hereabouts," Buster announced between breaths that burst from his mouth like puffs of steam in the cool, autumn air, and he pointed to the south, where above the trees could be seen clear azure and no mountains blocking the view. Buster knew cell phones operated on radio waves and he figured one needed an open sky. Telephone communication satellites in the silent, frigid darkness of space hovering in their locked orbits two hundred miles above the earth would always be in line of sight to the relay towers on earth. So, it was line of sight to an unseen distant cell phone relay tower that was the challenge for these refugees. Fortunately, the city of San Bernardino was to the south, which was the direction they were facing, so prospects were favorable.

"Give'er a go," Buster said as he pulled the collar of his wool jacket up around his ears and plopped his tired butt down on an embankment, allowing his two charges to wend their electronic ways with their little hand-held devices. Buster shook his head disapprovingly as he rested. Thank heaven he wasn't hooked on these connections to the world like so many men and women. What's wrong with people, he was thinking as he watched his two wards, that they cannot seem to live for twenty minutes without having to talk to somebody on a god damn phone! He was picturing automatons walking around in tony Old Town Pasadena with their flip phones slapped against the sides of their heads. It's a world gone mad, he was thinking.

Preston Cook and Bobby Skylar were on it right away, mad or not, with their cell phones out and their thick fingers tapping away at the tiny keyboards. They were each looking through the treetops at the sky as though they could help matters by actually catching glimpse of one of the orbiting telecommunications satellites tirelessly following their orders to catch signals projected from earthbound antennae. But staring at the sky didn't help. The whole exchange was supposed to occur in fractions of a second. That day, however, Preston and Bobby found themselves waiting and waiting. What happened to the speed of light?

But then, suddenly, a phone rang far away in Washington, D.C, as Bobby connected with his agency! Preston glanced jealously at this comrade when he heard the joy in Bobby's voice as he began explaining to Digger Mac Brown that they were still in operation but in a tight spot in the mountains. Preston also heard the federal agent say they might need some back-up because things were getting dicey, and hearing the word "dicey" did not make Preston feel any more secure. He was a man who had no idea where his wife and his son had finally landed in their rush to evacuate their Pasadena residence. Not a single aspect of the adventure that day was within his comfort zone.

After several minutes of frustration, Dr. Cook abandoned his efforts to contact Samantha, who so very often left her phone turned-off anyway. It may have been ringing but there was no answer.

Preston had no idea that while he was trying to call her, she was riding shotgun with Cain, a Desert Eagle lying prominently between them as they motored along in the assassin's big white BMW relentlessly zeroing in on Preston and his compatriots while they struggled with not-so-smart early iterations of cell phones, which were basically small walkie-talkies.

Neither of the two men trying to connect with the outside world, after having wandered down from the strangely imagined hide-away miles off of Old Mill Road, would have guessed that a well-intentioned local guy casually reading the *LA Times* at the Crestbear Store had given Cain enough information on the whereabouts of their cabin to put Cain and Samantha on a fateful collision course with where Preston and Bobby stood with their cell phones, looking at the vast blue sky above the proud and fragrant evergreens gently swaying in the San Gabriel Mountains. All Cain had to do was take the first rutted pathway beyond the falling-down bass fishing billboard on Old Mill Road. It was a cinch. Furthermore, he would find to his delight that the gravel trail was freshly upturned, clear evidence his target had come that way.

Preston, Bobby, and Buster would have no reason to rush that morning, to get their cell phone conversations completed and begin their assent toward the cabin, where they might be protected and hidden. Nor did, Buster, their host, know to advise them there was imminent danger as he sat to the side where the lunacy of modern-day electronic addiction was on display before his condescending gaze.

Following a frustrating fifteen minutes, when his wife did not answer, Preston turned to ringing up his son, Dalton, and with only a few moments of relays and electronic pulses flying at 180,000 miles per second from relay station to earth-orbiting satellite to another relay station, there was a solid connection and he heard Dalton's small, beautiful voice answer, "Hello?"

No one really telephoned odd and brilliant young Dalton Cook other than his mother or his father. Therefore, he was afire with excitement when his phone rang. His heart was nearly bursting.

Meanwhile, Martin and Samantha moved steadily up Old Mill Road at modest speed. It was significantly colder than when they had begun their journey in the valley, so Cain had donned a chocolate brown leather jacket, probably worth a thousand dollars. Sam was still wearing the sweater she had on when she was nabbed in Hollywood.

Cain scanned the shoulders of the worn two lane blacktop, shoulders that intermittently rose into granite walls on both sides of the road and then fell away to dense forest, left or right. Sometimes the vehicle was on a ribbon sliding between boulders on one side and a two hundred foot plunge on the other, with only a dilapidated guard rail to save them from going over the edge. It was when Martin Speck and Samantha Cook were surrounded by trees on the Old Mill Road that the landmark they were anticipating came into view. It was ten or twelve miles beyond the Crestbear Store and it was just like old wild-hair at the Crestbear Store had said, one could not miss it. Straight ahead was the dull billboard, leaning sadly. One proud leg tried desperately to keep the advertisement on its job convincing passing motorists that great fishing lay ahead. The faded large-mouth bass arching across the sign was hooked and leaping from what must have been crystal blue water many years ago. Samantha feared the fish on the billboard looked as moribund as her own future.

Ladd Graham

Dr. Day-Steiner's dulled mind was struggling through various scenarios while the big BMW slowed and Speck surveyed the opposing shoulder of Old Mill Road for a place to turn off.

As predicted, in less than a hundred yards after the billboard an easement-like break in the woods appeared on the left. There was dirt and gravel making an overgrown path of some kind that headed westward, somewhat down the mountain at first, but it veered abruptly to the right some twenty yards away and where the trail headed beyond that point was not clear. It wasn't much of a road, with visible potholes and the foliage leaning inward on both sides. Once again, old wild-hair at the Crestbear Store was correct. But Martin hadn't come all that way to back down. He didn't give a damn about the car. It was a BMW, for chrissakes, and it should be able to handle some abuse even if it wasn't built for off-road. So, Martin angled the nose of his clean white sedan across Old Mill Road gently toward the mouth of the roughly hewn route he'd spotted on the opposite side of the black top.

"Whoa! Whoa! Whoa, here!" spoke up Samantha impulsively, startling even herself with the energy in her words. Adrenalin can be a wonder drug, even for the terrified.

And Martin did stop, right there at the beginning of the turn-off. He looked over at her with some degree of incredulity quite visible in his usually non-committal eyes. It was in that millisecond of adrenalin fueled surprise, like a flash of light in her brain, Samantha realized that her own value as collateral to this madman was no good to him if she disappeared right there where they stopped! And that's *why* he stopped! He didn't want to mess things up at that point. Her value was only real if they wound up in front of her husband! Because they were tantalizingly close to the assassin's objective, Samantha gained leverage. Cain probably would not kill her *there*. He needed her. What was she to do? Her mind was racing.

"We won't make it through," she tried. "Let's go back and get something with four-wheel drive like you said."

He looked at her for a long beat. "So… you're giving advice now?"

"I'm just saying," pointing ahead at the narrow miserable passage, "this car is not going to go anywhere on this road!"

Martin studied what lay ahead of them. Tree limbs protruded on either side, only a few feet from the ground, reaching a third of the way across the trail, and the ruts, while graveled had not seen proper attention in decades. It wasn't inviting. But he could see the tire tracks of Skylar's rental, which had ground through there the day before.

"This automobile is one of the finest driving machines in the world," he said. "If a Ford Taurus can negotiate what lies ahead, then I think we should have no trouble." He looked at her again, as she shrank back again near her door.

Samantha was afraid. Should she jump from the car on impulse in that very instant, while they were stopped, and make a run for it? After all, she thought, he might need her alive. Do it now! Do it now! Run! She was shrieking inside her own skull. But the sight of that Desert Eagle near the gearshift, a nickel-plated monster of a handgun, convinced her in its own silent but compelling way to wait and see what happens. So, she slumped where she sat. The moment had passed. She was not going to make a break for it. But she did find herself contemplating what her role had been in the whole convoluted drama that led to that moment and she felt shame.

Then, as if he knew exactly what she was thinking, Martin Speck comfortably took his eyes from his hostage, shoved the transmission into low gear in the automatic's gated shifter and they moved forward amongst the trees, which immediately began scratching and screeching along the sides of the white sedan like a posse of vandals enthusiastically keying every inch of the exterior. It made one's skin crawl. But Martin didn't care as long as the wheels kept turning as they relentlessly moved onward to what lay ahead, toward his target and perhaps the conclusion of this much-too-drawn-out mission.

As they jostled along the ruts and bounced forward into the right hand turn they had seen waiting ahead, they found it was a change in their path which almost immediately led uphill on a grade that drew them into thicker vegetation and forest. Tires now began slipping a bit, sending dirt and gravel flying, but they kept moving. The noise and the spine-wrenching pounding of their ride became more and more intense as they pressed onward.

All the while, Martin was dreaming about getting back home and spending time in his bucolic garden. He had been away far too long. He could see his vibrant nasturtiums blooming right then and he imagined throwing a few of their peppery petals into a lunchtime salad while he relaxed on his veranda overlooking the diversity of his beauties in the slanting autumn light. Martin was thinking he really needed to be more selective about the assignments he accepted in the future. Money had long ago become the lesser imperative in the use of his time and his skills. This mission was not worthwhile to him. Maybe he was getting soft. Frankly, a portable energy source that might light up the Third World didn't seem all that heinous a prospect in his mind. But such thoughts and contemplations were not part of his job on that day, on that trip to America, nor were similar considerations part of his job on any other assignment. His role was not to judge. Martin Speck, or Cain, or whatever his real name was, the professional killer, always fulfilled his mission. Nothing was going to stop him, not even his own reservations.

Quite to the contrary during that minute, Dr. Samantha Day-Steiner, slouching against the right side door was absolutely *not* thinking about money, nasturtiums, the world-wide value of cold fusion, or even something as mundane as getting home to Pasadena.

She was thinking that she wanted to live to see tomorrow. She wanted to see and hug her family again. And she also prayed Preston would come out of this okay. He was a good and beautiful man who had done something wonderful for the world and did not deserve what was happening. She continued on a guilt-ridden and painful reflection about the affair she had with her husband's friend and partner, Maxwell Umberto. How in god's name had all this come about? Samantha felt like she was in a swamp of a dream, a nightmare bog, a surreal place. She scanned her life for answers, but nothing surprising came to mind. Dr. Day-Steiner had made her own decisions along the way and she knew why. She just didn't like the why.

If there was an oversight in Martin Speck's plan of attack, it was that he could not travel that backwoods route quietly in any kind of motor vehicle. Tires grind. They spit rocks. Labored engines surge and sputter. It was a noisy undertaking. A clandestine approach to Buster's and Cloud's hideaway, the remote cabin they had meticulously carved out in the deep mountain forest above Crestline to protect themselves from a rotting and corrupt world, was not really possible if someone was trying to arrive using a machine. Perhaps Martin could have had the vision to look ahead in his mind and see the problem. A more cautionary strategy by Cain might have involved leaving his BMW a mile downhill. But that also would have meant he foresaw Buster, Bobby, and Preston outside their hideaway seeking a position to connect their cell phones. No one had the faintest notion they were on a collision course that crisp October morning bursting with fragrances and the colors of a California autumn. Combat was imminent and none of the combatants knew how very close it was.

Cain and Samantha were being tossed about like mannequins as the hearty German sedan growled and clawed forward through the overgrown route, disregarding external damage with Bavarian determination. It was in those minutes, Buster and his charges had arrived at the juncture where the rutted trail leading to his cabin met the gravel pathway below and they were just beginning their cell phone search of the heavens.

CHAPTER 80

"Are you alright, Dalt?" yelled Preston, leaning forward into his call and turning slightly away from the others. He was overcome by having finally reached one of his family members.

"Yes, dad," said the boy, but his father knew instantly something was wrong, the way parents can magically sense a problem on nothing but the subtlest of inflection miles and years distanced from their children.

"What is it, son?" said Preston his breath pausing.

"I'm here with the policeman, Fitzy," Dalton said, trying to speak reasonably, in his attempt maintain composure like grown-ups do. "I'm okay, but that bad man, the one all the cops are after, he was here, Dad," said Dalton.

"He was *there*?" said Preston, wild eyed!

"I mean he was at Fitzy's apartment. We left and now we're at his mom's house. She's really nice."

"*The policeman's mom*?" This was a peculiar turn in the conversation that Preston did not anticipate in any way.

"Yes," said Dalton. "I like her."

"You're at Detective Jack's mother's house?" Preston asked one more time soberly, because he had to confirm what he had heard.

"Yes. She used to be a cop, too, a long time ago, and his mom and dad are going to help Ahmad get home."

"That's swell, Dalt," said Preston. "Ahmad seems like a decent young man. But let me speak with your own mom for a minute, okay? Can you put her on the phone?"

There was a long pause before Dalton said, "Mom's not here." And his voice trembled. "She tried to get away," he added weakly.

"Tried to get away?" This got Preston's attention. It sounded ominous. But he could also hear his son's anxiety and near-tears, so he didn't want to insert his own fearful and loosed imaginings about his wife into Dalton's story. "What happened, Dalton?" Preston said calmly. "Just take a deep breath and tell me. Okay?"

"That bad man came just when we were all leaving the policeman's apartment. He started shooting at us. Mom ran one way and we ran the other."

"Was anybody hurt?" said Preston, his heart in his throat.

"Nobody," said the boy.

"Thank god," said Preston. "Do you know where your mom went?" said Preston. "Did you see?"

"No. I didn't. I haven't heard anything since she ran down the stairs at the apartment. I'm scared, dad. I tried to look out for her." He started to cry. He felt responsible for his mother's disappearance, even though there was nothing he could have done. He remembered his dad telling him to look after his mom when they left.

"It's all good, Dalt. It's gonna be okay. You did a great job, 47! We're proud as the dickens of you. I'm sure your mom's alright. She knows her way around and she went to a safe place; I'm sure. You did the right thing." But even as he said this, trying to protect his son, Preston shivered with fear. She had not answered her cell phone. She had not returned the call. Preston knew something was quite adrift. Samantha wasn't great about keeping her cell phone turned on, but she would not have ignored her phone messages in this kind of situation.

"Is Detective Jack there?" asked Preston. "I'd like to speak with him for a second, okay? And then you can get back on the line. Okay?"

"Okay," Dalton said trying to choke back his tears, trying with all his young heart not to be a baby.

Preston could hear his son's small voice working to sound strong, "Fitzy, my dad wants to talk to you."

When Preston finally folded his Sanyo cell phone that morning in the mountains after his conversation with his son and with the LAPD detective, he looked up to find both Bobby Skylar and Big Buster Bernard staring at him. Preston was ashen with concern and they instantly knew there were problems. Things were not good, not good at all, Preston was thinking as he processed in his head the story he'd just heard from Fitzgerald Jack. It pretty much matched what young Dalton had reported about the shooting in Hollywood and Samantha's disappearance. The detective agreed they would sit tight in Brentwood until Preston could make his way safely back down the mountain, but he did not share his fear Dr. Day-Steiner had been taken hostage by Cain.

"What is it?" said Bobby to Preston.

"Sam… she's missing," Preston returned without elaborating. "I spoke with my son and with that LA police detective. Cain showed up at the cop's apartment and started blasting the place to hell. They were all outside, about to leave. They got separated. Right now Dalton is with the cop and he's safe. But we don't know where Sam is."

Buster, the neighbor and friend, was at Preston's side in three quick steps. He wrapped one of his beefy arms around Preston's shoulders and said, "Ya don't know what happened back there, man. Don't invent worries. Common, now. Sam is one tough broad! You know that. She's okay, just like yer boy!" Buster was treating Preston like Preston treated Dalton. It's what humans do.

Dr. Cook didn't know what to say. His thoughts and his words were bound up in his mind like they were in cement. So he simply deflected it all by looking at Bobby and asking, "Did you get to your people?"

"Yes, I did!" Bobby replied conclusively. "Now they've got an idea of what's goin' down." Then he said, "Cain smoked the cops back at your house."

And suddenly Bobby saw Preston's face muscles tighten beneath his skin and Bobby wished he hadn't been so graphic. It had been all over the news, he'd been told, but Bobby's comrades on the mountain knew nothing of the most sensational killings in the Crown City for decades, perhaps ever.

Bobby took a tardy stab at patching up his insensitivity by adding, "Remember, Preston, I told all of them not to confront this guy. But *your wife* is a smart, feisty woman. She would know when to get out of the way. She's a survivor, like Buster said. I know the type." And Bobby was right about that. Samantha *was* a survivor when she was up to it. That's what led her to Maxwell and it's what infuriated her about her husband's altruism. But Preston also knew she wasn't always quite so game. She had a soft side and he knew she was currently hurting. Like most men and women she became much more delicate and vulnerable when her confidence went south.

"Yeah," Preston nodded without a lot of moxie in his voice.

That's when Bobby launched into his newly hatched plan. "I'm going to leave my cell phone right here... at this location," he announced and he looked around at the forest that bent around them in all directions and the patch of blue sky to the south through which they seemed to have made their cell phone connections. "The little bugger is still online to Washington, as we speak," he said. "Probably heard everything we just said. The battery'll last a couple'a hours, I hope. Time for them to get support here. Like a beacon."

"Who are *they*?" asked Preston.

"Marines," most likely, said Bobby in a matter-of-fact way.

Preston did not know what to make of this turn. Only a handful of hours ago he was thinking about nothing but mathematical formulae and cold fusion possibilities and now he was in the San Gabriel Mountains overcome with worry about his family and the U. S. Marines were on the way.

"Excellent!" exclaimed Buster, who was more grounded in the moment. "Did ya tell 'em we're just up the trail from here?"

"Absolutely," said Bobby and he smiled. Buster grinned, too. It gave them some comfort to know the cavalry was summoned. And they both turned to Preston, who could not muster a grin at that time, given recent news, but he was aware of what had been said.

"Help is on the way," reassured Bobby and he walked over to the shoulder of the rough path, not far from where they had been making their frantic calls and quite close to where Buster had been relaxing in disdainful regard of their electronic world. Agent Skylar looked back to the clearest patch of wild blue yonder he could find above the trees, as if that made any difference at all to the radio waves. And he carefully situated his cell phone on a large mossy rock, propping the phone open against the base of a two hundred foot California redwood that was probably a sapling when Columbus made landfall. The little electronic device, a rectangular Motorola flip-phone common to those years, was lit in cobalt blue and it was trying its damnedest to support a non-existent conversation flowing through the ethers between that pin-point in the San Gabriel mountain wilderness and Washington, D.C.

Bobby stepped back and looked at his phone and he glanced over his shoulder at the sky one more time before saying, almost as though he could sense the presence of Cain, "Let's get our asses back to the cabin."

Just as Preston, Buster, and Bobby turned to slog their way up the rutted, narrow poor excuse for a trail that led back to their refuge, they heard an engine grinding its way along the gravel path behind them, the slightly wider but still miserable easement leading upward from Old Mill Road.

They immediately looked at one another, faces gone pale and eyes wide. Who would be coming this way? And they all came to the same answer on a beat. It was not the Marines.

"Let's get going!" yelled Bobby. And they instantly picked up the pace. Coming down-grade earlier that morning wasn't easy on the uneven trail, but for three out-of-shape middle-aged men, going uphill in a hurry was by far worse. In less than a hundred yards they were all panting and heaving and sweating and wondering if their hearts would explode, but they pressed onward. Their movement was such that the grinding sounds of the vehicle behind them did not get much closer, but the sounds did not fall away, either. The vehicle was relentlessly pursuing them on that very path. They continued stumbling and staggering, trying to get back to the cabin where the heavy log walls would offer some kind of protection from the cannon of a handgun the monster, Cain, favored. They all felt fear and they were all somewhat frantic, even the federal agent, Bobby Skylar.

Behind them down the path, the once pristine white and now beaten-to-pieces 745i BMW sedan carrying Martin Speck and his hostage roared and crashed through thicker brush on the smaller, tighter route leading to the cabin. The car had made the turn from the first gravel road and as the three men scrambled up the mountain they could hear limbs cracking as the vehicle kept coming after them

like a Third Reich Tiger tank and just as terrifying. Cain was probably already beyond Bobby's improvised cell phone homing beacon
by then and his BMW was crushing their fresh footprints with steel
belted Michelins. The three compatriots were trying to move as fast
as possible, but after another fifteen minutes up the hill there was no
more hurry left in the wheezing men and their worn out legs. And,
by then, the roar of the engine was definitely getting louder. They
were being gained upon and the cabin was not yet in sight ahead of
them up the mountain.

"Just around the bend up there," encouraged Buster, pointing
directly ahead. "Not far now!" he shouted. Preston could not even
see a bend in the path, with all the underbrush and trees.

"Wait!" shouted the federal agent suddenly. "Stop!"

Both the other men did come to a pause but were clearly confused and anxious about any delay. "What? What are we doing? We
have to keep moving?" said Big Buster.

"You keep going. I'm going to stay here and distract that bastard.
It's our only chance."

"No!" said Preston, like he knew what he was talking about, "We
can make it to the cabin!"

The BMW continued to growl, grind, and roar, coming ever
closer and now probably not a hundred yards behind them down
the grade.

"We can't get caught out in the open with this guy!" said Bobby.
"He's going to catch up to us! Somebody has to slow him down!" Then
from his jacket pocket Bobby produced a compact, 9 mm Walther
PPK, the handgun popularized by Ian Fleming's James Bond, and he
held it up in the air. "You see? I'm the only one with a weapon!" he
said conclusively, which was a very clear statement causing Preston
and Buster to regard one another soberly. Buster's Army issue .45

was nowhere to be seen because he had left it with Cloud Willow in case she needed a gun with a maniac in the neighborhood.

"You go on, now!" said Bobby to the other men. "I'll meet you later. Be sure to lock everything at the cabin tight as shit, okay?" he commanded.

They nodded, not liking the implication, but understanding what he was saying.

"Don't waste time! Get going!" yelled Bobby.

Preston and Buster looked at one another again and started uphill.

"Don't do anything stupid or heroic!" shouted Preston over his shoulder as they trudged onward toward the cabin.

"Not my style!" yelled Bobby as the two men moved up the trail away from him.

The oncoming vehicle was getting louder and nearer. Bobby looked down the trail toward the sound of the engine, but he could see nothing approaching him. He knew he only had a couple of minutes to find cover, but he did not panic. He glanced around purposefully and with focus to identify a vantage point at the side of the path from which he could initiate his ambush. He planned on getting off two or three quick rounds at the most. Bobby's goal was to halt Cain, if even shortly, and provide his exhausted comrades precious extra seconds to make it to the cabin. He sought a well-concealed low level position with a good angle and a rapid escape route, because he absolutely did not want to get into a firefight with Cain. Nonetheless, he was also morbidly fascinated with the prospect of once again actually laying eyes on this mysterious icon in the international world of hired guns, an assassin of nearly mythical proportions. He was already one of the few men or women in the world who could report having seen him in the flesh. Glimpsing the man again intrigued Bobby, but he knew it was an intrigue fraught with deadly danger.

CHAPTER 81

Thrown left and right, hanging on as the BMW sedan clawed between the trees and growled forward bottoming out every ten feet and then lurching over earthen moguls, Martin Speck, with teeth clenched as he gripped the leather-bound steering wheel glanced quickly toward a pale and terrified Samantha Day-Steiner, who clung with both hands to the overhead grip. They slowly approached the spot where Bobby Skylar was waiting. The stretch of trail lying ahead did not appear special in any way that would suggest caution to Cain. It was not wider, not brighter, and was thick with brush and massive pines interspersed by fallen trees moldering away. The trail at that point was undistinguished in any way except that among the dark forest shadows an unseen gunman was waiting.

Bobby had found the vantage point he wanted on the downhill side of the crude path, where a tree had toppled years earlier and was well into decay, but the trunk remained propped slightly on the sprawling heavy root system of a neighboring wide-bodied oak. A two foot, triangular, ground level aperture had been created by those two trees and Agent Skylar lay motionless in the moist leaves and soil peering through the opening, with his Walther PPK loaded and at the ready. He wouldn't be visible to Cain until the oncoming vehicle was directly in front of Bobby, providing the federal agent with a sweet clean shot. Behind Bobby the mountain fell away pretty

quickly but he had seen enough to know he could run thirty feet or
so into the thick of the flora to gain some kind of cover from anyone
who might be aiming to put a fifty caliber slug through his skull.
Even the maestro, Cain, needed to see his target. Where that downhill escape route would take Bobby, he had no clue, maybe off the
edge of a cliff. But there had been no time to explore options.

Bobby could hear that the intermittently roaring car was almost
on him. He lay still and held his pistol with both hands, the muzzle
not quite protruding through the opening between the tree trunks.

As he lay there in the damp earth, out of the corner of his eye
Bobby could see a bright green inchworm arching its back and scoot-
ing slowly ahead on the rotting surface of the decaying tree. And
Bobby was momentarily jealous of that worm which did not care a
hoot about assassins or nuclear energy. The creature was probably
just trying to get home. Bobby Skylar was reminded that his useful
years in Special Group were probably at an end. It was time for him
to inch his way homeward, too.

In the midst of that self-reflective moment the dirty, half-
wrecked BMW entered the ambush arena from Bobby's right and he
suddenly could see the man, Cain, at the wheel riveted on negotiating the uneven road. In that millisecond Bobby was again puzzled
by the ethnicity or nationality of the man. Was he European, Indian,
Asian, African?

Then in a recognition taking mere nanoseconds to process, he
heard himself say inside his head, "My god! That's Preston's wife
beside him!" Bobby had to pivot his plan in that fraction of an instant
while reconfigurations were speeding through his cranium. It was
all happening in subatomic time. He could not fire directly at Cain
with the car bouncing like it was. There was too much of a chance
an errant shot would strike Preston's wife. And in the only moment
of panic he'd experienced in this entire adventure, he realized that

before the vehicle moved too far along and he lost his angle of attack, he had to shoot! So, he pulled the trigger and let go a round at a front tire, which was not part of his original plan.

It happens, a 9 mm projectile is not a sure bet on blowing out a car tire, especially steel belted radials, and his first bullet did not do the trick, glancing off the wheel and ricocheting around inside the wheel well. But it did make a lot of noise and it did get Cain's very practiced attention as his head swiveled immediately in the direction of the shooter, toward the downhill side of the road. He couldn't locate Bobby right away, giving Agent Skylar another free shot, and this one hit the wall of the Michelin squarely, exploding the tire and pitching the moving BMW suddenly to its left, requiring Cain to stop before the car smashed into a wide evergreen at the trail's edge.

This time when Cain looked toward the shooter, in a flash of recognition his eyes met Bobby's eyes. Cain knew he had seen the shooter before, but the new position of the stopped vehicle gave Bobby the confidence to safely let go one more round directly at the bastard who had been driving the car, so he squeezed the trigger. The drivers' side window burst magnificently, glass showering across the earthen trail and inside the car. Unfortunately, Cain was unscathed. He had ducked immediately when he saw the Walther PPK. Still, that simple hesitation gave Bobby the moment he needed to spring onto his downhill escape route. Behind him he could hear the car door open and Bobby knew Cain was in pursuit.

The underbrush and forest rapidly enveloped Agent Skylar as he charged away from the scene of the ambush, slapping back the foliage, almost falling, as he ran down the steep slope. He struggled to keep his feet. Then Bobby heard the sound of a heavy bullet flying near his head. The projectile shoved aside leaves and tree limbs, zipping by him with a deeper hum than the high pitched buzz of most slugs from handheld weapons. He actually could feel a touch of

breeze on his hair as it passed him and in that same millisecond the
.50 caliber missile that had barely missed his head exploded a dinner
plate sized chunk of wood out of a pine tree not far ahead. Splinters
were flying and were accompanied by the jarring report of Cain's
un-silenced Desert Eagle back at the trail. A sliver of bark sliced a
crease across Bobby's left ear.

"Key-rist!' said Bobby to himself, putting a hand to the wound,
and he kept on running.

Preston and Big Buster were pressing onward toward the cabin
as fast as their exhausted legs would allow. The cabin was not in sight
when they heard three distinct pops back down the road and the men
knew right away it was gunshots. They looked at one another for a
beat and then glanced slowly over their shoulders; but they could see
nothing on the trail behind them other than the rocky path they had
just traversed and overgrown forest to either side. Then they heard
the great boom from Cain's Desert Eagle, which echoed off massive
granite cliffs to the north.

"Shit!" they said in unison. And the two men turned back to the
hill, eyes wide, finding a new adrenalin-fueled energy in their thighs
as they put their backs into climbing that last steep rise. Huffing and
groaning and clawing at roots and rocks they dragged themselves
up and around a small curve and there, a hundred yards ahead, sat
the squat heavy log cabin waiting quietly and darkly in the midst of
trees crowding it on all sides. The broken Taurus was just off to one
side near Buster's Harley. Preston was thinking how thankful he was
that his survivalist neighbors had elected to build their mountain
sanctuary like it was a small fort, because they sure as hell needed a
fort on that day.

Martin Speck stood at the edge of the roughly hewn pathway, his crippled BMW idling behind him. He was looking down the mountain in the direction his attacker had fled. But he knew as he stood there, he could not pursue. He was not a happy man and any discontent about this assignment before had just multiplied. Cain had his hostage to worry about. He looked quickly toward the car to see if she had stayed put, and he found that she had, curled up petrified against the front passenger's door. Obviously a visit to this hide-away in the mountains was not going to be a surprise. Still, the sooner he got to his objective the better, as there would be less time for his targets to prepare their defenses.

Cain didn't know precisely what lay ahead, but he was smart, savvy, and committed to his mission. He glanced once more down the shooter's escape route and sensed a fleeting curiosity about who had the balls to lay in wait for him and deign to take a shot. He recognized from his glimpse of the gunman's face that he was the same man who surprised him at CTU, who had appeared at Umberto's office door, and Cain knew it was the federal agent Skylar.

On that conclusive thought Martin Speck returned to his waiting and barely running, formerly white, BMW sedan with Dr. Day-Steiner cringing inside. But his nickel-plated Desert Eagle was hanging like a weight in his right hand, hanging like the weight of his thoughts. Perhaps it was fatigue and perhaps it was the unworthiness of the assignment, but as he stood there in the forest where he'd been ambushed, he realized that hubris had just led him into making one of the few miscalculations in his entire illustrious career. The ante had been upped. The shooter must be the seasoned government agent that Breadcrumbs had identified, and a federal agent presented a new set of threats. Speed became the key ingredient to Cain's operation.

Martin examined the front left tire that had been punctured by the gunman's shot. Happily for Cain, the Michelin was not just steel belted, but it was also a run-flat tire. So, although the exterior had been shredded by the bullet, it remained only half deflated and was quite serviceable for the short distance he needed.

CHAPTER 82

Panting like huskies in the Iditarod, Preston and Buster staggered up to the small stoop at the front of the cabin. Buster fumbled for keys and finally he managed to unlock the deadbolt, throwing back the thick redwood door and gesturing for Preston to go inside. Buster turned once again and looked back to carefully study the trail leading to his retreat from the world. The cool October air and the slightly yellowing leaves were picturesque behind him and lent little credence to what ugliness was to come. At that moment, there was no sign of anyone or anything abnormal on that wooded lane, as calm and undisturbed as such a forest trail might have appeared two centuries past. This particular adventure wasn't exactly part of Big Buster Bernard and Cloud Willow's original fantasy about how their retreat would come into play, a fantasy which predicted the inevitable and final collapse of western civilization with destitute half-starved mobs roaming and ravaging the streets of Los Angeles as well as other great cities around the globe. Still and all, true to their forecast, Buster *had* been driven up the mountain because of a social collapse of sorts, driven to this place he and Cloud had built as a refuge. It was a collapse of local civil order and a collapse of police protection to be sure, all of which was not so terribly far afield from the buckling of foundations in broader civilization that he and Cloud had envisioned. Buster reckoned on that day, perhaps he was experiencing an early tremor heralding the final catastrophic disintegration. In a peculiar turn of thinking that only a survivalist can follow or an evangelical Christian contemplating the coming of the rapture, Buster privately fanaticized their situation represented an early crack in society's fabric and the end was neigh.

By the time Big Buster was closing the thick door and disappearing into his cabin sanctuary, joining Preston Cook to await their fate, Martin Speck had climbed back into the drivers' seat of what was once a pristine and powerful BMW grand touring car. By then it more resembled a street junker with a nearly flat, left-front tire. Nonetheless, after sliding behind the wheel, Martin punched the accelerator without hesitation and the machine responded mightily, showing a young heart in a worn body. The automobile leapt forward into the chase, the flat tire's high-tech inner tube supported the lifeless, wobbly Michelin. Martin aimed the car away from the trees it had confronted and directed it back onto the main trail as he gave her the gas. The BMW jumped ahead up the mountain again, eager to please.

Where that gunman had gone Martin had no idea but he expected another assault was in his future, feeling what the American pioneers must have felt traversing these inhospitable mountains, not knowing when the natives would spring from the darkness of the forest to wreak havoc and death upon them. Those adventurous souls had to know danger was waiting. So, he too fully anticipated another round of bullets and he kept his eyes in their scan-mode to the left side of the pathway, the downhill side, where lay the dense wooded terrain into which his assailant had fled. Martin was not going to be surprised again. The scanning technique, even while he was occupied with other duties, was a skill he understood well and at which he was accomplished. There would be no more ambushes. The agent who had attempted the last attack would not survive another.

Samantha lay silently to the right, frightened. She could feel the air in the sedan grow as thick as Martin's resolve. His anger and his concentration swelled around him and filled their space like a tangible energy, a presence Dr. Day-Steiner could sense on her skin and in her lungs. It was hard to breathe. She was scared. The stakes had just been raised as the BMW growled forward like an animal, an extension of Martin Speck himself, a man who never backed down. A challenge like this one pushed his game to the next level. Sometimes a boxer needs to be hit in the face before he can really deliver the fight and Cain was like that, a characteristic he did not choose, yet he'd seen it in himself before. He had been hit now and he was infused with resolve to finish this job as his vehicle lurched ahead, resuming its momentum and doing its damnedest to disregard its injured foot and stay on track. Any questions or lingering doubts in Martin Speck's mind about his objective, the mind that loved gardens, natural beauty and nurturance, were completely quieted.

Cain glanced at Samantha one time, but no more than that, as he pressed his BMW forward. His eyes had gone robotic gray. She could not even remember what color they had been before. This was a man on a renewed mission and she knew it.

Big Buster Bernard took down the shotgun from above the fireplace in his cabin and looked strangely at it in his hands. He was wishing he had not left his Army issue .45 in Pasadena. Cloud Willow would never touch a gun, but he wanted it to be there for her because he knew a madman was on the loose.

"Twelve gage Remington, over and under, breach load. Three hundred and fifty bucks used, a one-owner," he said like he was talking about an automobile he'd purchased. He continued to study the weapon, sensing the heft of it. "This's all we have up here for guns."

"It sure as hell is better than nothing," said Preston, peeking out one of the two front windows' simple curtains toward the trail leading to the cabin. "Do you think we should wait or try and make a break for it?"

"Break for it? Break for where?" asked Buster incredulously. "It's cliffs on all sides... and going back down there with him coming up toward us... I don't think that's the A move."

"Maybe Mr. Skylar got him," said Preston weakly.

"I don't think so," said Buster. "The last shot we heard was Cain's."

Preston looked soberly at his host. He was hesitant to ask any more questions about what happened to the federal agent.

"How long do you think we can hold him off?" asked Preston.

Buster returned his attention to the twin barreled gun in his hands. "Not sure," he said with an unexpected and very odd inflection to his words. "Ya see," he added, "I've never actually fired this thing."

"*What*?" Preston said.

"Cloud and me figured we might need a gun, what with all the wild life up here and the occasional dim-witted brown bear on the prowl. So, we figured it'd be a good idea. But I never got around to shootin' the damn thing."

"Do you have bullets?" asked Preston, more exercised than he wanted to be.

"Ya don't call shotgun ammo, bullets," Buster said. "They're cartridges. Slugs or buckshot. And, yes, we picked up a box 'a cartridges to practice with. Slugs. Which is pretty much a wad, instead of a bunch 'a pellets scatterin' all over the damn place. S'easier to hit yer target with the buckshot, but we didn't have duck huntin' in mind. We was picturin' rabid bears or mountain lions or demented townies. So, we got slugs. They'll stop a big critter but they don't travel that far accurate."

"*How* far?" said Preston.

"Far enough to blow the shit out'a that bastard Cain, if he gets in this cabin!"

Preston gave his host a studied regard. "Do you know how to shoot that shotgun, Buster?" he said carefully.

"How hard can it be?" said Buster, putting the gun's butt to his shoulder and sighting down its barrel.

"Can you load it?" said Preston not finding any humor in their situation, with a professional assassin on his way up to the cabin and for their only defense they have a shotgun that nobody has used.

"Don't be stupid. I shot a lot'a guns in the Army," said Buster softly, but in spite of the man's imposing stature and the weapon he held in his hands, the very quizzical look on his face as he examined his Remington did not engender confidence.

CHAPTER 83

The Brentwood house where Fitzgerald Jack's mother lived was on a quiet and shaded affluent street, several social levels above the simple neighborhood in Pasadena where young Dalton Cook had been raised. But upscale mattered not a whit to him. He was missing his home. He wanted everything to be like it was before this bad man came around, yet he was old enough to sense it may never be like that again. He'd seen and heard on television what happened the day before in Pasadena, the deaths and the fire. So, after speaking on his cell phone with his dad that morning, his father became the brightest blip on the radar screen of his young and focused mind. He had to find his dad. He had to get back with his dad. Dalton wanted his mom, too, but he had no idea where she might have gone. At least he knew his dad was in the mountains near the Big Bear resort and he quickly hatched a plan.

"You said you wanted to find my father?" said Dalton suddenly to Fitzgerald, recalling Fitzgerald's statement, moments after Dalton had disconnected from his dad's call, a call that had been fired at the speed of light through trees, along mountain sides, on to base stations and to satellites, and in less than one second had located Dalton's phone hidden away in the Brentwood home of one-time detective Sally Jack. The communications possibilities had become mind-boggling.

Fitzgerald looked suspiciously at the youngster and said slowly, "Yes. That's right, Dalton. I want to help your father." He was very focused on Dalton's statement about his father because he knew the boy had both just spoken with this dad and the boy's question might be the lead he needed to intercept the assassin. "Do you know where your father is in the mountains right now?" said Detective Jack.

"Not exactly," said Dalton, "but close."

"What is 'close'?" said Fitzgerald moving from his chair to sitting beside Dalton on the chintz davenport that faced wide paned windows looking onto a spacious trimmed Brentwood front yard. Even in October it was alive with a robust and colorfully diverse floral display that would have made Martin Speck smile.

"They're near Big Bear, at Buster's cabin," said the young man to his host. "And I want to go get my dad."

"Yes," said the detective, "and I'd like to get your dad, too, but we don't know *exactly* where they are, do we?"

"We can fly up there and find them," said Dalton.

"Fly?" said Fitzgerald and he smiled, thinking this must be some super-hero fantasy the boy was contemplating. "My flying skills aren't what they used to be," he said and to show he cared Fitzgerald grinned and gave one light stroke to the mop of dark hair Dalton had inherited from his mother. "But I do like the idea."

Dalton was not to be so easily placated and he looked Fitzgerald Jack straight in the eyes and said, "I have an airplane."

"You do?" said Fitzy with some surprise, seeing the boy was serious; but then Dalton always tended to be a very serious young man, which made sense given that his primary playmate in life had been a grown-up, a world-class physicist.

"It's my dad's plane at the Van Nuys airport. A Cessna Skyhawk," he said.

"Well," said Detective Jack sympathetically, "we still need a pilot."

"I can fly it," said Dalton. "I've flown with my dad a lot."

Fitzgerald Jack could see immediately there was not an ounce of silly-business in this boy's words.

"Well," said Fitzgerald, "do you have a license?" The whole concept had come so completely out of left field that he didn't know exactly how to respond.

"I'm flying up there to get my dad," young Dalton said conclusively. "You can come with me or you can stay. But I'm going."

At the time Dalton was stunning Fitzgerald with plans of flying to Big Bear, Fitzy's mother, Sally Jack, was headed toward LAX to put Ahmad on an airplane as had been planned the night before. She was praying there would be assistance at the airport, assistance driven by this young man's influential father, influence that would get him past the enhanced post 9/11 security at Bradley International Terminal and onto his flight home. But that adventure still lay ahead as she angled her Volkswagen Passat onto the 105, the freeway that would take her to the doorstep of the airport.

Sally had once been a strong willed police officer herself and after a decade of retirement she didn't mind walking straight into tough situations, but she was nonetheless a little nervous as she escorted Ahmad Mulham into Bradley International Terminal at the Los Angeles Airport. In 2005, for both good reasons and bad ones, Middle-Easterners entering airports in the United States got long looks from tourists and from security officers alike and that is exactly what was happening as Ms. Sally Jack and Ahmad Mulham strode through the lobby of a very busy terminal toward the American Airlines ticket counter. Ahmad was a wanted man, wanted by the LAPD for a murder in Westwood only two days ago! An all-points-bulletin on him was still very active.

Ahmad, onetime "Skip" at the University of Miami and devoted "Hoorocane," was categorically westernized in his clothing, his style, and his manners. Yet that benefit didn't keep Sally from being wary as a bagman at a cop convention while they walked through the busy airport terminal. She was thinking ahead and since she didn't really know how the ticket purchase was supposed to occur, she already had her Visa card out and was poised to pay this young man's fare as quickly as possible. The faster the transaction the better, she figured. She didn't want to mess around in those circumstances. Ahmad was praying quietly to himself that his complete lack of identification or documents would have been patched over through his father's connections in some miraculous way.

Neither Sally nor Ahmad knew with certainty what had been arranged. Ms. Jack had no choice but to trust the young stranger when he reassured her on their drive to the airport that all would be okay when they arrived, yet in Sally's mind the whole enterprise was shakier than a novice on stilts. The influence and reach of Ahmad's father was not entirely appreciated by her in those extraordinarily tense early minutes at the airport, but the adrenalin kept her moving. Interestingly, on that strange day at LAX, the old cop recognized she missed the rush of the action even after more than a decade in retirement.

Bradley International Terminal's private security officers, the Airport Police, Homeland Security, TSA officers, as well as the ticket agents were already on the look-out for Ahmad Mulham long before he entered the building. True to their clandestine orders, law enforcement personnel and agents of every stripe held back and kept their distance when Ahmad and Sally Jack entered the terminal building.

Ahmad had been flagged on cameras and through radio messages in mere seconds after he and Ms. Jack appeared at the terminal entrance. There was no evidence of poor or bumbled communications at play among officers from various agencies on that morning but it took the invisible hand of a man on the other side of the globe, Mahudin Mulham, Ahmad's father, a man who knew a lot of people in the right places, to make it all happen. Debts were called in and old accounts were settled that day. And after barely coming to a halt at the end of a queue leading to the two reservations agents on duty at the American Airlines ticket counter, and while Ahmad and Sally were both working very hard to appear as innocuous as possible, they were suddenly plucked from the back of the line and ushered by a tall Scandinavian American Airlines employee to an unattended ticket window off to the side. They came to a halt twenty feet away from the long line of passengers.

Sally and Ahmad were afraid to speak and both of them thought they had been busted for sure as they glanced between themselves. Ahmad almost fainted where he stood and he went a bit pale. They assumed they would be encircled by a dozen armed airport police in only a heartbeat or two. But as it turned out, that wasn't the case.

"Mr. Mulham?" said a pretty, ebony-skinned young woman on the other side of the ticket counter who emerged through an "Employees Only" door behind the counter. "We've been expecting you," she added in a matter-of-fact sort of way and then she smiled at them warmly, which was not what happens typically when one is being arrested. Furthermore, no law enforcement agents were approaching from any direction. The only armed officer in the American Airlines boarding area stood off from them by some fifty feet and while he kept his eyes on the proceedings, he did not advance, nor did he threaten to do so.

"One ticket to Jeddah, Saudi Arabia, please," began Sally assertively and holding out her credit card, still reeling a bit, but assuming that some kind of negotiation had to take place.

The young reservations agent on the other side of the counter simply held up a smooth thin palm and said, "That's alright. It's all been arranged," and she smiled again. "Luggage?" she asked of Ahmad as if everything was business as usual.

"No luggage," stammered Ahmad, as lost as was Sally Jack. "Just this," he continued, finally realizing that things were falling into place, and he gestured to what he was wearing and he smiled. After all, handsome "Skip, the Hoorocane," had a magnetic and quite disarming grace, so the young ticket agent smiled back at him bigger and brighter than before.

"Okay," she said, "Please go with Vin," she added and gestured for Ahmad to follow the tall Scandinavian employee. She flashed another brilliant smile at Ahmad when he rounded the counter and came nearer to her.

Ahmad Mulham and Sally Jack made eye contact one more time when the ticket counter separated them. "Thank you for everything, Mrs. Jack," said Ahmad earnestly to her. "You and your husband are wonderful people."

"You're welcome, Ahmad" returned Sally. "Have a safe flight," she said and she winked at him before he disappeared through the "Employees Only" door.

A second later Sally glanced at the pretty ticket agent and said softly, "Thank you for your help."

"Thank *you* for choosing American Airlines," returned the young and pleasant agent like this had been an everyday ticket purchase, like nothing out of the ordinary had just occurred.

And on that strange thought Sally turned around and faced what she expected to be a random mob of tired travelers in the Bradley terminal headed for faraway places, but instead she found two hundred sets of eyes staring straight at her, strangers with carry-on bags moving in slow motion. The pretty American Airlines ticket agent might have behaved like the exchange that just occurred was routine, but apparently what transpired at the ticket counter that day must have looked a tad unusual to the gawking passengers all around.

Sally kicked-started herself on that beat and decided whatever it was that happened at the ticket counter with Ahmad and American Airlines was over. So, let's skedaddle, she said to herself, throwing back her shoulders and heading single-mindedly toward the very doors through which she and Ahmad had made what they mistakenly thought was a low-profile entrance. Nobody bothered her as she strode across the crowded lobby. Not a single question was asked. Yet all the way, she realized she was being scrutinized from every direction. It was one of the most surreal experiences she'd ever had in a long police career. And Sally Jack was a woman who had once rounded up a squeaky clean U.S. Senator while he was still under the sheets with metal-bedecked, identical-twin, teenage girls. Another time, Sally had survived a soured narcotics sting because a flaming Mexican drug lord her liked her shoes. Nonetheless, that peculiar day in 2005 at the Bradley International Terminal ranked right up there with all of it. Ahmad's father must be one influential son of a bitch, Sally thought, as she went out into the bright and cool October day, one amazingly connected human being.

But the complete scope of what her son had gotten himself into by protecting the Cook family was not on Sally's radar screen. She didn't know about the power structure that was involved, in spite of her glimpse of the power displayed by Ahmad's father at LAX. Sally did not know anything about Preston Cook's invention and the goldmines his invention would bury forever. She did not really comprehend from whence sprang the scary "Cain" character, she'd heard mentioned.

Through her narrow peephole on that one day at the airport, Sally Jack simply helped a young man she perceived to be innocent of charges against him to find his way home. She wasn't wearing a badge anymore and she knew very well the quagmire into which Ahmad would have tumbled if he had been apprehended in the United States, especially in those particularly dark days for Muslims in America. Fitzgerald's mom did not care to wade into things further, even though she could sense there were abundant possibilities slithering beneath the surface like moray eels. She reminded herself she had retired her desire for that level of curiosity years ago.

CHAPTER 84

A fifty caliber, 600 grain slug from Cain's Desert Eagle struck one of the cabin's front windows in a startling explosion of glass as it passed through the living room with its distinctive low-resonance hum, pursued by a storm of razor shards flying in every direction. When it happened, Preston had been contemplating his cell phone, again trying to figure out how to jury rig the damn thing to get a connection from where they were, tucked away on a mountain side. In that same moment Big Buster was studying the shotgun he had loaded a few minutes earlier and he was puzzling over its supposed poor accuracy. Both men instinctively hit the floor when the window shattered and glass shrapnel zipped around them. They each took several painful shards somewhere on their bodies and a pair of four-inch blades of window glass were sticking straight out from the farther wall like they had been thrown there by an expert with knives. The heavy bullet did not slow down exploding the window and it blew a pair of softball sized holes on a straight line through two interior walls made of white pine before the bullet embedded itself in a foot-thick log on the farther side of the cabin.

From where they were, prostrate on the floor, Buster and Preston stared at one another, paralyzed with shock. This was it! The bastard was there! They had smallish lacerations on their faces, Preston's on his brow and Buster's on his cheek. Preston looked at his left hand and gingerly removed an inch long piece of glass from just above his thumb. There were razor sharp bits of the window scattered all across the rough-weave American Indian carpet on which they had thrown themselves. They didn't know exactly what to do next because they hadn't really made a plan. This territory was not familiar to them. They both had previously imagined there might be a shootout of some kind.

But these two civilians could not possibly have known Cain did not participate in gun fights. To him, throwing a lot of hot lead back and forth was not the least bit efficient and the whole enterprise was far too unpredictable. Nor could the men have known that Cain didn't waste time, having learned long ago that the offensive must be swift and unhesitating. It's the kind of understanding a street fighter has that regular working stiffs do not. There can be no compunction when fists start to fly. Instinct always wins.

Even before Preston and Buster could climb to their feet, a blast from Cain's Desert Eagle blew the latch off the front door! He kicked it once and it flew open! Suddenly the monster was in the room with them, dragging Samantha Day-Steiner by her hair twisted into his left fist!

Preston and Buster were on their knees stunned at how quickly he had assaulted and overtaken the cabin. Only two shots had been fired! This wasn't at all what they pictured. Buster had not even raised his shotgun as both men stared with wide eyes at the muzzle of the large, nickel-plated handgun aimed their way. And the man holding that gun seemed totally unfazed by what had just transpired. It was business as usual for Martin Speck. Preston and Buster could not have known how very different this assignment had actually been for Cain and how unusually ruffled he was by the delays and complications. It surely didn't show. But those elements were grinding away slowly at Cain's sensibilities. He was not a happy man on that day, even though he was, in truth, the type of gentleman who could be quite jovial when fussing over his garden or enjoying a fine meal with a clever companion. But that was not now, and he had already vowed to himself that sooner or later someone would have to pay for his immense dissatisfaction.

Cain studied the two terrified men kneeling in front of him and he gestured toward Preston, saying carefully in his otherworldly, unidentifiable accent, "I would guess you are Dr. Cook. Is that true?"

"No!" interrupted Buster heroically and as earnestly as he was able. "*I'm* Dr. Cook!"

Cain smiled at the big man. Buster's gesture was charming, actually, to Cain. So, there was an extended pause while Martin Speck continued to hold Samantha in his tight grip at arm's length to his left side while he gazed curiously at these two strange allies. Then he said carefully to Buster, "I think you are *not* Spartacus. That would be your friend here. But let me suggest non-Spartacus, kindly rest your Remington on the floor in front of you, as gently as a baby, and raise your hands very slowly. *Both* of you please, if you don't mind," he concluded.

Buster reviewed the gun he held like he'd just then realized it was still clenched in his hands. There was a long hesitation at that moment which panicked Preston and he quickly interjected, "Put the damn gun *down*, Buster!" He was terrified that his neighbor would try something foolish.

Buster did look at Preston with crazy eyes. He had been contemplating a surprise attempt at killing this assassin in their midst. But instead, after Preston's words, he rested the shotgun on the Indian woven carpet and raised both of his hands as he had been instructed. Preston followed suit by raising his hands, too. They both remained there on the floor on their knees in front of this blondish, tall, athletic, attractive stranger who killed men and women for a living, and who held Preston's wife by her hair in one clenched hand like she was a lifeless doll.

Cain seemed to be looking at the Remington on the floor in front of Buster, but in fact he was noticing the littered-with-glass rug upon which the over-and-under shotgun had been placed. "Is this Apache?' he asked suddenly, gesturing toward the carpet with the muzzle of his Desert Eagle like a pointer in his hand.

Buster stammered. "Yes," he said.

American Indian weaves by tribe or nation are quite distinct from one another but not usually identifiable to U.S. citizens, even those from the southwest. Martin Speck, who sprang from god knows where, was an astute man and he always researched the culture and history of any terrain he was going to navigate on his assignments, mostly for the mere joy of it rather than to any strategic advantage. "Apache is not indigenous for this region, is it?" queried Cain quite seriously. "I would have expected Navajo. Or even Arapahoe... although west of the Mojave it would be peculiar."

"We got this rug in Santa Fe," shrugged Buster. He was not really conversant in these things. Cloud Willow chose the rug. She was part Indian.

"That would be you and the woman you live with?" probed Cain.

"Yes," said Buster very quietly.

Cain's face went reflective. "A very interesting lady," he said, recalling Cloud Willow's defiance in Pasadena before he let her walk. And then upon seeing the distinct flash of horror in the eyes of the big man on his knees, which was really quite disarming to Martin Speck, he added quickly, "Oh, she's safe, my friend. Don't worry." Speck was not a reckless murderer in his own mind. He was a man doing his job.

Seizing this relatively gentle moment to speak, Preston asked softly from his tension-dried throat, "Sam, are you okay?"

She had been standing under Martin Speck's outstretched hand, not struggling, not speaking, not trying to make problems, just cooperating, nothing more than a sack hanging inertly from Cain's left fist.

Cain had bound Samantha's wrists at her back with nylon hand-cuffs that he'd plucked from one of the Pasadena police officers he'd killed at the Cook's residence. One never knows how a prisoner will behave in the open. He glanced at Samantha curiously when her husband asked after her. "Aren't you going to answer?" Cain said toward her.

"I'm alright, Preston," came back her weak reply.

"And she'll be much better when I let her go," added Martin Speck, getting back to business. "And I'd like to do that sooner than later, if you don't mind." He saw no benefit in beating around the bush; so he moved directly to his mission. "Where is the device, Dr. Cook?"

The cold fusion instrument around which all of this horror was spinning happened to be hidden in plain sight, right there in the living room of this mountain survivalist hide-away, right there in the metal rolling case Preston had hauled with him from his workshop in Pasadena and loaded into the Taurus only the day before. It sat silently nestled up against the worn plaid, wing chair and in plain view, waiting patiently for a competent engineer to pick it up and go to work lighting the world. That was the instrument's mission. But who would look for a nuclear reactor in something the size of a smallish suitcase? It defies imagining, so Cain did not consider that possibility. He only had a vague notion of the object he was after, basically because few had ever seen it. He had no idea how large or small or complicated the contraption might be. Martin was an informed and literate man in many disciplines including science, but he certainly didn't picture the mechanism to be anything that small. He'd seen the carry-on suitcase already, of course. He recorded everything right away during his initial scan of the environment after bursting through the door; he was a professional. Still, he intuitively assumed that carry-on contained personal items, because it wasn't serious luggage. Yet Cain also knew from having been inside the garage laboratory before he burned it down, that the reactor – whatever its size – had been removed.

Preston opened his mouth to respond to Cain's question but he hesitated and that pause was just long enough. Before Preston had a chance to invent an answer, a 9 mm Walther PPK bullet zipped through the open doorway! There was a *pop* from somewhere outside even as the bullet creased Cain's left shoulder and caused him to let go of Samantha!

"Ouch!" he exclaimed as he jumped to the side. Blood immediately appeared on his shirt sleeve and a trickle began to crawl down his arm. He impulsively and solidly kicked the heavy door closed with a bang! "*Maird!*" Cain muttered, feeling like he had just left himself as vulnerable as an amateur.

This assignment was becoming less and less attractive to Martin Speck with every passing minute. He hadn't been touched by a bullet in at least fifteen years. In a flash, he remembered the last time he'd been wounded. It was when he put an end to a vocal and problematic Soviet Colonel in Germany just before the Berlin Wall came down. Cain had been commissioned by the KGB for that job and it was messy from the beginning, like this one. But now-a-days he really did try to avoid leaving his DNA around, like on his bed sheets at the Beverly Hills Hotel or on that American Indian rug where perhaps a splattering of his blood had just fallen. His attention to details had changed in many ways since that KGB fiasco years ago.

Outside the cabin, Bobby Skylar crept around behind the parked cars and the Harley-Davidson Fantail Classic waiting in front of the cabin. His government issued Walther PPK was in his hand and his clothes were torn and bedraggled from climbing around in the weeds and woods along the side of the mountain. One of the two sedans was Martin Speck's beat-to-pieces big white BMW and the other was Skylar's ruined Ford Taurus. Clearly, neither of the vehicles was reliable after their heroic efforts to bring passengers up the mountain. Those cars were finished. Transmission fluid and oil spread dark as blood in the leaves and dirt beneath each of them. Only the motorcycle appeared road-worthy.

Bobby had made it his mission to get back to the cabin after the ambush he had staged on the trail. He was as focused as a junky at that point and, like Cain, he was not without experience in these situations. He knew he had hit the mysterious bastard when he fired that one shot through the cabin doorway. He had not only seen the demon in the flesh twice, but he had now wounded the son of a bitch, too! It made Bobby's heart pump like mad. Yes! For the moment, it was as though he was in his first year with Special Group. He was twenty-eight years old again!

CHAPTER 85

At the Van Nuys Airport, the loyal Cessna Skyhawk was parked patiently just as Preston and Dalton had left her the last time they went flying. Like other machines she was as reliable as the attention she got from her owners and the attention Preston and his son had provided this Skyhawk over the years had been loving and ample. So, on that day Lucky 47, sporting her special and magical name boldly on her cowling, was ready to serve, ready to soar, and ready to satisfy.

Young Dalton was circling the Skyhawk at Van Nuys Airport giving the aircraft the standard careful visual inspection his father has so thoroughly engrained in him. He vigorously tested the flaps with hands and he examined the pavement underneath the airplane for oil stains and he looked for streaks of any wrong kind along the cowling and fuselage. Meanwhile, Fitzgerald Jack was tagging along like the family pooch. Never mind he was a forty-plus year-old Lieutenant in the Los Angeles Police Department's Detective Bureau, a lauded officer with a burgeoning reputation. That day in Van Nuys he was fairly much at a loss for words, looking befuddled as he watched a boy drag his fingertips tenderly along the skin of an airplane.

Fitzgerald had said he wasn't going to condone this adventure when they were at his mother's house in Brentwood, yet there he was at the Van Nuys Airport. When he insisted they get some kind of approval at air control for what they were about to do, he had been basically dismissed by the boy, because Dalton had no pilot's license and Dalton was not about to be dissuaded from his mission. That part was clear. Lieutenant Jack had already bristled and threatened to turn his young charge over to youth officers and Dalton called his bluff right away. Dalton did not believe Fitzgerald for an instant. He said simply, "I'm going to save my dad, detective. Please don't try to stop me. Help me." And then the boy went straight ahead and, in no time, they were at Van Nuys Airport checking out the Cessna for take-off.

Officer Jack had actually driven the boy to the airport, rather than release him to take a cab or hitch-hike. The Cain character was still out there somewhere and Fitzgerald was already up to his neck in potential legal complications regarding Ahmad Mulham, so he pressed forward for better or for worse in making sure the boy was safe. His original plan was slipping into uncharted territory and all the while he was praying he wasn't destroying his career along the way. The entire enterprise was so unlike Fitzgerald Jack and so unlike advice he would give to any rookie cop. On the other hand, he was tremendously encouraged by a short cell phone exchange with his mother, Sally Jack, in which she had expressed her astonishment at how smoothly undocumented Ahmad Mulham had been provided his passage out of the country at Bradley International Terminal. Maybe they were all doing the right thing after all, in spite of such a diverse collection of individuals who had fatefully converged at a modest home in Pasadena where deadly mayhem had later broken out. It was off-the-charts.

"Aren't we supposed to file a flight plan or something like that?" said Fitzgerald to the boy as they both ducked under the starboard wing struts and rounded the plane.

"Don't be silly," said Dalton, in a very adult matter-of-fact sort of way, without even looking at Lt. Jack. "We are going to take off. That is all."

"What about the control tower?" asked Fitzgerald getting more and more nervous, contributing any random imaginings he had about how airports operate. The experience was dragging him farther and farther afield, away from his comfort zone. He didn't know what in the world to say to the boy pilot at that point.

Dalton stopped and looked back at his companion. "The control tower?' he asked incredulously. "Do you mean that room over there?" and the boy pointed to a squat cinder block building that had a couple of plate glass windows facing the airfield. "That is air control. There is no tower. This is Van Nuys, not LAX."

"But what if another plane is landing or something?" said Fitzy desperately.

"There is only *one* runway, Detective Jack. We will look both ways very carefully before we taxi out onto it," said Dalton shaking his head at the inanity of the question, and then he returned to his inspection of the Cessna. "There is a wind sock over there, if that will make you feel any safer," he added and pointed toward a red tube of cloth hanging like a limp flag at the top of a pole near the cinder block air control building.

Fitzgerald Jack nodded but didn't bother to look, understanding this was the youngster's notion of humor. "Thank you for the reassurance," he said.

"You are welcome," said Dalton.

The dynamics of power at the mountain cabin had been altered when that bullet slit Cain's shoulder. Martin Speck was still in charge, but now he had two kneeling men with a shotgun lying before them, plus a handcuffed frightened woman who had run to her husband's side when Speck unintentionally released her the instant he was wounded. Cain also had to add to the equation an extra factor outside the cabin, a factor with a gun, and a factor that was a good shot, too. So, priorities had definitely shifted and Cain was recalculating. He understood what was happening. All of the action in Martin Speck's life was a matter of mathematics, algorithms, and probabilities. It was a strange calculus to most men and women, but it had come to be second nature to Cain, because that was his livelihood. He was a scientist, too, in a macabre fashion, using deductive reasoning and critical thinking on the fly.

Cain figured that outside the cabin was a guy who was looking to find an advantage, a weak spot, an opportunity, and his attack would more likely than not be swift. That was Cain's own formula and he had already deduced that the individual outside, throwing 9mm rounds through an open door, was the same Walther-toting US agent who had ambushed him earlier and had blown out a front tire on his BMW. Skylar was obviously someone who knew what he was doing. Cain recognized that such an adversary roaming around outside raised a new and different set of concerns. But Cain was convinced the agent was not a part of a larger force. His opponent was a lone operator for the present.

Martin Speck made no assumptions about weakness on the part of any enemy. He knew to respect his opposition and anticipate the worst. That was always his rule and it had served him well. So, for the moment, it was *he* who had to contemplate developments. But Cain was not usually one to hunker down and wait, while his enemies made their moves and he certainly was not without options. He had *three* hostages. In other words, he had collateral.

The trim, tanned, and square-jawed air controller at Van Nuys Airport, Dirk Stevens, was working overtime from his regular job not that far away at Burbank Airport, which had been rechristened the Bob Hope Airport in recent years. Dirk Stevens was a stage name, but his acting career and his ambitions at becoming a matinée idol had headed south years earlier, so he had gone to working around airplanes because they were a fascination of his since he was kid. Beyond a love for airplanes Dirk was also recently married to his other love, a Marilyn Monroe look-alike who managed to find work in the movie business here and there when blonde bombshells were needed. As it happened, Mr. and Mrs. Dirk Stevens were excitedly anticipating a baby in the spring, so any extra cash was welcome, meaning that Dirk would gladly fill in at Van Nuys air control anytime help was needed. The day that Dalton and Fitzgerald were appropriating Preston Cook's Cessna was just such a day.

Dirk did not really know the regular aviators who frequented the Van Nuys Airport. Consequently, he didn't notice anything unusual, off to his right, some hundred yards or so, well beyond the southern hanger, where a dozen private aircraft were tied down. He paid no particular attention to Dalton and Fitzgerald in the distance. He could see that a youngster and an adult were inspecting a Cessna Skyhawk but that notation made not the slightest blip on his risk management radar screen. People were out there all the time showing off their airplanes to family and friends. It was routine.

What wasn't routine was when the airplane started to move. Dirk Stevens quickly scanned his log of scheduled flights. He didn't think he had any take-offs queued at that time. Otherwise, he would have been ready and waiting. It was a quiet day, so he double-checked his records as the Cessna rolled forward and he finally confirmed for himself the records were void of any authorized flights. He had a problem.

Dirk went immediately to his radio microphone. "This is Van Nuys control, Lucky 47, please reply. Over." He doubled-checked the frequency, too, when he got no answer, but he found he was on the correct channel.

There was simply no response from the pilot of that aircraft.

"Come in, Lucky 47, you are *not* cleared for take-off! Abort immediately!" exclaimed Dirk.

He could see the airplane taxing toward the runway, where it stopped a couple of beats at the edge before moving forward, pausing while young Dalton was scrutinizing the sky in both directions for incoming aircraft, just as he had promised Fitzgerald. The boy knew from his dad that occasionally an airplane in distress will approach a landing strip unexpectedly from the wrong direction, so both the eastern and the western horizons were scanned thoroughly by Dalton and they were found to be clear.

"Lucky 47! Acknowledge! Over." said Dirk loudly into his microphone, coming completely off of his chair as he glared at the airplane pivoting out onto the single, primary runway. How could this be happening? "Do *not* proceed, Lucky 47!" he yelled. "Abort! Abort!"

But there was no stopping Dalton Cook at this point, as the detective had discovered earlier. The Cessna rolled another hundred meters to the eastern end of the runway and then it rotated 180 degrees to face a steady ocean-fed breeze and held its spot as it readied for take-off. Dalton was going through the preflight checklist in his mind, the one he had gone through so many times with his dad and he was trying not to panic. He'd never flown solo before.

Ashen Fitzgerald Jack was strapped into the right hand seat of the Skyhawk while young Dalton sat buckled into the pilot's seat mumbling and checking off items from his mental list. But mental lists were not difficult for Dalton.

Simultaneously, they both caught sight of a tall wild man, Dirk Stevens, running from the control building two hundred yards away waiving his hands in the air and screaming. Dalton realized in that moment he could not wait to finish the checklist and he pulled back on the throttle. The engine wound up in response and the small plane started vibrating and moving forward down the runway.

Dirk didn't know what to do. He had never had some maverick take off in an airplane on his watch. There was security at Van Nuys airport, but it consisted of a sixty-five-year old retired Air Force MP with a blue uniform and a walkie-talkie. So, Dirk just took it upon himself to try and stop a thief from stealing an airplane. He ran out of the control building and sprinted toward the runway screaming, "Stop! Stop right there! Stop! Abort!" He kept yelling at the airplane at the top of his voice as he ran toward the runway waving his arms and hands. But the Cessna Skyhawk swept past him ten yards away, roaring forward at increasing speed.

When it was too late, Dirk came to a stop and bent forward with his hands on his knees, desperately trying to catch his breath. He was shocked to have seen a mere boy at the controls, a slightly strange boy he would later report to authorities, after their eyes had connected for an instant. The adult he'd witnessed wandering around earlier was the passenger! Of course, some of the dots would be connected pretty quickly when the Van Nuys police found Fitzgerald Jack's black Jeep in the parking lot, but in so many ways it would also remain a mind-boggling puzzle. As events played out, most of the questions from that day would be answered and charges would not be lodged. But when that Cessna lifted into the wild blue yonder on that day in October of 2005, it certainly seemed as though an esteemed LAPD police detective had been party to stealing an airplane.

From his hands-on-knees perspective, and while he was still sucking air, Dirk Stevens turned his head and watched as the Cessna cruised smoothly away and lifted gently off the runway, rising into the cool autumn sky. It banked gently to the north and climbed. What was Dirk going to say to his boss?

CHAPTER 86

Cain stood stiffly near a cabin window, considering his options. His Desert Eagle hung to his side, a weight in his right hand. The three kneeling hostages were staring at him waiting on their next instructions. He walked slowly around to where he was behind Samantha Day-Steiner and with the same razor sharp knife he had used to slash the throat of the old woman standing at her doorway in Pasadena, Cain quickly cut the police handcuffs he had tightened around Sam's wrists. Then he rotated back to his station nearer the window.

"Dr. Day-Steiner?" said Martin Speck, as calmly as a man chairing a business meeting. "Please seek out some rope, cord, or wire from somewhere in the building. Three meters should be sufficient. If either of you gentlemen could give her some verbal guidance as to where she might find this, I would be grateful."

Both Preston and Samantha looked directly at Big Buster, who appeared to be reflecting on how such a request might be fulfilled. After a few seconds that dragged forward like pain filled minutes, he began to nod. Buster tried to recall as best he could where things were around the cabin. After all, he and Cloud Willow were not really there that often. It wasn't a weekend get-away to them, a vacation spot. The three hostages all imagined the rope or cord had something to do with them being tied-up, but they weren't the ones with the fifty caliber sidearm, and being tied-up was a preferable option to being plugged by one of those huge bullets. They all knew that either could occur.

"We have some rope in the kitchen," said Buster finally. Tall cupboard. Put some tools in it."

"Thank you," returned Martin Speck. "Dr." he said toward Samantha, "it would be good of you to go and find that rope. And when you rise from where you are, please put one hand behind you and then slowly pick up that shotgun with your free hand. Pick it up by its barrel and bring it over to me. Be careful to follow my instructions precisely."

Samantha looked at the Remington on the rug in front of Buster. She rose from where she had been crouched next to Preston and, as told, she put her left wrist at the small of her back and she picked up the shotgun from the floor with her right hand, gripping it in the middle. She carefully delivered the weapon to Cain, who took it from her with his left hand, as the Desert Eagle was in his right.

"Nicely done," he said. "Now locate that rope, please," he added.

Samantha Day-Steiner did as instructed and disappeared toward the kitchen or galley area of the cabin on other side of the broad stone fireplace. She wasn't really in a separate room, but she was out of sight.

Martin looked at the shotgun in his hand and he examined it. "This 12 gauge looks to be brand new to me," he said astonished, noticing its pristine condition, with nary a scratch or mark anywhere.

"What kind of ammunition do you have in it?" he inquired indifferently.

"Slugs," said Buster.

Cain nodded and he put his nostrils over the muzzle and sniffed. "Whoa! This shotgun has never been fired!" he said in amazement.

Martin Speck knew guns. Even though the Remington had been purchased as pre-owned, Speck knew it was fresh out of the box.

The Cessna Skyhawk was going to reach the San Gabriel Mountains pretty quickly after heading north from Van Nuys Airport, leaving behind a befuddled substitute air controller talking to himself. The small airplane buzzed along, less than two hundred feet above a sprawling flat valley made of tiled rooftops and swimming pools interrupted by ribbons of paved road that took the occupants of those houses to work and back. It was a flat-land of bedrooms and occasional strip mall. Below the Skyhawk normal lives were in the midst of normal activities as the airplane sped onward in a mission that was anything but normal. On the ground families like the Cooks' were going about family routines. They were happy. At least that was the fantasy that slipped so easily through Dalton's imagination when he glanced down and saw a man in a business suit getting out of a car and a pair of children running from a house to greet him. Dalton wanted that scene for himself; he wanted it back. In that moment, Dalton was painfully connected to his seemingly lost life through a millisecond of eye contact he made with one of those two surprised kids as Lucky 47 zoomed overhead almost close enough to touch.

Bringing Dalton back to reality his grown-up passenger, Detective Jack, was less philosophical as they raced toward the dry, October-gold San Gabriel mountain range directly ahead. At their modest altitude, to Fitzgerald a hundred knots felt like jet speed. Furthermore, the detective could not forget he was flying with a child at the controls. How in god's name did I get into this mess, he thought?

"Aren't we a little low?" Fitzy shouted, trying to be heard by Dalton over the wind noise and the pull of the airplane's engine.

Dalton pointed to a set of headphones with a mike attached to them, hanging from the control panel, identical to the pair of phones Dalton was wearing. Fitzgerald awkwardly pulled them across his head and he immediately found it made all the difference in the world. The ambient noise fell away and he clearly heard the very young pilot say, "What is it?"

"Well… aren't we flying kind of low?" Fitzy repeated.

"Yes," returned Dalton. "We are much harder to see down here. Dad taught me."

"It's illegal," said Fitzgerald.

"I know," said the boy pilot, "but not more illegal than stealing an airplane."

"Your dad wouldn't say we're stealing his airplane would he?" came back the detective becoming the student in the presence of his teacher.

"Relax" said Dalton. "You are too wound up."

Fitzgerald was sensing an uncomfortable trend and he asked, "Where are we headed right now? This is north and Big Bear is east."

"I want to get to the mountains as soon as I can, because it'll be harder for the cops to find us. When we cross the first mountains, we'll go east." Dalton did not even remember he was speaking to a cop.

Detective Jack asked, "Your dad taught you all of this hide-and-seek stuff?"

"I got some from the movies."

"How long will it take us?" asked Fitzgerald.

"Thirty minutes, if we don't crash."

"Let's leave the crashing part out."

"Mountain flying is hard," said Dalton and he didn't bat an eye. He was quite serious. "If we flew across the valley it would be faster and safer."

"Well, maybe we *should* fly the valley," came back the lieutenant.

"The police," said Dalton like he was a seasoned pilot, "we'd be made in two minutes."

"Made?" said Fitzgerald.

"Movies," said the boy.

The Los Angeles Police Detective could not have possibly conjured up the imaginary lives and movie scenarios that Dalton and his dad, the physicist and inventor of workable cold fusion, had played out for fun over the years, as they slipped in that Skyhawk low and unnoticed above the valleys and cities around LA County. They loved to throw in their favorite motion picture dialogue, too. It had all been entertainment for them and now it had become serious business.

And that was when the Skyhawk began to climb and strain up the side of the first mountain they reached on the north side of the San Fernando Valley, a steep climb that had the detective gripping his seat with white knuckles. Dalton pulled full throttle for fifteen seconds to make it happen, before they roared over the top of the first ridge and plunged down the farther side into a deserted wide gully, an arroyo, which they followed for half a mile before they would arrive at the next range of mountains. The wall-to-wall commuter housing of the San Fernando Valley had magically vanished below them leaving nothing but a desiccated earth with scrub and rocks flickering beneath the airplane's dark shadow. Detective Jack caught glimpse of a boney, skittish coyote interrupted while nosing around amongst sagebrush. Just like that, the second largest metropolitan area in the United States was beyond reach and they were surrounded by an arid mountain wilderness. It was one of the true marvels of living in Los Angeles. The desert was always nearby and waiting, biding its time to reclaim the land, as though humans were a temporary inconvenience to the natural order.

After twenty seconds of level flying, they began to climb again and Fitzgerald looked up to see the mountain ahead of them, which was significantly taller than the one they had just traversed.

"Oh, my god," Fitzy said quietly.

CHAPTER 87

Bobby Skylar knew the rules of engagement in a situation of this kind, just as did Cain. Don't hesitate. Strike as quickly as possible and disrupt your opponent's opportunity to regroup. He knew that bastard was inside the cabin getting ready. The son of a bitch would use any collateral at his disposal to gain an advantage and in that case the collateral might well be human lives. Clearly, Bobby Skylar and Martin Speck had been reading from the same manual.

But, of course, there was that other card Bobby was hoping to play in his game. While they were down the mountain an hour earlier trying to connect with their cellphones, he'd managed to deliver a fevered message directly to his boss, Digger Mac Brown in Washington, describing their life-and-death goings-on in California. After that call Bobby left his cell phone behind them in transmission mode like a tiny beacon. But how long would it take for reaction to his words to take place, if any would take place at all? Bobby's old and not-so-smart Motorola cell phone was pumping out its signal for as long as it could and as best it could where he left it resting against a tree. Perhaps it was silent already. In the worst way, Agent Skylar dreamed of a clarion call and a furious cavalry assault from the flank. It was his fantasy, anyway, and it was probably General Custer's fantasy, too. Whatever was going to happen that day had to happen soon or he was going to have to act on his own, with cavalry or with no cavalry. That was the reality. Do not delay. He knew the drill.

Bobby considered his pathetic options as he crouched against a tall, moldering redwood not far from the cars and motorcycle. Charge the door? Take pot shots and hope for a hit? Wait until dark? All choices seemed equally bleak. Burn them out? That was a favorite in some situations, but once a fire is started it's difficult to control. The cabin might go up like tinder. What if the three hostages are tied up and Cain leaves them inside as he fights his way out? What if the surrounding forest starts to burn? A fire could roar up and down those heavily wooded remote mountainsides in no time. So, burning the cabin to the ground in order to drive the creature out into the open did not seem like a good idea.

Agent Skylar took inventory on his ammunition. Two shots were fired back on the trail, and one had been used a few minutes ago. That meant four rounds remained in his Walther PPK and he always carried one spare clip in his pocket; so, he still had eleven chances to end the mysterious assassin's reign and Bobby well knew that with that particular adversary he had better make good use of each bullet and every opportunity. Strangely, he was quite electrified by his situation and his eyes were dilated. There weren't many circumstances that brought such a scintillating high to him anymore. It temporarily reminded Bobby of the old days, in his early years with the agency, when the world was full of excitement and the sky was the limit. Frankly, he didn't know until that moment that he still had a touch of it in him and he also realized he must be an adrenalin freak because at his age it no longer made sense.

Dr. Day-Steiner had uncovered a length of quarter-inch hemp rope in the kitchen, in the very cabinet that Buster had suggested. Speck cut the rope into a pair of meter length section and instructed Samantha to securely tie the hands of her husband and Big Buster

Bernard, behind their backs. She was unsure of herself while trying to tie-up the men, not having been a girl scout. Still, she did give the effort a good college try, inventing a set of very peculiar knots by the standards of a midshipman but they were sufficient for the assignment. With his Desert Eagle hanging in his right hand and the shotgun in the crook of his left arm, Martin Speck inspected the bindings when Samantha was done and he came away amused by them but satisfied they would hold.

When Cain had returned to his position like a sentry near the closed cabin front door, Samantha said meekly, standing behind the two men she had just tied up, "What now?"

That bullet crease near Cain's upper left shoulder was really getting sore, and it was not soothed by the weight of the Remington he cradled in that arm. It seemed the wheels had come fully off the cart on his mission. Carrying out an elongated cat and mouse game with a shooter outside had pretty much absorbed the last dram of his patience. A cowpoke gunfight in the backwoods of the American west was not what he signed up for, but it seemed more and more to be what he was facing.

The Cessna Skyhawk was flying above the tree line. Below her wings a dense pine forest passed by proudly holding its ground, its linage safe for the time being along the steep slopes and the difficult terrain in the more remote regions of the San Gabriel mountains. Civilization was still a rumor there even though the mountain resorts lay ahead like an invader's outpost. The airplane's occupants didn't experience so much diving and climbing by then, to Fitzgerald's gratitude, and at almost 7,000 feet they could glide gently above the crests of each ridge without having to plunge into the ravines separating them. Roads below the Cessna were rare and usually no more than winding rutted pathways between the ever-greens. Detective Jack did not spot a single car or truck after they left the San Fernando Valley. It was desolate but it was also beautiful as they drifted along under the cloudless October sky with the sun cutting dramatic angles across the shadowed forest floor. To the north there were emerald mountain slopes facing west, backed by mysterious dark and deep canyons hidden from light.

"Wow. This is beautiful," said Detective Jack absently to his young companion, while he leaned against the window and looked downward.

"It is very cool," said Dalton. He'd seen it many times, of course. "Day on one side of a hill and night on the other."

Fitzgerald had never flown in a private plane through the mountains before. He could see movement from the wind in the tall Sierra pines beneath him and he witnessed hundreds of birds in a single flock bank suddenly away, flashing from a sheet of gray to brilliant white in an instant. He didn't know sparrows from condors, but whatever they were they were magnificent.

Over the years when Fitzgerald had gazed dully out the window of a Southwest Airlines 727 at thirty thousand feet these same mountains were merely soft mounds of earth far below, a rumpled green blanket. They were not at all the dynamic and very alive wilderness that he witnessed on that day. His view from the Cessna was so different and so superior, like snorkeling among coral reefs rather than speeding in a motor boat above them.

But there was serious business ahead and the young pilot reeled Lieutenant Jack away from his daydreams by saying, "The approach to Big Bear is not something I have done before. It is over a lake and my dad says it is tricky."

"You haven't done this?" said Fitzy staggering back into reality.

"I have not done *any* of this before, Detective. I have only piloted Lucky 47 in a straight line across the San Fernando Valley with my dad."

Fitzgerald blanched. "What do you mean by 'tricky'?" he said carefully.

"There are winds and thermals and other things. There is the lake."

"What are the other things?"

"Big Bear air control does not know we are landing there. So that is an extra problem."

"Should we call ahead," said the detective, gesturing to the radio controls, which were right there in front of them. Once again he was showing how remarkably naive he could be when he was out of his element.

"I do not think so, Lieutenant. We do not want to be greeted by the Big Bear police, do we? My plan is we just land the plane and we make a run for it."

"*Run for it*?" queried the detective, taken-aback. His voice was actually faint. This was not what he expected. The whole idea was becoming more and more rickety as the conversation progressed.

"When we stop," said Dalton, "we need to contact my dad right away."

"How?" said the detective. "We don't know where he is, do we?"

"We'll triangulate."

Fitzgerald Jack knew what triangulation was but he didn't know how they were going to do it in this situation. "And how do we triangulate?" he asked.

"My dad fixed all our cell phones to do it. If we call a number from one place and then move to another place and call that number again, our phones will tell us where the other phone is and how far away it is, too."

"What?" said Lt. Jack. He'd never heard of such a thing. "You can't do that with a cell phone."

"My dad sometimes invents things that people say cannot be invented."

Fitzgerald Jack looked at the boy in the pilot's seat who was confident and relentlessly guiding the Cessna forward on its rescue mission. The detective knew this entire odyssey was the result of a creation that nobody thought was possible, cold fusion and unlimited energy for the entire world. Maybe the damn phones *could* triangulate.

Bobby Skylar made his way around to the rear of the cabin, where a back door led to a trash pit outside, a compost heap, and a wood shed at twenty paces. The ground was relatively level there, but the terrain took off like a rocket beyond the shed, following a mossy granite bluff toward the sky. Basically, the cabin had its backside against the base of a hundred foot cliff. There was no escape in that direction.

Inside the living room of Big Buster's and Cloud Willow's safe-haven, Martin Speck peeked through the window curtains adjacent to the front door. The curtains moved slightly in a chilly breeze because there was no glass in that part of the window after Cain's single shot earlier had sent jagged bits of glass flying. His three hostages were now sitting on the floor, two of them tied up. They all watched with wide eyes at every move their captor made. It was strangely quiet outside, not even birds could be heard as though they had headed for higher ground in anticipation of fireworks. The silence was getting under Cain's skin because he knew his opponents.

"Is there another entrance?" he said quickly to Buster, the proprietor of this mountain retreat.

"Yeah," said Buster, "in the galley area over there," and he nodded back to where Dr. Day-Steiner had retrieved the rope a few minutes earlier, "off the laundry room."

"Dr. Day-Steiner," Cain said. "Please, assure the rear entrance is bolted and please don't attempt any funny business back there that might prove to be fatal to people you care about."

Cain head-gestured for her to go about her assignment. She knew the man would put a bullet through Buster's head in a blink. Her husband was the valuable one, after all. At that point she understood they were all currencies of differing values and nothing more. Cain was not in an ambiguous frame of mind at that moment. Everything was concrete.

Samantha climbed to her feet and scurried like a trained dog toward the galley to find the one door leading outside toward the compost heap and wood shed which had been constructed away from the cabin, near the steep, rocky incline. She investigated the rear door and she found it had a pair of heavy deadbolts, both of which were open and both of which she secured quite audibly with quick twists of her wrist. *Click! Click!* Yet, as she was throwing the top bolt she happened to glance outside through the paned window in the back door and she made eye-contact with Bobby Skylar, who was crouched outside just to the left of the rear entrance! He was ragged and dirty, but he had a gun and she was taken breathless by the sight of him. Bobby thrust a finger to his lips to silence her on the spot. She knew right away what he was up to and it terrified her through-and-through to see him there. She was almost as quick as him, in shaking her head to say, No! Don't come this way! Sam understood Skylar wanted to get inside; but although she wasn't a federal agent or a police officer, she had already concluded it was not a good idea for Bobby to charge into that cabin and start shooting. There were other people inside and a scary guy with a very big gun of his own. She had spent time with the man and she believed Cain was not a character to be sneaked up on.

Of course, blindly charging into a gunfight would not have been Bobby's plan, but a conversation to disabuse Sam of her fears could not happen in that fleeting exchange because Samantha vanished from the back door window and left Bobby outside leaning against the cabin's rear wall, ruminating over developments. He didn't know what she thought and what she would do inside. He struggled in his mind to find a way to help them even at ultimate risk to himself. The risk part Samantha Day-Steiner grasped fully well as she walked back to the cabin's living room, yet it was primarily the fear of risk for herself, her husband and Buster that was pounding through her veins. When she returned to the living room she didn't know for sure what to do and she was rather pale in trying to maintain composure.

"It's locked," she said plainly to Martin Speak as she resumed sitting beside her husband, while her imagination swarmed with images of what might be coming.

"Are you alright, Dr. Day-Steiner?" said Cain, noticing her color and affect.

"You've got to be kidding," said Sam sarcastically.

Cain chuckled and he returned to his surveillance out the window.

Bobby Skylar rested his head against the outside wall of the cabin where he squatted out of sight. He understood the fear he saw in Dr. Day-Steiner's eyes. Very few men and women often find themselves in life-threatening situations, as did Agent Skylar and as did Cain. Such a world had its addictive moments and for a few minutes he had felt the adrenaline rush of his youth, but there, outside the cabin, he longed for home. The initial excitement had dissipated and reality had settled around him. He could smell the autumnal change in the woods. It didn't matter if he was in the forests of California or Virginia near where Bobby lived, the dense, moldy scent of decay and regrowth was unmistakable. He inhaled deeply and closed his eyes and he could see himself playing with his children in golden-leafed woods.

So, there Bobby Skylar was, momentarily side-tracked down fantasy lane and away from his professional objective, tired and leaning against a cabin wall with his enemy not fifty feet from him, inside. Climbing slowly back into reality, Bobby began to reassess how he was going to get into the cabin. There had to be a way. If Bobby were Cain, he would have blocked all outside entrances. Skylar understood Cain's behavior and Cain understood Skylar's. In many ways, they were quite alike in the arc of their careers. Undoubtedly the master gardener, Martin Speck, appreciated the cycle of life and these forest scents as much or more than did Bobby. Who would know, on that fateful day, they shared an appreciation for the fecund world around them? Martin Speck's obsession with gardening was certainly unknown to Bobby Skylar because not much at all was known about that infamous assassin. No commiseration around the woodsy fall aromas would take place between those two determined men before a lethal reckoning would come to pass.

Maybe a window was ajar somewhere around the cabin, thought Bobby, in spite of the crystal clear message from Dr. Day-Steiner through the back door that danger lay within. Evidently the assassin was prepared, not that Agent Skylar was surprised by the news. Cain was quite alive and he was functioning at full speed regardless of the bullet Bobby had sent his way not that many minutes earlier. If Cain had not made it a habit of being prepared during his career, he wouldn't have been there on that beautiful October afternoon in California. Cain's accomplishments and his unilateral preparation were what made him a legend in the world of secret service. *Of course* there was danger inside that cabin!

CHAPTER 88

When news reached Digger Mac Brown of the silent but relentlessly live connection to Bobby Skylar's cell phone somewhere in the San Gabriel mountains of southern California, he was instantly on high alert. It was old school resourcefulness. He recognized it in a nano-second. Special Group would never disconnect an open line to an agent in the field and Skylar knew that. Bobby needed back-up and he needed it right away. And god-damn it, back-up he was going to get it!

Telephone conversations were fast and furious in Washington. An hour after Agent Skylar's cell phone signals were traced, a helicopter loaded with Marines was on its way to Big Bear from the sprawling Marine Corps base at Twenty-Nine Palms in the desert north of the California mountain resorts, a military facility that had practically been emptied to fight the war in Iraq in those years. But a battalion of leathernecks remained to keep the lights on, and a Marine Corps UH-1E Huey, a fifteen seat rotary wing aircraft in service since the '60s, was dispatched and was pounding southward above the San Gabriel mountain ridges in response to Bobby's call for help.

The Huey was following the ever weakening signal from Skylar's abandon cell phone. The Corps was doing its best to trace the call with state-of-the-art equipment, but they were in a poor situation in the mountains and there was tremendous interference. Finding that bee-line on the origin of the transmission was intermittently successful.

Generally Marines weren't the optimum choice for an operation of that kind, but Digger's agency was small. He couldn't send back-up from Special Group. Plus the recalcitrant CIA and the fumbling FBI didn't really care about anyone outside their silos. Fantasies of unifying these entities into a workable seamless whole following their disconnected efforts on November 11, 2001 remained a dream in 2005 and would remain so for years to come. The local resort police were wholly unprepared for the kind of intervention that was needed with Cain in the picture, yet Digger Mac Brown understood that immediate response to Skylar's beacon was an imperative.

Digger was an ex-Marine himself and he knew the Corps was always ready for a challenge. It was their nature. So to help Special Group, he contacted a Colonel he'd known since Vietnam who was stationed at Twenty-Nine Palms and just like that he got whatever clearances were needed.

Whether the squad of Marines knew exactly what they were supposed to do as they began to power over the mountains toward Big Bear in their UH-1E Huey would never be clear. What was known about Marines then and now is that all of them would give one hundred percent to whatever mission lay ahead. There was no doubt.

Lieutenant Alfonse Sweeny led the helicopter command. He spent the early part of the flight with an earbud jammed into his left ear canal while a summary of their situation and their objectives was downloaded verbally into his brain to share with his men as soon as possible: A federal agent was missing in the mountains. Find him. There may be hostages and important equipment to be located and protected. Something was said about the equipment having to do with nuclear energy. And it was also said that foreign operatives hostile to U.S. interests would be present. That's what Lt. Sweeny remembered from the radio message. He heard no mention about the size or the shape of the apparatus they would be seeking. Then the entire message was repeated twice, per protocol.

The Lieutenant was six months out of Officer Candidate School at Quantico and fairly fresh to leadership. He was also a man with a lisp, a characteristic that was off-putting to many of the instructors at OCS. Yet in spite of those prejudices, he did become a commissioned officer in the U.S Marine Corps in April of 2005. But the bigotry haunted Sweeny. His commanders at Twenty-Nine Palms were no more open-minded about fair-play than the OCS crew at Quantico and that included Digger's Colonel-buddy who orchestrated the helicopter engagement. Lt. Sweeny would have been the Colonel's very last choice out of the battalion for the mission on that day. On any other afternoon Sweeny would have been relegated to shooting pool in the dayroom while the mission was being carried out by someone else. But on that unanticipated October afternoon adventure, Lt. Sweeny was tapped to lead the squad by default because the other Officer of the Day at the heavily depleted Marine base had come down with the flu.

Fifteen young men in desert warfare camouflage, helmets, Kevlar vests, and assault rifles between their knees, sat grimly in two rows facing one another as the helicopter carried them over the southern mountains in pursuit of Skylar's beckoning. Some of the young men had been to Iraq or Afghanistan and some had not; but that was typical for men and women in uniform in those years.

Sweeny was busy second-guessing himself while trying to appear in control sitting next to his men as he twice reviewed the mission message that was being run through his ear. What was green Marine Lieutenant Alfonse Sweeny to tell his squad, he was thinking, on this his first foray into what was potentially harm's way? They would be sliding down ropes into a mountain forest in only a few minutes. International agents may be in the picture. A nuclear reactor? Their mission was not some silly exercise dealing with a drunken surviv-alist gone nutty. That would have been for the local cops. Instead, Marines could actually get killed on that day because there was a real and lethal enemy at hand. What was Sweeny to say?

"Listen up," he began, standing as best he could, crouching and shouting at the top of his lungs to be heard above the roar of the engine and props. His men instantly gave him the attention his rank deserved, meaning they listened as best they could with the blades of the Huey hammering away at the thin mountain air outside and the turbines fiercely whining.

"We are currently following a cell phone signal from a point in these mountains and it looks like we'll soon be dropping down in wooded, steep terrain near that cell phone. Do not get tangled up in the trees, gentlemen, because we'll have to cut you loose from up top. We can't be havin' this bird tethered to a limb down there, *entienda*?' Sweeny saw his half-Hispanic California based squad nodding that they understood, and he went on. "So, keep that in mind. When your boots hit the ground, squat and wait. We'll check off after our bus leaves and then we will locate the transmission device. We'll proceed from there. Understood?"

The Marines nodded. "Yes, sir!" they all shouted.

"Another thing," went on the Lieutenant, "we're looking for some scientific equipment. There are foreign agents here after the same equipment. Insurgent activity. There may be a firefight. We don't know."

The men looked at each other. It was an odd and unex-pected development.

"What kind'a equipment, Lieutenant?" said the Lance Corporal nearest to where Alfonse stood swaying in front of his men, with one hand twisted into a loop above him.

"Has to do with atomic energy. All I can say," said Sweeny. "We've got to secure it first. Copy that?"

The men looked at one another again, eyes big as old fashioned silver dollars. Is it an atomic bomb, they were thinking?

"Do you *copy*?" demanded Lt. Sweeny.

"Yes, sir!" said the men together, a little more emphatically after an actual and lethal enemy had come onstage and the words "atomic energy" had been dropped into the equation. It had suddenly become a real mission to them.

"Okay, then," said Alfonse Sweeny to his squad. "Buckle up, Marines! We'll be hitting ground zero in fifteen minutes. Lock and load!"

And with those words fifteen live magazines were slammed into fifteen M-16s and the men tightened what had to be tightened to get ready for their descent on ropes. They were alert to the potential for hostile targets even if they didn't have a clear picture of what they were charging into. After all, they were Marines.

Unfortunately for those men the operation was not going to play out as imagined. The Corps had one frame of mind about insurgency and Martin Speck, alias Cain, had another entirely different frame of mind, which was well outside the box of conventional thinking.

CHAPTER 89

The Cessna banked sharply around the eastern end of Big Bear Lake, the left wing dipping steeply toward the ground, exposing an ever-expanding mountain community that swept directly below with A-frames, chalets, and log cabins separated by thin rows of pines and winding lanes. Detective Jack looked down at a long stretch of vacation homes carved along the side of the mountain near the lake. In spite of the evergreens left standing to add mountain character, overall he could see that Big Bear was not really a mountain resort anymore. It was a small city with a lingering rustic attitude and a thriving year-round population. Big Bear was to mountain life what a cruise ship was to sailing.

Suddenly, the plane leveled and the detective saw the lake stretching out in front of them, flat and dark, and they were descending so quickly he got shivers up his back because it looked like they were going to land in the water! But in that same moment, beyond the lake, he saw the airport's asphalt runway and he heard the radio crackling with Big Bear air control's sharp alarm, "Cessna, are you in distress?" Then after a beat, the request came again, "Cessna, are you in distress?" And upon receiving no reply from the incoming aircraft, control transmitted, "Abort your approach, Cessna! Abort your approach! Do you read? You are not cleared!"

Yet the little plane sped forward without hesitation. The youngster at the throttle was undeterred.

"What now?" said Fitzgerald as the runway relentlessly grew to greet them just beyond the farther shore. They were only twenty feet above the water and still descending over the cobalt lake where two fishermen in an aluminum outboard looked up shocked to see the approaching low flying Cessna and they crumpled instantly to the bottom of their small boat just as the plane zipped a few feet over their heads! The fishermen sat up goggle-eyed after the Skyhawk had passed.

"I am going to try and skid to a stop as quickly as possible," said the boy and he was confident. "So get ready. Then we will run for those trees off to the right."

Fitzgerald saw there were several buildings midway down the runway on each side, hangers to the north and the modest terminal and parking lot to the south. He also saw thick forest on the right hand side that ran parallel to the runway, continuing behind the hangers farther away. There looked to be fifty yards or more of rough flat ground to the right of the tarmac, tufts of weeds and grasses that spread out to where the trees created a perimeter for the airfield. And in that five second reconnaissance, Fitzgerald also noted the trees blended directly into rugged thick forest that scaled the mountainside just beyond to the north, but there wasn't time to study it all, because they were moving so quickly.

On the radio, the man in the squat Big Bear air control building continued to vehemently waive them off with more and more urgency. Fitzgerald could picture spittle flying from the lips of an invisible incredulous controller as he screamed into his microphone while Dalton deftly lifted the nose of the airplane and dropped her tail for touchdown.

"Here we go!" thought Detective Jack. It was pretty much how they left Van Nuys Airport with air control yelling at them. There they were, landing at Big Bear in the same unceremonious fashion.

In fact, right before they touched the tarmac, Fitzy could see a pair of security guards already running out to intercept them from the distant control building, maybe three hundred yards away. It was all too familiar.

Fitzgerald Jack nodded to himself at their predicament. What else could he do? Was he to start making suggestions while the Cessna's tires chirped sharply across the blacktop? They had barely settled all three landing gear when the boy aviator jammed the plane into full flaps on the starboard wing, causing the Cessna to swerve off the runway at such a severe angle to the right that it nearly careened out of control and flipped!

"Whoa!" shouted Detective Jack when the left landing gear lifted off the ground and the right wing tip sparked across the tarmac. Then he yelled, "Christ!" as the plane thudded back onto all three wheels and stabilized as it jostled rapidly across the stretch of grassy terrain directly toward the trees. Fitzgerald sat there clutching his seat cushion. The evergreens and forest underbrush rushed toward them at an alarming speed. All they could do was hang on! Fitzgerald thought they would both be killed for sure. But an instant before the Cessna's single prop chewed into the rough bark of a California pine directly in front of them, the aircraft jolted to a halt in the soft soil. Remarkably, after such a landing, the plane seemed to have remained entirely in one piece.

"Isn't she great?" said Dalton shutting down the Cessna's engine and he immediately yelled, "Let's go!" as he leapt out of his door. Fitzgerald regained himself as quickly as possible and he followed suit.

In the distance they could hear the men from the control building sprinting toward them and hollering, "Stop! Stop right there!"

What an odd place for an accomplished police officer to be, Detective Jack thought, as they dodged into the tree line and scampered around and through bushes, not looking back. Fitzgerald had become a bona fide *desperado* by then. It was dreamlike. He was running from the law and following a twelve year-old, Down syndrome youngster trying to save his father from an assassin.

On the back wall of Big Buster's cabin, Bobby Skylar noticed that one of the counter-balanced windows was open about a quarter of an inch at the sill. In fact it hadn't been closed completely since the last time Big Buster and Cloud Willow were up there. In July, Buster had been doing some work on a stubborn closet door in that very sleeping bay, one of two in the cabin, and he'd forgotten to fully secure the window as he finished up, when Cloud hurried him so they could get back down the mountain to Pasadena before nightfall. But on that cool October afternoon, one simple oversight dating back to the summer had become an opportunity for Agent Skylar.

Bobby examined the opening closely. It wasn't much. He couldn't get his fingers inserted sufficiently to lift the window and it was made more difficult by the awkward angle. From where Bobby's feet were planted in weeds along the cabin's backside and without something to stand on, the window sill was just too high.

The federal agent looked around for a lever of some kind to help jimmy the window open but there was nothing he could see at first. He was thinking he could find a stout stick but then he spotted a rusted axe head which had broken off its handle, laying some fifteen paces away near a stump were Buster had evidently been chopping wood when his axe handle snapped at the neck. It's not an uncommon occurrence cutting fire wood and there was substantial evidence of Buster's back-work with wood chips scattered liberally all around the stump curled and pale like hundreds of fingernail clippings in the weeds and grass. Given the big guy's goal for his house and his world vision, Bobby could see how building a substantial stockpile of fire wood for the future economic horrors, would be a priority for Buster Bernard and Cloud Willow. The nearby shed was filled with the results of Buster's labor.

Bobby rightly guessed there was no electricity in the cabin. Buster and his wife had decided to rely mostly on what nature provided. That's the way survivalists would plan, of course. They would anticipate the absence of creature comforts when the modern world caves in under its own weight, and they knew they needed fire wood. For a moment Bobby imagined the bomb shelters people from the fifties and sixties built. That was his parents' generation. And the survivalists of 2005 were very much like them. On some dystopian level, they all secretly hoped for the cataclysm to come, because without it, their carefully and fretfully constructed safe-havens were all for naught.

Agent Skylar retrieved the axe head from where it rested in the grass near the stump and he scampered back to the window with it. He immediately squatted next to the window and he listened patiently for any sounds or activity within the cabin that suggested his movements outside had drawn attention, but there was nothing.

So, he waited a minute until his breathing settled again, and then he turned to his task and quickly found he could wedge the cutting edge under the window frame sufficiently that with some wiggling up and down, the window began to lift. "Hot damn!" he thought. "Sometimes it takes serendipity, but I'm inside!"

Bobby knew that if he climbed through this window he was going to have to make each bullet in his Walther PPK count. In fact, he was thinking rather grimly, from a perspective honed by several decades of experience in tight situations and tempered by an appreciation for this particular adversary's near-mythical reputation, he had better make his *first* bullet count because he may not be firing any bullets after that one. That very serious turn of mind led him to recall again his children and his home back in Foggy Bottom. But Skylar shook his head quickly to dismiss those images, rid them from this mind, not wanting to be distracted by sentiment at this critical juncture. And with that, he began using the axe head to inch up the window as silently as he was able, pausing each time the window frame would issue a squeak and each time it would chill him to the bone.

It took Bobby fifteen long minutes of inching the window open, at first with the axe head, and then with his hands, to get it opened enough that he could pull himself up and look into the cabin. He peered inside only to find a dark sparse room with a pair of bunk beds and two simple dressers. The quarters looked more army than vacation; but then again the cabin had always been envisioned as a last stand, not a picturesque retreat.

And with that, Agent Skylar began to shimmy his way up and into the sleeping bay. He was not a large man, less than six feet tall, but very athletic for his years. He only halted once before ducking through the opening, when he thought he heard something. It wasn't inside the cabin actually; it was outside. He thought he picked up the sound of a helicopter pounding air low to the ground some distance off and Bobby had a lifetime of experience with helicopters, so he hesitated and listened carefully. But with the fickle wind redirecting sounds as it can, he didn't hear anything more, and so he pressed onward, climbing and slithering forward into the cabin and whatever future it held for him.

In the cabin's main living room while Cain contemplated next steps near the front door, he paused suddenly and froze on high alert! That momentary distant sound Bobby Skylar had heard, that distant atmospheric thumping, was a helicopter for sure. Cain recognized it in a heartbeat and he also guessed it had something to do with the shooter outside. Martin Speck began to prepare for increased resistance in his get-away and how that might look given whatever was happening beyond the cabin walls.

During those same moments, fifteen battle-ready US Marines were sliding down ropes near Bobby's pooped-out cell phone a quarter of a mile away from the cabin. The chopper's turbines screamed above the Marines who had been carried to that site. Until all boots were on the ground, the downdraft from the Huey raised a storm of dried leaves and dust along the rutted mountain path where lay the small telephone Agent Skylar had left behind in his call for reinforcements.

CHAPTER 90

Martin Speck was not a defensive player. That had never been his style and his style had made him a legend in the special services world, so he was not about to change his strategy. He knew things were happening out there, beyond the walls of the cabin and they were not good things for his operation and his objectives. He didn't know who fired that shot that grazed his left arm, but he knew it wasn't the first shot delivered by whomever it was. His instincts were clear on that count. It meant back-up had to be in the picture, as well. Sitting there in the cabin could not be his plan but he had too many hostages for travel, so he had a serious logistical problem. Both of the men and the one woman under his control were valuable commodities for negotiation should it come to that and he was loath to waste any of them. He knew he was in a pickle, as the Americans liked to say.

Outside the window he could see a blossom that was unusual to Southern California. It had captured his attention from the moment he assumed guard position by the doorway and for a few moments the flower lifted him away. The tall Sierra Blue Ceanothus was leaning gently against a tree some thirty feet from the cabin. Brilliant in color, the lilac was wild and rare for these parts, delivered to that spot by a migrating bird, perhaps. He suspected it was probably nothing much more than a large weed to his captives. They had no idea. But seeing the blossoms gave Martin Specks' heart a little rise and it projected him back into his own garden at home. He fantasized taking the plant with him, but he knew it was impossible. Such fantasies were not unusual in his travels where he found the beauty of the natural world would go largely unappreciated. He had observed it was a short-sightedness shared by all cultures.

Cain shook his head to rid himself of those thoughts. The Ceanothus was not part of his dilemma. The real problem for him was how he would get this cold fusion business back to his sponsor, or eliminate it altogether. Those were his options, his directives and his choices. He was to steal the device if possible, but if not possible, he was to eradicate both the device and its architect. It was neither a clear-cut nor an easy job he had taken. Martin's employer was wagering that because the scientist who gave birth to the strange new tool had not gone public with his discovery, then very few men or women understood how it worked. Killing the idea completely was quite possible, Cain's employer figured, and unfortunately his employer's calculations were catastrophically accurate.

Due to Preston's dogged long term insistence on privacy and his ongoing resistance to any premature discussions about the work, nobody at CTU or anywhere else really knew how cold fusion had been accomplished. After Maxwell Umberto died, none among Preston's colleagues knew for certain that cold fusion had really happened. Nothing had been published or publically discussed, all for the most egalitarian reasons and much to Samantha's dismay. Preston wanted to share the final success of his work unilaterally with the entire world! And the genius behind the device was sitting right there at gunpoint in front of Martin Speck.

The lab and materials related to the invention had all been destroyed, all the way back to the womanizing partner's residence and the quaint little home-made laboratory in Pasadena. All were ashes. So, the only plans for the device that existed anywhere in the world were inside the head of the brilliant but very stubborn cuckold right there in the cabin. Martin Speck wondered momentarily if the scientist even suspected his whore wife had been the lover of his friend Maxwell. But that was a sidebar in the drama. On center stage was cold fusion itself and how it had come to be.

"Dr. Cook," began Martin Speck as the pale and nervous Dr. Day-Steiner took her seat on the Apache rug next to her bound-up husband, "as I was saying when we were so rudely interrupted... where exactly *is* the prototype portable nuclear reactor that everyone is making such a fuss about? I noticed it was gone from your boutique laboratory in Pasadena."

Preston didn't want to respond. His eyes were wide and he tried to think of some ruse that would protect the device, but his mind was a wall. Deception was not his natural strength, but he was learning about it quickly as the unreal situation pressed onward.

"Perhaps I'm not making myself clear," said Cain, drawing back the hammer of the huge Desert Eagle, with a click. "Do you want one of these two individuals to suffer because of your bravura?"

"No," said Preston Cook quietly. "I'm not being brave."

"Then tell me, please, where is the reactor?" said Martin Speck.

"Well... it is right here," said Preston.

"Here?" said Cain. He had no idea what the contraption looked like.

"Yes," said Preston. "It's in that carry-on over there by the chair," he said tilting his head in the direction of the small aluminum suitcase against the wall behind him and adjacent to the wingchair. "It's wrapped in towels inside," he added reassuringly.

"*That*?" said Cain incredulously.

"Yes," returned Preston.

The assassin was clearly in disbelief. It was indeed small. Cain had been told it was portable, but he pictured something like a steamer trunk at the very least, probably larger, more like an armoire.

"My god, Dr. Cook," Cain said, genuinely taken aback. He was an educated man and he looked at the modest luggage and he was dumbfounded. "You have truly done something unbelievable."

"Thank you," said Preston softly. Comity was natural for him.

"So unbelievable. I think I should have to take a look," added Cain. "Kindly show me, sir." He could not help himself. He truly wanted to see this remarkable mechanism, a device that could change the world forever and fit within such a small container.

"I can't," said Preston Cook.

"Of course," came back Martin Speck, recalling that Dr. Cook's wrists were bound. "Dr. Day-Steiner would you please bring the case over here between us and open it?" he asked.

"That won't help," said Preston suddenly and on a whim, learning subterfuge on the fly.

"And why not?" said Cain, not one to readily embrace the unexplained.

"The case has a combination lock and I have only half the combination," said Preston, which was an absolute fabrication. Was there a combination on the case? Yes. Did he possess only half the combination? No.

"Who has the other half?" asked Cain.

"My son," returned Preston.

"Your son?" said Cain, surprised. This really went to a different place in their conversation than he expected.

"Yes. We sort of built this together," said Preston, which was oddly enough not entirely a lie and sufficiently off kilter to win credibility.

"Isn't your son a Down syndrome child?" inquired Cain, evidencing the homework that characterized his meticulous work ethic.

"He's a very intelligent boy," said Preston firmly and truthfully.

"Yes, he is," chimed in Samantha Day-Steiner, clutching her husband's bound arm.

"Okay, then" said Cain, raising his fifty caliber Desert Eagle for display, "I think we can solve the problem of a suitcase lock."

"There is fissionable material inside," said Preston Cook quickly. "I wouldn't fire a bullet anywhere near it," he offered soberly. "It is portable. That's true. But it remains rather sensitive, if you catch my drift. We could all be vaporized in a flash sufficiently intense to deforest the entire southern slope of this mountain." Again he was fabricating a danger that didn't exist, but he was getting the hang of this deceit business and it seemed to be working. In truth, the relatively inert quality of the fissionable material he used in his cold fusion reactor was one of the device's most compelling selling points. It was the "cold" in cold fusion. The instrument was not the least bit dangerous as an explosive. Unlike a big reactor and its potential for melt-down, the cold fusion device was not unstable in any way. It couldn't be converted into a bomb even by knowledgeable techni-cians. Cain's .50 caliber slug would just ricochet around wildly before crashing through the heavy floorboards of the cabin. There would be no mushroom cloud.

But Martin Speck didn't know what was true in this situation, and the possibility of an unplanned nuclear reaction struck a chord with the assassin, the way it had with many other smart but igno-rant men and women who heard about portable nuclear reactors and immediately thought of them as portable atomic bombs.

"Alright," Cain said after a beat of contemplation and coming to resignation. "I wouldn't know what I was looking at anyway. In any case, we are going to be abandoning this lovely sanctuary. I have no appetite for hostile company on such a lovely autumn afternoon. And I'd wager hostile company is well on its way." He touched his wounded left shoulder, which throbbed mercilessly and he surveyed his captives' faces.

Cain was pleased to see they all just stared back at him awaiting further orders and that was precisely the subservient response he was looking for. "But I thank you for your hospitality, Mr. Bernard," he said toward the big man. "You have constructed an impressive retreat... you and your partner," he added recalling the rather remarkable woman he'd met in Pasadena with her lovely dress flowing about her as she exited the Cook house.

Martin Speck then glanced back outside at the Sierra Blue Ceanothus snuggled up to a scrawny tree not far away and he wished again that he could rescue it from this American wilderness.

By then, the squad of Marines was fully deployed on the ground along the rutted narrow path leading to Big Buster's and Cloud's cabin. They were all silent and crouched as though they expected an ambush. Their M-16s were at the ready and their eyes and ears were on alert. Lt. Alfonse Sweeny raised one arm to orient his men as the helicopter, like a mother ship, pulled away into the October sky, hauling up the ropes the men had just used to slide down onto moist earth beneath the forest canopy. No one had become tangled in tree limbs, as was feared. They were all ready for action. Their squad leader, Lt. Sweeny, swirled one finger in the air, which meant his men should spread out and find the cell phone that was sending these signals. They all knew it was nearby and it only took a couple of minutes with their honing devices to zero in on the poor little Motorola whimpering away on its last breath. The phone lay, propped against a tree where Bobby Skylar had rested it, doing its damnedest to keep the signal going. It almost seemed disrespectful when Lt. Sweeny picked up the Motorola that had been leaning there in the forest, on the job, and he put the little phone to his ear to see if there was someone on the other end. "Hello?" he said. And hearing no response he abruptly snapped it shut, cutting the signal.

Sweeny looked around at the surrounding autumn forest and the gouged automobile tracks under his feet. The tire marks in the dirt were not that old. Then a private 1st class came up to him with a pair of 9 mm casings he'd found near a rotting log not far up the road. He had also found one .50 caliber casing there. Alfonse sniffed the cartridges and he realized they were all fresh. Clearly, there had been some gunplay at that spot and it was recent.

Instinctively, Lt. Alfonse Sweeny gestured uphill along the narrow trail in the direction of where the shell casings had been found, in the direction of the cabin, although he had no idea that a cabin existed. Nor did he know how far it would be before his Marines would encounter what they came all that way to encounter. Nonetheless, the Lieutenant signaled for his squad to fan out and move up the mountain. He knew something lay ahead. From that point onward, they were on silent tactical orders and no one spoke a word.

In the cabin, Bobby Skylar had slowly made his way to the short hallway between one of the cabin's sleeping bays and the main living room. It was only moments after he had jimmied open a window to snake his way inside. Now he was standing upright with his back to a hallway wall right next to a bullet hole that had been made by Cain's Dessert Eagle during his blitzkrieg assault on the cabin. Bobby was desperately trying to control his breathing and he could feel the sweat building up across his forehead as he listened to Cain's instructions just around an archway that was by then only a foot from Agent Skylar's shoulder. The cabin was not large. Bobby had moved a mere ten steps from the window through which he had crawled.

Even as he listened to Cain he could not help but notice the cabin smelled of lumber and varnish. Although basic, Skylar could see it had not been thrown together. There was nothing prefabricated about that cabin. Every window and doorway was finished carpentry and constructed with a craftsman's skill. There Bobby was, admiring the woodwork in that sturdy survivalist's refuge, with his Walther PPK at the ready while the scourge of the world's secret services was only a few feet away. If only he knew where everyone was positioned. Unfortunately, the federal agent did not know where his target and the hostages were on the other side of that archway. He didn't know if they were standing or sitting. It was a serious problem in that kind of situation. Bobby knew he would have to reconnoiter in the blink of an eye as he plunged into the room to get off his rounds. He understood clearly that the merest sliver of a single second consumed by aiming and firing would determine the outcome of the upcoming encounter. It was the kind of moment that defines the career of a man in Skylar's line of work and it was unlike any career moment known to most men or women. Life or death right now. At best, two shots were all that Bobby would have time to get off and he had to make them count.

All hell was about to break loose.

CHAPTER 91

In the cabin living room, Martin Speck had moved away from his station by the door, which was cracked an inch so he could watch for movement outside and he had eased from the window, too, abandoning his precious Sierra Blue Ceanothus, which had been courting him from its moist soil. Instead, Speck made his way around behind Preston and Buster who were still sitting up on the Apache rug. From there Cain faced the cabin's large central fireplace. The archway to the sleeping bays was in front of him and on his left. Standing behind his hostages, Cain instructed Samantha Day-Steiner to untie both of the men.

"We've had a change in our itinerary. We're going to have to move fast when I say it's time," said Martin. He didn't know at that point if he was going to have to put a bullet in two of his hostages or not. Eliminating a pair of them would entirely depend on whether one of the cars could be coaxed into taking them down the mountain. Both the Taurus and the BMW were in pretty bad shape and each had lost a lot of oil after pounding across rocks the size of basketballs and crashing into ruts as deep as a plumber's ditch during their determined struggles up to the cabin. If the motorcycle outside was the only other option for Cain, two of his hostages had to go. It wasn't his preference, to throw away collateral, nor was needless killing appealing to him, but he figured four adult humans cannot ride on one motorcycle unless they're circus clowns. He had noticed

Buster's black motorcycle helmet resting on a chest in a corner, and Cloud's white daisy covered helmet was there, as well.

Cain hated using human-shields in any way for his escapes. It was a compromise of his self-esteem, as he viewed it. It had only happened to him once before in Uganda when he had been hired by the Israelis to eliminate a child-prostitution trafficker cum arms dealer who linked Ida Amin to the PLO by selling hundreds of Soviet made shoulder launched ground-to-air rockets to the Palestinians. In that situation Cain was forced to rely on bribing an associate of President Amin's and many elements in Cain's plan went to pieces pretty quickly after that. Cain had managed to escape Uganda after offing his target, but only by holding a favored nephew of Amin's tight to his side for eighteen hours with his preferred weapon of that time, a Smith &Wesson .357, shoved into the boy's ribs. It was not a pleasant experience but Cain was younger in those years and he had gone out of his way afterward to avoid using hostages again. Yet, there he was in 2005.

Because Martin Speck had vowed to himself that hostage taking was no longer part of his strategic vocabulary, serious anger toward his newest employer was growing exponentially. In his later years, Cain was not accustomed to being in an uncontrolled situation. The cold fusion venture had been clumsy from the beginning. He was stuck in a mountain cabin with *three* hostages! In retrospect he realized he had not been provided sufficient intelligence about what he was confronting on this mission and his ego had him feeling that he looked like a rank amateur. That creeping sensation may have been the most galling aspect of the entire unhappy experience for him. His professional pride was injured. Beneath his relatively calm exterior, Cain was becoming one furious professional gunman who swore to himself that somebody was going to have to pay for all of his embarrassment. It certainly wasn't a good situation for bystanders.

And that was precisely the moment Bobby Skylar chose to make his move! He rolled around the archway and dove into the living room, pivoting to his right where he had calculated his target would be. Bobby's eyes were fully dilated and his heart was pounding like a drum. The agent's Walther PPK was raised as he rapidly sized up the small space. He instantly recognized and recorded the faces that stared at him in shock, as Bobby seemingly drifted laterally in slow motion through the air to his left, just as he had been trained so many years ago.

Through Bobby's eyes the action before him also transpired in stretched time, an amazing amount of detail was being processed at the speed of light through his adrenalin infused cortex. Samantha was just getting up from having untied Big Buster Bernard, but nearby, her husband's hands were still bound at his back. Both of the men were sitting on the floor and behind them stood that undefined, evil bastard Cain, with a shotgun in his left hand and his Desert Eagle in his right. Bleached blond hair? Agent Skylar questioned what he saw in a nanosecond of bizarre reflection as he continued to fall to his left toward the floor and as he leveled his Walther with both out-stretched hands and sighted down the barrel toward the assassin.

In those same elongated shards of time that Bobby was taking aim, Cain was hoisting the Remington with his unsteady wounded left arm and he quickly got off one round from the shotgun, blasting a chunk out of the arched doorway and throwing splinters of wood through the air while filling the room with the thick stench of gun-smoke. Bobby fired twice, in that same nearly frozen moment. Unfortunately, untied Big Buster was foolishly trying to stand up while bullets were flying. Cain instinctively shoved his prize hostage, Preston Cook, to the floor with a solid kick in the back to protect him from stray rounds. In that simultaneous exchange of shots, rather than taking out the assassin, one of Skylar's 9 mm slugs struck Buster in his thigh as he was climbing to his feet, and it was Big Buster who crumpled to floor crying out in pain and not Martin Speck! The second shot buzzed harmlessly past Cain, hitting the wall behind him.

Bobby Skylar made a jarring left-shoulder crash onto the hardwood just as he got off a third round from his Walther PPK, but the impact with the floor sent his bullet wildly off target and high. His effort to attempt a fourth shot from where he lay was interrupted by the sledge hammer-like thud of the fifty caliber Desert Eagle projectile that struck him directly in the chest, sliding him fully backward four feet across the hardwood floor into the base of the fireplace behind him. Skylar's gun was knocked from his grip by the blow from the large bullet that had just passed through his lung. When he came to rest against the heavy gray stones that comprised the foundation of the fireplace his Walther lay near to him with another precious cartridge waiting in the chamber and ready to go. He could hardly breathe, but he remained conscious and committed to his objective. He had to get off that fourth round!

Bobby Skylar lay crooked on the floor against the base of the central fireplace and he looked down at his chest where a profusion of blood matted his shirt breast. His clothes had become soaked so very quickly. Although Bobby didn't know it, there was also a wound the size of an orange in his back just below his right scapula, but his heart had been missed. Due to shock, Skylar wasn't really in severe pain, but he knew it wasn't good. With his Desert Eagle hanging by his right hip and that Remington by his left leg, Cain walked slowly over to Skylar and stood six feet away looking down at his adversary. Bobby's blood-covered hand crawled on the hardwood floor a couple of inches toward the Walther PPK that lay where it had fallen, with another bullet beckoning him from its chamber, wanting to be spent. Cain simply shook his head at Bobby as if to say, "Don't do it." And with that, agent Skylar stopped. He knew it was over. He knew he had been given a moment to collect his memories and make peace. He'd come to the end. Cain kicked the Walther across the floor and away from Skylar.

Bobby chose to picture his beautiful wife when they met in Georgetown, back in the days when he had been carousing with Maxwell Umberto. Upon meeting that woman his life had been turned around completely. As he lay bleeding in that cabin, he could smell her hair. She was so beautiful. She remained so beautiful all those years later. He pictured his children, too. And there was little Aubrey at her fifth year birthday party looking up at her father with unabashed joy and her small rosebud lips saying, "I love you, daddy." Bobby could actually hear his daughter's voice while he lay there dying. He *heard* her say those words like she was in the room! And on that recollection he drifted off to a sleep with no dreams.

Behind Cain, who was standing over Bobby Skylar watching him die, Preston Cook looked into his wife's eyes and he whispered, "Run! Run *now*!" He knew they were in a gift moment that could not be wasted.

She was hesitant but the opportunity was brief and she knew it, too. She saw the front door was open an inch and Cain's back was turned. It only took a couple of strides for Samantha to dash past Martin Speck as he stood over his fallen foe. Hearing something, Cain spun around on a foot to see what was happening behind him but he only caught a glimpse of Samantha as she dashed through the front door outside into the October late afternoon. Cain leaped after her, glancing quickly at the two men in the living room, the big guy wounded and writhing on the floor and the scientist still bound and now prostrate on his chest, wild-eyed and praying his wife was going to make it to safety.

Martin Speck took only two or three steps in pursuit off the front stoop onto the carpet of wet forest leaves, looking to his left and his right when he stopped among the towering evergreens surrounding the property. Dr. Samantha Day-Steiner was nowhere to be seen. She'd dodged around the side of the cabin, figuring Cain would not chase her very far leaving Buster and Preston alone inside. And as it turned out, she was absolutely correct. Once Cain saw that the woman was out of sight around the edge of the cabin, he slowly backed up the front stoop, backed away from the bright Sierra Blue Ceanothus nearby, into the living room and he quickly issued his freshly detailed orders for their get-away. He was far less disturbed by Samantha's escape than Preston had expected. Cain was not flustered nor, to any observation, concerned at all about this turn of events. It looked like he was relieved by Sam's disappearance, an outcome that was all very strange to Preston Cook.

Bobby Skylar had not killed Cain that day as he wanted to do, but he *had* managed to change the assassin's plans. He managed to disrupt Cain and, most importantly, in doing so he probably saved lives, given the bloody eliminations that Cain had contemplated moments before Bobby dove into the living room with his Walther PPK blazing. It was all so ironic and all so lethal. By his heroic actions the federal agent laid Martin Speck's choices into a framework that made them much easier to navigate. At that point, there was no need to kill off two of his captives, which had been a very real and present likelihood. The sullen, unfaithful wife had vanished into the mountain woods, so she was out of the equation. Furthermore, the huge biker had been shot in the leg and despite his size Cain knew the mountain man was not going to go far with that hemorrhaging wound in his thigh. Consequently, and fortuitously to Martin Speck, the remaining single healthy hostage was Dr. Preston Cook, who was Cain's primary objective from the beginning. It was serendipity!

Cain emptied the Remington of its remaining slugs and then he tossed the shotgun across the room, where it slid along the hardwood floor into the kitchen area near to Skylar's Walther PPK. Then Cain walked over to where Preston Cook lay, glancing only absently at the groaning big man, Buster. With a single swipe of the knife he extracted again from the sheath on his leg, Martin Speck cut the scientist free. "Let's get out of here," the assassin said to Preston Cook. "And bring your work," he added, pointing with his Desert Eagle to the aluminum carry-on waiting patiently nearby.

As Preston was climbing to his feet, dazed and not knowing what was coming next, Cain turned to Big Buster Bernard, who hadn't moved much from where he had fallen with blood oozing from his leg. "I'd suggest a tourniquet," said Martin Speck. "There's some rope left," he added and pointed at it with his Desert Eagle. "You would be dead by now if that bullet hit your femoral artery. You'll be okay. Staunch the bleeding. Help will be here soon," Cain said in reference to helicopter borne reinforcements he knew the dead agent had summoned.

CHAPTER 92

Lt. Alfonse Sweeny and his squad of Marines were trudging up the mountain following the treacherously uneven path that led toward Buster and Cloud's sanctuary. The Marines had fanned out creating a ten meter line that reached slightly into the woods on the high side of the trail and slightly into the woods on the downside, too. They had formed a combat front as best they could in the thick forest. They were focused and moving forward ready for anything hostile coming their way. Yet, that squad of Marines had no idea a bloody altercation had transpired not that far ahead of them in the last few minutes, with a federal agent surging into a cabin where there were hostages, with an exchange of gunfire and one captive escaping. Sounds from the altercation had been absorbed in the dense foliage all around and muffled within the heavy log walls of the cabin. The Marines did not even know there was a cabin somewhere up the trail. They had no reason to imagine a clandestine branch of the U.S. government was involved in their operation, nor could they imagine who it was they were looking for on that mountain. More often than not warfare turns on probabilities, sketchy information, and guesswork.

All those young leathernecks knew about their objective was that scientific equipment was missing and a research scientist of some stripe was to be rescued. There had also been a passing reference to a nuclear reactor, but jarheads are not drama queens and they don't usually ask a lot of questions. They just move ahead with their M-16s locked and loaded just as they were doing on that October afternoon in 2005, trying to be ready for whatever came their way.

The security guards at Big Bear Airport didn't know what to do with the Cessna Skyhawk left sitting in weeds off to the side of the runway, after a young pilot and a man had leaped out and dashed into the woods. There was no use chasing them. The guards were off-duty Big Bear police officers, collecting extra cash working at the air field now and then, but their jurisdiction on the job was a misty concept at best and they had no specific orders that applied to unauthorized aircraft landing, much less a procedure about what to do with an airplane abandon like that one, or what to do with its occupants for that matter. Chasing them down was not a compelling option and raised more questions than it resolved. Nothing like this had ever happened before at the Big Bear airport to their knowledge, which was a quiet resort facility for the most part, serving wealthy weekenders with private aircraft that would glide in on a Friday afternoon and drift away come Sunday. Only one commercial flight arrived and departed daily, and that was a sixteen passenger Golden State Airways turboprop out of Burbank. Frankly, the two guards were befuddled.

After kicking a tire on the renegade airplane like he was checking out a used car, one of the security guards looked at his partner and said he had a Deadbolt in his Chevy's trunk that he hadn't used in five or six years. A Deadbolt was basically a steel rod, a commercial device with rubberized hooks on each end that could extend like a trombone to various lengths and was invented to prevent car theft when one of the ends was hooked through the steering wheel and the other end was hooked around a floor pedal. Ratcheted tightly down, the contraption was supposed to make the vehicle undrivable.

"Let's lock the sombitch up!" the security guard with the Deadbolt said emphatically and rather proudly about his inventive solution. His partner had no better suggestions at the moment, so that's what they did. As it turned, out the Deadbolt didn't really fit the Cessna's controls all that well. It wasn't really created to lock-down an airplane. The steering wheel and pedals were too far apart and they were at an awkward angle, too, but the men did manage to tie up the controls by sticking one end of the Deadbolt out the pilot's window. Anybody flying the Cessna would have no rudder because they could not turn the steering gear very far, nor could he or she pull back or push forward, eliminating the aircraft's elevators. That would mean the Cessna's ability to climb or descend was seriously compromised. The plane would probably never get off the ground with the Deadbolt attached as it was, and it would certainly crash within seconds if someone did manage to get her airborne. The two security officers were quite proud of themselves as they waited for further instructions from the airport administration or from their colleagues on the Big Bear police force, all of whom had been notified.

Dalton and Fitzgerald watched this development from some fifty yards up the hillside in the mountain forest. They crouched behind trees and glanced back and forth between one another without speaking as the two security guards explored the interior of the Cessna, but there was nothing for them to find. Naturally, the young pilot and his passenger were concerned because they both felt the airplane might be their means of escape. When the one guard had run off momentarily and come back with his Deadbolt and proceeded to attach it to the steering gear, configuring it so the Deadbolt was protruding out the port window, Dalton saw Lt. Jack smile.

"What?" Dalton whispered intensely toward his companion.

"Piece 'a cake," said Fitzy, which gave Dalton immediate reassurance. The Deadbolt was no real deterrent to theft for cars *or* airplanes. It was an easily defeated device, a fact that would explain why it disappeared from the marketplace after a couple years of selling thousands of units to gullible customers.

"Okay," the boy said quickly. "'Then we have got to go", he added, relying totally on Fitzgerald Jack's assessment of the Deadbolt at Big Bear Airport.

"You lead," said Lt. Jack as though anything else could possibly happen at that point in their rescue mission, and they immediately began to scramble along the side of the mountain through thick underbrush and trees for two hundred yards, trying to discover a way to get back down and into the open where Dalton could activate his jury-rigged, Buck Rogers, triangulation cell phone. Fitzgerald was still skeptical. There were no downloadable applications for cell phones at that time to locate other people, no smart phones at all, and limited GPS for civilians, none of which was included in cell phone technology. That widespread magic would amaze the world a couple of years later. But to Lieutenant Jack in 2005, triangulating cell phones, like portable nuclear reactors, were the stuff of science fiction movies.

As the Marines trudged up the mountain in a battle line, they arrived at the exact spot where the trail was tightened by a ten foot bolder to their right and an extraordinarily steep grade in front of them. While the Marines puzzled over this obstacle, they saw crushed bushes and a less-steep narrow path near the boulder, which was streaked by metal fragments and paint from the doors of both the Taurus and the BMW. The earth beneath their feet had clearly been churned by the determined effort of automobile tires.

And it was at this very moment of their contemplation that a *roaring* Harley-Davidson carrying two men burst like a screaming demon from the crest of the rise in the road directly ahead of the squad! The full-throttle motorcycle was launched in a low arc above the camouflaged helmets of the spread-out Marines. The dense forest prevented the men from hearing the machine until the last second as Cain's Desert Eagle spit fire left and right while the smoking monster was gliding gracefully beyond the young, slack-jawed Marines, capturing them in surreal amazement. By the time the Fantail Classic dug into the ground again, ten meters farther down the slope, skidding sideways and heaving a wave of rocks and dirt back toward the Marines like shrapnel, Cain had already neutralized two of the leathernecks with fifty caliber bullets blowing holes in their Kevlar jackets, killing them instantly, lifting both men off their feet and slinging them into the nearby undergrowth. Cain's first shot was to his right and the second was to his left as they screamed past the squad. The last of Cain's three shots in the brief firefight was a no-look trick shot over his shoulder and behind him while he was still airborne, as he glanced for the briefest faction of a second into a rearview mirror on the motorcycle's handlebars. That final large slug ripped into a Marine's rotator cuff and basically separated his arm. If not so gruesome, it would have been worthy of a carnival.

After shock and hesitation the squad recovered and opened fire in a ferocious fusillade downhill in the direction of the receding Harley, but fortunately for Martin Speck and Preston Cook none of those reactionary rounds made it home. One ricocheted off Buster's purloined helmet, cracking it. Otherwise, the assassin and his captive were very lucky that day, although luck of that kind had long been a companion to Cain. Preston was scrunched low astride the bike in front of Cain, both of them leaning as far forward as they could, virtually turning them into a single rider with two heads. Cain was wearing Buster's black – now cracked – helmet and Preston was wearing Cloud Willow's white helmet with daisy stickers.

From the first moment he heard the helicopter, Cain had anticipated some kind of back-up arriving, summoned by the man who had invaded the cabin, but Cain had zero evidence to tell him he would be roaring through a squad of U.S. Marines during his bold motorcycle escape. In fact, the entire plan may have gone a different direction if he thought Marines were waiting on the road. Martin Speck had been thinking two or three comrades of the dead agent's may be lying in wait. As astonishing as it was, Cain's explosive display of marksmanship and bravado during that soaring encounter with the leathernecks was wholly impromptu.

It would be fair to say Cain had gambled and as was most always the case for him he won his gamble. A Harley-Davidson fantail classic is not an off-road bike and its suspension was damaged by its leap over the Marines. The motorcycle slid wildly as it growled forward down the mountain, grinding around a bend on the heavily wooded trail, leaving behind the dismayed Marine squad firing away in full automatic mode. A hundred M-16 bullets swarmed like hornets around Cain and Preston Cook, clipping leaves and thudding into tree trunks on all sides of the motorcycle, but that was before the assassin and his captive plunged further ahead on the trail, pounding across ruts and holes at a remarkable speed given the condition of their vehicle, powering straight down the fall-line like they were on a thrill ride. The zip of bullets disappeared behind them as they charged forward. Of course, Cain was no stranger to heavy Harley-Davidson motorcycles or to an abundance of hostile weapons fire. He was in his element again and his strategy of surprise had rescued him once more from his adversaries.

Beneath Cain's sternum, however, Preston was grim, ashen, and hanging on to the bike's chassis for dear life with the carry-on suitcase containing the cold fusion reactor wedged between his breast and the motorcycle's gas tank. The threesome had become an unhappy and unwilling but tightly-knit unit roaring, racing, pounding down that mountain trail. Preston was beginning to wish he had never become so obsessed with his research and cold fusion. It was the first time during the entire bloody storm of recent days that such a thought actually took significant form in his mind. He had only wanted to help the world and yet all of this horror had resulted. Police officers, Marines, a federal agent, and his friend Max were all dead. How could that have happened? He imagined Samantha out there somewhere in the forest. He knew it wasn't a good environment for her. She liked hot-water baths and creature comforts. She hated camping. Preston was losing his sense of the situation. And where was Dalton right then, his lovely boy? Was he safe? A weary and frightened Dr. Preston Cook was wishing he could undo it all. No more killing. No more mayhem.

CHAPTER 93

When the high-flying and fire-breathing Harley-Davidson was finally gone, churning its way down the mountain side, its sound gradually lost in the forest and rocky ravines below, Lt. Alfonse Sweeny stepped into the center of the trail down which the demon bike had disappeared and he looked around at his fragmented command. Two of his men were dead on the spot. Another had mostly lost an arm and was groaning terribly to the side of the pathway, bleeding profusely. It didn't look good for him at all. Sweeny's Marines were doing their best to attend to their wounded comrade in the wake of the sudden furious exchange of gunfire that has just occurred, but the squad did not bring a medic on their misbegotten operation. In no way had they anticipated such a level of casualty. Clearly they were not prepared properly for the kind of enemy they encountered, a classic military error as the ghost of General Custer would attest. They had no idea. In truth, they expected little serious opposition on their mission to rescue a scientist and recover some strange equipment. The notion that foreign agents might be engaged meant nothing to those men when they heard it in their briefing on the flight from Twenty-Nine Palms.

The squad leader studied the trail down which the Harley had vanished. He could still very faintly hear its grinding roar disappearing below them on the mountain, sounds giving way to the growing distance. Around him, Lt. Sweeny could also hear the understandable consternation of his men as they tended to the fallen and to one another. "Who the hell was that?" Sweeny said to himself just before his radio crackled into life with an acknowledgement from the helicopter that had been waiting a distance away and he soberly tendered his request for evacuation, "With dead and wounded," he added.

Almost a quarter of a mile from and above the Big Bear airport, Dalton Cook and Fitzgerald Jack stumbled out of the trees onto a paved blacktop highway and they instantly had to leap backward to avoid being crushed by a huge, high-riding Chevy SUV with oversized knobby tires that swerved to avoid them! It had a wiggling "Baby on Board" caution sign suction-cupped to the rear glass and the perturbed woman driving the SUV announced her annoyance as she roared away with a stretched blast from her horn and a middle finger pointed skyward out her window.

Other cars were approaching at speed from both directions. It appeared to Fitzy and Dalton they had happened upon a pretty significant stretch of road for a rural community. Dalton pointed to a sign identifying it as Route 38, but that meant nothing to Lt. Jack. He'd never been to Big Bear before. In truth, neither of them knew where they were but they could see they were standing beside a busy stretch of asphalt.

There were substantial homes all the way up the slope on the opposite side of that highway. The lieutenant could easily see they were not rustic little mountain retreats. Most of them were constructed from a combination of heavy gray stone and redwood. Many had French doors opening onto expansive second floor balconies that enjoyed spectacular views of expansive Big Bear Lake, the same lake over which Dalton and Fitzy had made their desperate approach an hour earlier before abandoning their brave little Cessna at the airport.

The nouvelle riche of Big Bear lived in those houses, reckoned Lt. Jack, as he scanned the wooded mountain rising before him on that fall afternoon. The first floors of the homes were obscured by evergreens intermingled with the gold and crimson leaves of liquidambars. A majority of the dwellings rose above the surrounding forest like a community of castles. Fitzgerald pictured the trendy occupants, a mix of pretenders and high-rollers sipping martinis while they watched the sun descend gloriously to the west. He imagined them having snowy Christmases with twelve foot professionally decorated trees in their cathedral ceilinged living rooms. Fitzgerald knew these images well because he remembered them from his time with homicide at the LAPD, not in the mountains but in Beverly Hills and in Brentwood where bloody murder had left its dark stains.

"Let's go this way," said Dalton jerking Fitzy out of his meanderings, as the boy wonder began walking determinedly away along the uneven shoulder of the road.

"Whoa, partner!" said Fitzgerald, tugging at the young man's shirt sleeve. "Do you have a clue where we're headed?"

Dalton stopped and looked seriously at his policeman companion. "No, but *that* is north," he said pointing up the mountain toward the countless, toney vacation homes among the trees. "Big Bear town is *there*," Dalton said and he pointed to the East. "Behind us," he added, gesturing down the slope from whence they had come, "is south and the airport. So, I think we should go *west* and find a place to triangulate." Then Dalton tossed in his family-honed sarcasm and said with as much sincerity as he could muster for being only twelve, "Do you want to get a souvenir in town?"

"Comical," said the lieutenant, not amused. "Those security guards have notified law enforcement by now. I know how this works. Soon a cruiser will be coming down this highway looking for us. It's time for you to do your magic with your phone." He looked at the boy for a beat and then threw in, "Do we need an umbrella covered in aluminum foil to phone home?"

"Umbrella?" asked Dalton.

Putting a hand on Dalton's shoulder, the lieutenant said, "*E.T.*?"

Then they started westward along the shoulder of the road, brushed back by fast moving vehicles two feet from where they trudged. Fitzy realized clearly in those moments that the drivers had an oddly indifferent regard for pedestrians. To the residents of Big Bear, maybe pedestrians were just worthless interlopers wandering around, a strange prejudice since nobody could be more out of place in a mountain forest than the ostentatious vacation houses above them.

With a tourniquet and a blood soaked bandage around his leg, pale and sweating in the October afternoon chill and partially supported by a grunting, exhausted middle-aged woman, Big Buster Bernard with Samantha Day-Steiner under his arm stumbled forward into the clearing where the squad of Marines was waiting for evacuation. The Marines were stunned at Buster's and Sam's sudden appearance. Big Buster was gaunt. Samantha, who had lain in wait near the cabin after her escape, had been struggling down the road beneath Buster's huge shoulder, trying to help him walk.

She had watched the cabin from hiding before re-entering it. Sam had seen Cain load her husband and his cold fusion suitcase onto the Harley-Davidson motorcycle before they spun off down the narrow and miserably rutted trail toward Crestline.

Samantha was not a Special Group agent, like dead Bobby Skylar lying slumped at the base of the fireplace inside the cabin with thoughts of his family vanished into his cold night. The distinguished mathematics professor, Dr. Day-Steiner, unfaithful wife, itinerant mother, and greedy opportunist, was scared to trembling as she hung out on that horrible day amongst the trees and critters of the California sierras. She was so totally inept. It was a revolutionary sensation. Her life had evolved during the last forty-eight hours in ways she could never have imagined. Her review of events went well beyond fear and finding herself hiding and alone in a mountain wilderness. She was a fundamentally changed woman. She was swarmed by an awareness of her own weaknesses and of what mattered most to her.

After the Harley had roared away, Samantha went back into the cabin where she found the dead federal agent and she found Big Buster bleeding with a length of rope making a tourniquet on his leg. Fortunately he was still alert and Sam quickly figured to fashion a bandage from a bed sheet. So, she shredded one into several substantial strips and wrapped Buster's leg tightly, tossing aside the bloodied rope. With a wad of cloth set against the bullet wound, the bandage staunched the blood flow. Samantha almost threw-up twice while she helped with the dressing, yet she got it done. Because of her, Buster was finally able to climb unsteadily to his feet. He was very weak. Yet, as unsteady as Big Buster was, they decided to try and head down the mountain together to find the help that Cain said was on the way. For some inscrutable reason, they both trusted the assassin's words.

CHAPTER 94

Buster and Samantha's stumbling entrance onto the trail was an adrenaline jolt to those green Marines. They were wired after what had happened and they swung around almost in unison with their M-16's leveled as that very strange couple staggered, leaning together, into the clearing out from the trees and scrub where they had found a more negotiable grade to make their way down the mountain. Hobbled as they were, Buster and Samantha had no interest at all in tumbling from the top of the steep rise that fronted the Marines on the trail, the same rocky ledge from which Cain's stolen Harley-Davidson had leapt twenty minutes earlier, gliding brilliantly with gunfire to each side before speeding onward, down the mountain. Instead, Buster and Samantha had elected to work their way around that precipice and were as startled as the Marines when they fell out of the brush directly into the gun sights of ten automatic weapons.

The two frightened Pasadena neighbors were milliseconds from being torn asunder by dozens of .22 magnum M-16 slugs, slicing them up and down from multiple angles. Those Marines were absolutely trigger-ready after their brief and deadly encounter with high-flying Cain and his passenger. It would have been a *Bonnie and Clyde* pulverization which was only narrowly averted by an instinctive instantaneous scream from Lt. Sweeny, "Hold your fire!"

He uttered the command on the spot when he saw the peculiar pair crumple forward into the clearing, because to him it was immediately apparent they were no threat, not the enemy, and they were unarmed. He also sensed the tension in his men, which prompted his lightening quick reaction.

Heaving with exhaustion the intruders collapsed on the dirt trail before the gun-wielding Marines. Buster was a huge man for Samantha to even attempt to assist, to half-carry, and that very point on the downward trail from the cabin would have been about as far as Dr. Day-Steiner could have possibly gone with Buster leaning on her, whether they had encountered the leathernecks or not. From where they had fallen on their hands and knees in the dirt, Samantha looked up at the Marine Lieutenant standing there flanked by his men and she said quietly toward him, "Thank you." She comprehended quite clearly that she and Buster had been a fraction of a second from obliteration.

A walloping roar from the evacuation helicopter enveloped them rather suddenly, arriving in cranked up decibels like a stereo's volume knob had been twirled all the way up. Tree limbs and undergrowth began whipping around, as dust rose into a swirl from the trail. The downdraft became quite oppressive and the noise rose to near deafening level. Nonetheless, Lt. Sweeny was fast to his radio, hunched over with one hand covering his exposed ear, yelling to the pilot above them that there were two more pick-ups, both of them civilian, and one was seriously wounded. Sweeny had to scream the message several times to be understood in the din of their retreat.

In later months, Lieutenant Sweeny labored over what had happened on that mountain. He believed he had failed miserably in his leadership on that day in October, returning with two dead Marines and one in the throes, but who would miraculously survive after an amputation. None of it should not have gone the way it did. But, at Twenty-Nine Palms Sweeny was never really in a good position to point out his superiors had grossly under-assessed the enemy, even though responsibility lay with his superiors. Higher-ups frantically began to cover their asses as the picture of what occurred emerged. The results of it all weighed heavily on Sweeny. Even so, he would try to bolster himself by arguing that through instinct alone he had saved the lives of two civilians. Unfortunately for Lieutenant Sweeny, his legitimate defenses would never truly be aired during the investigation which followed the operation, where the deaths of the Marines were laid entirely at Sweeny's feet in spite of the absence of reliable intelligence about what the squad was facing when it was sent aloft to rescue Dr. Cook and his invention. In truth, the whole operation had been run on the fly, prompted by influences in Washington, D.C. The salvation of the two civilians on that cool and tragic October day was of little consequence to the review board, whose disapproval and sanctions ultimately resulted in Sweeny's resignation from his command and his unceremonious voluntary departure from the Marine Corps one year later.

Alfonse Sweeny remained a moody man after leaving the Marines, which he had once tried to see as his real home. He was never able to fully comprehend the conspiracy of events and circumstance leading to what he felt was his disgrace. The lieutenant had been betrayed by the family he wanted to love. There was no way he could have possibly been aware of the sweeping international intrigue and the years of nuclear fusion research in a CTU scientist's garage that led to that day in the San Bernardino Mountains. And in a relentlessly depressed frame of mind on a rainy California afternoon a week before Thanksgiving in 2007, former Lt. Sweeny with the slight lisp, used a classic Korean War vintage Marine issue Colt .45, like the one owned by Big Buster, to end his torment, becoming the third fatality from that October day. *Semper fi.*

The Harley-Davidson fantail classic leaned around a bend on Old Mill Road and rumbled onward, leaving the faded and falling-down fishing billboard behind. With the chill October air racing around them, Cain was in his element and loving it. He didn't know where they were going exactly but he had his primary objectives right there on the bike in front of him, the scientist and his contraption. Plus, Cain was pretty good at improvisation when plans went awry, so he wasn't worried.

On the other hand, the physicist, Preston Cook, was pale with apprehension about what lay ahead. He was holding on to the motorcycle as best he could with his awkward cold fusion carry-on clutched to his chest, while they sped ahead. The two men were sitting more upright by then since no red-hot lead was slicing the thin air around them, but they were certainly an odd sight zooming down the mountain road, two men crowded onto a Harley-Davidson, one with a black helmet and one clutching a suitcase and wearing daisies.

The city of Big Bear was not their destination after they had made it to the highway. Cain was going to head *down* the mountain toward the valley, in the opposite direction of Big Bear. But when Preston answered an urgent and surprising cell phone call from his son, not long after the motorcycle had squealed onto Old Mill Road, the resort town of Big Bear would soon became their new destination. Very near the falling-down bass-fishing billboard is where reliable access to cell phone service magically reappeared for Preston and that was also where Cain chose to crank up the gas as the fantail Harley accelerated with an immense tailpipe growl along Old Mill Road toward Crestline. Preston could barely hear as he tried to answer his incoming call, holding on to his suitcase so it would not topple off the speeding motorcycle. Martin Speck found Preston's predicament on the bike quite amusing. He was not especially concerned about the cell phone call, guessing it was family, but he eavesdropped as best he could.

Not two minutes later the men had sped past the Crestbear general store where the tattoo girl was serving lattes to a pair of cheerful retirees wearing brand new "Lake Arrowhead" sweat shirts. The motorcycle pivoted onto Rim of the World Highway where Cain and his captive began racing south toward San Bernardino. All the while Preston was yelling into his cell phone, talking in amazement with young Dalton who was desperately trying to explain to his father that he was up there, in the mountains, at Big Bear, come to save his dad! It was all so unexpected for Preston. Plus they had to scream at each because of the motorcycle's roar and the wind, so it took a few minutes for the conversation to jell. And that's when the motorcycle's speed began to diminish.

"You flew here in the Cessna? Alone?" Preston shouted into his phone, while Martin Speck eavesdropped over the shoulder of his hostage.

"Lieutenant Jack is with me," said Dalton to his dad.

"Good. That's good," said his dad, although Preston wondered how the law enforcement officer would permit a mere boy to fly them all the way to Big Bear. On the other hand, he knew Dalton had the strong will and stubbornness of his mother.

The conversation between Preston and Dalton was happening while Martin was pulling in the reins on their descent toward the valley and in thirty seconds the bike had coasted to a complete stop on a scenic turnout overlooking a flat, picturesque expanse of California Inland Empire's agricultural plain, six thousand feet below them. Cain was already reimagining his plans around this unexpected development, because he was positive he heard reference to a Cessna. It seemed young Dalton had used the cell phone his father had jury-rigged to find his father, shifting locations according to the triangulation protocol taught to him by his dad and Dalton actually caught Preston on the way down the mountain. The phones and the improvised system worked precisely as it had been designed, to find a path for connection. Dalton had even calculated by his triangulation that his father was headed *away* from Big Bear and he knew pretty much how far away. In triangulation mode the modified cellphones spoke directly to one another via satellite and did not go through a relay tower. Preston's jury-rigged cell phones did not even have to be turned on for triangulation to work. All they needed was sufficient juice in each device.

Dalton had a map opened up on his lap and that's how he had figured out exactly where his father was at that very moment. Over the phone he implored his father to stay by pleading again, "Don't leave, dad. I've come to get you!" Of course, young Dalton did not know that Martin Speck was holding his father captive. He had no clue the assassin was right there, practically a third party to the call. Dalton hadn't thought through to that possibility. He was a boy and he was too happy to hear from his dad.

"Well… we were heading on down to San Berdu, Dalt," continued Preston figuring the availability of his aircraft was not a good thing at that particular moment but Preston was also trying to be as obscure as possible with regard to what his son had done. At the same time he felt Martin's intrusive presence near his ear, as they sat there at the turnout, both of them astride that Harley-Davidson, butt to groin. Preston also felt Cain's knuckles up against his ribs and he adjusted his report by saying, "Or somewhere in the valley… I'm not sure," corrected Preston to his son.

"Who is with you?" asked the boy frankly and innocently.

Again came those knuckles against Preston's ribs, a little firmer this time.

"Oh… I'm on Buster's motorcycle. It's kind of hard to hear. Are you okay?"

"I'm okay. Dad, come here, *please!*" returned his son without the least artfulness.

The two men on the Harley by the side of the highway, with the cold fusion case crosswise over the gas tank, certainly made a peculiar sight to passersby, thousands of feet above the plains of San Bernardino with a chilled October wind rising from below. And none of those curious passersby could have understood the seriousness of the close conversation they saw between the black and the flowered helmets, and what was really at stake for the entire planet. They were just a couple of guys on a motorcycle and one of them was wearing peculiar headgear for a man.

"Ask the lieutenant to help you get back to Cloud's house, Dalton. Do you think you can do that?" said Preston. Not really knowing what to say in this unexpected situation and understanding, it all must have sounded very strange to Dalton.

"Dad, did you hear me? I'm at *Big Bear airport!* I have the Cessna!" insisted Dalton, thinking his father did not understand.

Cain, however, *did* understand. He had his ear so close to the phone that he could hear quite clearly what the boy was saying and Cain suddenly covered Preston's mouth with one hand and whispered into Preston's ear, "Tell your son, you will meet him."

Preston froze momentarily until he heard Dalton's small voice from the phone. "Dad? Dad? Are you there?"

"Alright, Dalt," said Preston. "We'll come to where you are. Big Bear airport. What a brave young man you are. I'll be there soon," Preston added before Cain grabbed the phone out of his hand and rang off before any further odd conversation could take place. Even Martin Speck knew Preston did not sound normal toward the end.

"You are right, professor. Your son *is* brave," said Cain quite sincerely. "I thought he was just a boy."

"He's twelve," said Preston.

This caught even jaded Martin Speck by surprise. "*Twelve*? Well, as you Americans like to say, 'An acorn does not fall far from the tree.'"

"So, it's the Big Bear airport, is it?" Cain added quickly, with no further comment at that time as to the boy's remarkable accomplishment. "Let's be on our way," he said, and he cranked up the bike.

From a standing start, they spun around in a tight circle, hurling gravel and dirt ten yards to their stern. Cain's eyes were sparkling and Preston was terrified, as they roared back *up* the mountain *toward* Big Bear, beyond Crestline and the Crestbear general store, and beyond the community of Lake Arrowhead.

While they sped along the winding Rim of the World Highway, a United States Marine Corps helicopter hundreds of feet above them pounded through the cold air and banked northward toward Twenty-Nine Palms in the desert. It was carrying the remains of Sweeny's platoon, Prestons' wife, and Big Buster Bernard who had passed out from blood loss and lay on the floor of Huey. No Marine in that helicopter had bothered to look down, where they might have glimpsed the demon Harley-Davison tearing along the serpentine Rim of the World Highway far below them. They all just wanted to go home and get away from the nightmare they had experienced.

CHAPTER 95

After Dalton had triangulated and made the connection with his father and had made plans to rendezvous at the Big Bear Airport, Dalton carefully folded up the map he had on his lap. The boy didn't know anything was dangerously awry in speaking with his father. He assumed the "we" in his conversation with his dad meant his dad and Big Buster Bernard. They were on Buster's motorcycle. Dalton was overwhelmed to have finally connected with his father and he was ever so happy his dad agreed to turn back toward the Big Bear Airport. He was imagining he, his dad, and Fitzy could all fly home together in Lucky 47. Dalton was brimming with joy. All that stuff with airport security could be worked out, he was thinking. At the end of the day, he was just a boy after all.

Fitzgerald Jack stared at his young companion a bit dumbfounded that this triangulation business really worked using a tricked-out Sanyo and he said, "Well, I'll be damned. Your phones can actually do it."

Holding up one index finger for the lieutenant to see, Dalton looked squarely into the eyes of Lt. Jack and croaked in his very best *ET* voice, "Phone home!"

Fitzgerald was awash with amazement that this supposedly compromised Down syndrome boy could do all the things that Lt. Jack had witnessed during these last couple of days. A hardened cop's world view had been changed by his experience. "If your dad is coming *here* because we have an airplane," he continued carefully, "then

I suggest we'd better get back over to the airfield to make sure we really do have an airplane to use." Fitzgerald was not as starry-eyed as Dalton. Anything could happen. The police detective was significantly more grounded in the reality of their predicament. A team of regular on-duty Big Bear police were likely all over the airplane by then and flying it away may be out of the question.

Fitzgerald added soberly, "Remember, my young, very bright friend, that aircraft may be guarded by now." Immediately, he could see Dalton's spirits begin to sink. The boy's face was always an unchecked mirror of his feelings and the detective rapidly intervened by adding, "But... I *do* have a plan." When Fitzgerald threw in a little smile and he could see right away that he'd buoyed Dalton. Delight swept the boy. He was wonderfully transparent. Twelve-year old Dalton Cook was glowing again. He had absorbed the words from the Lieutenant like they were indisputably reliable, even though Fitzy's own confidence in the plan to which he alluded was far from rock solid.

In not much time, Lieutenant Fitzgerald Jack and Dalton found themselves crouched in the woods just up the mountain from Big Bear Airport looking down at the Cessna that sat silently on the wide grassy shoulder of the runway. They had hunkered down at pretty much the same spot where they were hiding an hour or so earlier, when they had first abandon the airplane and escaped up the slope. It was where they had knelt behind trees and watched as the rangier of the two security guards finagled his steel Deadbolt across the steering wheel of the Cessna and out its window. When done, they had seen the security guard step back with his fists on his hips, quite satisfied with his work. And the Deadbolt was still there as Dalton and Fitzgerald looked down from their vantage point. It protruded oddly from the pilot's window like the foot of a metal cane.

The better news was that the shorter, more corpulent, and hopefully slower of the two security guards remained alone on duty at the Cessna site as Fitzy and Dalton reviewed the situation. The guard had wandered off toward the runway, more than fifty yards from the airplane. The portly security guard was looking this way and that as though he was expecting someone, but from where Fitzy and Dalton were positioned, they could see no air traffic in either direction, no ground traffic either, and they had a very decent view from their position up the mountain above the airport.

"What's he doing out there?" whispered Dalton to his cop buddy.

"He's probably bored," said Fitzy, which was right on the money, as the job of airport security at Big Bear was fairly uneventful and neither of those guards imagined anything irregular happening on any day.

Lt. Jack was privately worrying why the local police weren't there. There was no evidence the Big Bear police had come and gone from the scene, which was very odd, indeed. The entire picture below them was all basically just as they had left it, which was not what one would expect when a rogue aircraft lands at an airport.

As it happened, the two security guards had elected to take turns at sentry near the airplane until local police arrived. They, too, were puzzled why it was taking so darn long for the Big Bear police to show up. They had put in a call right away. And because they were off-duty, deputized cops themselves, the two security guards personally knew every one of the local sworn peace officers. They were not off-the-radar yokels.

But in the midst of that day's spiraling haphazard events at both Big Bear and nearby Crestline, serendipity had lent a hand. All the local police officers had been captivated by an urgent message from the Marine Corps Base up at Twenty-Nine Palms asking local law enforcement to investigate a firefight near Crestline, a community too small to have a police department of its own.

News of gunplay heated up cop conversations all over the mountain that afternoon as word zipped between law enforcement venues faster than one of Preston Cook's subatomic particles. The San Bernardino County Sheriff's Office, Big Bear City Police, Lake Arrowhead City Police, and even the California Highway Patrol had all picked up the call-to-action and they had converged *en masse* at the turn-off from Old Mill Road where the narrow gravel path cut away through the woods and headed up to Big Buster and Cloud Willow's safe-haven. The obscure intersection near that falling down bass fishing billboard was quickly so congested with law enforcement sedans of every stripe that civilians could not get by, either up or down the mountain. The heavily wooded section of Old Mill Road was awhirl with colored lights and radio communications crackling through squad cars' open doors into the cool October air. There was more excitement than those men had seen in years. Two of the Sheriff's police cruisers had already tried to follow the torturous gravel road that angled away from the black asphalt, and those cruisers were stuck miserably and grinding away just out of sight around the first bend. It would have been embarrassing for the drivers to know that a rented Ford Taurus had banged and crunched up this grade not that long ago with nothing more than determination and abject disregard for damage. However, the local constabulary gathered together at that site did not know about the Taurus and the BMW, so they reasonably acquiesced to the challenges of the rutted route rather than destroy their vehicles. They elected, instead, to summon reinforcements in the way of two of the County Sheriff's moon-buggy, John Deer, all-terrain vehicles.

In the meantime, all the uniformed officers were gossiping with one another, speculating about the shootings, and not paying the least attention to the repeated report on their radios of goings-on at Big Bear Airport, where there had been an unscheduled landing and the abandonment of a private plane. For those pumped up minions of the law above Crestline that day, the two scenarios simply didn't equate.

There was official word that the United Sates Marines had come and gone and they had engaged armed resistance in the backwoods. Fantasy quickly bloomed in these officers' hearts and minds, a derivative of a rural cop's ruminations about everything that is wrong with America. In no time, they were telling each other a group of heavily armed anarchists were holed-up somewhere deep in the mountain forest with a hostile scheme to rain serious damage on the local resorts. One of the officers confirmed he had actually heard "hostages" were involved and the source was "reliable", as he put it.

Consequently, peacekeepers of every stripe figured they were mandated to help out in any way they could. It was shaping up to be something really big. Order had to be maintained; lives might be at stake. Those officers were mostly ex-military, after all, so they didn't blame the Marines for handing the situation off to them. Law enforcement was not the purview of the armed forces. Law enforcement was the role of sworn officers like the men gathered at that intersection on that day, and by god, they knew they were the ones to take care of the problem. They had seen far too many of those damn hippie-like, survivalist types gathering in that neck of the county in preceding years and it was high time to send them a message.

Eventually the peace officers would make their way up to the dark cabin squatting at the end of a gruelingly steep and stone-ridden dirt pathway. It would take more than two hours of trekking up hill. They would pass the spot at the base of a rise where the Marines had encountered Cain flying above them on a Harley-Davidson, his Desert Eagle blazing. The assorted law enforcement officers would finally make their way to Buster's and Cloud's sanctuary, hidden among tall evergreens and pressed against a gray granite bluff. With handguns tense in their fists the police would cautiously enter the cabin only to find the bloody body of Bobby Skylar inside, leaning against the fireplace where he'd fallen. And, of course, they had also seen the Taurus and BMW outside which fascinated them more than the dead federal agent, because the presence of the cars gave rise to a most exercised conversation. How did those vehicles manage to get up that damn trail?

Much to the gathered officers' chagrin, they did not find a band of survivalists hiding amongst the trees or in the cabin, ready to wage war. Nor, after that long march up the mountain, did they come upon a commune of latter-day hippies smoking marijuana and planning revolution, a scenario that had slowly evolved into the officers' last best hope of keeping their fantasy alive.

As it went, the law enforcement brigade ended the afternoon wandering silently back down the long gravel road two by two, empty handed, with heads hanging, thoroughly disappointed, while the long awaited and late arriving moon-buggy ATVs were bouncing along not far behind them like a pair of remote control toys, one of them carrying the remains of Agent Skylar in a black zipper bag.

As the cops involved in the Crestline adventure trudged quietly homeward, at Big Bear Airport where the unauthorized landing of a Cessna had occurred and gone totally ignored by the local police and everyone else, events were unfolding that were epic, that were irrevocably derailing a grand future for all of humanity.

CHAPTER 96

"Here's my idea," said Lieutenant Jack to his young compatriot as they gazed down at the abandon airplane from their high hiding spot among the trees and as they estimated the distances between the plane, the runway, and the squat security guard who was pacing back and forth yearning for reinforcements and befuddled by their absence. "*You* need to get into that airplane. *I* do not," said the Lieutenant frankly to Dalton.

"But we are a team!" came back the boy, more loudly and emotionally than Fitzgerald had expected and with a face instantly rife with anxiety.

Fitzy smiled at the boy and put a finger to his lips. "Hush," he whispered. "Let me finish. We need to work quietly."

Dalton nodded, kept his mouth shut, and continued to stare at the LAPD detective with whom he had begun the adventure and with whom he assumed he would complete it.

"As soon as we catch sight of your dad and Buster coming on the motorcycle, I'll get down there and knock that Deadbolt off. It's nothing, really. But the guard is going to start running toward me. I doubt he is too fast. I'll draw him away from the airplane at that point. Understand?"

Again Dalton nodded, but he was very worried about this turn in the conversation.

Fitzgerald added, as matter-of-factly as he could, "I'll sprint off, after I get rid of that Deadbolt," and he pointed toward the farther end of the runway past the nearer cement block hangars and Quonset huts flanking the north side of the runway, buildings that appeared to be deserted, although there were several small aircraft tied down in front of them. "I'm sure I can make it beyond those buildings," the detective said.

"But…" came back Dalton in protest, but he was immediately cut off.

"No!" said Lt. Jack emphatically, taking control for the first time during the boy's heroic excursion, finally acting like an adult in charge. "I'll outrun the chubby guy, Dalton. So, don't worry about me. He'll radio for his partner, but we'll be way down there by the time I let them catch me." Detective Jack pointed toward the farther end of the runway, several hundred yards to the west. "I'll flash my LAPD badge at him and it will create enough confusion that I'll be okay. Trust me. I've done this before. I'll be fine," he added.

"That's because they won't understand why a police officer is doing this?" asked Dalton, reluctantly accepting the assignment because he could see it made sense. Logic had always played a powerful role in his life. His father was a scientist.

"That's right, my brave young friend. You run down the hill after I've yanked out that Deadbolt. Wait until the fat guard is chasing me. Okay? You come down as fast as you can and climb inside that Cessna and crank her up! Do you understand? Get your dad and Buster in there and fly them out of here! Got it? That killer can't be far away."

"What about you?" said the boy.

"Don't worry, Dalton. I can find my way back to LA. Right now we have to hope your dad shows up pronto… before we have a regiment of police here. I don't know why they aren't here already. When it's time, we'll have to move quickly. Like comedy, timing is everything," added Fitzgerald in a reference that made no meaning whatsoever to Dalton.

That's when they heard the Harley-Davidson's growl and saw it bouncing over the parking lot curb adjacent to the squat terminal building a couple of hundred yards to the south. It plowed past cement pylons protecting the parking lot from the runway. The motorcycle shot cross a short stretch of landscaped lawn, heaving tufts of sod before roaring out onto the tarmac. At the same moment, the skinny security guard burst from the terminal building with four or five other employees shuffling curiously behind him like jetsam, gawking at the commotion. The lanky guard quickly left the others behind instantly on task, running and shouting after this motorcycle intruder who had ignored proper boundaries, churned up the lawn, and was now headed rapidly toward the interloper airplane! The skinny guard was livid, his Irish face cherry red with indignation.

Meanwhile, the chubbier, curly-haired guard was crouched like he was ready for action when he saw that Harley headed his way. His eyes were wide and his breathing was ramped up! He immediately put two and two together and figured it had something to do with the abandon Cessna, but he couldn't know what. He had his right hand on his service revolver while his mind was racing through the possibilities. He was not a deputized law enforcement officer when he was here at the airport. He was just a part-time security guard and he knew the use of lethal force was murkier territory in that role and it left him a bit uncertain as to what he should do in the situation. The short guard could see two men on the motorcycle racing across the runway in his direction, with a suitcase lodged on the lap of the guy in front. It was a strange sight to behold. Was this a drug operation? He could also make out his taller counterpart in the distance running in pursuit from the terminal building, well behind the Harley and rapidly losing ground. The situation didn't look good.

Why in god's name, the short guard was thinking as he witnessed the drama unfolding toward him, didn't he go to the Pumpkin Festival that day like his girlfriend had wanted?

"There they are!" said Detective Jack pointing across the field at the distant motorcycle charging toward them from the far away control building. "Get down there just as soon as I split and the guard chases me! Get your dad's or Buster's attention any way you can! And take off *right away* when they're on board! Do *not* hesitate!" And with no further words, Fitzgerald winked at Dalton, patted the boy's shoulder, and bolted down the mountain, swinging past pine trees to control his rapid descent and keep his feet underneath himself on the slippery leafy earth. In mere seconds Dalton could see the detective charging forward through the tall grass and into the clearing where the Cessna sat patiently, like it had been waiting on this very day for thirty years, as though history-altering events were its destiny.

Arriving at the airplane, Lt. Jack opened the pilot's door and with two swift blows from the heel of his right hand he quickly dislodged the Deadbolt from the airplane's steering column and he tossed it like junk away from the Cessna into the grass.

The squat, curly-headed security guard was after Fitzgerald right away as predicted, having heard the commotion behind him. And as anticipated he came shouting and running as fast as he could directly toward Lt. Jack even as the Deadbolt was cast aside. The detective immediately took it on the toe to the west. Fitzy started sprinting like a purse snatcher toward the father end of the runway beyond the tied down idle aircraft and the Quonset hut hangars. And, as expected, the curly headed guard was on his trail huffing and puffing and pushing his short legs to make up the distance. Fitzgerald was actually a pretty good runner, having been on the track team in high school, so to stay within his scheme he had to keep it in low gear. He couldn't be leaving the guard in the dust. Meanwhile, the chubby guard remained in hot pursuit doing his damnedest without the slightest suspicion that the runner glancing over his shoulder was pacing him. The guard kept his hand on the hilt of his gun all the way, just in case, but he was also judiciously reluctant to pull it out, which was to Fitzy's serendipitous good fortune.

"Halt!" screamed the guard. "Stop or I'll shoot!" he added, but shooting was not really an option for him, even though he figured the threat of it might get the runner to surrender. The guard had no clue as to what this guy was up to, aside from unlocking the airplane. In the squat guard's experience there was an unsettling quality about the whole abandon aircraft episode that felt more like a prank than a crime. But what was it? He was trying to figure that out as he chased his suspect, slowly falling behind.

Did the runner stop just then, look back, and wait a beat for him to catch up? That would be especially weird, the security guard thought, between gasps. But the part-time guard knew nothing about goings-on in the cold-fusion research world. He may have read or heard the news about the multiple killings and the burned-to-the-ground garage in Pasadena and he may have heard about a California Technological University professor somewhere in the thick of it, but the guard certainly didn't associate those events in Pasadena with what was going on at the Big Bear Airport that day. He could not have guessed he had become a player in events that would shape history, nor could he have guessed the CTU scientist from the news was on a motorcycle roaring into his world while he chased a trespasser along the one and only Big Bear airport runway, shouting for him to stop. International intrigue and the future of global energy were not on the security guard's radar screen that day or any other day. He was just an off-duty cop trying to make an extra buck working at a quiet, rural airport, and wishing he'd gone to the Pumpkin Festival because some really strange shit was happening.

CHAPTER 97

As Lieutenant Jack was running, as he was glancing back at his pursuer and glancing beyond him to the Cessna, he could see the Harley-Davidson motorcycle arriving with two passengers, sliding sideways to a stop right beside the waiting aircraft. Fitzgerald was calculating while he ran away that Preston Cook had arrived with Big Buster Bernard. He was hoping Dalton had already come down through the trees to the airplane as was planned. Fitzgerald Jack smiled inwardly as he turned and continued running. He had gambled the guard wasn't going to shoot him dead, and thus far it was paying off.

Huffing madly the short, curly-headed guard realized he had to let go of the problems back at the airplane because his rangy partner was at that very moment striding as fast as he could from the control building toward the Cessna. Unlike his shorter partner, the lanky, red-faced security guard was infused with indignation at the brazen intrusion of the motorcycle across airport property, ripping up a well-tended flowerbed in the process, which was an ironic sin for garden-sensitive Martin Speck.

Unfortunately, the leaner security guard had no compunction whatsoever about hauling out *his* service revolver, being far less disturbed by the complexity of the situation than his partner who was scampering off in hot pursuit of the Deadbolt cracker. In fact, the tall, thin guard brandished his Colt .38 police special as he ran forward toward the airplane and the Harley-Davidson motorcycle, yelling at the top of his lungs for everyone to "Stand still! Don't move!"

Right on time, Dalton had appeared from the tree line just before the motorcycle came to a sideways halt in the grass adjacent to the plane and he ran ecstatically toward the Cessna and his father. The boy was overcome with happiness to see his dad, even though the man with him was not Big Buster. There was no waving of Dalton's hands or yelling that was needed to capture Preston's full attention, because the scientist saw his son immediately. Climbing off the Harley, Dr. Cook dropped the cold fusion future-of-the-world suitcase in the raggedy grass and ran toward Dalton. They hugged in the shadow of the Cessna's wing and Martin Speck allowed them their moment.

After a few beats, he said, "That's enough, darlings."

Dalton and Preston turned toward Cain and tensely waited. "Who is that man?" asked Dalton to his dad, but Dalton got no immediate answer.

The three of them standing adjacent to the Cessna were interrupted at that moment by the shouting, tall, boney and red-faced security guard who had been galumphing directly toward them all the way from the control building, several hundred yards behind him. Just like his curly-headed colleague, the lanky guard had no inkling of what was going on that day or with whom he was dealing. Unfortunately, skinny-guard chose to waive his handgun around in a bizarre demonstration of authority. He obviously thought it was a good idea. With a loud *crack* he fired a warning shot into the air to get control of the situation. The rangy security guard loved being on the job at the airport whenever possible, because unlike his typical police-deputy routines, he was in control at the airport. He could tell people what to do and they would do it. The rangy guard figured he would get these motorcycle rowdies to understand who was in charge and a gunshot into the air had accomplished exactly that for him in the past when he was on regular duty. In those cases his peacekeeping usually involved inebriated locals shoving each other around outside a mountain tavern at two o'clock in the morning. But the control he sought on that cool day in October 2005 was not what he achieved.

"Stop right there!" shouted the guard following his warning shot into the air.

Preston and his son could hear the skinny security guard yelling, who unlike his curly-headed counterpart had no Pumpkin Festival options to have kept him away, nor did he want any.

"Put your hands up!" the guard shouted, still waiving his Colt revolver around like it was a baton. They could also see the guard had slowed to a walk at that point and he was breathing heavily from his pursuit. He was about twenty yards from them when he chose to level his service revolver in their direction as though he meant business, which was a major error in judgment.

"Don't even think about it, or you're dead meat!" the guard commanded as if he was a cop in a television show, figuring in a misbegotten way that he was in his element. But Cain's Desert Eagle was out from his backside clip and was discharged before the thin guard could even recognize that any one of them was armed. The fifty caliber slug hit the guard in his larynx and went right out the back of his neck tearing his spinal column apart at the third vertebrae. If the skinny, Irish guard had lived, he'd have been on life support from that moment on, so perhaps it was by the grace of fate that he died quickly, knocked flat on his back by the impact, where he twitched around in the tall grass for several seconds before he was gone.

Preston grabbed Dalton to his chest quickly and hugged him tightly. The boy was stunned rigid by what he had just witnessed. "It's going to be okay," whispered Preston into his son's hair, trying to calm him. "It's going to be okay," he repeated, because it was all he knew to say in the presence of such bloodshed, a level of graphic violence that had been totally unknown to the sensitive and loving boy. Before the last couple of days, it was a level unknown to Preston, as well.

Although he had whispered to his son that things were "going to be okay", the truth was Preston really had no earthly idea if things were going to be okay. Preston and Dalton were in the hands of an unpredictable professional killer, and at that moment, anything could happen.

While hugging his father with his cheek buried into Preston's side, Dalton looked at the stranger and said seriously, "You are an evil man!" which were probably the nastiest words the boy had ever issued to anyone in his life and they had come from the darkest place Dalton had ever sensed within himself.

Cain looked at the boy for a long moment. The possible truth of what Dalton said had wormed into his contemplations too often in recent years. "Perhaps I am," he replied softly. Martin Speck did not choose evil. He was just doing his job.

Toward the west end of the runway at the Big Bear airport, the curly-headed guard in hot pursuit heard the distant report of the Desert Eagle and he had to pause. He knew the sound of his partner's .38 police special, but that gunshot sounded more like a Howitzer. It echoed around the airport and up the mountain, so he turned and glanced back toward the renegade airplane to see what had happened. He knew any gunshot could mean nothing but trouble and immediately a chill raced up his spine when the short guard saw his partner lying in the grass. Oh, my god, he thought, not knowing in that moment whether to run back toward the Cessna or to continue his pursuit. He knew the dumb bastard must have pulled out his gun! Over the months they had actually compared notes while wasting away hours there at the airport, wrangling over the pros and cons of displaying firearms.

The entire scenario of the uninvited Cessna and a foot race down the runway had in a flash transformed itself from hijinks into something ice-cold and deadly. Everything had changed. The running man was now an accomplice to homicide, so the short guard resolved on the spot that he could not let the runner get away. He owed it to his partner.

The short guard knew that in his very brief pause to look back, the runner would have gained distance. Yet, when the curly guard swiveled back into the chase, he was shocked to find the runner had stopped dead in his tracks and put his hands in the air! What was that about? He was surrendering? The curly guard's imagination raced around searching for dangers and for reasons. Something was very, very fishy. This was not how hot pursuits go!

After a shooting in which his partner had been killed the curly guard had no choice but to draw his own Big Bear PD service revolver from its holster, just as his colleague had done, and he aimed it in both outstretched hands directly at the runner. Unlike his dead partner, the short curly guard chose to accomplish his maneuver in very slow motion and without dramatic flourish. He slowed his pace to a walk and he judiciously crouched as he approached the man he had been chasing, even though the man appeared to be giving himself up.

"I'm with the Los Angeles Police Department," said the runner calmly. "My name is Lieutenant Fitzgerald Jack."

"I don't care if you're J. Edgar Hoover," said the guard. "Get down on your knees and put your hands behind your head." He kept the business end of the Colt revolver pointed directly at Fitzy's chest.

Lt. Jack did exactly as he had been told and went to his knees, locking both hands at the back of his skull. He made no sudden moves and he did not attempt to provide identification. He was silent. He let this security guard take charge. Fitzgerald was not interested in being a threat, but he could not help but be interested in what was happening back at the Cessna, having heard the Desert Eagle's resounding report, too, and having also seen the lanky guard sprawled in the grass. Fitzgerald tried as best he could to look down the runway toward the airplane. He was very worried. Clearly, things were not going the way he had drawn them up. He calculated accurately in his mind that Big Buster was not with Preston Cook on the motorcycle as they were expecting, but the assassin was.

"There's a killer back there!" Fitzy tried on impulse with his captor.

"You bet there is," said the rigid guard, his revolver still aimed directly at his captive. And not knowing exactly what to do at this point, he simply said, "Stay still."

"A professional assassin! I'm *not* with him. I'm a *cop*," Fitzgerald said urgently, staring into the curly guard's large brown eyes.

But the guard's brown eyes merely stared back at Lt. Jack like he was a lunatic, even though what the suspect was saying could be true. What did the security guard know? That day had run completely off the tracks. "Be quiet," he said firmly to Fitzgerald, while still panting heavily. Then he hauled out his cell phone from a leg pocket on his cargo pants. Cell phones usually worked pretty well around the airport because it was an open area and it was in direct line of sight to a relay station near the terminal, a station busily chirping away to one of those satellites gliding silently far overhead in space, doing its job without distraction, which is exactly what the curly-headed short guard really wanted for himself at his airport gig.

CHAPTER 98

"What do you want from us?" Preston said soberly to Cain, as he held Dalton by his side with an arm around the boy although there was little he could really do in the face of Cain's capabilities. "Let my son go and I'll do whatever you want. The cold fusion reactor? Do you want it? It's yours," Preston said and he nodded toward the device, lying there in the tall grass, hidden snuggly within the unassuming aluminum carry-on. "Take it!" Both Preston and Cain glanced momentarily at the grip like it was crammed with millions of dollars from a bank heist gone wrong.

Dalton, however, was not at all interested in the suitcase. He was focused on his father. "Dad, you're coming with me aren't you?" he said ignoring the adults' conversation and suddenly terrified that they might be separated again. "We're getting out of here!"

Preston stroked Dalton's hair and said softly, "Shhhh. We'll see. If I can't stay right now, I won't be gone for long." And he turned fully back to Cain who stood his ground sternly, some ten paces away near the Harley while his Desert Eagle hung in his right hand. Even without the silencer the huge handgun's long barrel reached below Cain's knee. A trail of smoke rose from the weapon's muzzle, a wisp of evidence left behind by its deadly work.

"I don't want the reactor," said Cain flatly leaving Dr. Cook perplexed. Cain was not a simple man and he had a keen sense of the surreptitious world-wide attention the cold fusion creation had garnered, even by rumor, and he understood clearly why such attention would exist, including the white hot interest of his current employer. No one wanted this machine to upset the world's energy status quo… *unless* the interested party could *own* the machine! Possession changed the whole equation for each player in what had become an international competition. If the secret to a sea change in the delivery of energy to the world and the immeasurable wealth and power accompanying that secret was going to drop in someone's pocket, none of the power brokers wanted it to be in anyone's pocket but their own. Martin Speck had already concluded for himself that he was not going to deliver that fabulous instrument to the unsavory character who had hired him. It wasn't a contractual requirement and, knowing his employer like he did, handing over a miracle just didn't seem like the right thing to do. Notions of right and wrong did play an odd ancillary role in Cain's life, and when he was able to invoke what was right without it intruding upon his assignment for the day, he was pleased to do so.

Cain was personally quite amazed at what Dr. Cook had contrived in his private laboratory, humbled by it actually, to the degree that a man in Cain's line of work could be humbled. A different Martin Speck, a Martin Speck who was not hired to either capture the cold fusion concept or eliminate it from the planet altogether, might have joined forces with Preston Cook, might have aspired to a more altruistic goal. Such was not a difficult stretch for the high-minded side of Martin Speck that regaled in natural beauty. Comprehending the spectacle of a star nebula is not so far removed from comprehending the spectacle of a giant tiger orchid.

Yet, capturing or eliminating the cold fusion invention were the two options in Martin Speck's marching orders and he had already concluded that eliminating the device was going to be his choice. His contract regarding this new energy source was signed and sealed, so there would be no backing out. Cain had his business principles and he absolutely never violated the terms of an agreement. It was an iron law in his mind. He had to follow through. He always did. If it were any other way, there would be no further contracts coming to him in the rarified violent world in which he lived.

"Dalton?" said Martin Speck to Preston's son, trying his best to be as earnest and non-threatening as he was able in a highly charged circumstance. "Would you please come over here and stand by me? Don't be afraid. I'm not going to hurt you." Children did not play a large role in Cain's life and he was always uncomfortable around them. On the other hand, he knew that respect and honesty work well with most human beings and the young ones were likely no different. But honesty and respect weren't magical and the boy had just witnessed a true horror.

"No!" Dalton replied angrily and he clung to his father.

"I know that what you saw here was ugly and it was unfair," said Cain to the boy. Maintaining eye contact with Dalton, he gestured toward the dead security guard and added, "That is not what I want. I have seen many terrible things in my life, the kinds of things that I hope you will never see," he said. "I will not hurt you," said Speck truthfully. And in an odd connection of dots that strangely worked in the mind of Dalton, the boy regarded Cain differently after that was said. The boy's internal antennae were finely tuned and active.

Preston operated on a more rational level and he understood logically they were not in a negotiating position, so he bent down and whispered in Dalton's ear. "You have to do what this man says right now. He isn't going to do anything bad. Everything will be okay. You have always been brave, our beautiful Dalton." And with that he lifted his son's hands away from his waist, which was the most painful, single physical act he had ever performed in his entire life, and nudged his son in the direction of the assassin. "Go on. It'll be okay," he reassured to Dalton. Even though Dalton was not comfortable doing so, he did very tentatively move over next to Martin Speck while keeping his eyes glued on his father.

Cain looked at the boy and said sincerely, "Thank you, Dalton. I will take you home. I promise."

"Now," said Cain, returning to Dr. Cook, who was apprehensive, eyes open, and attentive. "Pick up your invention."

"Go on," Cain insisted after he saw no movement from the professor. And finally Preston did what he was told.

As Preston lifted the carry-on case from the tall grass where it had been dropped Cain said, "Put the device on the passenger seat of the airplane, please."

Preston Cook was getting the drill by then and he promptly did as he was instructed, opening the passenger door to the Cessna and shoving the baggage containing the much sought-after cold fusion instrument onto the seat.

"Good," said Cain. "Thank you. And now, this is what I want you to do, Dr. Cook," he continued matter-of-factly. "Get into your airplane, with your invention and take off. Fly directly toward that setting sun," he said pointing toward the blinding orb burning a path toward the horizon in the west. "Fly in a direct line. Follow the sun. Keep going and do not turn around."

Preston's eyes widened. In that moment he understood the objective.

"Where is he going?" said Dalton.

Cain ignored the youngster's question and Preston knew why.

"My job is either to bring home the item or erase it," said Cain. "I've looked for your engineering plans. There are none," he said recalling the razing of the garage laboratory and the ransacking of the dead, philandering partner's apartment. All related computers were in ashes and no public announcements had been made.

"We were careful about that," said Preston.

"I understand," said Cain. "It's safer to keep the plans in your head."

"Yes," said Preston, seeing where this was going.

"So, fly west and everything will take care of itself," said Cain. "Do you understand?"

Preston just stood there trying to absorb the task that had just befallen him and then he said, nodding, "Yes. I understand."

"I will escort your son home, as promised," said Martin Speck. "But if you do not follow my instructions and if I hear anything about a deviation from the plan, then I will come back and I will find you. I will find Dr. Day-Steiner. And I will find Dalton. Do you get my meaning? There will be no negotiating on that day."

"Yes," said Preston. "I get your point." He was absolutely convinced the man was telling him a gospel truth that was totally in keeping with the strange work he did in his very strange world. Cain would do exactly what he vowed he would do and he would succeed. Preston glimpsed the future. If he did not follow Cain's instructions to the letter, then the assassin would be back to do his dirty work on Preston's entire family.

"I pay attention. I track things. I am reliable," said Cain.

"Yes. I understand," repeated Preston coldly and looking straight into Martin Speck's unwavering gaze.

"Okay then," said Cain concluding they had come to an understanding. He glanced toward the sun which was already sinking in the west and casting long shadows across the mountain community of Big Bear, eventide shadows marking the end of the day. "You'd best be on your way," he said. "In an hour or so it will be dark."

Preston looked at Dalton and came over to him and knelt down in the tall grass to look him square in the eyes. "Go with this man," he said to Dalton, who was trembling, terrified, stiff, and uncertain as to what it all meant. "He will take you home," Preston said. "Your mother will be home soon. And I… I will be in touch later," he said. "Be a courageous young man right now. Okay? We're depending on you," Preston said.

"How much later?" asked Dalton.

"Not too much later. Not much. Don't worry."

The boy did not know what to say, but his eyes were welling up.

"I love you so much," Preston said and hugged his son who hugged him back tightly around his neck.

"I love you, too, Dad."

"You are such a brave guy to come here to help me. I am so very, very proud of you. And I will always be proud of you."

And then, once again, Preston had to remove the boy's hands from around him when he stood up.

"You take care of my son," he said to Cain. "He has done nothing wrong."

"I keep my word," said Cain and it was absolutely true.

So, Preston went to his Cessna, an aircraft that had probably flown him an equivalent of around the world a couple of times over the years and he climbed on board and he cranked up the engine. Lucky 47 roared into life immediately, dust flying backward from the tall grasses in the props' wake. Preston glanced out the window to where Dalton stood looking back at him, so alone and so small next to a dangerous stranger with a large gun. Tears were brimming in Dalton's eyes.

Dr. Cook smiled and gave a thumbs-up toward his son. "The center of stars!" he shouted above the roar of the engine.

And Dalton shouted back and gave a thumbs-up while trying to hold his tears, "The center of stars!"

Then Preston pulled on the throttle and the plane rolled around and bounced across the rough turf toward the runway.

Martin Speck and Dalton watched as the Cessna made its way to the tarmac and pivot toward the west. Preston cranked up the engine at that point and the aircraft provided its customary take-off shiver before it began to roll forward along the black pavement picking up speed, heading down the runway with the sun a blinding disk in the sky straight ahead. The airplane roared ahead, screaming past the place where the short security guard was leaning into a conversation on his cell phone and where Fitzgerald Jack knelt with his hands behind his head. Preston's eyes and Lt. Jack's eyes made fleeting contact as the Cessna lifted into the chilly October sky.

Fitzgerald knew things had not gone right. He didn't have a clue as to why Preston Cook would be flying away alone like he was, but it wasn't according to plan and the Lieutenant was absolutely sure it could not be good. His heart felt like a rock in the center of his chest.

CHAPTER 99

After Preston had taken off, Fitzgerald glanced once again toward the farther end of the runway to where the Cessna had been parked and he could see the Harley-Davidson motorcycle cranking up with two riders astride her again, only a few yards from the dead security officer lying in the grass. Lt. Jack could clearly make out one of the riders as young Dalton which meant the motorcycle driver must be the assassin, Cain. And at that very moment, the bike took off as fast as the Cessna, retracing its own tire tracks across the runway toward the previously gouged flower bed adjacent to the terminal and streaking past the gawking witnesses who had followed the skinny guard out of the terminal building, speeding away from the scene of the crime to race down the mountain prior to the delayed arrival of Big Bear city police.

Fitzgerald Jack felt a painful hopelessness as he watched the Harley depart. He imagined that everything had gone totally awry and it was entirely his fault. Why had he suggested the plan he did to that boy? He recognized he could not quickly untangle himself from his immediate predicament to intercept the motorcycle and rescue Dalton, but he had to at least try something!

"The killer is getting away!" Fitzgerald cried out desperately and as fervently as he could, nodding toward the escaping assassin and his captive. "Do you have a car?"

The curly-haired security guard, while on his phone, did turn and glance toward the escaping Harley racing across the runway and then grinding up the flower bed next to the terminal building before vanishing from sight, but in that glance the guard also revisited the sight of his partner lying dead in the weeds.

"Shut up," he said to Lt. Jack and he leaned back into his call, futilely attempting to locate any manner of police support.

For Preston Cook everything in the universe had turned upside down. He was in the process of discovering just how easily a human being can slide toward insanity. The future that he envisioned for himself and his family and for the world, too, had disappeared down a trap door. Madness entangled his brain like Alzheimer's plaques, changing his priorities and perceptions, and painting a horrific and bleak denouement. This new reality huddled coldly around him in his small Cessna cockpit like whispering ciphers. He was chilled by the voices so much that he shivered where he sat, eyes roaming the empty sky and sea that spread ahead of him as he flew past the coastline. He tried to steel himself for what was coming because his situation was completely surreal and totally unimaginable to an awakened mind, to the mind he had possessed earlier that very day. In fact, he ran through mathematical equations to confirm his mental trajectory. He was a scientist, so he did the arithmetic, balancing probabilities on one side of the equation against probabilities on the other side, proving again and again to himself that his decision was inevitable. His flight *had* to happen. Turning the airplane around and *not* chasing the sun to an unreachable horizon would be unacceptable in his topsy-turvy situation. Preston Cook had no choice but to do what he was doing, fly straight ahead. He could not figure any angle out of it, any silent escape route or missed loophole in the agreement. Cain made for an iron clad contract.

Gallows humor bubbled up like lava in the absurdity of developments and Preston laughed out loud at himself. "Ha!" The discoverer of sub-atomic secrets, the finder of the hidden keys to practical, workable, safe and affordable cold fusion, the man who was born to save humanity from its own energy gluttony, Dr. Preston Cook, was now choosing to erase any evidence of his monumental work by plunging a little, one-engine airplane directly into the Pacific Ocean more than a hundred miles from land! To most people, if any act could define madness, this would be it!

He'd gone through the dialogue in his head repeatedly after lifting off from the Big Bear airport and leaving his son behind with that man, that murderer. Yet in spite of Cain's reputation and actions, Preston completely believed Dalton *would* be delivered to his home as promised, a bizarre positive outcome in the strangely twisted new landscape that had arisen. Martin Speck was a monster to be sure, but he was a monster with a sense of responsibility and commitment, as oddly defined as they were. Sadly enough, Preston knew many men and women with less true commitment, men and women with a much weaker sense of responsibility, who lived acclaimed lives at CTU. His dead research partner, Maxwell Umberto, was an exemplar of misbegotten commitments. Dr. Cook had seen enough of Speck's values to believe he would be true to his word. Cain had said he would take Dalton home and Preston was convinced Cain *would* take Dalton safely home, someway, somehow. Likewise, he also realized that Sam would find her way out of the mountains and down to Pasadena, safely home, someway, somehow. She was a resourceful woman. Those twin firm beliefs in Cain and in Sam were all that kept Preston from losing his ability to function within an emotional whirlwind inside the small airplane. As he sat at the controls, guiding the Cessna straight ahead, his trust in the safety of his son and his wife were the only protections he had from the all-consuming horror that confronted him.

Cain was absolutely capable of locating Preston's entire family if the agreed upon flight plan was not followed on that October day, no matter where the Cook family eventually turned up. Martin Speck – under some new pseudonym – would exact his pound of flesh, just as he promised. In Preston's world, one had always used empirical evidence to make decisions, data driven decision-making, they call it. And Preston, the physicist, was as sure retribution would come his way if he reneged on his agreement with Cain as he was sure cold fusion was possible when he began his speculations about it years ago. There were doubters then, but he was doggedly sure in those days and he was doggedly sure on the day he flew over the Pacific Ocean. Grotesquely enough, it was also his faith in Cain the assassin's wrath that kept Preston going.

When it was all over and done with, people would routinely ask, "What if that missing professor flew north instead? What if he flew south? What if he hid his airplane at this place or at that place?" For a short period after the crash there would be *LA Times* articles about Dr. Cook's very strange choice for suicide and there would be suspicions that it wasn't on the up and up. "What if he jumped to safety and let the plane go?" people would ask. But none of those schemes would have worked, Preston concluded on his last day in the air, certainly they would not have worked with sufficient assurance that his wife and son would be safe to live out the long, happy lives they both deserved. None of those latter-day speculators and doubters reading the *LA Times* editorials about Preston Cook's disappearance at sea could possibly have comprehended in their imaginings the presence of a menace like Cain and what was truly at stake.

Dr. Cook was flying out over open water, almost a hundred miles from the coast with his invention propped silently on the seat next to him like a snoozing passenger in his trusty Cessna Skyhawk. Land was nowhere to be seen. Only vast stretches of a sparkling and dark sea lay around him. The plane's engine droned and pulled and did its job, staying on course toward the setting sun. All of Preston's hopes were gone at that point, gone into the void. Almost no one in the world would ever know how very close the entire planet had been to a new order of limitless energy. Hunger and the swollen bellies of starving children may have well have become a phenomenon of history, like leprosy. Humanity was on the doorstep to energy salvation in 2005. Everything could have been so very different… *forever*! But none of it was to be. Then Preston laughed again, "Ha!" And he said out loud, "Well, at least nobody is going to miss cold fusion! Nobody even knew it was here!"

Then, out of the corner of his eye, Preston caught glimpse of a Boeing 747. The jet was about fifteen thousand feet above him. He leaned forward and looked up at it, all silvery, streaming along the same flight path as his own, but that son of a bitch had somewhere to land. Hawaii? Japan? Who might be aboard that soaring "heavy," as they liked to call jumbo jets in the flight controllers' game? He imagined himself up there, forehead pressed against the plastic inner window looking down at a tiny, tiny Cessna wandering westward far below. Would he have said to himself, "Where does that little guy think he's going?" Probably not. Like all those other souls jetting overhead, he would be too absorbed in the prospects of his own adventure to give that speck of an airplane way down there a second thought.

The lunacy of his situation was near to overwhelming but Dr. Cook steadfastly continued on his final mission. In the end, that quality of determination had fairly defined his life. He knew unequivocally on that day of destiny gliding above the dark and deep Pacific Ocean what had always been true in his heart. He would never sacrifice his family in exchange for his work in spite of how obsessed with it he may have seemed. He had to let himself and cold fusion disappear forever to save the people he loved more than life. There was no other option.

CHAPTER 100

After having been deposited by Martin Speck at an intersection half a block north of his home in Pasadena, Dalton Cook walked at a careful pace carrying the flowered helmet he had worn. He moved slowly along the shaded avenue where he had sometimes played late into the evening during his young life. His face was tight with worry about what he would find when he reached his home. Dalton's heroic flight to save his father notwithstanding, in the end he was only a twelve year-old boy who wanted his life with his mom and dad to return to normal. He looked up at the Chinese elms that were still full of leaves in October despite recent chilly weather. It was reassuring for Dalton to see those friendly trees.

Dalton had been instructed to go straight to Cloud Willow's house and that is precisely where he was heading. All the while, Speck sat patiently watching Dalton from Buster's idling Fantail Classic, well behind the youngster in the long shadows of the elms. The assassin was fulfilling his promise to Dr. Cook to deliver his son to the boy's home and Cain was waiting until Dalton completed the mission. Cloud Willow's house, the Cook family's neighbor in Pasadena, had been specified as the rendezvous site two hours earlier when his mother spoke with Dalton through the boy's cell phone just as he and Cain commenced their descent down the Rim of World Highway toward San Bernardino. Like everything else in those very strange days, events were transpiring like a close order drill.

Not having had her special Cook family cell phone with her at the moment of abduction outside Lt. Jack's apartment in Hollywood, Samantha had to ultimately connect with her son through an old-fashioned land line at the Marine base in Twenty-Nine Palms.

The sprawling desert facility was characterized by barracks, by wind and dust, and not much else. There had been a nominal effort to make the buildings, entrance, and commissary appealing to families and guests, but it didn't work. It was no wonder the locals referred to the base as Twenty-Nine Stumps. To call her son, Dr. Day-Steiner used a square, black Ma Bell push-button telephone from a by-gone era sitting heavily on a nurse's desk in the sparse but ample emergence room at the base infirmary.

When Samantha finally spoke to Dalton she could feel stress and horrific pressure lift from her shoulders and vanish into the cold, dry desert air. She was then able to regroup sufficiently to tell Dalton that she would collect him at Cloud Willow's house as soon as she could get back into town. She had no confidence in the condition of the Cook house in Pasadena after what had transpired there with the police and the fire.

Cain had advised Dalton to tell his mother only that he would be there soon and avoid mentioning with whom he was riding, because Cain assumed that at the mention of his name things would start to unravel. Fortunately, Samantha did not pursue it. Simply hearing her son's voice was such a tremendous relief to her heart and mind. Dalton was safe and that covered her primary worry. She pictured his young, honest face and she was so eager to kiss him and hold him. Although Samantha had always loved Dalton in her own way, while she was talking with Dalton on the black, desk telephone at the Marine base she was swamped with emotions and she started to cry. For the first time since Dalton was born, Dr. Day-Steiner's son had become for her a wholly adequate and independent reason for being alive, regardless of her career, her status, or her wealth. That unique and bright boy alone brought sufficient meaning for her to be satisfied and happy. It was the first time Dalton had ever heard his mother weep and he did his best to comfort her. "Mom? Mom, it's going to be alright. I'm fine," he had said. He was confused by her tears but he loved her.

While Dalton was walking toward Cloud and Buster's house in Pasadena, beneath the Chinese elms, his mother was finding her way home from Twenty-Nine Palms riding in a Dodge minivan with Sister Josephine, a nun who had been at the base that day to deliver sacraments to servicemen waiting to deploy to Iraq.

After the helicopter evacuation from their mountain confrontation with Cain, Big Buster and Samantha had both been treated in top-notch order at what proved to be an up-to-the-minute medical facility packed inside the infirmary at the Marine base. With Bobby Skylar's 9 mm slug removed from his leg, Buster had received blood and antibiotics and stitches, as well as the strong recommendation from his physician that he remain at the base at least twenty-four hours. While politely acknowledging the Marine doctor's concerns and his experience with bullet wounds and blood loss, Buster opted to head home with Samantha when the opportunity presented itself.

On the other hand, sitting upright proved to be a different proposition for Buster and he fainted dead away the first time he attempted it. After that episode he concluded perhaps another day at Twenty-Nine Palms was the better plan. So, Dr. Day-Steiner gave her large, wounded neighbor a peck on the cheek, thanked her Marine Corps benefactors for all of their good will and their excellent care and she caught a ride home with Sister Josephine.

Sister Josephine was bone skinny, looking comical in a habit that hung around her like she'd borrowed it from someone twice her size. Yet she was more than willing to drop Samantha off at Cloud Willow's house in Pasadena on her way back to Eagle Rock where she lived in a two-bedroom apartment with another nun. The drop-off was on her way.

In truth, Sister Josephine didn't really take to being alone while driving down from Twenty-Nine Palms, which may have been an odd characteristic for someone with her calling. And the ride back to Pasadena for Dr. Day-Steiner was more than paid for by her having to answer a parade of questions from Sister Josephine whose thin, sharp jaw would not stop moving. She was up to the minute on all the juicy news and the goings-on around a missing scientist, a murdered CTU professor, and a possible connection to a murdered UCLA med student, too! She'd seen much of it on television, including the immolated garage laboratory at the house in Pasadena and she basically would not shut up during a ride of more than three hours all the way from the Marine Corps base in the desert to Pasadena. Early in their shared ride she discovered she had the *actual wife* of the vanished professor sitting right next to her! It was manna from heaven for Sister Josephine! She could barely contain herself!

"As I understand it" Sister Josephine said to Samantha like they were new best friends, "there was this playboy physicist who was murdered and is somehow involved. Is that right?" Sister Josephine asked the question and she pushed her starched white coif upward from her forehead because it tended to slip forward. She glanced with a toothy grin eagerly at Dr. Day-Steiner, anticipating a truthful answer.

"Watch the road," advised Samantha.

Then Samantha studied the emaciated driver beside her, wrapped in loose black cloth. Their eyes did play together for a moment as

Sister Josephine waited with an expectant grin that she could not contain, while Sam was concluding in that very same moment the crazy broad at the wheel shouldn't be tending to souls, she should be working for the *National Enquirer*.

CHAPTER 101

When the fuel finally ran out, when the prop sputtered and came to a stop directly in front of Preston's eyes, it was unreal. It was in slow motion. He could see the black blades whip around and jerk to a halt, one straight up silhouetted against a pale yellow sky surrounding the setting sun. Impulsively he pulled on the throttle. Just a pint more gas! An ounce, for god's sake, to have final thoughts! It was an impulse that didn't last long. His fuel gage read empty. He was done for.

There was nothing but silence and wind whistling around the cockpit as the Cessna began its descent. It was graceful at first as Preston took a deep breath and he pulled back on the yoke, trying to keep the nose upright, but soon the dropping airspeed would not allow for lifting the nose. He knew in moments he would go into a stall and lose control, which was perhaps a strange concern, given the inevitability of what the next ninety seconds would bring. Yet in that moment, Preston realized he did not want to hit the water at a steep angle and in a spin. He did not want his flesh to be mingled in the disastrous rending of his precious Skyhawk's light metal skin, airframe, and engine as it hit a water surface as impenetrable as cement. Consequently, he calculated he could bring the old girl in on a level angle of attack if he went into a dive, using his altitude to collect airspeed and then pull out of the dive toward the end and level out. So, that's what he did. He aimed straight down at the delicately laced white-caps licked by sea breezes in mid-ocean. Even as those frothy white-caps grew larger in his eyes he waited by seat-of-the-pants reckoning until the time was right. Then Preston pulled back as hard as he could on the control wheel. He gritted his teeth and by will power alone he hauled that son of a bitch back toward his chest! It was not easy at the nearly 100 knots he'd earned in free fall, but with that fresh velocity available the nose of the Cessna did rise toward the horizon. And as she leveled out, the plane was only meters above the waves. Sea water was misting across the windshield as Preston piloted his descent in a proper landing path to the ocean's surface. He raced through his memory for any pointers he'd received along the way about water landings, but he could not recall even one; so he just guesstimated at what to do. He was a physicist after all! The basics were right there around him. How does one maintain stability in a situation where landing gear will dig into water first? A quick forward flip and an upside-down smash into the drink would likely be the result.

Preston chose full flaps toward the end, for maximum lift. Fortunately for the outcome on his very last science experiment, the surface of the Pacific Ocean was rather smooth for deep water, displaying shallow swells crested by seraphim. He approached his touch-down just as he would on an asphalt runway; but in this case he planned to pull back viciously at the very last instant to drop his tail wings directly into the sea as a brake. Preston hoped the plane would then slap down onto the water upright, slowed sufficiently by the tail that it would not tumble as the landing gear and fuselage dove beneath the surface and brought the aircraft to a stop. At least, that was his plan. He was down to less than fifty knots. The overhead wings would hit the water last, he calculated, after the cockpit was submerged. Maybe the wings would provide enough resistance to keep the Cessna from going further down right away if they didn't rip away from their struts, but the cockpit would surely be mostly underwater. Lucky 47 was probably not that buoyant, he reckoned, and she would not remain on the surface for long. Sea water would be pouring in immediately from everywhere and Preston knew he would not be able to open a door until the pressure inside the plane equaled the pressure outside, which meant he had to let the cockpit fill up. According to his best guess, the plane would be tipping forward and heading toward the bottom before he could escape… if escaping and then slowly drowning after bobbing around the middle of the ocean was the way he preferred to die.

Right at that moment, in those last bizarre seconds, Preston noticed a school of bottle-nosed dolphins diving and swimming parallel to his descent. The dolphins seemed to be having a grand old time, cavorting there, racing the airplane. It was all just good fun to them. It is peculiar what one will consider when one has only sufficient time remaining in life to think about two or three things and Preston would never have guessed the motives of dolphins would have been one of them.

Preston hauled his attention back to the crisis at hand and rather than thoughts of dolphins he began to retrieve from memory images of his son and his wife. For reasons unknown to him, he recalled a day when they were on vacation two years ago at Disney World in Florida. It was a serendipitous day, magnificent beyond planning, one of the most wonderful days of his entire life. They were all in good spirits and joyful. And in those fractions of a second as the Cessna finally touched the ocean's frothy surface, Preston managed to magically connect with the contentment and happiness he had known on that special day. He recognized in those micro-moments as the landing gear bit into the sea that one particular afternoon in Florida two years past truly defined his adventure on earth. It was not cold fusion, not CTU, not his publications, and not his acclaim that had made his life worthwhile. Instead, it was one simple, sunny day on a family vacation when all he felt was a circle of devotion. That was the center of stars for him.

Dalton walked forward in his old neighborhood, following Cain's instructions, but he was terribly frightened, worrying about his mom and worrying about his dad, too, out there somewhere in Lucky 47 chasing the sun. The boy didn't understand the meaning of his dad's flight. He didn't understand the meaning of any of the chaos that had commandeered his comfortable young boy's life, but understand it or not, he knew he did not like what was happening around him.

He glanced over his shoulder as he neared his own house, just to check, and he saw Cain sitting there on the Harley watching him, watching him walk all the way to his destination. It was parental in an unexpected sort of way. Cain was waiting to confirm that Cloud Willow was actually home and that the boy would be delivered to his mother through Cloud Willow. That was the covenant he had made to the physicist, Preston Cook, prior to his take-off at Big Bear airport and by proxy to the mathematician, Samantha Day-Steiner, via Dalton's conversation with her not that long ago. Cain was nothing if he was not a man who embraced a covenant.

Dalton approached and then gingerly passed his own house which at first appeared strangely normal while eerily quiet, deserted and dark. The boy didn't like the feeling it engendered. He went cautiously by the house, where yellow crime-scene tape marked-off the entire property and a Pasadena policeman snoozed in a patrol car at the opposite curb with an open copy of *Guns & Ammo* on his lap. Dalton walked slowly to where the house's long driveway led to the back of the property, to where the garage laboratory had once modestly stood and that's when the boy's heart sank in his chest.

He suddenly saw the ashen remains of the place where he and his dad had been partners in taking a deep dive into the center of stars, the origins of life, the origins of all things. By then the garage was nothing more than a pile of charcoal, with unidentifiable lumps here and there and the sharp edges of metal equipment still visible in the midst of black rubble. It had all been so totally destroyed by the powdered napalm Cain had used that it was startling to see. But it was also amazing to observe how untouched the main house was, merely twenty feet away from what must have been a furiously focused conflagration.

The boy did not have the privilege of sifting through Maxwell Umberto's incinerated town home, nor sifting through his equally immolated office at CTU to know how powdered napalm works. Nonetheless, while inquisitive Dalton could see there was evidence of smoke damage on the main house, with slight burns on the wall nearest to an outrageously intense fire, he also could see it was a miracle the actual house had not been consumed along with the garage. And although Dalton had been scrupulously instructed by his mother to eschew any belief in miracles, his father had said he saw miracles in everything they did together. The entire universe was a miracle.

When Dalton approached the perimeter of Cloud's and Buster's property next door to his house in Pasadena, he took off and ran the rest of the way. The stress of it all was just too much. He scampered right up to the front door of Cloud's house and he rang the bell and he pounded as hard as he could. Cloud Willow's old pick-up truck was in the driveway, so Dalton knew she was home. And in a matter of seconds Cloud, flowing in colorful cotton, opened the door. She was overjoyed to see Dalton and she immediately swept him up into her arms, and she swung the boy left and right, and she hugged him and kissed his face.

"Dalton! Dalton, my love! You're here. You're alright, aren't you? Thank God! Thank God! How… did you get here?" she said gushing, and almost in tears herself.

"That man brought me," said Dalton and he pointed back toward the northern end of the street where Cain sat astride Buster Bernard's rumbling hog.

Cloud had already heard from Big Buster, who called from Twenty-Nine Palms on the same black, desk telephone Samantha had used, so she knew Buster was okay. Otherwise the sight of that Harley-Davidson Fantail Classic in those particular circumstances would have sent a flow of ice through her veins.

Even at that distance, some two hundred yards away, Cloud Willow's eyes were able to find and connect with Cain's. They had looked into one another's determined gazes once before. And at that moment of recognition, she saw him toss a very slight two-fingered salute in her direction, clearly acknowledging the boy was now in her care. Then Cain put the Harley into gear, rolled back on the gas, and he took off with a growl, disappearing almost instantly.

CHAPTER 102

Water logged, groggy, flat on his back and coughing up brine, Preston Cook opened his eyes onto clear early-evening October sky with clouds edged in gold high above him. They were magnificent. And even though Preston was having difficulty breathing, he could hear the sweet sound of gulls diving and swarming nearby and he knew in that moment he was not dead, but quite alive. He could smell the sea. He could feel a solid boat deck rocking gracefully beneath where he lay, lifted on the long Pacific Ocean deep-water swells.

Preston was a wasted, thoroughly exhausted man, and in those first moments he could not remember what had happened. He was disoriented and unsure of everything. Vaguely he remembered crashing his Cessna into the ocean. He remembered water pouring through a smashed window to his right and he remembered the airplane listing rapidly and dramatically. He had scrambled to unfasten his seat belt as the Cessna began to sink, foam and ocean water flooding the cabin. Then he faintly remembered a photograph of Sam and Dalton floating near his chin, but after that it all went dark. He could recall nothing more.

He lifted his hand to touch a very tender spot on his forehead and Preston's fingertips came back with wet blood on them. And in that semi-conscious minute, while he was trying to figure out what had happened, Preston looked to his right and he was struck by the sight of a large, faded 47 painted long ago on a weathered boat cabin. Was it his imagination? He knew better than to completely trust his senses at that point. He also smelled fish, lots of fish, and Preston's eyes rolled around in his skull as he struggled to regain full consciousness, as he tried to investigate his totally unexpected environment. There were booms overhead with block and tackle, and heavy black nets hanging near where he lay. He then realized his head was propped up against a thick coil of wet rope. And he came to see there were three very stout men staring at him, three men who had crept cautiously forward as Preston slowly rallied. They were not five feet away by then, looking down at him like he was a space alien hauled up from the sea. They were all darkly tanned and unshaven, wearing rubber overalls and knit caps. They looked rather alike, actually, strangely so, with mustaches, tattoos on their arms, and round bellies. Central casting couldn't have provided a more uniform trio.

Later Preston would discover the men were triplets who owned a fishing boat and when they realized Preston' eyes were open they all began speaking at once, jabbering toward Dr. Cook in frenetic Mexican Spanish, asking questions, pointing here and there, seemingly telling him what happened, hand gesturing about a crashing airplane and its sinking, sound effects and all, but none of their narrative was coordinated, organized, and none of it was comprehensible to Preston, whose Spanish was only passible at Mijares, a Mexican restaurant in Pasadena where "*Fajitas, pour favor*" covered it.

In Preston Cook's state of disorientation and exhaustion, the boat and the brothers' chorus of concern quickly became overwhelming for his frazzled nerves. He desperately wanted to figure out how he ended up where he was, on the deck of what was evidently a commercial trawler. Yet, the scene rather quickly began to spin and it slipped away as Preston succumbed to his bone-deep fatigue. The river of fervent Spanish provided only a fading backdrop to his loss of consciousness.

The triplets did not know what to do with this Yankee they had exhumed from a watery grave, after having witnessed the crash of his small airplane. Shortly after Preston lost consciousness again and they observed his shivering, the three fishermen lugged Preston from where he lay soaked and exhausted at the stern of their boat, into the cabin, which was not that much more comfortable, but at least it provided a sheltered wooden bench on which to place him. Then one of the brothers threw an old, dark and dense woolen blanket over their sleeping guest. It was the only blanket they had on board and the men tucked it around Preston while he slept. The blanket had not been laundered in years and had its own complex aroma, but it did provide warmth. There were not many items on board the trawler that did not have a unique and pungent scent, the very understandable consequence of a daily routine involving a thousand slippery fish freshly hauled from the Pacific Ocean and piled onto a bed of ice in the bowels of the vessel.

One of the brothers folded his well-worn fleece jacket and placed it beneath Preston's head as a pillow and then the triplets stood there watching the stranger sleep. Their attitudes had clearly changed since their first sight of the unexpected passenger. He was more human by then and so were they. After Preston was in the cabin, they hovered around him like he was a newborn and they were as dumbfounded as first-time fathers. None of it was ideal for Preston's recovery, of course, but there wasn't much in the way of creature comforts on that work-worn fishing trawler, chugging homeward through open seawater after the sun had been swallowed up to the west and night had swarmed around them. Those fishermen did all they could to protect the American pilot they happened upon that day, whose aircraft dropped from the sky. They were not formally educated men but they understood life and death at sea and they knew what hypothermia looked like and they knew the basics of how to deal with it.

The crash itself was startling enough as the three brothers would relate it to authorities when they returned to their fishing village, Baja Sur, in Mexico. They were two kilometers away, they said, when they saw an airplane plunge toward the ocean's surface. Then, quite suddenly, at the end of the airplane's fall, when it was very low above the waves, the small airplane pulled up and it leveled out. It actually seemed to be landing on the water! They could not believe their eyes.

They headed as quickly as their old trawler could take them toward the site of the crash. It had not been a good day for their nets and they had already dragged them out of the sea. Given the late hour, the fishermen were looking forward to going home rather than trolling on into the night, which they did routinely when the harvest was robust. On that particular afternoon, they had enough of their nets. But when the plane came down, the men knew immediately they had to help. No one comprehends the meaning of distress and urgency like fisherman. The sea can be cruel and unforgiving and response to crisis goes beyond obligation, it is second-nature.

Of course, on that cool late October afternoon none of those fishermen knew the pilot was out of gas when he ditched and they could not have known anything about his mission to destroy himself and his invention. They did not know about cold fusion and the international implications of what they were witnessing out in deep water. They assumed Preston was an American who lost control of his airplane and crashed. None of the fishermen spoke a word of English but they nonetheless dragged the *gringo* pilot onto the deck of their boat after having witnessed the very odd sight of his landing on the water. The brothers had to first consider the real possibility that Preston was a totally insane and dangerous American, as many Americans were to them. Therefore, they were well advised to be cautious around the pilot after they pulled him up.

When the trawler finally reached Baja Sur toward midnight, the most remarkable thing the three fishermen reported to the authorities, as they handed an enervated, wobbly Preston Cook over to them, was that it took them more than half an hour to reach the site of the Cessna's crash. They said they had to secure their nets and rigging on w47 before launching into their rescue mission. They said they saw the whole thing through binoculars. When that little aircraft slapped down after dragging its tail on the surface of the ocean, it tipped abruptly nose-down and listed to its right. The brothers said the Cessna leaned further starboard and appeared to be taking on water when its tail lifted and it headed to the bottom just like that. The airplane didn't float much over one minute. The brothers were sure they would find no one to rescue after such a swift disappearance of the aircraft beneath the waves, after they had chugged across two kilometers of ocean to the crash site, plowing forward at an agonizingly slow pace.

But when they arrived, they said, they found Preston unconscious and floating face up in the water! There was no debris of any kind at the site. How they found him on an open rolling sea was miraculous in itself. The airplane was completely gone but its pilot was there, bobbing in the seraphim, with his arms and legs stretched out and he was bleeding badly from his scalp. And most amazingly, he was being nudged to the surface where he could continue to breathe, by a school of dolphins! The animals were taking turns flanking his body and keeping him afloat like they could understand Preston needed air. It was an absolutely unbelievable sight! The three fishermen said they had heard stories of dolphins saving men in this way, mistaking a drowning man for another injured dolphin, perhaps, but they had never actually seen it. They said God must have chosen Preston to live.

Dr. Cook comprehended none of that exchange in Spanish, as he stood there with two very unhappy state police officers who had been summoned by the port master to take Preston into custody. They were dispatched to the waterfront on thankless middle-of-the-night duty because of some wayward *gringo*. After taking Preston into custody, the two officers shuffled him down the pier into the small disheveled office of the *Administración Portuaria Integral*, the port administration, to begin questioning the American survivor. One of the officers had become the de facto interpreter, too, since no one else understood English beyond "Okay."

The gendarmes were positioned on each side of Preston as the three fishermen held forth on their peculiar rescue. Preston could clearly see the amazed looks on the officers' faces as the story was told. In fact, the way the officers regarded him afterward was a little bit creepy. He had the odd and unexpected sensation he was a side-show attraction, but Preston didn't really understand.

In the moments following the fishermen brothers' explanation that the American's life had been saved by dolphins after his airplane crashed in the sea, Preston found the presence of mind to inquire, via the one policeman who spoke broken English, what had been said by the fishermen. And upon hearing the tale of the dolphins at his crash site, Preston became momentarily weak in the knees with incredulity. Then, after catching his breath, he followed up by asking why there was a large 47 painted on the cabin of the trawler that had dragged him out of the water. And when the question was passed on to the three brothers, one of them simply said that 47 was always their lucky number! The fisherman added quickly with hearty laughter, that it must be the *gringo's* lucky number, too!

If the dolphin story did not cause Preston to collapse, the number 47 added to the story almost finished the job. He went pale and weak. The officers actually had to hold him up by his elbows, not knowing what was happening, but Preston managed to right himself, drag up a smile and say cordially, "Yes. Yes. You're right. It is my lucky number. You have no idea."

The entire episode was overwhelming and unbelievable. Preston immediately envisioned young Dalton and himself in the garage laboratory behind their Pasadena house trying to uncover the secrets of the universe, the unimaginable magic that happens in the center of stars, magic that obviously exists far beyond the stars and into everyday life on earth. Preston had not planned on being saved that chilly afternoon in 2005. He hit the water figuring he would be dead in a matter of minutes. But having been hoisted away from the yawning maw of darkness the way he was, so very strangely, he wondered briefly if what people call miracles actually do occur in everyday life.

Would he see his wife and his brilliant boy again? Anything was possible, he thought, just like cold fusion was possible. But on that weary and uncertain night in Baja Sur, Mexico, Preston also recognized the unresolvable truth that being with his family again could not be soon. The invention was gone, yet Cain was still a powerful reality.

CHAPTER 103

"Where is the deposit?" came the voice suddenly from shadowed darkness in Buckley Wick's expansive private study, within his expansive stately home outside Washington, D.C.

"Jesus Christ!" yelled Buckley, spinning around wildly, his eyes wide and his glasses slipping down his nose, which he clumsily straightened. He was not an athletic man and certainly not graceful. As he collected his startled and frightened self, he began to see a specter coalescing before him out of the ethers in the room. Buckley began to make out the image of Cain sitting with his legs crossed and relaxing in Buckley's floral Pierre Deux reading chair, not ten paces away and only dimly lit from the brass desk lamp Buckley had just opened on that black, moonless night. "How... how the hell did you get in here?" said Buckley, trying to recover but still at a loss and shocked into trembling where he stood.

"The deposit?" said Cain calmly again, returning to the point of his visit.

"Well, hey... Mr. Speck! Christ, I wasn't expecting you. Let me see here," Buckley said as he stumbled around in his confused cranium trying to orient himself right there in his own house, while he looked at the man in the chair, illuminated only faintly by the one desk lamp. Even though there was not much light cast through that deeply hued study in the Wicks' mansion, Buckley had managed to figure out the specter was in fact his contract gunman, currently going by "Martin Speck". They had met face to face once before.

"The deposit?" repeated Cain, a touch more sternly this time.

"Oh, yes… well… you know… I was waiting… I wanted to be absolutely sure *you* would get the money and not some Swiss banker middle-man!"

"So, you were going to keep it, if I was killed," said Cain.

"No! No! Not at all! I wanted to hear from you. That's it!"

"I sent you the trigger message we had agreed upon," said Cain.

"But you were in a very difficult situation back there! I didn't know what had happened!"

Unexpectedly, Cain gestured to an oil painting above and behind Buckley's wide heavy desk on which rested the dim, brass lamp. The painting depicted two bare-breasted brown Polynesian women carrying baskets of fruit in a colorful and lush jungle. "Gauguin?" Cain asked.

Buckley Wicks was confused, not caring for a change of direction right at that moment. "Uh… yes, it is. That's his teenage mistress."

"I would like you to think of this evening's scenario, Mr. Wicks, not as Gauguin would have floridly rendered it but more as a pastel. You would be well advised to understand I am capable of delivering vivid scenes, too."

Buckley Wicks didn't care for abstract references, terrified as he was, but he stumbled ahead guessing at Cain's meaning, "I understand," Buckley said. "Yes, I've always intended to pay you, Mr. Speck. Trust me. As you can see, I am a man of means. There's no need for vivid work here." And he tried a chuckle, to show good humor but his efforts gained no traction with the assassin.

"I do see," said Cain.

"Your money will be in your account first thing in the morning. Absolutely!" said Buckley Wicks.

"That's best for you," said Cain and he rose gently from the chintz Pierre Deux reading chair and he walked slowly toward the study's entrance with its tall carved doors, imported from Portugal, which were open onto the house's polished marble foyer. Buckley's dilated eyes followed Cain all the way to those doors.

"Don't call anyone for fifteen minutes after I leave," said Cain not looking at Buckley Wicks.

"I won't! Believe me, I won't!" came the quick and compliant response.

But as Cain arrived at those Portuguese doors, he turned back toward his employer and without comment or warning he smoothly extracted his Desert Eagle from the clip at his back. And just like that, he swept the silenced muzzle of the long weapon directly toward one of Buckley Wicks' expensive loafers and pulled the trigger, firing an unanticipated and accurate fifty caliber round that pulverized all the metacarpals in Buckley Wick's right foot! "Arrrrgh!" cried Buckley loudly, dropping to the carpet like a sack of spuds.

Upstairs in the master bedroom suite Arvella Wicks was sitting at her sprawling vanity counter and she halted from her careful facial cleansing for just a moment when her husband was shot. Did she hear something? She waited and listened. But no other sounds followed, so she contentedly returned to her self-indulgences before the mirror.

That heavy .50 caliber bullet went straight through Buckley's fragile foot bones and straight through the thick hardwood floor beneath them, through the ceiling of the wine cellar below and in scattered fragments that same bullet exploded half a dozen bottles of decades-old cabernets, which in the dampness and quiet of the basement spilled their rich contents like blood across the cement floor beneath the antique wine rack.

"Christ almighty!" Buckley Wicks exclaimed, crumpled on the floor, on the twenty-five thousand dollar bullet-punctured silk

Persian rug in his study, beneath Gauguin's brown-skinned bare-breasted girl lover.

"Oh, my God! Shit-fuck!" Buckley said, as he clutched his bloody and shattered foot with both hands. It was the most excruciating physical experience of his entire life and he was at a total loss as to why it happened. Buckley would never walk correctly again. It wasn't fair! After all, he had just promised the man that he was going to pay him, and it was a damn fortune, too!

"Holy Jesus! This was not necessary!" Buckley Wicks pled. "Why did you do this?" he said looking up at Cain. Buckley found himself in waves of the most intense agony and fire resonating from his destroyed foot.

Unfazed and quite relaxed, Cain looked down at the wounded man, a crippled, devastated, very wealthy and powerful man, who was at that moment rocking back and forth on the floor with a crushed and oozing foot in his hands, a mangled foot snug inside a thousand-dollar piece of soft, tasseled, and shredded Italian leather. And as Cain returned his large pistol to the clip at the small of his back, hidden beneath his thick dark and flowing flannel shirt, he said simply to Buckley Wicks, "Because you deserve it. I'll be looking for full payment tomorrow."

Then he walked out.

CHAPTER 104

Soon after Preston Cook heard that 47 was the lucky number of the fishermen triplets, he realized that an interrogation from the two weary state policy officers was about to commence. And that was also precisely when the CTU physicist chose to retreat into a loss-of-memory scenario. He sensed things might run strange with the frustrated and unhappy constabulary at the scene, if he was forthcoming. They wanted to draw their middle-of-the-night adventure to a close as soon as possible. And although the amnesia angle was not a carefully planned strategy by Preston, it did provide the needed refuge for him to think things through. It was a plan of action snatched on impulse by Preston, resurrected from a B-movie he'd seen decades earlier in which a blow to the heroine's head resulted in lost recall. It was half true for Preston because he really did not remember the dolphins or specifics about the crash.

The former Preston Cook would never choose to fly by seat-of-his-pants during a police interrogation but his situation in Mexico had traveled completely off the edge of his life map. Any strategy should be considered. Assassins, nuclear energy, secret agents, and a suicide mission? He could see that *truth* would have been completely unworkable for the Mexican state police officers in Baja Sur on that bizarre October night. Saved by dolphins was enough of the outrageous. So, Preston conveniently forgot the rest.

The one police officer who spoke broken English asked Preston his name and Preston indicated that he had hit his head during the crash and he didn't remember. Fortunately for Preston, there in the port master's office, he had the scalp laceration and dried blood on his face to support his story. He had actually been knocked-out soon after his Cessna hit the water and started to sink. He indicated in rudimentary exchanges with the one officer, exchanges that hung somewhere between Spanish, English, and pantomime, that he wasn't able to remember anything, including his own name, where he came from, why he was flying out that far, or anything else. Preston donned the very best perplexed face he was able to muster in front of the suspicious eyes and scrutiny of these grumpy and inconvenienced Mexican cops.

After some unproductive questioning, the policemen didn't know what to do with their damp, tired, and mysterious American specimen. So, they asked Preston, who was weak and genuinely compromised by what had happened to him, to rest and wait on a bench off to the side for few minutes while they conferred. The short, padded bench was out of their way, yet still inside the port master's quarters. The one quasi English-speaking officer explained to Preston that they had some phone calls to make.

When he sat down and glanced through the brine-fogged windows toward the rows of boats moored at five piers, Preston noticed his new seat wasn't that far away from fishing trawler 47. Obviously, Baja Sur's harbor was where the trawler that rescued Preston rested when she was not harvesting tuna and aviators from Davy Jones' Locker. "Isn't there something called a pilot fish?" Preston whispered to himself. Dalton would have enjoyed that.

And while Preston sat waiting on the bench in the port master's office, the two policemen were soon leaning into their cell phones, feverishly trying to contact headquarters and get some guidance as to next steps. The whole episode was definitely not business as usual for the only two law enforcement officers anywhere near that fishing village. Even to Preston, who could not comprehend a drop of meaning in the river of Spanish those men poured into their phones, they were clearly a pair of frustrated civil servants who did not know exactly what to do with their new prisoner. That night in October was not one they wanted or expected for themselves when they went on duty.

While the two state cops huddled together on their phones and waived their hands around in the air, struggling to find anyone at their agency willing to help with their predicament, Preston absently discovered his own cell phone buried in his buttoned cargo pants' thigh pocket! It was a revelation for him! He didn't have much in the way of personal items remaining on him at that point. His not-buttoned-down wallet and his personal identification were all gone, washed away during the crash and the mugging he had received from the sea in those few chaotic moments of awareness when water poured furiously into the starboard side of the Cessna's cabin, as he tried desperately to gather himself sufficiently to get out. That was when he struck his head and consciousness abandoned him. By all rights he should have drowned.

Sitting there on the bench in the port master's office ignored by everyone, Preston nostalgically flipped open his Sanyo clamshell phone. He fully expected the phone to be dead after it was submerged for half an hour or more in sea water while he floated amongst the life-guarding dolphins that he could never thank. But the Sanyo's small screen lit right up right away! Christ! The damn thing still worked! He was shocked.

Preston quickly snapped the phone shut, fearing it might be confiscated to identify him, and he surreptitiously slipped it back into his buttoned pocket. He glanced around but no one was paying him the slightest attention. The trio of fishermen brothers was long gone by then, carrying their amazing story to share with girlfriends, wives, or pals at the local cantina. The port master was back on his watch at his marine radio coordinating the late night return of two more fishing trawlers. Meanwhile, both of the exhausted but determined state police officers were caught up in their demands for clear directions from superiors. Their task that night was not an easy one, given that law enforcement around Baja Sur was typically expeditious. But in a sensitive situation involving an American pilot dragged out of the ocean, nobody on the other end of the line wanted to commit to offering any kind of advice.

After discovering his phone still worked, Preston could feel a small smile forming on his lips, a smile he had to suppress immediately. A functioning cell phone in his pocket changed everything for him! It gave Dr. Cook access to his former life, to money, and to his family. At first, as he sat there on the cushioned bench digesting what he had just discovered. He could not imagine how in hell his cell phone would still operate! It was truly a day of miracles. Water and electronics do not mix, not in the early days of radio and not in 2005. They are fundamental enemies to one another. But then Preston remembered that when he had jury-rigged his family's phones by soldering in a chip for triangulation and other features, Preston also filled the phones with melted paraffin knowing it was harmless to circuitry and maybe it would help absorb shocks if the phones were dropped. He'd done it on a lark, never calculating the wax would also render the innards waterproof. It was total luck!

He knew right away he would have to be very stingy with his phone's use, mindful of the limited charge that remained in its battery. Plus calls could be tracked, so the damn thing had to be retired quickly if his survival was going to be a secret. His calls would have to cease within hours or sooner. But if being judicious with resources was a virtue in a man, Dr. Preston Cook was a saint. After all, he had already conjured up salvation for the world's energy crisis by working out of his garage with copper wire and a thermos bottle.

The two state police officers were clearly mired in more bureaucratic muck than they ever anticipated. Preston could see they were wildly frustrated in their conversations, looking at one another in disbelief at whatever it was they were hearing and tossing their hands in bald-faced dismay. All that while, they never glanced toward the object of their aggravation, the American who had been found floating in the middle of the ocean, a nameless lost American who sat fifteen feet from them, a mere spectator to their animated conversations.

Preston looked left and he looked right. He had become invisible where he sat to the side, while the cops drilled ahead in rat-a-tat-tat Spanish and the port master was keenly into his ship-to-shore transmissions as trawler captains on their way home in the dark negotiated the harbor's protective reefs. Preston comprehended none of what was being said by anyone.

So, rising gently from his place on the bench, doing his best to draw as little attention to himself as possible, Preston slowly walked away from where the police officers were conferencing on their cell phones and the port master was taking care of business. Preston ambled toward the open door that led toward the main street of the fishing village. No one inside the port master's office said a word or even noticed that Preston was leaving and in less than a minute the physicist was completely outside into the balmy Baja California night.

On the ramshackle street running past the embarcadero, there were only half a dozen distantly situated streetlight poles, linked by a long assortment drooping black electrical wires, some of which leeched into buildings on either side of the road. The old bulbs on the few streetlamps threw a pleasant amber glow along the unpaved gravel road and the handful of dark storefronts on both sides of the street. It was not bright by any means and it was very quiet. Preston saw no one at all, one way or the other. The street was deserted.

Then, as serendipitously as the appearance of a school of bottle-nosed dolphins, a rusting and faded, full-sized 1975 Ford Galaxie taxi cab lumbered around a corner fifty yards away and came rolling slowly along the gravel, main drag toward Preston. The car had one set of cock-eyed headlights from some past adventure that lit up the closed shops on the opposite side of the road, but on that particular night in Mexico, the past-its-prime, wide Ford crunching gently down the main street in Baja Sur was the most beautiful automobile Preston had ever seen. So, he seized the moment and he lifted a hand to hail that cab.

As it happened, aside from the working cell phone in his left buttoned pants pocket, Preston Cook also had a number of soaked U.S. bills, maybe a hundred dollars all told. Standing at the car's passenger window, Preston said nothing but showed half the cash to the balding, skinny unshaven cabbie who smelled of tequila and who leaned over to get a good look at what was offered. Upon seeing the money, the skinny cabbie nodded and said, "Si," and Preston opened the front passenger door and slid inside.

CHAPTER 105

Preston didn't know how far he could go on fifty bucks in Mexico, but he figured it would be far enough to get away from the two state policemen and it turned out to be much farther. Actually Preston rode with the skinny, bald cabbie all the way to Cabo San Lucas, down to the southern tip of Baja California. Fifty American dollars was not close to sufficient for that long ride. Cabo was more than a twenty-hour, non-stop, grueling undertaking. But, as it happened, the cabbie had a lot on his mind that night and he was determined to push his old Ford all the way to Cabo San Lucas so he could shoot the boy-friend of his ex-wife right between the eyes. Shoot his ex, too. And the skinny cabbie rather fancied some company on his fateful journey. He even had serviceable English that could keep the conversation going.

Since Cabo San Lucas was where Pico, the cabbie, was already headed, Preston's fifty bucks was simply found-money to the cab driver. Consequently, it wasn't half bad between them on the journey. Pico confessed he had a revolver in his glove compartment to take care of his business when they got to Cabo and Preston appreciated the information but encouraged his driver to keep the gun where it was. Its unseen presence right there in front of where Preston sat on the front seat made him nervous enough.

By the time the two Mexican state police officers back in Baja Sur came charging out of the port master's office on the night Preston escaped, realizing the fallen American pilot was gone, by the time they ran onto the quiet, dimly lit, night-time gravel street fronting the embarcadero, wild-eyed with their cell phones still squawking in their hands, the officers quickly discovered their prisoner was well over the hill and down the road. And with that truth they realized they were really, truly stuck. After more than an hour-long fuss over their phones with their bosses and with others, too, about this American, they would then have to go back and say, "Never mind. He's gone."

There would be detailed reports for them to write. There would be hard questions to answer and there would be scapegoating for sure. The night the American aviator was fished from the sea did not start out very well for these two unfortunate and distressed state police officers who were called to the scene, and it was not ending much better. Sometimes everything goes wrong A to Z and that was one of those nights for the Baja Sur cops.

As Preston came to understand it in the following weeks, while he was quietly attempting to secure a foothold in Cabo, the cab driver's bloody revenge on his wife and her lover never took place. In fact Pico, the cabbie, stayed in close touch with Preston during the following months and he became Preston's interpreter in key situations where Preston needed assistance in that community. Pico said he was eternally grateful to Preston for the advice Preston had provided during their ride together, advice that steered Pico away from ruining his life by using that pistol in his glove compartment and he felt there was a debt to be paid. Preston was likewise enormously grateful to Pico for the long, nearly free, ride to Cabo San Lucas.

After Preston had been resurrected from everlasting death in the Pacific Ocean, the big rusty car and inebriated Pico seemed to appear from nowhere as welcome as the trawler and as magical as the dolphins. No single day in Preston's entire life would ever hold such serendipity and wonder as the one in which the assassin, Cain, had ordered him to fly west and lose forever the world-changing gift that Preston had dreamed of offering to humanity. But even on that miraculous day cosmic balance was in play. Preston Cook may have survived his flight but the dearest element in his life – his family – was gone from him.

Cabo San Lucas turned out to be the right place for Dr. Cook in his strange and unanticipated situation since it was a remote setting, yet far from undeveloped. Cabo was a tourist destination, so it had an active airport. There was also reliable electricity and the Internet, too.

When Preston was bouncing along Mexican Highway #1 southward in the dark with the taxi's cock-eyed headlamps illuminating the scrub trees along the hills to the left and Pico was babbling away about how he had been done wrong by his ex-wife, Preston was finally beginning to accept that his tomorrow would be very, very different for him than the endless dark cold he had believed was his destiny while flying westward above the Pacific earlier that day. The cabbie was bent on his sad and angry prospects in Cabo San Lucas while Preston's future was looking brighter by the mile. He calculated that if he acted quickly he could safely use his cell phone *one time only* and transfer some cash out of his account at Pasadena Federal Credit Union to somewhere in Cabo as long as it wasn't a suspiciously high figure. If his withdrawal didn't earn anyone's immediate attention then it may not be noticed later and no one would ever see that the dates didn't line up with his disappearance. And as things turned out, nobody bothered to check. Preston withdrew his customary thousand bucks from his credit union account the day after he died and he had the discipline to never go back for more. Consequently, no one blinked.

During their long drive, after listening to Pico's story of betrayal and revenge, Preston eventually said earnestly to the cabbie that if you truly love a woman, you have to be ready to forgive her for anything, and if she loves you back, rest assured at some point she will have to forgive you equally. It works out, he said. Maybe Preston knew about Maxwell Umberto and his wife when he offered that advice to the Mexican cab driver and maybe he didn't, but it was the best advice he could muster in the moment and as events played out in the following weeks it apparently saved the lives of a woman and a man Preston did not know and would never see. It also made Pico, the cabbie, an invaluable asset to Preston in Cabo San Lucas and a friend for life.

That Dr. Preston Cook's rescue and his survival had neither been orchestrated by him nor even faintly imagined by him were facts that worked advantageously for Preston in light of his concerns about Cain's promise to exact retribution for the slightest betrayal of their original agreement on the runway at Big Bear. It might be that Cain was brutal but he was also strangely just, as Preston read him. Most importantly, Cain was very real and Preston knew he would absolutely follow through on his promises.

In the darkness of the big Ford, as it jostled along that rather poor excuse for a highway southward toward Cabo San Lucas in Mexico on the day Preston had been rescued from the sea, it began to appear to Dr. Cook that it may be possible for him to both die *and* live. As brilliant as he was, he could never have engineered what had happened.

Preston was forced to picture a future for himself in a Mexican resort town – which had its leisurely appeal – but it was not a life he had ever envisioned before or truly wanted. He was resourceful and he figured that with a working cell phone in his pocket he could quickly parlay what little energy it had left into an existence of sorts. He was stridently confident about that. Preston had already parlayed subatomic energy into the possibility of a new life for billions of people around the globe. Creating nominal energy for himself in Mexico should be a cinch, he thought, and as it turned out with a little help from his friend Pico, Preston succeeded.

With some money in his pocket and fresh clothes on his back, Preston slid without too many questions into the role of science teacher at a small parochial girls' school in Cabo, where the affluent students and most of the staff spoke solid English. He observed their facility with English was partly a byproduct of omnipresent American television and otherwise a byproduct the students' cosmopolitan lives. Most of them would routinely travel to the United States with their families. For those well-to-do Mexican Catholic families, English was not optional. They were rather European in their regard for practical multilingual skills.

There would be time to contact his son and his wife. Preston Cook understood it could not be right away and it would have to be carefully timed and carefully arranged. After all, to them he was dead and complicated things were in motion, a memorial service and life insurance settlements. But while Preston built his quiet life in Cabo San Lucas, he came to patiently believe he could eventually fix whatever transpired while he was supposedly dead and he could make his life whole again in the U.S. someday. He could make it work. He *would* be with his family, he affirmed within himself.

The intense Pasadena garage fire and the police killings associated with it did create a heightened buzz in the news and more than minor involvement of local authorities. Big Buster Bernard was interrogated numerous times about the mysterious foreign agent called Cain who pursued him and Preston to the mountains, yet Buster could provide no real leads. Yes, he'd briefly seen the assassin, but after that what he knew he'd learned from Agent Skylar. And true to its nature, Special Group shut the door quickly and tightly on discussing any agent's involvement in what had happened in California. The federal government would admit to nothing.

Buster did share with the press that his neighbor had invented a safe, atomic generator of some kind, but he didn't know how it worked and his stories about that miracle were quickly chalked up as the scrambled whimsy of an aging, dope-smoking hippy biker.

In spite of her time with Cain in his car as his hostage, Samantha Day-Steiner tip-toed gingerly around all of the questions that came her way during the weeks that followed Preston's disappearance at sea. She understood quite clearly there were powerful and dangerous forces at play in what had happened and she also wanted to keep her tryst with Maxwell out of the conversation. Therefore, she chose to shrug off as much as she could when asked about those events, including her husband's research. She knew very little, she said, and she kept it that way. She wanted only to protect her son to help him get beyond the horror of what had happened, if that was possible at all. She also had chosen to honor Preston for Dalton's sake in ways that she wished she had done much earlier, when Preston was alive.

Lt. Jack, although a police officer himself, was unable to provide much help in the Pasadena investigations. He never actually saw the alleged assassin except from a great distance at the Big Bear airport. And Fitzgerald's boss at LAPD wanted him back on duty at the precinct right away after events went down. "That's Pasadena business," the Captain had said extricating Fitzgerald the very next day. Fitzy would later admit to friends there was something artificially urgent in the way his supervisor yanked him out of the picture in Pasadena that made the lieutenant believe serious outside pressures were in the mix, pressures from very high up. It just didn't feel right. For instance, Fitzy wanted to get in touch with Dalton – to see if the boy was okay – but Lt. Jack was told in no uncertain terms that he was to abandon any connection to the Pasadena case and he was to make no attempt to intervene or contact any of the principles. It was an atypically prescriptive set of rules Fitzgerald received, but his boss was deadly serious when he outlined them.

The political noise around what had happened was intense in the beginning, but dead ends were everywhere as reporters, detectives, and agents of other stripes quickly discovered, and soon more sensational happenings elsewhere in the world drew away the public's attention as the very strange events in Pasadena in October of 2005 began to fade from the public memory.

But Lt. Jack was his mother's son. In spite of what he had been told, he had to find out about the Down syndrome boy who had opened the officer's mind to the limitless possibilities that can be driven by human determination and by love. So, Fitzy eventually did contact Dalton and was pleased to find the boy was doing well, pleased to find Dalton was vehemently convinced his dad was alive somewhere and that his dad would eventually return. Neither of them knew at that time Preston was in fact alive, but the spirit of hope was burning in Dalton. Fitzgerald Jack didn't know in the beginning if it was healthy for the boy to be so sure about something so unlikely, but ultimately the Lieutenant decided Dalton's faith was so intensely bright he should leave it alone, and in what was at that time a seemingly out-of-character move, Dalton's mother had made the same decision. Samantha even fostered the possibility with her son. "Your dad is good at miracles," she would say, which was perhaps the first irrational concept she had actually embraced since she and Preston were wide-eyed graduate students bent on changing the world.

From Mexico, Preston witnessed none of the scrutiny that was laid upon Sam and Big Buster in the wake of Lucky 47's crash into the sea, but Preston knew the prying had to be excruciating, it had to be intense, and it had to be unrelenting for a time. He understood there must have been many difficult hours of questioning for Samantha to endure, but he also was convinced that she among all the men and women he knew had the mettle for it. She would protect Dalton. She would not cave. And with each passing day in Mexico Preston grew increasingly confident he would not only see his family again, he would find a way to be with them again beyond Cain's watch. A better life for them all would be born. It became Preston's mission, his new obsession, and few men or women knew obsession like Preston Cook.

CHAPTER 106

After destroying Buckley Wicks' right foot, Cain strode casually through the grand marble foyer of the lovely Wicks' home toward the heavy ebony gate-like front doors through which he had easily managed his entrance an hour earlier. Emerging into the quiet and chilly October Washington, D.C. evening, Cain glanced around at an exceptionally well-tended autumnal garden circling the sumptuous house he was leaving. He wanted to wander in that garden, investigating any lovely surprises he might find, but at that point he heard a tortured cry from Buckley Wicks, where he lay bloodied in his richly-appointed study, "Arvella! Help! Help me!"

Cain could also hear from somewhere upstairs in the mansion, Buckley's wife, the true brains of their enterprise, as she shouted a genuinely worried reply to her husband's call, as she realized in that moment that she probably had heard a muffled gunshot a few minutes earlier. "What is it, Buckley, honey? Are you okay?" she yelled back toward her husband as she rose from her boudoir. All the servants had gone home for the night, so the two Wicks were alone in their stately house.

It had not been the fifteen minutes of silence Buckley Wicks had agreed to, or even three minutes of silence, but Cain concluded it didn't matter. Instead, he strode across the expansive manicured lawn toward a gigantic water oak at the perimeter of the property that was probably two-hundred years old or more, with a gnarled gray trunk five feet in diameter and great limbs that spread for twenty paces all around and reached down like a mother's arms. As Cain passed beneath the canopy of that weathered, durable tree he could smell the age, the mold of centuries. He loved the scent and he drew the fragrance deeply into his lungs. He walked straight ahead beyond the ancient tree and he vanished into the night.